ROMA

ROMA

THE NOVEL OF ANCIENT ROME

STEVEN SAYLOR

St. Martin's Griffin
New York

This is a work of fiction. All of the characters, organizations, and events portrayed in this novel are either products of the author's imagination or are used fictitiously.

www.stmartins.com

Book design by Susan Walsh
Family tree illustration by Jackie Aher

The Library of Congress has cataloged the hardcover edition as follows:

Saylor, Steven, 1956–
      Roma : the novel of ancient Rome / Steven Saylor.
        p. cm.
      ISBN 978-0-312-32831-3
      1. Rome—History—Fiction. I. Title.

      PS3569.A96 R57 2007
      813'.54—dc22

                                2006051179

ISBN 978-1-250-00060-6 (trade paperback)

Second St. Martin's Griffin Edition: June 2011

10   9   8   7   6   5   4   3   2

To the shade of Titus Livius,
known in English as Livy,
who preserved for us
the earliest tales
of earliest Rome

CONTENTS

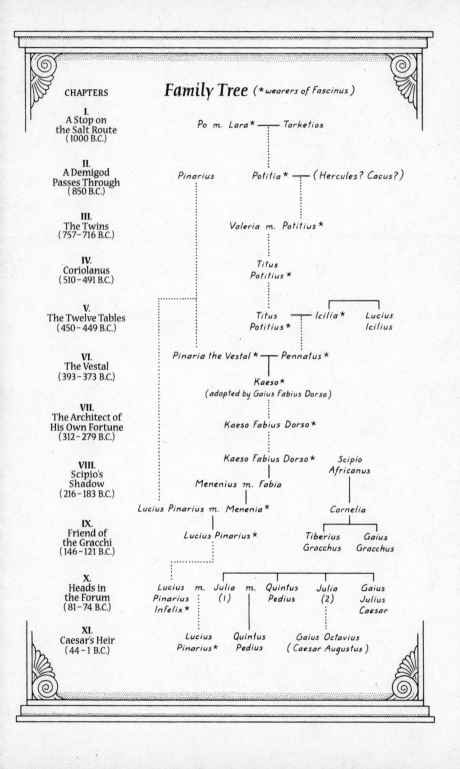

CHAPTERS

I.
A Stop on
the Salt Route
(1000 B.C.)

II.
A Demigod
Passes Through
(850 B.C.)

III.
The Twins
(757–716 B.C.)

IV.
Coriolanus
(510–491 B.C.)

V.
The Twelve Tables
(450–449 B.C.)

VI.
The Vestal
(393–373 B.C.)

VII.
The Architect of
His Own Fortune
(312–279 B.C.)

VIII.
Scipio's
Shadow
(216–183 B.C.)

IX.
Friend of
the Gracchi
(146–121 B.C.)

X.
Heads in
the Forum
(81–74 B.C.)

XI.
Caesar's Heir
(44–1 B.C.)

Family Tree (*wearers of Fascinus*)

Po m. Lara* —— Tarketios

Pinarius   Potitia * —— (Hercules? Cacus?)

Valeria m. Potitius *

Titus
Potitius *

Titus —— Icilia *   Lucius
Potitius *   Icilius

Pinaria the Vestal * —— Pennatus *

Kaeso*
(adopted by Gaius Fabius Dorso)

Kaeso Fabius Dorso *

Kaeso Fabius Dorso *   Scipio
                          Africanus

Menenius m. Fabia

Lucius Pinarius m. Menenia *   Cornelia

Lucius Pinarius *

Tiberius   Gaius
Gracchus   Gracchus

Lucius   m. Julia   m. Quintus   Julia   Gaius
Pinarius   (1)   Pedius   (2)   Julius
Infelix *   Caesar

Lucius   Quintus   Gaius Octavius
Pinarius *   Pedius   (Caesar Augustus)

Roman months and days

The names of the Roman months were Januarius, Februarius, Martius, Aprilis, Maius, Junius, Quinctilis (later Julius, to honor Julius Caesar), Sextilis (later Augustus, to honor Caesar Augustus), September, October, November, and December.

The first day of each month was called the Kalends. The Ides fell on the 15th day of Martius, Maius, Quinctilis, and October, and on the 13th day of the other months. The Nones fell nine days before the Ides.

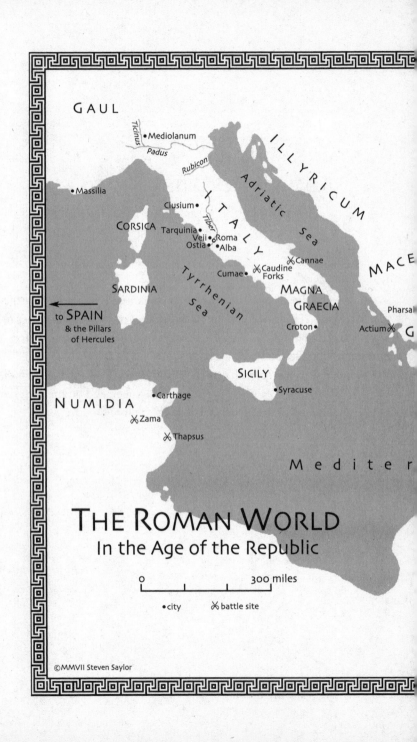

GAUL

Ticinus
•Mediolanum

Padus

Rubicon

I L L Y R I C U M

Adriatic Sea

•Massilia

CORSICA

Clusium•

I T A L Y

Tarquinia•
Veii•
Ostia•
•Roma
•Alba

Tiber

⚔Cannae

MACE

SARDINIA

Tyrrhenian Sea

Cumae•
⚔Caudine Forks

MAGNA GRAECIA

Pharsal

← to SPAIN
& the Pillars
of Hercules

Croton•

Actium⚔

G

NUMIDIA

•Carthage

⚔Zama

SICILY

•Syracuse

⚔Thapsus

M e d i t e r r

THE ROMAN WORLD
In the Age of the Republic

0   300 miles

•city   ⚔ battle site

©MMVII Steven Saylor

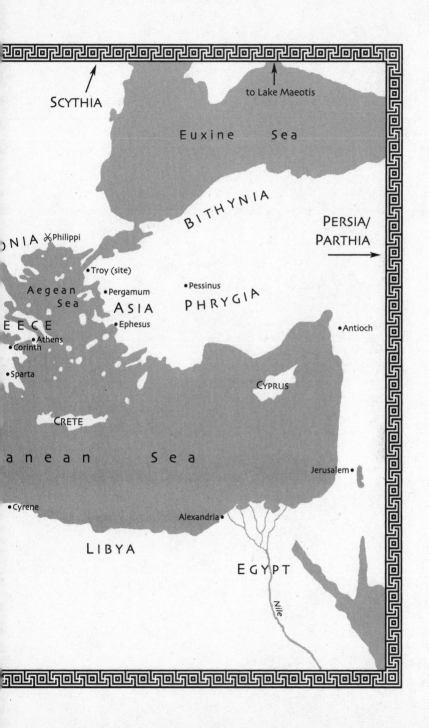

LEGEND IS HISTORICAL, JUST AS HISTORY IS LEGENDARY.
Alexandre Grandazzi, *The Foundation of Rome*

ROMA

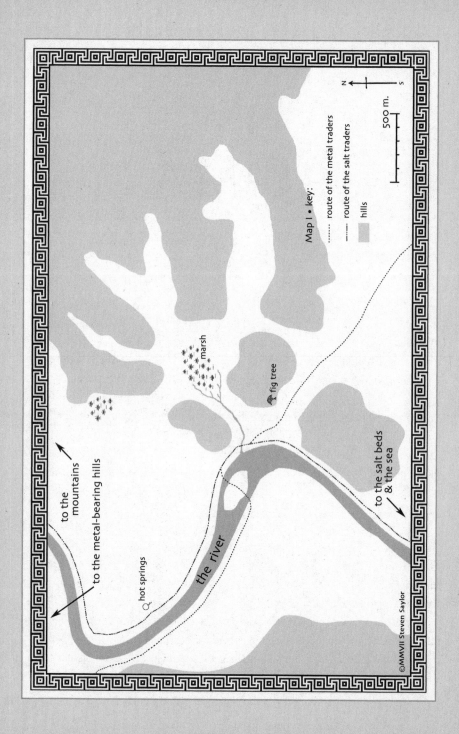

N

S

500 m.

Map I • key:

.... route of the metal traders

—·—·— route of the salt traders

hills

to the
mountains

to the metal-bearing hills

hot springs

the river

marsh

fig tree

to the salt beds
& the sea

©MMVII Steven Saylor

A STOP ON THE SALT ROUTE

1000 B.C.

As they rounded a bend in the path that ran beside the river, Lara recognized the silhouette of a fig tree atop a nearby hill. The weather was hot and the days were long. The fig tree was in full leaf, but not yet bearing fruit.

Soon Lara spotted other landmarks—an outcropping of limestone beside the path that had a silhouette like a man's face, a marshy spot beside the river where the waterfowl were easily startled, a tall tree that looked like a man with his arms upraised. They were drawing near to the place where there was an island in the river. The island was a good spot to make camp. They would sleep on the island tonight.

Lara had been back and forth along the river path many times in her short life. Her people had not created the path—it had always been there, like the river—but their deerskin-shod feet and the wooden wheels of their handcarts kept the path well worn. Lara's people were salt traders, and their livelihood took them on a continual journey.

At the mouth of the river, the little group of half a dozen intermingled families gathered salt from the great salt beds beside the sea. They groomed and sifted the salt and loaded it into handcarts. When the carts were full, most of the group would stay behind, taking shelter amid rocks and simple lean-tos, while a band of fifteen or so of the heartier members set out on the path that ran alongside the river.

With their precious cargo of salt, the travelers crossed the coastal lowlands and traveled toward the mountains. But Lara's people never reached the mountaintops; they traveled only as far as the foothills. Many people lived in the forests and grassy meadows of the foothills, gathered in small villages. In return for salt, these people would give Lara's people dried meat, animal skins, cloth spun from wool, clay pots, needles and scraping tools carved from bone, and little toys made of wood.

Their bartering done, Lara and her people would travel back down the river path to the sea. The cycle would begin again.

It had always been like this. Lara knew no other life. She traveled back and forth, up and down the river path. No single place was home. She liked the seaside, where there was always fish to eat, and the gentle lapping of the waves lulled her to sleep at night. She was less fond of the foothills, where the path grew steep, the nights could be cold, and views of great distances made her dizzy. She felt uneasy in the villages, and was often shy around strangers. The path itself was where she felt most at home. She loved the smell of the river on a hot day, and the croaking of frogs at night. Vines grew amid the lush foliage along the river, with berries that were good to eat. Even on the hottest day, sundown brought a cool breeze off the water, which sighed and sang amid the reeds and tall grasses.

Of all the places along the path, the area they were approaching, with the island in the river, was Lara's favorite.

The terrain along this stretch of the river was mostly flat, but in the immediate vicinity of the island, the land on the sunrise side was like a rumpled cloth, with hills and ridges and valleys. Among Lara's people, there was a wooden baby's crib, suitable for strapping to a cart, that had been passed down for generations. The island was shaped like that crib, longer than it was wide and pointed at the upriver end, where the flow had eroded both banks. The island was like a crib, and the group of hills on the sunrise side of the river were like old women mantled in heavy cloaks gathered to have a look at the baby in the crib—that was how Lara's father had once described the lay of the land.

Larth spoke like that all the time, conjuring images of giants and monsters in the landscape. He could perceive the spirits, called numina, that dwelled in rocks and trees. Sometimes he could speak to them and hear what they had to say. The river was his oldest friend and told him where the fishing would be best. From whispers in the wind he could foretell the next day's weather. Because of such skills, Larth was the leader of the group.

"We're close to the island, aren't we, Papa?" said Lara.

"How did you know?"

"The hills. First we start to see the hills, off to the right. The hills grow bigger. And just before we come to the island, we can see the silhouette of that fig tree up there, along the crest of that hill."

"Good girl!" said Larth, proud of his daughter's memory and powers of observation. He was a strong, handsome man with flecks of gray in his black beard. His wife had borne several children, but all had died very young except Lara, the last, whom his wife had died bearing. Lara was very precious to him. Like her mother, she had golden hair. Now that she had reached the age of childbearing, Lara was beginning to display the fullness of a woman's hips and breasts. It was Larth's greatest wish that he might live to see his own grandchildren. Not every man lived that long, but Larth was hopeful. He had been healthy all his life, partly, he believed, because he had always been careful to show respect to the numina he encountered on his journeys.

Respecting the numina was important. The numen of the river could suck a man under and drown him. The numen of a tree could trip a man with its roots, or drop a rotten branch on his head. Rocks could give way underfoot, chuckling with amusement at their own treachery. Even the sky, with a roar of fury, sometimes sent down fingers of fire that could roast a man like a rabbit on a spit, or worse, leave him alive but robbed of his senses. Larth had heard that the earth itself could open and swallow a man; though he had never actually seen such a thing, he nevertheless performed a ritual each morning, asking the earth's permission before he went striding across it.

"There's something so special about this place," said Lara, gazing at the sparkling river to her left and then at the rocky, tree-spotted hills ahead and to her right. "How was it made? Who made it?"

Larth frowned. The question made no sense to him. A place was never *made,* it simply *was.* Small features might change over time. Uprooted by a storm, a tree might fall into the river. A boulder might decide to tumble down the hillside. The numina that animated all things went about re-shaping the landscape from day to day, but the essential things never changed, and had always existed: the river, the hills, the sky, the sun, the sea, the salt beds at the mouth of the river.

He was trying to think of some way to express these thoughts to Lara, when a deer, drinking at the river, was startled by their approach. The deer bolted up the brushy bank and onto the path. Instead of running to safety, the creature stood and stared at them. As clearly as if the animal had whis-pered aloud, Larth heard the words "Eat me." The deer was offering her-self.

Larth turned to shout an order, but the most skilled hunter of the group, a youth called Po, was already in motion. Po ran forward, raised the sharpened stick he always carried and hurled it whistling through the air between Larth and Lara.

A heartbeat later, the spear struck the deer's breast with such force that the creature was knocked to the ground. Unable to rise, she thrashed her neck and flailed her long, slender legs. Po ran past Larth and Lara. When he reached the deer, he pulled the spear free and stabbed the creature again. The deer released a stifled noise, like a gasp, and stopped moving.

There was a cheer from the group. Instead of yet another dinner of fish from the river, tonight there would be venison.

The distance from the riverbank to the island was not great, but at this time of year—early summer—the river was too high to wade across. Lara's people had long ago made simple rafts of branches lashed together with leather thongs, which they left on the riverbanks, repairing and replacing them as needed. When they last passed this way, there had been three rafts, all in good condition, left on the east bank. Two of the rafts were still there, but one was missing.

"I see it! There—pulled up on the bank of the island, almost hidden among those leaves," said Po, whose eyes were sharp. "Someone must have used it to cross over."

"Perhaps they're still on the island," said Larth. He did not begrudge others the use of the rafts, and the island was large enough to share. Nonetheless, the situation required caution. He cupped his hands to his mouth and gave a shout. It was not long before a man appeared on the bank of the island. The man waved.

"Do we know him?" said Larth, squinting.

"I don't think so," said Po. "He's young—my age or younger, I'd say. He looks strong."

"Very strong!" said Lara. Even from this distance, the young stranger's brawniness was impressive. He wore a short tunic without sleeves, and Lara had never seen such arms on a man.

Po, who was small and wiry, looked at Lara sidelong and frowned. "I'm not sure I like the look of this stranger."

"Why not?" said Lara. "He's smiling at us."

In fact, the young man was smiling at Lara, and Lara alone.

His name was Tarketios. Much more than that, Larth could not tell, for the stranger spoke a language which Larth did not recognize, in which each word seemed as long and convoluted as the man's name. Understanding the deer had been easier than understanding the strange noises uttered by this man and his two companions! Even so, they seemed friendly, and the three of them presented no threat to the more numerous salt traders.

Tarketios and his two older companions were skilled metalworkers from a region some two hundred miles to the north, where the hills were rich with iron, copper, and lead. They had been on a trading journey to the south and were returning home. Just as the river path carried Larth's people from the seashore to the hills, so another path, perpendicular to the river, traversed the long coastal plain. Because the island provided an easy place to ford the river, it was here that the two paths intersected. On this occasion, the salt traders and the metal traders happened to arrive at the island on the same day. Now they met for the first time.

The two groups made separate camps at opposite ends of the island. As a gesture of friendship, speaking with his hands, Larth invited Tarketios and the others to share the venison that night. As the hosts and their guests feasted around the roasting fire, Tarketios tried to explain something of his craft. Firelight glittered in Lara's eyes as she watched Tarketios point at the flames and mime the act of hammering. Firelight danced across the flexing muscles of his arms and shoulders. When he smiled at her, his grin was like a boast. She had never seen teeth so white and so perfect.

Po saw the looks the two exchanged and frowned. Lara's father saw the same looks and smiled.

❖

The meal was over. The metal traders, after many gestures of gratitude for the venison, withdrew to their camp at the far side of the island. Before he disappeared into the shadows, Tarketios looked over his shoulder and gave Lara a parting grin.

While the others settled down to sleep, Larth stayed awake a while longer, as was his habit. He liked to watch the fire. Like all other things, fire possessed a numen that sometimes communicated with him, showing him visions. As the last of the embers faded into darkness, Larth fell asleep.

Larth blinked. The flames, which had dwindled to almost nothing, suddenly shot up again. Hot air rushed over his face. His eyes were seared by white flames brighter than the sun.

Amid the dazzling brightness, he perceived a thing that levitated above the flames. It was a masculine member, disembodied but nonetheless rampant and upright. It bore wings, like a bird, and hovered in midair. Though it seemed to be made of flesh, it was impervious to the flames.

Larth had seen the winged phallus before, always in such circumstances, when he stared at a fire and entered a dream state. He had even given it a name, or more precisely, the thing had planted its name in his mind: Fascinus.

Fascinus was not like the numina that animated trees, stones, or rivers. Those numina existed without names. Each was bound to the object in which it resided, and there was little to differentiate one from another. When such numina spoke, they could not always be trusted. Sometimes they were friendly, but at other times they were mischievous or even hostile.

Fascinus was different. It was unique. It existed in and of itself, without beginning or end. Clearly, from its form, it had something to do with life and the origin of life, yet it seemed to come from a place beyond this world, slipping for a few moments through a breach opened by the heat of the dancing flames. An appearance by Fascinus was always significant. The winged phallus never appeared without giving Larth an answer to a dilemma that had been troubling him, or planting an important new thought in his mind. The guidance given to him by Fascinus had never led Larth astray.

Elsewhere, in distant lands—Greece, Israel, Egypt—men and women worshiped gods and goddesses. Those people made images of their gods, told stories about them, and worshiped them in temples. Larth had never met such people. He had never even heard of the lands where they lived, and he had never encountered or conceived of a god. The very concept of a deity such as those other men worshiped was unknown to Larth, but the closest thing to a god in his imagination and experience was Fascinus.

With a start, he blinked again.

The flames had died. In place of intolerable brightness there was only the darkness of a warm summer night lit by the faintest sliver of a moon. The air on his face was no longer hot but fresh and cool.

Fascinus had vanished—but not without planting a thought in Larth's mind. He hurried to the leafy bower beside the river where Lara liked to sleep, thinking to himself, *It must be made so, because Fascinus says it must!*

He knelt beside her, but there was no need to wake her. She was already awake.

"Papa? What is it?"

"Go to him!"

She did not need to ask for an explanation. It was what she had been yearning to do, lying restless and eager in the dark.

"Are you sure, Papa?"

"Fascinus . . . ," He did not finish the thought, but she understood. She had never seen Fascinus, but he had told her about it. Many times in the past, Fascinus had given guidance to her father. Now, once again, Fascinus had made its will known.

The darkness did not deter her. She knew every twist and turn of every path on the little island. When she came to the metal trader's camp, she found Tarketios lying in a leafy nook secluded from the others; she recognized him by his brawny silhouette. He was awake and waiting, just as she had been lying awake, waiting, when her father came to her.

At her approach, Tarketios rose onto his elbows. He spoke her name in a whisper. There was a quiver of something like desperation in his voice; his neediness made her smile. She sighed and lowered herself beside him. By the faint moonlight, she saw that he wore an amulet of some sort, suspended from a strap of leather around his neck. Nestled amid the hair on his chest, the bit of shapeless metal seemed to capture and concentrate the faint moonlight, casting back a radiance brighter than the moon itself.

His arms—the arms she had so admired earlier—reached out and closed around her in a surprisingly gentle embrace. His body was as warm and naked as her own, but much bigger and much harder. She wondered if Fascinus was with them in the darkness, for she seemed to feel the beating of wings between their legs as she was entered by the thing that gave origin to life.

⁂

The next morning, when the others began to wake and stir, Larth saw that Lara was back in the bower where she usually slept. He wondered if she had disobeyed him. Then he saw, by the look in her eyes and the smile on her face as she woke, that she had not.

While the others broke camp and made ready to depart, Larth called Po to his side. The youth was uncharacteristically slow to respond and kept his eyes averted while Larth spoke to him.

"Before we set out this morning, Po, I want you return to the place where you killed the deer yesterday. Rake the earth and cover any traces of blood on the path. If blood was spattered on leaves or loose stones, throw them in the river. This should have been done yesterday, but the light was fading and there was much work to do, skinning and roasting the deer. Do it now, before we set out. We can't leave blood on the trail."

"Why not?" said Po.

Larth was taken aback. Po had never used such a surly tone with him before. "Blood will attract vermin and predators. Blood on the trail may offend the numina that reside along the river, no matter that the deer freely offered herself. But I needn't explain these things to you. Do as I tell you!"

Po stared at the ground. Larth was about to speak again, more harshly, when he was distracted by the arrival of the metal traders, who had come to see them off.

Tarketios stepped forward. He made a great show of offering Larth a gift. It was an object made of iron, small enough to hold in the palm of one hand, with an opening at one end and a very sharp point at the other. It was a spearpoint made of iron—a very useful thing for bringing down the next deer that should cross the river path. Tarketios made it clear that he expected nothing in return.

Larth's people possessed a few crudely fashioned knives and scraping tools made of iron, but nothing as finely wrought as the spearpoint. He was very impressed. He showed it to Po. "What do you think of that?" he said. Before Po could answer, Larth reached for Po's spear and took it from his grasp. "You're the best hunter among us. You should have this. We'll let Tarketios show us how to fix the point to the shaft."

While Po stood dumbly by, Larth handed the spear and the iron point to Tarketios. Tarketios smiled at both men. The sight of his perfect teeth made Po's fingers twitch. With a small hammer and nails, Tarketios set about fixing the point to the shaft. Larth watched him work, fascinated, and took no notice of the deep red blush that spread across Po's face.

When the work was done, Tarketios handed the spear back to Po. The new point was heavier than Po had realized. The spear tilted forward in his hand and the iron point struck the ground with a thud.

"The balance is different," said Larth, laughing at the younger man's consternation. "You'll have to learn how to aim and throw all over again. But the new point should allow for a cleaner kill, don't you think? You won't need to throw as hard."

Po hurriedly shifted his grip and held the spear firmly upright again, grasping the shaft so tightly that his knuckles turned white.

A little later, as the salt traders were getting ready to depart from the island on the rafts, Tarketios approached Lara. He led her to a secluded spot. There were no words they could share to express what they were feeling. For a while they simply touched and held each other, then drew apart. In the same instant, each read the intention of the other: to offer a parting gift. The moment of shared understanding and the likeness of their intentions made them both laugh.

To Tarketios, Lara offered the most precious thing she could: a small clay vessel with a cork stopper, filled with pure white salt.

Tarketios accepted the gift, then set it aside. Over his head he lifted the leather strap around his neck, along with the amulet that hung from it. It was strange because it had no discernible shape; it appeared to be nothing more than small lump of unworked metal. But it was a metal such as she had never seen before, very heavy in the palm of her hand, and of a most unusual color, a pure yellow like the light of the sun. The only work that had been done on the metal was a small piercing that allowed it to be hung from the leather necklace.

Tarketios placed it over her head. He uttered something, naming the thing he had given her, but the word was only a strange sound in her ear. Lara had no way of knowing how precious the little lump was; it was the only metal that never tarnished. But by the look in Tarketios's eyes, she could see that he treasured it, and that by giving it, he honored her.

Although she did not yet know it, already he had given her another gift. A new life was quickening in her womb.

The sun was well up in the sky by the time the little band set out. Upriver from the island, the hills to their right receded and the river made a sweeping bend around a low, flat promontory. The first landmark they came to was a little path that led to some hot springs near the river. In cooler weather the springs were a favorite place to make camp, but not at this season.

Larth was settling into the rhythm of the walk when he suddenly remembered the task he had assigned to Po before they set out. He looked over his shoulder. "Did you clean the blood from the path?" he said.

By the look on Po's face he could see at once that his order had been ignored.

"Go back, then, and do it now!" he said, exasperated. "We won't wait for you. You'll have to run to catch up with us."

Without a word, Po stopped in his tracks. He let the others pass him. He watched as the band continued onward, until the last straggler disappeared from sight.

The spear in his hand seemed to quiver. He looked down and saw that his hands were trembling. It was one thing to act on impulse—to see a deer and instantly spring into action, to cast his spear and then stab the creature until it was dead, with hardly a thought until the deed was over. To do what he was now contemplating was something altogether different.

Po remained standing on the path for a long time. Finally he turned and headed back in the direction of the island, running at a steady trot, hefting the spear in his hand and judging its weight.

The terrain along the path steadily rose as the band proceeded upriver. Several times, at places which afforded a view, Larth paused and asked Lara, whose eyes were better than his, to look back the way they had come. She saw no sign of Po, or of anyone else on the trail. The sun began to sink, and still Po had not rejoined the group. Larth grew fearful. He should not have sent the youth alone. Because Po had disobeyed him, anger had clouded his judgment.

But just as the group stopped to make camp for the night, Po appeared. He strode toward them at a steady pace, not rushed or out of breath. Instead he seemed calm and relaxed.

"You took your time!" said Larth.

"What was the hurry? A man can't get lost, following the river path."

"You did as I told you?"

"Of course."

Larth's eyes had weakened, but he retained a sharp sense of smell. He looked at Po more closely, especially at his hair and his hands. They were very clean—unusually so. "You have the smell of the hot springs on you."

For several heartbeats, Po did not answer. "Yes. I stopped to bathe in the springs."

"You even washed this." Larth touched the youth's woolen tunic. It was freshly rinsed and still slightly damp.

"I felt . . . the blood of the deer on me. You said to cover all traces. The numina along the trail . . ." Po lowered his eyes. "I felt the need to wash myself."

Larth nodded. He said no more.

※

The place where they camped was near a high, steep hill. From past journeys, when his eyes had been sharper, Larth knew that from the summit of the hill a man could see a great distance. He found Lara and told her to come with him.

"Where are we going, Papa?"

"To the top of the hill. Quickly, while there's still daylight."

She followed, puzzled by his urgency. When they reached the top, Larth took a moment to catch his breath, then pointed in the downriver direction. The sinking sun was in their eyes. It cast a red glow across the land and turned the winding river into a ribbon of flame. Even with his poor eyesight, Larth could discern the hilly region near the island, though the island itself was hidden. He pointed toward it.

"There, daughter. Where the island lies. Do you see anything?"

She shrugged. "Hills, water, trees."

"Something moving?"

She narrowed her eyes and shielded her brow. Silhouetted against the red haze of the sunset, she saw a multitude of tiny flecks of black above the island, slowly circling and riding the wind, as bits of cinder spin above a fire.

"Vultures," she said. "I see many vultures."

※

Later, while the others slept, Larth remained awake, as was his habit. He watched the fire for a while, then rose and walked stealthily to the place where Po lay. The youth was sleeping by himself, away from the others, as if he wanted to keep his distance from them. His spear lay close beside him. To take it, Larth had to be very careful not to wake him.

By the firelight, he looked very closely at the iron point. Even in the hot springs, it must have been impossible to scrub every bit of blood from the hammered metal. In tiny, jagged fissures, traces of blood yet remained.

He returned to Po and stood over him. He pressed the spearpoint to the youth's throat and gave him a kick.

Po stirred, gave a start, then was instantly awake. A bead of blood appeared around the spearpoint pressed to his neck. He gasped and gripped the shaft with both hands, but Larth exerted all his strength to hold it steady.

"Speak in a whisper!" he said, not wanting to wake the others. "Remove your hands from the spear! Put your arms at your side! That's better. Now tell me the truth. All three of them—or only Tarketios?"

For a long time, Po did not answer. Larth saw his eyes flash in the darkness and heard his ragged breathing. Though Po lay very still, Larth could feel the quivering tension of the youth's body transmitted through the shaft of the spear.

"All of them," Po said at last.

Larth felt a great coldness descend upon him. Until that moment, he had not been sure of the truth. "Their bodies?"

"In the river."

My oldest friend, fouled with blood! thought Larth. What would the numen of the river think of him and his people now?

"They'll flow to the sea," Po said. "I left no trace—"

"No! At least one of the bodies must have grounded on the riverbank."

"How can you know that?"

"Vultures!" Larth could picture the scene—blood in the water, a corpse amid the rushes, the vultures circling overhead.

Larth shook his head. What a hunter the boy must be, to stalk and kill three men! And what a fool! Could the people afford to lose him? Could they afford to keep him? It was in Larth's power to kill him, here and now, but he would have to justify his action to the others. More than that, he would have to justify the action to himself.

At last, Larth sighed. "I know everything you do, Po. Remember that!" He lifted the spearpoint from the youth's throat. He let the spear fall to the ground. He turned away and went back to his place by the fire.

It might have been worse. If the boy had been such a fool that he killed only Tarketios, then the other two would surely have come after him, seeking vengeance. They would have taken the news back to their people. The knowledge that one of the salt traders had done such a thing would have spread. The consequences and recriminations could have continued for a lifetime, perhaps for generations.

As it was, only the numina along the trail would know, and the river, and the vultures. And Larth.

He gazed at the fire and wished, more fervently than he had ever wished before, that Fascinus would appear to him that night. Fascinus could put in his mind the proper thing to do. But the fire died to darkness, and Fascinus did not appear.

It would never appear to him again.

That night, except for the vultures, whose gullets were stuffed with carrion, the little island in the river was deserted.

As long as Larth lived, the salt traders never camped there again. He told them that lemures—shades of the restless dead—had come to dwell upon the island. Because Larth was known to possess a deep knowledge of such things, the others accepted what he said without question.

As winter turned to spring, Lara gave birth to a son. The birth was difficult, and Lara very nearly died. But when her suffering was most acute, for the first and only time in her life, she had a vision of Fascinus, and a voice in her head assured her that she and her child would both survive. All the while, she clutched the lump of gold that hung from the necklace around her neck, and the cool metal seemed to absorb her pain. In her delirium, the gold and Fascinus became one and the same. Afterward, she told her father that the numen of the wingèd phallus had come to dwell in the gold.

Shortly after the birth, in a simple ceremony near the salt beds beside the sea, Lara was wedded to Po. Though he knew better, Po claimed the child as his own. He did this because Larth told him he must, and he could see that Larth was right. Po would never be as wise in the ways of the numina as was his father-in-law, but even he could sense that his act of violence on the island demanded an act of contrition. By accepting the son of the man he had killed, Po made restitution to the lemur of Tarketios. He also appeased any numina which had witnessed and been offended by the blood he had deliberately shed.

Over the years, Lara's memories of Tarketios grew dim, but the gold amulet he had given her, which she now believed to house the numen of Fascinus, never lost its luster. Before she died, she gave the amulet to her son. Her explanation of its origin was not true, but was not a lie either, for Lara had come to believe less in her dim memories than in the fanciful stories she had invented to take their place. "The gold came from the fire," she told her son, "the same fire above which your grandfather saw Fascinus on the last night we camped on the island. Without Fascinus, my son, you would never have been conceived. Without Fascinus, neither you nor I would have survived your birth."

Fascinus inspired conception. Fascinus safeguarded birth. It had another power, as well: Fascinus could avert the evil eye. Lara knew this from experience, because after her son was born, she had heard other women whisper behind her back, and had caught them looking at her strangely. In truth, they looked at her with curiosity and suspicion, but she interpreted their gazes as envy. The gazes of the envious, as her father had taught her, could cause illness, misfortune, even death. But with Fascinus hanging from her neck, Lara had felt safe, confident that the dazzling luster of the gold could deflect even the most dangerous gaze.

As the amulet and the story of its origin were passed down to succeeding generations, it was left to Lara's descendents to ponder the exact role played by Fascinus in the continuation of the family line. Had the winged phallus itself emerged from the flames to impregnate Lara? Had such an instance of intercourse between numina and humankind ever occurred before, or since? Was it because a numen had fathered her child that the other women had been suspicious and envious of Lara? Had Fascinus made a gift of the gold knowing that Lara would need it to protect herself, and to safeguard his own offspring?

The gold amulet, its true origin forgotten, was passed down through the generations.

Many years passed. Larth's warning of restless lemures on the island in the river was forgotten, and the salt traders once again camped there. Still, the island and the surrounding area remained nothing more than a stopping place. Deer, rabbits, and wolves roamed the seven nearby hills. Frogs and dragonflies dwelled in the marshy lowlands between the hills. Birds passed overhead and saw below them no sign of human occupation.

Elsewhere in the world, men built great cities, made war, consecrated temples to gods, sang of heroes, and dreamed of empires. In faraway Egypt, the dynasties of the Pharaohs had already reigned for millennia; the Great Pyramid of Giza was more than 1,500 years old. The war of the Greeks against Troy was two hundred years in the past; the taking of Helen and the wrath of Achilles had already passed into legend. In Israel, King David had captured the old city of Jerusalem and made it his capital, and his son Solomon was building the first temple to the god Yahweh. Further to the east, migrating Aryans were founding the kingdoms of Media and Parsa, forerunners of the great Persian empire.

But the island in the river, and the seven nearby hills, remained unsettled by men and overlooked by the gods, a place where nothing of particular importance had ever happened.

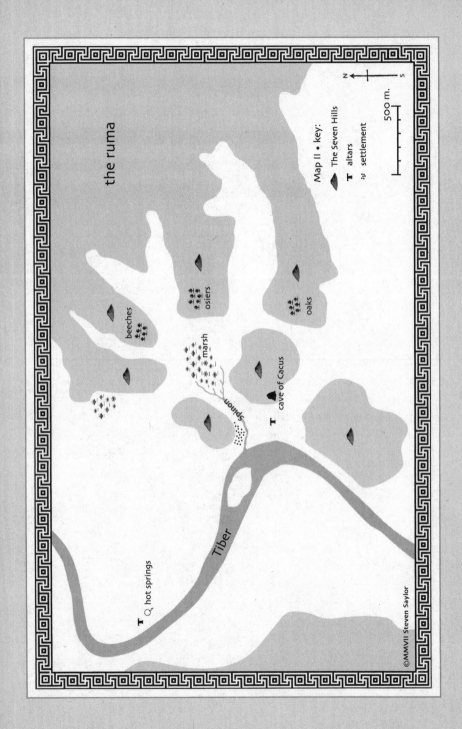

the ruma

Tiber

Spinon

marsh

beeches

osiers

oaks

cave of Cacus

hot springs

Map II • key:
The Seven Hills
altars
settlement

500 m.

N
S

©MMVII Steven Saylor

A DEMIGOD PASSES THROUGH

850 B.C.

It seemed to Cacus that, once upon a time, he had been human.

Cacus had been born in a village high in the mountains. Like the others in the village, he possessed two arms and two hands, and he walked upright on two feet. Clearly, he had not been born an animal, like the timid sheep or the wild wolves, but a human being.

But Cacus had always been different from the others. They walked with an even gait; Cacus shambled, because one of his legs was too short and oddly bent. The others could stand tall and straight with their arms at their sides; Cacus's back was hunched and his arms mismatched. His eyes were sharp, but there seemed to be something wrong with his mouth; he never learned to speak, and could make only a garbled noise which sounded like "cacus"; it was from this noise that he acquired his name. His face was grossly misshapen; another child once told him that a potter made his face out of clay, then threw it down and stepped on it.

Few people ever looked at him directly. Those who knew him looked away out of pity; strangers drew back in fear. His deformities should have marked him for death in the hour of his birth, but his mother had contrived to spare him, pleading that the infant's prodigious size—he was so big that she very nearly died in bearing him—was a promise of future strength. She had been correct. While still a child, Cacus grew to be bigger and stronger than even the biggest, strongest man in the village.

When that happened, the villagers who had pitied him began to fear him.

Then came the Hunger.

The winter was dry and cold. The spring was dry and hot. The summer was drier and hotter still. Streams dwindled to a trickle, then to nothing. Crops withered and died. The sheep could not be fed. When it seemed that things could not become worse, one night the mountain shook so severely that some of the huts collapsed. Not long after that, black clouds came from the west; they promised rain, but sent down only lightning bolts. A lightning strike started a fire that swept across the mountainside and destroyed the hut in which the grain was stored.

The villagers turned to the elders for advice. Had things ever gone so badly before? What could be done?

One of the elders recalled a similar time from his childhood, when the number of villagers had grown too large and a series of bad years led to hunger and desperation. There was a ritual handed down from a time before his birth, called the rite of sacred spring. A pact was made with the great numina of the sky and the earth: If the village could survive the winter, then, when spring came, a group of children would be driven away from the village, sent forth to survive in the world beyond as best they could.

It seemed a harsh remedy, but times were harsh. The elders advised that there must be a rite of sacred spring. The villagers agreed.

The number of children to be sent away was decided by portent. On a still day, the elders climbed up to a stone promontory on the mountainside above the village. There they set fire to a bundle of dry branches, then stood back and waited until the rising smoke formed a column in the air, so that the sky was separated into two regions, one to either side of the smoke. The elders watched the sky and counted the number of birds that flew from one region to the other, crossing the line defined by the smoke. By the time the branches burned to ashes and the column of smoke dispersed, seven birds were seen to cross. Seven children had to be chosen.

The choosing was done by lottery. It was important that everyone in the village could see that the numina of chance, not the scheming of any parent, dictated the outcome. While everyone in the village watched, the children stood in a line. A pot full of small pebbles, all white except for seven black ones, was passed before them. One by one, the children reached inside and took a pebble. When all of them were done, together they opened their palms to show the stone they had chosen. When it was seen which children had chosen the black pebbles, there was much weeping; but when Cacus's claw of a hand opened to show a black pebble, even his mother seemed relieved.

That winter was milder than the year before. Despite hunger and hardship, no one in the village died. It seemed that the rite of sacred spring had placated the numina and preserved the village. When spring came, and the first buds opened on the trees, it was decided that the children must set out.

According to the ritual, an animal would guide the children to their new home. All the elders agreed on this, but none of them could quite remember how this animal was to be chosen. The eldest among them said that the animal would make itself known, and sure enough, the night before the children were to set out, several of the elders had a dream in which they saw a vulture.

The next morning, the seven children were taken from their homes. The other children and all the women of the village were shut away; from the huts, their weeping could be heard all over the mountainside. The elder with the keenest eyes climbed up to the promontory and watched. At last he gave a shout and pointed to the southwest, where he saw a vulture circling just above the horizon.

The men took up cudgels. Beating drums and shaking rattles, the elders led them in a chant meant to summon their courage and harden their hearts. The chant grew faster and faster, louder and louder. At last, screaming and brandishing their cudgels, they ran toward the seven children and drove them from the village.

The days after that had been very hard. Each morning the children searched the sky for a vulture. If they saw one, they headed toward it. Sometimes the vulture led them to carrion that was still fit to eat; sometimes it led them to a carcass so foul that even the vulture would not touch it. Desperation taught them to hunt and fish and to sample every plant that might be edible; even so, on many days, the children went hungry. Cacus was too clumsy to be of much use as a hunter, and the others resented him because he needed more to eat. But he was the strongest by far, and when predators howled at night, it was to Cacus that the others looked for protection.

The first to die was a girl. Faint from hunger, she fell from a high place and struck her head. The children debated what they should do with her body. It was not Cacus who suggested the unthinkable, but another boy. The rest agreed, and Cacus did as the others did. Was that when he began to become something that was not human, when he first ate human flesh?

Little by little, their wanderings took them to the lower lands to the south and west of the mountains. Here the land offered more game and the rivers more fish, and the plants were more fit to eat. Still, they were hungry.

The next child to die was a boy with an injured foot. When the children came upon a bear and scattered in panic, the boy lagged behind. The bear caught him and mauled him badly, then lumbered off when Cacus came running back, screaming and brandishing a branch. The boy was already dead.

When the children ate that night, it seemed only proper that Cacus should have the largest portion.

Summer passed, and still they found no home. One of the children died after eating a mushroom. Another died after several days of sickness and fever. Despite their hunger, the survivors feared to eat the bodies of those who had died of poison or fever, and so they buried them in shallow graves.

Only Cacus and two others remained. That winter was unusually bitter and cold. Trees shivered naked in the wind. The earth turned as hard as stone. The animals vanished. Even the most skillful hunter would have found it impossible to survive without the desperate solution to which Cacus resorted.

Was that when the change occurred in Cacus—when he decided not to wait for a fall or a bear, or some other chance event? Instead, he did it himself. He did what he had to do, and for the most basic reason: He needed to eat. But he did not act rashly. He did not kill them both at once. First he killed the stronger one, and let the weaker one live a little longer. More than once, that child, his final companion, tried to escape from him. Cacus waited as long as he could, until his hunger was so great that no man could have endured it. He waited because he knew, as soon as the other child was gone, that the only thing worse than hunger would follow: loneliness.

Spring came. Cacus was alone. At night he could not sleep, but lay awake listening to the sounds of the wilderness, entering more and more into a world bereft of human reason.

He continued to wander. Eventually he encountered travelers, and came upon villages, but no humans would have anything to do with him. They feared him, and rightly so; more than once, he stole a child and ate it. When that happened, the humans pursued Cacus. A few times they came close to capturing him, but always Cacus escaped and left the hunters behind, their bones picked clean. Surviving in the wild had taught him cunning and stealth. Physically, no man was his match; Cacus had grown bigger and stronger than any man he had ever seen.

The wheel of the seasons passed again and again. Cacus survived the dry summers and the harsh winters, always alone, always wandering.

One day, he saw a vulture cross the sky. The season was early spring. The green of the earth and the soft warmth of the air stirred in his mind a dim recollection of the beginning of his journey. He set about following the vulture.

Eventually, he found himself on a path beside a river. Around a great bend in the river, he saw ahead of him a region of hills, and beyond one of the hills, a plume of smoke. He lost sight of the vulture, but decided that the path he was following was as good as any other. Paths led to villages; in villages, there was food to be stolen. This time, he told himself, he would stay hidden and go raiding only at night. The longer he could go without being seen, the longer it would be before the villagers ran him off.

Suddenly, Cacus felt a great sadness. Once he had lived in a village himself. The others had sometimes teased and taunted him, but they had accepted him as one of their own, despite the fact that he was so different. Then they had driven him off. Why? Because the earth and the sky themselves demanded it; that was what his mother had told him. Before he left the village, he had never harmed anyone, yet the world and everything in it had become his enemy. The sadness he felt swelled inside him and turned into rage.

He rounded a corner and saw ahead of him a young girl on the path. She was carrying a basket of clothes, heading to the river. Her hair was golden, and around her neck, suspended from a simple strip of leather, was a small amulet made of gold that flashed in the sunlight. The girl saw him and screamed. She dropped her basket and ran away.

Furious, suddenly weeping, he ran after her, shouting his name: "Cacus! Cacus!"

He followed her only a short distance, for up ahead, he saw the first signs of a settlement. Wishing he could disappear, he stepped off the path, into the brush. From the settlement, he could hear the girl still screaming, then the shouts of others as they ran to her side, asking what she had seen.

What *had* the girl seen, when she looked at him? Not a human like herself, that was certain. And not an animal, either; no animal, except perhaps a snake, inspired such revulsion and fear. It was a monster she saw. Only a monster could wrench such a scream from the girl's throat.

He had become a monster. When had this happened? It seemed to Cacus that, once upon a time, he had been human. . . .

The settlement by the river started as a trading post. Traffic along the river path, and up and down the route used by the metal traders, had increased to such an extent that there always seemed to be people coming and going through the region of the Seven Hills. It was an enterprising descendent of Po and Lara who hit upon the idea of settling permanently at the crossroads and setting up a marketplace for the exchange of goods. Why should the salt traders transport their salt all the way to the mountains, when they need bring it only as far as the trading post, exchange it there for the goods they wanted, then head back to the mouth of the river for more salt?

A place that had been a crossroads became a destination and, for the handful of settlers at the trading post, a home. By acting as middlemen and providing accommodations for travelers, the settlers thrived.

The settlement of twenty or so huts was located at the foot of a steep cliff, where a broad, flat meadow beside the river offered easy access to the path and provided plenty of space for setting up the market. A seasonal stream, called the Spinon, cut through the meadow and emptied into the river, which men now called the Tiber.

The huts were round with a single large room, made of intertwined twigs and branches daubed with mud, with peaked roofs made of rushes and reeds. For a doorway, sturdy upright poles, in some cases elaborately carved, supported a wooden lintel; a flap of stitched animal skins provided a covering for the doorway. The huts, furnished with simple pallets for sitting or sleeping, were intended strictly for shelter from the elements or for privacy. All cooking and most social activities took place outside.

The marketplace, on the other side of the Spinon and nearer the river, consisted of a few thatched sheds for storing salt, pens for livestock, and an open area where traders could park their wagons and carts and offer their goods for sale. The livestock included oxen, cattle, swine, sheep, and goats. On any given day, the various commodities might include dyed wool, fur rugs, hats made of straw or felt, bags made of leather, clay vessels, woven baskets, combs and clasps made from tortoiseshell or amber, bronze ornaments and buckles, and axes and ploughshares made of iron. There were pine nuts from the mountains, crayfish from the river, succulent frogs from the marshy lake, pots of honey, bowls of cheese, pitchers of fresh milk, and, in season, chestnuts, berries, grapes, apples, and figs. Some of the traders arrived at regular intervals and became old friends to the settlers and to each other, but new faces were always appearing, men from far away who had heard of the trading post and were eager to see for themselves the variety of goods to be found there.

The trading post was also a place to exchange news and gossip, to hear stories from faraway places, and to listen to traveling singers. Men who knew magic passed through, offering their services. Some could cure the sick or make a barren woman fertile. Some could see the future. Some could commune with the numina that animated the nonhuman realm.

By far the most exotic visitors to the settlement were the traders who arrived by boat, paddling upriver from the sea, where they arrived on larger ships, which they left moored at the mouth of the Tiber. Those huge, splendid ships—some of the settlers had once made a journey downriver to look at one—carried the traders up and down the coast and even, so they

claimed, across the great sea. These seafarers called themselves Phoenicians. They spoke many languages, wore brightly colored clothes and finely
wrought jewelry, and brought with them extraordinary things to barter,
made in unimaginably distant lands, including small images of men, made
of metal or clay. At first, misunderstanding, the settlers thought that numina
lived in the images, just as numina lived inside trees and rocks, though the
idea that a numen would reside in even the most splendid man-made object seemed to many of them far-fetched. The Phoenicians tried to explain
that an idol did not house a numen, but stood as a representation of something called a god; but this concept was too abstract for the settlers to
follow.

The latest descendent in the line of Po and Lara was a girl called Potitia,
daughter of Potitius. Growing up at the trading post, Potitia had been allowed from earliest childhood to roam the surrounding countryside. For a
long distance upriver and down, she knew every steep embankment and
muddy beach along the riverbank. She had waded across the Tiber when it
was low, and had swum across when it was high.

She had also explored the Spinon, which ran in front of the settlement,
following it up through a little valley flanked by steep hillsides to its
source, a marshy lake surrounded by hills. The marsh teemed with living
creatures—frogs, lizards, dragonflies, spiders, snakes, and all sort of birds.
It was exhilarating to see a flock of startled geese take flight from the reeds,
or to watch the swans make circles in the sky before landing on the water
with effortless grace.

As she grew older, Potitia's explorations had taken her farther and farther from the settlement. One day, venturing upriver, she had discovered
the hot springs. Greatly excited, she had run all the way home to tell the
others, and was chagrined to learn that her father already knew about the
springs. Where did the bubbling water come from? Potitius said it flowed
up from a fiery place deep underground. Curious, Potitia had searched all
around the hot springs for an entrance to the underworld, but had never
found one. On one occasion, the hot springs dried up, but then returned.
Alarmed that such a thing might happen again, the settlers decided to
build an altar at the springs, and to make offerings to appease the fiery numina in the earth. Potitius had built the altar himself, using oxen to drag a

large stone to the spot, then chiseling the stone into a shape that seemed suitable to him. Once a year, an offering of salt was spread upon the altar, then scattered over the hot springs. So far, they had not run dry again.

As her explorations took her outward from the village, so they also took her upward. The first of the Seven Hills which Potitia conquered was the one directly behind her family's hut. On the side that faced the settlement, the hill presented a sheer cliff that was impossible for even the most determined child to climb, but on the far side of the hill, by trial and error, Potitia discovered a route that led all the way to the top. The view was astounding. Circling the crest of the summit she could look down on the marshy lake, on the settlement below, and on the region of the hot springs, which she now could see were situated at the edge of a large plain that lay in an elbow of the Tiber. Gazing beyond these familiar places, she realized that the world was much vaster than she had previously imagined. The river stretched on in either direction for as far as she could see. Wherever she looked, the impossibly distant horizon faded to a smudge of purple.

One by one, Potitia conquered all the Seven Hills. Most of them were bigger than the one closest to home, but were easier to climb, once you knew the best place to begin the ascent and which route to take. Each hill had something to distinguish it. One was covered with a beech forest, another was crowned with a ring of ancient oaks, another was populated by osier trees, and so on. The hills had not yet been given individual names. Collectively, for longer than anyone could remember, men called them the Seven Hills. More recently, a visitor passing through had jokingly referred to the region as the *ruma,* which was the same word men used to refer to a woman's breasts, or the teats of a cow, and now, as often as not, *ruma* was the word people used for the hilly region. To the settlers, it seemed perfectly natural to liken the features of the earth to the parts of a body.

In a cliff directly across from the settlement, beyond the meadow on the far side of the Spinon, Potitia had discovered the cave. Situated in a cleft of the steep hill and concealed by scrubby bushes that clung tenaciously to the rocks, the mouth of the cave was hard to discern from the ground directly below; it might have been nothing more than a shadow cast by a lip of rock. Through trial and error, Potitia determined that it was impossible to climb down to the cave from above. Climbing up from below would require considerable skill and daring. Her first few attempts over the course of a summer resulted in one nasty fall after another, and repeated scoldings from her mother, who disapproved of Potitia's scraped hands, bloody knees, and torn tunics.

Eventually, Potitia discovered a way to reach the cave. When she stepped inside for the first time, she knew that all her efforts had been worthwhile. To a child's eyes, the space seemed enormous, almost as big as her family's hut. She sat upon an outcropping of rock that formed a natural bench, and rested her arm on a ledge that provided a shelf. The cave was like a house made of stone, just waiting for her to claim it. Unlike the hot springs, the cave was unknown to the others at the settlement. Potitia was the first human being ever to set foot in it.

The cave became her secret haven. On hot summer days she escaped there to take a nap. On wet winter days she sat inside, comfortable and dry, and listened to the rain.

As Potitia grew older, roaming the woods and exploring the *ruma* grew less important to her. She became more interested in learning the skills her mother could teach her, such as cooking and weaving baskets from the reeds that grew around the marsh. Her mother told her that she should begin to consider which of the boys in the settlement she might wish to marry; by various signs, Potitia's body had begun to manifest the advent of her womanhood.

To celebrate her maturity, Potitia's father gave her a precious gift. It was an amulet made of the yellow metal called gold.

For ten generations, the lump of gold which Tarketios had given to Lara had been left in its natural state; nothing had been fashioned from it, for the metal seemed too soft to be properly worked. It was a visiting Phoenician who had shown Potitia's grandfather that gold could be alloyed with another precious metal called silver, and for a great price the Phoenician smith had crafted the resulting ingot into a shape specified by Potitia's grandfather. By the highest Phoenician standards, the workmanship of the amulet was crude, but to Potitia's eyes, it was a thing of wonder. Made to be hung upon a leather necklace, the little amulet was in the shape of a winged phallus. Her father called it Fascinus—bringer of fertility, protector of women and infants in childbirth, guardian against the evil eye.

Although she had questioned her father on the subject and listened carefully to his answers, Potitia could not quite understand whether the amulet actually *was* Fascinus, or contained Fascinus, or only represented Fascinus, in the way that the idols of the Phoenicians were said to represent their gods. Despite her lack of clear understanding, Potitia nonetheless felt very grown-up when she wore the amulet. She was no longer the girl with skinned knees and muddy feet, the child who wandered carefree across the little world of the *ruma*. Even so, she carried within her a child's sense of wonder and the sweet nostalgia of having grown up in a world where there was little to fear and much to discover.

Until very recently, that world had remained unchanged—a place where strangers met in good company and where Potitia might expect to raise her own children with little concern for their safety, allowing them to wander at will, as she had done. But now, all that had changed. The world had become dark and dangerous. Families kept their children always in sight. Even grown men did not dare to wander alone across the *ruma*.

The coming of the monster Cacus had changed everything.

It was Potitia who had seen him first, that day she headed down to the river to wash a basket of clothes. At the sight of him, she screamed, dropped the basket, and fled. The creature ran after her, making a hideous noise that made the hair rise on the back of Potitia's neck: "Cacus! Cacus!"

Just when her energy flagged and he might have caught her, the monster gave up the chase. Potitia reached the settlement unharmed. She was convinced that Fascinus, and Fascinus alone, had saved her. All the way back to the village, she ran with one hand at her throat, grasping the amulet tightly, begging for Fascinus's protection, whispering aloud, "Save me! Save me, Fascinus!" Afterward, trembling with relief, she whispered again to the amulet, giving it her thanks and pledging her devotion. It was a prayer that Potitia uttered, in just such a manner as the Phoenicians would have understood, made not to a nameless numen that inhabited a thing or place, but to a powerful, superhuman entity that possessed the intelligence to understand her words. She had not offered ritual propitiation to a numen, but had prayed directly to a god. In that moment, although Potitia acted with no idea of the significance of what she had done, Fascinus became the first native god to be worshiped in the land of the *ruma*.

For a long time, no one but Potitia had seen the monster, and there were those in the settlement, listening to her description of Cacus, who thought that she must have imagined the encounter on the path. Her family, after all, were known for their fanciful beliefs, showing off the amulet they called Fascinus and hinting that their line had sprung from the union of a numen and a woman—as if such a thing were possible!

Then, little by little, it became evident that some malicious creature was indeed among them. Bits of food went missing, along with small objects that no one had cause to steal. Now and again, objects of value were found broken—a spinning wheel, a clay pot, a toy wagon made of wood—as if some overgrown, immensely strong child smashed them out of spite. The troublemaker struck at night and left no trail; Cacus had grown skillful at covering his tracks.

The settlers were angry and frightened. Their fear of the monster was compounded by another: that the traders who came to the market would learn about Cacus and be frightened away. If traders stopped coming, the settlers would lose their livelihood, and the settlement might vanish altogether.

One morning, during the busiest cattle market of the year, everyone in the settlement was awakened by a lowing among the cattle. Outside the pen, a cow was found dead, its body torn open and much of the flesh missing. The cow could not have climbed over the fence, and the gate remained shut. What sort of man could possess the strength to lift a cow up and over the rough-hewn fence, and then to kill the beast and tear it open with his bare hands? A thrill of panic ran through the settlement. Some of the cattle-traders rounded up their herds and drove them homeward at once.

Armed with knives and spears, hunting in pairs, the settlers combed the Seven Hills. Two of the hunters must have found the monster. Their bodies were eventually discovered on the hill of the osier trees, broken and eviscerated, much as the cow's body had been.

It did not take long for word to spread up and down the trails that led to the *ruma*: The monster that was stalking the trading post had an appetite for human flesh. Traders did not merely stop doing business at the settlement; they made great detours to avoid passing anywhere near it.

With most of the traders gone and traffic so greatly reduced on the trails, the monster grew even bolder. An infant went missing. Her remains were found only a short distance from the settlement, at the foot of the steep hill on the far side of the Spinon. One of the searchers, looking up to avert his eyes from the horrible sight, glimpsed a movement on the hillside above. From behind a bramble-covered lip of stone, a hideous face peered down for a moment, then disappeared. A moment later, a shower of rocks rained down on the searchers, who fled. Peering up at the hillside from a safe distance, they discerned what appeared to be a cave, its opening obscured by brambles. None of them could see a way to scale the hillside. Even if it could be scaled, none of them could imagine what would await them once they reached the mouth of the cave.

Back at the settlement, the searchers told what they had discovered. To her horror, Potitia realized that the monster had taken up residence in her secret cave, which was a secret no longer.

From his hole high up in the side of the hill, Cacus ventured out at night to terrorize the settlement. During the day, he stayed hidden in the cave.

More than once, the settlers attempted to scale the hillside and attack him in his lair. Bellowing his name, Cacus dropped stones on them. One settler fell and broke his neck. Another was struck in the eye and blinded. Another managed to draw closer to the mouth of the cave than anyone else, but was killed instantly by a stone that struck his forehead. Instead of falling, his limp body became caught on sharp rocks and brambles. No one dared to climb up and retrieve it. There it hung for several days and nights, a horrifying rebuke to those who had sought to destroy the monster. One morning, the body was no longer there. Cacus had claimed it. The man's bones, picked clean, appeared one by one at the foot of the hill as Cacus tossed them out.

It was Potitius who suggested that the hillside be set afire. If the flames and smoke did not kill the monster outright, they might at least drive him from his lair. The brambles at the foot of the hill were set on fire. The flames spread upward, heading directly for the cave. Then a wind blew up from the Tiber and drove the flame this way and that. Embers spiraled high in the air, blew across the Spinon, and ignited the thatched roof of a hut. The flames spread from hut to hut. The settlers worked desperately to douse the flames with buckets of water from the river. When the fire at last burned itself out, the face of the hillside was scorched and black, but the cave was untouched and the monster unharmed.

❈

It was decided that a watch should be set upon the cave, so that, if the monster descended, an alarm could be raised. Men and boys took turns throughout the day and night, training their eyes upon what little could be seen of the mouth of the cave from below.

One of Potitia's cousins, a burly, hotheaded youth named Pinarius, boasted to her that he would put an end to Cacus once and for all. Caught up in his enthusiasm, Potitia confessed to her cousin that she had climbed to the cave many times. Scarcely believing her, Pinarius nonetheless accepted her explanation of how it could be done.

On the afternoon that it was his turn to keep watch on the cave, Pinarius decided to act. The day was hot and the air was heavy with sleep. The rest of the settlers dozed, except for Potitia, who knew of her cousin's plan and gave him a kiss for luck before he began the climb.

From above, there came a faint noise that they took to be the sound of the monster snoring. Perhaps it was the buzzing of flies, drawn to the cave by blood and gore. Potitia remembered summer afternoons when she had dozed in the shadowy coolness of the cave. She could picture the monster asleep in that familiar, beloved place. The image made her shiver, yet it also pierced her with a sadness that she could not explain. For the first time she wondered where the monster came from. Were there others of his kind? Surely a mother had given birth to him. What fate had led him to the *ruma,* to become the most wretched of all living things?

Pinarius made the ascent quietly and quickly, but as he drew close to the cave he reached for a handhold that would have taken him in the wrong direction. Watching from below, Potitia corrected his course with a loud whisper.

The sound that might have been the monster's snoring abruptly stopped. Potitia felt a shiver of dread.

Pinarius reached the mouth of the cave. He pulled himself onto the lip of stone, gained his balance, and grinned down at her. He pulled out his knife and showed her the blade, then disappeared into the cave.

The scream that followed was like nothing she had ever heard, so loud that it woke every sleeper in the village. A rending noise followed, then silence. A few moments later, Pinarius's head came flying from the hole in the hillside. It landed with a thud in the grass just beyond Potitia, who fell to the ground in a faint. Dazed, with the sun in her eyes and swooning from the heat, she looked up and saw Cacus standing on the lip of stone high above, staring down at her. His hulking, misshapen body was covered with blood and gore. The sound that came from his throat—"Cacus? Cacus?"—had a low, urgent, questioning quality, as if he gazed at a thing which fascinated him, from which he desired a reply.

"Cacus?" he uttered again, cocking his head and staring down at her.

Potitia scrambled to her feet. Running blindly, she tripped over the head of Pinarius. She gave a shriek and staggered back to the settlement, weeping.

The death of Pinarius drove many of the settlers to the limit of their endurance. His father, also named Pinarius, argued that the time had come to abandon the settlement. The monster had inflicted great suffering, and against him they were powerless; but more than this, the arrival of the creature had unleashed a great evil in the land of the *ruma*. The numina all around them had turned against the settlers. The worst of the misfortunes had been the burning of the huts by treacherous winds and flames, but there had been many other, smaller misfortunes in recent days. The settlers must move on, argued the elder Pinarius. The only questions to be debated were when and to where, and whether they should stay together or go their separate ways.

"If we leave, cousin, what will keep the monster here?" asked Potitius.

"I think he'll follow us. He'll stalk us on the trail. Our children will be his prey."

"Maybe," acknowledged Pinarius. "But in the open, away from his cave, we might at least have a chance to kill the thing."

Potitius shook his head. "This creature is a far more skillful hunter than any of us. We'd have no chance against him in the wild. One by one, he would take us."

"That's what he's doing now!" Pinarius wept, grieving for his son.

The argument was not settled, but it seemed to Potitia that it was only a matter of time until Pinarius would prevail. The *ruma* had become a place of sadness and despair. Still, it broke her heart to think of leaving the hills of her childhood.

Then the stranger arrived.

It was the lowing of oxen that woke Potitia that morning. There had been no oxen in the market for a long time. At first, she thought she must be dreaming of the old days before the coming of Cacus. But as she stirred and rose, the sound of the oxen continued. She hurried from the hut to see what was happening.

Sure enough, a small herd of oxen was standing in the slanting sunlight in the meadow on the far side of the Spinon, peacefully eating the grass that grew near the foot of the hill where Cacus dwelled. Near the herd, sitting on the ground and leaning against a tree trunk, was the ox-driver. His eyes were closed and his head was tilted to one side; he appeared to be asleep. Even at a glance, and at such a distance, Potitia was quite certain she had never seen him before. For one thing, he was much larger than any other man she had ever seen, except Cacus, if Cacus could be called a man. Unlike Cacus, he was not at all ugly or frightening to look at. Indeed, he was quite the opposite. She found herself crossing the steppingstones that traversed the Spinon and walking toward him.

"Potitia! What are you doing?" Her father, along with most of the other settlers, had gathered near the empty cattle pen. They were watching the stranger from a safe distance, trying to decide whether he should be approached, and who should do it. Potitia realized that they were afraid of the stranger, but she did not share their fear.

As she stepped closer, she saw that his mouth was slightly open, and she heard him softly snoring. His hair was long and black. His beard was thick. Everything about him was oversized. His strong, rugged face was a match for his brawny shoulders and arms. Potitia decided that he was by far the most handsome man she had ever seen, even though he looked slightly ridiculous, sitting there snoring.

Over his shoulders he wore a pelt of some sort, tied across his chest by the animal's forelegs. The fur was a tawny gold, and the paws were tipped with formidable claws. Potitia realized that it was the pelt of a lion, and she regarded the stranger with even greater curiosity.

He must have sucked in a flying insect, for suddenly he bolted forward, instantly awake. He made a face and spat convulsively. The group gathered across the stream let out a collective gasp of alarm, but Potitia laughed. To her, the ox-driver looked more ridiculous—and more appealing—than ever.

He picked a fly from his mouth, gave a shrug, then looked up at her and smiled.

Potitia sighed. "You can't stay here."

He frowned.

"Your oxen aren't safe here," she explained.

His gaze was uncomprehending. Could it be that he had not heard of Cacus? He must have come from very far away, she thought. When he spoke, her suspicion was confirmed. She could not understand a word he said.

A dog that had been lying near the oxen rose to its feet and ambled toward them, wagging its tail. The ox-driver shook his head. He wagged his finger at the dog and said something in a gently chiding tone. Clearly, it was the dog's job to wake him if anyone approached the oxen while he was sleeping, and the dog had not done its duty.

The ox-driver stood and stretched his massive arms above his head. He was even taller than Potitia had thought. Craning her neck to look up at him, she felt very small, like a child. Unconsciously, she reached to her throat and touched the gold amulet. The ox-driver gazed at Fascinus for a moment, then looked into her eyes. His gaze stirred certain feelings in her, and Potitia knew that she was not a child any longer but a woman.

※

Try as they might, the settlers seemed unable to communicate to the stranger the peril he faced by staying in the meadow so near the cave of Cacus. They pointed, they mimed, they spoke in all the various dialects they had learned from traders. The man did not understand.

"I'm not sure he has all his wits," said Potitia's father.

"We shall wake tomorrow to find his dead body lying at the foot of the hill," grumbled Pinarius.

"What terrible things to say! I think you're both wrong," said Potitia. She smiled at the ox-driver, who smiled back.

Pinarius exchanged a sidelong glance with his cousin and lowered his voice. "On many important things we disagree, Potitius, but I think one thing is evident to us both. Your daughter is smitten by this stranger."

"He *is* impressive," said Potitius, looking the man up and down. "How do you think he came by that lion's skin he wears? If Potitia finds him suitable—"

Pinarius shook his head and spat. "It shall come to grief. Mark my words!"

※

The afternoon became sweltering as the midsummer sun beat down upon the *ruma*. A warm breeze, smelling of mud and decay, rose from the marshes and followed the Spinon down to the Tiber. The droning of cicadas filled the meadow, where the oxen lay dozing in the shade.

As the settlers believed there were numina in places and objects, so they also believed that numina informed certain phenomena, such as sleep. Like other numina, those of sleep could be friendly or unfriendly. Sleep could heal the weary and the sick and give comfort to the grieving. Sleep could also render even the strongest man utterly helpless.

That afternoon, the numina of sleep descended upon the settlement like a hand upon the brow of an infant, shutting the eyes of the settlers whether they wished to close them or not. Men fought to stay awake, and lost the battle without even knowing it.

The oxen slept. The dog slept. The ox-driver also slept, leaning back against the tree where Potitia had first seen him.

Potitia did not sleep. She sat in the shade of an oak tree and studied the stranger, wondering what the future might hold for her.

There was another who did not sleep. With his long arms and immense strength, Cacus had found a way to climb down from the cave that even Potitia did not know about. Brambles kept him hidden at almost every point as he descended. If he exercised great stealth and did not cause a single leaf to tremble or a shard of stone to give way underfoot, his movement down the face of the cliff was very nearly invisible. Even if the boy who had been set to watch the cave that day had not been dozing, Cacus probably would have descended unseen.

Cacus was not aware of the coming of the stranger, but he had heard the lowing of the oxen. He had not eaten beast-flesh in many days.

Across the meadow, he caught sight of the oxen. He took no notice of the ox-driver or Potitia. Both were nearby, but both were very still, and obscured by the dappled shade of the trees. He chose the smallest of the oxen and made his way toward it. Not a single twig broke beneath his feet; it was a remarkable thing that a creature so large and ungainly could move so quietly upon the earth. Nonetheless, the ox sensed danger. It swished its tail, rose to its feet, and uttered a low bleat. The beast saw Cacus, took a step back, then froze.

When he reached the ox, Cacus did not hesitate. He clamped his fists together, raised them in the air, and landed a hammer-like blow upon the ox's forehead.

The ox snorted once, shuddered, and fell dead. It struck the earth with a heavy thud. The other oxen stirred and began to mill about. The dog's ears twitched, but he remained asleep.

Potitia, who had just nodded off, gave a start. She opened her eyes and saw that the monster was no more than ten paces away. She sucked in a breath and would have screamed, but her throat was suddenly so tight that no sound would come out.

She jumped to her feet. Her first thought was to wake to the ox-driver, but to do that, she would have to run past the monster. She turned and ran in the other direction, away from the settlement, toward the cave.

Cacus's eye was drawn by the movement. He caught a glimpse of her amid the high grass, and recognized her at once. He ran after her.

His legs were mismatched, but very long and powerful. When it suited him, he could run with incredible speed. The flies that had been buzzing about the oxen followed after him in a swarm, drawn by the odors of blood and rotting flesh that clung to him.

Potitia's foot struck an exposed root and she went flying. Perhaps it was as the elder Pinarius said: All the numina of the *ruma* had turned against them, and even the roots of the trees were conspiring with the monster. What a fool she had been to think that the arrival of the ox-driver was a sign of a better times to come! As she tumbled against the hard, sun-baked earth, she reached up to touch Fascinus at her neck, and whispered a prayer that the monster might kill her swiftly.

But Cacus had no intention of killing her.

The ox-driver slept, dreaming of the faraway land of his childhood. It was a dream of sunshine and warm meadows, lowing oxen and singing cicadas.

Then, in an instant, he was awake.

One of the oxen stood over him, urgently pressing its cold, wet snout against his cheek. The stranger grunted with disgust, wiped his face with the back of his hand, and looked about.

At once he saw the cause of the ox's distress. One of its companions was lying in the grass nearby, utterly still and in a most unnatural position. Where was the dog? He saw it curled up on the grass not far away. The dog yawned, briefly opened its eyes, then shut them again and resettled itself more comfortably.

The ox-driver cursed and jumped to his feet.

He heard a muffled sound that might have been a woman's scream and ran toward it.

What he saw first was a swarm of flies above a depression in the high grass. Then he caught a glimpse of bare, hairy flesh—the hunched back of

Cacus, moving up and down and this way and that. The ox-driver moved forward more cautiously, not sure what sort of man or beast he was approaching. Punctuating the gasps and groans and slavering noises was a curious, guttural sound: Cacus . . . cacus . . . cacus!

Then he heard a sound that chilled his blood—the scream he had heard before, from a woman in great distress.

The ox-driver gave a shout. The hunched back suddenly ceased moving. A face, shockingly hideous, rose above the high grass and peered at him. The creature snarled, gave a cry of indignation—"Cacus!"—then rose to its full height. That the creature was male became evident by the virile member displayed between its legs. Beneath the creature, still hidden by the grass, the woman let out a plaintive sob.

The ox-driver was not used to encountering anything that walked on two legs that was as big as himself; this creature was bigger. Nor had he ever encountered a creature as loathsome to look at as Cacus. Revulsion rose in his throat, and an unaccustomed emotion washed over him—the cold prickle of fear. The lion whose skin he wore he had killed with his bare hands, but a lion seemed a minor menace compared to Cacus.

The ox-driver braced himself and gave another shout, challenging the creature to fight. A moment later, with a deafening roar, Cacus hurtled toward him.

The sheer mass of the creature struck the ox-driver with bruising force, knocking him to the ground. The stench of the creature's breath filled his nostrils. The taste of the creature's foul sweat mingled on his tongue with the bitter flavor of dirt as they tumbled on the ground. The flies that swarmed around the creature buzzed in the ox-driver's ears and flew into his nostrils and eyes, tormenting and distracting him.

With the creature atop him, crushing him, the ox-driver frantically reached for anything that might serve as a weapon. His hand closed on a fallen branch. He swung it with all his might. A shuddering impact ran through his arm as the branch broke against the creature's skull. The piece that remained in his fist was jagged and sharp; he stabbed it against the creature's flank. A scream pierced his ears. Hot blood ran over his hand, causing him to lose his grip on the weapon. The creature bolted up and away from him.

The ox-driver staggered to his feet. He watched the creature pull the shard of wood from his bleeding flesh and cast it aside. For a moment he thought the creature might flee. Instead, Cacus hurtled toward him and knocked him to the ground. The ox-driver managed to wriggle free and scamper back to his feet. A short distance away, amid the high grass, he saw a stone the size of newborn ox, and ran toward it. He surprised even himself when he lifted the stone over his head. He hurled it toward the pursuing Cacus.

Cacus managed to dodge the stone, but only barely; it grazed his shoulder and sent him reeling. Enraged, he picked up an even larger stone and hurled it. The ox-driver dove to one side. The stone struck a towering oak tree and shattered the trunk. The whole tree came crashing to the ground.

Amid a din of creaking and cracking, a host of shrieking birds took flight, and then all was still. The ox-driver struggled to catch his breath. The creature was nowhere to be seen. Had he fled? Was he pinned beneath the branches of the tree? For an instant the ox-driver let down his guard—then he caught a whiff of the creature's stench, and heard the buzzing of flies. He whirled about, and in the next instant felt two hands grip his throat.

Spots swam before his eyes. The meadow grew dim, as if night had suddenly fallen. His head seemed to swell like a bloated wineskin, until he felt sure it would burst.

His struggled to pry Cacus's hands from his throat. The creature's grip was unshakable. The ox-driver sought desperately to gain a purchase with his fingertips, and at last managed to grasp one of Cacus's fingers and slowly bend it backward. He heard the finger snap, and was sickened by the noise, but Cacus held fast. He broke another finger, on the creature's other hand, and another. As a fourth finger snapped, Cacus gave an unearthly scream and relented. His grip was broken.

Before Cacus could escape, the ox-driver deftly slipped behind him and caught the creature's neck in the vise of his elbow. With his other hand he gripped his wrist, tightening the vise. Cacus struggled to draw a breath, but could not. Nor could he wrench the arm away from his throat, for his fingers were broken, his hands useless.

Mustering all his remaining strength, the ox-driver wrenched the creature's head to one side and gave it a hard twist. Cacus's neck was broken. He thrashed and convulsed. The huge weight of his body slipped from the ox-driver's grasp. He tumbled to the ground with his head cocked at an impossible angle and his limbs akimbo.

Utterly exhausted, the ox-driver dropped to his knees, fighting back nausea and gasping for breath. His vision was blurred. Flies buzzed in his ears.

The dog, wide awake now, suddenly arrived at a gallop, barking ferociously and baring his fangs at the sight of the corpse. He pounced atop the limp body of Cacus, stood stiffly upright, perked his ears, and alerted the people of the *ruma* with a long howl of triumph.

In feverish glimpses, Potitia had witnessed the entire struggle.

When the stranger's challenge drew Cacus's attention, she had managed to scramble to her feet and to flee. Stumbling and staggering, she repeatedly looked back. It seemed to her that she saw not two men but two entities greater than human engaged in a fight to the death. She felt the earth shake beneath their stamping feet. She saw them lift stones that no mortal could lift. She saw a great tree fall to the ground, destroyed by their combat. She saw Cacus fall dead, and the ox-driver drop to his knees.

In a daze, she made her way to river. No matter how vigorously she scrubbed her flesh, rubbing until it was red and raw, the stench of the monster clung to her.

When she staggered back to the settlement, no one remarked on the smell. Indeed, they took no notice of her. Learning of the monster's demise, the ecstatic settlers had circled the ox-driver and were loudly praising him, shyly touching him, trying to lift him onto their shoulders and laughing when he proved to be too big and heavy.

No one realized what had happened to Potitia except the ox-driver, who shot her a look of mingled relief and remorse. She herself said nothing about it, not even to her father.

The body of Cacus was dragged a great distance from the settlement. Repeatedly, vultures tried to land upon it. The people drove them off, until the ox-driver made it clear that they should desist and allow the vultures to snatch whatever delicacies they could. When the vultures flew off with Cacus's eyes and tongue, the ox-driver applauded them.

"It seems the fellow has a high regard for vultures," noted Potitius. "And why not? Whenever he sees a vulture, it's probably because another of his enemies is dead!"

Satisfied that the vultures had been propitiated, the people pelted the corpse of Cacus with stones, then set it aflame. A wind from the southwest carried the foul smoke high into the air and away from the *ruma*. The numina of fire and air were seen to be in accord with the people, who could only hope, with the monster's baleful influence removed, that the other numina of the region would again show kindness and favor to them.

That night, there was rejoicing in the settlement. The ox that had been killed by Cacus was butchered. The flesh was roasted for a great feast in honor of the stranger who had delivered them. His hunger was voracious; he ate everything they set before him.

Potitius felt moved to make a speech. "Nothing so terrible as the coming of the monster has ever occurred in living memory. Nothing so wonderful has ever occurred as the monster's destruction. We were on the verge of abandoning this place in despair." Here he looked sidelong at his cousin Pinarius. "Then we were saved by an occurrence which none of us possibly could have foreseen—the arrival of a stranger who was every bit a match for the monster. This is a sign that we were meant to reside always in the land of the *ruma*. Whatever happens, we must have faith that ours is a special destiny. Even in our darkest moments, we must remember that we are guarded by friendly numina of great power."

Wine had always been a rare and precious commodity in the settlement; it had become even more so after the traders stopped coming. Still, the store that remained, mixed with water, was enough to provide a serving to everyone at the feast, with extra portions—unwatered and as much as he could drink, which proved to be a great quantity—for the ox-driver. Encouraged by raucous laughter and shouting, he repeatedly mimed his battle with Cacus, laughing and stumbling around the roasting pit until at last he lay down exhausted and fell into a deep sleep.

The settlers were drunk and stuffed with food. Many had not enjoyed a proper sleep since the coming of Cacus, and they happily followed the stranger into the land of dreams.

All slept—except Potitia, who feared that sleep would bring only nightmares.

She found a spot to herself, away from the others, and lay on a woolen mat beneath the stars. The night was warm and lit by a bright moon. On such a night, when she was girl, she might have climbed up to her cave and slept there, safe and secluded. That could never happen again. The monster had ruined the cave and her memories of it forever.

Potitia hugged herself and wept—then gave a start when she sensed the presence of another. She smelled his breath, heavy with wine. His massive silhouette blocked the moon. She shuddered, but when he knelt and touched her gently, she stopped sobbing. He stroked her brow. He kissed the tears that ran down her cheeks.

He loomed over her, as Cacus had loomed, yet was different in every way. The smell of his body was strong but pleasing to her. Cacus had been brutal and demanding, but the ox-driver's touch was gentle and soothing. Cacus had caused her pain, but the stranger's touch brought only pleasure. When he drew back, fearful that his sheer bulk might overwhelm her, she gripped him like a child might grip a parent and pulled him closer to her.

When the paroxysm of their first coupling passed, for a time she lay quiet and felt utterly relaxed, as if she floated on air. Then she suddenly began to tremble. She shuddered and began to weep again. He held her tightly. He knew she had suffered an ordeal beyond his understanding, and he strove, awkwardly but with exquisite gentleness, to comfort her.

But the cause of her weeping was beyond even Potitia's understanding. She was remembering something she had been trying to forget. At the moment of her utmost loathing and despair—while Cacus was inside her, squeezing and crushing her from all sides—she had looked into his eyes. They were not the eyes of a beast, but of a human like herself. In that instant, she had seen that Cacus was full of more suffering and fear than she could imagine. Amid her loathing and disgust, she felt something else: pity. It stabbed her like a knife. Now, with all her defenses down, she found herself weeping, not because of what Cacus had done to her, but for Cacus himself and the awfulness of his existence.

The next day, when the hung-over settlers awoke, the stranger was gone. So were his oxen and his dog.

Pinarius said that someone should be sent after him, to ask him to return. Potitius argued against this; as the coming of the stranger had been unforeseen, so it had been with his leaving, and the people of the settlement should do nothing to interfere with the comings or goings of their deliverer.

Word of Cacus's demise spread. One by one, the traders began to come back to the settlement. When they heard the tale of the ox-driver, they put forward many notions about who he might have been and where he might have come from.

It was the Phoenician seafarers, the most widely traveled of all the traders, who made the most compelling case. They declared that the ox-driver was the strongman of their own legends, the demigod named Melkart. A demigod, they explained, was the offspring of a god and a human. The settlers were inclined to agree that the stranger had exhibited a strength beyond the merely mortal.

"Oh, yes, the hero who saved you was most certainly Melkart," the Phoenician captain declared. "Every Phoenician knows of him; a few have met him. The fact that he wore a lion's skin proves his identity. The killing of a lion was one of Melkart's most famous exploits; he wears the skin as a trophy. Yes, it was Melkart who killed this monster of yours, most assuredly. You should set up an altar to him, as you set up an altar to the numina who inhabit the hot springs. Surely Melkart did more for you than ever those hot springs did! You should make sacrifices to him. You should pray for his continued protection."

"But how did this . . . demigod . . . come to be here, so far from the lands where he's known?" asked Potitius.

"Melkart is a great traveler. He's known in many lands, by many names. The Greeks call him Heracles. They say his father was the sky god they call Zeus."

The settlers had only a vague notion of who the Greeks might be, but the name Heracles was more pleasing to their ears than Melkart, though the captain's pronunciation of the Greek was a bit garbled. They decided to call the ox-driver Hercules.

As the Phoenician captain had suggested, an altar was erected to Hercules, very near the spot where Potitia had first seen him sleeping. Since the Phoenicians knew more about god-worship than the settlers, they were consulted about the best ways to show honor to Hercules. It was decided that dogs and flies must be kept away from his altar, since, during the battle, his ally the dog had failed him and the flies had fought against him. Vultures he had favored, so it was decided that the vulture would be sacred to his memory. It was also decided that when an offering was made, every part of the sacrificed animal should be eaten, in the way that Hercules himself had exhibited such a hearty and unbridled appetite.

Thus, although Fascinus was the first native god and the first god to receive the prayers of a settler, it was a deity already worshiped in other lands who received the first altar dedicated to a divinity in the land of the *ruma*.

Potitia grew big with child. Her father had suspected that something beyond flirtation might have transpired between his daughter and the stranger, and her pregnancy seemed to confirm his suspicion. Potitius was pleased. According to family legend, long ago an ancestress had experienced intercourse with a numen; Potitia was partly descended from Fascinus, whose amulet she wore. Had the demigod Hercules seen this spark of the otherworldly in Potitia? Was that why he had found her worthy to bear his child? And would that child not be something new and special upon the earth, containing the mingled essence of numen, demigod, and human in his veins? Potitius mused on such ideas, and was pleased.

Potitia fell prey to darker thoughts, for she knew there was an equal chance that the child might have a different father: Cacus. If the thing that came from her womb was a hideous monster, everyone would know her shame. Would they kill the child at once and her as well? Was the thing stirring inside her a god or a monster? She was torn by many emotions. Her father was puzzled and dismayed by her misery.

It was decided to celebrate the very first sacrifice to Hercules not on the anniversary of his arrival, as would later become the custom, but on the day that Cacus had first been seen, in the springtime; thus the first Feast of Hercules could expunge the bitter memory of Cacus's arrival. Potitius and Pinarius squabbled over who should assume the duty of slaying an ox, roasting the meat, and placing the offerings upon the stone altar before consuming them. Finally they decided to share the duty and perform the rites together. The feast would be shared equally by their families.

But on the day chosen for the sacrifice, Pinarius was absent. He had gone to visit relatives at a farm upriver, and had not yet returned. Potitius decided to begin the ritual without him.

Dogs were driven off, and an oxtail whisk was used to banish flies. The ox was sacrificed, butchered, and roasted, and the offering placed upon the altar. A prayer of supplication was chanted, using phrases suggested by the Phoenician captain. Potitius summoned the members of his extended family to share in the feast. "We must eat it all," he told them, "not just the meat, but also the organs and the entrails—the heart, kidneys, liver, lungs, and spleen—for that was the example Hercules set for us with his voracious appetite. To eat these parts of the sacrificed beast is our privilege, and we should begin with them. Here, daughter—to you I give a portion of the liver."

As Potitia ate, she remembered the first time she had seen Cacus, and the prayer she had uttered to Fascinus; she also remembered the terror she had felt when Cacus attacked her, and the gentleness of the man they now called Hercules. She was very near to giving birth, and subject to powerful extremes of elation and despair. She often laughed and wept at the same time. Potitius, watching her, seeing how pale and drawn she was, wondered if his daughter had been too delicate a vessel to receive the seed of a demigod.

The feast was very nearly finished when Pinarius arrived, bringing his family with him.

"You're late, cousin—very late! I'm afraid we proceeded without you," said Potitius. A full belly and a portion of wine, only slightly mixed with water, had put him in good spirits. "I'm afraid we've already finished the entrails, but there are some choice cuts of meat remaining for you."

Pinarius, angry at himself for missing the ceremony, grew furious at this further indignity. "This is an outrage! We agreed that I was to serve equally as a priest of the Altar of Hercules, and that the eating of the entrails was a sacred duty—yet you've left none for me and my family!"

"You were late," said Potitius, his good mood spoiled. "You'll eat what the god left for you!"

Their squabbling grew louder and their words more belligerent. Relatives began to gather behind each man. It seemed that the first sacrifice to Hercules might turn into a brawl.

The argument was suddenly interrupted by a loud cry. It came from Potitia. Her labor had begun.

The delivery took place before the Altar of Hercules, for Potitia was in too much distress to be moved. The labor was short but intense, and there was something not right about it. The baby was too big to come out; the midwives were thrown into a panic. Along with her physical pain, Potitia was in an agony of suspense.

At last the baby emerged from her womb. It was a man-child. Potitia reached for him. The midwives placed him in her arms. He was big, very big, yes—but not a monster. All his limbs were intact, and his proportions were no different from any other baby's. Still, Potitia was uncertain. She gazed into the baby's eyes, as she had gazed into the eyes of Cacus, and also into the eyes of the ox-driver. She could not be sure! The eyes that now gazed back at her might be the eyes of either man.

Potitia did not care. Whoever his father might be, the child was precious to her, and precious to Fascinus. Weak and exhausted, but filled with joy, Potitia lifted the necklace bearing Fascinus over her neck and placed it around the neck of her newborn baby.

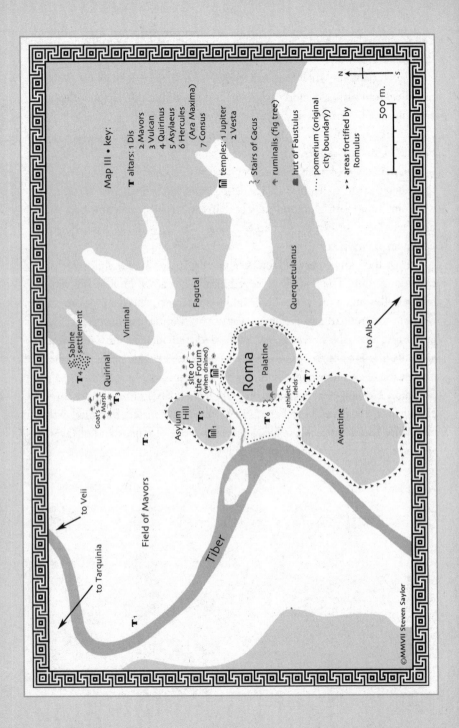

Map III • key:

T altars: 1 Dis
2 Mavors
3 Vulcan
4 Quirinus
5 Asylaeus
6 Hercules
(Ara Maxima)
7 Consus

🏛 temples: 1 Jupiter
2 Vesta

Stairs of Cacus

🌳 ruminalis (fig tree)

hut of Faustulus

...... pomerium (original
city boundary)

▸▸ areas fortified by
Romulus

N
S

500 m.

Sabine
settlement

Quirinal

Viminal

Fagutal

Goat's
Marsh

T₄

T₃

Asylum
Hill

T₅

🏛₁

T₂

site of
the Forum
(when drained)

🏛₂

Roma

Palatine

athletic
fields

T₆

T₇

Querquetulanus

Aventine

to Alba

Field of Mavors

to Veii

to Tarquinia

Tiber

T₁

©MMVII Steven Saylor

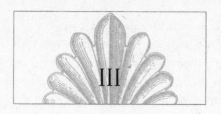

THE TWINS

757 B.C.

The day was an important one for Potitius—the most important day so far in his young life. From infancy, he had been a witness to the ritual. Later, he became a participant in the feast. Now, for the first time, at the age of fourteen, he was assisting his father in performing the annual rites of sacrifice at the Altar of Hercules.

While the assembled family members of the Potitii and the Pinarii watched, Potitius's father stood before the altar and recited the tale of the god's visit, telling how Hercules appeared in the peoples' time of greatest need and killed the monster Cacus, then just as suddenly disappeared. Meanwhile, young Potitius slowly circled the altar and waved the sacred whisk, fashioned of an oxtail with a wooden handle, to drive away any flies that might come near. His distant cousin Pinarius, who was the same age and was also performing for the first time in the ritual, circled the altar in a wider orbit, walking in the opposite direction; his job was to drive away any dog that might come near.

Potitius's father finished the story. He turned to the father of Pinarius, who stood beside him. For generations, the two families had jointly tended to the altar and performed the ceremony, trading duties from year to year. This year, it fell to the elder Pinarius to recite the prayer for Hercules's protection.

An ox was slain and butchered. While it was being roasted, a portion of raw flesh was placed on the altar. The priests and their sons searched the sky. It was young Potitius, with a cry of excitement, who first saw the vulture fly overhead and begin to circle above them. The vulture was favored by Hercules; its appearance was a sign that the god was pleased by the offering and accepted it.

The priests and their families gathered to feast on the ox. In every other matter relating to the ceremony, the families shared precisely equal duties; but, following tradition, the eating of the entrails remained a privilege accorded solely to the Potitii. It had become a tradition as well for the various Pinarii to grumble good-naturedly about this—"Where is our portion? Why are we given no entrails?"—to which their cousins would give the traditional reply: "No entrails for you! You arrived late for the feast!"

Young Potitius took all his duties very seriously. He even attempted to banter with young Pinarius about the entrails, but received only a sullen look and a grunt in reply. The two boys had never been friends.

After the feast, his father took Potitius aside. "I'm proud of you, son. You did well."

"Thank you, Father."

"Only one more ritual remains to complete the day."

Potitius frowned. "I thought we were done, Father."

"Not quite. I think you know, son, although we seldom talk about it—no need to make the Pinarii more jealous of us than they are already!—that our ancestry can be traced back directly to Hercules himself."

"Yes, Father."

"You also know that the ancestors of the Potitii include a god even more ancient than Hercules." He reached up to touch the amulet of Fascinus which hung from a leather strap around his neck.

Potitius could count on his fingers the times he had seen the amulet. His father wore it only on very important occasions. He gazed at it, fascinated by the luster of the gold.

His father smiled. "When I was your age, I took part for the first time in the rites of the Altar of Hercules, doing just as you did today, whisking the flies away. When the feast was done, my father took me aside. He told me that I had done well. On that day, he said, I was no longer a boy, but had become a man. Do you know what he did then, son?"

Potitius gravely shook his head. "No, Father. What did he do?"

In answer, his father raised the leather strap over his head, then solemnly placed it around Potitius's neck. He smiled and ran his hand over his son's silky blond hair, a gesture of affection to seal the last moment of his boyhood.

"You are a man now, my son. I pass the amulet of Fascinus to you."

Potitius might now be a man, but after the feast, when the day's duties were done and he was at last free to do whatever he pleased, he reverted to behaving like a boy. There were many hours of midsummer sunlight remaining. He had promised to visit his two best friends after the feast, and he was eager to join them.

Since the days of Cacus, the little settlement by the Tiber had continued to prosper and grow. The market by the river saw a thriving traffic in salt, fish, and livestock; these three commodities arrived separately, but after being treated with salt, the preserved fish and meat could be transported great distances, or traded for other goods that flowed into the busy market. The oldest and most prosperous families, like the Potitii and the Pinarii, continued to live in the original settlement near the Spinon and the market grounds, in huts not very different from those of preceding generations, though the number of huts had increased greatly and they were now built much closer together. Numerous other, smaller settlements, some consisting of hardly more than a single family, had sprung up across the *ruma,* some in the valleys and some on the hilltops. Well-worn footpaths linked all the settlements together.

The word *ruma* itself, as a reference to the region of the Seven Hills, had changed subtly in pronunciation over the years and by repeated usage had acquired the status of a proper name, so that people now called the area "Roma." The name had a quaintness and a coziness about it, conveying the sense of a hilly place that lovingly nurtured its inhabitants.

With more settlements and more people had come the tendency to formalize the names of various locales amid the Seven Hills, often naming places for the trees which lived there. Thus the hill of oak trees came to be called Querquetulanus—"Oak Hill"—while the hill of osiers was the Viminal, and the hill of beeches was the Fagutal.

Shepherds and swineherds now lived and tended their livestock atop the hill above the old cave of Cacus. That hill was called the Palatine, after the goddess whom the shepherds worshiped, Pales. Of gods, once unknown in Roma, there now were many. As the population of mortals had grown, so had the number of deities, and each of the little communities scattered across the Seven Hills acknowledged a local divinity to whom they paid homage. Some of these divinities retained the nameless, nebulous character of the ancient numina, but others had acquired names and well-defined attributes after the fashion of gods and goddesses. Among these deities, the primacy of Hercules was recognized by everyone in Roma, and thus his altar had come to be called the Ara Maxima, or Greatest of Altars. It was agreed that his father was the sky-god known locally by the name Jupiter. The role of the Potitii and the Pinarii in tending to the Ara Maxima gave them great status among the people of Roma.

Potitius took pride in carrying on his family's traditions; but now, his duties done, he was eager to join his two friends, who lived on the Palatine. He quickly returned to his family's home, a compound of interconnected huts, where he threw off the finely woven woolen robe he had worn for the ceremony and put on an old tunic, more suitable for rough play. He kept the amulet of Fascinus around his neck, for he wanted to show it off to his friends.

Potitius strode through the busy marketplace and crossed a wooden footbridge that spanned the muddy Spinon. He walked past the Ara Maxima, where a few of his wine-befuddled relatives still loitered at the scene of the feast. He continued on to the foot of the Palatine, where he scaled a steep stairway hewn from the rocky hillside. The stairway had been made long ago, after the demise of the monster Cacus, to remove the threat of what had been an inaccessible cave. The hillside was no longer unscalable, thanks to the stairway, and the cave itself, an accursed place, had been filled in with stones and dirt. Brambles and clinging bushes had grown over the spot, so that little trace of the cave remained—nothing more than a bare outline that could be discerned only by someone looking for it. Potitius knew the history of the Stairs of Cacus, as people called the steep trail, and his father had shown him exactly where the cave had been located; whenever he passed it, Potitius uttered a prayer of thanksgiving to Hercules. But the Stairs of Cacus also served a purely practical function; it was the shortest route to the top of the Palatine.

At the top of the Stairs grew a fig tree. It was older than Potitius and, for a fig tree, very large, with branches that formed a wide canopy. After scaling the steps, Potitius welcomed the cool shade offered by its dense foliage. He paused to catch his breath, then gave a cry when something struck his head. The projectile was soft enough to cause no damage to his scalp, but hard enough to sting. Potitius was struck again, and then again.

From above, Potitius heard laughter. Rubbing his smarting head, he looked up and saw his two friends sitting on a high branch, grinning down at him. Remus began to laugh so hard that it appeared he might fall from his perch. Romulus hefted a green, unripe fig in his hand.

"Stop it, you two!" cried Potitius. He saw Romulus cock his arm to hurl the fig. Potitius dodged, but too late. He yelped as the fig struck his forehead. Romulus was known for a sure aim and a strong arm.

"Stop it, I said!" Potitius jumped up and grabbed the end of the branch upon with the brothers were sitting. Using the full weight of his body, he swung back and forth. The soft wood yielded without breaking, and the motion was violent enough to upset the twins from their perches. With shrieks of laughter, they both came tumbling down.

The two of them recovered at once, tackled Potitius, and used their combined weight to pin him down. All three were gasping, barely able to breathe for laughing.

"What's this?" said Romulus. He reached for the amulet of Fascinus and held it up, so that the leather necklace was pulled taut. A shaft of sunlight, piercing the fig leaves, glinted off the gold. His brother joined him in gazing at it.

Potitius smiled. "It's the image of the god we call Fascinus. My father gave it to me, after the feast. He's says that—"

"And where did your father acquire such a thing?" asked Remus. "Stole it from a Phoenician trader?"

"Don't be ridiculous! Fascinus is our family god. My father received this amulet from his father, who received it from his father, and so on, back to the beginning of time. Father says—"

"Must be nice!" said Romulus curtly, no longer laughing but still holding the amulet and gazing at it. Potitius suddenly felt self-conscious, as he sometimes did with his two friends. Potitius came from one of the oldest and most respected families in Roma. Romulus and Remus had been foundlings; the swineherd who had raised them was a man of little account and the swineherd's wife had a bad reputation. Potitius's father disapproved of the twins, and it was only behind his father's back that Potitius was able to associate with them. Potitius dearly loved them both, but sometimes, as now, he acutely felt the difference between their status and his own.

"And what does this Fascinus do?" said Romulus.

Remus laughed. "I know what I'd do, if my manhood had wings!" He flapped his arms, then made a lewd gesture.

Potitius was beginning to regret having worn the amulet. It had been a mistake to think that the twins could understand what it meant to him. "Fascinus protects us," he said.

"Not from flying figs!" said Remus.

"Or from boys who are stronger than you," added Romulus, regaining his high spirits. He released the amulet, reached for Potitius's arm, and twisted it behind his back.

"You are *not* stronger than me!" protested Potitius. "I can take either one of you, as long as you come at me one at a time."

"But why should we do that, when there are two of us?" Remus seized Potitius's other arm and gave it a twist. Potitius yowled in pain.

It was always thus with the twins: They acted in concert, as if they shared a single mind. Their harmony was one of the things that Potitius, who had no brothers, admired most about them. What did it matter if no one knew their lineage?

The infant twins had been discovered by the swineherd Faustulus in the aftermath of a great flood. The Tiber often flooded, but that flood had been by far the worst than anyone could remember. The river had risen so high that it submerged the marketplace. The marshly lake that fed the Spinon became a little sea, and the Seven Hills became seven islands. After the water receded, the swineherd Faustulus had found, among the flotsam, two infants in a wooden cradle on the slope of the Palatine. Many people who lived upriver had died in the flood. Since no one ever claimed the twins, it was assumed that their parents must be dead. Faustulus, who lived only a stone's throw away from the fig tree in a squalid little hut surrounded by pigsties, raised them as his sons.

Faustulus's wife was named Acca Larentia. An unkind joke told behind the twins' backs claimed that they had been suckled by a she-wolf. As a small boy, when Potitius first heard this joke—told with a leer and a wink by his cousin Pinarius—he thought it was literally true; only later did he realize that "she-wolf" was another term for a whore, and thus an insult to Acca Larentia. Pinarius had also told him that the names given to the twins by Faustulus were a rude play on words—Romulus and Remus referring to the two *ruma* of Acca Larentia, whom Faustulus delighted in watching when she suckled both infants at once. Because her favorite place to suckle them was beneath the shade of the fig tree, Faustulus had named it the *ruminalis,* or suckling-tree.

"A vulgar, dirty man, hardly better than the pigs he raises!" That had been the pronouncement of Potitius's father about Faustulus. "As for Acca Larentia, the less said, the better. They're hardly fit to be called parents, the way they let those boys run wild. Romulus and Remus are none the better for it—a pair of wolves, raised in a pigsty!"

But even those who most disapproved of the twins could not deny that they were uncommonly handsome. "Only Romulus is better looking than Remus," went the local saying, in which the names could as easily be reversed. "And only Remus can compete with Romulus," went the response, for the twins were by far the fastest and strongest of all the local boys, and delighted in any opportunity to prove it. To Potitius, it seemed that the twins were everything a boy could wish to be—good-looking, athletic, and unfettered by a father's control. Even when they ganged up to inflict a bit of misery on him, Potitius found it exciting to be in their company.

In unison, the twins released him. Potitius groaned and rubbed his shoulders to relieve the ache.

"So?" said Romulus, looking at his brother. "Should we tell him, or not?"

"You said we should."

"But I'm having second thoughts. He's all high and mighty with his fancy amulet from his father. He looks down on nobodies like us."

"I do not!" protested Potitius. "Tell me what?"

Remus looked at him slyly. "We're hatching a plot, my brother and I. We're going to have some fun. People will talk about nothing else for days afterward."

"Days? Years!" said Romulus.

"And you can join us—if you dare," said Remus.

"Of course I dare to," said Potitius. His shoulders ached so badly he could barely lift his arms, but he was determined to show no pain. "What is this scheme you're hatching?"

"You know what people say about us—what they call us behind our backs?" said Romulus.

Not sure how to respond, Potitius shrugged, and tried not to wince at the pain.

"They call us wolves. Romulus and Remus are a pair of wolves, they say, suckled by a she-wolf."

"People are stupid," said Potitius.

"People are frightened by wolves, that's what they are," said Remus.

"Especially girls," added his brother. "Here, look at this." He reached for something at the base of the fig tree and drew it over his head. It was a wolf's pelt, fashioned so that the head of the wolf fit over his face and formed a mask, leaving his mouth uncovered. "What do you think?"

With his hands on his hips and the face of the wolf taking the place of his own, Romulus presented a fearsome image. Potitius gazed up at him, speechless. Remus produced another pelt, fitted it over his head, and stood beside his brother.

Romulus smirked, pleased by the look of amazement on Potitius's face. "Of course, if it's just Remus and me, everyone will know it's us. That's why there has to be a third wolf in the pack—to throw people off the scent."

"A third wolf?" said Potitius.

Remus tossed something to him. Potitius gave a start but managed to catch it. "Put it on," Remus said.

It was another wolfskin. With trembling hands, Potitius fitted the head over his face. A rank odor filled his nostrils. Looking through the eye-

holes, he felt strangely concealed from the world and curiously transformed.

Romulus smiled. "You look very fierce, Potitius."

"Do I?"

Remus laughed. "But you sound like a little boy. You must learn to
growl—like this." He demonstrated. Romulus joined him. After a moment's hesitation, Potitius did his best to emulate them.

"And you must learn to howl." Remus threw back his head. The sound
that came from his throat sent a shiver up Potitius's spine. Romulus joined
him, and the harmony produced by their baying was so uncanny that Potitius was covered with gooseflesh. But when he himself let out a howl, the
other two broke into laughter.

"Obviously, this will take some practice," said Romulus. "You're not
ready yet. You must learn to howl like a wolf, Potitius. You must learn to
move like a wolf, and to think like a wolf. You must *become* a wolf!"

"And when that day arrives, you must be sure to remove that amulet,"
added his brother. "Otherwise, someone is bound to recognize it and report us to your father."

Potitius shrugged. The pain in his shoulders was gone. "I could always
wear Fascinus inside my tunic, where no one would see."

"Your tunic?" Romulus laughed. "Wolves don't wear tunics!"

"But—what will we be wearing?"

Romulus and Remus looked at each other and laughed, then threw back
their heads and howled.

Winter came before the twins felt that Potitius had sufficiently mastered
the ways of a wolf. It would not do to carry out their scheme when the
weather was cold and wet. They waited until the weather turned warm
again. At last the perfect day arrived—a clear, mild day when everyone
across the Seven Hills would be out and about.

Very early that morning they went hunting. The twins had been tracking a wolf for several days, watching its movements to discover its lair.
Shortly after sunrise They flushed it out and hunted it down. It was Romulus who killed the beast with his spear.

On a makeshift altar—a simple slab of rock—they skinned the wolf and bathed their hands in its blood. They cut the skin into strips and tied these around their wrists, ankles, thighs, and arms. Other strips they carried in their hands. It seemed to Potitius that he could feel the life force of the beast still emanating from the warm, supple hide.

It no longer felt strange to Potitius to run naked across the hills. He had done it many times with Romulus and Remus, though usually at night and away from the settlements. What still felt strange was the mask of wolf hide that covered his face. Peering out the eye-holes, knowing he was hidden, imagining his ferocious appearance—all this gave him a feeling of power and a sense that his relationship to everything around him was changed, as if the mask truly bestowed on him faculties that were other than human.

They ran over the hills and across the valleys, from settlement to settlement, howling and yelping and brandishing their straps. Whenever they encountered a young female, they ran straight toward her, competing to see who could reach her first and give her a smack with his strap. They were the wolves, and the girls might have been sheep; like sheep, most of them were out in groups, going about their morning chores, fetching water or carrying burdens. Some cried out in alarm at the sight of them. Others shrieked with laughter.

Potitius had never done anything so exhilarating in all his life. He became physically aroused. Many of the girls seemed more alarmed by the sight of his swaying sex than by the threat of his wolfhide strap, although some of them seemed amused, tittering behind their hands and averting their eyes. Romulus and Remus, seeing his excitation, converged on him. Laughing and yelping, they took aim at his sex with their wolf-hide straps.

"Too bad you left that amulet at home today," whispered Romulus. "You've no phallus at your neck to protect the one between your legs!"

"Stop trying to cover yourself," said Remus, shaking with laughter. "A good strapping with one of these will make you more potent than ever! You'll have the power of the wolf between your legs!"

At last the twins relented, and the three of them returned to their pursuit of screaming girls.

As the twins had predicted, the incident became the talk of all Roma. That evening, Potitius's father gathered the immediate family—Potitius, his mother, and sisters—to discuss it.

"Three youths, naked except for wolfskins concealing their cowardly faces, running all over the Seven Hills, terrifying everyone they met—such behavior is an outrage!"

"Did no one try to stop them?" said Potitius's mother.

"A few elders dared to berate them for their behavior; the scoundrels ran circles around the poor fellows, howling like animals, scaring them half to death. A few of the younger men gave chase, but the troublemakers outran them."

"But what did they look like, husband? Was there nothing to distinguish them?"

"I didn't see them myself. Did any of you?"

Potitius averted his eyes and said nothing. He nervously bit his lip when one of his sisters, who was a little younger than himself, meekly spoke up. "I saw them, father. I was visiting a friend over on the Viminal when they came tearing through the village, howling and growling."

Her father's face stiffened. "Did they molest you in any way?"

She blushed. "No, Father! Except . . ."

"Speak, daughter!"

"Each of them carried a thing in his hand; I think it must have been a long, narrow strip of wolf hide. They snapped them in the air, like little whips. And they . . ."

"Go on."

"Whenever they came to a girl or a young woman, they struck her with it."

"Struck her?"

"Yes, Father." She blushed more furiously than ever. "On her bottom."

"And did they strike you, daughter—on your bottom?"

"I—I don't really remember, Father. It was all so frightening, I can't recall."

Liar! Potitius wanted to say. He remembered the moment quite clearly. So, he was sure, did his sister. It was Remus who had slapped her bottom, and, far from being frightened, she had run after them, giggling and trying to give Remus's naked bottom a slap in return. Despite his nervousness, Potitius had to force the grin from his face.

Potitius's father shook his head. "As I said, an outrage! What's even more outrageous is the fact that not everyone thinks as we do about this matter."

"What do you mean, Father?" asked Potitius.

"I was just talking to the elder Pinarius. He seems to be amused by the incident! He says it's only the older people who find such behavior scandalous. He says that all the young men envy these savage wolflings, and all the young women admire them. You don't envy them, do you, Potitius?"

"Me? Of course not, Father." Nervously, Potitius touched the amulet at his neck. He had put on the necklace as soon as he returned home that evening, wanting Fascinus to be near him. To be sure, he was not exactly lying to his father; a man could not envy himself.

"And you, daughter—you don't admire these troublemakers, do you?"

"Of course I don't, Father. I despise them!"

"Good. Others may praise these savages, but in this family, there are standards to be upheld. The Potitii set an example for all of Roma. So should the Pinarii, but I fear that our cousins may have forgotten their special standing among the people." He shook his head. "The identities of two of these wolflings is only too obvious—those scoundrels Romulus and Remus. But who was the third wolfling? What innocent youth did the swineherd's boys lure into playing this disgusting game with them?" He stared directly at Potitius, who turned pale. "Do you think, my son . . . do you think it might have been your cousin, young Pinarius?"

Potitius swallowed a lump in his throat. "No, Father. I'm quite sure that it wasn't Pinarius."

His father grunted and gave him a shrewd look. "Very well. Enough of this matter. I have something much more important to discuss. It involves you, my son."

"Yes, Father?" said Potitius, relieved at the change of subject.

The elder Potitius cleared his throat. "As priests of Hercules, we play a very important role among the people. Our judgment in matters of the divine is greatly respected. But there is much that we could still learn when it comes to reading the will of gods and numina. Tell me, my son: When a farmer's well runs dry, whom does he call upon to pacify the spiteful numen that blocked the spring? When a fisherman wants to find a new fishing spot, whom does he call to mark boundaries in the river and say a prayer to placate the water numina? When a bolt of lightning kills an ox, whom does the oxherd consult to determine whether the blasted flesh is cursed and should be consumed by fire upon an altar, or blessed and should be eaten with rejoicing?"

"If they can afford it, people call for an Etruscan diviner—what the Etruscans call a haruspex."

"Exactly. Our good neighbors to the north, the Etruscans, are very wise in the ways of divination—and Etruscan haruspices make a very good living at it. But divination is simply a skill, like any other. It can be taught, and it can be learned. There is a school of divination in the Etruscan town of Tarquinia. I am assured that it is the finest of all such schools. I have arranged for you to study there, my son."

Potitius was silent for a long moment. "But Father, I don't speak Etruscan."

"Of course you do."

"Only enough to barter with Etruscan traders in the market."

"Then you shall learn to speak Etruscan fluently, and then you shall learn all the Etruscans can teach you about divination. When your studies are done, you will return to Roma as a haruspex, and you will become an important man among the people."

Potitius felt torn between excitement and a fear of leaving family and friends. "How long will I be gone?"

"I'm told that your studies will take three years."

"Such a long time! When do I leave, Father?"

"Tomorrow."

"So soon!"

"The sooner the better. As today's incident of the wolflings demonstrated all too clearly, there are bad influences among us. I have every faith in your character, my son. Nonetheless, I think it would be best to remove you from those influences, and the sooner the better."

"But Father, you don't think—"

"I think that Romulus and Remus must be very persuasive young men. I think their harmful influence might draw even the most upstanding youth into serious trouble. It is my duty as your father to see that such a thing does not happen to you, my son. You will go to Tarquinia. You will obey your instructors in all matters. You will master the Etruscan arts of divination. I suspect you have an aptitude for such things, and the learning will come easily to you. And you will think no more about Romulus and Remus. The swineherd's brats are good for only one thing—making trouble. They came from nothing and they shall amount to nothing!"

754 B.C.

About his love of learning and his natural aptitude for divination, Potitius's father proved correct. About the fate of the twins, he could not have been more mistaken.

Potitius had been the first youth to fall under the spell of the twins, but he was not the last. The incident of the wolflings greatly elevated their standing among the restless young men of Roma, many of whom were eager to become their companions. Romulus and Remus soon attracted a considerable following, especially among those whom Potitius's father would have labeled disreputable—young men of obscure family and little means who were not above stealing the occasional cow or shearing a sheep and bartering the wool without its owner's knowledge.

"They shall come to a bad end," declared Potitius's father, glad that his son was away in Tarquinia pursuing his studies. "Romulus and Remus and their little gang think their activities are harmless, that the men they rob are either too wealthy to care or too timid to strike back. But sooner or later, they will cross the wrong man, and that will be the last we see of Romulus and Remus!"

His prediction very nearly came true on the day that Remus and a few companions, venturing farther afield than usual, fell into a skirmish with some shepherds in the vicinity of Alba, a town in a hilly region to the southeast of Roma. Unlike the Romans, the Albans had long ago been subjugated to the strongest man among them, who called himself their king and wore an iron crown. The current king of Alba, Amulius, had accumulated a great store of wealth—precious metals, finely wrought jewelry, exotic clay vessels, and woven goods of the highest quality—which he kept inside a gated compound surrounded by high wooden pickets and guarded by mercenary warriors. He lived not in a hut but in a great hall made of wood.

The cause of the skirmish was later a subject of much debate. Many assumed that Remus and his men were trying to steal some sheep and the Alban shepherds caught them; Remus would later declare that it was the shepherds who picked a fight with his men, taunting them with insults to their manhood and slurs against the people of Roma. Whatever the cause, it was Remus who got the worst of the skirmish. Some of his men were killed, some were captured, and a few managed to escape. Remus himself was taken prisoner, bound with iron chains, and led before King Amulius. Remus's attitude was defiant. The king, who was not used to being crossed, ordered Remus to be hung from a rafter and set about torturing him, using hot irons, sharp blades, and leather whips.

When word of Remus's captivity reached his brother on the Palatine, Romulus set about mustering all the young men of the Seven Hills, calling on them not only to rescue Remus but to defend the pride of Roma. Even men of upstanding families who had never consorted with the twins joined the cause. Knowing the mercenaries of Amulius would be well armed, they gathered whatever weapons they could find—shepherd's crooks that might serve as staves, butchering knives, slingshots, hunter's bows and arrows—and set out.

Before the walls of Alba, Romulus demanded that the king release his brother and the other captives. Amulius, flanked by his mercenaries on the parapet, peered down at the motley band and refused.

"Is it ransom you want?" asked Romulus.

Amulius laughed. "What could the likes of you afford to pay? A few moth-eaten sheepskins? No, when I'm done torturing your brother and his friends, I shall cut off their heads and mount them on this picket wall, as a warning to others of their ilk. And if you're still in my kingdom when morning comes, young fool, your head will end up next to your brother's!"

Romulus and his men withdrew. The height of the pickets which surrounded the king's compound at first daunted them, as did the archers who guarded the wall. There seemed no way to storm the compound without being struck down by a hail of arrows. But that night, under cover of darkness, Romulus managed to set fire to a poorly guarded section of the wall. The fire spread quickly. In the chaos that followed, his men proved braver and more bloodthirsty than the mercenaries of Amulius. The king's guards were slaughtered.

Striding into the great hall, Romulus seized Amulius and demanded to see his brother. The king, shaking with fear, took him to the room where Remus hung in chains, then produced a key and released him from his shackles. Too weak to stand, Remus sank to his knees. While Remus watched, Romulus knocked Amulius to the ground, kicked and beat him until he was senseless, then cut his throat. The king's crown, a simple circle of iron, went rolling across the floor, spun on its edge, and with a clatter came to rest on the floor before Remus.

"Pick it up, brother," said Romulus. "It belongs to us now!"

But Remus, his naked body scarred by burns and cuts, was too weak even to lift the iron crown. Weeping to see his brother in such a state, Romulus knelt before him, picked up the crown, and began to place it on Remus's head.

Then he hesitated. He withdrew the crown from his brother's brow.

"This crown belongs to us both, brother, equally. But only one can wear it at a time. Let me wear it first, so that I can appear before those who fought with me today and show them that the crown of Alba belongs to us now." Romulus put the iron crown on his own head, then rose and strode out to declare victory to his men.

By seizing the treasure of Alba, Romulus and Remus made themselves wealthy men, far wealthier than any other man in all of Roma. When Remus had recovered sufficiently to travel, they returned home in triumph, surrounded by their loyal companions and followed by wagons loaded with booty.

Not everyone in Roma was pleased by their success. The father of Potitius met with the other elders and voiced his doubts. "If Remus was captured by the shepherds of Amulius while trying to steal their sheep, then King Amulius was in his rights to hold him captive, pending a ransom. In that case, Romulus's attack upon Alba was unjustified. His killing of the king was murder, and his seizure of the treasure was theft. Are we to make brigands into heroes?"

The elder Pinarius disagreed. "Was Remus up to no good in Alba? It doesn't matter. After he was taken prisoner, Amulius didn't demand a ransom or restitution; instead, he proceeded to torture Remus, and plainly stated his intention to kill him. To save his brother, Romulus had no choice but to take up arms. Amulius was a fool, and he died a fool's death. The wealth that Romulus seized in Alba is his by right."

"The Albans may not think so," said the elder Potitius. "Such an incident may set off a blood feud that could last for generations. And the twins may have offended the gods, as well. We should consult a haruspex, to determine the will of the gods in this matter."

"Pardon me, while I ask an Etruscan if I can take a piss!" said Pinarius, his voice dripping with sarcasm.

"As it happens, cousin, we have no need for an Etruscan haruspex. My son has completed his studies. He should arrive home any day now. Potitius can perform the proper rites."

"How fortunate for the boy, that he was conveniently absent when the battle at Alba took place, and so avoided all danger," said Pinarius, whose son had fought beside Romulus.

"Those words are uncalled for, Pinarius, and unworthy of a priest of Hercules!" In fact, the elder Potitius was relieved that his son had not returned in time to be recruited by Romulus, but Pinarius's insinuation of cowardice was unfair. He took a breath to calm himself. "A divination must be taken to determine the will of the gods."

"And if the divination goes against Romulus? What then?" asked Pinarius. "No, I think there must be some better way to make sure that all concerned, even the Albans, can see that it was just and proper for Romulus to seize the crown and the treasure of King Amulius." By the shrewd glint in his eyes, Potitius could see that the man had some scheme already in motion.

Potitius arrived home from Tarquinia the next day. The family greeted him with much rejoicing and not a little curiosity, for he was attired in the costume of an Etruscan haruspex. Over a yellow tunic he wore a long, pleated cloak fixed at his shoulder with a bronze clasp, and on his head he wore a conical cap held in place by a strap under his chin. His father noted with pride that he also wore the amulet of Fascinus. When he had given Potitius the amulet, he had told him that he was a man, though in his heart he had not quite believed it. But Potitius had matured greatly in the years he had been away. His confident bearing and his thoughtful way of speaking were those of a man, not a boy.

His father told him about the siege at Alba and the triumphant return of the twins. Rather than exhibiting excitement at the tale, Potitius seemed most concerned about the injuries that Remus had suffered, and this further display of maturity again pleased his father.

"I know you were their friend, my son, despite my disapproval. Go and see them. Talk sense to them. Show them the will of the gods. At the moment, everyone in Roma is singing their praises. Fools like Pinarius will only encourage them to carry out more escapades. They shall grow more and more reckless, until they bring the wrath of some warlord down upon us all. Roma has no walls, like those Amulius built at Alba. Our safety depends entirely upon the good will and self-interest of those who come here to do business. If the twins continue to shed blood and loot their victims—if they turn the local youths into a band of brigands—sooner or later they'll bite the tail of a wolf bigger than themselves, and the people of Roma will pay a terrible price."

The next morning, Potitius went to visit his old friends. Despite their newfound wealth, the twins were still living in the swineherd's hut on the Palatine. Waves of nostalgia swept over Potitius as he scaled the Stairs of Cacus, uttering a prayer of thanksgiving to Hercules as he passed the site of the cave. He reached the top and stepped under the fig tree. The branches hung low with ripe fruit. The shade was so dense that at first he did not see the three figures who sat in a circle near the trunk.

He heard a low whisper: "You see, I told you he was back. And haughtier than ever—look at that fancy hat he's wearing!"

As his eyes adjusted to the darkness, Potitius realized that it was neither of the twins who had been whispering; it was his cousin, Pinarius.

Romulus jumped up. He had grown a thick beard and was brawnier than ever, but his bright smile was the same. He feigned wonderment at Potitius's exotic garments, cocking an eyebrow and flicking his finger against the conical hat. Potitius likewise lifted an eyebrow and pointed at the crown on Romulus's head. They both broke into laughter.

Remus rose slowly to his feet. His smile was weak and he walked with a slight limp. He opened his arms and embraced Potitius.

Pinarius hung back, gazing at Potitius with his arms crossed and a sardonic expression on his face. "Good to have you back, cousin. Did your studies go well?"

"Extremely well, once my teachers beat enough Etruscan into my head so that I could follow their lessons."

"Good for your teachers. Around these parts, the twins have been teaching us all a different sort of lesson—how to throw down a king and take his crown!"

"Yes, my father told me. I thank Hercules that you're still alive, Remus."

"Hercules may have helped, but it was my brother who slit that bastard Amulius's throat."

Romulus smiled. "Yes, we were just discussing that, with Pinarius."

Pinarius looked warily at Potitius. "Perhaps I should go now, and we can continue our discussion later."

"No need for that! Potitius can join us," said Romulus.

"Are you sure that's a good idea?" His cousin's gaze was so frosty that Potitius turned to leave, but Remus reached for his arm.

"Stay, Potitius. We need your advice."

The four of them sat in the shade of the fig tree. Romulus resumed the discussion. "This is the problem: There are some who say that what we did in Alba was wrong, that killing Amulius was murder and taking his treasure was theft. Never mind that such talk is stupid; if people think ill of us, it's likely to cause us problems in the future. Nobody wants a blood feud with Amulius's kinsmen, or more trouble between Alba and Roma. Don't mistake me: I'll fight any man who cares to fight us, and I'll kill any man who crosses us. But it would all be easier if people could see that we were in the right. If they don't already see it that way, how can we convince them? Remus and I have been pondering the question for days, getting nowhere, and then, bright and early this morning, here comes Pinarius with an idea that's so brilliant it lights up the sky. Isn't it brilliant, Remus?"

"Perhaps." His tone was less enthusiastic than his brother's.

"Remus and I aren't thinkers, we're doers. That's why a fellow like Pinarius is such a valuable friend. He fought like a lion at Alba—*and* he's got a head on his shoulders, as well!"

Pinarius looked at Potitius smugly.

Potitius frowned. "Romulus, what are you talking about?"

"Pinarius's plan! Or should I say, the truth that Pinarius has revealed to us, which we shall reveal to the rest of the world. Shall I tell him the tale, or shall you, Remus?"

Remus smiled weakly. "You tell him, brother. I'm afraid I'll forget something."

"Very well. Do you remember the story of how Faustulus found us? It was the year of the great flood. Remus and I were set adrift in a wooden cradle that settled on the slope of the Palatine, right over there. That's where Faustulus found us. Because so many people were drowned, everyone thought we were just two more orphans, so why not let Faustulus and his wife raise us as their own? They've always been good to us, no one can deny that. I call them father and mother, and I'm proud to do so."

Averting his face from the twins, Pinarius flashed a grin. Potitius knew he was thinking of the rude joke about the brothers being suckled by a she-wolf.

"But here's something that Pinarius has discovered from asking a few questions down in Alba," Romulus continued. "Remember: All this happened *in the year of the great flood.* Back then, Amulius wasn't king of Alba; his brother Numitor was king. But Amulius, bloodthirsty bastard that he always was, killed his brother and took his crown. Now *that* was murder; *that* was theft. I think there must be no crime worse than that—a man killing his own brother! The only person who remained who might make trouble for Amulius was his brother's daughter, Rhea Silvia. What if she had a son, and what if that son someday decided to avenge his grandfather and take back the crown? To keep that from happening, Amulius forced Rhea Silvia to become a priestess of Vesta—Vesta being the hearth goddess they worship in Alba. Her priestesses are called Vestals, and they take a sacred vow to remain virgins, upon penalty of death. Amulius must have thought he was being very clever. He let his niece live, and so avoided staining his hands with more blood, but he found a way to keep her from bearing a possible rival, and did so in a way that he could claim was pleasing to the goddess.

"But something went wrong with Amulius's plan. Despite her vow, despite being kept in seclusion in a grove sacred to the war god, Mavors, Rhea Silvia became pregnant. Some people in Alba say that Amulius must have raped her, since he was the only man to have access to her, and any man who'd murder his own brother wouldn't be above raping his own niece. But other people in Alba tell a more curious tale. They think it must have been Mavors who ravished Rhea Silvia, since it was in his grove that she was kept secluded.

"Whoever the father was, Rhea Silvia managed to hide her pregnancy until her labor began. When Amulius was informed, he was furious. Rhea Silvia gave birth—but very soon thereafter she was dead. It may be that Amulius murdered her; it may be that she died in childbirth. But now the tale becomes even more interesting, because the people of Alba say that Rhea Silvia gave birth to *twins*. And you have to ask yourself: Whatever happened to those two boys, the grandsons of the murdered King Numitor?"

Potitius looked at him dubiously. "Romulus, what are you suggesting?"

"Remember, Potitius, all this happened in the year of the great flood—the very year that Remus and I were found by Faustulus."

"And you think . . . ?"

"The newborn twins vanished—but how did Amulius dispose of them? He could claim a right to kill Rhea Silvia, you see, because she had broken her vow of chastity, but even Amulius didn't want the blood of two innocent newborns on his hands. According to the talk in Alba, he did what people usually do when they want to get rid of a deformed or unwanted newborn—he ordered a servant to take the twins to some remote spot and abandon them."

Potitius nodded gravely. "No one is held responsible for killing babies exposed in the wild. They die by the will of the gods."

"But do they always die? Everyone has heard tales of exposed infants raised by wild animals, or otherwise rescued because gods or numina saw fit to help them. Who's to say those two babies, laid side by side in a wooden cradle on some remote hillside, weren't carried away by the great flood to a place far from Alba, where no one knew them, where they were raised in quiet, humble circumstances, safe from Amulius until the time the gods saw fit to guide them to their destiny?"

Potitius shook his head. "Romulus, this sort of talk is nonsense. It's mad."

"Of course it is—brilliantly mad! I give all the credit to Pinarius, who uncovered the tale, saw the obvious connection, and came here today to lay the facts before us."

Remus stirred. He winced. Was he in pain, or made uncomfortable by his brother's enthusiasm? "These are hardly facts, Romulus. They're wild speculations."

"Perhaps. But isn't it just the sort of story that people like to believe?"

"Do *you* believe it, Romulus?" said Potitius. His training as a haruspex had instilled in him a great respect for truth-seeking. Finding the truth was often a difficult business; a man's own eyes and ears were unreliable, as were the tales of others, and even in the best circumstances the will of the gods could be obscure and open to interpretation. His friend's glib way of toying with the truth made him uneasy, as he could see it made Remus uneasy.

"Perhaps I do believe it," answered Romulus. "Can you tell me the name of the woman who gave birth to me and to Remus, Potitius? No. Then why not say it was Rhea Silvia?"

"But . . . that would make Amulius your father—the man you killed for a crown!"

"Perhaps. Or was it the war god Mavors who fathered us? Don't scoff, Potitius! You say you're descended from that god that hangs from your neck, and you claim that the blood of Hercules runs in your veins. Why shouldn't Remus and I be the sons of Mavors? Either way, the story makes us out to be the grandsons and heirs of old King Numitor. When we got rid of Amulius and took his treasury, we were doing nothing more than avenging our grandfather's murder and reclaiming what was rightfully ours!"

There was a long silence, until Remus finally spoke. "Like Potitius, I have reservations about this idea. But I must admit, claiming a royal bloodline for ourselves might solve a great many problems for us, not only now, to pacify the people in Alba, but later on as well, if people hereabouts waver in their loyalty to us, or grow jealous of our good fortune."

Romulus placed a hand on Remus's shoulder and smiled. "My brother is the wisest of men. And you, Pinarius, are the most clever." Pinarius grinned back at him. "And how lucky we are, on this day, to welcome back our oldest and most loyal friend, after so many years away." He gazed at Potitius with a look of such warmth and affection that Potitius's feelings of uneasiness vanished, as morning mist on the Tiber vanishes beneath the rising sun.

753 B.C.

In the months that followed, the twins continued to build on their success at Alba. Scattered across the countryside within a few day's ride of Roma were numerous men who had accumulated enough wealth and power to rule over their neighbors, surround themselves with warriors, and call themselves kings. One by one, Romulus and Remus found reasons to challenge those men, and one by one they defeated them in battle, claimed their wealth, and invited their warriors to join them at Roma. The twins were ferocious and fearless fighters. As their victories mounted, they acquired a reputation for invincibility. Men found it easy to credit that they were the offspring of Mavors.

As their fame spread, more men flocked to join them, drawn by the chance for adventure and a share of the booty. Every day, new strangers appeared in the marketplace, asking for the twins. These men were very different from the honest traders who had been visiting the market for generations, or the hard-working laborers who passed through, looking for seasonal employment in the butchering pens and meat-salting operations. These newcomers were rough-looking men. Some carried weapons, wore bronze helmets or mismatched pieces of armor, and bore the scars of previous battles. Some arrived with nothing more than the rags they wore, and many of these were shifty-eyed and secretive about their pasts. A few were innocent and starry-eyed, adventure-hungry youths smitten by tales of the twins and eager to serve under them.

"What have they done to our Roma?" moaned the elder Potitius. "I can remember a time when you could circle the Seven Hills and not meet a single person you didn't know by name. You knew your neighbor; you knew his grandparents, and who his cousins were, and which of the gods were most sacred to his household. Every family among us had been here for generations. Now, every time I leave the hut, I feel I've stumbled into a gathering of cast-offs and cattle-thieves! It was bad enough when these strangers began showing up among us, straggling in, uninvited. Now the twins have put out a call for such men to come to Roma! 'Come, join us!' they say. 'It doesn't matter who you are, or where you've been, or what you're running from. If you're fit to fight and willing to take an oath of loyalty, then take up arms and go looting with us!' Every cutthroat and bandit from the mountains to the sea can find a home in Roma, up on Asylum Hill. And why not? Cutthroats and bandits are just the sort of men Romulus and Remus are looking for!"

Potitius, who had his own hut now, living near the twins on the Palatine, had come home merely to pay a brief visit, but had found himself trapped by his father's rantings. His father's reference to Asylum Hill was particularly stinging. As the number of the twins' followers had grown larger and larger, room to lodge them had been found atop the high hill directly above the market. It was a natural spot to lodge an army; the two highest points at opposite ends of the hill afforded commanding views of the surrounding countryside, and steep flanks on every side made the hill the most defensible location in Roma. The name which people had lately given to the hill, Asylum, came from the altar which the twins had erected there, dedicated to Asylaeus, the patron god of vagabonds, fugitives, and exiles, who offered sanctuary to those who could find it nowhere else. As a haruspex, and because of his training as a priest of Hercules, Potitius had presided at the consecration of the Altar of Asylaeus. His father's harsh words about the Asylum and its inhabitants struck Potitius as a personal rebuke.

But the elder Potitius was only beginning his tirade. "And you, my son—you go on these raids with them. You join in the looting!"

"I travel with Romulus and Remus as their haruspex, father. At river crossings, I ask the numina for safe passage. Before each battle, I take the auspices, reading the entrails of birds to determine if the day is propitious for victory. During storms, I study the lightning for signs of the gods' will.

These are the things I was trained to do, during my schooling in Tarquinia."

"Before you became a haruspex, you were a priest of Hercules, my son. First and foremost, you are the keeper of the Ara Maxima."

"I know that, Father. But consider: Hercules was the son of a god, and a hero to the people. So are Romulus and Remus."

"No! The twins are nothing more than orphans raised by a pig farmer and his whore of a wife. They're more like Cacus than like Hercules."

"Father!"

"Think, my son. Hercules rescued the people and moved on, asking for nothing. Cacus killed and stole without remorse. Which of those two do your beloved twins more closely resemble?"

Potitius gasped at the recklessness of his father's words. If he himself had ever harbored such thoughts, he had banished them once he made the decision to stand by the twins and to bind his fortunes to theirs.

"And now," his father went on, "they plan to encircle a good portion of Roma with a wall, even higher and stronger than the pickets that surrounded the great house of Amulius at Alba."

"But surely, Father, a wall is a good thing. Roma will become a proper city. If we're attacked, people can find safety inside the walls."

"And why should anyone wish to attack the good, honest people of Roma—except for the fact that the twins have wrought bloodshed and misery on others, and brought home more loot than they have any need for? There are two ways of making a way in the world, my son. One is the way that your ancestors pursued—trading with others peacefully and fairly, offering hospitality to strangers, accumulating no more wealth then is needed to live comfortably, and diligently seeking to offend neither men nor gods. People must barter for the things they need; Roma provided a safe, honest place to do so, and thus it was to everyone's advantage to leave Roma unmolested. And because we did not pile up riches, we did not attract the envy of greedy, violent men.

"But there is another way of living, the way of men like Amulius, and of Romulus and Remus—to take by force that which other men have accumulated by hard work. Yes, their way leads quickly to great wealth—and just as surely to bloodshed and ruin. It is all very well to bully and rob your neighbors, then use the treasure you've stolen to pay strangers to help you bully and rob yet more neighbors. But what will happen when those neighbors unite and come looking for vengeance, or a stronger bully appears on the scene and comes looking to steal the twins' treasure?

"Ah, but if that happens, you say, there will be a *wall* to keep us safe. What nonsense! Did the twins learn nothing from their victory over Amulius? Did walls keep Amulius safe? Did his mercenary warriors save him? Did all his treasure buy him even a single breath when Romulus cut his throat?"

Potitius shook his head. "All you say would make perfect sense, Father, except for one great difference between Amulius and the twins. Amulius lost the favor of the gods; fortune turned against him. But the gods love Romulus and Remus."

"You mean to say that *you* love them, my son!"

"No, father. I speak not as their friend, but as a priest and a haruspex. The gods love the twins. It is a manifest fact. In every battle, especially a battle to the death, there must be a winner and a loser. Romulus and Remus always win. That could not happen unless the gods willed it to be so. You speak with scorn of the path they've chosen, but I tell you that their path is blessed by the gods. How else can you account for their success? That is why I follow them, and why I use all the skills I possess to shed light on the way ahead of them."

His father, unable to refute these words, fell silent.

⁂

The twins agreed that a wall should be built, but they did not agree about its location.

Romulus favored a wall that would encircle the Palatine. Remus thought the wall should be built around the Aventine, further south. Day after day, Potitius listened to them argue.

"Your reasons are purely sentimental, brother" said Remus. "We were raised here on the Palatine, therefore you wish to make it the center of Roma. But no one lives on the Palatine except a few herders and their livestock. Why build a wall around a city of sheep? Or do you intend to drive away the herders and cover the Palatine with buildings? I say, leave this hill wild and open, as it was when we were boys, and build up the city elsewhere. South of the Spinon is the natural place to expand, close to the riverfront. The marketplace, the salt bins, and the slaughtering yards are already pushing against the foot of the Aventine. That is the hill we should encircle with a wall, upon which we should begin to build a proper city."

"How perfectly reasonable you sound, brother!" Romulus laughed. The two brothers, along with Potitius and Pinarius, were strolling across the Palatine. The sky was dazzling blue with white clouds heaped against the horizon. The hill was covered with green grass and spangled with spring flowers, but there was not a single grazing sheep to be seen; the sheep had all been gathered into their pens, which were adorned with juniper boughs and wreaths of laurel leaves. This was the day of the Palilia, the festival of the goddess Pales. Here and there, streamers of smoke trailed into the sky. Each family had set up its own altar to Pales, and upon these raised stones they were burning various substances: for purification, handfuls of sulfur, which emitted sky-blue smoke, followed by twigs of fragrant rosemary, laurel, and Sabine juniper, then an offering compounded of beanstalks mixed with the ashes of calves already burned, sprinkled with horse blood. With juniper branches, the shepherds wafted the smoke across the penned animals; the sacred smoke of Pales would keep the herd healthy and fertile. Afterward, the shepherds would feast on millet cakes and drink bowls of warm milk sprinkled with purple must.

"Perfectly reasonable," Romulus said again. "But this is not about reason, brother. It's about creating a city fit for two kings. You say I favor the Palatine because I'm sentimental. Indeed, I am! How can you walk across this hill on the day of the Palilia and not feel the specialness of this place? There was a reason the gods left our cradle on the slope of the Palatine. Truly, this is the very heart of Roma! It's around the Palatine that we must build a wall, to honor the home that nurtured us. The gods will bless our enterprise."

"Ridiculous!" snapped Remus, with a harshness that startled them all. "If you can't listen to reason, how do you expect to rule a city?"

Romulus strained to keep an even tone. "I've done a good enough job so far, brother, building an army and leading them in battle."

"Running a city will be a different matter. Are you such a fool you can't see that?"

"*You* dare to call *me* a fool, Remus? I wasn't the fool who got himself captured by Amulius and needed rescuing—"

"How dare you throw that in my face! Or do you enjoy reminding me of the hours I spent suffering, needlessly, because you wasted time here in Roma—"

"Unfair, brother! Untrue!"

"And because *you* strangled Amulius, *you* wear the crown every day, even though you promised it would be shared equally between us."

"Is that what this is about? Take it! Wear it!" Romulus lifted the iron crown from his head, cast it to the ground, and stalked away. Pinarius ran after him.

When they were boys, the twins had never argued. Now they seemed to argue all the time, and their arguments grew more and more heated. From childhood, Romulus had been the more headstrong and impulsive, and Remus had been the one to restrain his brother. But the torture he had received at the hands of Amulius had wrought changes in Remus. His body had never fully recovered; he still walked with a slight limp. More than that, his even temper had deserted him; he had become as quick to anger as his brother. Romulus had changed as well since Alba. He remained as high-spirited as before but was more disciplined and purposeful, and more self-assured and arrogant than ever.

At Alba, Remus had suffered the tortures of Amulius; Romulus had enjoyed the glow of triumph and the satisfaction of rescuing his brother. One had been a victim and the other a hero. This disparity had created a rift between them, small at first but constantly growing. Potitius knew that the argument he had just witnessed was not about the wall, but about something that had gone terribly wrong between the twins, which neither could put a name to or knew how to set right.

The castoff crown had landed at Potitius's feet. He stooped to lift it from the grass, and was surprised at how heavy it was. He offered it to Remus, who took it but did not place it on his head.

"This matter of the wall must be settled once and for all," said Remus quietly, staring at the crown. "What do you think, Potitius?" He saw the troubled look on his friend's face and laughed ruefully. "No, I'm not asking you to take sides. I'm asking your advice as a haruspex. How might we settle this matter by consulting the will of the gods?"

As quick as a blink, a shadow passed over them. Potitius looked up to see a vulture high above. "I think I know a way," he said.

The contest was held the next day. It was not Potitius who called it a contest, but the twins, for clearly, that was how they thought of it. To Potitius, it was a very solemn rite, calling upon all the wisdom he had learned in Tarquinia.

The rite was conducted simultaneously upon each of the contesting hills. Romulus stood at a high spot on the Palatine, looking north; beside him was Pinarius, in his role as a priest of Hercules. Remus, with Potitius, stood on the Aventine, looking south. At each site, an iron blade had been driven upright into the earth, so that by its shadow the exact moment of midday could be determined. A mark had been made in the ground a set distance from the blade, to mark by the blade's moving shadow the passing of a precise measure of time. Within that span of time, each brother and his priest would watch the sky for vultures in flight. The priests would keep count of each vulture that was sighted by scraping a furrow in the dirt with a spear.

Why vultures? Potitius had explained his reasoning to the brothers: "The vulture is sacred to Hercules, who was always joyful at the sight of one. Among all creatures, it is the least harmful; it damages neither crops, nor fruit trees, nor cattle. It never kills or hurts any living thing, but preys only upon carrion, and even then it will not prey upon other birds; whereas eagles, hawks, and owls will attack and kill their own kind. Of all birds, it is the most rarely seen, and few men claim ever to have seen its young. Because of this, the Etruscans believe that vultures come from some other world. Therefore, let it be the sighting of vultures that determines the will of heaven in situating the city of Roma."

Midday arrived. Upon the Aventine, Remus raised his arm and pointed. "There's one!"

Potitius suppressed a smile. His training as a haruspex had taught him to recognize every sort of bird at a great distance. "I believe that is a hawk, Remus."

Remus squinted. "So it is."

They continued to watch. The time seemed to pass very slowly.

"I see one, over there," said Potitius. Remus followed his gaze and nodded. Potitius pressed his spear to the ground and scraped a furrow.

"And there's another!" cried Remus. Potitius agreed, and scraped a second furrow.

So it went, until the shadow of the blade reached the mark that signaled the end of the contest. There were six furrows in the ground, to mark the six vultures seen by Remus. He smiled and clapped his hands and seemed pleased. Potitius agreed that it was a considerable number and boded well.

They descended from the Aventine. They were to meet Romulus and Pinarius at the footbridge over the Spinon, but after a long wait, Remus became impatient. He headed for the Stairs of Cacus, with Potitius following him. As Remus ascended, he tripped on some of the steps. Potitius noted that his friend's limp was very bad that day.

They found Romulus and Pinarius sitting on a fallen tree not far from the spot where they had kept watch on the Palatine. The two of them were laughing and conversing, obviously in high spirits.

"We were to meet at the Spinon," said Remus. "Why are you still here?"

Romulus rose. He smiled broadly. "Why should the king of Roma leave the very center of his kingdom? I told you that the Palatine is the heart of Roma, and today the gods have made it clear that they agree."

"What are saying?"

"Go see for yourself." Romulus pointed to the place where Pinarius had marked furrows in the ground.

When Potitius saw the number of furrows, he drew a sharp breath. "Impossible!" he whispered.

There were so many furrows that they could not be numbered at a glance. Remus counted them aloud. ". . . ten, eleven, twelve. Twelve!" He turned to confront Romulus. "Are you saying that you saw twelve vultures, brother?"

"Indeed, I did."

"Not sparrows, not eagles, not hawks?"

"Vultures, my brother. The bird most sacred to Hercules, and most rare. Within the allotted measure of time, I saw and counted twelve vultures in the sky."

Remus opened his mouth to say something, then shut it, dumbfounded. Potitius stared at Pinarius. "Is this true, cousin? You verified the count with your own eyes? You made each of these furrows in the earth? You performed the ritual openly and honestly before the gods, as befits a priest of Hercules?"

Pinarius stared back at him coldly. "Of course, cousin. All was done in a proper manner. Romulus saw twelve vultures, and I made twelve marks. How many vultures did Remus see?"

If Pinarius was lying, then Romulus was lying as well, deceiving his own brother and smiling as he did so. Potitius looked at Remus; his friend's jaw quivered and he blinked rapidly. Since his torture by Amulius, Remus's face was sometimes subject to a violent twitching, but this was something else. Remus was fighting back tears. Shaking his head, unable to speak, he hurriedly walked away, limping badly.

"How many did Remus see?" Pinarius asked again.

"Six," whispered Potitius.

Pinarius nodded. "Then the will of the gods is clear. Do you not agree, cousin?"

When Romulus later took him aside and asked for his counsel, as a haruspex, regarding the making of the city boundaries, Potitius resisted him. He stopped short of accusing Romulus of lying, but Romulus read his thought. Never admitting deceit, he dismissed Potitius's doubts about the counting of the vultures. There had been a disagreement, the disagreement had to be settled somehow, it had been settled, and now they must all move on.

By subtle flattery, Romulus convinced Potitius that his participation was essential to the establishment of the city. There was a right way and a wrong way to do such a thing, and surely, for the sake of the people of Roma and their descendents, all should be done in accordance with the will of the gods—and who but Potitius could reliably divine their will? Romulus stated his earnest desire that Remus should perform an equal share of the ritual, and persuaded Potitius to play peacemaker between them.

Thanks to Potitius, when the day arrived to establish the pomerium—the sacred boundary of the new city—all was done properly, and both twins took part.

The ritual was performed in accordance with ancient traditions handed down from the Etruscans. At the place which Potitius determined to be the exact center of the Palatine, and thus the center of the new city, Romulus and Remus broke ground and dug a deep pit, using a spade they passed back and forth. All those who wished to be citizens came forward one by one and cast a handful of dirt into the pit, saying, "Here is a handful of dirt from . . ." and speaking the name of the place they came from. Those who had lived in Roma for generations performed the ritual as well as those who were newcomers, and the mixing of the soil symbolized the melding of the citizenry. Even the father of Potitius, despite his reservations about the twins, took part in the ceremony, casting into the pit a handful of dirt he had scooped from the ground before the threshold of his family's hut.

When the pit was filled, a stone altar was placed in the soil. Potitius called upon the sky-god Jupiter, father of Hercules, to look down upon the foundation of the city. Romulus and Remus invited Mavors and Vesta to pay witness—the war god rumored to be their father and the hearth goddess to whom their reputed mother, Rhea Silvia, had been consecrated.

Ahead of time, the twins had circled the Palatine and decided upon the best course for an encircling network of fortifications. Now they descended to the foot of the hill, where a bronze plough had been hitched to a yoke drawn by a white bull and a white cow. Taking turns, the brothers ploughed a continuous furrow to mark the boundary of the new city. While one plowed, the other walked beside him and wore the iron crown. Romulus began the furrow; Remus took the last turn and joined the furrow's end to its beginning.

The throng that had followed every step of their progress cheered, laughed, and wept with joy. The brothers lifted their weary arms to heaven, then turned to each other and embraced. At that moment, it seemed to Potitius that the twins were truly beloved by the gods, and that no power on earth could lay them low.

On that day, in the month that would later be named Aprilis, in the year that would later be known as 753 B.C., the city of Roma was born.

The building of fortifications commenced at once. Compared to the great walls that had been built elsewhere in the world, such as those of ancient Troy, it was a very modest project. The plan was not to build a wall of stone blocks; that would have been impossible, as there were no quarries to supply the stone, no skilled masons to shape and set the blocks, and no one with the engineering skills to design such a wall. Instead, the new city would be defended by a network of ditches, earthen ramparts, and wooden pickets. In some places, the steep slope of the hillside itself would supply an adequate defense.

As modest, or even primitive, as the project would have appeared to a Greek tyrant or an Egyptian temple builder, the first fortifications of Roma were an undertaking on a scale never previously attempted in the region of the Seven Hills. For manpower, Romulus and Remus called upon the dwellers on Asylum Hill who had gone raiding with them, as well as the local youths with whom they had grown up. Few from either group had much experience at the tasks the twins set them. Frequent mistakes and a great deal of wasted effort led to much squabbling at the work site.

Whenever something went wrong, it was Romulus rather than Remus who gave way to fits of anger. He shouted at the workers, threatened them, and sometimes even struck them. The more the workers protested that they were blameless, the more furious Romulus would become, while Remus stood back and watched his brother's outbursts with barely veiled amusement. It seemed to Potitius, at first, that things were simply getting back to normal, with Romulus showing himself to be the more hot-tempered of the twins and Remus the more easy-going. But after this scene was repeated numerous times—a failure in the fortifications, expressions of outrage from Romulus, the workers protesting their blamelessness, and Remus silently observing the incident—Potitius began to harbor an uneasy suspicion.

He was not alone. Pinarius was also present each day, and there was little that escaped his notice. One afternoon he drew Potitius aside.

"Cousin, this situation cannot go on. I think you should have a word with Remus—unless, of course, you're the one who's putting him up to this."

"What are you talking about, Pinarius?"

"So far, I've said nothing to Romulus about my suspicions. I have no wish to make more trouble between the twins."

"Speak plainly!" said Potitius.

"Very well. There have been too many problems with the construction of these fortifications. The men may not be skilled builders, but they're not stupid. Nor are they all such shirkers and cowards that none of them would take responsibility for an honest mistake. Yet mistakes keep happening, with no one to take the blame. Romulus grows more vexed every day, while Remus can barely contain his laughter. A bit of harmless mischief is one thing. Deliberate treachery is another."

"Are you saying that someone is sabotaging the construction?"

"Perhaps it's nothing more than a series of practical jokes. The intention may be to infuriate Romulus, but the harm goes beyond that. Romulus is being made to look foolish. His authority is being undermined. The morale of the men is being damaged. Someone very clever is behind this. Is it you, cousin?"

"Of course not!"

"Who, then? Someone close to Remus—someone who can speak to him freely—needs to discuss this matter very seriously with him. Not I; he thinks I'm Romulus's man. Perhaps you should talk to him, cousin?"

"And accuse him of treachery?"

"Use whatever words you think best. Just make sure that Remus understands that this situation must not continue."

But when Potitius spoke to Remus—in a very careful and roundabout way, accusing him of nothing but suggesting that someone was hampering the progress of the fortifications—Remus shrugged off the idea. "Who would do such a thing? Certainly no one that I can think of. But have you considered, good Potitius, that the whole project is cursed? If there's a will at work to thwart construction, might it not be a will other than human?"

Potitius shook his head. "Everything was done to appease the numina and appeal to the gods for their blessing. You yourself invoked Mavors and Vesta—"

"Yes, but was the original divination properly conducted?"

Potitius felt personally affronted. "The contest for sighting the vultures was soundly conceived. I called upon every principle of divination I learned in Tarquinia—"

"I find no fault with you, Potitius, or with your skills as a haruspex. But were the vultures properly—and honestly—counted? If not, then the selection of the Palatine was based upon a falsehood, and the city conceived by my brother Romulus is an offense to the gods—who have ways of making their will known."

Potitius shook his head. "But if you believe this, Remus—"

"I didn't say I believe it. I only suggest it as a possibility. It's at least as credible as your suggestion that someone is maliciously causing damage. Again I ask you, Potitius: Who would do such a thing? Who would wish to stir up so much trouble, and have the daring and the guile to do so?"

Remus raised an eyebrow and gave him an indulgent smile to show that, as far as he was concerned, his friend's idea had been put to rest. But Potitius, more uneasy than ever, found himself harboring a new suspicion. He now was certain that Remus had done nothing to hinder the construction, no matter that he showed bitter amusement at his brother's vexation. If there was a troublemaker among them, a person who said one thing and meant another, who seemed always to have his own ulterior motives, was that person not his cousin Pinarius?

Of this new suspicion, Potitius said nothing. He decided to watch and to wait, and meanwhile to keep silent. Later he would wish that he had spoken out, not only to Remus but to Romulus as well; but perhaps nothing he might have done could have altered the course of events.

Summer came, and with it long, sweltering days. Work on the fortifications proceeded, but slowly and with repeated setbacks. The men grew tired of so much hard work and restless; they wanted to go raiding again. It was on a particularly hot, humid day, when tempers were already short, that the worst of all mishaps occurred.

The men were working along a section of the perimeter where the terrain was largely flat, and therefore required considerable fortification. First a picket wall was constructed in sections. Each section was made of sharpened stakes laid side by side, then lashed together with leather thongs. A narrow trench was dug, into which the picket sections were set upright and secured together, so that when the trench was filled with tightly packed earth the picket wall was steadfast. But Romulus was dissatisfied with the height of the completed wall. Many of the tree trunks and branches that had been used for the pickets were hardly taller than a man, and once they had been buried in the trench they were shorter still; if enough debris—or dead bodies—were to be piled before the wall, an attacker with long legs and strong nerves might dare to leap over the pickets. Along that section, Romulus decided that another layer of defense was called for, so he ordered the men to dig an outer trench, knee-deep, which would be lined with spikes.

Digging was the job the men despised most, especially in the hard, sun-baked earth. They dripped sweat, grumbled under their breaths, and spoke of how much sweeter it would be to mount a horse and go riding with the warm wind in their faces, looking for booty and bloodshed and women.

Suddenly, first in a few places and then along the whole length of the ditch, the bank of earth between the wall and the trench began to crumble. The men had dug too close to the pickets. The packed earth that anchored the wall gave way. All at once, the entire wall tumbled forward, directly on top of the men digging the trench.

Romulus was nearby, discussing the next stretch of fortifications with Remus, Potitius, and Pinarius. At the sound of men screaming, they all came running, and witnessed a scene of despair. The fallen wall was too heavy to be shifted. The men trapped beneath it had to be dragged clear. Where that was impossible, the rescuers set about disassembling the wall, hacking with knives at the leather bindings and pulling the pickets away. Many of the men had been seriously injured, with crushed fingers, broken bones, and cracked skulls. They clutched their wounds and wailed in pain.

Amid the chaos, Potitius saw that Pinarius had drawn Remus aside and was speaking in his ear. Potitius had never seen a look of such fury on Remus's face. What was Pinarius saying to him?

Potitius drew nearer and overheard Pinarius, who spoke in a hoarse whisper: "It was never my idea, I swear to you! Romulus insisted, and I was afraid to refuse him—"

"I knew it!" cried Remus. "I suspected it, but until now I never knew for sure. The liar!" His knife in his hand, he pushed Pinarius aside and strode toward his brother. Romulus rose from assisting a wounded worker and saw him coming. He blanched at the look on Remus's face and jumped back.

Remus did not attack him. Instead he pointed to the fallen wall with his knife. "There, brother, do you see what your scheming and your lies have accomplished? Are you happy now?"

Romulus stared back at him, dumbfounded.

"You complained that the wall wasn't high enough," said Remus. "Look at it now! Any man could jump over it, even a man with a limp." He took a running start and bounded over the fallen wall, then turned to taunt Romulus further. "What good is a wall, if it won't stand up? And why won't it stand? Because the gods are having a joke on you, brother. You've angered them. You can lie to me, you can lie to everyone in Roma, but you can't deceive the gods. They're laughing at you, brother, just as I'm laughing at you!"

"The gods are on my side!" shouted Romulus. "You're the one who's been wrecking all my hard work. How dare you commit treachery behind my back, then blame it on the gods? How dare you laugh at me?" Romulus cried out in fury, picked up an iron shovel, and rushed at his brother.

The twins were too evenly matched for the fight to quickly go one way or the other. Since his torture, Remus had become the weaker, but he wielded a superior weapon. Romulus's anger made him clumsy and he swung the shovel wildly, opening himself to Remus's knife. The glancing cuts he received made him more furious than before, but also more reckless, and the pain sapped his strength. A few times he managed to strike Remus soundly with his shovel, hitting him across the shoulders and hips hard enough to knock him down, but Remus quickly scrambled up, regained his balance, and deftly wielded his knife. At last Romulus struck a blow to Remus's hand and the blade went flying through the air.

Romulus raised the shovel and stood poised to strike the defenseless Remus with all his strength. As one, those watching drew a sharp breath. But instead of striking, Romulus cried out and cast the shovel aside. He fell on Remus, reaching for his throat, and the two tumbled to the ground.

Potitius clutched his chest. Until that moment, he had truly feared that one of the brothers might kill the other. But now, locked together and fighting with bare hands, they would surely exhaust their fury and come to their senses. He opened his palms to heaven and whispered a prayer to Hercules. As he mouthed the god's name, he thought he heard it uttered aloud, and turned to see that Pinarius also stood with open palms, whispering a prayer. But for what outcome did Pinarius pray?

The twins rolled on the ground. The advantage shifted back and forth as they savagely pummeled each other, choked each other, and gouged at one another's eyes.

That day, it was Remus's turn to wear the iron crown. It was a tight fit. It stayed on his head throughout the combat, until Romulus suddenly reached for it and wrenched it from his brother's brow. Remus gave a cry and tried to snatch it back. Each twin gripped the crown with both hands. They twisted this way and that until they struggled to their knees, each pulling with all his might at the circle of iron, which seemed to be suspended motionless in the air between them. Their knuckles turned white. Blood oozed from their fingers' staining the crown red.

Remus lost his grip. His arms flew up and he fell backward. Romulus likewise recoiled, but scrambled back onto his knees. Before Remus could rise again, Romulus raised the crown high in the air and brought it down with all his strength.

Potitius, who had never ceased his fervent, whispered prayers, heard the shattering of bone beneath the broken flesh. The sound was as sharp and earsplitting as the snapping of a branch on a winter day. The blow to Remus's head was so powerful that it left a dent the size of a man's fist in his skull.

Romulus was breathing hard, trembling from exhaustion. He stared at his brother's ruined face for a moment, then staggered to his feet. He fitted the bloody crown on his head. He circled his brother's body, stamping and shambling like a drunken man, glaring at the circle of shocked faces around him.

He pointed down at Remus. "There! Do you all see? That is what happens to any man who dares to jump over *my* walls!"

Some in the crowd gasped. Some wept. A few, the most ruthless and bloodthirsty of the vagabonds who had come to Roma to seek Asylum, grunted in savage approval. In the background, Potitius heard the wailing of men still trapped beneath the fallen wall.

Potitius saw great oily spots before his eyes and felt light-headed. The moment became unreal. Somehow the waking world had vanished, and this nightmare had taken its place.

Romulus came to an abrupt halt. His shoulders slumped. His gaze followed the line of his own arm down to his bloody, pointing finger, then down to the crushed face of his brother. His chest began to rise and fall convulsively. He threw back his head, dropped to his knees, and let out a wail such as no man present had ever heard before. Men covered their ears to shut it out. Hearing that wail, it seemed to Potitius that his heart ceased to beat and his blood turned to ice.

Romulus collapsed upon his brother's corpse, weeping uncontrollably.

Potitius averted his face. He found himself looking at Pinarius, who gazed unblinking at the spectacle of Romulus's grief. More than ever, Potitius knew that he must be in a nightmare, for how could any man look upon the horror of what Romulus had done and react, as did Pinarius, with a faint smile?

Remus was buried at the summit of the Aventine, at the site where he had searched the sky for vultures. Potitius oversaw the funeral rites. Romulus stood among the mourners. He did not weep. Nor did he speak; it was Potitius who delivered the eulogy. Indeed, Romulus would never speak of his brother again, nor, after the funeral, would he ever allow anyone else to speak the name of Remus in his presence.

It was a curious fact, noted by everyone, that after the death of Remus, the series of setbacks stopped. Construction of the fortifications continued with no further mishaps, and the grand project was quickly finished.

Had Remus been lying to Potitius when he disclaimed responsibility for the mischief? No. Potitius believed that someone else had been responsible, and stopped after the death of Remus so as to make it seem that Remus had been the culprit. That same person had worked to poison the mind of Romulus against his brother, and likewise had incited Remus against Romulus by telling him, on the day of his death, that the contest of vultures had been a sham.

But Potitius had no way of proving these suspicions, and without proof, his ideas counted for nothing; his influence with the king had waned. After the death of Remus, Romulus relied more than ever on the counsel of Pinarius.

It was on the advice of Pinarius that Romulus, as king of Roma, took on more and more of the religious duties of the city—duties which otherwise would have fallen to Potitius. Potitius remained hereditary priest of Hercules and keeper of the Ara Maxima, and would be so for the rest of his life, and from time to time King Romulus still called upon his skills as a haruspex; but more often it was the king, not Potitius, who read the sky for signs of the gods' favor and determined the will of heaven. And why not? Romulus himself was the son of a god.

717 B.C.

Romulus was only eighteen years old when he founded the city and became its king. Thirty-six years later, he was still king of Roma.

Much had been accomplished in those years. Many battles had been fought. Most of these had been little more than seasonal raiding parties to take booty from neighbors and to establish Romulus's dominance over other men who called themselves kings. A more important series of battles recently had been waged against the nearby town of Veii, which tried to claim ownership of the salt beds at the mouth of the Tiber and take control of the salt trade. By force of arms, Romulus forced the Veiians to give up their claims. He established Roma's supremacy as a salt emporium beyond dispute and assured her continuing prosperity. But Veii had only been bested, not conquered; the city would continue to engage in warfare with Roma for many generations to come.

Altars to many gods and goddesses had been erected, and temples had also been built. The very first temple in Roma was built by Romulus atop Asylum Hill and dedicated to the king of the gods, Jupiter. It was a small, rectangular wooden building—its longest side measured only fifteen paces—and its facade was quite plain, with an unadorned pediment supported by two pillars. It contained no statue, only an altar, but it housed the spoils of war which Romulus had taken from other kings.

In honor of Rhea Silvia, his mother, he built a temple to the goddess Vesta. It was a round building with wicker walls and a thatched roof; in shape, it was not unlike the hut Romulus had grown up in, but much larger. It contained a hearth in which burned a sacred flame, tended by virgin priestesses. In honor of Mavors, his father, he erected an altar upon the broad plain enclosed by the arm of the Tiber, which provided a suitable training ground for his soldiers. That area became known as the Field of Mavors.

As he had fortified the Palatine, so Romulus eventually fortified Asylum Hill, and also the Aventine, fulfilling the ambition of his brother. The marshy lake which fed the Spinon he drained and filled with rubble and hard-packed earth. The resulting valley, accessible to all the Seven Hills, became a natural crossroads and meeting place; men called it the Forum.

For himself, Romulus built a royal dwelling, bigger and grander than the hall of Amulius in Alba. The hut in which he had grown up was consecrated as a sacred site, to be preserved for posterity in its humble condition as a monument to the founder's origins. Likewise, the tree beneath which he had been suckled was made sacred, and it was declared that a fig tree should always be located there and called the ruminalis, or suckling-tree.

To reward his bravest warriors and most steadfast supporters, he established an elite body called the Senate. To its one hundred members he granted special privileges and delegated special duties. Potitius was among the first senators. So was Pinarius.

Romulus altered and added to the calendar of festivals. The Palilia had been celebrated every spring since a time beyond memory; because of the holiday's proximity to the groundbreaking ceremony for Roma, the Palilia had also become the occasion to celebrate the birth of the city. Only old men in their fifties, like Potitius, could remember a time when the Palilia had been a festival unto itself, with no connection to the founding of Roma.

The running of the wolflings had also become an annual event, which greatly amused Potitius. How his late father, in his dotage, had railed against this development! Each winter, on the anniversary of the occasion when Romulus, Remus, and Potitius had run naked around the Seven Hills, the Romans celebrated the Lupercalia, a festival in honor of Lupercus, god of flocks. A goat was sacrificed. The young sons of senators caroused naked, but instead of adorning themselves with wolf skins and brandishing wolf-hide straps, they carried strips of hide from the sacrificed goat. Young women offered their wrists to be slapped, believing that contact with the sacred fleece enhanced their fertility; to be sure, a great many babies were born nine months after the Lupercalia. The ritual which began as a celebration of predators now celebrated the flock, as befitted a civilized people who lived within a protective enclosure under the rule of a king.

Other traditions remained intact and unchanged throughout the king's long reign. The Feast of Hercules was still performed at the Ara Maxima each year exactly as it had been for generations, with the Pinarii pretending to arrive late for the feast and the Potitii claiming the exclusive privilege of eating of the entrails offered to the god.

For the fifty-fourth time in his life—and, though he did not know it, the last time—Potitius had taken part in the Feast of Hercules. His eldest grandson, for the first time, had joined in the ritual, waving the sacred ox-tail whisk to keep flies away from the Ara Maxima. The boy had done a good job. Potitius was proud of him, and had been in a good mood all day, despite the heat, and despite the unavoidable, annual unpleasantness of having to deal with his fellow priest and cousin Pinarius.

Now the feast was over. Potitius had retired to his hut on the Palatine and was lying down for a nap. Valeria, his wife of many years, lay beside him, her eyes closed. She had eaten her fill at the feast and was also sleepy.

Potitius gazed at his wife and felt a great swelling of love and tenderness. Her hair was almost as gray and her face as wrinkled as his own, but he still found pleasure in looking at her. She had been a loyal wife, a wise and patient mother, and a good partner. If nothing else, life had given him Valeria. Or, to give proper credit: If nothing else, Romulus had given him Valeria.

In a few days, the people of Roma would celebrate the great midsummer festival, the Consualia. Potitius could not think of Valeria without thinking of the Consualia; he could not think of the Consualia without thinking of Valeria, and remembering . . .

The very first Consualia—though the festival would only later receive its name—had been celebrated by Romulus early in his reign. He had decreed a festival of athletic contests to be held in the long valley between the Palatine and the Aventine—foot races, somersaulting, demonstrations of daring on horseback, and stone-hurling competitions. To join in friendly competition with the youths of Roma, Romulus invited some of the city's neighbors—members of a tribe called the Sabines who had settled on the most northern of the Seven Hills. The Sabines called this hill the Quirinal, after their chief god, Quirinus.

The ostensible purpose of that first Consualia had been athletic competitions; but Romulus had a surprise in store for the unsuspecting visitors.

Potitius, when he had been made aware of Romulus's secret plan, had strongly protested. Hospitality to visitors was a law decreed by the gods. Every priest in every land agreed: A traveler with honest intentions must always be welcomed, and it was the duty of his host to keep him safe. What Romulus was plotting—encouraged, Potitius had no doubt, by his counselor, Pinarius—went against every law of hospitality.

Potitius tried to dissuade him, but the king was adamant. "There are too many men in Roma, and not enough women, and more men arrive every day," he insisted. "The Sabines on the Quirinal have a surplus of young women. I've made overtures to their leader, Titus Tatius, inviting him to send brides for my men, but he refuses; their mothers complain that the Romans are too uncouth. They want their daughters to marry other Sabines, even if it means they must leave the Quirinal to go live with the tribes in the mountains. This is nonsense! My men deserve wives. Are they not good enough for the Sabine women? As for impiety, I have prayed to the god Consus for guidance on this matter."

"The god of secret counsels?"

"Yes. And by various signs he has shown his favor."

Romulus had carried out his design. The Sabine youths arrived to take part in the competitions. The Sabine elders and women came to watch; it was easy to tell which of the women were unmarried, for the matrons stayed in one group and the virgins in another. All the Sabines arrived unarmed, as befitted invited guests. The contests proceeded. The Sabine youths exerted themselves to the utmost, exhausting themselves, while the Romans held back and saved their strength. At a signal from Romulus, some of the Romans seized the unmarried Sabine women and carried them off, into the fortified city, while others took up arms. The Sabine men, unarmed and exhausted, were easily driven off.

That had not been the end of the matter. Titus Tatius, at first determined to take back the women, called upon his relatives among the Sabine tribes to help him, but he could not muster enough manpower to seriously lay siege to Roma. Many a skirmish and ambush followed; meanwhile, Romulus encouraged his men to court the captive women and win them over without force. Many of the women eventually married their suitors, willingly, and gave birth to children; even those who were unhappy in Roma began to realize that they could not return to their homes on the Quirinal, for the other Sabines would consider them compromised and unfit for marriage. Eventually, Titus Tatius decided to make the best of a bad situation and to end the dispute by negotiation. Romulus made a settlement of goods to the families of the seized women, and in return the Sabines recognized the marriages and agreed to resume peaceful relations. Some hard feelings lingered, but in the end, the intermarriage of the two groups drew them closer together, and Romulus and Titus Tatius formed a long-lasting alliance.

Potitius had never stopped protesting the plan to seize the Sabine women—until the moment he laid eyes on Valeria. She had been among the other Sabine virgins being held against her will in the walled courtyard of the king's house. Looking frightened and miserable, she had not been the most beautiful of the Sabines, but some quality about her attracted Potitius's gaze, and he could not look away. Pinarius saw him staring and whispered in his ear, "Do you want her, cousin? Take her—or else I will!" As the two men approached her, Valeria cowered at the predatory gleam in Pinarius's eyes, but when she saw Potitius, who looked as miserable as herself, a very different emotion lit her face. In that moment, a bond was forged between them that was to last a lifetime. Of all the Sabine women, Valeria had been the very first to marry one of the captors willingly. Their child had been the first to be born to a Roman and a Sabine.

Romulus himself married one of the Sabines, Hersilia. Their marriage was happy, but barren. Potitius, who had many children, wondered if the gods had cursed Romulus to remain childless because he had so flagrantly violated the sacred laws of hospitality to capture the Sabine women. If the king himself harbored such thoughts, he never spoke them aloud.

Romulus did, however, develop strong ideas about marriage and family life. As king, he made his ideas into law. No marriage could ever be dissolved, although a husband had the right to put his wife to death if she committed adultery or drank wine (because drinking wine, Romulus believed, led women to adultery). Over his children and their children, a father wielded absolute control during his entire life; he could hire them out to others as laborers, imprison them, beat them, or even put them to death. No son ever outgrew the legal authority of his father. This was the law of the paterfamilias—the supreme head of the household—and it was to remain absolute and unquestioned in Roma for centuries to come.

These things Potitius remembered and pondered, thinking of Valeria, and the first Consualia, and the so-called rape of the Sabine women. If nothing else, Romulus had given him Valeria . . .

Beside him, Valeria slept. Potitius could tell, because she was gently snoring. Studying her face, remembering all their years together, he decided that their marriage would have been a successful one with or without the stern laws of Romulus, just as their children would have grown up to be respectful and obedient whether or not the king had decreed the law of paterfamilias. Potitius's own father had often disapproved of his decisions, but would never have invoked a law to punish him or to break his will. What did Romulus—who had no sons or daughters, who claimed to have no human father—know about raising children or respecting a father? And yet, the world that came after Romulus would be different from the world that came before him, because of the laws he imposed on the families of Roma.

There was a rapping at the door to his hut. Moving quickly but carefully so as not to wake Valeria, Potitius went to answer the door. The afternoon sunlight dazzled his eyes and made a silhouette of his visitor, and Potitius did not recognize him until he spoke.

"Good afternoon, cousin."

"Pinarius! What are you doing here? The feast is over. I thought I wouldn't have to see your face again for at least a year!"

"Unkind words, cousin. Will you not invite me in?"

"What do we have to say to one another?"

"Invite me in, and find out."

Potitius frowned, but stepped aside to let Pinarius enter. He shut the door. "Keep your voice low. Valeria is asleep." From behind the wicker screen that hid their bed, he could hear her quiet snoring.

"I took a good look at her at the feast today," said Pinarius. "She's still a handsome woman. If only I had moved a bit faster than you, all those years ago—"

"Why are you here?"

Pinarius lowered his voice even more. "A change is coming, cousin. Some of us will survive it. Others will not."

"Speak plainly."

"You've always had differences with the king. Over and over you've opposed him, since the very beginning of his reign. If I were to tell you that his reign will soon be over, would you shed a tear?"

"Nonsense! Romulus is as fit as a man half his age. He still leads his warriors into battle and fights in the front rank. He'll live to be a hundred."

Pinarius sighed and shook his head. "You really have no idea of what's going on, do you, cousin?"

This was how Pinarius always spoke to him—in riddles, with a mixture of pity and scorn. But Potitius realized that his cousin was serious, and speaking of something very grave. "Tell me, then. What's going on behind the king's back?"

"The senators grumble that the king has become too arrogant, that he's reigned too long, that he takes his power for granted and abuses it. You've seen how he strides across the Palatine in his scarlet tunic and purple-bordered robe, surrounded by his coterie of surly young warriors. Lictors, he calls them, using the Etruscan word for a royal bodyguard—yet another of his affectations. The other day, when he deigned to attend a meeting of the Senate, he sat on his plush throne and gazed down on us, not even paying attention; he laughed and joked with his lictors instead. His ears perked up only when some wastrel, a lazy swineherd, appeared before him with a trumped-up complaint against a respectable man of property. And how did Romulus rule? For the swineherd and against the senator! While we were still gaping at that outrage, he announced that he would divvy up a newly conquered parcel of prime farmland among his soldiers, without consulting us—or giving us a share. What's next? Will the king start throwing his old comrades out of the Senate and replacing us with swineherds and nobodies who arrived in Roma yesterday?"

Potitius laughed. "Romulus loves the common people, and they love him. And why not? He was raised by a swineherd! He may live in a palace, but his heart is in the pigsty. He loves his soldiers, too, and they love him. He was born to be a troublemaker and a rabble-rouser. Pity the poor senators who've grown too greedy and too fat to keep the king's love! You complain that he's arrogant, but what do you care if Romulus parades about in a purple robe? You care only about protecting your own privileges against newcomers and common folk who don't know their place."

Pinarius thrust out his jaw. "Maybe so, cousin, but things cannot go on as they are. A day of reckoning approaches, a day marked in the calendar of the heavens."

Potitius grunted. "There have always been plots against Romulus—and Romulus has always put a stop to them. Are you here to tell me that another plot is being hatched? Are you asking me to take part?"

"Cousin, you always see though me!" Pinarius smiled. "To you I never tell the truth—yet from you I have no secrets."

Potitius shook his head. "I'll have nothing to do with any plot to harm the king." Behind the screen, Valeria sighed and turned in her sleep. "I'll hear no more of this. You should go."

"You're a fool, Potitius. You always have been."

"Maybe so. But I won't be a traitor as well."

"Then at least keep your distance from the king, if you want to keep your head. What's the Etruscan saying? 'When the scythe cuts the weed, the grass is cropped as well.' You'll know the time of reckoning has arrived when the light of the sun fails, and day turns to night."

"What are you talking about?"

"Your Etruscans taught you much about divination, Potitius, but they taught you nothing about celestial phenomena. That study was left to me. Years ago, Romulus charged me with finding wise men who could predict the movements of the sun and moon and stars, so that we could better chart the seasons and fix the days of the festivals. There are ways of knowing in advance when certain rare events will occur. A day is coming when, for a brief while, the light of the sun will go out, and the gods will withdraw their favor from the king. Romulus will leave this earth, along with anyone who stands too close to him. Do you understand?"

"I understand that you're even madder than I thought!"

"You've been warned, cousin. I've done my best to save you. But if you breathe a word of this to anyone, the lovely Valeria will become a widow before she needs to."

"Get out of my home, cousin!"

Without another word, Pinarius departed.

After his visit from Pinarius, Potitius suffered sleepless nights. He had no doubt that his cousin's knowledge of a plot against the king was genuine; nor did he doubt that Pinarius's parting threat was sincere. Should he warn Romulus? Over and over in his mind Potitius imagined doing so, yet he could not find the will to act. Was it because he feared Pinarius? Or was it because, despite his protestations of loyalty, his relations with the king had grown as strained as those of the other senators?

Pinarius had left him with the impression that an attack on Romulus was imminent. Only a few days later, Roma celebrated the festival of Consualia, with rituals and competitions to commemorate the first athletic games and the taking of the Sabine women. Potitius's duties as a haruspex required his attendance on the king, and he spent the day of the Consualia in an agony of suspense. First, a sacrifice was made to Consus, the god of secret deliberations, to whom Romulus had prayed when formulating his plan to seize the Sabine women, and to whom Romulus had erected an altar after his success. The Altar of Consus was kept buried during the rest of the year and uncovered only for the Consualia, when the king asked for the god's continued blessing for his covert schemes. What more appropriate day could there be for an attack on Romulus, plotted in secret? Pinarius, too, attended the king, and Potitius watched him closely; but Pinarius showed no signs of strain or high emotion. The sacrifice to Consus was propitious, the games were blessed with splendid weather, and the day passed without incident.

More days came and went with no attack on Romulus, yet Potitius felt no respite from the anxiety that spoiled his sleep. He found himself watching the king and the senators with fresh eyes. Everything Pinarius had said was true. The king had grown arrogant and careless; he blatantly favored young warriors and newcomers, and just as blatantly showed contempt to his old comrades. The senators concealed their anger in the king's presence, but after he and his young lictors passed by, hatred erupted on their faces and they fell to whispering among themselves—whispers that ceased the moment Potitius drew close enough to hear.

716 B.C.

Summer passed to fall, fall to winter, and winter to spring. Another summer approached, and still the senators did not act. The reign of the king seemed as unshakable as ever. Had the conspirators changed their minds? Had the celestial phenomenon predicted by Pinarius failed to occur? Or had his cousin's overture to join the plot, and Potitius's refusal, been reason enough for its cancellation? Potitius had no way of knowing, for the other senators barred him from their counsels. He had forfeited any chance to warn the king by waiting too long; how could he explain to Romulus his procrastination in the face of such a threat? Potitius found himself friendless and alone.

He told himself that the plot against Romulus, like every previous plot, had come to nothing. Nevertheless, a feeling of impending doom settled over him. He could not shake its grip.

Long ago, Potitius had made a decision to break with an old family tradition. Instead of passing the amulet of Fascinus to his son when the boy reached manhood, he had kept the amulet for himself, intending to wear it, on special occasions, until his death. This was in keeping, he reasoned, with the law of paterfamilias decreed by Romulus, whereby Potitius would remain supreme head of his household as long as he lived.

But now, goaded by a premonition of dread, Potitius decided to pass the amulet to his eldest grandson. At first, he thought to honor tradition and do so at the next Feast of Hercules, but his premonition grew so urgent that he called the family together a full month before the festival. He wept to see them all in one place, feeling certain that it was for the last time; they wondered at his tears, which he made no effort to explain.

He made a solemn ceremony of removing the talisman from his neck and placing it over the neck of his grandson. Once this was done, Potitius felt greatly relieved. Fascinus was the oldest god of his family, even older than Hercules, and now that Potitius had safely passed on the god's amulet, the most ancient obligation laid down by his ancestors had been fulfilled.

The next day, Potitius was called upon to take the auspices at the dedication of the Altar to Vulcan, god of the fiery regions underground. The place was the Goat's Marsh, at the western end of the Field of Mavors, where a streamlet that ran through the valley north of the Quirinal terminated in a pit of hot, bubbling quicksand. Over the years, many a wandering goat had been lost in the treacherous pit; hence its name, and the notion that the site must be sacred to Vulcan. Here the god claimed sacrifices, whether men offered them or not.

Romulus had decided to attach great pomp to the occasion. He ordered all the senators and citizens of Roma to attend. Throughout the morning, people gathered on the Field of Mavors, arriving from their homes scattered across the Seven Hills. The warriors who had fought in the king's many campaigns wore the trophies they had captured in battle—finely wrought bronze armor, helmets decorated with brightly dyed plumes of horsehair, belts of tooled leather with iron clasps. Even the poorest citizens wore their best, if only a tunic without a hole in it.

At the appointed hour, the king and his retinue came striding though the crowd. Potitius wore his ceremonial yellow cloak and conical cap. The king wore a new cloak upon which the dye was barely dry; Potitius could smell the distinctive scent of the red stain obtained from the madder plant. The king's young lictors were outfitted in newly minted armor that shone brightly beneath the midday sun. In a tradition borrowed from Etruscan royalty, the weapons they carried were bundles of rods and axes—rods for scourging anyone who offended the king, and axes for executing on the spot any man the king declared to be his enemy.

The new altar had been cut from blocks of limestone and erected on a high mound of earth. It was decorated with elaborate carvings that depicted scenes of battle from the recent war against Veii, and Romulus's triumphal procession, on foot, through the streets of Roma. The best Etruscan artisans had been hired to carve the altar. Gazing at the results of their intricate workmanship, Potitius thought how simple and plain the unadorned Ara Maxima seemed in comparison.

Nearby, the goat intended for the sacrifice bleated plaintively, as if aware of its fate. Romulus himself would perform the sacrifice, slaying the goat with a ritual knife upon the altar. Potitius's role was to examine the animal first, to make sure that it was without defects. He checked that the goat's eyes were clear, its orifices without discharge, its coat unblemished, its limbs whole, its hooves sound. Potitius declared to Romulus that the goat was suitable for sacrifice. While the goat was being bound, Potitius glanced at the faces of the senators in the front ranks of the crowd. His eyes connected with those of Pinarius.

His cousin wore a strange expression. His smiled, but his eyes were grim. With a prickle of apprehension, Potitius knew that the day of which Pinarius had spoken had finally arrived. And yet, how could anyone dare to attack the king in such a place, at such a time? His lictors were all around, the whole population of Roma was assembled to pay witness, and the occasion was sacred.

Bound and bleating, the goat was placed upon the altar. Romulus held up the sacrificial knife and turned to face the great multitude that had gathered on the Field of Mavors. "So many!" he murmured. His voice was so low that only Potitius was close enough to hear. "Did you ever think, when we were young, that such a day as this would come? That they would all stand before us and call us king, that only gods would stand above us?"

Potitius heard the king's words, but knew they were not intended for him; it was to Remus that Romulus spoke. In that instant, Potitius knew why he had never warned the king of the plot against him—not because he feared Pinarius, and not because of his own small grievances against the king. In the deepest recesses of his heart, he had never forgiven Romulus for the murder of Remus. Nor had Romulus ever forgiven himself.

The murmur that rose from the crowd grew hushed in anticipation of the king's invocation to Vulcan. Potitius gazed out at the sea of faces. It seemed to him that there had been a gradual change in the light, an increasing dimness that was most peculiar, almost uncanny. Others had noticed the change, as well. A few in the crowd turned their faces up to the sun.

What they saw was bizarre and inexplicable. A great portion of the sun had turned as black as coal, as if a portion of its flame had gone out.

Men pointed and shouted in alarm. Soon everyone was gazing at the sun. Its fire dwindled until it appeared to be a blackened ball of coal rimmed with flame. People in the crowd gasped in wonder and awe, then began to scream in of panic.

At the same time, Potitius felt a strong wind on his face. The day had been almost cloudless; now, from the west, vast heaps of black clouds tumbled across the already darkened sky. The wind snatched the conical cap from Potitius's head. He reached in vain to snatch it back and watched it go spinning though the air. An invisible hand seemed to lift it over the altar, crumple it, then throw it down onto the glistening surface of the Goat's Marsh. The cap weighed very little, yet the bubbling quicksand sucked it under in the blink of an eye.

Potitius turned to face the crowd again. By a spectral light which grew dimmer with each heartbeat, he saw that the Field of Mavors had become a scene of chaos. Above the howling of the wind, he heard screams of pain and fear. People ran this way and that, trampling and tripping over those who fell. Romulus's young lictors were as frightened as the rest; instead of forming a cordon around the king, they scattered like leaves. A jagged bolt of lightning tore across the black sky and struck Asylum Hill. The crack of thunder that followed split his ears and almost knocked him down. The flash had completely blinded him, so that when he stepped forward, thinking to find the king, Potitius groped the empty air like a man without eyes.

Raindrops as hard as jagged pebbles pelted his face. He smelled the dye of the madder, and knew that Romulus was near. His fingers touched another man's garments. He gripped the wool and held it tightly. Another bolt of lightning tore the sky. By its unearthly white light, he saw before him not Romulus, but Pinarius. In one hand his cousin held a bloody sword. In the other, gripping it by a tuft of hair, he held a severed head. Its face was turned away from him, but upon the head Potitius saw the iron crown of Romulus.

When Remus had died, Potitius had felt as if he were in a nightmare. Now, despite the stark horror of the moment, he felt acutely, supremely clearheaded, as if he were waking from a dream. Another bolt of lightning lit the scene. He watched, with curious detachment, as Pinarius drew back his sword. Potitius reached up reflexively to touch the amulet of Fascinus at his neck, but the talisman was not there; he had given it to his grandson the day before. The amulet, at least, was safe.

With a great shout, Pinarius swung the red blade toward his neck.

Jupiter himself had sanctioned what he had done. Or so Pinarius reasoned, for although he had long ago predicted the eclipse and planned to take advantage of the awe and confusion it would inevitably inspire, he could not have foreseen the magnificent storm that accompanied it. Lightning was the hand of Jupiter. Thunder was his voice. The god himself had lighted Pinarius's way to the altar. The god had roared with approval when Pinarius severed the head from Romulus's shoulders.

Pinarius had warned his cousin not to stand too close to the king. Everyone else, even Romulus's lictors, had fled from the scene, and yet, in the first moment after the deed was done, there was Potitius, gripping his robes and staring at him. The decision to kill him had been instantaneous, and correct. Jupiter had roared approval with a deafening peal of thunder.

Very quickly, Pinarius and his accomplices stripped the headless body of Romulus, then threw it into the Goat's Marsh, where it sank without a trace. They did the same with the body of Potitius. Even if the marsh should ever give up its secrets, who could identify two naked bodies, each without a head? Various of the senators departed with pieces of the clothing hidden under their robes, vowing to burn these bits of incriminating evidence as soon as they reached their homes.

Pinarius removed the crown from Romulus's head and placed the circle of iron upon the altar, where it could easily be found. He had intended to dispose of the head of Romulus himself, but instead he handed it to one of his accomplices and ordered the man to bury it in a secret location. The death of Potitius presented him with a more pressing obligation. The man had been a fool, but he was also Pinarius's relative and his fellow priest of Hercules; to dispose of his severed head was the least and the last favor that Pinarius could perform for Potitius.

The eclipse was passing. The darkness lessened by small degrees, but the storm raged on. The Field of Mavors was abandoned, but Pinarius nonetheless kept the head concealed beneath his robes as he made his way toward Asylum Hill. He hurried up the steep path. Newcomers still made camps before the Altar of Asylaeus, but the storm's fury had driven them all elsewhere. Pinarius proceeded to the Temple of Jupiter. To give thanks to the god for blessing the events of the day, Pinarius would bury his cousin's head in the shadow of Jupiter's temple.

He knelt in the mud and took a last look at his cousin's face. Then, using his bare hands, he set about digging a deep hole in the soft, wet earth.

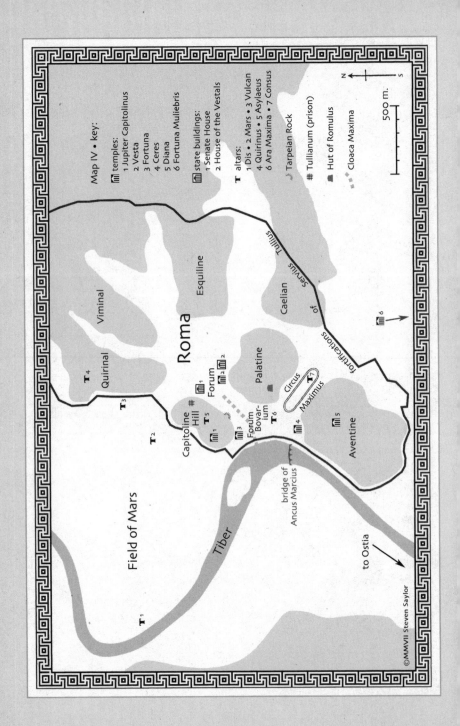

Map IV • key:

temples:
1 Jupiter Capitolinus
2 Vesta
3 Fortuna
4 Ceres
5 Diana
6 Fortuna Muliebris

state buildings:
1 Senate House
2 House of the Vestals

altars:
1 Dis • 2 Mars • 3 Vulcan
4 Quirinus • 5 Asylaeus
6 Ara Maxima • 7 Consus

Tarpeian Rock

Tullianum (prison)

Hut of Romulus

Cloaca Maxima

500 m.

N — S

Roma

Field of Mars

Tiber

Quirinal

Viminal

Esquiline

Capitoline Hill

Forum

Palatine

Caelian

Circus Maximus

Forum Boarium

Aventine

fortifications of Servius Tullius

bridge of Ancus Marcius

to Ostia

©MMVII Steven Saylor

CORIOLANUS

510 B.C.

The twelve-year-old boy sat cross-legged on the floor, reciting his lessons. His grandfather sat before him on a simple wooden folding chair with bronze hinges. Despite the fact that the chair had no back, the old man sat rigidly erect, setting an example for the boy.

"Now tell me, Titus, upon what day did King Romulus depart from this earth?"

"Upon the Nones of Quinctilis, two hundred and six years ago."

"How old was he?"

"Fifty-five."

"And where did this occur?"

"At the Altar of Vulcan that stands before the Goat's Marsh, at the western end of the Field of Mars."

"Ah, yes, but was it called the Field of Mars in those days?"

The boy frowned. Then, remembering what he had been taught, his face brightened. "No, grandfather. In King Romulus's day, people called it the Field of Mavors, because that's what they called Mars in olden times—Mavors."

"And what do we learn from this example?"

"That words and names can change over time—they usually grow shorter and simpler—but that the gods are eternal."

The old man smiled. "Very good! Now, describe the ascension of King Romulus."

"There was an eclipse of the sun and also a great storm, and the people fled in fear. That's why the festival each year held on that day is called the Populifugia, 'the flight of the people.' But one man, an ancestor of the Pinarii, remained. His name was just Pinarius; back then, most people only had one name, not two, as we do now. Pinarius witnessed the miracle that occurred. The sky opened and a funnel-shaped whirlwind came down. It was the hand of Jupiter, and it lifted King Romulus into the sky. Before he left, the king removed his iron crown and placed it on the Altar of Vulcan, for his successor. Thus King Romulus became the only man in all history who never died. He simply left the earth, to go live as a god among the gods."

"Very good, Titus! You've been studying hard, haven't you?"

"Yes, grandfather." Pleased with himself, young Titus Potitius reached up and touched the amulet of Fascinus that hung from a gold chain around his neck. His father had given it to him at the last Feast of Hercules, when Titus had assisted for the first time as a priest at the altar.

"Now tell me: who were the kings who followed Romulus, and what were their greatest achievements?"

"King Romulus had no son, so after he departed, the senators met and debated who should succeed him. This set a precedent that would be followed forever after, that the succession of the kings is not hereditary; instead, a king is chosen, to serve for life, by the Senate. They chose Numa Pompilius, a man of Sabine blood who had never even set foot in Roma. This set another wise precedent—that the new king could be an outsider, and should not come from the ranks of the Senate, else the senators might fight among themselves to seize the crown. The reign of Numa was long and peaceful. He was very pious, and he did much to organize the colleges of priests and the worship of the gods."

"Then came Tullus Hostilius. He was as warlike as Numa had been peaceable. By destroying her rivals, he made Roma the chief city of all the Latin-speaking people of Italy. Tullus Hostilius built the great assembly hall in the Forum where the Senate meets.

"Then came Ancus Marcius, who was Numa's grandson. He built the first bridge across the Tiber. He also founded the city of Ostia at the mouth of the river, to serve as a seaport for Roma.

"The fifth king was the first King Tarquinius. He was of Greek blood but came from the Etruscan city of Tarquinia, from which he took his name. He was both a great warrior and a great builder. He constructed the great underground sewer, the Cloaca Maxima, that follows the ancient course of the Spinon and drains the Forum. He laid out the great horse-racing track in the long valley between the Palatine and the Aventine, which we call the Circus Maximus, and built the first viewing stands. And he drew up the plans and began the foundations for the greatest building ever conceived anywhere on earth, the new Temple of Jupiter on the Capitoline Hill."

Titus rose from the floor and strode to the window, where the shutters were open to let in the warm breeze. The house of the Potitii was situated high on the Palatine, so that the window afforded a splendid view of the massive construction project on the neighboring Capitoline Hill. Surrounded by scaffolds swarming with artisans and laborers, the new temple had begun to take shape. It was of an Etruscan design called araeostyle, with a broad, decorated pediment set atop widely spaced columns and a single grand entrance from the recessed porch. Titus gazed at the sight, fascinated.

His grandfather, ever the pedagogue, prompted a digression. "Was the hill always called the Capitoline?"

"No. Since the days of King Romulus it was called Asylum Hill, but now people have started calling it the Capitoline—'Head Hill.'"

"And why is that?"

"Because of the amazing thing the diggers found when they started work on the new temple foundations, back in the reign of the first King Tarquinius. They uncovered the head of a man, which appeared to be very ancient but was remarkably well preserved. The priests called it a sign from the gods, and a most excellent one, portending that Roma would become the head of the world." Titus frowned. "How could such a thing have happened, grandfather? Who would have buried a head with no body on the Capitoline, and how was it preserved?"

The old man cleared his throat. "There are mysteries which no man can explain, which are nonetheless true, for tradition tells us so. If you doubt the veracity of the tale, I can assure that I myself, as a young man, was privileged to see the head not long after it was found. The man's features were somewhat decayed, but one could see very clearly that his hair was blond, mixed with gray, as was his beard."

"He sounds like you, grandfather."

The old man raised an eyebrow. "I'm not as far gone as that! Now, back to the list of the kings. After the first Tarquinius . . ."

"The first Tarquinius was succeeded by Servius Tullius. He had been a slave in the royal household, but he rose to such prominence that when Tarquinius died, he was put forward by Tarquinius's widow to succeed him. He greatly reinforced and extended the fortifications of the city until all the Seven Hills were enclosed by pickets, walls, embankments, and trenches. He also excavated the underground cell in the state prison at the foot of the Capitoline, which we call the Tullianum, where the enemies of the king are executed by strangulation. He put these projects first, so that work on the new temple came to a standstill."

"And after Servius Tullius comes the present king, the son of Tarquinius, also named Tarquinius. Our king is famous for acquiring the Sibylline Books, which are full of prophecies that guide the people in times of crisis."

"And how did that come about?"

Titus smiled, for this was one of his favorite stories. "The Sibyl lives in a cave down in Cumae, on the coast. The god Apollo compelled her to write hundreds of strange verses on palm leaves. She stitched together all the palm leaves into nine scrolls, which she brought to Roma and offered to sell to King Tarquinius, saying that if a man could interpret her verses rightly, he could foretell the future. Tarquinius was tempted, but he told her that the price was too steep, whereupon she waved her hand and three of the scrolls burst into flames. Then she offered to sell him the remaining six—for the original asking price of the nine! Tarquinius was angry and again refused, whereupon the Sibyl burned three more scrolls, then named the same price once again. King Tarquinius, thinking of all the knowledge that had already been lost, gave in. He paid the price she had asked for nine books and got only three. The Sibylline Books are very sacred. They must be consulted only in the direst emergency. To house them, Tarquinius set about completing the great temple which his father began."

Again Titus gazed out the window. For most of his life, work on the temple had been progressing. With the huge columns and massive pediment finally in place, its final form was becoming more evident with each passing month. Even men who had traveled far beyond Roma, to the great cities of Greece and Egypt, said they had never seen a building so grand. "No wonder they call him Tarquinius the Proud," murmured Titus.

The old man stiffened. "What did you say?"

"Tarquinius the Proud—that's what I've heard men call the king."

"What men? Where?"

Titus shrugged. "Strangers. Shopkeepers. People passing in the Forum or on the street."

"Don't listen to them. And don't repeat what they say!"

"But why not?"

"Just do as I say!"

Titus bowed his head. His grandfather was the eldest of the Potitii, the paterfamilias. His will within the family was law, and it was not Titus's place ever to question him.

The old man sighed. "I will explain, but only once. When men use that word about the king, they do not mean it as a compliment. Quite the opposite; they mean that he is arrogant, stubborn, and vain. So do not say such a thing aloud, not even to me. Words can be dangerous, especially words meant to wound a king."

Titus nodded gravely, then frowned. "One thing puzzles me, grandfather. You say the monarchy is not hereditary, but the present King Tarquinius's father was also king."

"Yes, but the crown did not pass directly from father to son."

"I know; Servius Tullius came between. But didn't Tarquinius kill him, and that's how he became king?"

The old man drew a quick breath, but did not reply. Titus was old enough to be taught the list of kings and their principal achievements, but not yet old enough to be taught about the political machinations that had brought each king to the throne and the scandals that had attended each reign. To a young man who could not yet understand the importance of discretion, one hesitated to speak ill even of kings long dead; one certainly did not speak ill of a living king. About Tarquinius and the murders that had brought him to the throne, and all the murders that had followed, there was little to say that was fit for the boy's ears.

Ambitious to become a king like his father, Tarquinius had married one of the two daughters of his father's successor, Servius Tullius, but when she proved to be more loyal to her father than to Tarquinius, he decided he preferred her more ruthless sister. When Tarquinius's wife conveniently died, as did the husband of his sister-in-law, and the two bereaved spouses married one another, the word "poison" was whispered all over Roma. In short order, Tarquinius and his new wife murdered her father, and Tarquinius declared himself king, dispensing with the formalities of election by the people and confirmation by the Senate.

Having seized the throne by force, Tarquinius ruled by fear. Previous kings had consulted the Senate on important matters and called upon them to act as jurors. Tarquinius showed only contempt for the Senate. He claimed sole authority to judge capital cases, and used that authority to punish innocent men with death or exile; he confiscated his victims' property to pay for his grand schemes, including the new temple. The Senate had grown to include three hundred members, but its numbers diminished as the king destroyed one after another of its wealthiest, most prominent men. His sons grew to be as arrogant as their father, and there were rumors that Tarquinius planned to name one of them as his heir, abolishing outright the ancient rules of nonhereditary succession and election by the people.

The old man sighed and changed the subject. "Fetch your stylus and wax tablet. You shall practice your writing skills."

Titus dutifully took the instruments from a special box in which they were kept. The tablet was a framed piece of flat wood upon which a thick coating of wax had been laid down. The stylus was a heavy iron rod with a sharpened tip, of a circumference to comfortably fit a boy's hand. The wax had been written on only a few times, then rubbed flat afterward for the next lesson.

"Write the name of the seven kings, in order," said his grandfather. Writing was a skill the Romans had learned from the Etruscans; the Etruscans had learned it from the people of Magna Graecia—Greeks who in recent generations had colonized southern Italy, bringing with them the advantages of a culture more advanced and refined than those of the native Italians. Writing, especially, had proven to be of great value. Records and lists could be kept, royal proclamations and laws could be written down, corrections and additions could be made to the calendar, and messages could be sent from one place to another. To master the skill required great diligence, and it was best learned at an early age. As a hereditary priest of Hercules, and as a member of the patrician class—a descendent of one of Roma's founding families—with the prospect of someday becoming a senator like his grandfather, it was very much to young Titus's advantage to learn to read and to write.

Usually, Titus was very conscientious about forming letters, but on this day he seemed unable to concentrate. He kept making mistakes, rubbing them clear, then starting over. Repeatedly, he looked toward the window. His grandfather smiled. To capture a boy's imagination, the making of letters in wax could not hope to compete with the construction of the new temple. Titus's fascination with the project was perhaps not a bad thing; a knowledge of how such a building was made might serve him well someday.

He waited until Titus had painstakingly written the "s" at the end of Tarquinius, then patted him on the head. "Good enough," he said. "Your lessons are over for today. You may go now."

Titus looked up at him in surprise.

"Did I not tell you to go?" said his grandfather. "I'm a bit tired today. Being compared to that head discovered on the Capitoline has made me feel my age! Smooth the wax, put away your stylus, and then be off. And say hello to that fellow Vulca for me!"

The afternoon was warm and sunny, with hours of daylight left. Titus ran all the way from his family's house on the Palatine down to the Forum, then uphill again to the top of the Capitoline. He didn't stop until he reached the Tarpeian Rock, the sheer summit from which traitors were hurled to their death. The rock also provided a panoramic view of the city below. His friend Gnaeus Marcius loved to play with miniature wooden soldiers, pretending to be their commander; Titus preferred to gaze down at the city of Roma as if its buildings were toys, and to imagine rearranging them and constructing new ones.

Roma had changed much since the days of Romulus. Where once the Seven Hills had been covered by forests and pastures, and the settlements had been small and scattered, now there were buildings everywhere one looked, built close together with dirt and gravel streets running between them. Some citizens still lived in thatched huts and kept animals in pens, but many homes were now made of wood, some rising to two stories, and the houses of wealthy families—such as the Potitii—were grand affairs made of brick and stone with shuttered windows, interior courtyards, terraces, and tile roofs. The Forum had become the civic center of Roma, with a paved street called the Sacred Way running through it; it was the site of numerous temples and shrines and also of the Senate House. The marketplace beside the river was now called the Forum Bovarium, from the word *bovinus,* referring to its ancient and continuing role as a cattle market; it had become the great emporium of central Italy. The original settlement at the foot of the Capitoline, including the ancestral hut of the Potitii, had long ago been cleared away and built over to make room for the expanding marketplace. At the heart of the Forum Bovarium stood the ancient Ara Maxima, where once a year Titus and his family, along with the Pinarii, celebrated the Feast of Hercules.

Roma under the kings had prospered and grown. Now the grandest sign of the city's progress was rising on the summit of the Capitoline. Turning his back on the panoramic view, Titus gazed up at the magnificent project which each day drew nearer to completion. Since his last visit to the site, a new section of scaffolding had gone up along the front of the temple. The workers on the top tier were applying plaster to the recessed surface of the pediment.

"Titus, my friend! I haven't you seen for a while." The speaker was a tall man with strands of gray in his beard, about the age of Titus's father. There was plaster dust on his blue tunic. He carried a stylus and a small wax tablet for making sketches.

"Vulca! I've been very busy with my studies lately. But my grandfather let me go early today."

"Excellent! I have something very special to show you." The man smiled and gestured for him to follow.

Vulca was an Etruscan, famous all over Italy as an architect and artist. King Tarquinius had employed him not only to oversee construction of the temple, but to decorate it inside and out. The building was made of common materials—wood, brick, and plaster—but when Vulca was done painting, it would be dazzling: yellow, black, and white for the walls and columns, red for the capitals and the bases of the columns, more red to trim the pediment, and many shades of green and blue to highlight the small architectural details.

But the most impressive of Vulca's creations would be the statues of the gods. Properly speaking, the statues were not ornaments; they would not decorate the temple, but rather, the temple would exist to house the sacred statues. Vulca had described his intentions to Titus many times, and had drawn sketches on his wax tablet to illustrate, but Titus had not yet seen them; the terra-cotta statues were being made in great secrecy in a concealed workshop on the Capitoline, to which only Vulca and his most skilled artisans had access. Titus was greatly surprised when the artist led him though a makeshift doorway into a walled-off area beside the temple, and even more surprised when they rounded a corner and a statue of Jupiter confronted them.

Titus gasped. The statue was of red terra-cotta, not yet painted, but the impression that the god was physically present was nonetheless overwhelming. Seated on a throne, the bearded, powerfully built father of gods looked down on him with a serene countenance. Jupiter was dressed in a toga, much like the royal garment the king wore, and in his right hand, instead of a scepter, he held a thunderbolt.

"The toga will be painted purple, with a border of gold foil," Vulca explained. "The thunderbolt will be gold, as well. The king balked when he learned the expense of the gold foil, until I pointed out what a thunderbolt made from solid gold would cost him."

Titus was awed. "Magnificent!" he whispered. "I never imagined . . . I mean, you've described to me what the statue would look like, but in my imagination I could never really . . . it's so . . . so much more . . ." His shook his head. Words failed him.

"Of course, no one will ever see the god this close. Jupiter will be positioned on a suitably ornate pedestal at the back of the main chamber, so as to gaze down on everyone who enters. The other two will be placed in their own, smaller chambers, Juno to the right and Minerva to the left."

Tearing his eyes from the Jupiter, Titus saw the other two figures beyond. These were not as far advanced. The Juno had not yet been given a head. The Minerva was little more than an armature that suggested the shape to come.

Then his eyes fell on a sight even more fantastic than the Jupiter. His gasp of astonishment was so loud that Vulca laughed.

The piece was huge, and so complex that it boggled Titus's imagination. It was a larger-than-life-size statue of Jupiter in a quadriga—a chariot pulled by four horses. The standing Jupiter, holding his thunderbolt aloft, was even more impressive than the Jupiter enthroned. The four horses, each different, were sculpted with remarkable detail, from the flashing eyes and flaring nostrils to the muscular limbs and magnificent tails. The chariot was made of wood and bronze, like a real vehicle, but of giant size, with extravagant designs and decorations on every surface.

"It all comes apart, of course, so that it can be reassembled atop the pediment," explained Vulca. "The horses will be painted white—four magnificent, snow-white steeds worthy of the king of the gods. The attachment of this sculpture to the pediment will be the final step in the construction. Once Jupiter and the quadriga are firmly in place and fully painted, the temple will be ready to be dedicated."

Titus gaped. "Vulca, I can't believe you're showing me this. Who else has seen it?"

"Only my workmen. And the king, of course, since he's paying for it."

"But why are you showing me?"

Vulca said something in Etruscan, then translated it into Latin: "If the flea hangs around long enough, sooner or later he'll see the dog's balls." When Titus looked at him blankly, Vulca laughed. "That's a very old, very vulgar Etruscan saying, young man, of which your staid grandfather would doubtless disapprove. How many times did I see you skulking about the work site before I called you over and asked your name? And how many times have you been back since then? And how many questions have you asked me about the tools and the materials and all the processes? I don't think I can count that high! I daresay there's not a man in all Roma, outside myself, who knows this building better than you do, Titus Potitius. If I were to die tomorrow, you could tell the workmen what remains to be done."

"But you won't die, Vulca! Jupiter would never allow it!"

"Nor would the king, not until I'm done with his temple."

Titus walked up to one of the horses and dared to touch it. "I never imagined they would be so big, and so beautiful. This will be the greatest temple ever built, anywhere."

"I'd like to think so," said Vulca.

Abruptly, Titus gave a yelp. He reached up to rub the spot where a pebble had struck his head. He caught a glimpse of another stone descending on him from the sky and jumped aside.

From beyond the wall which hid the works in progress came the sound of boyish giggling.

Vulca raised an eyebrow. "I believe that must be your two friends, Titus. I'm afraid they are *not* invited to see the statues, so if you want to join them, you'll have to step outside."

"Titus!" called one of the boys outside, in a loud whisper. "What are you doing in there? Is that crazy old Etruscan molesting you?" There was more giggling.

Titus blushed. Vulca tousled the boy's blond hair and smiled. "Don't worry, Titus. I long ago stopped taking offense at schoolboy taunts. Run along now, and see what those two want from you."

Reluctantly, Titus took his leave of Vulca and made his way out of the enclosure. From behind a stack of bricks, his friends Publius Pinarius and Gnaeus Marcius staged a playful ambush, one of them grabbing his arms while the other tickled him. Titus broke free. The others chased him all the way to the Tarpeian Rock, where they all came to an abrupt halt, laughing hard and gasping for breath.

"What was the Etruscan showing you in there?" demanded Gnaeus.

"I think they were playing a game," said Publius. "The Etruscan said, 'I'll show you my measuring rod, if you'll show me your Fascinus.'" He flicked his finger against the amulet at Titus's neck.

"Not much of a game," said Gnaeus. "Anyone can see Titus's Fascinus!"

Titus made a face and tucked the amulet inside his tunic, out of sight. "You two aren't worthy to look on the god, anyway."

"*I* am!" protested Publius. "Am I not your fellow priest of Hercules? And am I not as much a patrician as you? Last February, did I not run beside you in the Lupercalia? Whereas our friend Gnaeus here . . ."

Gnaeus shot him an angry look. Publius had touched on a subject about which Gnaeus was increasingly sensitive. Publius and Titus were both of the patrician class, descendents of the first senators whom Romulus had called the fathers, or *patres,* of Roma. The patricians jealously guarded the ancient privileges of their class. The rest of the citizenry, rich and poor alike, were simply the common people, or plebeians. Plebeians could attain wealth through commerce and distinction on the battlefield. They could even attain great power—Gnaeus's distant relative, Ancus Marcius, had become king—but they could never claim the prestige which attached to the patricians.

To be sure, Gnaeus's mother was a patrician; Veturia came from a family almost as old as the Potitii and the Pinarii. But his deceased father had been a plebeian, and, following the law of paterfamilias, a son was assigned to the class of the father. To Titus and Publius, their friend's plebeian status was of little consequence; Gnaeus was the best athlete, the most skilled equestrian, and the handsomest and smartest boy they knew. But to Gnaeus, class mattered a great deal. His father had died in battle when he was quite young, and he identified more closely with his mother and her family. Veturia had raised him to be as proud as any patrician, and it vexed him greatly that a patrician was the one thing he could never be. Perversely, he had no sympathy with plebeians who argued that class distinctions should be erased; Gnaeus always took the patrician side and showed nothing but contempt for what he called "upstart plebs."

Gnaeus usually carried himself with aloof self-confidence, a trait which Titus greatly admired; his demeanor matched his haughty good looks. But the irony of his class loyalty was the flaw in his armor; Publius, who enjoyed getting a rise from him, could not resist alluding now and then to Gnaeus's plebeian status. On this occasion, Gnaeus hardly blinked. He fixed the other boy with a steely gaze.

"Very soon, Publius Pinarius, we three shall be of fighting age. Every Roman fights; it is the highest duty that Roma demands of her citizens, that they train every spring and go forth every summer in search of fresh booty. But not every Roman achieves the same degree of glory. The poorer plebs, with their rusty swords and ramshackle armor, who must fight on foot because they cannot afford a horse, have a hard time of it; we can only pity them, and expect little glory from their bloodshed. But from men of property, like ourselves, who can afford the very best weapons and armor, who have time to train and opportunity to master the fine art of horsemanship, Roma expects much more. Glory is what matters in this world. Only the greatest warrior attains the highest glory. That is what I intend to become, if only to make my mother proud of me: the greatest warrior that Roma has ever seen. For now, Publius, you can taunt me all you want, because as yet we're still only boys, without glory. But soon we will be men. Then the gods will see which of us can more proudly call himself a Roman."

Publius shook his head. "Upstart! Pompous little pleb!"

Gnaeus turned and strode away, his head held high.

Titus reacted to Gnaeus's speech much as he had when he beheld Vulca's statue, and, gazing after his friend, he muttered the same word: "Magnificent!"

Publius looked at him sidelong and slapped the back of his head. "I think you're more in love with Gnaeus than you are with your Etruscan pederast." Publius had just learned this word, Greek in origin, and enjoyed using it.

"Shut up, Publius!"

That night, Titus's grandfather presided at a large family dinner, which included Titus's father and uncles and their families. There were two guests, as well: a young cousin of King Tarquinius, named Collatinus, and his wife, Lucretia. The women dined alongside the men, but, after the meal, when a serving girl brought a pitcher of wine, the women were offered no cups. When Collatinus made a toast to the health of the king, the women merely observed.

He was a pleasant-looking young man with a cheerful disposition, a bit loud and overbearing but not as arrogant as the sons of Tarquinius. His approachable manner was the chief reason the elder Potitius had decided to cultivate a relationship with him, thinking that Collatinus might offer access to the king without the unpleasantness of dealing with the king's sons.

After the toast, rather than taking only a sip, Collatinus drained his cup. "A most excellent wine," he declared, then smacked his lips and looked sidelong at his wife. "A pity you can't taste it, my dear."

Lucretia lowered her eyes and blushed. In that moment, the gaze of every man in the room was on her, including that of Titus, who thought he had never seen another woman half as beautiful. The blush only served to accentuate the perfection of her milky skin. Her hair was dark and lustrous, and so long that it might never have been cut. Though she was modestly dressed in a long-sleeved stola of dark blue wool, the lines of the gown suggested a body of exquisite proportions. As the blush subsided, she smiled and looked up again. Titus's heart missed a beat when her green eyes briefly met his. Then Lucretia looked at Collatinus.

"Sometimes when you kiss me, husband, I receive a faint taste of wine from your lips. That is enough for me."

Collatinus grinned and reached for her hand. "Lucretia, Lucretia! What a woman you are!" He addressed the others. "It was a wise law of King Romulus that forbade women to drink wine. They say the Greeks who live to the south let their women drink, and it causes no end of strife. There are even some here in Roma who have grown lax and allow such a thing, men of the very highest rank, who should know better." Titus sensed that Collatinus was referring to his royal cousins. "But no good can come of it, and I'm glad to see that old-fashioned virtue and common sense is practiced by the Potitii, in keeping with your status as one of Roma's oldest families."

Titus's grandfather nodded to acknowledge the compliment, then suggested another toast. "To old-fashioned virtue!"

Collatinus drained his cup again. Titus, being a boy, was given wine mixed with water, but Collatinus drank his wine undiluted, and was feeling its effects.

"If virtue is to be toasted," he said, "then a special toast should be drunk to the most virtuous among us—my wife Lucretia. There is no finer woman in all Roma! After the toast, I'll tell you a story to prove my point. To Lucretia!"

"To Lucretia!" said Titus.

She blushed and lowered her eyes again.

"A few nights ago," said Collatinus, "I was at the house of my cousin Sextus. His two brothers were present as well, so there we were, all the king's sons and myself. We were drinking, perhaps a bit more than we should have—those Tarquinius boys do everything in excess!—and a debate arose as to which of us had the most virtuous wife. Well, I say 'a debate arose'; in fact, perhaps it was I who brought up the subject, and why not? When a man is proud of a thing, should he keep silent? My wife Lucretia, I told them, is the most virtuous of women. No, no, they said, their own wives were every bit as virtuous. Nonsense, I said. Do you dare to make a wager on it? The Tarquinii can't resist a wager!

"So, one by one, we paid a visit to our spouses. We found Sextus's wife off in her wing of the house, playing a board game and gossiping with one of her servants. Not much virtue there! Off we went to the house of Titus. His wife—she must be three times the size of Lucretia!—was lying on a dining couch, eating one honey cake after another, surrounded by a mountain of crumbs. Not much virtue in gluttony! Then we called on the wife of Arruns. I regret to tell you that we found her, with some of her friends, actually *drinking wine*. When Arruns pretended to be shocked, she told him not to be silly and to pour her another cup! Clearly, she does it all the time, without the least fear of being punished. 'It helps me sleep,' she said. Can you imagine!

"Then we called on Lucretia. The hour was growing late. I assumed she might be asleep already, but do you know what we found her doing? She was sitting at her spinning wheel, busily working while she sang a lullaby to our new baby, who lay in his crib nearby. I tell you, there was never a prouder moment in my life! Not only did I win the wager, but you should have seen the look on the faces of the Tarquinius brothers when they saw Lucretia. She's always beautiful, but sitting there at her wheel, wearing a simple, sleeveless white gown so as to leave her arms free, with the glow of the lamplight on her face, she took my breath away. Those Tarquinius boys were so jealous! You made me very proud, my dear."

Collatinus took his wife's hand and kissed it. Titus sighed, imagining the sight of Lucretia by lamplight with bare shoulders and arms, but his grandfather frowned and shifted uneasily.

The old man quickly changed the subject, and the talk turned to politics. By cautious degrees, the elder Potitius sought to determine how candidly he could speak before Collatinus. As Collatinus drank more wine, it became evident that he was not overly fond of his cousin the king. The aristocratic bent of his politics, if not the specifics, reminded Titus of his haughty friend Gnaeus Marcius.

"All this coddling of the plebs by the king—and not the better sort of plebs, respectable people you or I might have to dinner, but ordinary laborers and lay-abouts; it's not to my liking, I can tell you," said Collatinus. "Of course, it's very clever of the king, to grind down the power of the Senate even as he curries favor with the mob. He prosecutes rich men, confiscates their wealth, then uses that wealth to build massive public works, which gives employment to the rabble; that monstrosity of a temple is the most obvious example. He sends the bravest and boldest of the patricians into battle against Roma's neighbors; the territory that's won is made into colonies where the landless plebs can settle. The blood of Roma's finest warriors is spilled so that some beggar can be given his own turnip patch!

"If he'd become king the old-fashioned way, by election, then no one could complain. They say the senators of old had to go down on their knees and beg King Numa to take the job; cousin Tarquinius has senators begging him not to take their property! Even the wise Numa needed the Senate to advise him, but not Tarquinius; he has a higher source of knowledge. Whenever there's a question about public policy, whether it's making war on a neighbor or fixing a crack in the Cloaca Maxima, Tarquinius whips out the Sibylline Books, picks a verse at random, reads it aloud in the Forum, and declares that it's proof that the gods are on his side. Tarquinius the Proud, indeed! My mouth is awfully dry. Could we have more wine?"

"Perhaps you'd rather drink some water," suggested Titus's grandfather.

"I can't imagine why, when you have such good wine in this house. Ah, there's the serving girl. By all means, fill it to the brim! Excellent; this tastes better than the last. Now what was I saying? Ah yes—the Sibylline Books. Well, at least the king paid the Sibyl for those, fair and square, even if he did get the bad end of the bargain. Usually he just takes whatever he wants, even from members of his own family. Look what he's done to his nephew, Brutus. People love Brutus; in whispers they'll tell you that he would have made a far better king than his uncle. He's one of the few men Tarquinius doesn't dare to destroy outright. Instead, he's gradually stripped Brutus of all his wealth, bit by bit, reducing him to a pauper. Yet Brutus has endured every indignity without saying one word against his uncle the king. People respect him all the more for showing so much fortitude and restraint."

Collatinus's speech was slurred and his eyelids drooped; he abruptly seemed to run out of energy. Titus's grandfather, who felt that too much had already been said, saw an opportunity to bring the evening to a close. He began to rise, but before he could wish his visitors farewell, Collatinus spoke again.

"Cousin Tarquinius could take everything from me, as well, just as he took everything from Brutus. He could do it like that!" He snapped his fingers. "Quick as a thunderbolt from Jupiter! Ruinous as an earthquake sent by Neptune! I could lose everything, except the one thing—thank the gods!—that the king and his sons can never take from me, the most perfect and most precious of all my possessions: my Lucretia!"

All though the evening, she had listened to him patiently, laughed softly at his jokes, shown no embarrassment when he spoke too loudly, and blushed sweetly when he complimented her. Now she graciously took his hand in hers and rose to her feet, bringing him with her. She had seen that it was time to go, and effortlessly assisted her inebriated husband to make a graceful exit.

Titus, observing her, thought that she must be very wise and very loving, as well as beautiful.

A few days later, Titus, with his friends Publius and Gnaeus, sat on an outcropping of stone near the Tarpeian Rock, watching the workers on the scaffolding that surrounded the new temple. Titus was explaining how the quadriga with Jupiter would be hoisted atop the pediment—Vulca had described the procedure to him at length—when Gnaeus abruptly interrupted. Gnaeus had a habit of changing the subject when he grew bored.

"My mother says there's going to be a revolution."

"What do you mean?" said Publius, who was also bored by Titus's talk about the temple.

"The days of King Tarquinius are numbered. That's what my mother says. People—at least the people who count—are fed up with him. They'll take his crown and give it to someone more worthy."

"Oh, and I suppose Tarquinius will humbly bow his head so that they can remove his crown?" Publius snorted. "What does your mother know, anyway? She's just a woman. My great-grandfather says quite the opposite." Publius was proud of the fact that his great-grandfather was still alive and had all his senses, and was very much the paterfamilias of the Pinarius family. "He says that Tarquinius has cut the legs off of anyone who might have opposed him—men like his nephew Brutus—and we'd better get used to the idea that one of his sons will take his place after he's gone. 'There may be a Tarquinius on the throne for as long as there's a Pinarius tending the Ara Maxima'—that's what my paterfamilias says. How about your grandfather, Titus? When you're not putting him to sleep with talk of temple construction, what does the head of the Potitii say about our beloved king?"

Titus didn't like to admit that his grandfather avoided talking to him directly about such serious matters. While he had some idea of his grandfather's opinions, he also knew that his grandfather wouldn't want him to discuss them openly with the loose-tongued Publius. "My grandfather would probably say that boys our age shouldn't indulge in dangerous gossip."

"It's only gossip when ill-informed women like Gnaeus's mother are talking. When it's men of affairs like ourselves, it's a serious discussion of politics," said Publius.

Titus laughed and was about to say something scornful about Publius's inflated ego, when Gnaeus abruptly threw himself onto the other boy.

Publius was no match for Gnaeus, especially when caught by surprise. In the blink of an eye, he was on his back on the ground, his limbs flailing helplessly.

"You will apologize for insulting my mother!" demanded Gnaeus.

Titus tried to pull him off, but his friend's arms were as unyielding as stone. "Gnaeus, let go of him! How can he say anything while you're squeezing his throat? Gnaeus, let go! You'll choke him to death!" Titus was genuinely alarmed. At the same time, he couldn't help laughing. Publius's face was as red as the king's toga, and the sputtering noises he made sounded as though they should be coming out of the other end of his body.

Titus laughed harder and harder, until his sides ached. Gnaeus, trying to keep a scowl on his face, suddenly burst out laughing and lost his grip. Publius jerked free and rolled away. He clutched his throat and glared at Gnaeus. Between coughing and wheezing, he managed a croak of protest. "You're mad, Gnaeus Marcius! You could have killed me!"

"I *should* have killed you, for insulting my mother and impugning my honor."

"Your honor!" Publius shook his head. "There should be a law forbidding a plebeian like you to even lay a finger on a patrician like me."

Gnaeus did not fly at him, but stood absolutely still. His face turned crimson. "How dare you say such a thing to me?"

"How dare I call you a plebeian? It's what you are, Gnaeus Marcius! Only a fool can't accept his fate, that's what my paterfamilias says."

Titus shook his head. Why was Publius still taunting Gnaeus? Did he want to be thrown from the Tarpeian Rock? Titus was wondering whether he should run to find help, when he heard a noise from the city below.

"What's that?" he said.

"What?" Publius kept a wary eye on Gnaeus.

"That sound. Don't you hear it? Like a great moan . . ."

"Or a roar. Yes, I hear it. Like the sound you hear from inside a seashell."

The noise distracted even Gnaeus from his rage. "Or a sob," he said. "The sound of a great many women all sobbing at once," he said.

"Something's happened," said Titus. "It's coming from the Forum."

Together, they strode to the verge of the cliff and looked down. The workers on the temple had also heard the noise. Men climbed from the scaffolding onto the roof of the temple to get a better view.

A great crowd had gathered in the Forum. More people were arriving from all directions. A group of senators, dressed in their togas, stood on the porch of the Senate House. Among them, even at such a great distance, Titus recognized the king's gaunt-faced nephew. Instead of a toga, Brutus wore a ragged tunic hardly fit for a beggar—a demonstration of the poverty to which the king had reduced him. He was speaking to the crowd.

"Can you hear what he's saying?" said Titus.

"He's too far away, and the crowd's too noisy," said Gnaeus. "Why won't they shut up?"

Those in the crowd nearest to the Senate House were quiet and attentive and all turned in one direction, listening to Brutus. It was the people at the back of the crowd who were moving about with their hands in the air, shouting and weeping. They were parting to make way for someone trying to pass through on his way to the Senate House.

"Who's that man, and what's he carrying?" said Titus.

"What man?" said Publius hoarsely, rubbing his throat.

"I can't see who it is, but I can see what he's carrying," said Gnaeus. "A woman. He's carrying a woman in his arms. She's completely limp. People are stepping back to make way for him. I think I see blood on his tunic. I think the woman must be . . ."

"Dead," said Titus, who felt a cold, hard knot in the pit of his stomach.

The man worked his way through the crowd, step by step. Wherever he passed, there was a commotion, followed by an awestruck silence. By the time he reached the steps of the Senate House, the entire crowd had fallen eerily silent. Staggering, as if the burden he carried had become intolerably heavy, he mounted the steps to the porch. Brutus and the senators bowed their heads and drew aside. The man turned to face the crowd.

"I knew it!" whispered Titus. "It's Collatinus. That means the woman in his arms . . ."

The lifeless body was dressed in a long-sleeved stola of dark blue, stained with blood at the breast. Her head was thrown back, hiding her face. Her dark hair hung straight down, so long that it brushed her husband's feet.

Brutus stepped forward. Now, in the utter silence, Titus could hear him clearly. "Tell them, Collatinus. They won't believe me. They don't want to believe such a terrible thing. Tell them what's happened."

Collatinus's wrenching sob reverberated around the Forum and sent a shiver through the crowd. For a long moment he seemed unable to compose himself. When he finally spoke, his words rang loud and clear. "Sextus Tarquinius did this. The king's son! He raped my wife, my beloved Lucretia. While I was away, he came to my house. He was welcomed as an honored guest, invited to dine, given a room. In the middle of the night, he came to her. He forced his way into her bed—our bed! He held a dagger to her throat—you can see where the blade scored her flesh! A servant heard her beg for mercy, but one of Sextus's men guarded the door. The servant sent for me, but by the time I arrived, Sextus was gone. Lucretia was weeping, inconsolable, mad with grief. Sextus left behind the knife he used to threaten her. Before I could stop her, she plunged it into her heart. She died in my arms!"

As if the weight suddenly grew too heavy, Collatinus dropped to his knees, still cradling the body in his arms. He hung his head and wept.

Brutus stepped forward and held up a bloody dagger. "This is the knife!" he cried. "The very blade that Sextus Tarquinius used when he raped Lucretia, the blade she used to kill herself." He waited for the gasps from the crowd to die down. "How much longer will we stand for this? What else will we allow the tyrant and his sons to take from us? This intolerable state of affairs ends here and now, today!" Brutus held the knife high in the air and turned to face the Capitoline, as if he were addressing Jupiter in the unfinished temple atop the hill. To Titus, it seemed as if the stern-looking, gaunt-faced man had abruptly turned to look directly at him and his friends. The sensation was unsettling, and Titus shivered.

"By the innocent blood on this knife," declared Brutus, "and by the gods, I swear that with fire and sword, and whatever else can lend strength to my arm, I will pursue Tarquinius the Proud, his wicked wife, and all his children, not one of whom deserves to live in the company of decent men, much less rule over them. I will drive them out, and never again will I let them or any other man be king in Roma!"

The crowd erupted in a tumult of shouting. Women tore at their hair. Men shook their fists. A mob surged up the steps of the Senate House and lifted Brutus onto their shoulders. He seemed to float above the crowd, his arm upraised to thrust the bloody knife toward heaven.

Even from the safety of the Capitoline, Titus felt a prickle of fear. He had never seen such a spectacle; the fury of the mob was like a force of nature unleashed. His heart pounded in his chest. His mouth was too dry to speak.

"What do you think he meant by that?" said Gnaeus. His voice seemed impossibly calm.

"He couldn't have said it more plainly," said Publius, his voice breaking. "Brutus means to drive Tarquinius out of Roma."

"Yes. And then what?"

Publius snorted with exasperation. "Brutus will take his place, of course."

"No, Publius, that's not what he said. 'Never again will I let them *or any other man* be king in Roma.' Brutus means to cast out the king, and put no one in his place."

Publius frowned. "But if there's no king, who will rule the city?"

Like his friends, Titus was puzzled. He was frightened and exhilarated, all at once, and struck dumb with grief that Lucretia—beautiful, wise, loving Lucretia—should have suffered such a horrible fate. He was overwhelmed by what he had just witnessed. Something had ended that day, and something else had begun, and all their lives would be changed forever.

509 B.C.

Dressed in his priestly robes and proudly wearing the talisman of Fascinus—for today he was present both in his ancestral role as a priest of Hercules and as the scion of the Potitii—Titus stood between his father and grandfather in the front ranks of the crowd that had gathered on the Capitoline before the new Temple of Jupiter. The Pinarii were there as well, in a place of equal honor. Publius's great-grandfather was looking very frail and more than a little confused; but whose head was not in a spin, after the tumultuous events of the last year?

The occasion was the dedication of the temple. Up to the last minute, Vulca had been frantically putting finishing touches here and there— daubing paint on the scuffed elbow of Minerva, polishing the great bronze hinges of the doors, instructing his men to move the throne of Jupiter a finger's width to the left because the statue was not precisely centered atop its pedestal. It did not matter that Vulca still perceived tiny imperfections everywhere; to Titus, there had never been anything as beautiful as the temple. It was truly worthy of its commanding position atop the Capitoline, which made it the most prominent building in all of Roma, dominating the skyline from every vantage point. With the scaffolding gone at last, Titus could fully appreciate the perfection of its proportions and the soaring line of the columns that supported the pediment. Atop the pediment, the statue of Jupiter in his chariot drawn by four white horses majestically evoked the supreme king of gods and men. The temple was a thing of earthly beauty that inspired religious awe.

Standing side by side on the porch of the temple, overseeing the dedication, were the two consuls, Brutus and Collatinus. Though his face was as gaunt as ever, Brutus no longer dressed in beggar's rags. Like Collatinus, he wore a toga with a purple stripe to denote his status as one of the two highest magistrates of the new republic.

Republic—the word was still new to Titus and fell strangely on his ear. It came from the words *res* (a thing, circumstance, state of being) and *publica* (of the people). *Res publica*: the people's state. In the wake of Tarquinius's sudden downfall and departure—the uprising had been so overwhelming that the revolution occurred almost without bloodshed— the leading men of the Senate had decided to run the state themselves, without a king. The common people had loudly insisted they must be given an assembly of their own, and laws to protect them, because the favor of the king had been their only bulwark against the whims of wealthy, powerful patricians.

"Rules, rules, rules!" complained Titus's grandfather, after attending the first raucous meetings of the new government. "When no man is king, every man is king, and thinks he should have his own way, or at least his own say. The result is chaos! Endless arguments and no agreement about anything, except that there must be new rules to override any old rules that were previously agreed upon. No one is satisfied. Everyone thinks everyone else is getting a better deal. It's *almost* enough to make a man nostalgic for the one we called Proud!"

Despite all the problems that plagued the new state, this was a day of celebration. The dedication of the new temple, which was to have been

King Tarquinius's crowning achievement, would serve instead to mark the first year of the new republic. Indeed, to Titus, the magnificence of Vulca's brightly painted statues and the breathless perfection of his architecture exemplified a bold new spirit in the city of Roma.

To a visitor, it might have appeared that the two magistrates on the porch of the temple were co-rulers, little different from kings. Their dress set them apart from and above the rest, and like kings they were guarded by lictors armed with rods and axes. Even the fact that they had been elected to office did not differentiate them from kings, for all the kings of Roma, except Tarquinius, had been elected to the post, even if some had been more freely chosen than others. But the two consuls, ruling side by side so that one might serve as a check on the other, were to serve for only a year, and then to relinquish their office to the next two consuls to win election. By dividing the powers of the consuls and holding annual elections, it was hoped that the state could be made to serve the people, and that Roma would never again fall under the sway of a tyrant like Tarquinius.

The public ceremony came to an end. The great doors of the temple were opened. The consuls entered, followed by a very select group of citizens, for the sanctuary could accommodate only a small portion of the crowd. Titus's grandfather was among them, as was the great-grandfather of Publius, who ascended the steps with difficulty, leaning upon the arm of his fellow senior priest of Hercules. Titus was not permitted to attend the more exclusive ceremony within the sanctuary, but, thanks to Vulca, he had already seen the finished chambers, which housed the statues of Jupiter, Juno, and Minerva, and been allowed to gaze upon the gods at his leisure.

The milling throng began to disperse. There was a joyous mood in the air. Men greeted one another with embraces and laughter. Titus felt inspired and uplifted.

When he saw Gnaeus nearby, his spirits rose even more, until Publius muttered into his ear, "Look there! It's your plebeian friend, Gnaeus Marcius. How did he get so near the front of the crowd? He must be posing as a Veturius today, pretending his mother's blood makes him one of us."

"Shut up, Publius! Say nothing to insult him. Deliberately causing dissension on such a day shows disrespect to Jupiter."

Publius laughed. "By all the gods, I should hate to offend your religious sensibilities, Titus! I'll simply move along, then. Greet the pompous little pleb in whatever fashion you imagine would please Jupiter."

After Publius disappeared, Titus called to Gnaeus, who returned his smile.

"You were right all along about Vulca and the temple," said Gnaeus. "Foreigner or not, he's given us a truly magnificent building, something all Roma can be proud of. I look forward to seeing the statues inside."

Titus merely nodded. To Publius, he proudly would have boasted that he had seen the statues already, but Gnaeus might think he was acting superior and take offense.

Gnaeus's smile faded. "You were standing closer to the consuls than I was. Did Brutus look rather haggard?"

"Perhaps. My grandfather says there's a rumor that he's unwell."

"If it were only that!"

"What do you mean?"

Gnaeus took Titus's arm and pulled him away from the crowd. He spoke in a low voice. "Have you not heard the rumors about Brutus's sons?"

The consul's two sons were a few years older than Titus, who knew them just well enough to greet them by name when he saw them in the Forum. "Rumors?"

Gnaeus shook his head. "Just because your grandfather still treats you like a boy doesn't mean you have to think like a boy, Titus. We're too old for that. The times are too dangerous. You need to take a greater interest in what's going on around you."

Titus smiled crookedly and fingered the talisman of Fascinus at his throat. "All I really care about is learning to be a builder, like Vulca."

"You should leave such matters to hired artisans. Men like us were born to be warriors."

"But temples bring us closer to the gods. Building a temple is as important as winning a battle."

Gnaeus snorted. "I won't even reply to that! But we were talking about Brutus and his sons. Since you seem unaware of the situation, I'll inform you. This precarious state of affairs—this so-called republic—is hanging by a thread. Our neighbors are making alliances to wage war against us. Without a king, they think we're weak, and they're right. All this strife and bickering has sapped our strength. The worthless rabble of the city was placated for a while, after the usurpers allowed them to plunder the Tarquinius family estates—shame on Brutus and Collatinus for permitting such an outrage!—but now the mob is growing suspicious of the new magistrates, and they think their own assembly should take the place of the Senate. May the gods help Roma if that should happen! And now . . ." He lowered his voice even further. "Now there's a plot to restore the king to the throne. Some of the most respected men in Roma are involved."

Titus drew a sharp breath. "Is such a thing possible?"

"Not without a great deal of bloodshed. But yes, it's possible. As long as Tarquinius and his sons are alive, they'll never stop scheming to take back the throne. I know I wouldn't!"

"But who would help them to do such a thing? After what Sextus Tarquinius did to Lucretia—"

"What of it? A man raped another man's wife, not for the first time, and not for the last. It was a crime, to be sure—but not a reason to abolish the whole system of kingship that made Roma a strong city. Don't forget, it was a king who gave us that temple you're so proud of. The enemies of Tarquinius merely used the rape as a means to stir up anger against the king, so that they could take his place."

Titus felt a prickle of dread. "Gnaeus, *you're* not involved in this plot to bring back the king, are you? Gnaeus, answer me!"

Gnaeus affected an aloof, mysterious expression, and Titus could see that his friend was enjoying his consternation. "No, I am not," he finally said. "But nor am I completely unsympathetic to those who think Roma was better with a king."

"But, Gnaeus, even for one such as you . . ." Titus realized he must speak carefully, so as not to offend his friend; at the same time, he wanted to show that he was not as ignorant of politics as Gnaeus seemed to think. "Collatinus is a patrician, but Brutus isn't; his mother was the king's sister, but his father was a plebeian. By winning election to the consulship, these two have set a precedent for the future. In the republic, any man of worth—patrician *or* plebeian—will have a chance to rule the state."

Gnaeus snorted. "For a year! What good is that?"

Titus pressed on. "New men have been added to the Senate, as well. Tarquinius killed off so many senators that Brutus and Collatinus are nominating new members every day, to bring the number back to three hundred. Not only patricians, but plebeians, as well."

"Even worse! Is that the best a man can hope for? To become one of three hundred?"

Titus frowned, genuinely puzzled. "Gnaeus, I think you miss the point." He could not help but imagine how bluntly Publius would have stated the case: *There may be a place for you yet in the new republic, Gnaeus, even though you're just a lowly plebeian!*

"No, Titus, *you* miss the point. This republic, this government by the people—what can it offer a man except the chance to become a mere senator, one of three hundred, or at best a consul, the first among equals, and one of a pair at that, elected for only a year? So long as Roma had a king, there was hope; there was something a man could strive for."

"I don't understand."

"Hope, Titus! An ambitious man, a great man, a fierce warrior—a man head and shoulders above all other men—such a man, in the old days, might hope someday to occupy the throne, to become a true ruler of men, to be king of Roma. But now, with the monarchy gone, replaced by this pathetic republic, what hope remains for such a man?"

Titus gazed at his friend, fascinated and appalled. Had Gnaeus truly imagined that he might someday be king of Roma? Where had such unbridled ambition come from? Was it to be feared or admired? He almost wished that Publius were present, to deflate Gnaeus's fantastical notions with a snide comment.

Titus shook his head. "How did we come to speak of such things? You were going to tell me something about Brutus . . . and his sons . . ."

"Never mind," said Gnaeus. He hid his face, but in his voice Titus heard all the anger, pain, and exasperation of a youth whose dreams are understood by no one else, not even his closest friend.

Gnaeus strode away without another word.

Just as his grandfather had stressed to Titus the importance of mastering letters, so, too, had Brutus made sure that his two sons could read and write. It was this ability that doomed them.

The younger brother of Brutus's wife was deep in the plot to restore the king. It was this man, Vitellius, who convinced his nephews to join the conspiracy, with promises that they would be greatly rewarded in the second reign of Tarquinius. Secret envoys carried messages back and forth between the king and the conspirators. As the date for Tarquinius's planned return grew closer—a day that would turn the Forum into a lake of blood—the nervous king pressed for greater assurances from his supporters. He demanded letters of express intent, with explicit pledges of loyalty, signed by their own hands. The two sons of Brutus, Titus and Tiberius, signed such a letter, and placed it into the hands of a slave owned by their uncle Vitellius.

The slave had been bribed by Brutus to keep him informed of the plot. Brutus knew that his brother-in-law was involved; having no love for Vitellius, he was determined to expose him. Brutus did not know of the involvement of his own sons.

If he could produce proof of the conspiracy, the slave had been promised freedom and all the rights of citizenship in the new republic. With mingled dread and excitement, he strode into the presence of the two consuls to deliver the letters with which he had been entrusted.

"How many?" said Brutus.

"Twenty letters," said the slave, "signed by twenty-one men."

Brutus frowned. "One of the letters bears two names?"

"Yes, consul."

One by one, Brutus took the letters and read them, then passed them to Collatinus. Some of the names came as no surprise to Brutus; others shocked him. Acutely conscious of the gravity of the moment, he kept all expression from his face.

The slave averted his eyes when he handed Brutus the last letter. The consul stared at it for a such a long time, maintaining such an unnaturally rigid posture, that Collatinus, waiting for the letter to be passed to him, wondered if Brutus had been stricken by some form of paralysis. Growing impatient, he took the letter from Brutus's hands. When he saw the two names upon it, he let out a gasp.

Still, Brutus showed no reaction. His voice was devoid of emotion. "We have their names now. We have proof of their guilt. We know where all these men reside. We must send our lictors to apprehend them as quickly as possible, so that none can warn the others."

"And then?" said Collatinus in a whisper.

"There is no need for a trial. The Senate has entrusted us with emergency powers to deal with just such a circumstance. We will act swiftly and surely to save the republic."

The next day, the citizens were called to assemble on the Field of Mars, where the consuls took their seats upon a raised platform.

The condemned men were brought before them. They had been stripped of all clothing. They were all young, and all from respectable families. From a distance, they might have appeared to be naked athletes parading before the crowd in the Circus Maximus, except for the fact that athletes would wave to the crowd, and these men had their hands bound behind them.

All eyes were on the sons of Brutus. If they had learned nothing else from their father, they had learned composure. While some of the conspirators shouted curses, or begged for mercy, or wept, or struggled against the lictors, Titus and Tiberius stood rigidly upright with their mouths shut and their eyes straight ahead.

Thick tree trunks had been laid in a continuous row before the tribunal. The prisoners were made to stand side by side before the trunks, then to kneel in the sand and to lean forward until their chests rested upon the wood. A long rope was wound once around each man's neck, linking them all together; the slack portions of rope between each man were secured by iron cleats hammered into the ground. Thus the prisoners were restrained and made ready for punishment.

First they were flogged. The lictors took their time. The sons of Brutus and their uncle Vitellius were beaten no more and no less than the others. The flogging continued until the sand was red with blood. Some of the prisoners fainted. They were doused with water to revive them.

Had the prisoners been the captured warriors of another city, or common criminals, or rebellious slaves, the crowd would have jeered and laughed; as it was, there was hardly a noise to be heard, except, here and there, the sound of muffled weeping from men who hid their faces and could not bear to watch. Most in the crowd did their best to emulate Brutus, who sat in his chair of state as rigid as a statue and observed the punishment of the traitors without flinching.

One by one, the prisoners were beheaded. The lictors shared the duty, passing the axe from man to man, wiping it free of blood and gore before using it again. The sons of Brutus were near the middle of the line, side by side. When the lictors came to Titus, ten men had already been executed; their heads lay where they had fallen on the sand in pools of blood that poured from their severed necks. Some of the men farther up the line were weeping; some, in fits of panic, were struggling frantically against their bonds. Some had lost control of their bowels and their bladders; the stench of urine and feces was added to the odor of blood. Vitellius, who was at the very end of the line, had begun to scream incessantly. One of the lictors, unable to stand the noise, gagged his mouth with a bloody rag.

The axe was passed. The lictor wiped the blade, raised it in the air, and brought it down on the neck of Titus. Tiberius, who kept his eyes tightly shut, was beheaded next. Nine more prisoners remained. The lictors continued with their work.

Gazing down from the tribunal, the face of Brutus was no less impassive after his sons' execution than it had been before. The citizens in the crowd looked at him in awe.

When his turn arrived, Vitellius managed to spit the gag from his mouth and began to scream again. The axe rose and fell. His screaming abruptly stopped. The Field of Mars was utterly silent.

Collatinus stood. His bearing was stiff; only by the repeated clenching and unclenching of his fists did he betray his agitation. Next to him, Brutus rose from his chair. For a brief instant, he appeared to falter. As one, the crowd drew a sharp breath, fearful that his legs would give way beneath him. Collatinus instinctively reached out to grasp his fellow consul's arm, but stopped short of touching him and drew back his hand.

Collatinus spoke to him in a low voice; he was offering to perform a duty which previously they had agreed would fall to Brutus. Brutus shook his head, declining the offer. He extended his right arm. One of the lictors delivered a staff into his open hand.

"Vindicius, come forward!" Brutus cried.

The slave who had exposed his master Vitellius and the other conspirators approached the tribunal. Brutus looked down at him.

"For your role in saving the republic from its enemies, a reward was promised to you, Vindicius. In the brief life of our republic, never before has a slave become a citizen. You shall be the first. By the touch of this staff, I grant you the rights, duties, and privileges of a free man of Roma."

Vindicius bowed his head. Brutus touched the crown of his head with the staff.

Brutus's voice, raised to orator's pitch, had a shrill edge, but it did not break. "Let it be seen that a slave can become a citizen by serving the republic. And let it be seen that any citizen who betrays the republic will be shown no mercy. All the men executed here today were guilty of treason. They betrayed their city and their fellow citizens. Some of them were guilty of another crime: They betrayed their father. Disloyalty to father, or to fatherland—for either crime, there can be only one punishment, which you saw carried out today. This we have done upon the Field of Mars, with nothing to hide us from the eye of heaven. Let the gods pay witness. By their continuing favor, let them affirm that what we have done was well and rightly done."

Brutus stepped down from the tribunal, his head held high. His gait was steady, but he leaned heavily upon the staff in his right hand. Never before had he needed a staff to help him walk; never again would he be able to walk without it.

Among those in the front of the crowd, watching the consul's departure, were Titus Potitius and Gnaeus Marcius.

Titus, thanks to his family's status, was used to being at the front of any assembly; on this day, he might have wished to be anywhere else. Several times, especially during the beheadings, he had grown faint and nauseated, but with his grandfather standing close by, he had not dared to look away. His friend Gnaeus, who was used to being further back in any crowd, had on this occasion pleaded with Titus to allow him a place beside him, so that he could have the best possible view of the proceedings. When Titus had grown weak, he had touched Fascinus with one hand and with the other had reached, like a child, for Gnaeus's hand. Gnaeus, though it made him feel slightly foolish, had held his friend's hand without protesting; he owed his place at the front of the crowd to Titus, after all.

Gnaeus was not squeamish; the sight of so much blood had not sickened him. Nor had he felt pity for the prisoners. They had taken a terrible risk, knowing the possible consequences. Had they succeeded, they would have shown no more mercy to their victims than had been shown to them.

About Brutus, Gnaeus was not sure what to think. The man had a will of iron; if any mortal was worthy to be a king, it must be Brutus, and yet the man had no interest in claiming the throne; his hatred of monarchy seemed to be entirely genuine. Brutus had invested all his hopes and dreams in the curious notion of *res publica,* the people's state. *Res publica* had claimed his own sons, and had demanded that he carry out the punishment himself. Even a god who required such a cruel sacrifice might find himself spurned, yet Brutus still worshiped *res publica*!

Gnaeus had seen the birth of a new world, one in which patriots, not kings, held sway. The world had changed, but Gnaeus had not; he was still determined to be first among men, held in esteem above all others. How this might be accomplished in the new world, he did not know, but he had faith in his destiny. Time and the gods would show him the way.

504 B.C.

The arrival of Attus Clausus in Roma was an occasion of great pomp and celebration. All concerned recognized that it was a momentous event, though none could have realized just how far-reaching its effects would be.

The first five years of the new republic had been marked by many setbacks and challenges. Enemies from within had conspired to restore the king. Enemies from without had sought to conquer and subjugate the city. The citizens roiled with discontent, as power shifted from one faction to another in a relentless contest of wills.

Among the external enemies of the city were the Sabine tribes to the south and east, who had long been unified in their hostility to Roma. When one of their leaders, Attus Clausus, began to argue for peace between the Sabines and Roma, his fellow warlords turned against him and Clausus found himself in imminent danger. He made an urgent request to the Senate that he should be allowed to emigrate to Roma, along with a small army of warriors and their families. The Senate debated the issue and empowered the consuls to negotiate with Clausus. In return for a substantial contribution to the exhausted state treasury and the induction of his warriors into the Roman ranks, Clausus was welcomed to Roma. His dependents were promised land on the Anio river, and Clausus himself was enlisted among the patricians and given a seat in the Senate.

On the day of his arrival, a great crowd of well-wishers thronged the Forum and cheered him as he strolled up the Sacred Way with his family. Flower petals were strewn in their path. Horns and pipes played the festive melody of an old song about Romulus, his acquisition of the Sabine brides, and its happy result. The procession reached the Senate House. While his wife and children remained at the foot of the steps, Clausus ascended to the porch.

As usual, Titus Potitius stood near the front of the crowd, where he was able to get a good look at the famous Sabine warlord. He was impressed by the man's distinguished bearing and his regal mane of black hair shot with silver. Titus's grandfather stood among the magistrates and senators on the porch who welcomed Clausus and presented him with a senatorial toga. The Sabine tunic Clausus wore was a splendid green garment with sumptuous gold embroidery, but he made a show of good-naturedly raising his arms and allowing the toga to be wrapped around him and properly draped. He wore it well, and looked as if he had been born to the Roman Senate.

Speeches followed. Titus's attention began to wander and he found himself studying the members of the Clausus family who were positioned nearby. The new senator's wife was a striking woman, and their children were the offspring of two very good-looking parents. One of the daughters in particular caught Titus's eye. She was a dark beauty with a long nose, sensual lips, and flashing green eyes. Titus was unable to look away. She felt his eyes upon her and returned his gaze, appraising him for a long moment before she smiled and looked away; up on the porch, her father had begun to speak. Titus's heart was stirred as it had not been stirred since he first saw the doomed Lucretia.

Clausus spoke Latin with a charming Sabine accent. He expressed gratitude to the Senate of Roma—making no mention of the common people, Titus noticed—and he promised to continue his efforts to convince the other Sabine leaders that a peace accord should be struck with Roma. "But if they cannot be pacified in the counsel chamber, then they shall have to be crushed on the battlefield, and in that endeavor I shall do my part. The Sabine warriors I brought with me are now proud Roman warriors, just as I am now a proud Roman senator. Indeed, even as I put on this toga, I put aside my Sabine name. This morning I awoke as Attus Clausus, but as of this moment, I declare myself Appius Claudius. I think the name suits me, just as this toga suits me!" He smiled and slowly turned around to show off his new garment, eliciting applause and friendly laughter. The crowd loved him.

Titus, too, felt a surge of love, and also of hope, for now he knew what to call the object of his desire. The daughter of any man named Claudius would bear the name Claudia.

Claudia! he thought. *I am in love with the most beautiful girl in the world, and her name is Claudia!*

"According to Appius Claudius, he will leave the decision to the girl herself. What a strange character that man is!"

"Yes, grandfather," said Titus, nodding nervously. "And?"

"And what?"

"What was her decision?"

"By Hercules, young man, I have no idea. I spent the whole visit talking to her father. I didn't even see the girl. If she's anything like your grandmother, she won't make up her mind on the spot. Give her time to think it over!"

In the days following their arrival in Roma, Appius Claudius and his family had been invited to the homes of all the city's foremost families. Among their first hosts had been the Potitii, for Titus had encouraged his grandfather to invite them to dinner as soon as possible. Titus had seized the chance to meet Claudia, and managed to speak to her privately for a few moments. She proved to be more fascinating than he could have imagined; her voice was like music, and the words she uttered took him into a realm of magic. Claudius, whom the Romans were beginning to consider a bit eccentric as they got to know him, had seen to the education of his daughters as well as his sons. Claudia could actually read and write, and when Titus mentioned his interest in architecture, she spoke of how impressed she was by the great Temple of Jupiter atop the Capitoline.

"Imagine that, grandfather," Titus had said afterward. "A female who can read and write! Such a woman might be a great helpmate to her husband."

"Or a positive menace! A wife who could read her husband's private papers? What a dreadful idea! But what are you saying, Titus? Do you want this girl for your wife?"

So had begun Titus's courtship of Claudia. He was allowed to see her on a few more occasions, always with Claudia's maidservant present to act as chaperone. His enchantment with her grew with each brief visit. The marriage negotiations had been conducted mostly by the patresfamilias of the two households; Titus's grandfather sent inquiries to Appius Claudius, who responded with a positive reply. A marriage bond would offer advantages to both families. Claudius was immensely wealthy; his daughter would bring a considerable dowry, and the Potitii were in need of an infusion of wealth. They, in turn, were one of Roma's oldest and most distinguished families; a marriage union with a Potitius would grant the Claudii instant legitimacy among the patricians of the city.

The marriage negotiations went very well, until the day Titus's grandfather came home with unsettling news. Titus was not the only suitor interested in young Claudia.

"Who else?" demanded Titus. "Whoever he is, I shall . . . I shall . . ." He was not certain what he would do, but he felt a wave of aggression such as he had never experienced.

"It's your friend Publius Pinarius," said his grandfather. "Can you imagine that! Apparently, Publius saw the girl that first day before the Senate House, just as you did, and the Pinarii had the Claudii to dinner the very day after we did. Publius has been courting the girl ever since, just as assiduously as you have. This puts Appius Claudius in a bit of a spot. He argues—and I cannot deny it—that there is very little to distinguish the Potitii and the Pinarii when it comes to a good match for his household. Our bloodlines are equally ancient, equally distinguished in the history of the city."

"Except that the Pinarii came late to the Feast of Hercules!"

His grandfather laughed. "Yes, there is that, but I don't think a blunder made a few hundred years ago is enough to tip the scales in our favor. With all things being equal between you and Publius, Claudius says he shall leave the decision to the girl herself."

"When will she decide?"

"My dear boy, as I've already told you, I have no idea. I didn't give the man a deadline."

"Perhaps you should have. I don't think I can stand the waiting! This is worse than the first time I went into battle. At least then I felt it was all up to me, whether I made a good showing of myself or not. But this is terrible; I've done all I can, and now all I can do is wait. I'm totally at her mercy!"

Titus began to pace. They were in the small garden in the courtyard at the center of the house. Rose bushes stood at each corner of the garden. Titus paced from one to the other, taking no notice of the blooms or their scent. His grandfather shook his head and smiled, recalling, vaguely, what it had been like to feel the passionate longings of a young man not yet married.

"Fretting will accomplish nothing," he said. "Perhaps you should—"

A slave approached and announced that a visitor was at the door.

The old man raised an eyebrow. "This could be our answer. Claudius said he would send a messenger as soon as the girl made her decision."

"It's not a messenger," said the slave. "It's the young lady who's visited before."

"Claudia?" Titus, suddenly short of breath, strode past the slave. A short hallway led to the vestibule at the front of the house. From the open skylight above, a beam of midday sunlight lit the impluvium, the little pool for catching rainwater. Flashes of reflected light danced across Claudia and her chaperone.

"You've come!" Titus said, striding past the maidservant and daring to take the girl's hands in his own.

Claudia lowered her eyes. "Yes. I had to send my regrets . . ."

Titus's heart sank.

". . . to Publius Pinarius. My father's messenger should be at his door now. But to you I wanted to come myself, so that I could say to you: Yes! I will be your wife, Titus Potitius."

Titus threw back his head and laughed, then took her in his arms. The maidservant discreetly turned her face away, but Titus's grandfather, from the shadows, watched the young couple's first kiss with a smile of satisfaction at having conducted the marriage negotiations so successfully. He only hoped that young Publius Pinarius would not take his rejection too bitterly.

The marriage ceremonies of most Romans were simple family affairs, without religious rites. Many couples entered into matrimony with hardly any ceremony at all; a man and woman needed only to state that they were married and to live together for their union to be recognized.

The marriage of two patricians was another matter.

First, Titus's grandfather took the auspices to determine a favorable day for the ceremony. Because the bride would need to perform certain religious rites in her new household on the day after her marriage, various days of the calendar with conflicting religious rites were immediately excluded from consideration. Likewise, from long tradition, the entire months of Februarius and Maius were thought to be inauspicious. Upon the Ara Maxima, Titus's grandfather placed a parchment on which he had written five possible dates. One by one, he placed a stone upon each date, watched the flight of birds in the sky for signs of heaven's favor, and determined the most auspicious day for the ceremony.

This was the first Roman wedding in the family of Appius Claudius, and he was determined to observe all the local traditions. When he inquired about the origins of each custom, the Romans could explain some but not others, which had been handed down from a time beyond memory.

On the appointed day, at sundown, the wedding party departed from the house of Appius Claudius. The procession was led by the youngest boy in the household—Claudia's little brother—who carried a pine torch lit from the family's hearthfire; its flame would be added to the hearthfire of the bridegroom when they arrived at the house of Titus Potitius.

Following the torchbearer was a Vestal virgin, wearing the linen vestments of her order, with a narrow headband of twined red and white wool tied around her closely shorn hair. She carried a cake made from consecrated grain and sprinkled with holy salt; a few bites would be taken by the couple during the ceremony, after which the cake would be shared with their guests.

Next came the bride. Claudia's veil was bright yellow, as were her shoes. Her long white robe was cinched at the waist with a purple sash tied at the back in a special configuration called the Hercules knot; later, it would be the bridegroom's privilege, and challenge, to untie the knot. In her hands she carried the implements of spinning, a distaff and a spindle with wool. Flanking her, making a show of offering support to her arms, were two of the bride's cousins, little boys hardly older than the torchbearer. At first, these escorts took their duty very seriously and set out with somber expressions, but when the torchbearer stumbled, they broke into giggles so infectious that even the Vestal virgin began to laugh.

Following the bride were her mother and father and the rest of the bridal party, who sang a very old Roman wedding song called "Tallasius." The foreign-born Claudii had to learn this song from scratch, but the words were charmingly appropriate considering the circumstances. When the Sabine women were taken by Romulus and his men, the most beautiful of the women was captured by the henchmen of a certain Tallasius, a loyal lieutenant of the king, who had observed and selected her in advance. As she was carried off, the Sabine woman begged to know where the men were taking her, and so the song went:

> *Where do you take me?*
> *To Tallasius the dutiful!*
> *Why do you take me?*
> *Because he thinks you're beautiful!*
> *What will my fate be?*
> *To marry him, to be his mate!*
> *What god will save me?*
> *All the gods have blessed this date!*

The wedding party arrived at the home of Titus Potitius. Before the house, under the open sky, by the light of tapers soaked in wax, a sheep was sacrificed upon an altar and skinned. Its pelt was thrown over two chairs, upon which the bride and groom sat. The auspices were taken, and declared to be good. The gods were called upon to bless the union.

Still carrying her distaff and spindle, Claudia rose from her chair and was escorted by her mother to the door of the house, which was decorated with garlands and flowers. Her mother embraced her. Miming an attack, Titus stepped forward and pulled his bride from her mother's arms. This was another echo of the abduction of the Sabines, as was what came next: Titus, blushing furiously, picked her up, kicked open the door, and carried her like a captive over the threshold.

Claudia's mother wept. Her father fought back tears with laughter. The wedding party cheered and applauded.

Inside the house, Titus set Claudia down on a sheepskin rug. She put aside her distaff and spindle. He handed her the keys to the house, and asked, with breathless excitement, "Who is this newcomer in my house?"

Claudia answered as the ancient ritual prescribed: "When and where you are Titus, then and there I shall be Titia." Thus the bride gave herself a first name, the feminine form of her husband's first name—something that did not exist for women in the world at large, and would only ever be used in private between the two of them.

The wedding banquet was mostly a family affair, but certain close friends of the bride and groom were invited. Titus had thought long and hard about whether to invite Publius Pinarius. In the end, he had taken his grandfather's advice and had done so, and as his grandfather had predicted, Publius had spared everyone from embarrassment by sending his regrets, saying he could not attend because his family would be visiting relatives in the countryside.

Gnaeus Marcius, however, did accept Titus's invitation. He had recently become betrothed himself, to a plebeian girl named Volumnia. If he was disappointed not to have arranged a marriage with a patrician girl, he did not admit it. His demeanor was as haughty as ever; if anything, his self-assurance had increased, bolstered by his first forays into battle. As yet, Gnaeus was still some distance from achieving his lofty goal—to become the greatest warrior that Roma had ever seen—but he had made a good start, coming to the attention of his commanders by repeatedly proving his bravery in combat.

Busy accepting the good wishes of all the other guests, Titus was able to pay only passing attention to Gnaeus. He worried that his friend might feel a bit out of place amid so many Claudii and Potitii, or, given his sensitivities, might experience a bit of envy, perhaps even resentment, at seeing the trappings of the patrician wedding he himself would never experience. Then Titus saw, across the crowd, that Gnaeus was deep in conversation with Appius Claudius. The two of them looked very serious one moment, burst out laughing the next, then returned to their sober discussion.

What were they talking about? Titus worked his way across the crowd until he was close enough to overhear.

"And yet," Claudius was saying, "it's my understanding that even before the coming of the republic, there was considerable friction between the best families and the common people. It seems unfair to blame Brutus for stirring a hornet's next. His intention, surely, was to spread the powers which Tarquinius hoarded to himself among the senators, so that all the best men could take a turn at the rudder, so to speak."

"The revolution that Brutus began still continues, and could veer out of control at any moment," said Gnaeus. "Revolutions begin at the top, then work their way down. The trick is to arrest the process before the worst people kill the best and gain control."

"But the republic appears to be working," said Claudius. "It's true, and perhaps unfortunate, that even the lowliest citizens are allowed to vote for the magistrates; on the other hand, only the best men are eligible to run for office. And citizens vote not as individuals but in tribal units, and those votes are weighted; the units which include the best families and their dependents count for much more than those of the rabble. It seems a reasonable system."

"Perhaps, if the common people would be satisfied with it. But have you listened to the rabble-rousers in the Forum? They say the debts of the poor should be forgiven. Can you imagine the chaos if that should happen? They say the plebeians must be allowed to elect their own magistrates, to 'protect' them from the patricians. They want two governments instead of one! They say the common people should consider seceding from the city altogether—go off and found their own city, and leave Roma to fend for herself against her enemies. That's traitor's talk!"

"Serious matters, indeed," said Claudius. "Thank the gods that Roma has clear-headed young men such as yourself, Gnaeus Marcius, who can recognize that some beasts were born to pull a plow and others to guide it."

"And thank the gods, Appius Claudius, that a man as wise and honorable as you has chosen to join his destiny with that of our beloved Roma."

Titus smiled and moved away, pleased but not entirely surprised that his aristocratic father-in-law and his elitist best friend had each found a kindred spirit in the other.

493 B.C.

The slave entered his master's study, bearing a large, rolled parchment. He cleared his throat. "Excuse me, Senator. I believe these were the plans you requested."

Titus Potitius, who stood bent over a table, studying a similar parchment by the bright sunlight from the window, looked up and nodded absently. "What? Oh, yes, the plans for the Temple of Jupiter on the Capitoline! I've been wanting to see Vulca's old drawings. They may help me solve a problem I've encountered with the design of the new Temple of Ceres. Put the scroll there, in that corner. I'll look at it later."

The slave obeyed, then returned to Titus and cleared his throat again.

"Yes? Is there something else?"

"You asked me to remind you, master, when the time for the triumph drew near."

"Of course! I've been so busy, I entirely forgot! I mustn't be late. I daresay old Cominius wouldn't care whether I showed up or not, but Gnaeus would never forgive me if I wasn't present to witness his moment of glory. Go fetch my toga and help me put it on."

An hour later, Titus stood among his colleagues on the steps of the Senate House. His grandfather had died not long after Titus's marriage; his father had died three years ago. Now, at the age of twenty-nine, Titus was paterfamilias of the family and one of the youngest members of the Senate. As always, throughout his life, his pedigree gave him claim to a place of honor—in this case, on one of the upper steps that afforded a splendid view. On the step above Titus stood his father-in-law, Appius Claudius, who had risen to great prominence in the Senate; only the consuls and the other magistrates stood higher, on the porch of the building. On the step below stood his old friend Publius Pinarius. Across from the Senate House, Titus's son stood in the very spot where he had stood as a boy, at the front of the crowd of patricians who had gathered to watch the triumphal procession on the Sacred Way.

The occasion for the triumph was the successful conclusion of a war against a people called the Volsci, south of Roma. The consul Postumius Cominius had led the campaign. In short order, his troops had seized the Volscian cities of Antium, Longula, Polusca, and the greatest prize of all, Corioli. A grateful Senate had enthusiastically voted to award Cominius a triumph, an honor once given exclusively by the kings to themselves, but which now was granted by the Senate to those consuls who achieved a great military victory.

Titus heard the shrill piping of flutes playing a military air. Surrounded by the musicians, a white ox led the parade. It would later be sacrificed, along with a portion of the spoils of battle, on an altar before the Temple of Jupiter atop the Capitoline.

Following the ox came the Volscian warriors who had been captured in battle. They had been stripped of their armor and were dressed in rags. Filthy and unkempt, they shuffled forward in shackles, hanging their heads. The crowd laughed and jeered at them. Boys threw pebbles to make them flinch. A grizzled, toothless Roman soldier stepped from the crowd to spit on them. At the conclusion of the triumph, having served their purpose as ornaments, the luckiest of the prisoners might be returned to their families, if an adequate ransom had been offered. The others would be sold into slavery.

Next came the elite prisoners, those who had been the chief men of the captured cities. For them, neither freedom nor slavery waited. While the priests sacrificed the ox to Jupiter, these prisoners would be lowered into the Tullianum, the prison cell at the foot of the Capitoline, and strangled by executioners. According to the priests, offerings were more pleasing to the god when accompanied by the death of those who had been the leaders of Roma's enemies.

Next came the spoils of battle: the captured arms and insignia of the Voscians, as well as wagons full of precious metals, jewels, and fine objects including vases and etched silver mirrors—all the portable items of value that had been seized when the fallen cities were sacked. Greatest of all was the booty of Corioli, where the wealthiest of the Volsci had lived in great luxury.

After the spoils of war came the general's lictors wearing red tunics, marching in single file with their axes raised high, shouting the Latin victory chant. "*Io triumphe! Io triumphe! Io triumphe!*" The general himself followed in a chariot pulled by four horses and decorated with bronze plates embossed with images of winged victories. Watching the chariot approach, Titus smiled. He could hear in his head the lecturing voice of his grandfather: "Romulus *walked* up the Sacred Way for his triumphs; his feet were good enough for him! This business of riding in a quadriga began only with the elder Tarquinius." The clatter of the horses' hooves was added to the chant of the lictors, then both were drowned by roar of the crowd.

Cominius was dressed in a tunic sewn with flowers and a gold-embroidered robe. On his head he wore a laurel crown. In his right hand he carried a laurel bough, and in his left a scepter surmounted by an eagle. His youngest son rode beside him in the chariot and handled the reins.

In commemoration of the enemy blood spilled under his command, the hands and face of Cominius were stained bright red with cinnabar. He raised his scepter in salutation to the senators, who saluted back.

Following the general marched the soldiers who had fought under him. At their head, in a place of honor, was Titus's old friend, Gnaeus Marcius, the hero of the battle of Corioli.

For years, in battle after battle, Gnaeus had been gaining a reputation as a fearless fighter, but at Corioli, where he had served as second in command to Cominius, his exploits had elevated him to a new level of glory. At a critical moment during the siege, the defenders had boldly opened the gates and sent forth their fiercest fighters. The bloodshed that followed was horrific, but one Roman never wavered as he slew enemy after enemy: Gnaeus Marcius. Driven by a force that seemed more than human, he fought his way to the open gates and ran into the city, alone. The soldiers and citizens of Corioli swarmed around him, determined to kill him, but

Gnaeus could not be stopped. After surrounding himself with corpses, he seized a torch and set aflame anything that could burn. The conflagration so terrified and distracted the defenders that the gates were left unmanned. The Romans rushed into the city and a mass slaughter followed.

After the battle, Cominius praised Gnaeus's heroism before the assembled troops. He presented him with a magnificent war-horse with trappings worthy of a general. He also promised Gnaeus as much of the silver of Corioli as he could carry and his choice of any ten captives to become his slaves. Gnaeus accepted the horse, saying it would help him to fight Roma's enemies, and one captive, a man he recognized for having fought bravely against him, whom he then released. The other gifts he rejected, saying that he had done no more and no less than any Roman soldier should. The conquest of Corioli itself was the only reward he desired.

Gnaeus Marcius had become a hero to his fellow soldiers that day. Now, marching behind him in the triumphal procession, they began to chant, quietly at first, then louder and louder: "Coriolanus! Coriolanus! Coriolanus!"—an honorific title to hail him as the conqueror of Corioli.

Because such a title would more properly be given to a commander, Titus thought the men must be referring to Cominius. The general apparently thought the same thing, for he smiled broadly, turned around in the chariot to face his troops, and raised his scepter to them. But in the next instant, it became evident for whom the troops were crying out. A band of them broke ranks, rushed forward, and raised Gnaeus Marcius onto their shoulders. They spun him about, all the while shouting: "Coriolanus! Coriolanus! Coriolanus!"

A lesser man might have betrayed a flash of jealousy at seeing a subordinate so honored on the day of his own triumph, but Cominius was as canny a politician as he was a commander. His unwavering grin became a smile bestowed on Gnaeus Marcius. His raised scepter became a salute to the hero of Corioli. When the crowd began to take up the chant as well, Cominius seized the moment. He beckoned to the soldiers bearing Gnaeus aloft. They trotted forward, laughing like boys, and deposited their comrade onto the chariot alongside the commander.

A few in the crowd were taken aback at this breach of decorum. Below him, Titus heard Publius Pinarius let out a gasp and mutter, "By Hercules, did you ever see anything so audacious?" But a far greater number of spectators were roused to cheering and even moved to tears, especially when Cominius warmly embraced Gnaeus, then placed Gnaeus's hand upon the scepter next to his own and raised it high.

"People of Roma, I give you Gnaeus Marcius, the hero of Corioli! All hail Coriolanus!"

"Coriolanus!" the people chanted. The name reverberated around the Forum like rolling thunder.

From the step above, Appius Claudius leaned over and spoke into Titus's ear. "I always knew that friend of yours would make a name for himself. Today he has, and everyone in Roma is shouting it." Claudius stood upright, cupped his hands to his mouth, and joined the others: "Coriolanus! All hail Coriolanus!"

"The temple will be dedicated very soon, then?" said Gnaeus Marcius.

Titus laughed. "Yes, very soon. It's polite of you to inquire, Gnaeus—or should I call you Coriolanus now? But we both know you have very little interest in temples, and even less in architecture for its own sake. We see each other so seldom nowadays, it seems to me that we should speak of matters that interest us both."

They were dining, alone, in the garden of the house on the Palatine where Gnaeus lived with his mother and wife. The previous day, various citizens had organized private feasts to follow the triumph. The food had been so sumptuous, and Titus had eaten so much, that he had thought he would never be hungry again. Yet, a day later, his stomach was empty again and he found himself craving a simple meal. Even more, he craved the company of his old friend Gnaeus, just the two of them alone, away from the swarms of strangers and well-wishers who had surrounded Gnaeus the previous day with their incessant cries of "Hail Coriolanus!" And so, when Gnaeus invited him to a private dinner to enjoy his mother's chickpea and millet porridge, Titus had eagerly accepted.

"It's true that our lives have taken different paths in recent years," said Gnaeus. "But that may be about to change."

"How so? Am I to leave the Senate, and the construction projects they've entrusted to me, and join you in battle? I was never very good at it.

I suppose I could be your spearbearer, or hold open the gate of an enemy city while you rush inside."

"I mean quite the opposite. I shall be invading your domain."

"My construction projects?"

"No! I mean the Senate."

"What are you saying?"

Gnaeus smiled. "Cominius promised me as much, yesterday, after he invited me onto his chariot. As we passed all those cheering people, he whispered in my ear, 'See how they love you, my boy! Amazing! I've never seen anything like it! A man like you belongs in the Senate, where you can do even more good for Roma than you did at Corioli. I shall make a special appointment, and for that alone, men will say my year as consul was well spent.' "

"But Gnaeus, this is wonderful! Except that now I truly have no idea what I should call you. Senator? Coriolanus? Senator Gnaeus Marcius Coriolanus—that's a mouthful!"

"Then stuff your mouth with chickpeas and millet instead," said Gnaeus. He laughed, but a moment later Titus saw that Gnaeus's lips were silently mouthing his impressive new title, and that it pleased him.

"How the gods must love you! You always said you'd become Roma's greatest warrior, and so you have. Now you can become Roma's most beloved politician. Cominius is no fool. He wouldn't appoint you to the Senate if he didn't see great potential in you. Appius Claudius sees it, too. Mark my words, in due course, you shall be elected consul."

"Perhaps. In the meantime, I shall need someone to teach me the ins and outs of the Senate. You're the man for that, Titus."

"I hardly think so! Appius Claudius is your man. He took me under his wing when I entered the Senate. It was thanks to his influence that I was put in charge of building the Temple of Ceres. He'll do the same for you, insofar as such a capable fellow needs to be taken under anyone's wing."

"Claudius is a good man to know. But nothing takes the place of a boyhood friend. When the odds are against me, it's to you I'll turn, Titus." Gnaeus put his hand on Titus's shoulder.

Titus nodded. "Coriolanus honors me."

Gnaeus leaned back and smiled. "So—how goes the work on the Temple of Ceres?"

"A subject in which you have no interest!"

"No interest as a soldier, perhaps. But as a senator, I may have a great deal of interest in the project."

"Then tomorrow you shall come and see for yourself. It's a prominent location, quite spectacular—a spur of the Aventine that looms above the starting gates of the Circus Maximus. It's in the Etruscan araeostyle, just like the Temple of Jupiter on the Capitoline. Not as large, but it will be quite grandly decorated. Vulca is no longer with us, alas, but we've employed the very best Etruscan sculptors for the terra-cotta statue of Ceres. To execute the frescoes and reliefs on the walls, we've brought in two Greek artists, Gorgasus and Damophilus. They're almost done, and their work is amazing! And . . ." Titus realized that Gnaeus was not paying attention. He was staring into the middle distance with a distracted look.

Gnaeus noticed that Titus had stopped speaking, and flashed a wry smile. "You're right, Titus. I care nothing about the temple's architecture or its adornments. But I do care about the politics behind it."

"Famine," said Titus bluntly. "It was the famine three years ago that inspired the building of the temple. So many men were called to war that there was no one to sow the crops that year, and the fields that were sown were devastated by more warfare. Roma had insufficient stores in reserve, and people starved—the poorer people, anyway. My father also died that year—not directly from the famine, because our sort never went hungry, but from a fever; disease goes hand in hand with famine, and from a fever no man is safe. The Sibylline Books were consulted. It was decreed that a temple should be dedicated to Ceres. To prevent another famine, we would appeal to the goddess of the harvest. Sometimes the advice of the Sibylline verses actually makes sense!"

"Or was there another agenda?" said Gnaeus. His tone was suddenly grave. "Ceres is a favorite deity of the plebeians. Is it not true that the annual festival to commemorate her temple will be organized exclusively by plebeians, just as the annual festival to commemorate the Temple of Jupiter is organized by patricians?"

"Yes. Thus we'll have a new plebeian festival to match the old patrician festival. What's wrong with that?" asked Titus, with a sigh. He knew where Gnaeus's argument was leading, for he had heard it before, from Appius Claudius; it was really quite amazing, how closely Gnaeus's attitudes matched those of Titus's father-in-law. Both men were endlessly suspicious of anything that might advance the political power of the plebeians. Claudius had maneuvered to have Titus oversee construction of the Temple of Ceres not because he approved of the project, but for reasons quite the opposite: "If it must be done, then better we put you in charge of the project, my boy, rather than some sycophant who wishes only to curry favor with the mob!"

Titus himself was largely apathetic about politics; if anything, he was sympathetic to the struggles of the plebs. His chief priorities were to determine the best design for any given project, to employ the best artists and artisans at the best prices, and to see the building progress from imagination to splendid reality.

Gnaeus shook his head. "If the plebeians continue to have their way, Titus, one morning you may wake up in a world you no longer recognize, where the lowest have usurped the highest, and the age-old prestige of a name like Potitius counts for nothing. Can you not see that the new plebeian festival indicates a dangerous shift in the balance of power? Since the birth of the republic, by this means and that, in small ways and large, the plebeian masses have ceaselessly conspired to wrest power from the patricians, always to the detriment of Roma's security and prosperity."

"Some would say they've merely been trying to wriggle out from under the patrician heel," said Titus.

"They've refused to pay their debts, which is robbery! Some have refused military service, which is treason! And last year, they pulled the most outrageous stunt of all, their so-called 'secession' from the city. Thousands of them—men, women, and children—packed their things and left Roma altogether. They brought the city to a standstill, and refused to come back until their demands were met."

"Were their demands unreasonable?"

"Of course they were! Appius Claudius fought like a lion to stop his fellow senators from capitulating, but they did. The plebs were granted their demands and that ended the secession. Now they're allowed to elect their own magistrates. And what will these so-called aediles of the plebs do?"

"Their primary function is sacred—to guard the new Temple of Ceres."

"And what will be kept in the temple? An archive of the Senate's decrees. That was another of the plebs' demands, that all the decrees of the

Senate should be written down, so anyone who wishes may search them for discrepancies and scrutinize them for unfair treatment of the plebs."

"Is it a bad thing, Gnaeus, that laws and proclamations should be written down? The kings ruled by spoken words. They could make promises with one breath and take them back with another. They could ruin a man's life on a whim, then disclaim all responsibility. My grandfather, may Hercules bless him, taught me to respect the written word. That the laws should be duly and precisely recorded is not a bad thing."

Gnaeus was unswayed. "Even worse than the aediles—much worse— are these other officers whom the plebeians can now elect, the so-called tribunes. From ancient times the people have been divided into tribes, so they call these representatives their tribunes—but I call them bullies and upstarts! Under the pretext of protecting common citizens from the alleged abuses of magistrates and senators, these tribunes of the plebs can summarily confiscate the property of anyone—anyone!—who they deem has threatened the physical well-being of a citizen. And where will the confiscated goods be deposited? In the Temple of Ceres, under guard of the aediles! And if any man should dare to threaten or in any way interfere with a tribune, that man can be exiled or even put to death!"

Titus sighed. "There *have* been abuses against the plebs. Once, in the year of the famine, I saw an old veteran being hounded by the hired ruffians of a senator. The veteran was crippled and in rags. He may have owed the senator money, but he clearly had no means to repay the debt, nor was he fit to work it off, no matter how much the ruffians shoved him about. The old man begged them for mercy. He finally tore off his tunic to show his battle scars—the wounds he had received fighting for Roma. If the tribunes had existed then, they could have put a stop to that shameful spectacle! And if the Temple of Ceres had existed, the veteran could have gone there for protection, because, among its other functions, it will serve as an asylum for the plebs."

Gnaeus snorted. "I've heard that tired story about the abused veteran a hundred times before, and I've never believed it. No man worthy to be called a Roman veteran would show off his scars to escape paying a debt."

Titus shook his head. "The temple will also house a center for distributing food to the poor. Does that offend you?"

"Indeed it does! How will the aediles purchase that food? With the confiscated wealth of patricians who've dared to offend the tribunes!" Gnaeus raised an eyebrow, then leaned back and crossed his arms. He exhaled a long breath. "Titus, dear Titus. I think I liked it better when I was a warrior and you were a builder, and we had no interests in common."

"Membership in the Senate does not necessarily draw men together," said Titus wryly. "But if my father-in-law and I can get along, despite our differences, then so can we, Gnaeus. You'll find that I have few fixed opinions; in matter of politics, I follow the consensus. The only thing I truly care about is my passion for building."

The conversation was joined by a feminine voice. "Did I hear you say something about distributing my food to the poor, Titus Potitius? Is my chickpea and millet porridge too common for your taste?"

Titus stood to acknowledge the appearance of Gnaeus's mother in the garden. One needed to look no further than the graceful Veturia to see the model which had inspired her son's erect posture and haughty demeanor. "Veturia! You misheard my comments. For your porridge, I have only the highest praise!"

"Good! I made it myself. No slave's cooking will do for my son, on the rare occasion that finds him home from fighting Roma's enemies!" From behind, she leaned over to embrace Gnaeus, who remained seated and reached up to grasp her hands and give her a kiss. The widow Veturia was still a very handsome woman, and Gnaeus unabashedly adored her. *If only to make my mother proud of me,* Gnaeus had once said, declaring his boyhood ambition to become Roma's greatest warrior. At that moment, the mother of Coriolanus looked very proud indeed.

It was not every senator whose first speech before the august body set off a near-riot inside the chamber, and a full-scale riot outside.

The special appointment of the hero Coriolanus to the Senate was swiftly done. He was outfitted with a senatorial toga, and the day of his induction, if not as momentous as that of Appius Claudius, was nonetheless marked by all the proper ceremonies and speeches of welcome.

The fact that Gnaeus was a plebeian was not an impediment to his admission. A number of wealthy, powerful plebeians had been admitted into the ranks of the Senate. A small handful had even been elected consul, beginning with the great Brutus himself, though for any man not of patrician rank the attainment of the consulship posed a steep challenge. It was one thing to achieve *nobilitas,* the status of being among "the known," which membership in the Senate conferred to a man and his descendents; it was quite another thing to attain the nobility's highest honors. As Publius Pinarius had once remarked to Titus, approvingly, "To reach the very top in our brave new republic, it's not enough merely to be noble; it's necessary for that nobility to be covered with purple must like old wine, to be ancient and rusty like iron. That sort of status comes only with generations of breeding!"

If anyone might have opposed Gnaeus's appointment to their ranks, it would have been the plebeian minority in the Senate who regularly put forth radical legislation and who knew very well where Gnaeus's allegiances lay; but the plebs bided their time and did not speak against him. It was Gnaeus who spoke against them.

The more conservative senators had always opposed the establishment of the tribunes as protectors of the plebs. Some who had acquiesced to the necessity, in order to end the secession of the plebs, now regretted it. Yet no one, not even the reactionary Appius Claudius, dared to call publicly for the abolition of the tribunes. There was some question as to whether it would be even legal to do so; to interfere with the work of the tribunes was a crime punishable by exile or death, and could it not be argued that calling for their abolition amounted to interference with their work?

It was left to a man who knew no fear to do what Appius Claudius and his colleagues were afraid to do.

On the morning that Gnaeus was inducted into their ranks, the business of the Senate was commonplace. Funds needed to be appropriated to repair a section of the Cloaca Maxima. More funds were needed to rebuild a portion of a road south of the city rendered impassable by heavy rains. A section of the wall protecting the Aventine needed repair. There was debate as to who should receive these contracts; certain senators were notorious for getting the most lucrative contracts, and for overcharging, as well. After some acrimonious exchanges, the matter of funding was tabled and scheduled for further debate.

Titus Potitius was asked about progress on the Temple of Ceres. "I am happy to report that the work of the Greek artists Gorgasus and Damophilus is very nearly complete. Some of you have seen the results already. I believe I can say without exaggeration that our grandchildren, and their grandchildren, when they look upon this temple, will praise their ancestors for having created a gift of such exquisite beauty to the goddess. In years of bounty, we shall have a place to thank her. In lean years, we shall have a place to appeal to her favor."

There was a murmur of approval throughout the chamber. Titus was well liked, and his competence was beyond dispute.

The attention of the Senate turned to its newest member, who had put in a request to speak. Gnaeus, who was sitting between Appius Claudius and Titus, rose to his feet and strode to the center of the chamber, so that he could move about freely and face all the senators in turn.

"My colleagues, let me tell you straight out that I am not a man of delicate words. My oratorical skills, such as they are, were not learned on the Field of Mars where the men standing for consul beg for votes. I am not accustomed to flattering anyone, least of all my inferiors. I learned to speak on the battlefield, exhorting other men to fight and to spill their blood for Roma. Today, I find myself on another battlefield, where the fate of Roma hangs in the balance. You, senators, are the warriors I must rally to take up arms and fight for Roma!

"Not long ago, when the plebs staged their so-called secession, one of your number, the distinguished Menenius Agrippa, made an impassioned speech to the people, trying to make them see reason. He told them a fable which went something like this: Long ago, the parts of the human body were not all in harmony, as they are now, but each had its own thoughts and ideas. The hard-working limbs and the vigilant eyes and ears noticed that the belly seemed to do nothing but lay idle and wait for the other parts to feed it. 'We all work hard to satisfy the belly, but what does the belly do for us?' they said. 'Let us teach the belly a lesson!' So they conspired to withhold all nourishment from it. The limbs refused to gather grain, the eyes refused to watch for game, the hands refused to take food to the mouth, the mouth refused to open. When the empty belly began to grumble—not a selfish demand, but a warning of danger!—the other parts merely laughed. How simpleminded, how spiteful were these resentful parts! Because, quite soon, the limbs began to wither, the hands began to tremble, the eyes and ears grew dull. The weakened parts fell prey to every manner of disease. Finally, they realized that the belly, too, had its essential part to play in the great scheme of things, for it was the belly that sustained the rest of the body, and without it the other parts could not continue to exist! The rebellion ceased. The natural order was restored. The body gradually returned to health, and the other parts never again conspired against the belly. When it asked to be fed, they all worked together to do so, without questioning.

"If only the fable told by Agrippa had sufficed to make those malcontents see the error of their ways! A city must be ruled by the best and wisest of its men, and to those men must be given the respect and privileges they deserve. The other citizens have their purpose, but it is *not* to rule the city! They exist to fill the ranks of the army, to settle new colonies so as to spread the power of Roma and encircle her with obedient allies, to harvest the crops, and to build the roads. It is not the rabble's place to rule, yet they persist in their reckless attempts to pull down their betters and take their place! They can only fail, because, like the limbs who rebelled against the belly, what they are attempting goes against the natural order of the universe, against the will of the gods.

"And yet, these malcontents have already done great damage to the state, and they have done so with the craven cooperation of a majority within this very chamber! This appeasement must stop. More than that, it must be rolled back, before the damage becomes irreparable. This is not merely an internal matter, a disagreement among citizens. Never forget that Roma is surrounded by enemies, and those enemies are always watching. How gleeful they must be, to see our predicament! One by one, the best men of Roma will be pulled down by the rabble. Who then will defend the city against her foes? Just as the lesser men will destroy the greater men in Roma, so lesser cities will unite to destroy Roma herself. Your fortunes and your land will be taken from you. Your families shall be sold into slavery. Our beloved Roma shall cease to exist—and men will say that her destruction began with the creation of the tribunes of the plebs!"

There was an uproar in the chamber. Members cried out, "This issue has already been settled!" and "The plebs are not the enemy!" But others were exhilarated by Gnaeus's words, including Appius Claudius, who sprang to his feet and shouted, "Hail Coriolanus, the man who dares to speak the truth!"

Gnaeus raised his hands. As the din subsided, one senator shouted, "What exactly do you propose, Gnaeus Marcius?"

"What do you think? I propose that the tribunes must be abolished."

"The proposal is illegal!" shouted a senator. "Withdraw it at once!"

"I will not! I stand by my words, and I ask you, my colleagues, to stand by me. A grave mistake was made and it must be rectified, for the sake of Roma!"

If Gnaeus had hoped to put forward a formal proposal and to call for a vote, he was thwarted. All over the chamber, senators sprang to their feet and loudly demanded to be recognized. Shouting led to name-calling, and then to shoving matches. Amid the chaos, Gnaeus, who was used to the discipline of the army and its clear lines of authority, threw up his hands in disgust and strode out of the chamber.

Titus caught up with him as he descended the steps of the Senate House. "Gnaeus, where are you going?"

"Anywhere to escape that tumult. The Senate is just what I expected— all kings and no crown. How they ever accomplish anything, I can't imagine. Would you believe it, just this morning, Cominius was telling me that I should consider a run for consul. Can you see me currying favor with that lot *and* the common rabble? I think not!"

"It's usually not quite so . . . disorderly." Titus laughed. "You certainly riled them up."

"I did, didn't I? Because they needed it!" Gnaeus's smile abruptly faded. In the middle of the Forum, he found himself confronted by a large group of men. One of the men stepped forward.

"Are you Gnaeus Marcius, called Coriolanus?"

"You know I am. Who are you?"

"Spurius Icilius, tribune of the plebs. I've been informed of a threat made against myself and the well-being of all plebeians."

"What are you talking about?"

"Did you not, only moments ago, make a proposal on the floor of the Senate that the tribunate of the plebs should be abolished, therefore threatening the safety and protection of all plebeians?"

"How would you know about that? Do you have spies in the Senate?"

"The eyes and the ears of the tribunes are everywhere. We are the protectors of the people."

"You're nothing more than hooligans."

"Did you or did you not threaten the tribunes?"

"What I said before the Senate, I'll say to your face: For the survival of Roma, the tribunes must be abolished!"

"Gnaeus Marcius, I place you under arrest for threatening a tribune of the plebs and for interfering with his mission. Your fate will be decided by a vote of the people's assembly."

"This is ridiculous!"

"You will come with me."

"I will not! Take your hands off me!" Gnaeus repulsed the tribune so forcefully that the man stumbled and fell backward.

Some of the men with Icilius produced cudgels and brandished them. Gnaeus struck one of them squarely in the nose and sent him reeling, then adroitly ducked a cudgel swung at his head. He struck another man and knocked him down. Titus, caught up in the excitement, joined the fight just as more men with cudgels arrived.

"We must run, Titus!" shouted Gnaeus.

"Run? Surely Coriolanus never runs!" Titus ducked a cudgel.

"When he's unarmed and outnumbered, even Coriolanus makes a strategic retreat!"

The tribune's men blocked the way back to the Senate House. Titus and Gnaeus ran in the opposite direction, toward the Capitoline, with the tribune and his men in pursuit. The last time the two of them had ascended the hill had been on the day of the triumph, when Gnaeus had received his title by the acclamation of the people. It occurred to Titus that some of the men pursuing them had probably been among those who shouted "Coriolanus!" How they had loved Gnaeus on that day; how they hated him now! Gnaeus was right, he thought. The rabble were fickle and foolish and did not deserve to have a warrior like Coriolanus to fight their battles.

They sprinted up the winding pathway and approached the summit. "Has it occurred to you," asked Titus, breathing hard, "that we shall have nowhere to go when we reach the top?"

"There is no strategic retreat without a strategy!" said Gnaeus. "I shall enter the Temple of Jupiter and demand asylum. If the rabble can find asylum in your Temple of Ceres, then surely Jupiter can shield a senator!"

But as they approached the temple steps, they were blocked by a group of men who had somehow circled ahead of them. There was no choice but to keep running, until they came to the Tarpeian Rock and could run no more.

The swiftest of the pursuers, almost upon them, shouted back to the others, "Can you believe it? The gods have led them straight to the place of execution!"

"Stand back!" cried the tribune Icilius. "No one will be executed today. This man is under arrest."

But as the mob approached, there were cries of "Swift justice!" and "Push him over!" and "Kill him now!"

Titus, already light-headed from running, glanced over the precipice and staggered back. He was dizzy and his heart was pounding.

"Now we see what sort of men you really are," said Gnaeus. "Cold-blooded murderers!"

"No one will be murdered!" insisted Icilius. He pushed his way to the front of the crowd. The mob surged behind him. He lowered his voice. "Senator, I am barely able to restrain these men. Do nothing to provoke them further! For your own safety, Senator, you must come with me."

"I will not! I recognize the authority of no man to arrest a Roman citizen simply for speaking his mind. Call off your curs, tribune, and leave me in peace!"

"You dare to call us dogs?" One of the men behind Icilius threw his cudgel. It missed Gnaeus but struck a glancing blow to Titus's temple. Titus staggered back and tottered on the precipice. Gnaeus leaped to catch him, and for an instant it appeared that both of them would fall. Gnaeus at last gained his balance and pulled Titus to safety.

The mob, which had watched in breathless excitement, now roared with disappointment and surged forward. Icilius held out his arms to restrain them, but there were too many.

Suddenly, there was a commotion at the back of the crowd. The consul Cominius had arrived with his lictors. The cudgels of the mob were no match for the axes of the lictors, who cleared a path through the crowd.

"Tribune, what is happening here?" demanded Cominius.

"I am placing this man under arrest."

"That's a lie!" shouted Gnaeus. "These hooligans chased my colleague and me all the way from the Forum, with the clear intention of murdering us. Before you arrived, they were about to throw us from the Tarpeian Rock."

"A traitor's death is what you deserve!" shouted one of the men. "Death to any man who tries to take away the protectors of the people!"

"Stand down!" cried Cominius. "Spurius Icilius, stop this madness. Call off your men. Retract the arrest."

"Do you dare to interfere with the lawful duties of a tribune, Consul?" Icilius locked his gaze on Cominius, who eventually lowered his eyes.

"Let there be a trial, if you insist," said Cominius. "But in the meantime, let Coriolanus go free."

Icilius stared for a long moment at Gnaeus, then nodded. "Very well. Let the people decide his fate."

Gradually, grumbling and spitting contemptuously at the feet of the lictors, the mob dispersed, and Icilius withdrew. Gnaeus burst out laughing and strode forward to hug his old commander, but the consul's expression was grim.

Titus, feeling a bit sick from the blow to his head, sat down on the Tarpeian Rock. The others seemed like phantoms from a dream. He found himself staring at the temple and the magnificent quadriga of Jupiter atop the pediment. How he loved the building that Vulca had made!

***

"Sometimes I think that even the gods have turned against me," whispered Gnaeus. He paced back and forth across the moonlit garden. His face was in shadow, as were the faces of those who had come in answer to his summons. No lamps had been lit; the least flicker of light might alert his enemies to the midnight meeting in the house of Gnaeus Marcius.

Titus was there. So were Appius Claudius and the consul Cominius. There were also a number of men dressed in full armor, as if ready to ride into battle. There seemed to be a great many of them, pressed together under the colonnade that surrounded the garden. By the light of the full moon upon their limbs Titus could see that most were young, and by the quality of their armor, he could see that all were men of means.

In recent days, Gnaeus had attracted a large following of young warriors, most of them patricians, or men like himself, of plebeian rank but with patrician blood. Their devotion to Gnaeus—or Coriolanus, as they always called him—was fanatical. No less fanatical was the determination of the tribune Icilius and his plebeian followers to see Gnaeus destroyed. The raging dispute over his fate had torn Roma apart. His trial was to be held the next day.

"The gods have nothing to do with this farce," said Appius Claudius bitterly. "Men are to blame. Weak and foolish men! You should have been applauded as a hero by the Senate, Gnaeus. Instead, they've abandoned you."

"The matter was never that simple," said Cominius with a sigh. "The right to elect the tribunes was won by the plebs only after a fierce struggle. Gnaeus stepped into the path of a raging bull when he decided to take them on."

"And are we to do nothing while that bull tramples the best man in Roma?" said Titus, his voice breaking. The day the mob chased them to the Tarpeian Rock had marked a turning point in his life. A great anger had welled up inside him; it hardened Titus's heart against the plebs and drew him closer than ever to his boyhood friend. How had he been blind for so long to the threat posed by the plebs? How had he failed to see that Gnaeus was right all along? Titus felt guilty for not having supported Gnaeus more enthusiastically from the beginning. When Gnaeus was booed by weaker men for speaking the truth in the Senate, Titus should have been ready with his own speech to back him up.

"Don't worry about the rampaging bull, Titus," said Gnaeus. He placed his hand on his friend's shoulder. "The beast will never touch me! I'll sooner die by my own sword than submit to the punishment of that rabble."

"That 'rabble,' as you call it, is the people's assembly," said Cominius, "and I fear that their right to try you is beyond dispute. The matter has been fully debated in the Senate—"

"Shameful!" muttered Appius Claudius. "I did my best to sway them, but to no avail!"

"And so this mockery of justice, this so-called trial, will take place tomorrow," said Gnaeus. "Is there truly no hope, Cominius?"

"None. Icilius has stirred the plebs into a frenzy. I had hoped the influence of their betters might serve to cool their thirst for your blood, but even outright bribery has failed. Tomorrow you'll be tried before the people's assembly and found guilty of impugning the dignity and endangering the persons of the tribunes. Your property will be confiscated and auctioned; the proceeds will be donated to the fund for the poor in the Temple of Ceres. Your mother and wife will be left with nothing."

"And I?"

Cominius hung his head. "You will be publicly scourged and executed."

"No! Never!" cried one of the young warriors from the shadows of the colonnade. His colleagues joined him with cries of outrage.

Gnaeus raised his hands to quiet them. He turned to Cominius. "And if I leave Roma tonight, of my own volition? If I flee into exile?"

Cominius drew a deep breath. "Icilius could try you in absentia, but I think I can convince him not to. He will have scored the victory he seeks, establishing the inviolability of the tribunes. If there is no trial, your property will remain intact. Your mother and wife will be provided for."

"I care nothing for my own life," said Gnaeus. "Let them flay me and eat my flesh, if they wish. But I will never allow my property to be put into the hands of the aediles, to feed the lazy rabble of Roma!" He turned his face up to stare at the full moon. By its white light, his handsome features looked as though they had been sculpted from marble. "Exile!" he whispered. "After all I've done for Roma!" He lowered his face, so that it was once again in shadow. He addressed the warriors who surrounded him.

"Some of you, when last we met, made a pledge that you would raise a sword and spill plebeian blood rather than see me executed, or, failing that, that you would follow me into exile. But now that the moment of decision has arrived, I do not hold any man to that pledge."

"We made a vow!" objected one of the men. "A Roman never breaks his oath!"

"But if we leave Roma, never to return, are we still Romans? Think what it means to be a man without a city! This fate was thrust upon me. I cannot thrust it upon anyone else."

One of the men stepped forward. "We all came here tonight armed and ready to fight—ready to die, if necessary. If your decision as our commander is to withdraw instead of engaging the enemy, we go with you, Coriolanus!"

"Even beyond the gates of Roma?"

"Yes, just as we followed you inside the gates of Corioli! That day, you fought your way inside, alone, and the rest of us trailed after you, like tardy schoolboys. Not so, on this day! We remain at your side, Coriolanus!"

"So say you all?"

"So say we all!" shouted the warriors.

Gnaeus laughed. "With that cry, you've awaked the whole Palatine! All Roma will soon be wondering what's afoot at the house of Gnaeus Marcius. We have no choice now, but to leave at once!"

While the others made ready, Gnaeus said farewell to Cominius and Claudius. He saw Titus standing in the shadows and went to his side. "I've already said farewell to my mother and my wife. Look after them, Titus, as carefully as you look after Claudia."

"I should go with you."

Gnaeus shook his head. "You heard what I told my warriors. This is a sacrifice I can demand of no man."

"Yet they follow you."

"That is their choice."

"It should be my choice, as well."

Gnaeus was silent for a long moment. Shadows hid his face, but Titus felt the man's eyes upon him. "You have a temple to complete, Titus."

"Damn the Temple of Ceres, and all it stands for!"

Gnaeus frowned. "A man must have something to believe in."

"As you once believed in Roma?"

"Believe in Roma, Titus. Believe in the Temple of Ceres. Forget that Coriolanus ever lived." Gnaeus turned and walked away. His followers encircled him. The entourage departed from the garden.

Titus's house was only a short distance away. Claudius offered to go with him, but Titus preferred to walk alone.

The night was warm. The shutters were open. Moonlight flooded the chamber where Claudia was sleeping. Titus gazed upon her face for a long time. He walked to the room where his son slept, and gazed upon his face for an even longer time.

He kept thinking of the image which Cominius had planted in his mind, of Gnaeus confronted by a stampeding bull. Hercules, whose altar had been in the keeping of Titus's family for generations, had once fought a bull on the faraway island of Crete. Gods demanded sacrifice; heroes deserved loyalty. Was not Coriolanus just such a hero as Hercules had been?

In his study, by moonlight—for he feared that lighting a lamp might wake those who slept—he wrote a message to Appius Claudius: *Father-in-law, I beseech you, look after your daughter and your grandson. I have done what I know to be right.*

He entered his son's room. He lifted the talisman of Fascinus over his neck and slipped it, carefully and quietly, over his son's neck. Deep in slumber, the boy reached up and touched the talisman, but never woke.

If Titus hurried, he might catch up with Coriolanus and his men before they passed beyond the city gates.

491 B.C.

"It's a long road that's brought us here," said Gnaeus.

"A very long road indeed," said Titus, smiling ruefully. He knew that his friend did not literally mean the road beneath their feet, which brought them, with each clop of the horses' hooves, closer to Roma. Gnaeus was speaking of the curious twists and turns their lives had taken since the night they fled the city, two years ago.

A man such as Gnaeus, with his knowledge of warfare and his reputation for bravery, and with a company of fanatically devoted warriors at his side, would have been welcomed in many cities. It was ironic, but perhaps predictable, that he chose to make an overture to the Volsci. True, he had spilled much Volscian blood, but always in honorable combat, and who was more likely than the Volsci to recognize his true worth? It was a curious thing, puzzling at first to Titus, that those whom Gnaeus had fought so ferociously could welcome him into their rank so enthusiastically. This was the way of the warrior: By a simple twist of fate, and in the blink of an eye, an enemy could become an ally.

Of course, Gnaeus, being Gnaeus, had become much more than an ally. He quickly became the Volsci's leading warrior, and then, just as quickly, commander of the whole army. The campaign to wreak vengeance on Roma had not been his idea, but that of the Volscian elders, who had to argue long and hard to overcome his resistance. Who better to anticipate and foil every Roman strategy than the man who been Roma's greatest warrior? What greater triumph for the Volsci than to see Coriolanus do to Roma what he had done to Corioli? What sweeter revenge for Gnaeus Marcius than to bring the city that had spurned him to its knees?

In the campaign against Roma, Gnaeus had transcended himself. The man who had proclaimed his desire to become Roma's greatest warrior had become the greatest warrior in all of Italy, and the boldest general as well. It seemed to Titus, who fought at Gnaeus's side in battle after battle, that the gods themselves must have taken a hand in delivering so many victories to his friend. The men under Gnaeus developed a superstitious belief in his leadership; the magic of his presence, not their bravery, was the key to victory. It was Titus's private conviction that the ancient spirit of Hercules now lived again in Coriolanus, the hero of the age. This religious conviction was a great solace to Titus in those moments when homesickness for Roma and his family threatened to overwhelm him.

Now the final battle drew near. Every clop of the horses' hooves along the road brought Gnaeus and the army of the Volsci closer to the very gate by which he had fled the city. In battle after battle, the armies of Roma had been defeated. Their ranks were depleted, their stores of arms captured and confiscated. The people were weakened as well. Crops had been burned, Roman colonies had been looted, and emergency supplies of grain from Sicily had been intercepted. As Roma grew more enfeebled, all the enemies whom she had humiliated in recent years flocked to join Gnaeus and the Volsci. The force led by Coriolanus was invincible.

While the invaders were still two days south of Roma, envoys had ridden out from the city to meet with Gnaeus. They reminded him of his Roman lineage. They pleaded with him to turn back his army. Gnaeus treated them with scorn, but allowed them to return to Roma with their heads. "The fact that the Romans beg for peace shows they're certain of defeat," he said to Titus.

The next day, two more envoys arrived. The dust from their chariot rose high in the still air and could be seen for a long time before they drew near enough to be recognized. Titus drew a sharp breath when he saw the haggard faces of Appius Claudius and Postumius Cominius.

Gnaeus ordered his men to stay back while he rode forward to meet the two senators. Titus accompanied him. While Gnaeus acknowledged the two men's greeting, Titus stayed to one side, unwilling to look his father-in-law in the eye.

Cominius first assured Gnaeus that his wife and mother were well; despite Gnaeus's betrayal, no one had taken vengeance on his family, and now no one would dare to do so. "My daughter Claudia and young Titus Potitius are also well," added Claudius, though Titus still averted his eyes. Speaking for the consuls and the Senate, the two men acknowledged the great wrong that had been done to Gnaeus. They promised the restoration of his citizenship and his place in the Senate, and full immunity from prosecution by the tribunes.

Gnaeus listened respectfully to his two old mentors, then asked, "And what of the tribunes of the plebs, and the aediles? Will they be abolished? Will the Temple of Ceres be pulled to the ground?"

Cominius and Claudius lowered their eyes. Their silence provided the answer.

Gnaeus laughed. "You think to turn back Coriolanus with a few words, yet with all the power of the Senate you cannot even bend the plebs to your will! No empty promises will stop me now. If you truly love Roma, go back and advise your colleagues to surrender the city. I have no wish to spill more blood than is necessary, and my men's craving for plunder will be easier to control if they take the city without a fight. Whether you resist me or not, by this time tomorrow Roma will belong to me."

"A bitter homecoming!" said Cominius.

"But a homecoming, nonetheless."

"And if you take the city—Jupiter forbid!—what will you do then?" asked Claudius.

Gnaeus drew a deep breath. "If they haven't already killed themselves, certain of my old enemies will receive the retribution they deserve. I think you know who heads the list."

"The tribune Spurius Icilius," said Cominius.

"What a pleasure it will be to cast him from the Tarpeian Rock!"

"What of the Senate?" said Claudius.

"Perhaps I will allow it to remain in existence, restored to the role it played under the kings, to give advice and assistance to the royal power. Its less useful members will be purged and replaced by new members of Volscian blood."

Cominius stifled a cry of despair. Claudius cast a piercing gaze at Titus. "What do you have to say about this, son-in-law?"

Titus stared back, his gaze steady. "When I was a boy, my grandfather taught me the list of kings: Romulus, Numa Pompilius, Tullus Hostilius, Ancus Marcius, Tarquinius the Elder, Servius Tullius. Tarquinius the Proud was to be the last, the very last, cast out and replaced forever by something called a republic. A mockery! A mistake! An experiment that failed! Today is the republic's final day. Tomorrow, men will shout in the Forum, 'All hail King Coriolanus!'"

He drew his sword and raised his arm to Gnaeus. His horse rose on its hind legs. "All hail King Coriolanus!" he cried.

The coterie of loyal warriors who had left Roma with Gnaeus, who always rode at the head of the army, heard Titus's cry and took it up. "All hail King Coriolanus!"

The cry spread through the ranks of the vast army: "All hail King Coriolanus!" Men raised their swords in salute, then beat them upon their shields, creating a frightful din as they shouted, over and over, "All hail King Coriolanus!"

Claudius seemed to wither. Cominius turned the chariot about. A cloud of dust rose behind them as they hurried back to Roma.

At that spot, a few miles south of the city, the army of Coriolanus made camp.

The next morning the army rose at dawn and made ready to march to battle.

As always, Coriolanus rode at the head of the army, with Titus beside him and his mounted Roman warriors immediately behind him. With each step, they drew closer to Roma.

They approached the crest of a low hill. Once they reached it, the hills of Roma would be visible in the distance.

Above the sound of hooves and the rustle created by a vast army on the march, Titus heard another sound, low at first and then louder. It came from beyond the crest of the hill. Something was on the other side, not yet visible, something that made a horrible, wrenching, frightening sound, a sound such as a man might hear on his descent to the realms of Pluto, a sound of utter hopelessness and despair.

Gnaeus heard it, too. He frowned and turned one ear forward. "What is *that*?" he whispered.

"I don't know," said Titus, "but it raises hackles on the back of my neck." A superstitious fear swept over him. What if the gods loved Roma more than they loved Coriolanus? What if, by betraying Roma, Titus and Gnaeus had sinned against the gods? What sort of unearthly creature of doom might the gods have conjured to meet them on the road to Roma? Or had a vast pit opened in the earth, into which they would all be cast down, never to return? That was what the noise sounded like—the shrieking and moaning of a vast chorus of the dead.

Once they reached the crest of the hill, they would know.

Gripping the reins of his horse, Gnaeus's knuckles turned white. Titus swallowed hard. He glanced behind him. Even the battle-hardened warriors in the front ranks had blanched, hearing that unnerving noise.

They came to the crest.

Before them, like a gigantic black snake upon the straight road, stretching all the way back to the city gate in the far distance, was a procession of women dressed in mourning. It appeared that all the women in Roma had come forth from the city

The unearthly sound was the collective noise of their lamentation. Some softly wept. Some were wrenched by sobs. Some swayed and moaned. A few shrieked with laughter, like madwomen. Some walked stiffly, as if in a dream, while others thrashed about in a kind of frenzy and swept the road underfoot with their unbound hair.

In contrast to the others, the women at the very front of the procession strode forward with great dignity. They were silent and held their heads high. Among them, by their headbands of twined red and white wool and their cropped hair, Titus recognized the Vestal virgins. Five of them were present, one having been left behind, as always, to tend to the sacred hearth in the Temple of Vesta; at a time of such crisis, it was more vital than ever than the flame should not be extinguished. Ahead of the Vestals were three women who, despite their proud, upright bearing, were dressed in dark, tattered rags, like beggars in mourning. They even went barefoot, but clearly were not accustomed to doing so, for their feet were bleeding. Despite the agony they must have felt, they never stumbled or missed a step.

As he had when the senators approached the previous day, Gnaeus signaled the army to halt while he rode forward with Titus beside him.

"Shame on the Senate!" said Titus. "The city's envoys failed to stop you, so now they stoop to sending women!"

When Gnaeus made no answer, Titus glanced at him. Instead of a sardonic expression to match his own, the look on his friend's face was troubled and his eyes glistened. Titus's heart sank. He felt a premonition of what was to come.

At a signal from the Vestals, the women behind them shambled to a stop. The three woman in rags who led the procession continued to stride forward, and stopped only when the two horsemen were almost upon them. In the center, Titus recognized Veturia, Gnaeus's mother. She looked much older than when he had last seen her. Though she stood rigidly upright, it appeared that she required some assistance to do so from the two women flanking her. To her right was Gnaeus's wife, Volumnia. When Titus saw the third woman, he let out a gasp. He had not seen Claudia since the day he left Roma. Her face was worn with care. She lowered her eyes and would not look at him.

Veturia, on the other hand, fixed her gaze on her son. "Gnaeus!" she cried out.

"Mother!" he whispered.

"Would you loom above your mother, like a master looking down on a slave?"

Gnaeus at once dismounted. Titus did likewise. But when Gnaeus stepped forward, Titus hung back. He clutched the reins, more to support himself than to restrain the horses. He suddenly felt light-headed. It was like the feeling he had experienced on the Tarpeian Rock when he was struck a blow on the head. Everything between that moment and this seemed a dream, and he feared he was about to be rudely awakened. His heart pounded in his chest.

When Gnaeus reached his mother, he raised his arms, but she refused his embrace. He stepped back. "Why do you not embrace me, mother? Why do you stand so stiffly?"

"If I were to lift my elbows free from the support that Volumnia and Claudia give me, I would fall to the ground."

"I would catch you."

"Liar!"

"Mother!"

She glared at him. "I always thought, if ever I reached an age when I could not stand upright on my own, that the strong arm of my son would be there for me to lean on. But when I came to need your arm, Gnaeus, it was not there for me. I had to lean on others—to my shame! May the gods cripple me completely if ever I should lean on your arm!"

"Harsh words, Mother!"

"Not half as harsh as the fate you've thrust upon me."

"What I've done, I was forced to do. For the sake of my dignity—"

"You cast away your dignity the day you took up arms against Roma. That day, you put a knife against your mother's breast. Today, you seem determined to thrust that knife into her heart."

"No, Mother. What I've done, I did for you. You always taught me—"

"I never taught my son to be a traitor! If I hear you say such a thing, I'll pull the sword from your scabbard and fall upon it, rather than draw another breath!"

"Mother, Mother—"

Veturia suddenly pulled her arm from her daughter-in-law's grasp. With all her strength, she slapped Gnaeus across the face. The crack of the blow was startlingly loud. The horses whinnied and wrenched sharply at their reins, burning Titus's palms.

Veturia began to fall forward, but the women caught her. Gnaeus was stunned. After a long moment, he signaled for Titus to come to him. He whispered in his ear. "Tell the men I've ordered a halt. Set up my tent beside the road. Too many eyes are upon us. I must meet with my mother in private."

What was said in that tent? What promises or threats were made, what memories or dreams rekindled? None would ever know but Coriolanus and his mother.

Veturia was the first to emerge from the tent. Volumnia and Claudia— who still had never met Titus's eyes—quickly stepped forward to assist her. Without a word, the three returned to where the Vestals waited. Veturia spoke to the virgins in a low voice, and they in turn made gestures to the women behind them to turn around and return to the city. As the vast procession retreated, the multitude of women neither wept nor were jubilant, but maintained an eerie silence.

Gnaeus remained alone in the tent for a very long time. When he finally emerged, he wore upon his face a look of determination such as Titus had never seen before.

Gnaeus mounted his steed, then summoned his Roman vanguard. The mounted warriors assembled before him. Titus was among them, dreading what he was about to hear.

"There will be no attack on Roma," said Gnaeus.

The men were dumbfounded.

"When we left Roma, we set out to meet our destiny. Destiny has led us very nearly in a circle. We have come this close to Roma—but we will come no closer. Over the mountains, across the seas, there is a vast world beyond the lands of the Romans and the Volsci. Out there, perhaps, is where our destiny now lies."

The men looked at one another anxiously, but such was their degree of discipline that not one of them spoke a word of protest.

"We shall now ride back through the Volscian ranks. When we reach the rear of the army, we shall simply keep riding."

"And the Volsci?" said Titus.

"If they wish to attack Roma, let them."

"They'll never do it! You're their talisman. Only Coriolanus can lead them to victory."

"Then I suppose they'll turn back, as well." Gnaeus snapped his reins and rode forward. The Roman vanguard followed. Titus caught up and rode beside Gnaeus. The Volscian foot soldiers stepped back to make way, gazing up at them in wonder and confusion.

"It's that woman's doing!" shouted one of them. "She's turned her son against us!"

"Coriolanus is deserting us!"

"Impossible!"

"Look for yourself!"

"But why did he lead us here?"

"It's a trap! Coriolanus lured us to this place, and now the Romans must have a terrible trick in store!"

Consternation spread through the ranks. It seemed to Titus that they rode above a sea of angry faces. The roar of that sea grew louder and louder. Its currents surged this way and that with ever greater violence.

"Turn back, Coriolanus!" cried the Volsci. "Turn back! Lead us! Or else—"

A stone struck Titus's helmet. The noise reverberated though his skull. Again, he was reminded of the day the cudgel had struck him on the Tarpeian Rock, and Gnaeus had saved his life. More and more, the world around him seemed strange and dreamlike, muted and distant.

More stones pelted his armor. Titus hardly felt them. The Volsci began with stones, but soon enough they drew their swords. The Romans on horseback did likewise. To Titus's ears, the clash of iron was oddly muffled. A blur of motion followed. It was with some surprise that he saw blood upon his own sword, then felt a burning pain in his side. The world spun about and turned upside down. Titus vaguely knew that he must be tumbling from his horse, but never felt himself hit the ground.

In the days that followed, the Senate of Roma decreed that the day of the city's salvation from Coriolanus should be a day of thanksgiving, and that special honors should be given to the courageous women of Roma, who had achieved what neither force of arms nor diplomacy could have achieved.

Those decisions were easy. Harder decisions followed.

Considerable acrimony attended the debate regarding the Ara Maxima. Since the dawn of time, the Altar of Hercules had been kept by the fami-

lies of the Pinarii and the Potitii, the hereditary priests who jointly celebrated the Feast of Hercules. In light of the dishonor brought upon his
family by Titus Potitius, should that family be allowed to continue as
keepers of the altar, or should they be stripped of their role, and should it
be given to another family, or to priests appointed by the state?

Appius Claudius was among those who argued that the state had no
right to interfere in a religious arrangement that predated the state itself.
Hercules himself had chosen the two families to keep his shrine. No act of
the state could undo what a god had willed in a time before memory. This
was his public stance. Privately, Claudius told his colleagues that the
shame brought upon him by his son-in-law was a torment hardly to be
borne; he disowned his daughter and grandchild, and declared that so
long as he or any descendent bearing his name held any influence in the
state, no man with the name Potitius would ever be elected to high office.

Claudius's argument carried the Senate. The keeping of the Ara Maxima would remain in family hands, unchanged. But the newly elected consul, Publius Pinarius, protested that his family would no longer carry out
its traditional duties alongside the disgraced Potitii. "After too many generations to count, we relinquish our place in the keeping of the altar. Let
the Potitii do it all by themselves!"

There was much talk among the elite of Roma regarding these two ancient patrician families, and the curious twists of fate which had brought
Publius Pinarius to the consulship, the pinnacle of his family's fortunes,
even as the Potitii reached their nadir with the disgrace of Titus Potitius.

Years later, a ragged drifter happened to find himself a few miles south of
Roma. He was a man with no city or tribe, doomed to perpetually wander,
surviving by his wits, which were often befuddled, and dependent on the
mercy of strangers; a broken man, without hopes or dreams. He had not
passed this way in many years.

He only vaguely realized where he was, but he knew that the small temple beside the road had not been there before. It was of simple design, but
handsomely executed and beautifully decorated. A young shepherd was
resting on the steps.

"Tell me, boy," said the vagrant, "what is this temple? To what god is it dedicated?"

The boy looked at the drifter warily at first, then saw that the grizzled stranger was harmless. "Not a god, but a goddess—Fortuna, the first daughter of Jupiter. She decides the ups and downs of life."

"I seem to recall that there are many temples to Fortuna in Roma," remarked the drifter, his voice dreamy.

"Yes, but this one is different. They call it the Temple of Fortuna Muliebris, Fortuna of the Women."

"Why is that?"

"Because the women of Roma paid to build it, if you can believe that. This is the very spot, you see, where the villain Coriolanus was turned back."

"Is it?" said the drifter, with a quaver in his voice.

"Indeed it is. And afterward, the women thought there should be a temple here, to mark the spot. The Senate and the priests approved, and the women themselves raised the money to build it. It's a beautiful building, isn't it?"

"Yes." The drifter gazed admiringly at the structure. "I used to be a builder myself."

"You?" The shepherd looked at him dubiously, then slapped his thigh and laughed. "And I used to be a senator! But look at me now, herding these dirty sheep!"

So this was the very spot. Titus's mind was flooded by memories long suppressed. Dimly he remembered witnessing Gnaeus's gory end; even the greatest warrior in Italy could not take on the whole of an army he himself had trained for combat. At least Gnaeus had died fighting. Dimly—thank the gods, only dimly!—Titus recalled the tortures to which the Volsci had subjected him before they let him go.

It all seemed very distant, like a dream almost forgotten. All the days of his life seemed like that, even yesterday, even today.

"If you like looking at temples," said the shepherd, "walk on a little ways to the crest of the hill. From there you can see the city. The highest thing you see is the Temple of Jupiter. Now that's a temple! It sits on the Capitoline like a crown on the head of a king. Even from here, you can see how grand it is. Go on, have a look."

Titus's heart pounded in his chest. As he was still wont to do in moments of great emotion, even after all these years, Titus reached up to finger the talisman of Fascinus at this throat. Of course, it was not there. He had given it to his sleeping son on the night he left Roma. How was the boy? Did he still live? Did he prosper? Did he keep the ancient rites of Hercules, as had his ancestors before him?

"Go ahead," said the shepherd. "Walk to the rise and have a look at the city."

The ragged wanderer, saying nothing, turned around and walked in the opposite direction.

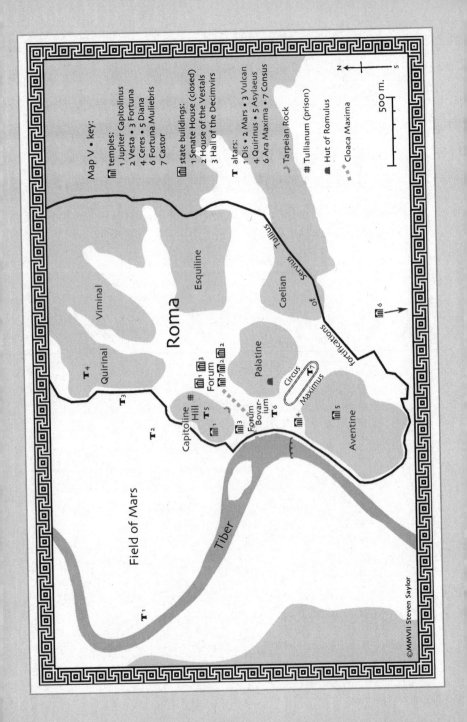

THE TWELVE TABLES

450 B.C.

"Another toast!" declared Lucius Icilius.

"What? Surely not another!" Lucius Verginius laughed heartily. He was a broad-shouldered bear of a man who greatly enjoyed wine, and his protest was purely for show.

"As your host, I must insist," said Icilius. With a wave of his long, bony arm, he beckoned to the serving girl to refill the cups.

The occasion was a joyful one—a dinner party to celebrate the upcoming wedding of the son of Icilius, young Lucius, to Verginia, the daughter of Verginius. The marriage would unite two of the most distinguished plebeian families in Roma. The Verginii had been prominent in the city nearly as long as some patrician families. The branch of Lucius Verginius, while not wealthy, was famed for prowess in battle; in recent campaigns against the Sabines and the Aequi, Lucius Verginius had upheld the standards of bravery set by his ancestors. The Icilii were well-to-do, politically active, and full of vitality and ambition. Men from both families had served as tribunes of the plebs.

The marriage bond between the Icilii and the Verginii would strengthen both clans. It was a love match, as well; Lucius and Verginia had fallen for each other at first sight. Tonight, with the wedding only a few days away, the two families dined together under the roof of Icilius to celebrate their impending union.

Icilius raised his cup. "A toast to the mothers! We must never underestimate the power of a Roman matron. More than forty years ago, when the traitor Coriolanus marched on Roma, what was the only thing that could turn him back? Not swords, not walls, not even the abject groveling of the senators. Only a mother's plea was powerful enough to save Roma. To the mothers of the bride and groom!"

"To the mothers!" agreed Verginius, raising his cup.

"Yes, to our mothers!" said young Lucius, his eyes sparkling from having drunk more wine than he was used to.

The subjects of the toast demurely lowered their eyes, and did not join in the drinking. Nor did the bridegroom's younger sister, the darkly beautiful Icilia. Nor did young Verginia, who had never tasted wine. She needed no intoxicant to make her blue eyes sparkle or to add color to her cheeks, which were as smooth as rose petals. Verginia was as fair as Lucius was dark; she was short and voluptuous rather than tall and lean like her betrothed. Their physical differences only served to complement each other's beauty; everyone agreed that they made a lovely couple.

Icilius drained his cup and wiped his mouth. "Now, you may wonder why, in such congenial company, I should mention the foul name of Coriolanus, which inspires loathing in the breast of any patriot."

"Because it brings up the subject of your toast—a mother's influence!" said Verginius, slurring his words slightly.

"Ah, yes, but more than that, I mention that accursed name to remind us of the great boon to Roma which was done by one of my relatives, the great tribune Spurius Icilius. It was Spurius who ran Coriolanus out of Roma. A mother may have kept the villain out, but an Icilius drove him away in the first place. I mention this, Verginius, to show you that the family into which your daughter is marrying, while it may not have a history as long as yours, has nonetheless *made* history. With an upstanding young scion like my boy Lucius, this family will continue to do so!"

"And why not, with the fine sons that my Verginia will give him!" cried Verginius.

Verginia blushed. So did Lucius, though he attempted a manly laugh to cover his self-consciousness. Icilia, whose skin was even darker than her brother's, did not easily show a blush, but such talk clearly disturbed her; the others, if they noticed, ascribed the pained look on her face to maidenly modesty.

"But, more seriously—" Icilius paused; all his concentration was momentarily required to suppress a belch. The critical moment passed. "As I was saying, on a more serious note: Forty years have passed since the wicked Coriolanus dared to threaten the tribunes, and for that crime he was duly punished; and yet, in many ways, the strife between the classes is now fiercer than ever. Only rarely, these days, is a plebeian elected to the consulship, and this is no accident. The patricians grow more jealous of their privileges, not less. They lay down every possible impediment in order to prevent even the most qualified plebeian from attaining the higher magistracies. You know this is true, good Verginius."

The other man nodded. "Regrettably, good Icilius, it is the truth."

Lucius groaned. "No, Papa. No politics tonight!"

Icilius shushed him. "This is not politics, my boy. This is serious family talk. The Verginii and the Icilii represent the very best of the plebeians. The union of our families is much more than the betrothal of a beautiful girl and a fine young man; this marriage represents the hope of the future.

"Will there ever be lasting peace between the patricians and ourselves? We must start by admitting that there have been abuses on both sides. Since the days of Coriolanus, we plebs have staged no more secessions, but sometimes, perhaps, we have been too eager to use the power of the tribunes to punish arrogant patricians. Some tribunes have stirred up the populace unnecessarily, and have wielded their power recklessly. To be sure, more than a few patricians, through devious means, have eluded punishment and cheated justice. Failures and abuses on both sides have led to further recriminations, which in turn have led to more strife and discord.

"In these dark days, despite the best efforts of honest men, the two classes seem to be drawing further and further apart. We can only hope that the children of Lucius and Verginia will inherit a better Roma than the one in which their parents were born!"

"Hear, hear!" agreed Verginius. "Well said, Icilius! The Decemvirs themselves should be here tonight, to hear you speak."

Young Lucius, feeling tipsy, raised his cup. "To the Decemvirs!"

His elders abruptly shot him a look that made Lucius feel quite small.

But the mood was too jovial for the tense moment to prevail. Verginius smiled first, then Icilius.

"A toast to the Decemvirs, my son?" Icilius clucked his tongue. "A toast implies congratulations, and in the case of the Decemvirs, that would be premature. No one has yet seen the fruit of their labors, though our ten little Tarquinii have already put a bitter taste in the mouths of many good citizens."

"The ten Tarquinii? That's a bit harsh, isn't it?" said Verginius.

"Is it?" Icilius raised an eyebrow.

Two years earlier the discord in Roma had grown so extreme that patricians and plebeians alike had agreed to an extraordinary measure. Elections were cancelled, the Senate was disbanded, and the magistrates, including the tribunes, were relieved of their offices. A board of ten men—the Decemvirs—was given temporary power to rule the state and charged with the task of writing a comprehensive code of laws. It had sounded like a good idea at the time: Roma's ten wisest men would determine why the state had come to a standstill, wield whatever power was necessary to resolve the problems, devise fair laws, and chisel those laws into stone for all to see. The plebs had long agitated for a written law code, believing that a clear list of offenses and an enumeration of citizens' rights would do more than anything else to put an end to the arbitrary abuses of the patricians. But the process had dragged on for two years, without visible results, and the Decemvirs had grown careless and abusive with their power.

Icilius clucked his tongue. "We all hoped—optimistically, perhaps foolishly—that the Decemvirs would follow the example of Cincinnatus—"

"Good old Cincinnatus! A toast to Cincinnatus!" cried Verginius, who had served under the famous commander. Eight years before, when a Roman army had been trapped by the Aequi and faced certain destruction, the general-turned-farmer Lucius Quinctius Cincinnatus had been called from retirement; he was named dictator and given total power over the state for the duration of the crisis. Begrudgingly, Cincinnatus left his plow, led a force to rescue the army, soundly defeated the Aequi, resigned his office, and returned to his farm—all in the span of fifteen days. It was said that his plow was exactly where he had left it, and he set about finishing the furrow he had begun, as if there had been no interruption. Expeditious and self-effacing, Cincinnatus had become a living legend.

But the Decemvirs had not followed the example of Cincinnatus. By devious means they had extended their original terms of office and continued to rule as absolute dictators while the people still awaited publication of the new law code. In recent months, their abuses had grown more flagrant as they ruthlessly suppressed anyone who questioned their authority. Men had died for opposing them; but the Decemvirs, so long as they held office, were immune from charges of murder.

"The good news," said Icilius, "is that the new law code should be made public any day now. The Decemvirs call it the Twelve Tables. Let's hope they've done such an outstanding job that the virtues of the Twelve Tables will make us forget the vices of the ten Tarquinii."

Young Lucius furrowed his brow. "I heard a rumor the other day, about these new laws."

"A rumor?" said his father.

"My tutor, Xenon, says they plan to outlaw marriage between patricians and plebeians."

"A terrible idea!" said Verginius.

Icilius's face grew long. "What would your Greek tutor know about such things?"

Lucius shrugged. "Xenon tutors other boys, including some of the Decemvirs' grandsons. He hears all sorts of things."

Icilius peered into his empty cup. "To be sure, there are those, patrician and plebeian alike, who believe that *more* separation of the classes, not less, is the answer to Roma's social ills. A ban on intermarriage might not be a bad thing."

"I suppose I should consider myself lucky, then," said Lucius, "that the most beautiful girl in all of Roma happens to be a plebeian, and she happens to be betrothed to me." He beamed at Verginia, who grinned and lowered her eyes.

No one was looking at Lucius's sister, Icilia, whose dark beauty was abruptly marred by a deep frown.

Verginius grunted. " 'Ten Tarquinii,' you called the Decemvirs. Appius Claudius must be the worst of the lot! A few generations back, the Claudii weren't even Romans. They weren't even the Claudii! What was that uncouth Sabine name his grandfather was born with?"

"Attus Clausus," said Icilius.

"Ah, yes! And now the grandson is chief among the Decemvirs. A thoroughly unpleasant fellow, always swaggering about, surrounded by lictors, wearing a purple toga and expecting everyone he meets to do his bidding. That man enjoys being a Decemvir entirely too much! And now he proposes to ban intermarriage. The patrician hypocrite! Only a few months ago, he asked me for Verginia's hand."

"Papa!" Verginia spoke up. "I don't think you should mention—"

"Why not? It's not as if either you or I led the old goat on in any way. Let Jupiter strike me down if I tell a lie! A few months ago, Appius Claudius asked if he might marry Verginia."

"And what did you say?" asked Icilia.

"I told him no, of course! Not that the match would have been unsuitable; Appius Claudius, a widower with grown children, may be a bit old for Verginia, but the Claudii have made quite a name for themselves in three short generations, and they *are* patricians, however newly minted." Verginius said this in an offhand way, but clearly, he didn't mind letting Icilius know that his daughter could have married a patrician, if Verginius had so chosen. "I rejected Appius Claudius as a suitor because I don't like the fellow—it's as simple as that! Couldn't stand the idea of having him be my son-in-law, or the father of my grandchildren. I much prefer you, Lucius. And more importantly, so does Verginia!"

Verginius laughed heartily and rose from his dining couch to give his daughter a kiss. She turned her face to offer her cheek. By doing so, she also hid her expression from everyone in the room.

"Another toast, then!" said Icilius.

"Another?" Verginius fell back on his couch and pretended to groan.

"Yes! A toast to love."

"To love, indeed!" said Verginius. "To Venus, the goddess of love, who has clearly blessed this union with the spark of mutual desire. What could be better than a genuine love match of which both fathers approve?"

The men drank more wine, then burst out laughing. The mothers laughed as well, caught up in the men's exuberance. Even dark Icilia ceased frowning, threw back her head, and laughed.

Only Verginia failed to laugh. From the moment her father had mentioned Appius Claudius the Decemvir, and the man's thwarted desire to marry her, an uneasy look had settled on her face.

The next day, Icilia and Verginia went shopping together in the market, chaperoned by their mothers.

The two girls had been raised in different circles, and had few acquaintances in common; yet, since they were soon to be sisters-in-law, everyone expected them to begin acting as if they were already old friends. Their recent outings together, since the announcement of Verginia's betrothal to Lucius, felt forced and artificial to both of them; their mothers, endlessly preoccupied with wedding details, had more to talk about than they did. To complicate matters, each of the girls had a problem that weighed upon her, but as yet felt unready to share her secret with the other. They moved though the market side by side, sporadically making conversation, each wrapped up in her own private thoughts.

"What do you think of this, Verginia?" Icilia ran her fingers over a bolt of finely woven yellow linen.

The merchant grinned. "From Syracuse, on the island of Sicily. All the best things come from Syracuse, and I offer them at the best prices!"

Syracuse had originally been founded by colonists from Corinth, and was nearly as old as Roma. It was one of many Greek colonies, not only on Sicily but across the southern part of Italy, a region so heavily settled by Greeks that the Romans called it Magna Graecia, "Great Greece." Romans had traded with these cities for generations, and had so far avoided becoming embroiled in the endless wars they fought against one another. In recent years, Syracuse had emerged as the most brilliant, the most free, and the most prosperous city in all of the western Mediterranean. The Syracusan fleet dominated the Tyrrhenian Sea. Syracusan merchants built warehouses in Ostia, at the mouth of the Tiber, to house the goods they traded with Roma and her neighbors. Syracusan grain more than once had saved Roma from famine. Syracusan scholars taught in the best Roman households; Icilius's tutor, Xenon, came from Syracuse.

"It's alright, I suppose," said Verginia, hardly looking at the fabric. Her thoughts were clearly elsewhere.

"Perhaps the young ladies would be more interested in pottery and earthenware," suggested the merchant. "The young ladies may as yet have no households of their own, but soon enough two such pretty girls will find themselves married, and will be requiring cups and pitchers for entertaining." The merchant could see by their simple, long-sleeved tunicae that the girls were still unmarried; they had not yet graduated to the more complicated stolas worn by their mothers. He held up a black pitcher. "This pattern is particularly beautiful. The red border is an unusual variation on a traditional Greek key design—"

Icilia, who had frowned and turned aside as soon as the man mentioned marriage, suddenly saw a familiar face across the crowded market. Her heart leapt into her throat. Looking over her shoulder, she saw that their mothers, deep in conversation, had strolled on ahead. Impulsively, Icilia gripped Verginia's arm, pulled her away from the nattering merchant, and whispered in her ear.

"Verginia, you must do me a favor!"

"What is it, Icilia?"

"Please, I beg of you—"

"Icilia, what's the matter?"

"Nothing is the matter. But I must leave you for a moment—only a moment, I promise! If our mothers come back and miss me, say . . . say that I had to step into the women's lavatory above the Cloaca Maxima."

"And if they ask why I didn't go with you, or if they decide to go looking for you?"

"Then say . . . oh, I don't know what!"

Verginia smiled. She was not sure what Icilia was up to, but from various small signs, she had come to suspect that Lucius's sister must have a secret suitor; perhaps this had something to do with him. If Icilia was still not ready to tell her the details, here was an opportunity for Verginia to earn her trust, and for the two girls to become closer. Was that not exactly what their mothers desired?

"Of course I'll help you, Icilia. Do what you must—but don't be too long! I don't have much experience at telling falsehoods to my mother."

"Fortuna bless you, Verginia! I shall be very quick, I promise." Casting a final glance at their mothers, who had ambled further ahead, she vanished into the crowd.

He had glimpsed her at the same instant she glimpsed him. He was waiting for her just around the corner from where she had seen him, with an anxious grin on his face.

"Icilia!"

"Titus! Oh, Titus!" It was all she could do not to kiss him, right there; but although they were away from the heavy traffic of the market, they were still visible. Eagerly, he took her arm and led her around another corner, into a narrow space between two buildings that was shielded from view by the foliage of a cypress tree.

He held her body against his and kissed her for a long time. Icilia was not shy; the very impossibility of their relationship encouraged her to abandon all restraint during the rare, fleeting moments she was with him. She ran her hands over his strong shoulders, inside the neck of his tunic and onto his chest, which was covered by fine blond hair. Her fingers encountered the talisman he wore. "Fascinus," he called the curious pendant, saying it was a god that had protected his family for centuries.

Icilia could not help thinking that Fascinus had fallen down on the job in recent generations. It was hard to believe that the Potitii had once been wealthy; even Titus's best tunics were threadbare. The first time Icilia had seen him, he was wearing the one garment he owned that was not covered with patches, the priestly robe he wore at the Ara Maxima. Watching him officiate at the altar with his father, she had been swept away by his good looks. Afterward, it had taken considerable ingenuity on her part to make his acquaintance. The passion that had stirred between them was so immediate and so overwhelming it must have been the hand of Venus that guided them to one another. Yet, when Icilia mentioned Titus Potitius in a very roundabout way to her father, he had reacted with a vehemence that startled her.

Icilia at first assumed it was Titus's poverty, or simply his patrician status, that offended her father, and hoped these barriers might be overcome. It was her brother Lucius who had explained to her the reason for the declining fortunes of the Potitii—the fact that Titus's grandfather had fought alongside Coriolanus. No wonder her father had reacted so violently! The name of Coriolanus was accursed in their house, and so would be the name of any traitor who had been his ally. Never would her father agree to let her marry a Potitius; nor would Titus's father approve such a match, for it had been an Icilius who engineered the exile of Coriolanus and, by extension, the ruin of Titus's grandfather.

The situation was impossible. These brief, stolen moments were all she would ever have with Titus, yet her craving for these encounters was almost more than she could bear, and in the days between them she thought of little else. When Titus began to lift the hem of his tunic as well as her own, and to press his hardness between her legs, she offered no resistance. Instead, she clutched him as hard as she could, praying that the gods would stop time and make this moment last forever.

Titus entered her. He moved inside her. His breath was hot in her ear. A fire was ignited at the very core of her being and radiated outward, building toward an ecstatic release. The rapture reached its pinnacle; the pleasure was so intense, so perfect, how she could doubt the rightness of their union? That she should love Titus must be the will of the gods, which superseded the objections of all petty mortals, including her father.

Afterward, as he was gasping for breath, Titus whispered in her ear. "We must try again. We must go to our fathers and beg them to let us marry. There must be a way to convince them."

"No! My father will never . . ." Icilia left the sentence unfinished and shook her head. The sensation of ecstasy quickly waned and was replaced by hopelessness and despair. "Even if he did approve, it wouldn't matter. The new laws . . . such a terrible rumor . . ."

"What are you saying?"

"My brother heard it from his tutor. The new laws from the Decemvirs—they want to outlaw marriage between patricians and plebeians. If that happens, there's no hope at all!"

Titus clenched his jaw. "I've heard the rumor, as well. The whole world conspires against us!" He sighed and kissed her lips.

Icilia stiffened. "Titus, I have to go."

"Now? Are you afraid Verginia will tell on you?"

"No, but our mothers are with us. They're probably missing me right now. If—"

Titus silenced her by pressing his mouth over hers and drawing her breath away. But when she pushed against him, he released her. She slipped away from him. Her final touch was a fingertip pressed to the talisman at his breast, and then she was gone.

✥

"Go away, you horrible man!"

Back in the market, Verginia found herself accosted, not for the first time, by the wheedling little man who called himself Marcus Claudius. The creature certainly hadn't been born a Claudius, she thought; he must have been a slave who took his master's family name when he was manumitted, as was the custom. Marcus Claudius had the cringing, ingratiating manner of a slave, continuously titling his head to one side as if to duck a blow, licking his lips, and giving her a sidelong leer.

"But why won't you come, dear girl? He merely wishes to talk to you."

"I have nothing to say to Appius Claudius."

"But there's so much he wants to say to you."

"I don't want to hear it!"

"It will take only a moment. He's just over there." The man pointed to a building on the far side of the market.

"In the spice shop?"

"He owns it. There's a cozy little apartment in the upper story. Do you see that window with the shutters ajar? He's watching you even now."

Verginia gazed above the awnings of the market, at the building across the way. Bright sunlight made her squint and shield her eyes. Not much of the dark interior of the room could be seen, but she thought she could discern, just barely, a shadowy figure standing at the window.

"Please, go away!" she said. "I shall tell my father—"

"That would be unwise. The *Decemvir* would not wish it," said Marcus, emphasizing Appius's Claudius title. "The Decemvir is a powerful man."

Verginia was suddenly short of breath. "Do you threaten my father?"

"Not I, young lady, not I! Who is lowly Marcus Claudius, to think he could ever do harm to a great warrior like Verginius? Oh, no, it would take a powerful man to bring about your father's ruin, a very powerful man, indeed; a Decemvir, perhaps."

Verginia looked at the window. She could definitely see the shadowy figure of a bearded man.

"Look, do you see?" said Marcus. "He has a gift for you!"

The figure drew closer to the window; its outlines became clearer. The man was holding something. When he extended his hand, a bit of sunlight glittered on the object.

Marcus whispered in her ear. "Do you see it? A pretty gift for a pretty girl—a silver necklace with baubles of lapis lazuli. How pretty those blue jewels would look against your white throat!" The man giggled. "I think he has another gift for you, in his other hand!"

While the figure at the window held up the necklace, his other hand appeared to be pressing and kneading something beneath his tunic, near the middle of his body.

Verginia stifled a cry and tore herself away from Marcus. She ran headlong into Icilia.

"Where have you been?" she cried. "I looked and looked for you, and then that horrible man—"

"Ah, there they are!" Icilia's mother, standing on tiptoe, called out and waved to them from across the crowd.

"What man?" whispered Icilia.

Verginia looked behind her. Marcus had melted into the crowd. She looked at the window above the spice shop. The shutters were closed.

Then their mothers were upon them, and even if the two girls had wanted to confide in each other, they could not.

⁑

A few days later, scrolls containing the first portion of the Twelve Tables were nailed to the posting wall in the Forum.

A great crowd gathered, made up of both patricians and plebeians. A man with good eyes and a clear voice volunteered to read the scrolls aloud so that the rest could hear, including the great majority who could not read. He was frequently interrupted by exclamations and questions, and when he was done, the crowd engaged in a lively discussion in which many voices were raised:

"Clearly, the new laws affirm the traditional rights of the paterfamilias. Very good! For as long as there's a breath in his body, a man *should* have control over his wife and his offspring, and over their wives and offspring as well."

"But what of this right for the head of a household to sell his sons and grandsons into bondage, and later buy them back?"

"It's already being done, every day. A man falls into debt, so he barters his son for a period of servitude. The new law merely codifies the common practice—and sets a limit on how many times a man can do it, which is a good thing for the sons and grandsons."

"And what about the law giving freed slaves full rights of citizenship?"

"Why not? As often as not, a slave is the bastard child of his master, the offspring of a slave girl in the household; if the master sees fit to free the bastard, then the fellow ought to become a citizen just like the rest of the man's sons."

"Perhaps the Decemvirs haven't done such a bad job, after all."

"Now, if only they would see fit to lay down their offices, call back the Senate, and let us elect new consuls!"

"And don't forget the tribunes of the plebs, the people's protectors!"

"The people's bullies, you mean."

"Please, citizens, please! Let us not be drawn into that old argument! The very purpose of the Twelve Tables is to heal the rifts within the city and allow us to move forward . . ."

Standing a little away from the crowd, Icilia strained to hear what the men were saying. It would not do for a young woman to stride into their midst or shout a question, yet she was desperate to know if the rumored ban on intermarriage was among the posted laws. She and Verginia had been on their way to the Temple of Fortuna to consult an auspex who would pick a new date for Verginia's nuptials. Verginius had abruptly been called away on military duty, and the wedding would have to be postponed for at least a month. Their mothers, chattering away, had gotten a little ahead of them, and when Icilia saw the crowd and realized what they were talking about, she begged Verginia to tarry with her for a moment.

"It's no good," she finally muttered, shaking her head. "None of them is discussing marriage; it's all about slavery and powers of the paterfamilias. We can go, now, Verginia. Verginia?"

She looked about. Verginia was nowhere to be seen.

The two mothers had missed them, and were heading back, looking displeased. "Icilia!" cried her mother. "You must keep up. No dawdling! We have too much to do today. Where is Verginia?"

"I don't know."

"Was she not with you?"

"Yes, but we stopped for just a moment. I turned away, and when I looked back—"

Icilia was interrupted by a man who came running up to them, looking alarmed.

"Aren't you the wife of Verginius?" he said.

Verginia's mother nodded.

"Where is your husband? He must come at once!"

"He's not in the city."

"Where is he?"

"Away, on military duty. What's happening?"

"I'm not sure, but it's very strange. Your daughter, Verginia—"

"What about her?"

"Come and see!"

The man led them across the Forum, toward the building where the Decemvirs met. A small crowd had gathered in front of the building. At the center of the crowd, flanked by the lictors who customarily guarded the entrance, was Marcus Claudius. In his fist he held a rope, the end of which was tied around the neck of Verginia, who stood trembling beside him with downcast eyes and a red face.

Verginia's mother gasped in horror. "What is the meaning of this?" she cried, pushing her way through the crowd. Men stepped back to make way for her, but when she attempted to remove the rope from her daughter's neck, the lictors brandished their axes and cudgels.

She shrieked and started back. "Who are you? What have you done to my daughter?"

"My name is Marcus Claudius." He looked down his nose at her. "And this female is *not* your child."

"Or course she is. This is my daughter, Verginia."

"You lie! This female was born in my household, a slave. Years ago, she disappeared, stolen in the night. Only now have I discovered that she was taken into the household of a certain Lucius Verginius. Apparently, the scoundrel has been passing her off as his daughter, and is even now con-spiring to arrange a marriage for her under false pretenses."

Verginia's mother was stupefied. "This is madness! Of course Verginia is my daughter. I gave birth to her. This is my child! Let her go at once!"

Marcus Claudius smirked. "Stealing another man's slave and perpetrating a fraudulent marriage are serious crimes under the new laws decreed by the Decemvirs. What do you have to say for yourself, woman?"

Verginia's mother sputtered and began to weep. "When my husband—"

"Yes, where is the scoundrel?"

"Away from the city—"

"I see! He must have gotten wind that I had discovered his ruse, and he's made his escape."

"That's ridiculous! This is absurd!" Verginia's mother looked pleadingly at the crowd around her. Some of the men looked at her with pity, but some with scorn. Some openly leered, excited by the spectacle of a purportedly well-born girl revealed as a slave and exhibited with a rope around her neck, while the woman claiming to be her mother dashed about in a frenzy.

Icilia's mother strode forward to try to calm her, but Icilia noticed that her manner was strained and her expression was hard to read. Had the man called Marcus Claudius sparked a doubt in her mind? He claimed that Verginius was deliberately perpetuating a fraud; if that was true, the victims of that fraud were the Icilii. What sort of man would offer a daughter in marriage, and deliver a slave instead, and a stolen slave at that?

Icilia could think of only one thing to do: find her brother. She headed home, running as fast as she could.

Marcus Claudius crossed his arms. "Clearly, wife of Verginius, since you will not confess to the theft of my slave, and instead persist in claiming that she's your daughter, her identity will have to be determined by a court of law. The court normally in charge of handling such disputes is currently suspended; the Decemvirs handle all such cases. I believe the Decemvir in charge of this particular kind of dispute is—"

"Then call on the Decemvirs, at once!" cried Verginia's mother. "But in the meantime, give her back to me!"

Marcus stroked his chin and pursed his lips. "I think not. If her purported father were present, I might be persuaded to give her up to him—but not to a woman, who can have no legal standing."

"I'm her mother!"

"So you say, but where is the man to vouch for that assertion? Since Verginius is not present, I will relinquish possession of this female only to a proper authority."

A number of men in the crowd, even those who appeared to sympathize with Verginia's mother, nodded and grunted their approval, swayed by Marcus's legal reasoning.

"I will give her up only to a Decemvir. Ah, look there! Here's just the man to take responsibility. This is the Decemvir in charge of deciding such cases."

Appius Claudius had appeared, seemingly by chance. He wore the purple toga with a gold border which the Decemvirs affected as their official dress, and was accompanied by a bodyguard of lictors. He carried himself with great dignity. His graying hair and well-trimmed beard gave him a distinguished look. With an expression of innocent curiosity, he strode through the crowd.

Verginia, who had stood motionless for a long time, paralyzed by shame, hugged herself and began to tremble violently. The girl's mother fell at Appius Claudius's feet. "Decemvir, help us!" she cried.

"Of course I'll help you, good woman," he said quietly, reaching down to touch her brow. He addressed Marcus. "Citizen, what's happening here?" His voice was low and steady; there was the slightest quaver, almost imperceptible, to match the fire of excitement that blazed behind his eyes.

"Let me explain, Decemvir," said Marcus. "I've just retrieved this wayward slave girl, who escaped from my household years ago."

Verginia suddenly clutched the rope around her neck and tried to bolt away; but Marcus, reacting at once, tightened his grip on the rope, and when she reached the limit of the tether Verginia was wrenched to the ground. Her mother gave a scream of horror.

Appius Claudius raised an eyebrow. "It seems that I've arrived just in time. Clearly, this situation demands the wisdom and authority that only a Decemvir can provide."

At that moment, Icilia returned, accompanied by her brother, both of them breathing hard from running at full speed.

"Let her go!" shouted Lucius.

"And who are you, young man?" said Appius Claudius.

"Lucius Icilius. That girl is to be my wife."

Marcus grunted and gave him a scathing look. "The female is my slave.

A slave cannot be any man's wife. Now, if I should decided to breed the bitch—"

Lucius ran toward him, bellowing with rage and swinging his fists. The lictors held him back.

"Stop this outrage at once!" shouted Appius Claudius. "You're disturbing the peace."

"This man is trying to abduct a freeborn girl!" shouted Lucius. "*That's* the outrage! If only we still had tribunes to protect us—"

"Ah, now I know who you are," said Appius Claudius. "The scion of the Icilii, a family famous for firebrands and rabble-rousers. Well, young man, bemoan the absence of the tribunes all you like; the Decemvirs are the only officers of state, and it is by a Decemvir that this matter must be decided. Since I happen to be the Decemvir in charge of such property disputes—"

"This is not a property dispute! It's an abduction!"

"Perhaps, young man; but that is for me to decide."

"Decemvir, you know this girl. This is Verginia, the daughter of Lucius Verginius. Did you yourself not ask for . . ." Lucius stopped himself. That fact that Appius Claudius had asked to wed Verginia—a fact revealed by Verginius after drinking too much wine—was not a matter Lucius would discuss in public.

"Young man, if you persist in this agitation, inciting the crowd to violence, I shall have no choice but to order my lictors to stop you. I shall empower them to use all necessary force. Once I give that order, you may be killed on the spot."

Icilia gripped his arm. "Brother, do as he says. Calm yourself."

Lucius shook free of her grip. His rage turned to tears. "Decemvir, don't you see what this man is up to? Don't you realize what he intends to do to Verginia? The girl is a virgin. She's to be my bride. For the sake of decency, she cannot spend a night under any man's roof except her father's!"

"I see your worry," said Appius Claudius, who used the opportunity to gaze openly at Verginia. She remained where she had fallen, on her hands and knees with the rope around her neck, blushing and trembling, utterly terrified. The Decemvir's lips parted. His eyes narrowed. Every man in the crowd was staring at Verginia; no one noticed the look of lust on Appius Claudius's face. Even Lucius, seeing Verginia in such a shameful position, turned his face away.

Appius Claudius squared his shoulders and lifted his chin. "Despite his hotheadedness, the young Icilius is correct: Until she is determined to be his property, the female cannot be left in the possession of Marcus Claudius. Pending the return of Verginius, when an informed judgment can be made regarding the female's status, I myself shall take her into custody. In the meeting hall of the Decemvirs, I have a private chamber. The girl will be perfectly safe there. Citizen, hand me the rope."

Marcus, bowing and cocking his head, handed the tether to Appius Claudius.

The Decemvir bent down to touch Verginia's cheek, which was wet with tears. "On your feet, girl. Come with me." He took her arm to help her up. Few saw just how hard he gripped her, digging his fingers into her flesh until she whimpered in pain. Quaking with fear, Verginia stumbled forward. Appius Claudius put his arm around her shoulder and whispered in her ear. An onlooker might assume he was speaking words of reassurance and comfort. In fact, no longer able to restrain himself, he was saying the things he had long dreamed of saying to her, telling her exactly what he intended to do to her as soon as they were alone in his room. Verginia stiffened and opened her mouth in shock, but no sound came out.

As Appius Claudius led her into the building, Verginia gripped the doorway and managed a faint cry for help. Lucius gave a cry of anguish and ran after them.

The lictors converged on him. They knocked him to the ground and struck him with their cudgels. Angered at seeing one of their own receive a public beating, a group of young plebs in the crowd rushed at the lictors and helped Lucius to his feet. Screams rent the air and blood was spilled on the paving stones.

More lictors emerged from the building. The crowd quickly dispersed.

Shaken and bleeding, Lucius limped home, assisted by his mother and sister. Verginia's mother followed them, weeping uncontrollably.

※

The actions taken by Appius Claudius that day, and in the days that followed, would be speculated upon long afterward.

When the full story came to light, it was widely thought that the Decemvir must have fallen prey to a kind of madness. Surely no reasonable man would have thought that the ruse put forth by Marcus Claudius would withstand scrutiny, or that the people of Roma simply would not care about Verginia's fate. And yet, at all times, Appius Claudius exercised a kind of reasoning, for each step of his scheme had to have been planned in advance and carefully executed; even the order calling Verginius to military service, it turned out, had originated with the Decemvir. Appius Claudius had not merely taken advantage of a situation that arose, or submitted to a sudden temptation that overwhelmed his better judgment; he deliberately orchestrated the situation and exploited it with unswerving ruthlessness.

Within an hour of Verginia's abduction, Lucius sent a messenger to the military camp outside the city where Verginius had been posted. Verginius rode through the night and returned to Roma the next morning.

The two men, Verginia's father and her betrothed, at once set out for the Forum, where they told their story to any who would listen. Overnight, word of the incident had spread throughout the city, making Verginia's plight the talk of Roma. When people learned that Lucius and Verginius were speaking publicly, they flocked to hear them.

The two men presented a pitiful sight. After an anxious, sleepless night of riding, Verginius was haggard and hoarse. Lucius had received a severe beating from the lictors; his head was wrapped with a bloody bandage and his face was badly bruised, with one eye swollen shut. His right shoulder had been dislocated and his arm was in a sling.

"Citizens!" cried Verginius. "Many of you know me. Many more have heard my name. I've fought in many battles for Roma. I fought the Aequi under Cincinnatus! If any man has earned your respect as a soldier, it's me. But what is it that we fight for when we risk our lives in battle? We fight to keep our wives and our children safe! Yet look what's happened. Even while I was in the field, preparing for battle, the very thing I fear most took place, right here in the Forum—my daughter, a virgin as pure as any Vestal, was taken from her mother and kept overnight against her will. Was it done by some savage invader? No! She was taken by a patrician, a man many of you admire and respect, although you wouldn't be far wrong if you called him a Sabine invader. Attus Clausus was his grandfather's name, and I curse the day that Sabine pig was admitted to the Senate!"

Some cheered at this, but others booed. One man shouted, "The girl isn't even your daughter! She's another man's slave!"

"That's a lie! There is no question whatsoever about my daughter's identity. She was abducted, in broad daylight, and for one purpose only— to satisfy the lusts of the Decemvir Appius Claudius. Citizens, can you imagine how painful it is for me to even speak of this, the shame I feel, that I should have to beg for your help in such a matter? Are there no fathers among you who can imagine what I fear?"

"This is ludicrous!" shouted another man. "I was there. I saw what happened. For you to suggest that the Decemvir plotted the whole thing—it's too far-fetched. A man like Appius Claudius has too much to lose to ever behave in such a reckless fashion. Now, it's possible this shady character Marcus Claudius was perpetrating a scheme—"

"Or maybe Marcus's story is true," said the man who had first interrupted Verginius. "Stranger things have happened! Romulus and Remus were princes, but they were raised by a swineherd. What's to stop a stolen slave girl being raised as a citizen's daughter?"

"Verginia *is* my daughter, my own flesh and blood!"

"Maybe so," said the man. "And maybe Marcus Claudius made an honest mistake. In that case, the Decemvir was absolutely right to take charge of the situation. Instead of tearing your hair and making terrible accusations against Appius Claudius, you should be thanking the man!"

"This is insane!" cried Lucius. "Don't you see what's happened? A patrician has taken a plebeian girl against her will, and against the will of her father and her betrothed. Who knows what he's done to her overnight? It drives me mad to think about it!"

A group of plebeians in the crowd, roused by Lucius's tears, became so infuriated that they began to strike the men who had argued against Verginius, accusing them of being agents in the pay of Appius Claudius. But, whether paid or not, there were more adherents of the Decemvir in the crowd than the hotheads realized. Once violence erupted, the two sides appeared to be evenly matched. Eventually, lictors emerged from the Decemvirs' hall and dispersed the crowd.

All day, Verginius and Lucius remained in the Forum, speaking to all who would listen. Again and again crowds gathered and erupted in violence. The unruly mobs were repeatedly dispersed, but came back in greater numbers each time.

At last, late in the afternoon, Appius Claudius emerged from the Decemvirs' hall, protected by lictors. He looked utterly serene; indeed, he looked quite pleased with himself.

"I am ready to render judgment in the matter of the identity of the female known as Verginia," he announced. "Erect a tribunal!"

A platform was set up and a chair of state placed upon it. Appius Claudius mounted the tribunal and sat, resplendent in his purple toga. Lucius pushed his way to the front of the crowd. The Decemvir's smug expression sickened him. Lictors surrounded the tribunal. One of the men who had beaten him the previous day smirked at him. Lucius trembled with rage.

Appius Claudius cleared his throat. "I've already heard the arguments put forth by Marcus Claudius, privately, in my chamber. His case is persuasive. He mentioned a certain physical characteristic of the slave girl who was stolen from him. I was able to ascertain with my own eyes the presence of this distinguishing mark, by examining the girl myself."

"What mark?" cried Lucius.

"There is no need to reveal that information."

"What mark?" demanded Lucius.

The Decemvir smiled coyly. "I would prefer to be less explicit, but since you insist on knowing, there is a small birthmark on the inside of the girl's left thigh. The location of the mark is such that no man could possibly have seen it, except a husband, or, as in the case of Marcus Claudius, a citizen who had occasion to intimately examine his slaves."

Lucius covered his face and wept.

"Nonetheless," said Appius Claudius, "it remains for me to hear what this fellow Verginius has to say for himself. The charge of abducting another man's slave and trying to marry her off as a freeborn girl is quite serious."

"This is a mockery of justice!" cried Lucius. "You stripped her naked! You saw what there was to see, and whatever you saw Marcus Claudius could claim to be the 'distinguishing mark' by which he could identify her!"

"Be quiet, young man, unless you desire another beating. I don't think you would survive it. In fact, I'm certain you would not."

The smirking lictor suddenly struck Lucius's bandaged head with his cudgel. Lucius screamed and dropped to his knees.

"Step forward, Verginius!"

Looking like the ghost of himself, Verginius made his way to the tribunal. Beside him stood an elderly woman wearing a simple tunica.

"Who is this woman?" said Appius Claudius.

Verginius's voice was very hoarse. "Decemvir, this is one of my slaves, the nurse who cared for Verginia when she was a baby. She still resides in my household. As you can see, she is very old, but her memory is sharp. I called her here because . . ." He hesitated, like a man telling a story who has lost his place. "I brought her because it occurs to me that . . . that there is a possibility . . . that perhaps, when my daughter was still very young, she was taken from me and a slave was left in her place. My newborn daughter, too, had a distinguishing mark. If the woman who nursed her could now examine Verginia . . . as you yourself were able to examine her . . ." He gritted his teeth. "If you will allow this, Decemvir, then perhaps, after all, I might be persuaded that the girl, whom I thought to be my daughter, is not."

Appius Claudius shook his head. "I can't give you custody of the girl for such a purpose. You might abscond with her."

"I don't ask for custody, Decemvir. If the nurse and I could simply be allowed to see Verginia, briefly, in a private place . . ."

The Decemvir stroked his beard and said nothing.

The crowd grew restive. A citizen cried out, "Let him see the girl!"

Others joined him: "Yes, let Verginius see her!"

At last, Appius Claudius nodded. "Very well. You and the nurse may enter my chambers and examine the female. Two of my lictors will escort you."

Verginius and the woman made their way to the entrance of the building. Lucius rushed to join them, but Verginius shook his head.

"No, Lucius. This task is not for you."

"But I must see her!"

"No! Verginia is my daughter, not your wife. This duty falls to me, and to me alone."

Verginius and the nurse stepped inside the building. The meeting room was empty. One of the lictors led them down a long hallway to the chamber of Appius Claudius. The lictor allowed Verginius and the nurse to enter the room alone, but he would not allow them to close the door behind them.

"Then avert your eyes!" demanded Verginius.

The lictor glowered at him, but turned his face away.

The room was small and dark, and far enough from the crowded Forum that no sound from outside could be heard. While Verginius and Lucius had harangued the citizenry all day, this was where Appius Claudius had kept himself shut away, alone with Verginia.

Verginius wrinkled his nose.

The lictor grunted. "Smells like a whorehouse, doesn't it?"

Verginia was sitting on a couch strewn with rumpled coverlets. She rose and clutched her breasts. Her face was red from weeping. "Papa! Thank the gods, at last!"

Verginius turned his face away. "Nurse, examine her. Lictor, keep your eyes averted!"

The old nurse stepped forward. At the sight of her, Verginia seemed to become a child. She stood passively and made no resistance as the woman lifted her tunica and stooped over to peer between her legs.

Verginius's voice was a hoarse whisper, barely audible. "What do you see?"

"Master, the child is no longer a virgin." The old woman shuddered and began to sob. The lictor snickered.

Verginia stepped back from the nurse and pushed down her tunica. Her lips quivered. "Papa?" she said. She looked at the floor, not at her father, and her voice trembled with fear.

Verginius moved quickly toward her. She abruptly threw open her arms in the posture of a woman expecting an embrace or surrendering to a blow.

Verginius reached into his tunic and drew out a dagger. With the last of his voice, he gave a cry of anguish. The sound that emerged was ghastly— a hoarse, stifled croak. It was the last sound Verginia would hear.

Only moments after he had entered the building, Verginius emerged, carrying his daughter in his arms.

The red-faced lictor ran out after him. "Decemvir, it happened before I could stop it! I never thought—"

Appius Claudius rose from his chair of state. He clenched his fists, but his face registered no expression.

Like a warm wind through a wheat field, a murmur passed through the crowd, traveling from those who could see Verginius back to those who could not. The murmur was followed by gasps and stifled cries as men rushed forward to see for themselves. A few, catching only a glimpse of the girl's body, thought that she was alive and being carried like a child; they cried out in triumph that Verginius had rescued his daughter. Then they saw how the girl's arm swayed with each step, as limp and lifeless as her hair; they saw the red stain on her breast. Cries of joy turned to cries of anguish.

Marcus Claudius appeared, spreading his arms to block Verginius's way. He glanced over his shoulder at the Decemvir with a look of panic in his eyes. Appius Claudius barely raised an eyebrow.

"What have you done, you fool?" shouted Marcus Claudius. "The girl—my property—"

"This is your doing," said Verginius. "Yours, and the Decemvir's. You gave me no choice. She was my daughter. I did the only thing a father could do. Let the gods judge me. Let them look down and judge you, as well." He faced the tribunal and raised the body in his arms. "And let the gods judge you, Appius Claudius!"

The Decemvir's face might have been made of stone. Only his eyes showed a flicker of emotion, which some interpreted as fear, but other as derision.

The crowd was startled by a cry of agony. Lucius appeared, his hands clutching his head, his face contorted almost beyond recognition. He dropped to his knees before Verginius. He seized Verginia's hand, clutching it desperately. He pressed it to his lips, then let it drop, horrified by the lifeless flesh. He gathered handfuls of her hair, sobbed, and hid his face amid her tresses.

Up on the tribunal, anticipating what was to come, Appius Claudius called for his lictors to gather around him. All Roma seemed to draw a final breath, and then the riot began.

All the violence that had come before was as nothing compared to the fury that swept through the Forum and spilled into the streets beyond. The whole city descended into a kind of madness. The mob's outrage at the fate of Verginia unleashed vast stores of anger and resentment that had nothing to do with the singular villainies perpetrated on her by Appius Claudius. Amid the uproar, men acted on their most reckless impulses and indulged their darkest cravings for vengeance and retribution. Men were chased through the streets and beaten without mercy. Houses were broken into and vandalized. Old scores were settled with unrestrained violence.

Much blood was spilled in Roma that day—but not the blood of Appius Claudius. Only his death could have satisfied the angry mob; only the sight of his corpse next to that of Verginia could have calmed the riot. The chair of state was smashed and the tribunal was torn down; Appius Claudius was not amid the wreckage. Men pushed past the lictors, broke into the meeting hall and ran through every room; the Decemvir was nowhere to be found. His inexplicable escape was like a spiteful trick played upon the mob, a deliberate insult to their righteous fury.

Almost forgotten amid the chaos, Verginius lowered the body of his daughter to the ground and knelt over her, joined by Lucius. Father and lover wept uncontrollably, adding their tears to the blood that stained Verginia's breast.

449 B.C.

By the time Icilia's pregnancy began to show, many things had changed in Roma.

The change that most intimately affected her was the death of her father. Walking through the Forum one day, Icilius had clutched his chest and fallen. By the time he arrived home, carried on a litter, his heart had stopped beating.

Upon their father's death, Icilia's brother Lucius became paterfamilias. It was Lucius who would decide Icilia's fate, and the fate of her unborn child.

Great changes had also taken place in the city.

The tragic end of Verginia had shaken Roma to its foundations. Had Appius Claudius possessed any idea of the forces his mad scheme would unleash? It was hard to imagine how any man, however blinded by lust or arrogance, could have proceeded on such a reckless course. For generations to come, his name would be a synonym for that which the Greeks called *hubris*—a pride so overbearing that the gods themselves are compelled to annihilate the offender.

Did Appius Claudius anticipate Verginius's intention to kill his daughter? Did he deliberately allow it to happen, having cold-bloodedly determined that this was his best course of action? In the aftermath of the upheaval, some put forth this opinion. They argued that Appius Claudius had already had his way with the girl, and thus had no further use for her. She had become a liability to him; her death would relieve him of the responsibility to determine her identity, and what better solution than to goad her father into committing the act? Appius Claudius thought he had found a way to take what he wanted without paying a price. If a man had power, and was clever, and was brazen enough to follow through on a ruthless scheme, then even for the most terrible crime he might hope to avoid punishment.

Others said that even Appius Claudius could not be that cold and calculating. Having desired Verginia so desperately that he would carry out such a dangerous plot, surely a single night and day had not exhausted his appetite for her. The fact that his face showed no reaction to her death was because he was utterly stunned by what Verginius had done.

Whatever his intentions, the Decemvir's desire for Verginia had nothing to do with politics, yet the girl's father and betrothed managed to convince their fellow plebeians otherwise. A merciless patrician had despoiled a plebeian virgin, beaten and humiliated her outraged plebeian suitor, and driven her distraught plebeian father to an act of uttermost shame and desperation.

All the discontent sewn by the Decemvirs' tyranny came to a head over the outrage committed against Verginia. For the first time in a generation, the plebeians staged a secession, such as the one which had won them the right to elect tribunes. Plebeian city-dwellers withdrew from the city; plebeian farmers put aside their plows; plebeian soldiers refused to fight. Their demand was the end of the Decemvirs, and in particular, the arrest, trial, and punishment of Appius Claudius.

In the end, after much bombast and negotiation, all ten Decemvirs resigned. Some managed to escape trial. Others were charged with misconduct and forbidden to leave the city, including Appius Claudius, who barricaded himself in his well-guarded house and refused to come out. His abuses were the most egregious of the Decemvirs, yet he seemed to be the least repentant.

Bitter and unwavering to the end, Appius Claudius hanged himself rather than face the judgment of the court.

Marcus Claudius, the accomplice of the Decemvir, was too cowardly to follow his master's example; he was brought to trial and condemned. Verginius himself requested that the villain be spared the penalty of death, and Marcus was allowed to flee into exile. It was said that on the day he left Roma, the ghost of Verginia, which for months had wandered from house to house across the Seven Hills, weeping and moaning in the night, terrifying children and rending the hearts of their parents, at last found peace and ceased to haunt the city.

The Senate reassembled. New magistrates were elected. Among the new tribunes of the plebs were Verginius and young Lucius Icilius.

The bitterness felt toward the Decemvirs as men and as tyrants was almost universal, but their labor as lawmakers was widely respected. The Twelve Tables were accepted by a consensus of both patricians and plebeians, and became the law of the land.

The new laws were cast in tablets of bronze, which were posted in the Forum, where any citizen could read them, or have them read aloud to him. No longer would Roman law be a matter of oral tradition—an accretion of moldering precedents, momentary whims, hazy surmises, and recondite deductions—known only to experienced senators and jurists; instead, the Twelve Tables were there for all to see. Virtually every citizen had a quibble or two with some provision of the new laws, but these objections were swept aside by the overwhelming value of the Twelve Tables as a whole. Once the spoken word of kings had been the highest authority, then that of the elected consuls; now the written word was king, to which each citizen had access.

On the day the bronze tablets were posted, Icilia dressed in the plain tunica of one of her slave girls and slipped away from her house. She waited in the secluded place near the market where her child had been conceived. Titus was to meet her there. He did not yet know of the child's existence.

Titus arrived late. As he slipped past the dense foliage of the cypress tree, he managed to smile. He kissed her. When he drew back, the smile had vanished. The grimness on his face mirrored her own.

"I came from the Forum," he said. "They've posted the Twelve Tables."

"You've read them?"

"Not all. But I read the part about marriage." He lowered his eyes. "It's just as we feared. There can be no marriage between a patrician and a plebeian."

Icilia drew a sharp breath. She had been hoping against hope that, somehow, a marriage to Titus might still be possible. She had clung desperately to this fantasy for as long as she could; now it was gone. She felt frightened and utterly alone, despite the arms that encircled her.

"Titus, there's something I must tell you."

He brushed a strand of hair from her cheek, and felt warm tears on this fingertips. "What must you tell me, Icilia? Whatever it is, it can't be as bad as what I've just told you."

"Titus, there's a child growing inside me. Your child."

His arms stiffened. After a moment, he hugged her fiercely, and then, just as abruptly, drew back, as if afraid he might harm her. On his face was an expression she had never seen on anyone before, joyful and despairing at the same time.

"Your brother?"

"Lucius doesn't know yet. No one knows—except you. I've hidden it from everyone. But I can't hide it much longer."

"When? How soon?"

"I'm not sure. I don't know about such things . . . and there's no one I can ask!" Fresh tears streamed down her cheeks.

"Icilia, Icilia! What are we to do? You'll have to tell Lucius. The two of you have always been close. Perhaps—"

"Not anymore! I'm afraid of him now. Ever since Verginia died, he's a different person. He suffers from the beatings he took from the lictors; one of his eyes will never be the same. There's so much anger in him, so much bitterness. He never used to hate patricians; now he's more vengeful than Father ever was. He talks of nothing but harming those he hates. We can't look to him for help, Titus."

"But he'll have to know, sooner or later. The decision will be his to make."

"Decision?" She was not sure what he meant.

He drew back from her, just enough to reach up and lift the necklace over his head. A bit of sunlight glittered on the golden talisman he called Fascinus.

"For our child," he said, placing it over her neck.

"But Titus, this belongs to your family. It's your birthright!"

"Yes, passed from generation to generation, since the beginning of time. The child inside you is mine, Icilia. I give this talisman to my child. The law prevents our marriage. Even if the law allowed it, your brother would forbid it. But no law, no man—not even the gods—can stop us from loving one another. The life inside you is the proof of that. I give Fascinus to you, and you will give it to the child you bear."

The pendant was cold against her flesh, and surprisingly heavy. Titus had claimed it brought good fortune, but Icilia remembered her doubts.

"Oh, Titus, what's to become of us?"

"I don't know. I only know I love you," he whispered. He thought she meant the two of them, but Icilia was thinking of herself and the helpless life within her. At that moment, she felt the baby stir and give a kick, as if pricked by its mother's fear.

The midwives, when Lucius angrily consulted them, all agreed: while there existed means by which a pregnancy could be ended—the insertion of a slender willow branch, or the ingestion of the poison called ergot—it was much too late to do so without gravely endangering Icilia herself. Unless he cared nothing for his sister's life, she must be allowed to bear the child.

The news clearly displeased Lucius. The oldest and most wizened of the midwives, who had witnessed every possible circumstance attending the birth of child, drew him aside. "Calm yourself, Tribune. Once the baby is delivered, it can easily be disposed of. If you wish to save your sister and avoid gossip, this is what I advise . . ."

Icilia was sent away from Roma, to stay with a relative of the midwife who lived in a fishing camp outside Ostia. There was no need for Lucius to invent excuses for his sister's absence. A young, unmarried woman had little public life; few people missed Icilia, and those who did readily accepted the explanation that she was in seclusion, still mourning her father.

Icilia's labor was long and difficult. The ordeal stretched over a day and a night—time for word to reach her brother in Roma, and time for him to arrive in the fishing camp even as the baby was being born.

Afterward, when Icilia came to her senses, the first thing she saw was Lucius standing over her in the darkened room. Her heart leaped with sudden hope. Surely he would not have come all the way from Roma if he simply intended to have the baby drowned in the Tiber, or cast into the sea.

"Brother! I was in such pain . . ."

He nodded. "I saw the sheets. The blood."

"The baby—"

"A boy. Strong and healthy." His voice was flat. It was hard to read any expression on his face. He no longer ever smiled, and the upper lid of his bad eye drooped.

"Please, brother, bring him to me!" Icilia reached up with her arms.

Lucius shook his head. "It's best if you never see the child again."

"What are you saying?"

"Titus Potitius came to me a few days ago. He asked me—no, *begged* me—to allow him to adopt your child. 'No one need know where it came from,' he said. 'I'll say it was an orphan from the wars, or the child of a distant cousin. I've asked my father to let me do this thing, and he gave his permission.'" Lucius shook his head. "I told Titus Potitius, 'It will still be a bastard.' 'That doesn't matter,' he said. 'If it's a boy, he shall have my name and I shall raise him as my son.' That's why I came today, sister."

"So that you can give the boy to Titus?" Icilia sobbed, partly from relief, partly from sadness.

Lucius grunted. "To the contrary! I told the patrician scum that under no circumstances would he ever come into possession of the child. That's why I'm here. I feared Potitius might discover your whereabouts and try to lay his hands on the baby. I will make sure that doesn't happen."

Icilia clutched his arm. "No, brother—you mustn't kill him!"

Lucius raised an eyebrow, causing the other to droop even more. "That *was* my intention. But now that I've seen the child, I have an even better idea. I shall take him with me back to Roma, where I shall raise him as a slave, to serve me and my household. Imagine that! A patrician's bastard, serving as a whipping boy in a plebeian household!" He smiled grimly, pleased at the idea.

"But Lucius, the child is your nephew."

"No! The child is my slave."

"And what of me, brother?"

"I know a Greek trader from Croton, at the furthest ends of Magna Graecia. He's agreed to take you for his wife. You set sail from Ostia tomorrow. You must never speak of the child. You must never return to Roma. Your life will be whatever you make of it. You and I shall not speak again."

"Lucius! Such cruelty—"

"The Fates are cruel, Icilia. Fortuna is cruel. They robbed me of Verginia—"

"So now you rob me of my child?"

"The child is a bastard and doesn't deserve to live. This is an act of clemency, sister."

"Let me see him!"

"No."

Icilia saw that he would not be swayed. "Do one thing for me, brother. I ask only one thing! Give him this, from me." With trembling hands, she raised the necklace over her head.

Lucius snatched it from her and studied at it angrily. "What is this? Some sort of talisman? It didn't come from anyone in our family. Titus Potitius gave it to you, didn't he?"

"Yes."

Lucius stared at it for a long moment, then slowly nodded. "Why not? It seems to be made of gold; I could just as easily take it for myself and melt it down for the value, but I'll do as you ask. I shall let the slave boy have it, as a gaudy trinket to decorate his neck. It will serve to remind me of his origin. Let the ancient bloodline of the Potitii continue in the veins of a slave, and let the slave wear this talisman as a mark of shame!"

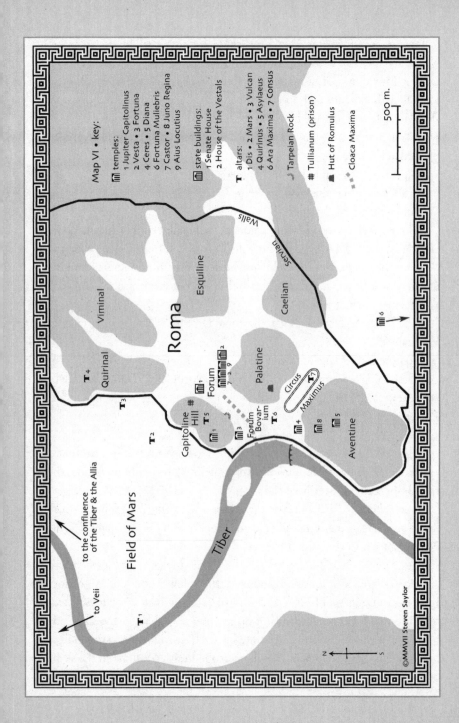

Map VI • key:

temples:
1 Jupiter Capitolinus
2 Vesta • 3 Fortuna
4 Ceres • 5 Diana
6 Fortuna Muliebris
7 Castor • 8 Juno Regina
9 Aius Locutius

state buildings:
1 Senate House
2 House of the Vestals

altars:
1 Dis • 2 Mars • 3 Vulcan
4 Quirinus • 5 Asylaeus
6 Ara Maxima • 7 Consus

Tarpeian Rock

Tullianum (prison)

Hut of Romulus

Cloaca Maxima

500 m.

Roma

Field of Mars

Tiber

to the confluence
of the Tiber & the Allia

to Veii

Quirinal

Viminal

Esquiline

Caelian

Capitoline Hill

Forum

Palatine

Forum
Bovarium

Circus
Maximus

Aventine

Servian
Walls

©MMVII Steven Saylor

VI

THE VESTAL

393 B.C.

On the eve of the greatest catastrophe yet to befall the city, the unsuspecting people of Roma celebrated their greatest triumph. One of the city's oldest rivals had at last been vanquished.

The city of Veii was scarcely twenty miles from Roma. A man with strong legs could walk the distance in a single day. A rider on horseback could journey there and back in a matter of hours. Yet, for generation after generation, even as Roma conquered more distant enemies, Veii remained proudly independent, sometimes at peace with Roma, sometimes at war with her. In recent generations, Veii had grown immensely wealthy. Her alliances with other cities in the region began to threaten Roma's dominance of the salt route and traffic on the Tiber.

For ten summers in a row, Roma's armies laid siege to Veii, yet with the coming of each winter and the cessation of warfare, Veii remained unconquered. It would take a very great general to put an end to Veii, men said. At last such a general appeared. His name was Marcus Furius Camillus.

No one who witnessed it would ever forget the triumphal parade of Camillus. All agreed that it was by far the grandest triumph in memory; the number of captives, the sheer magnificence of the booty displayed (thanks to the opulence of Veii), and the joyous spirit of the event outstripped all previous triumphs. But, impressive as they were, it was not these details that made the event unforgettable; it was the sight of Camillus in a chariot pulled by four white horses.

Standing on the viewing platform reserved for religious dignitaries, the Vestal Pinaria let out a gasp. She whispered to the Vestal standing next to her, "Foslia, have you ever seen such a thing?"

"I should think not. No one has seen such a thing! Four white horses!"

Pinaria shook her head in wonder. "Just like the quadriga of Jupiter atop the temple on the Capitoline."

"No general has ever done such a thing before," declared Foslia. At seventeen, Pinaria was the youngest of the six Vestals. Foslia was only five years older, but was very studious, and something of a know-it-all. She was especially well versed in the history of religious observances, and, like every public act in Roma, a triumph was a religious rite. "Romulus walked on foot for his triumphs. Tarquinius the Elder was the first to ride in a quadriga. But no general has ever dared to emulate Jupiter and hitch four white horses to his chariot!"

"Do you think it's an impious act?" asked Pinaria.

"That would not be for me to judge," said Foslia, primly.

"Still, it's quite a sight."

"It is, indeed." Foslia smiled. "And the general is so handsome—even with his face painted red!"

The two young women looked at one another and laughed. The Virgo Maxima did not approve of such talk, but all the Vestals indulged in it. It seemed to Pinaria that when they were not discussing religious matters, they were usually talking about men, and as often as not, about Camillus. In his fifties, the general was more robust than many a man in his thirties, with a magnificent mane of white hair, a broad chest, and powerful limbs.

"Do you think he knows how strikingly the white horses set off his white hair?" asked Foslia.

"Surely the man who conquered Veii has no time for vanity," said Pinaria.

"Nonsense! Who is vainer than a general, especially on the day of his triumph? But look there, coming up behind him—it's the statue of Juno Regina!"

Of all the objects taken from Veii, this was the most prized: the massive statue of the city's divine patroness, the queen-mother of the gods, Juno, in

whose honor the grandest temple in all Veii had been built. For generations, Juno Regina had protected the Veiians. On the eve of the final battle,
Camillus had vowed that if Veii fell, he would bring Juno Regina to Roma
and built an even grander temple for her. Now he was making good on the
first part of his pledge.

Men who had grown hoarse cheering Camillus raised their voices even
louder at the sight of the statue. It was transported on a massive cart pulled
by Veiian captives, among them the former priests of Juno, who had been
stripped of their robes and put in shackles. The statue was made of wood,
but no joinery was visible; the surface had been carved and smoothed by
the finest Etruscan sculptors, and covered with bright paint and precious
gilt. Juno Regina sat upon a throne, grasping a scepter in one hand and
holding a libation bowl in the other, with a peacock at her feet.

"Magnificent!" declared Foslia. "There can be no other image of Juno
to rival it. Even the statue made by the great Vulca for the Temple of
Jupiter can't compare. This one is so much larger—three times the size of
any mortal! The look on the goddess's face is truly sublime! And that giant
peacock, with its wings spread—did you ever see such a riot of colors?"

While they watched, a boy, egged on by his friends, darted from the
crowd. He grabbed hold of the loincloth of a captive priest, yanked it off,
and ran back into the crowd, whooping and waving the loincloth like a trophy. The priest, a middle-aged man already stumbling from exhaustion,
turned red and wept from shame, unable to cover himself because his
hands were shackled to the rope across his shoulder. Pinaria gasped, and
Foslia raised an eyebrow, but neither looked away.

"I wonder what the goddess thinks of that?" said Pinaria.

"Keep watching. She might speak at any moment!"

"Are you serious?"

"Why not? You know the story: When Camillus sent soldiers to take the
statue from her temple in Veii, one of the men, just to be funny, bowed and
asked the goddess if she would like to be taken to her new home. What a
shock those fellows had when the statue actually nodded—and then spoke
out loud! They thought someone was pulling a prank, so they asked her
again, and, as clearly as I'm speaking to you now, she said, 'Yes, take me to
Roma at once!' They say she sounded angry; Juno Regina doesn't like to
repeat herself. Of course she wanted to come here. If she hadn't lost affec-

tion for the Veiians, they would never have been conquered. Camillus has ordered the building of a new temple on the Aventine especially to house the statue. Veiian wealth will pay for materials. Veiian slaves will supply the labor. That naked priest can stop blushing. A slave doesn't need clothing to dig a trench or carry bricks."

"Do you think the Greeks treated the Trojans this way, after they conquered them?" asked Pinaria. Among the Vestals, there had been many discussions of late comparing the fall of Veii to the fall of Troy, a tale that the Romans had learned from the Greek colonists to the south. Just as the siege of Troy had lasted for ten years, so had the siege of Veii. Just as the Greeks finally took the city by guile—using the famous Trojan horse devised by Odysseus—so too had the Romans finally triumphed by a clever stratagem, tunneling under the walls so that Roman soldiers could steal inside by night and open the gates.

"Of course they did," said Foslia. "The Trojan women, including Queen Hecuba and the princesses, were taken as slaves. So were the men, at least the ones who weren't killed. No city is conquered unless its people have offended the gods; for the conquerors to kill or enslave the inhabitants is pleasing to the gods. The people of Roma have always known this. The humiliation of our enemies is one of the ways by which we please the gods, and by pleasing the gods, we continue to prosper."

As usual, Foslia's religious logic was irrefutable, and Pinaria gladly deferred to her, yet the sight of the disgraced Veiian priest disturbed her. She turned her head and looked instead at the triumphal chariot, which was now receding from them in the direction of the Capitoline. Camillus, turning this way and that to wave to the crowd, happened to look over his shoulder. His gaze abruptly settled on Pinaria. He ceased waving, tilted his head at a quizzical angle, and flashed an enigmatic smile.

Foslia grabbed her arm and squealed with delight. "Pinaria, he's looking straight at you! And why not? You're so lovely, even with your hair cut short. Oh, if he should look at me that way, I think I would die!"

Pinaria's face turned hot and she lowered her eyes. When she dared to look up again, the chariot had rounded a corner and was no longer in sight.

She heard a sudden burst of laughter and applause from the crowd. Following the statue of Juno Regina came a flock of geese. The white birds strutted forward, stretching and flapping their wings, craning their necks and honking. These were the sacred geese of Juno, captured from the Veiians along with her statue, objects of religious veneration but also of good-natured humor. The pampered creatures seemed to understand their exalted position; they gazed back at the crowd with haughty heads held high. One of the geese suddenly raced forward, toward the priest who had been stripped naked, and bit the man on the ankle. The priest let out a plaintive howl.

"Getting back at her former keeper for some transgression, I have no doubt," whispered Foslia.

The crowd roared with laughter.

In the last hour of daylight, after the sacrifice of a white ox upon an altar before the Temple of Jupiter and the ritual strangulation of high-born captives in the Tullianum, as the feasting and dancing in the streets began to die down, the Vestals convened at the Temple of Vesta.

While the others had watched the triumph, one of their number, as always, had been left to tend to the sacred hearthfire within the round temple. Now her five sister virgins rejoined her for the recitation of evening prayers, led by the eldest of them, Postumia, the Virgo Maxima. The keeping of the sacred hearthfire was the primary obligation of their order. Should the fire ever go out, catastrophe and misfortune for Roma would surely follow.

The keeping of their vows of chastity was an equally important obligation. Should a Vestal ever break that vow, she might conceal the crime from other mortals but never from the goddess. Vesta would know, and in consequence the hearthfire would sputter and dwindle. Only a pure virgin could maintain a steady flame in Vesta's hearth.

The Vestals linked hands and stood in a circle around the flame. While the others swayed gently and hummed in harmony, the Virgo Maxima intoned the evening prayer. "Goddess Vesta, hear us. We have kept your flame for another day, and now another night descends, its darkness illuminated, as always, by your undying light. You warm us. You light our way. The same unwavering fire that comforted the baby Romulus at his birth comforts us here in your temple."

Postumia was the eldest, but her short gray hair still had strands of black in it, and her voice was strong, without a quaver. She hummed and swayed with the other virgins for a moment, gazing at the flame, then recommenced the prayer. "For thirty years, each of us vows to serve you, goddess Vesta. We come to you before the age of ten; for ten years we learn; for ten years we perform the public rites; for ten years we teach the newcomers. Then we are free to go—or stay.

"Bless me, goddess Vesta! My thirty years passed years ago, but I chose to remain in your service. Permit me to stay, goddess, as long as I have eyes to witness the holy flame and strength to tend it, as long as I have words and wisdom sufficient to teach the younger virgins.

"Bless us all, goddess Vesta, but especially open your embrace to the youngest of us, Pinaria. Seven years she has been among us. Now that Foslia has entered her tenth year, Pinaria is the only novice. She still has much to learn. Give her special guidance, goddess Vesta."

Pinaria, who had entered a kind of trance while humming and watching the flame, gave a tiny start at the mention of her name. It was not often that the Virgo Maxima mentioned the Vestals by name in her prayers. Why was she doing so now, and why for Pinaria? What she said next unsettled Pinaria even more.

"We pray, goddess, that you will remember all the Vestals who have come before us, going back to the days of King Romulus, who named the first four Vestals in Roma, and King Tarquinius the Elder, who raised our number to six, and who, in his wisdom, imposed a punishment far more terrible than simple death for any Vestal who should break her vows—the punishment that remains in force to this day."

Pinaria drew a sharp breath, as did all the Vestals, their serene thoughts suddenly invaded by images of that most dreadful of all deaths. The humming and swaying stopped. The little temple became utterly silent except for the crackling of the hearthfire. Pinaria's heart was beating so hard that she thought the others must be able to hear it. Why had the Virgo Maxima mentioned her in the prayer, and in the very next breath spoken of the terrible punishment for those who strayed?

"Give all of us strength, goddess Vesta," whispered Postumia. "The way of the Vestal is not always easy, and harder for some than for others. Only the presence of your hearthfire within our hearts can keep us pure."

The prayer ended. The Vestals released each other's hands. Beyond the open doorway of the temple, twilight had turned to darkness.

"You may each ignite a taper from the sacred flame, to light your way safely back to the House of the Vestals. It's Pinaria's turn to tend the flame for the next four hours. Since she's a novice, I'll stay with her for a while."

"But Virgo Maxima, I've tended the flame plenty of times before, all by myself. I know how to—" Pinaria saw Postumia's withering gaze, and lowered her eyes. "Of course, Virgo Maxima. I'm honored that you'll stay with me."

The others filed out, carrying their tapers. Foslia, the last to leave, glanced back at Pinaria with a guilty look on her face before she shut the door behind her.

For a long time, Postumia stared at the flame and said nothing. At last she took a deep breath. "You may find this hard to imagine, Pinaria, but once upon a time, I was your age. I was not as beautiful as you—oh, no, not nearly as beautiful! For better or worse, Pinaria, with your auburn hair and your bright green eyes, you are an exceptionally lovely girl. But I was young, and passably pretty, and very, very vain, as only a young girl can be. I took my vow of chastity very seriously, but nonetheless, I saw no harm in adorning myself. I wore bracelets made of silver, and sometimes a necklace of carnelian that had belonged to my grandmother; I told people that I thought the red stone went very well with the red and white fillet we wear around our heads, but in fact, I thought it set off the pink glow of my cheeks. I anointed my hands and face with a scented oil that came all the way from Egypt—or so claimed the merchant who came once a month to the House of the Vestals to offer us such things."

"The Virgo Maxima allowed this?" said Pinaria. Postumia never permitted any of the Vestals to wear jewelry or to use any sort of perfume or unguent, and while men were allowed to enter the House of the Vestals during daylight hours—never after dark—they could do so only if they had official or family business with one of the virgins. A seller of scented oils would never be permitted inside!

"The Virgo Maxima in those days was very permissive. She doted on the younger Vestals. She doted particularly on me; I was her favorite. She encouraged me. 'How pretty that necklace looks on you, Postumia,' she would say, or, 'My, what lovely skin you have, so flawless and smooth!' I can't blame her for my vanity, but she certainly did nothing to discourage it. Nor did she discourage my flirtatious nature. Vanity leads to flirtation, you see. What good is being pretty if no one notices? And how can a girl know that she's noticed unless she looks others in the eye? First, she accepts their admiring gazes, and after that, she accepts their spoken compliments, and after that . . ." Postumia shook her head. "Such behavior is dangerous for a Vestal. Very dangerous! And it all begins with the eyes. A man gazes at us, and we accept his gaze with pleasure, and that pleasure, which seems so innocent, leads us to desire other pleasures."

Pinaria frowned. "Virgo Maxima, I don't understand why you're telling me this. I never wear jewelry; you don't allow it, and even if you did, I have no desire—"

"Camillus looked at you today."

Pinaria blinked. "Perhaps."

"He looked at you with pleasure."

Pinaria shrugged. "Did he? I couldn't say whether—"

"And it gave you pleasure, did it not? That such a great man, the hero of the hour, so strong and handsome, should desire to look at you."

Pinaria's face grew hot. "I did nothing wrong, Virgo Maxima."

"You returned his gaze."

"Perhaps, but only for an instant!" Pinaria furrowed her brow. For a brief, irreverent moment, she imagined that the Virgo Maxima was jealous of the look Camillus had given her. "Virgo Maxima, surely Camillus is a pious man. No Roman is more respectful of the gods, or more beloved by them. Before the final siege of Veii, he pledged to build a grand new temple for Juno Regina, and in return, the goddess allowed him to capture the city. As well, he pledged a tenth portion of all the booty to the god Apollo—"

"I don't question the piety of Camillus. But a pious man is a man, nonetheless. Pinaria, Pinaria! I don't mean that Camillus himself poses a threat to you—unless you were to lead him on. The threat comes from within yourself."

"But, Virgo Maxima—"

"Silence!" Postumia's bosom rose and fell in a sudden access of emotion. She watched the flames until she grew calmer. "Listen to me, Pinaria. As I told you, when I was your age, I was very vain. I adorned myself. I accepted the gazes of men—and returned them. I laughed when they said amusing things. I tried to be witty in return, and when men laughed, I felt a flush of excitement. I did nothing wrong—certainly nothing that betrayed my vow to Vesta. But my behavior attracted attention.

"The year that I was elevated from novice to full-fledged priestess, a series of bad omens occurred. A goat was born with two heads. A summer hailstorm rained tiny frogs. Worst of all, one augury after another indicated misfortune on the battlefield. The people were alarmed. They wanted to know the cause. Had the military commanders failed to make proper sacrifices to the gods? Was the Pontifex Maximus at fault—had the highest authority of the state religion been derelict in his duties? Or had the priests who keep the Sibylline Books misread the prophecies and led the people astray? All these possibilities were investigated, yet no fault could be found with the performance of any of the sacred rites, and no impurity was detected in those charged with carrying out those rites. And then . . . the investigation turned to me."

Again, Postumia fell silent for a long time, staring at the flame. "Do you know the penalty imposed on a Vestal who is found to have lost her virginity?"

Pinaria was barely able to speak about a whisper. "Of course I do, Virgo Maxima."

"Then tell me."

Pinaria swallowed hard. "If a Vestal is charged with breaking her vow of chastity, the Pontifex Maximus himself investigates the matter. A board of priests renders judgment. If they find her guilty . . ."

"Go on."

"The priests strip her of her vestments. The man with whom she broke her vows is brought before her in chains, and beaten to death before her eyes. Then the priests turn their fury on the Vestal. They scourge her with whips until she can no longer stand. They dress her like a corpse, all in black, and tie her with leather straps to a funeral bier, so tightly that she can't cry out. They place the bier upon a funeral wagon, draped in black, and the wagon is paraded through the city for all to see, just as if the Vestal were already dead and being taken to her funeral . . ."

"Go on."

"They take her to a place where a crypt has been dug beneath the city wall. They remove her from the wagon, and lower her into the crypt. They seal the entrance and cover it with a mound of earth. No funeral rites are conducted for her. She is never spoken of again." Pinaria's mouth was so dry that she could hardly speak. "No man kills her. No man sees her die. What happens to her in the tomb is known only to Vesta."

Postumia nodded gravely. "Who was the last Vestal to receive this punishment?"

Pinaria furrowed her brow.

"Come, come, Pinaria! Foslia would answer in a heartbeat."

"I remember now. It was almost a hundred years ago—"

"It was exactly seventy-nine years ago," said Postumia harshly, "in the days of my grandmother."

"As you say, Virgo Maxima."

"What were the circumstances? What was the Vestal's name?"

"She was called Urbinia. The women of Roma had fallen prey to a pestilence, especially women who were pregnant; there was one miscarriage after another. The Pontifex Maximus suspected impurity. It was found that Urbinia had given herself not to one man, but two, and yet she still dared to tend the sacred flame. Urbinia was tried and found guilty. After she was punished, the pestilence ceased, and the women once again bore healthy babies."

Postumia nodded. "Urbinia was the most recent Vestal to be found guilty of impurity and punished. But she was not the first. You come from a very old family, do you not, Pinaria?"

"Yes, Virgo Maxima."

"A family older than the republic, older than the kings; a family that has given Roma many consuls and magistrates, many warriors and priests, and not a few Vestals. But even the most respectable families have stains on their history. It was King Tarquinius the Elder who initiated the method by which Vestals are punished. And what was the name of the very first Vestal to be punished according to that practice?"

"Her name . . ." Pinaria's heart skipped a beat.

"Come, child! You know the answer."

"Her name was the same as my own: Pinaria. An ancestress of mine was the first Vestal to be . . ."

"Buried alive!" whispered Postumia. She drew a deep breath. "Buried alive—that's what they did to Pinaria, and to Urbinia. That's what they wanted to do to me. Even now, I can't speak of it with a steady voice."

"But surely you were innocent."

"Of course I was, you stupid girl! Had I been less than innocent, I wouldn't be here today! In the end, thank the goddess, I was able to convince the Pontifex Maximus of that fact. But the investigation itself . . . the fear I felt . . . the humiliation . . . the terror . . . the nightmares I still experience, after all these years!" Postumia cleared her throat. "When I became Virgo Maxima, I promised myself that no Vestal in my charge would ever suffer such an ordeal. To keep your vow is not enough. Innocence is not enough! A Vestal must be above temptation, yes—but she must also be above suspicion. Do you understand, Pinaria?"

"Yes, Virgo Maxima. I understand." Pinaria shivered and began to weep.

Postumia embraced her, holding her tightly and stroking her closely shorn hair. "There, there! I've frightened you, child. But I do it for your own good. I do it for the good of us all."

Though the door was shut, a sudden draft passed through the chamber, as if the temple itself drew a breath. The sacred hearthfire leaped this way and that, wavered, and for an instant appeared to vanish altogether.

390 B.C.

"Of course, the ban on intermarriage between plebeians and patricians should never have been repealed," said Postumia.

Foslia laughed out loud. "But Virgo Maxima, what can that possibly have to do with the so-called Veii Question?"

Postumia, who was about to take a bite from a stuffed grape leaf held delicately between her forefinger and thumb, put down the delicacy and cleared her throat. She was slightly flustered by Foslia's disrespectful laughter. "*All* questions of right and wrong impinge on one another. In matters of religion—and there are no matters unrelated to religion—every subject is relevant to every other."

Foslia was skeptical. "A ban on marriage between the classes—wasn't that in force only briefly, because it was so unpopular? And it was all so very long ago. People my age are hardly aware that such a ban ever existed!"

The occasion was dinner in the House of the Vestals. The weather was mild. The priestesses dined in the garden under the open sky, reclining on couches. The couch of the Virgo Maxima was at the head of the group. Dining on a couch opposite the Virgo Maxima was the youngest—still Pinaria, for in the three years since the triumph of Camillus, no Vestal had retired or died, and so no new novices had been inducted.

Female servants moved silently among them, delivering fresh dishes and taking away empty ones. "The eyes and ears of the Pontifex Maximus," Foslia called their servants. "They watch us like hawks," she had once remarked to Pinaria. "They listen to every word we say. If ever a Vestal should stray, the Pontifex Maximus will know about it even before the goddess does, thanks to his vigilant spies!" Foslia said such things in jest, but Pinaria was not amused.

Nor was the Virgo Maxima amused by Foslia's dismissal of her comment on marriage.

"May I remind you, Foslia, that a marriage between two patricians requires a religious rite, while any marriage involving a plebeian is purely a civil matter. In the time of the Decemvirs, this fact was one of the strongest arguments against intermarriage. In any mixed union, the patrician partner is deprived of religious ceremony—a state of affairs that must surely offend the gods. A patrician should marry only another patrician, and do so in accordance with the sacred rites. Yes, the ban was rescinded—but that doesn't mean it won't come back."

Postumia took a bite of the stuffed grape leaf, then returned the remainder to a small silver plate and waved for a servant to remove it. She was finished eating and ready to pontificate for the benefit of the younger Vestals. "Times of piety and of impiety occur in cycles. I grew up in a permissive era, but we now live in an age not so very different from that of the

Decemvirs. In recent years, due to the press of constant warfare, the election of consuls has been suspended, and Roma is ruled instead by six military tribunes. As for the conflict between the classes, if anything, it may be worse than in the days of the Decemvirs, because the patricians continually retreat and the plebeians continually demand more concessions—more land to settle, more debt-relief, more voting rights. If our leaders would use their power to reinstate the intermarriage ban, in that sphere at least Roma would again be in harmony with the will of the gods, and the classes might resume their rightful roles in the state. Such an idea did not originate with me; it comes from our sacred father, the Pontifex Maximus, who told me only yesterday that he intends to petition the military tribunes for a return of the intermarriage ban. And in this house, we do not contradict the Pontifex Maximus. If you have a conflicting opinion, Foslia, keep it to yourself."

"Of course, Virgo Maxima." Foslia's sardonic tone seemed to indicate that, while she might keep her opinions private, she would keep them, nonetheless. "And of course you're right to say marriage, at least any marriage involving a patrician, is a religious matter. But we were discussing the Veii Question, and surely that is about only two things: money and politics."

Postumia shook her head. "To the contrary, Foslia, can you not see that the Veii Question is very much a religious matter? Pinaria, you're very quiet this evening. You may still be the youngest, but you're no longer a novice. Speak up."

Pinaria swallowed an olive stuffed with goat cheese. "Very well, Virgo Maxima. It seems to me, more than ever, that Roma's conquest of Veii is a mirror of the Greeks' conquest of Troy. First, it took ten years. Second, it came about by a clever stratagem rather than by brute strength. Third, while it seemed to solve all our problems at the time, instead, like the Greeks after Troy, we discovered that the conquest merely led to more dissention at home."

Postumia nodded thoughtfully. "Continue."

"Veii was so rich, people thought the capture of so much booty would relieve the tensions between the classes. Surely, they thought, there would be enough, and more than enough, for everyone in Roma. But when the time came for the division of the spoils, no one was pleased. The temple to Juno Regina, and the ceremonies to dedicate the temple, cost a great deal more than anyone expected. Added to that was the tenth portion promised by Camillus to Apollo and his priesthood. The plebeians said they were being robbed of booty for which they had spilled their blood. In reply to that, the patricians said it was sacrilegious of the plebeians to try to claim booty that had been promised to the gods."

"And the result?"

"Bitter accusations of unfairness and greed from both sides."

"Which is certainly nothing new," said Foslia, who could never stay out of any discussion for long. "For generations patricians have argued, quite reasonably, that everyone must pull together for the common good. We must be united under our leaders, all willing to sacrifice in the face of so many threats from so many enemies. And for just as long, selfish, short-sighted plebeians have done nothing but complain. At times, they've even refused military service!"

"Of course . . ." Pinaria said, then hesitated. Certain ideas which she overheard outside the House of the Vestals were not always welcomed by her fellow Vestals, especially the Virgo Maxima.

"Go on," said Postumia.

"Yes, go on," said Foslia, with a mischievous glint in her eye, hoping to see the Virgo Maxima provoked.

Pinaria spoke slowly and carefully. "These are not my ideas, you understand; but one does hear things. For instance, there are some who argue that, while the temple itself honors Juno Regina, the money to build the temple actually goes into the pockets of the contractors chosen by the state. Most of those contractors are patricians and are already quite rich. And because those contractors tend to use slaves—men captured in war and sold to them cheaply by the state—plebeian workers see no profit at all from such a project."

"Their profit is the good will of the goddess, who is pleased by her temple!" declared the Virgo Maxima. "To reduce the building of a temple, a sacred act, to a squabble over money is nothing less than sacrilege, of the sort spewed by the worst rabble-rousers. Really, Pinaria, you must learn to allow such talk to go in one ear and out the other. Think about it: Simple reason dictates that the gods must always be given the first and greatest portion of the spoils. Otherwise, we might lose their favor, and then where would we be? Veii would have conquered us, instead of the other way around! After the gods, our responsible, hard-working leaders, the men who ensure the proper worship of the gods, must be given their rightful share. And after that, the plebeian rabble should be satisfied with whatever spoils may remain—just as they should be satisfied to marry within their own class! Instead of nurturing wild notions that they themselves are fit to rule the state, they should submit to those whose families have proved themselves best able to guide the destiny of Roma. This is a dangerous world, full of enemies. Only proven leadership that is pleasing to the gods can preserve us from catastrophe."

Pinaria bowed her head. "The Virgo Maxima speaks wisely."

The other Vestals, including Foslia, nodded and echoed her words: "The Virgo Maxima speaks wisely!"

"And yet . . ." Postumia's voice trembled with emotion. "And yet it sometimes seems that our worst enemies are inside the city, not outside. The rabble may be unfit to rule, but they still have their tribunes and other powerful men who cater to them, as we have seen demonstrated only too well in recent days."

The other Vestals put aside their food. The Virgo Maxima was alluding to a topic painful to them all.

Foslia broke the uncomfortable silence. "Is there no hope for Camillus, Virgo Maxima?"

Postumia sighed. "The situation remains unchanged. Even as we speak, Marcus Furius Camillus is making ready to leave Roma. Rather than face trial, he will go into exile. We all know how this lamentable state of affairs came about: In their fury over the spoils of Veii, the rabble decided to vent their spite on the man most responsible for dispensing those spoils. They accused Camillus of breaking the law. They claim he wrongfully enriched his friends and family members."

"But surely he isn't guilty," said one of the Vestals.

The Virgo Maxima shook her head. "Alas, men wise in the ways of the courts tell me otherwise. By the strict letter of the law, Camillus did indeed commit improprieties. He is unable to account for all the wealth that was dispensed. The courts take such matters very seriously and cannot look the other way. Really, these laws are written as if they were intentionally fashioned to give a weapon to the enemies of any man in public life. The higher a man rises, and the more far-ranging his decisions, the more vulnerable he becomes to charges of corruption. And so, Camillus—our beloved Camillus!—is being driven from Roma. Only three years ago, every man, woman, and child was shouting his name in the streets, praising him as our savior. And now, this! Vesta forgive me for saying such a thing, but if Camillus were to raise arms against us, as Coriolanus did, I should hardly be able to deny that the city deserved it! But of course, he will never do that. Camillus is too great a man, and too loyal a Roman, no matter that his enemies have made him an outcast. Tonight, when we gather at the temple, we must all remember him in our prayers. May Camillus be comforted and kept warm by Vesta's fire, however far he may journey from the hearth."

"May Vesta's fire keep him warm!" echoed the other Vestals, and some quietly began to weep; many tears had been shed in the House of the Vestals over the misfortunes of Camillus in recent days. In the years since his triumph, all the Vestals, including the Virgo Maxima, had come to regard the conqueror of Veii with a certain awe. In reverent tones they spoke of his military triumphs and his grandiose public works; in whispers they spoke of his chiseled features and brawny bearing, the exemplar of Roman manliness. The Vestals had built a veritable cult around Camillus, and his fall had devastated them.

Pinaria did not weep. She was remembering the day of Camillus's triumph, and the shock she had felt at seeing the four white horses that pulled his chariot. Surely Jupiter, who saw everything from the clouds, had seen those white horses as well. Had the god believed that a mortal was mocking him? The Virgo Maxima saw the will of the gods in all things, so why not in the downfall of Camillus? But Pinaria had already provoked the Virgo Maxima once this evening; she did not care to do so again by imputing any fault to a man whom the Vestals held in such esteem.

It occurred to Pinaria that, in the course of the evening's digressions, the topic that had originally been brought up was the very topic no one had discussed: the Veii Question.

The spoils of Veii had been claimed; the people had been sold into slavery and the conquered city had been stripped of every ornament, as vultures strip a carcass of its flesh. But even the most ravenous vultures leave bones behind, and the bones of Veii remained: its houses, walls, wells, fountains, assembly halls, streets, gardens, and temples. The houses of Veii stood empty. Veii was a city without citizens.

What was to be done with Veii?

One faction, led by a tribune of the plebs named Sicinius, argued that half the population of Roma should leave their homes and move to Veii, taking up residence in the empty houses there. Renters could become owners; men mired in debt could make a fresh start. Farmers who had been promised small homesteads in distant, conquered Volscian territory could instead receive lots outside Veii, enjoying the amenities of a city already built and living close to their family and friends in Roma. With two complete cities to accommodate the population of one, much of the disparity between the haves and have-nots of Roma could be eliminated overnight.

The supporters of Sicinius's proposal were wildly enthusiastic, but the opposition was fierce. The landlords and moneylenders of Roma had everything to lose and nothing to gain. Those who ran the city foresaw a dilution of their authority; what if Veii became not an annex of Roma but a rival city, with its own magistrates and priesthoods? Opponents accused Sicinius of scheming to make himself rich by controlling the distribution of properties in Veii; perhaps he even intended to become king of Veii. To the opposition, the proposed migration was nothing less than another secession of the plebs—only this time, the secession would be permanent. The gods had shown favor to one city, Roma, and Roma should remain as it was. Veii should be utterly destroyed, it walls pulled down and its buildings burned to the ground.

Camillus had been among those who spoke most vehemently against the move to occupy Veii. In a speech to the Senate, he had uttered a phrase which became the rallying cry of the opposition: "Any city abandoned by the gods must never be inhabited by men!" Some said his exile was the price he paid for opposing Sicinius and his faction. They had brought charges of corruption against which Camillus had been unable to defend himself, but the real issue had been Camillus's stand on the Veii Question.

Should Roma be one city or two? Should Veii be inhabited or destroyed? The unresolved issue overshadowed every other concern facing the city. The debate was fierce and unrelenting, and often descended to open violence in the Forum. There seemed to be no middle ground; migration either promised the solution to all problems, or threatened the annihilation of Roma. The stakes were incredibly high. No wonder Foslia had laughed at the Virgo Maxima's quaint digression on intermarriage when the Veii Question was raised!

And yet, as Postumia had argued, all such questions were at some level related to one another. Politics split each question into many different questions, all of them vexed and insoluble: Every man asserted his own will, and whoever was strongest at a given moment prevailed. Religion unified all questions into one, to which there was a single answer: the will of the gods.

It often seemed to Pinaria that the world outside the House of the Vestals was a swirling chaos of violence and uncertainty. The enemies of Roma sought her destruction, as she sought theirs. The citizens of Roma endlessly struggled against one another for wealth and power; even within families, sons contested against one another and sometimes disobeyed their paterfamilias, and wives rebelled against their husbands. But these struggles were mere shadows of something far greater, and yet hard to see, as a temple by its vastness must be hard for an ant to discern: the will of the gods. Wisdom came not from within, or from other mortals; wisdom came from determining the desire of the gods. But how was this to be done? Even after her many years of study, the path often seemed obscure to Pinaria.

She was glad the dinner was over, and conversation had ceased; now the Vestals would make their way to the temple of the goddess for the evening's thanksgiving. No matter how much delight the play of words gave to clever people like Foslia, or to teachers like the Virgo Maxima, talking never resolved anything. Peace came only in the performance of ritual, and the greatest peace came in those precious moments when Pinaria could gaze, uninterrupted and free from all extraneous thoughts, into the hearthfire of Vesta, knowing it to be the one thing in all the world that was pure and everlasting.

"They are on their way! They are on their way! I must warn everyone! They are on their way!"

The madman had forced his way past the servants at the entrance of the House of the Vestals. He had rushed though the vestibule and into the atrium, where he now stood in the center of the impluvium. It was high noon and the sun shone directly down on him. When he stamped his feet in the ankle-deep water, like a child throwing a tantrum, the sunlight sparkled and lit rainbows amid the splashing water.

"They are on their way!" he cried, clenching his fists at his sides and drawing his eyebrows to a point. "Why will no one listen?"

The Vestals and their huddled servants kept their distance and watched him, fascinated. Foslia, who had just arrived, whispered in Pinaria's ear. "Who is this creature?"

"I don't know. But I've seen him before, in the street between here and the Temple of Vesta."

"He looks like a beggar, to judge by those rags. And that awful unkempt hair and beard! Has he threatened anyone?"

"No. He seems to be trying to warn us about something. The Virgo Maxima has gone to find the Pontifex Maximus—"

"You must be joking! I should think she'd fetch some armed lictors to take the man away in chains."

"She seemed to take him rather seriously."

There was a commotion at the entrance. Postumia and the Pontifex Maximus appeared in the vestibule and strode into the atrium, followed by a retinue of priests and augurs.

The madman dropped to his knees with a splash. "Pontifex Maximus! At last! *You* will hear the truth of what I say."

The high priest wore a toga distinctive for its many folds gathered and tucked in a loop just above his waist; the cowl that would have covered his head at ceremonies was pushed back to reveal a bald crown fringed with white hair. He stroked his long white beard and looked down his nose at the man in the impluvium. "Marcus Caedicius! How far you've fallen in the world—and I don't just mean to your knees."

"Pontifex Maximus, do you know this man?" said Postumia.

"I do. Caedicius used to be a respectable plebeian, a fuller who washed and dyed wool; observe the dark stains behind his fingernails. But some time ago he gave up his shop and became a vagrant. He frequents a particular spot in the street above the Temple of Vesta. Have you not seen him pacing this way and that, muttering to himself? Well, Caecidius, what is this nonsense? What can you be thinking, forcing your way into this sacred dwelling and terrifying the holy virgins! What do you have to say for yourself?"

"Oh, Pontifex Maximus, you must listen to me!"

"I *am* listening, you fool. Speak!"

"I heard a voice. I was in the street, alone—there wasn't another mortal in sight, I swear—and a voice spoke to me, as clearly and distinctly as I'm speaking to you now. A voice from nowhere!" Caedicius wrung his hands and chewed his lower lip.

"By Hercules, man, spit it out! Do you think I have nothing better to do? What did this voice say?"

"It said: 'The Gauls are coming!' That's what it said, as clearly as you hear me now: 'The Gauls are coming!' "

The Pontifex Maximus wrinkled his brow. "The Gauls?"

One of his subordinates drew alongside him. "A tribe of savages who come from a land far to the north, Pontifex Maximus, beyond a great mountain range called the Alps. Some years ago, they discovered a pass across the Alps. Some of them moved into Italy and founded a city called Mediolanum. Poets say it was a craving for wine that drew the Gauls to Italy; in their native land they have nothing like it. Their language is said to be a combination of grunts, very uncouth and grating to the ear."

"Yes, I've heard of these Gauls," said the Pontifex Maximus. "Why should they come here, Marcus Caedicius, and why should we care?"

Caedicius splashed his hands in the shallow water, close to weeping. "The Gauls are coming! Do you not understand? Their arrival shall be terrible, the most terrible thing that has ever happened! Doom! Death! Destruction! Warn the magistrates! Flee at once, and take the Vestals with you! Pray to the gods for our salvation!"

For quite some time, a rotund little priest in the retinue behind the Pontifex Maximus had been searching through a scroll, rotating the cylinders with both hands and scanning the text. The man gave a sudden jerk, which caught Pinaria's attention.

Foslia also noticed. She gripped Pinaria's arm and whispered into her ear. "Do you realize what that priest is holding? It's one of the Sibylline Books!"

"Surely not," whispered Pinaria. "Aren't they kept on the Capitoline, in a vault beneath the Temple of Jupiter?"

"Of course; that's where the priests study the Greek verses, translate them into Latin, and debate their meaning. That roly-poly little fellow must be one of the priests, and that must be one of the Sibylline Books!"

"I never thought that I should ever actually see one," said Pinaria, feeling a tremor of dread. The arcane verses were consulted only in times of dire crisis.

The priest gave another jerk and uttered a cry of excitement. "Pontifex Maximus, I've found something! I knew I had seen the reference before; at last I've located it. The Sibyl herself foresaw this moment. She wrote a verse to guide us."

"What does it say? Read the oracle aloud."

The little priest looked up from the scroll. He stared wide-eyed at Marcus Caecidius for a long moment, blinked and cleared his throat, and read:

> *A man kneels on water and does not sink.*
> *He speaks to the wise to make them think.*
> *From his warning they must not shrink.*

The little priest lowered the scroll. Everyone in the room gazed at the man who knelt in the shallow water, who claimed to have heard a warning from a disembodied voice that proclaimed, "The Gauls are coming!"

Not long after Caedicius delivered his warning, word arrived that a vast army of Gauls had swept down from the north and was laying siege to the city of Clusium, located on a tributary of the Tiber, a hundred miles upriver from Roma.

The city fathers conferred. The prophecy of Caedicius and the words of the Sibyl were debated. It was decided that a delegation should be sent to Clusium to observe the Gauls at first hand. If they were as numerous as rumor asserted, and as menacing as Caedicius believed, then the envoys should attempt to use diplomacy—promises, pacts, or threats—to turn the Gauls back from Clusium, or at the very least to dissuade them from moving further south and setting their sights on Roma.

The Roman ambassadors were three brothers of the distinguished Fabius family. The Gauls received them courteously, for they had heard of Roma and knew the city was a force to be reckoned with. But when the Fabii asked what injury the Clusians had done to the Gauls that they should attack their city, and if making war unjustly was not an offense to the gods, the chieftain of the Gauls merely laughed at them. Brennus was a big-jawed man with a bristling red beard and a shaggy red mane, so massive and ruggedly muscled that he seemed to have been hewn from a block of granite. The Gauls were very nearly a race of giants, and Brennus towered over the Roman ambassadors. Even though he spoke with a kind of rough humor, it seemed to the Romans that he was belittling them.

"How have the Clusians offended us?" Brennus asked. "By having too much, while we have too little! By being so few, while we number so many! As for offending the gods, yours may be different from ours, but the law of nature is the same everywhere: The weak submit to the strong. So it is among gods, beasts, and men alike. From everything I've heard about you, you Romans are no different. Haven't you done your share of taking what belongs to others, making free men into slaves simply because you're stronger than they are and because it suits you? I thought so! So don't ask us to pity the Clusians. Instead, maybe we should pity the people *you've* conquered and oppressed. Maybe we should go about setting them free and restoring their goods. How would you like that, Romans? What do you say? Ha!"

Brennus laughed in their faces. The Fabii were greatly insulted, but kept their mouths shut.

The matter might have ended there, but Quintus Fabius, the youngest and most hotheaded of the brothers, was determined to draw some Gallic blood. All races, including the Gauls, recognized the divinely protected status of envoys; it was universally agreed that ambassadors must be afforded hospitality and must not be harmed, and in return must not take up arms against their hosts. Quintus Fabius violated this sacred law. The next day, putting on the armor of a Clusian, he joined the forces of the besieged

city and rode into battle against the Gauls. Picking out a Gaul of particularly large stature, he rode straight toward the man and killed him with a
single blow of his sword. Wanting a trophy, Quintus Fabius jumped from
his horse and set about stripping the dead man of his armor, and in doing
so his Clusian helmet fell from his head. Brennus, fighting nearby, saw his
face and recognized him at once.

The Gallic chief was outraged. Had he been able to confront Quintus
Fabius there on the battlefield, the death of one or the other might have
ended the matter, but the press of the battle carried the two men apart, and
both ended the day unscathed.

The Fabii headed back to Roma. Brennus, an impulsive, prideful man,
brooded all night. In the morning, he announced that the siege of Clusium
was ended. For grossly insulting him—first by suggesting that he had offended the gods, then by flagrantly breaking divine law to take up arms
against him—the Romans must be punished. Brennus declared that the
entire force of the Gauls—more than 40,000 fighting men—would march
south at once.

In Roma, the Pontifex Maximus called for the punishment of Quintus
Fabius, saying that all guilt should rest on one man so as to exonerate the
rest of the citizens and spare them from divine retribution. But popular
opinion applauded Quintus Fabius for his recklessness. The people scoffed
at retribution from either gods or Gauls; had not Quintus proved how easily
a Gaul could be killed, no matter how gigantic, and had not the gods seen
him safely home? Election time was at hand, and rather than punishing
Quintus Fabius, the people elected him and his brothers military tribunes.
Brennus, hearing this, grew even more enraged. His speeches whipped the
Gauls into a frenzy. The vast horde rushed down the valley of the Tiber and
rapidly drew nearer to Roma.

One man had the proven ability to unify the Roman forces and lead
them to victory, even in the face of overwhelming odds, but that man was
in exile: Camillus. Nightly, the Vestals prayed for his return, even as they
saw omens everywhere that foretold disaster. But Camillus was not recalled from exile, and no dictator was appointed to deal with the emergency; instead, the Fabii and the three other military tribunes saw fit to
split the command between themselves. Though they managed to muster
an army to match the Gauls in numbers, the vast majority of these soldiers

were raw recruits. Many had never held a sword or cast a spear; full of bravado like their leaders, they were unruly, undisciplined, and overconfident. On the eve of battle, still at odds with the priesthood that had demanded the punishment of Quintus Fabius, the commanders neglected to take the auspices or make sacrifices to the gods. Roma was to face Brennus without Camillus, without a sufficiently trained army, and without the favor of the gods.

The battle took place on the summer solstice. The longest day of the year became the most miserable day in the history of Roma.

The Roman forces were advancing upriver beside the Tiber, poorly massed and in disarray thanks to conflicting instructions from their commanders. As they approached the confluence where the river Allia ran through a steep ravine to join with the Tiber, about ten miles upriver from the city, they heard a noise like a multitude of animals braying. The noise grew louder and nearer, until the Romans began to realize it must be a marching song sung by the Gauls in their uncouth language. The scouts had given no warning, and it seemed impossible that the Gauls could have come so far so quickly. A tremor of fear ran through the front ranks. In the next instant, they came face to face with the enemy.

The Romans panicked, broke ranks, and ran. Thousands were pushed into the river and drowned. Thousands more fled into the narrow ravine; those who were not trampled by their own men were slaughtered by the Gauls. Those who survived the battle did so only because Brennus, amazed at the ease of his victory, suspected a trap. He kept his men from advancing as quickly as they might have, which allowed the Romans who threw down their weapons and cast off their armor to outrun their pursuers, saving themselves while shedding every vestige of their dignity. Because it was closer, most fled to Veii, not to Roma. Only a handful made it back to the city with news of the disaster.

The Roman army was destroyed. Its remnants were disarmed and scattered. Elated by their good fortune but exhausted from so much slaughter, the Gauls rested that night. The next day they stripped booty from the fallen dead; so many Romans had been killed that the process took all day.

The next morning the Gauls pressed on toward Roma. When they arrived, at nightfall, they beheld a city with open gates and not a single sentry on the walls. All was silent and still. So eerie was the sight that Brennus camped outside the walls that night, again fearing a trap. He waited until morning to venture into the defenseless city.

※

Alone in the Temple of Vesta, Pinaria slept. Not even the goddess was present, for the sacred fire of Vesta was gone. Only ashes remained in the hearth.

The previous day, while the others made ready to flee, racing about the House of the Vestals in a panic, Pinaria had been overcome by a desire to spend a few more moments, however fleeting, in Vesta's temple. She had meant to steal quickly to the temple and just as quickly back again, but the masses of people in the street thwarted her intentions. By the thousands, Roma's citizens were abandoning her. Some fled on foot with nothing more than the clothes they wore. Some pushed carts loaded high with belongings. Some hitched donkeys to wagons and attempted to take all their possessions with them.

As Pinaria threaded her way through the throng, others, seeing her holy vestments, tried to make way for her, but in many places the crowd was simply too thick. Pinaria was jostled this way and that. The heat of the midsummer day was stifling and oppressive. People moaned in misery. A woman screamed and cried out that her child had fallen and was being trampled underfoot. Pinaria turned to look, but the crowd carried her forward against her will.

At last she reached the temple. She broke away from the crowd and rushed up the empty steps. The doors stood open. There was no one inside. Pinaria closed the doors behind her and took a deep breath.

Why had she come? Vesta was no longer here; wherever the hearthfire was, that was the place where the goddess might be found, and the eternal flame had been transferred to a portable brazier to be transported away from Roma, to a place of safety. The Pontifex Maximus and the Virgo Maxima had overseen the grim ceremony while the Vestals looked on and wept; as long as Vesta's hearthfire could be preserved, there remained a chance, however slender, that the city of Roma might endure.

The circular sanctum was dark and empty. The chamber was surprisingly quiet; the heavy doors muffled the hubbub of the crowd outside. As she stood alone in the Temple of Vesta, a sense of calm descended on Pinaria.

"What use is prophecy?" she said aloud, though there was no one to hear.

Marcus Caedicius had warned the magistrates and the priests about the Gauls, yet his warning had done no good. Despite their efforts to prevent the coming of the Gauls—indeed, because of those very efforts!—the Gauls were now marching on Roma, with nothing to stop them. The prophecy of Caedicius had proved no more useful than the prophecies of the Trojan princess Cassandra, who foresaw her city's doom and yet could do nothing to prevent it. Was the fate of Troy to become the fate of Roma?

Pinaria shuddered and shut her eyes. She suddenly felt very weary. She knelt on the floor and leaned against the empty hearth.

She had not meant to fall asleep. Indeed, she would have thought it impossible to do so, considering the overwrought state of both the city and herself. Somnus, the god of sleep, overwhelmed her, accompanied by his son Morpheus, the shaper of dreams.

Pinaria woke. She did so suddenly, with a jarring sense of dislocation in time and space.

Where was she? Blinking, she realized that she was in the Temple of Vesta. She felt a stab of panic. Had she fallen asleep while tending the sacred flame? She looked at the hearth. It was cold and dark, the fire extinguished! Her heart raced and she felt lightheaded, then she remembered: The Gauls were coming. The flame had been removed so that it could be carried to safety.

She sensed that many hours had passed since she entered the temple. The murmur of the crowd no longer penetrated the heavy doors; no sound at all came from outside. It was not nighttime; bright sunlight leaked in from the narrow gap beneath the doors.

Pinaria opened the doors and shielded her eyes, dazzled by bright morning light. The hand of Somnus must have been very heavy upon her, to make her sleep from one day's light until the next.

Morpheus had visited her as well, for now she remembered a dream that had haunted her sleep. Foslia was in the dream, nattering on and on, showing off her erudition. Everything she said irritated Pinaria and made her more distressed . . .

"Romulus walked on foot for his triumphs. Do you suppose Brennus will ride a quadriga through Roma, like Camillus? I wonder if Brennus is as handsome . . . "

There was more, though in the dream Pinaria protested and tried to stop her ears.

"The Trojan women were taken as slaves. Do you suppose we Vestals will become slaves? I don't imagine the Gauls will allow us to remain virgins for long . . . "

And though Pinaria howled in protest, still Foslia continued, determined to show off her irrefutable religious logic.

"No city is conquered unless its people have offended the gods. Killing or enslaving the inhabitants of a conquered city pleases the gods. Now the Gauls have conquered Roma. What do you think that means, Pinaria? What does it say about Roma?"

What a terrible nightmare! Pinaria shivered, despite the warmth of the day. As she descended the steps and looked around her, what she saw was as disquieting as the dream, and just as strange.

The street was littered with castoff items, all the things that people had thought they could carry while they fled but had abandoned when panic or common sense overcame them: pieces of pottery, sacks full of clothing, boxes stuffed with trinkets and mementos, toys made of wood or straw, even chairs and small tripod tables. Forsaken wagons and handcarts had been knocked on their sides, with their contents strewn beside them.

Not a single person was to be seen, nor the sound of a single voice to be heard. Pinaria had lived her whole life in the city; she was used to its teeming energy, its loud, brash crowds. To see the city without people was bizarre. Roma was like an empty shell. It was like a tomb without a body.

Even the gods were gone. Before fleeing, the Romans had stripped their temples of every sacred object. The hearthfire of Vesta, statues of the gods, sacred talismans of the kings, the Sibylline Books—all been taken away for safekeeping or buried in secret places throughout the city. Only Somnus and Morpheus remained; perhaps they hovered over her still, for Pinaria felt as though she were walking through the strange, unreal landscape of a nightmare.

She wandered about the Forum, sometimes startled by the echo of her footsteps in the empty public spaces. Rounding a corner, she drew a sharp breath. She was not alone, after all. On a backless chair before the entrance to his official residence sat the Pontifex Maximus. He heard her gasp, gave a start and turned his head, as surprised to see her as she was to see him.

She ran to him. He stayed where he was, sitting stiffly upright and furrowing his brow. "Pinaria! What are you doing here? All the Vestals left yesterday."

She knelt beside his chair. "Yes, Pontifex Maximus, and I was to go with them. But I wanted to visit the Temple of Vesta, one last time. I meant to stay only a moment, but somehow—"

"Shhhh! Do you hear?"

Pinaria cocked her head. The sound was distant and vague at first, then grew closer and more distinct. It was the sound of men talking, punctuated by shouts and raucous laughter.

"The Gauls," whispered the Pontifex Maximus. "They've come at last!"

"But Pontifex Maximus, why are you still here? Why have you not fled?"

"Because some among us are still Romans. Flee the city? Never!"

"But when the Gauls find you—"

"I'm not the only one. Walk across the city and you'll see the others who remain. Mostly old men, like myself; men who have never in their lives fled from an enemy and have no intention of doing so now. Nor will we cower inside our houses. Each of us has drawn a chair before his domicile, to sit and await whatever is to come, with our Roman dignity intact."

"But the Gauls are monsters! They're giants, twice as big as normal men. They drink human blood, and sacrifice babies, and burn their victims alive!"

"They may destroy my body, but they shall not rob me of my dignity. But listen, Pinaria—they're drawing closer! You must flee!"

"Where?"

"Cross the street, quickly! Hide among the branches of that yew tree, and don't make a sound, no matter what you see. Go!"

Reluctantly, Pinaria left him. She hid herself just before a troop of Gauls came striding up the street, laughing and swinging their swords for the thrill of hearing the blades cut the air. They were indeed large, though not as gigantic as Pinaria had expected. Nor were they as ugly as she had thought; some might even be called handsome, despite their strangely braided hair and untrimmed beards.

The Gauls saw the Pontifex Maximus and fell silent for a moment. They drew closer, peering at him curiously. He sat so still, with his hands on his knees and his eyes staring straight ahead, that perhaps they thought he was a painted statue. They slowly circled him, grunted to one another in their savage language, laughed, and pretended to poke at him with their swords. He did not react in any way; he did not even blink. At last, one of the Gauls—a redheaded giant from whom the others took orders—stooped down and peered at the Pontifex Maximus, eye to eye and nose to nose. He grabbed hold of the long white beard, grinned, and gave it a sharp tug.

The reaction of the Pontifex Maximus was instant: He slapped the Gaul across the face. The crack of the blow echoed up and down the street. Pinaria gasped.

The Gaul sprang back and roared. He drew a long sword and swung it in a circle in the air. The Pontifex Maximus did not move, but his face became as white as salt. With all his strength, the Gaul swung his blade against the neck of the Pontifex Maximus. There was a sickening sound, and then the priest's head went flying through the air, the white beard trailing behind it like a comet's tail. It landed in the street, bounced once, then rolled to a stop only a few steps from the place where Pinaria was hidden.

Despite herself, she opened her mouth to scream, but from behind a hand slipped over her mouth, and an arm embraced her so tightly that she had no breath to cry out.

The decapitated body of the Pontifex Maximus became a fountain of blood. The limbs jerked in a spastic fashion and the fingers madly twitched. The Gauls laughed and seemed refreshed by the rain of blood upon them. The sight was so horrible that Pinaria struggled wildly against the arms embracing her, desperate to flee, but the man held her fast. Against her back, she could feel that his heart was beating as rapidly as her own. The body of a Vestal was sacrosanct; Pinaria was not used to being touched. The sensation of being held so tightly was at once terrifying and strangely comforting.

The Gauls knocked the body of the Pontifex Maximus from its chair, kicked it a few times, then began to move on. Their leader barked an order at one of his men, who ran back to fetch the severed head. The man came so close to Pinaria that he might easily have seen her, had he peered into the foliage of the yew tree, but he kept his eyes on the head as he grabbed it by the beard and ran off, swinging it over his head.

The Gauls moved out of sight.

Slowly, the man loosened his grip on Pinaria. She slipped free and spun around to see a youth no older than herself. He was dressed in a tattered tunic. His shoes were mere scraps of leather, so worn as to be hardly worth wearing. Pinaria glanced at the hand that had covered her mouth, then at the one that had touched her breast.

"Where is your ring?" she said.

The youth merely raised an eyebrow. He had bright blue eyes and was very handsome, despite a haircut so ragged that his fair hair poked this way and that like tufts of straw.

"Your citizen's ring?" demanded Pinaria. "Where is it?" Following a custom of the Greeks, every Roman citizen wore a ring, usually a simple band of iron. Sometimes such rings were carved with identifying initials or symbols; those who had cause to send letters or documents used their rings to impress their insignia on the sealing wax.

"I don't have a ring," said the youth. "But I do have this." He indicated an amulet that hung from a leather strap around his neck. It appeared to be made of lead, very crudely molded in the form of a male member with wings.

Pinaria blanched. "You're a slave, aren't you?"

"Yes."

"A slave dared to touch me!"

The youth laughed. "Had you rather I'd let you cry out? Those Gauls would have found you, for sure, and then they'd have found me, as well. And since I'm prettier than you, who knows which of us they would have ravished? I don't know about you, but I don't fancy becoming a plaything for one of those bloodthirsty giants."

Pinaria stared at him, dumbfounded. No man had ever spoken to her in such a crude fashion. Few slaves had ever spoken to her at all, except in response to her orders. No one had ever looked her in the eye and grinned at her in such a brazen way.

The slave looked her up and down. "You must be a Vestal."

"I am!"

"What are you still doing here? I should have thought you'd have left yesterday."

Pinaria was suddenly on the verge of tears. She drew a breath to steady herself. "You're very impertinent."

"Is that what you'll say to Brennus when he has you staked spread-eagled in the middle of the Forum, and the line of Gauls queued up to make your acquaintance runs all the way to the Aventine?"

Pinaria slapped him across the face, then began to weep uncontrollably. The slave made no move to touch her, but stepped back and crossed his arms. "Have I frightened you?"

"Yes."

"Good! Because more Gauls will be here at any moment, and this is not a very good place to hide."

Pinaria fought back her tears. "I must get out of the city."

"Impossible."

"Then where can I go?"

"Take my hand."

"What?"

"More Gauls are coming. Can't you hear them?"

Pinaria listened. From nearby, she heard men braying a marching song in the ugly language of the Gauls. They sounded drunk.

"My name is Pennatus, by the way. Now take my hand, and don't let go. We're going to run, very fast."

"Where?"

"How should I know? We'll trust the gods to guide us."

"The gods have left Roma," said Pinaria, but she took his hand nonetheless.

This way and that they ran, uphill and downhill, heading nowhere, striving only to avoid the Gauls. As more and more Gauls appeared, overrunning the city like rats overrunning a ship, eluding them became harder. Sometimes they were seen, and the Gauls cried out and ran after them, but each time they escaped. Pennatus seemed to know each winding alley and every hole in every wall in the city.

They saw many terrible things. Like the Pontifex Maximus, others had decided to greet the Gauls fearlessly, seated like statues before their houses. Some, like the Pontifex Maximus, had been beheaded. Others had been strangled or stabbed to death. Some had been hanged from trees.

There seemed to be a surprising number of Romans in the city who, like Pinaria, had intended to flee but had failed to do so before the Gauls arrived. The city became a killing field; the Gauls were the hunters, the Romans the prey. Men were slaughtered and women and children were raped while Pinaria watched.

Shops were looted. Buildings were set on fire. The Gauls gawked at the opulent houses on the Palatine, and gawked even more at the crude Hut of Romulus, preserved as a rustic monument in the midst of the city's finest dwellings. Could such unfeeling, half-human creatures understand what the sacred hut represented? While Pinaria watched from the shadows, a group of drunken Gauls stood in a circle around the hut and urinated on it, whooping and making a contest of their desecration. No other sight that day offended Pinaria as deeply, or made her feel more desperately that the history of Roma was finished forever.

The dreadful day seemed endless. At last, passing below the Tarpeian Rock, Pinaria and Pennatus heard voices calling from above. "Here! Up here! You'll be safe if you can get to the top of the Capitoline!"

Looking up, they saw tiny figures peering over the rock. The figures beckoned to them, then frantically pointed.

"Gauls! Very near you, just behind that building! Run! Hurry! If you can get to the path that winds up the Capitoline—"

Pinaria was too frightened to think, too weary to move. It was Pennatus who dragged her forward, holding her by the hand. Crossing the Forum, they were spotted by the same troop of Gauls who had beheaded the Pontifex Maximus; one of the giants still toted the priest's head as a trophy, carrying it by the beard. Pinaria screamed. The Gauls laughed and ran after them.

They came to the path which would take them to the top of Capitoline, the same route by which every triumphal procession reached the Temple of Jupiter. Drained by grief, immobilized by terror, Pinaria had reached the end of her endurance, yet, with Pennatus pulling her along, she seemed almost to fly up the winding path. Truly, she thought, the slave must have wings, as his name suggested, for how else was she being transported when her limbs had failed and her will was utterly spent?

With its steep slopes, the Capitoline had always presented one of the most naturally defensible positions among the Seven Hills. Over the generations, an accretion of monuments and buildings linked by walls and ramparts had essentially made it into a fortress. The defenders at the top had only to fill a few openings and passageways with rubble to secure the perimeter. They were doing so even as Pennatus and Pinaria reached the top of the winding path.

A narrow gap still remained amid the stones and bits of timber that were being hastily piled up to block the passage. A man stood in the breach, waving frantically. "The Gauls are right behind you!" he cried. Another Roman appeared atop the barrier, raised a bow, and let fly an arrow that very nearly parted Pinaria's scalp. The buzzing of the arrow was followed by a scream, so close behind her that Pinaria flinched. The pursuers were very near, practically breathing on her neck.

Pennatus rushed through the breach, pulling her behind him. She tripped on the rubble and scraped her shoulder against a jagged bit of wood as she passed through to safety.

More arrows whizzed through the air, even as men rushed to fill in the breach. The archer gave a whoop of triumph. "They're retreating! I got one in the eye, and another in the shoulder. Even giants turn tail and run if you show them who's in charge."

The archer jumped down from the barricade, rattling his armor. He removed his helmet to reveal a clean-shaven face, bright green eyes, and a shock of black hair. He squared his broad shoulders and stood stiffly erect. "Gaius Fabius Dorso," he announced in a deep voice, taking such pleasure in enunciating his name that the effect was almost comical. He glanced at her vestments. "Can it be possible that you're one of the Vestals?"

"My name is Pinaria," she said, trying to steady her voice.

"What's this?" Dorso peered at her shoulder. The fabric of her gown had been torn. The pale flesh was marred by a scrape and bright red speckles of blood. He averted his eyes, conscious of the sanctity of her body. "How did such a thing happen? The slave must have treated you very carelessly! If he needs to be punished—"

"Don't be ridiculous," said Pinaria. "The wound is nothing, and the slave saved my life."

She covered the exposed scrape with her hand and winced, suddenly aware of the pain. She looked at Pennatus. Perhaps he was not as handsome as she had thought; seeing him next to Gaius Fabius Dorso, he looked slightly ridiculous, with his badly cropped hair and shabby clothes. Nonetheless, when he grinned at her—such cheek, from a slave!—she could not help but return his smile. Her face grew hot and she lowered her eyes.

"If you truly had wings, you could fly away from here," said Pinaria. "If only . . ."

She stood behind a rampart on the Capitoline, overlooking the Forum and the hills that surrounded it. Many days had passed since the coming of the Gauls. The sight of Roma occupied by savages—horrifying and bizarre at first, almost beyond comprehension—had now become commonplace. Rarely now did the beleaguered Romans atop the Capitoline hear the screams of some hapless citizen being rousted from a hiding place by the Gauls to be tortured and raped. Most of those in hiding had been discovered in the very first days of the occupation; a lucky few had made their way to the Capitoline. Nonetheless, the Gauls' assaults upon the city itself continued, day after day. After a house was ransacked, the Gauls often set it on fire, apparently for no reason other than to delight in its destruction or to infuriate the Romans watching from the Capitoline. On this day, from all over the city, great plumes of smoke rose into the air. High above the hills, the smoke coalesced into a grey miasma that obscured the midsummer sun and turned midday into twilight.

The handful of defenders atop the Capitoline—Gaius Fabius Dorso insisted that they think of themselves thus, and not as captives, for they were Romans and stood upon Roman soil—had, for the time being, enough to eat and drink. In the first days of the occupation, they stayed busy strengthening their defenses. They erected pickets, dug trenches, and even chipped away some of the hillsides to make them even steeper. So long as they kept watch day and night, their position was virtually impregnable. And yet, despair was always near. The sight of their beloved city being demolished house by house, the loss of all contact with those who had fled, the fear that the gods had abandoned them—these anxieties preyed on their waking thoughts and colored their nightmares.

If only one had wings; if only one could fly away . . .

Beside her, Pennatus smiled. He was always smiling, despite the grimness of their situation. He was quite unlike anyone Pinaria had ever encountered. Most of the slaves she had met were quiet and self-effacing, desirous of nothing except to go unnoticed. Most of the free men she had known were self-consciously deferential in her company, awkward or aloof. Pennatus was none of these things. He was constantly joking and making light of their situation, and her exalted status seemed to mean nothing to him. He appeared to be utterly without religious scruples or even religious belief. He often said things that went beyond sacrilege, not so much disparaging the gods as disavowing their existence.

Pinaria had never met such a person, or even imagined that such a person could exist. It seemed there was nothing Pennatus feared to say to her. Sometimes she thought he must be flirting with her, though she had so little experience in such matters that she couldn't quite tell. If only Foslia were with her, so that Pinaria might have someone to talk to about the unfamiliar feelings stirred in her by this peculiar slave!

"For better or worse," said Pennatus, "despite my name, I do not have, nor have I ever had, wings. Did I not tell you already how I came by my name?"

Pinaria shook her head.

"It was given to me by my master when I was an infant. He owned my mother as well."

"What about your father?"

Pennatus shrugged. "I never knew him. For all I know, the old master sired me."

Pinaria blushed. Pennatus clucked his tongue. "Really, do they teach you Vestals nothing about the facts of procreation? Well, of course they don't. To what practical purpose could a Vestal virgin put such knowledge?"

She blushed more deeply. "Really, Pennatus! I shall pray to Vesta that you may become more respectful of her servants."

"Why bother? I'm only a slave. I should think your goddess has no more interest in me than I have in her."

Pinaria sighed, exasperated. "You were telling me how you acquired your name."

"From this pendant I wear. As you see, it has wings. My mother wore it. It protected her in childbirth, but afterward, she wanted me to have it. She placed it on a cord around my neck not long after I was born. The old master's eyesight was poor, and all he could tell about the talisman was that it had wings, and so he called me Pennatus: 'winged.' I was still quite small when my mother died. Her gift helps me to remember her."

Pinaria gazed at the black object, which nestled in the cleft of Pennatus's chest. His tunic was crudely made, and the wide opening for his head exposed a considerable portion of his chest, so that the talisman was always visible. Not for the first time, Pinaria noticed that the muscularity of his chest was quite pronounced, and the firm, sunburned flesh was covered with soft golden hair. "What is the amulet made of?"

He smiled oddly, as if at some private joke. "What does it look like?"

She shrugged. "Lead?"

He hummed and nodded. "And what master would bother to take a worthless lead pendant from a slave? Now, if it were made of some precious metal—silver, or even gold—many a master would take the talisman for himself, either to wear it or to sell it. Even a kindly, indulgent, slightly doddering old master might do so."

"I suppose," said Pinaria, who seldom thought about the lives of slaves and the problems and humiliations they faced. The world was as the gods had made it, and one did not question such arrangements. But if one were like Pennatus, who seemed not to believe in the gods, how very different the world and the people in it must appear . . .

Pennatus had been lucky. His master treated him well, and in return, Pennatus had been very loyal to the old man, who needed constant looking after. When the Gauls came, the master was too frail to be moved. Pennatus stayed with him, and by doing so missed the chance to flee the city. The shock of events proved too much for the old man. His heart stopped beating the very morning the Gauls arrived, leaving Pennatus to fend for himself. That was how Pennatus came to be wandering the city when he encountered Pinaria.

Pinaria sighed and gazed at the plumes of smoke that rose from all over the city. A noise from below drew her attention. Down in the Forum, a group of drunken Gauls were attacking a marble statue of Hercules with wooden staves. Their staves kept breaking against the stone, but the red-faced, maniacally laughing Gauls stubbornly kept up their assault. At last a finger broke off the statue and went clattering across the paving stones. The Gauls pranced about and howled in triumph.

Pennatus laughed. "What idiots!"

"What monsters!" Pinaria was not amused. The sorry spectacle made her feel disheartened and full of sorrow. She raised her eyes to the vast nimbus of smoke that veiled the dark red sun. "If you truly had wings, Pennatus, would you not fly away from here at once? Far, far away?"

He raised an eyebrow. "I might. Or I might keep my wings folded and stay here with you."

"What a silly thing to say!" muttered Pinaria, but suddenly she felt less sorrowful.

They looked at each other for a long moment, then both turned at the sound of approaching footsteps. Gaius Fabius Dorso strode toward them. As always, he carried himself with an erect military bearing, but he was not clad in armor. He wore a toga with a ceremonial belt of gold and purple cloth and a headband of the same material, as if he were about to take part in some religious rite. In his hands, a bit awkwardly, he carried several small vessels made of hammered copper.

"Are you ready, Pennatus? I can carry the vessels of wine and oil myself, but I shall need you to carry the bowls of salt and ground millet."

Pennatus nodded. He stepped forward to relieve Dorso of the bowls.

"What's happening?" asked Pinaria.

Dorso stood tall before her and raised his chin. "This is the day of the annual sacrifice of the Fabii on the Quirinal. Since I am the only Fabius left in Roma, I shall tend to the ritual."

"But where will you offer this sacrifice?"

"At the ancient altar on the Quirinal, of course."

"But how? There must be a thousand Gauls between here and there."

"Yes, and another thousand swarming over the Quirinal like rats.

Nonetheless, it is incumbent upon me to perform the ritual, and so I shall."

"But Dorso, it isn't possible!"

"The ritual has been performed on this day every year, without fail, for many generations. Long ago, during the very first war against Veii, an army made up entirely of Fabii—three hundred seven in all—went to fight for Roma. There was a terrible ambush, from which only a single Fabius returned. To avert the recurrence of such a disaster, each year we make an offering to Father Romulus in his divine guise as the god Quirinus. Today is the day."

"But Dorso, to leave the Capitoline would be madness!"

"Perhaps. But to neglect the sacrifice would be a greater madness, surely. Dear Vestal, I should think that you, of all people, would understand that. I shall walk across the city, directly to the altar. I shall perform the ritual. I shall walk directly back again. If the Gauls challenge me, I shall tell them they are standing in the way of a sacred procession. These Gauls are a peculiar people. They appear to possess little knowledge of the gods, but they are very superstitious and can easily be overawed."

"But you don't even speak their language!"

"They will see that I carry sacred vessels. From my face they will know that my purpose is a holy one. The god Quirinus will protect me."

Pinaria shook her head. She glanced at Pennatus, and swallowed a lump in her throat. "Must you take Pennatus with you?"

"A slave customarily accompanies the Fabius who performs the ritual, to help carry the vessels."

"But Pennatus is not your slave."

"No, he is not, and I am not compelling him to go with me. I asked him to go, and he agreed."

"Pennatus, is this true?"

The slave shrugged and flashed a crooked smile. "It seemed reasonable at the time. I'm getting bored, trapped up here day after day. I think it may be a great adventure."

Pinaria shook her head. "No, this isn't right. Pennatus . . . Pennatus is impious! He can't be part of such a ritual. He has no more respect for the gods than the Gauls do."

"All the better!" declared Dorso. "If I fail to overawe them, perhaps the Gauls will see in Pennatus a kindred spirit, and leave us alone for his sake." He smiled at Pennatus, who smiled back at him.

The unlikely friendship that had developed between the two young men was a great puzzlement to Pinaria. Two mortals could hardly be more different. Gaius Fabius Dorso was a pious, upright patrician warrior; he was oddly likeable, despite being more than a little vain and self-important. Pennatus was an impious slave who seemed to respect nothing and no one. And yet, thrown together atop the Capitoline, in a situation where the normal constraints of society were undone, the two men had discovered a pleasure in each other's company that grew deeper every day. Now, to Pinaria's amazement and dismay, they were about to set out together on a mad venture that would surely put an end to both of them.

Pinaria stepped forward and laid her hand on Dorso's arm. "Please, I implore you, don't do this thing! Forgo the ritual. The gods—if they still have any love for us—will understand and forgive."

Her touch humbled Dorso. He lowered his eyes. "Please, Vestal, I need your blessing, not words of discouragement. The truth is this: I returned to the city from the battle at the River Allia and I remained here, despite the coming of the Gauls, for the express purpose of performing this ritual. I am . . ." He drew a deep breath and lowered his voice to a whisper. "I am all too aware of the role played by my kinsmen in drawing the wrath of the Gauls, and perhaps the wrath of the gods, upon Roma. I cannot turn back time and reverse the damage that was done by my impetuous, impious cousin, Quintus. For his crime, Quintus should have been punished—the Pontifex Maximus himself said so—but instead he was commended by the people of Roma and made a commander of the legions. Now disaster has overwhelmed us, and it falls to me to honor the gods and my ancestors by performing this ancient ritual. If . . ." Again he drew a deep breath. "If I should die in attempting to do so, perhaps my blood will assuage the gods. Perhaps they will accept my sacrifice in place of my cousin Quintus, and return their favor to Roma."

Pinaria was so moved that for a long moment she could not speak. She fought back tears, and finally said, "If the Virgo Maxima were here, she would bless you—but the Virgo Maxima is gone, and so are the other

Vestals. I'm the only one left in Roma, so I will bless you, Gaius Fabius Dorso. Go and make the sacrifice—and come back safely!"

Dorso bowed his head to her, then turned and strode toward the barricade, carrying the vessels of wine and oil.

Pennatus lingered behind for a moment. He gave Pinaria an odd look; his eyes seemed to smile even though his lips did not. He looked down at the vessels of millet and salt, frowned and furrowed his brow, then puffed out his cheeks and seemed to reach a decision. "Well, then! I told him I would go with him, and so I shall."

"Come back safely, Pennatus!" she whispered. She very nearly touched his arm, as she had touched the arm of Dorso, but at the last moment she drew back her hand. It would hardly be pleasing to the goddess, for a Vestal to touch a slave.

Pennatus squared his shoulders and took a deep breath. "Of course I'll come back. Will your gods not protect me? If the Gauls menace us, I shall simply sprout wings and come flying back to you!"

With Dorso leading and Pennatus walking behind him, the two men strode across the Capitoline. Word of Dorso's intentions had spread, and a crowd gathered to watch them depart. Soldiers rushed forward to help the two men keep their balance as they climbed over the barricade, holding the ritual vessels aloft. Not a grain of salt or millet or a drop of wine or oil was spilled, and this was seen to be a good omen. The soldiers crowded together along the top of the barricade to watch Dorso and Pennatus descend the winding path.

Heads turned and a hush fell over the spectators as Pinaria climbed up to join the soldiers. They drew aside to make room for the Vestal. She gazed at the receding procession of two and began to move her lips without making a sound. Thinking to join her in prayer, men muttered pleas to the god Quirinus for the safekeeping of his worshippers, but the words shaped by Pinaria's lips were not addressed to any god.

"Come back!" she begged silently. "Come back to me, Pennatus!"

The hours passed slowly. The afternoon sun suffused the smoky sky with a lurid glow, and began to descend toward the distant hills beyond the Tiber.

On the barricade, sharp-eyed lookouts kept a watch on the Quirinal, but saw nothing to indicate the fate of Dorso and Pennatus.

Pinaria paced back and forth across the open spaces of the Capitoline. Reflexively, she muttered prayers to Vesta, but in her heart she felt she was speaking to empty air. The hearthfire of the goddess was gone from Roma and her temple had been desecrated by godless savages. Vesta must be far, far away, thought Pinaria, beyond the reach of even the most devoted Vestal. Even if the goddess was still present, and could hear her, would she not see into Pinaria's heart and know that her prayer was profane? For a Vestal to pray for the safe passage of Dorso was one thing; he was a Roman citizen on a holy mission. But the prayer that came unbidden to Pinaria's lips was not for Dorso, and had nothing to do with the fulfillment of sacred rites. What would the goddess think, to hear one of her virgins plead so desperately for the return of a slave? It was better that the goddess was absent, unable to hear Pinaria's prayer, than that Vesta should hear it and perceive the longing in Pinaria's heart.

She was shaken from her gloomy reverie by a shout from one of the lookouts.

"There! At the foot of the Capitoline! I see them! Dorso and the slave—and Gauls, hundreds of Gauls . . ."

The words gave Pinaria a momentary flash of hope, then plunged her into despair. She imagined Dorso and Pennatus running at top speed, pursued by warriors; she pictured their severed heads borne aloft on stakes by taunting Gauls. She ran to the barricade, climbed to the top, and peered down the steep hillside.

"There!" said the lookout. "On the path, coming toward us."

What she saw was the last thing she expected. Walking proudly erect, bearing in their upturned hands the now empty sacrificial vessels, Dorso and Pennatus were ascending the winding path at a steady, unhurried pace. A huge crowd of Gauls followed them, bearing swords and spears but keeping at a distance and doing nothing to impede their progress.

The officer in charge of the barricade shook his head. "These Gauls and their cruel games! They'll wait until Dorso is almost to the barricade, then strike him down while we watch. Vile creatures! We should fire upon them now, while Dorso still has a chance to break and run. Archers! Raise your bows!"

"No!" cried Pinaria. "Can't you see their faces? It's just as Dorso predicted. The Gauls are in awe of him. See how they hang back? See how they whisper among themselves and jostle one another, trying to get a better look at him? He's put a kind of spell on them. If you fire on them, you'll break the spell. Lower your bows! Do nothing! Say nothing!"

The men on the barricade unnotched their arrows and fell silent.

Following the winding path, Dorso and Pennatus drew closer and closer. The Gauls followed doggedly behind them. Pinaria's heart pounded in her chest. The wait was excruciating. Why did they walk so slowly? She caught a glimpse of Dorso's face as he rounded the final bend; she saw the serene expression of a man at peace with himself and his fate, ready to live or die, as the gods saw fit. Then she saw Pennatus. Her heart leaped as his eyes met hers. He smiled—and then winked at her!

The two men reached the barricade. Hands stretched down to take the vessels and help them climb up. Dorso clambered atop the barricade and looked over his shoulder. "Stupid Gauls," he muttered. "Archers! Here's your chance to kill a few of those fools. Take aim and fire at once, before they can run!"

Arrows whistled though the air, followed by screams and the chaotic sounds of the Gauls retreating in a sudden panic.

Dorso quickly escorted Pinaria away from the barricade, out of harm's way. "It was your blessing, Vestal, that did the trick," he whispered. "I felt the goddess of the hearth looking over us every step of the way."

"Did you? Did you truly feel Vesta's presence?" Pinaria looked from Dorso to Pennatus.

"Something must have protected us," said Pennatus. "It was amazing! The Gauls were dumbfounded. They fell back on all sides, like grain cut by a scythe. Not one of them dared to approach us. Not one of them even raised his voice."

Dorso and Pennatus looked at each other and spontaneously embraced, laughing like two boys after a great adventure. Pinaria longed to join their embrace. Especially she longed to hold Pennatus and to be held by him, to reassure herself that he still lived and breathed, to feel the warmth of his body, to touch his hairy chest, where the black pendant hung between the firm muscles. Such thoughts made her feel weak and flushed, but she could not control them.

Could it be as Dorso said? Could it be that Vesta had watched over and protected both men, despite Pinaria's impure feelings? Or had Pennatus survived only because—or precisely because—the goddess was absent, no longer present to punish an erring Vestal and the object of her desire?

Either Vesta knew of Pinaria's passion for the slave, and approved of it—mad thought!—or Vesta was gone, perhaps forever, and no longer held sway over her devoted virgin—another mad thought! In either case, Pinaria knew, in a blinding flash, that no impediment remained to hold her feelings in check. The realization dazzled her. The ground gave way beneath her and the sky cracked open.

She looked at Pennatus. He looked back at her. Their eyes spoke a secret language. She knew he felt the same.

In that moment, Pinaria was lost, and she knew it. She burst into tears. Those who had gathered to welcome Dorso assumed they were tears of joy and relief, and men bowed their heads at the sight of a sacred virgin so deeply moved by the evidence of the gods' continuing favor for the people of Roma.

There was little privacy to be had among the defenders atop the Capitoline, but such privacy as could be arranged was given to the Vestal who dwelled among them. While others slept in the open, or crowded together inside the temples and public buildings, a small chamber in the foundations of the Temple of Jupiter was given to Pinaria for her sole use.

The entrance to Pinaria's room was at the back of the temple, out of sight. It was Pennatus who suggested to Dorso that it would be proper to install a simple lock on the inside of the door, so that no one could possibly walk in on the Vestal unannounced or by accident. As Pennatus knew how to fashion such a lock, he was given the job of making it himself. "What a clever fellow you are!" remarked Dorso, after the lock was installed.

One night, there came a soft knocking on Pinaria's door.

The hour was late, but Pinaria was not asleep. She rose from her bed and went to the door at once. She did not bother to ask who was knocking.

She opened the door and saw his head and shoulders silhouetted by moonlight. Her first thought was that he was mad to come to her on a night when the moon was so bright and might cast such a glaring light on his movements. What if he had been observed?

In the next instant he was inside, shutting the door behind him. Then his arms were around her and his body was pressed against hers. It was Pinaria who initiated the kiss, pressing her mouth to his. She had never kissed a man before. It seemed to her that they drew the same breath and shared the same heartbeat.

She was not accustomed to being naked, even among the other Vestals, but that was the way he wanted her. She allowed him to disrobe her, then helped him to take off his own tunic; she wanted no pretense that anything was being done solely at his behest, or against her will. Whatever might happen, it would not occur because she merely allowed it, but because she made it happen.

She knew a little about the basic act of sex, but she could not have imagined the sensations that accompanied it. The touch of his flesh against her own was thrilling, but nothing compared to the feeling when a part of his body actually entered her own and began to move inside her. There was a sharp pain at first, but it seemed a small thing to bear, compared to the pleasure that followed. The rhythm of the act was like a complicated dance, or a song of unearthly beauty, sometimes slow and languid, sometimes rushed and breathless. His rhythm inspired her to find a rhythm inside herself; she struggled to match his movements, cried out in frustration at the sudden awkwardness of it, and then, laughing breathlessly, clutching his hips, she demanded that his rhythm match her own. He submitted, resisted, submitted again. They seemed to be in competition for a while, and then almost at odds, and then, without warning, in perfect, ecstatic harmony.

They reached the pinnacle in the same instant. She felt him shudder and convulse inside her, and at the same time a wave of exquisite pleasure washed over her entire body.

The thing was done. There could be no turning back.

⁂

The occupation of the Gauls continued throughout the hot summer and into the autumn. Cooler days brought some relief to the defenders atop the

Capitoline, but their hunger increased. Rations were reduced to a handful of bread and a cup of wine a day.

House by house, the Gauls continued to pillage and burn the city below, poisoning the air with smoke. After the failure of their initial attempts, the Gauls stopped laying siege to the Capitoline, but sentries still kept constant watch around the perimeter.

On an autumn night when the air was cool but acrid with smoke, Pinaria and Pennatus lay naked upon her bed. A shaft of moonlight from a high, small window illuminated their sweat-glazed bodies. The hour was midnight, but neither of the lovers slept; there was still too much pleasure to be had from each other's bodies to think of sleep.

Pinaria had been delighted but not surprised to discover that Pennatus was such an insatiable lover. What had surprised her was the depth of her own craving, which was as great as his, if not greater. The devotion she had once given to tending the sacred hearthfire she now gave to the tending the fire that flared up inside them each time their bodies met. When she joined with Pennatus, it seemed to her that she was taken to a place beyond the mortal world, to a mystical realm such as that where the gods must dwell. She worshiped his body, the vehicle that transported her to that divine place; she adored his sex, that part of him, so potent yet so exposed and vulnerable, which he eagerly placed into her safekeeping. Such thoughts were blasphemous, surely; but the gods were gone, and the Vestal was no longer a virgin, and a slave had become her master. The world was a mad, broken place, but Pinaria had never before felt so alive and complete.

Through the little window, very faintly, they heard the cry of "All clear!" from the nearest sentry. The cry was echoed from various points around the perimeter of the barricades and cliffs. In the silence that followed, a goose let out a single, plaintive honk. To save them from the Gauls, the sacred geese of Juno had been brought from the goddess's new temple on the Aventine and were being kept in an enclosure beside the Temple of Jupiter.

"We shall have to eat them soon," said Pennatus.

"The geese? They're sacred to Juno," said Pinaria.

"But what good are geese to a goddess if all her worshipers die of starvation?"

"No one would dare to touch them."

"Yet I've noticed that their ration of grain has been cut. Those geese are getting awfully skinny. Soon there'll be no meat on them worth eating. Better to eat them now, while they can still give us some sustenance."

"People would sooner eat the dogs!"

"But the dogs at least serve a function. They keep vigil at night, along with the sentries. My old master was especially fond of goose liver. He said it was quite delicious."

"Pennatus, what terrible things you say!"

He snuggled close. "Like the things I whisper in your ear when I'm inside you?"

She shivered, and clutched his sex, which was full and firm in her hand. They had finished only moments ago, and already he was stiff again. He cupped her breast and kissed her nipple. A wave of sheer pleasure rippled through her.

She sighed. "Long before anyone considers eating the sacred geese, Camillus will come."

This was the hope on everyone's lips. Only a few days earlier, an intrepid soldier from the outside, Pontius Cominius, had managed to pass through the Gaul's defenses and reach the defenders on the Capitoline. He had filled his tunic with bits of cork and floated down the Tiber, and then, by night, stole through the streets and scaled the Capitoline at a point so craggy and steep that the Gauls kept no watch on it. The Roman sentry who witnessed his arrival had been amazed to see a human scrambling like a spider up the sheer rock face, and even more amazed when the man called out to him in Latin. Pontius Cominius brought word that the Roman forces were gradually regrouping under the leadership of the exiled Camillus, who requested that the handful of senators trapped atop the Capitoline should formally invest him with the powers of a dictator. The senators had sent Pontius Cominius back to Camillus with a pledge of their full support and promises to pray for his victory. Had the messenger passed safely through the Gallic forces to return to Camillus? No one knew, but the news from outside had brought fresh hope to the Capitoline. Camillus was on the march and might arrive any day. Camillus, the conqueror of Veii, would rescue them and drive the Gauls from Roma!

Pennatus rolled away from her, onto his back. His member became noticeably more pliant in her hand. "And then what? You shall go back to being a Vestal, and I shall go back to being a slave."

The sweat turned cold on Pinaria's body. She released his sex and pulled the coverlet over her breasts. The future that Pennatus suggested—a resumption of the way things had been before the Gauls came—was far less horrible than the one she envisioned. Pinaria knew all too well what was done to a Vestal found guilty of breaking her vow, and what was done to the Vestal's lover.

"Who can say what the future will bring?" she whispered. "Who knew that Camillus would be exiled, or that Brennus and the Gauls would come and change everything? Who knew that you would become my lover—who could imagine such a thing! Who knew that I . . ."

The sudden break in her voice caused him to furrow his brow. "Go on, Pinaria. What were you about to say?"

She drew a sharp breath. "I may be mistaken. It may be the strain of the siege that caused the interruption. I think that this happens to women sometimes—when there's a terrible crisis, or if they go hungry . . ."

"Pinaria, what are you saying?"

"The full moon has come and gone, and come again, and yet . . . no blood flowed from inside me. I don't know much about such things—but even I know what it means when a woman's menses is interrupted!"

He rose onto his elbows and stared at her. Shadows hid his face. "Are you with child?"

"I don't know, not for certain. As I said, perhaps there's another explanation . . ."

He moved closer. The moonlight revealed his awestruck expression. "But this is wonderful! Terrible and wonderful, at the same time!"

Pinaria shivered and hugged herself. "Sooner or later, it will begin to show. What will I do then?"

"Perhaps no one will notice."

"Not notice? I shall grow fatter while everyone else grows thinner!"

"You can loosen your robes. You can say that you need seclusion. I'll wait on you, and not let anyone else approach. And maybe Camillus will come soon, and set us free, and we can leave the Capitoline—"

"And go where? I could never hide my condition among the others in the House of the Vestals."

"Then we shall go into hiding. Or run away. We'll flee up to Gaul and live among godless savages! I don't know what we'll do, Pinaria, but we'll think of something. It's just as you said, no one can know what the future will bring."

He slipped beneath the coverlet and lay next to her. His hand sought hers and held it tightly. Together, they stared into the dark corners of the room. "I know you're afraid," he said. "Afraid of what the others will do to us if they find out. But . . . is it more than that?"

"What do you mean?"

"Are you unhappy because . . . because it's the child of a slave inside you?"

"Pennatus! I never expected to carry any man's child. I don't know what I'm feeling. I never said I was unhappy—"

"Because . . . because there's something about me that you don't know. It might make a difference."

She turned to face him. She touched his cheek and looked into his eyes, which reflected the pale moonlight. "I know that you're very brave, Pennatus. And very funny. And wicked sometimes—the things you say! I know that you're not like anyone else I've ever met, and that I love you. And I know that you love me. Such a precious thing, this love between us! Sometimes I think it must be a gift from the goddess, even though I know that's impossible. I could never regret that you've given me a child, Pennatus. I only wish—"

"I wish things were different, too. I wish that you weren't a Vestal. I wish that I wasn't born a slave! If it weren't for the bitterness of fate, I might have been as high-born as you, Pinaria. I have the blood of patricians in me."

"What do you mean?"

"This talisman I wear—it's more than it appears to be. And so am I!" He held up the image of Fascinus. The black amulet gleamed dully in the moonlight. "It's not made of lead, Pinaria. It's only been dipped in lead, to hide what's beneath, so that no master would bother to take it. If you scratch through the lead, you can see the pure yellow gleam underneath. It's made of gold, Pinaria. It's an heirloom. It's very ancient, older than

Roma itself—older than all the gods and goddesses of Roma! Fascinus was here first, even before Jupiter."

She shook her head. "More blasphemy, Pennatus? This isn't funny."

"It's neither blasphemy nor a joke. It's the truth, Pinaria. Before she died, my mother told me where I came from and who I really am. I was born a slave, yes, and so was she, but her father was the son of Titus Potitius, a Roman of the most ancient patrician blood, and Icilia, the sister of Lucius Icilius, who was a tribune of the plebs. The son of Titus Potitius and Icilia was illegitimate, and he was made a slave at birth because of the spite of his uncle. But even as a slave, he wore the talisman of the Potitii around his neck, and Titus Potitius himself, in secret, told him the tale of his birth. That slave passed the talisman on to his daughter, my mother. She was born a slave in the household of Icilius, but was later sold to my master, in whose house I was born. Before she died, she passed the talisman to me. It represents the god Fascinus, the most ancient deity worshipped by mortals in Roma. Fascinus was known even before Hercules and Jupiter, and long before the gods who came to us by way of the Greeks."

Pinaria was silent for a long time. "You never told me this before."

"It's my deepest secret, Pinaria."

"You scoff at the gods."

"I believe in Fascinus!"

"You mock the freeborn. You laugh at the vanity of patricians."

"I *am* a patrician—by blood if not by birth! Titus Potitius was my great-grandfather. Don't you see, Pinaria, the child inside you isn't the offspring of a nobody, a slave who came from nowhere, who has no ancestors worthy of remembrance. The child inside you carries the blood of the first settlers of Roma, from both his mother *and* his father. Whatever others may say, and whatever the law may call me, you need not be ashamed of the child. You can be proud, even if you must be proud in secret!"

"Pennatus! I feel no shame for what we've done, or what's resulted from it. Perhaps it's not even sinful. If Vesta is truly gone, and all the gods have left their temples here on the Capitoline, it may be that your god Fascinus holds sway in Roma, all alone, as he once did long ago, and you and I are doing his bidding, and everything is proper. Who can say, in a world where everything can change in the blink of an eye? No, Pennatus, I'm not ashamed. But I am fearful, for you, and for me, and for the child." She shook her head. "I didn't mean to tell you. Some impulse came over me and made me speak. I had thought to keep it to myself, until I was sure, or else . . ."

She bit her tongue and said no more. Why tell Pennatus where her thoughts had led whenever she considered the child that might be growing inside her? There were ways to rid a woman's womb of an unwanted baby. Pinaria had a vague notion that there were potions that could be drunk, some of them dangerously poisonous, or that a slender wand, perhaps made of supple willow, might be inserted into her body to bring about the desired expulsion. But Pinaria had no sure knowledge of such matters, and there was no one she could ask for advice or assistance, and there was no way to obtain such a potion. There was not a single willow tree on the Capitoline! And now that she had told Pennatus about the child, and he had responded by sharing his deepest secret with her, and had shown an almost fierce pride in the act of giving her a child . . .

She shook her head. The voice of the holy Vestal that still dwelled inside her whispered, *What a thing, that a slave should be proud of his offspring! What a world, where a Vestal could delude herself into thinking that her pregnancy might please a god!*

Suddenly, in the quiet stillness of the night, one of Juno's sacred geese let out a loud, blaring honk. The unexpected noise broke the tension between them. Pennatus laughed. Pinaria managed a crooked smile.

The goose honked again, and then again.

"If that keeps up, a certain goose is likely to get plucked, sacred to Juno or not," muttered Pennatus. He brought his lips to hers. They kissed. He moved to embrace her, then drew back. The single goose had been joined by others making the same abrupt, braying racket. "A good thing we're not trying to sleep!"

"It's the sentry's fault, waking them up by calling the all-clear," said Pinaria.

"But that was a long time ago. Long enough for the geese to fall asleep again." Pennatus frowned. "Maybe long enough for the sentry to fall asleep . . ."

The honking of the geese continued.

"Stay here," whispered Pennatus. "Lock the door after I leave. There'll be others up, awakened by the geese. I may not be able to return tonight without being seen. Kiss me, Pinaria!"

Pennatus tore himself from her arms, reached for his sword—Dorso had insisted on arming him, despite his status—and slipped out the door. He waited until he heard her drop the lock into place, then hurried toward the sentry post beyond the goose pen.

The rocky face of the Capitoline was very steep at that point—indeed, it was the very place where Pontius Cominius had made his impossible ascent. But of course, the ascent of Pontius Cominius had not been impossible; if he could do it, so could others. On a moonlit night, might a company of Gauls be able to find the footholds and handholds by which Pontius Cominius had reached the top of the Capitoline?

It seemed impossible. And surely, in the stillness of the night, a sentry would hear anyone making such an ascent, and peer over the side to see them long before they reached the top. Unless . . .

The geese continued to honk.

Pennatus saw the sentry, standing at his post at the cliff's edge—then realized that the figure dimly lit by the moon was not the sentry, but a Gaul! While Pennatus watched, two other Gauls appeared, clambering over the ledge and standing upright.

His blood froze. He tightened his grip on the sword. He had never actually used such a weapon, except in practice with Dorso. He gripped the image of Fascinus and did something he had never done before: He whispered a prayer for courage and strength.

"Out of my way, slave!" An armor-clad figure knocked him aside and rushed past him. Pennatus recognized Marcus Manlius, a friend of Dorso's and a former consul. The grizzled veteran rushed headlong toward the Gauls. Giving a great shout, he struck the foremost with his shield. The man staggered back and fell screaming from the cliff, taking the other two with him.

More Gauls scrambled over the edge. Manlius struck with his shield and stabbed with his sword. Pennatus gave a cry and ran to join him.

His sword struck metal with a deafening clang. He lunged again and struck flesh. The sickening impact seemed to travel into his arm and all through his body. Pennatus had scarcely ever caused another man to bleed, much less killed a man. Under moonlight, the blood on the paving stones was glistening and black.

He heard a shout, turned, and saw Dorso. The warrior slashed his sword against the exposed neck of a Gaul with such force that he nearly decapitated the man. A fountain of blood erupted from the wound. The look on Dorso's face was ferocious and frightening, filled with utter hatred. The Gauls had destroyed his city, driven away his gods, ruined his world. Now, at last, Dorso had a chance to bring death and suffering on at least a few of the Gauls in return.

What had the Gauls done to Pennatus? Their invasion had brought him unexpected freedom, a friendship he could never have known before, and a love he would never have dared to imagine. He feared the Gauls, but he could never hate them as Dorso did. Then he thought of Pinaria. If the Capitoline was taken, all would be lost. Pinaria, the most exquisite and perfect thing in all the world—what might they do to Pinaria?

Miraculously, the Gaul who had been struck by Dorso was still alive, staggering this way and that. With a great cry, Pennatus ran toward him, raised his blade, and finished what Dorso had started. The Gaul's head went flying through space. It disappeared beyond the precipice, where yet more Gauls were climbing over the edge.

The geese cackled madly. Men shouted and screamed. Suddenly there were many more Gauls and just as many Romans. What started as a skirmish abruptly became a battle, with clanging swords all around and blood everywhere. The moonlit battle seemed incredibly intense and yet utterly unreal to Pennatus, like a strange dream; yet it was no stranger—and no more dangerous—than the waking dream in which Pennatus had become the secret lover of a fallen Vestal.

✦

The Gauls were repulsed. For being the first to rush to the Romans' defense, Marcus Manlius was declared a hero, and rewarded with extra rations of bread and wine. A full ration of grain was also restored to the sacred geese, whose honking had alerted the defenders.

As for the sentries on duty that night, the military commanders at first declared that all would be put to death for negligence. So would the dogs who kept vigil with them. It was presumed they had all fallen asleep at their posts, including the dogs, since not a single dog barked. The geese had proven to be better sentinels!

Dorso argued against the mass punishment, pointing out that the Romans could ill afford to lose so many men, and among the common soldiers there was a great outcry. It was decided that only the sentry responsible for the area where the assault took place would be punished.

The man denied that he had fallen asleep. In the stillness of the night, he said, he had heard a man and a woman talking. Distracted and bored, he wandered from his post, toward the Temple of Jupiter, trying to figure out where the voices came from. His excuse gained him no sympathy. He was hurled to his death from the ledge where the Gauls had staged their attack. As a token punishment, a single guard dog was also thrown from the cliff.

The Romans increased their vigilance. So did the Gauls, who were determined that no more messengers should reach the Capitoline from the outside world.

❋

Throughout the winter, the occupation and the siege continued. Rain brought fresh drinking water to the Romans, but food grew scarcer.

"If only it would rain fish," said Pennatus one day, watching a downpour from beneath the pediment of the Temple of Jupiter.

"Or honey cakes!" said Dorso.

"Or bits of dried beef!" said Marcus Manlius, who had a fondness for military rations.

The situation atop the Capitoline grew more and more desperate, but so did the circumstances of the Gauls. Having never dwelled in a city, they understood nothing about sanitation and the disposal of their own wastes. They made a pigsty of Roma, and a plague broke out among them. So many died so quickly that the survivors gave up on burying the bodies separately, but instead piled the corpses in heaps and set fire to them.

Once again, as earlier in the siege, flames and columns of smoke surrounded the Capitoline. The sight of the flaming pyres was ghastly. The smoke and the stench from the burning bodies was stifling. As Pennatus wryly commented to Dorso, "These Gauls have a madness for burning. Having torched all the houses, now they set fire to each other!"

The Gauls also grew hungry. Early in the siege, they carelessly burned several warehouses full of grain. They sorely missed that grain now. Though the Romans on the Capitoline could not know it, the forces of Camillus had taken control of much of the countryside, and the Gauls could no longer go raiding at will to replenish their stores. The city which they had claimed as a prize was becoming a trap and a tomb.

Publicly, Pinaria joined in the daily prayers that Camillus would soon arrive and rescue them. Privately, she lived in constant fear. She did everything she could to hide the visible evidence of her pregnancy. She had so far succeeded, perhaps because the child growing inside her was small and undernourished. But what would happen when she gave birth? Even if she could hide in her room and deliver the child in secret, how could she conceal a crying baby? Could she bear to kill the child immediately after it was born? Babies were allowed to die every day, especially if they were imperfect, but even the most unfeeling mother did not kill an unwanted baby with her own hands; it was taken from her and left in an open place to die from exposure to the elements or wild beasts. The quickest and easiest way to dispose of the child would be to throw it from the Capitoline, but even that might prove impossible, because such a close watch was kept at all points of the perimeter. Would Pennatus do it, if she asked him? What a terrible thing, to ask a father to murder his own child!

And yet, if the child were born and allowed to live, it would surely be discovered—the proof of their crime—and they would all three be put to death. Many times, Pinaria woke from nightmares in which she saw Pennatus beaten to death, and then was sealed in a chamber underground, without light or air. The baby was buried along with her, and in the utter darkness of the crypt its wailing was the last sound she could hear.

In dark moments, she allowed herself to imagine that the baby would be born dead. That would end the fear and dread—but what a thing for a mother to wish for, to give birth to a dead child! Perhaps it would be better for Pinaria to jump from the precipice herself, and to do so soon, before the child inside her grew any larger. Let the Gauls find her broken body and burn it on a pyre. Men would honor her memory, then; they would say she had offered herself, a pure Vestal, as a sacrifice to the gods. The unborn child would die with her, and Pennatus's guilt would never be known. Slave or not, such a clever fellow surely had a life worth living ahead of him. He would soon forget her and the child that had resulted from their crime. It would be as if Pinaria had never lived . . .

The one outcome that she would not allow herself to imagine—because it was impossible, and thus too painful—was that the baby would be born healthy and whole, and that she would be able to look upon its face, and proudly show it off, and cherish it with all the devotion and affection of any normal mother. Such a thing could never happen.

These desperate thoughts consumed her. She grew distant from Pennatus. They ceased to make love. The act that had given her such delight she now saw to be a treacherous thing, a trap into which she had foolishly fallen. For a while, they still met in secret, and instead of making love, they conversed—but what was there to talk about except the suffering inflicted on them by the siege, and the even greater suffering that awaited them? Eventually she forbade Pennatus to come to her private chamber again, saying she did so for his own safety, when in fact she simply could not bear to be alone with him.

She grew closer to Dorso, who treated her always with deference and respect. Pennatus, as Dorso's friend, was often present in their company, but he knew better than to treat her with too much familiarity. He hid his pain and confusion by making wry comments and bitter jokes, and no one noticed that his behavior was any different than before. People did notice a change in Pinaria, and commented on it. Men called her the melancholy Vestal, but they thought her suffering was for their sake and they honored her sadness as a sign of her piety.

For seven months the Gauls occupied Roma, from midsummer to midwinter. It was on the Ides of Februarius that Pinaria, crossing the Capitoline, her head clouded by dark thoughts, was given the news by Dorso.

He ran up to her. He said something. She was so distracted that she did not hear his words, but from his animated expression she realized that something of great importance had happened. From the corner of her eye she perceived movement. She looked around and saw that all of the Capitoline was in a great commotion. People hurried this way and that, gripped one another, spoke in whispers and shouts, laughed, wept.

"What's happening, Dorso?"

"A messenger has come—a Roman! The Gauls allowed him to pass. He came right up the pathway."

"A messenger? Who sent him?"

"Camillus, of course! Come, let's hear what the man has to say." He led her to the Temple of Jupiter, where a soldier, dressed in armor but carrying no weapons, stood on the top step to address the crowd. People shuffled aside to allow Pinaria to move to the front of the crowd.

Men were shouting questions at the messenger, who raised his hand. "Be patient!" he said. "Wait until everyone has gathered. Otherwise, I shall have to repeat myself a hundred times."

"But look here!" shouted Marcus Manlius. "Gaius Fabius Dorso has arrived with the melancholy Vestal. That's everyone who counts! Say what you have to say!"

People in the crowd laughed. The mood was cheerful, for everyone could see by the messenger's face that he came with good news.

"Very well. Over the last few months, our armies have regrouped under the leadership of the dictator Marcus Furius Camillus—"

There was a great cheer.

"—who has met with the Gauls in a number of minor engagements. We cannot claim to have defeated the enemy, but we have stung them repeatedly, and the Gauls have had enough. They're ready to leave Roma."

The cheer was deafening. The messenger motioned for quiet.

"But the Gauls will not leave without a ransom."

"A ransom?" shouted Manlius. "Haven't they looted everything that was of any value in Roma?"

"They have, but they demand still more. There is to be a payment of jewels and precious metals. Camillus has gathered everything he can from the Romans in exile, and appealed to our friends for contributions—"

"The people of Clusium should pay the ransom!" shouted Manlius. "Did we not sacrifice ourselves to save them from being sacked by the Gauls?"

"The Clusians have contributed, very generously, and so have many others," said the messenger, "but there is still not enough. Camillus looks to you here on the Capitoline, who never left Roma, to help make up the final measure of the ransom."

There were shouts of protest. "Us?" said Manlius. "For months we've eaten fly-blown flour and drunk nothing but rainwater! These people have nothing left to give!"

"Are you sure? Perhaps some of you know where treasure was buried, to hide it from the Gauls. Perhaps some of the women still have a few pieces of jewelry. All the Roman women in exile have already contributed every piece of jewelry they possessed."

"This is wrong!" shouted Manlius. "Our women should not be stripped of every ornament, simply to satisfy the greed of Brennus."

"There is no other way," said the messenger. "The Gauls must be paid. Once they leave, the city will be ours again, and we can begin to rebuild."

Dorso looked over his shoulder at Pennatus and grinned. "Perhaps you should donate that little talisman you wear so proudly."

Pennatus gripped the image of Fascinus. He scowled and clutched it so hard that his knuckles grew pale.

Dorso laughed. "Relax, Pennatus! I was only joking. Not even a Gaul would want that worthless piece of lead!"

The ransom was paid in the Forum.

Brennus insisted on a formal ceremony at which Camillus himself was present. Those on the Capitoline watched the transaction with mingled dismay and relief. The Gauls produced a huge set of scales, large enough to weigh a whole ox. Lead weights were placed on one tray. The Roman emissaries piled the ransom onto the other. The treasure of ingots, coins, and jewels rose higher and higher, until at last the lead weights began to rise.

The two sides of the scale reached equilibrium. A sigh passed through the crowd watching from the Capitoline, to see such a fortune paid to recover the city that was theirs by birthright.

Down in the Forum, Brennus strutted before the scales and laughed. "Not quite enough!" he shouted.

Camillus looked at him darkly. "What are you saying? The scales are balanced."

"I forgot to include *this*. You want me to put it aside, do you not?" Brennus drew his sword and tossed it atop the lead weights.

Groans of anger and disgust rose from the Roman delegation. Some of the officers reached for their swords, but Camillus held up his hand to stay them. "We have yet a little more treasure in reserve. Place it on the scales."

More was added to the ransom, until the two sides were balanced again. Brennus let out a roar of triumph and clapped his hands. The Gauls broke into raucous cheering and laughter. Even from the Capitoline, the watchers could see Camillus's face turn dark red from fury and chagrin.

Pinaria, watching with the rest, suddenly felt the presence of Pennatus beside her. His hand sought hers. She submitted to linking her fingers with his. "Whatever may happen, Pinaria, I love you!" he whispered.

"And I . . ." She could not bring herself to say the words. She let out a gasp, drew back her hand, and placed it on her belly. The baby was kicking inside her. She sensed that the time was drawing very near.

Like a ruinous floodtide receding, the Gauls withdrew from Roma. The process took several days; there were a great many of them, and they were not in a hurry. They continued to rummage for loot and set fires until the final hour of their occupation.

The Romans on the Capitoline, despite their impatience, waited until the last Gaul had departed before they began to climb over the barricades and descend the winding path. Elated to be free at last, but horrified at the wreckage of their beloved city, they dispersed across the Seven Hills, each seeking a remnant of home, and awaited the return of Camillus and the exiles.

Dorso, with Pennatus at his side, accompanied Pinaria to the doorway of the House of the Vestals. The structure appeared to be intact, though the doors had been broken open and hung crookedly from their hinges.

Trembling, Pinaria stepped inside. Dorso moved to follow her, but Pinaria shook her head. "No, stay back. What I must do here, I must do alone."

"But we can't be sure it's safe. I can't leave you, Vestal."

"Of course you can! Do you think the goddess has protected me this long, only to allow some misfortune to befall me in the House of the Vestals? Go, Dorso. Leave me, so that I can set about purifying the house before the other Vestals return. Aren't you eager to see what's become of your own house?"

Dorso frowned. "And you, Pennatus? Where will you go?"

He shrugged. "Back to my old master's house, I suppose—if there's anything left of it."

"Very well, then," said Dorso. The three parted company.

Only moments after Pinaria crossed the threshold, her water broke, and then the pains began. Staggering, she made her way to her bedchamber. The room was filthy, the bed disheveled; a Gaul had slept there in her absence. She felt a wave of revulsion, but had no other choice than to collapse onto the bed.

A little later, she opened her eyes. Pennatus stood over her. In her delirium, she thought he was an image sent by Vesta to taunt her with her guilt, but then Pennatus smiled, and she knew he was real. He took the cord from his neck and placed it over her head.

"Fascinus protects women in childbirth," he whispered. "Don't worry, Pinaria! I'll stay with you."

"But what do you know about childbirth?"

He grinned. "What do I *not* know? When I was small, I watched slave girls give birth to my master's bastards. When I grew older, I carried and fetched for the midwives. I know what to do, Pinaria. You'll be safe with me, and so will the baby."

"Pennatus, Pennatus! Will you never cease to amaze me?"

"Never! I love you, Pinaria."

"That amazes me most of all."

⁂

It was an early birth and the baby was small, but nonetheless healthy; he gave a great cry when Pennatus held him up to examine him for defects. For an hour Pinaria held him.

The winter day was short, and shadows were already growing long.

There were voices from the street. The first of the exiles had already entered the city. At any moment, the Vestals might arrive.

"Pennatus, what shall we do with the child?"

"He was born whole and healthy. That means the gods want him to live."

"Do you really think so?"

"*I* want him to live, no matter what the gods intend."

"Blasphemy, Pennatus!" She shook her head and managed a rueful laugh. "How absurd, that I should chide you. I've just given birth to a child, in the House of the Vestals!"

"Will you stay here, Pinaria?"

"There's nowhere else for me to go."

"The baby can't stay here with you."

"No."

"Can you bear to give him up, Pinaria?"

She gazed at the child in her arms. "Where will you take him, Pennatus? What will you do with him?"

"I have a plan."

"You always do! My clever Pennatus . . ."

Gently, he took the child from her. Tears ran down her cheeks. She touched the talisman at her breast. "You must take this as well, for the baby."

Pennatus shook his head. "Fascinus is for you. It averts the evil eye. It will protect you from the scrutiny of the other Vestals."

"No, Pennatus—"

"Fascinus is my gift to you. Let it remind you of me, Pinaria, as it served to remind me of my mother."

"Your mother is dead, Pennatus."

"And so am I, in the world to which you must return. We will never see one another again, Pinaria, at least not like this. We will never again be alone together, never speak words of love. But you will know that our child is alive and well, proof of the love we shared on the Capitoline. I promise you that!"

She closed her eyes and wept. When she opened them again, Pennatus and the baby were gone. The room grew dark. Time passed, and more time, and the room slowly grew light again. From within the house, she heard voices, indistinguishable at first, then growing closer and louder. They were the voices of women, talking with great excitement.

She recognized the voice of the Virgo Maxima, and of Foslia. They called her name aloud: "Pinaria! Pinaria! Are you here?"

The Vestals had returned.

⁜

"Tell me again, where and when you found this infant?" said Dorso, frowning.

"Yesterday, abandoned in the bushes outside the ruins of my old master's house," said Pennatus. "Clearly, the mother had just given birth."

"And who might the mother have been?"

"Not a Gaul, surely. The child is too handsome to be a Gaul, don't you think?"

Dorso scrutinized the baby. "He *is* a good-looking fellow. And too tiny to be a Gaul! The child of a returning Roman, then?"

"My intuition tells me so. No doubt the mother experienced great hardship during the occupation, and when she returned to the city to find that all she knew was burned or in ruins, the prospect of caring for the newborn was simply too much for her. Another harsh legacy of the Gauls, that the women of Roma should be so beset by fear and uncertainty that they abandon their children! And such a beautiful child as this little fellow!"

"You appear to be very fond of this infant, Pennatus."

"There is something very special about him. Can you not sense it? I think it was a sign, that I should have found this child on the very day the Gauls departed and the Romans returned—a pledge from the gods that the city is to be reborn, that its best years lie ahead."

"Words of piety and optimism from *you,* Pennatus?"

"I am a changed man since my months on the Capitoline."

"And you will be a free man, as well, if I have any say in the matter. You accompanied me when I made the sacrifice on the Quirinal. You fought beside us when the Gauls gained the summit and frightened the geese. You've more than earned your freedom, and your master is dead and no longer needs you. I intend to approach his heirs, pay them a reasonable sum, and see that they set you free. What do you say to that, Pennatus?"

"The gods are surely smiling upon me, that I should rescue this child, and receive such a pledge from you, in the space of two days! But . . ."

"What is it, Pennatus? Speak!"

"If you truly wish to reward a humble slave for his service on the Capitoline, I have a different request to make. Not so much for myself—for what am I except a broken thread in the great tapestry woven by of the Fates?—but for the sake of this helpless, innocent child."

Dorso pursed his lips. "Go on."

"What use is freedom to me? On my own, in such a devastated city, a dull fellow like me would probably starve. I would much prefer that you purchase me outright and keep me as your slave. I promise that I shall strive every day to prove my worthiness to be your trusted servant. I shall be honored to be the slave of the bravest descendent of the bravest of all Roman houses, the Fabii. And if someday, after my years of service, you should see fit to manumit me, I will proudly bear a freedman's name that honors my former master: Gaius Fabius Dorso Pennatus."

Dorso was not immune to flattery, even from a slave. "I see your point. I will be glad to honor this request. You shall be the most senior of the slaves in my household, and my trusted friend."

"And also—though I know this is an extraordinary request, still I feel compelled to make it—I ask that you adopt this foundling, and raise him as your own son." Seeing the look of surprise on Dorso's face, Pennatus pressed on. "Is there not an ancient precedent for such an act? Romulus and Remus were foundlings, the flotsam left behind by a great flood; so, too, this child was left behind when the Gauls at last receded. Faustulus adopted the Twins and never had cause to regret it, for the gods meant him to do so, and surely you shall not regret it if you adopt this foundling."

Dorso raised an eyebrow. Why was Pennatus so interested in the child? He claimed to see the newborn as an omen, but seeing omens and bowing to the will of the gods was not in character for Pennatus, unless his captivity on the Capitoline had truly transformed him. Was it not more likely that Pennatus's concern for the newborn sprang from a more personal reason? In his head, Dorso had already done some simple arithmetic. The occupation and siege had lasted seven months; a normal pregnancy lasted about nine months. It was not hard to imagine that Pennatus had enjoyed a dalliance shortly before the arrival of the Gauls, and then, during the occupation, had became separated from his lover—probably a slave girl, but possibly a free woman, perhaps even high-born, for such things did happen. Now Pennatus had descended from the Capitoline to discover that he was the father of a newborn. Whether slave or free, the mother felt obliged to relinquish the child rather than keep it—and now the wily slave sought, by this gambit, to make his own bastard the son of a Fabius!

Dorso felt an impulse to call Pennatus's bluff and demand the truth from him. And yet . . . the gods worked their will in mysterious ways, using doubters and disbelievers and even slaves as their unwitting vessels. Pennatus might think he was getting the better of his new master; but in fact, it might be that the gods were guiding both men to do exactly what the gods desired.

Dorso recalled the long walk from the Capitoline to the Quirinal, with Pennatus following behind him. In retrospect, the mad boldness of the act took his breath away, yet it had proved to be the best thing he had ever done, or probably ever would do. That action had made him a famous man; his name would be spoken and revered long after he died. On that day, Dorso had become immortal—and Pennatus had been there with him, every step of the way, helping him keep up his courage simply by showing no fear. Pennatus had done no less than Dorso, yet he would be forgotten by posterity. Did Dorso not owe a debt to Pennatus—a debt so great that it demanded a repayment as bold as the walk to the Quirinal itself?

Dorso nodded gravely. "Very well, Pennatus. I will adopt your . . . I will adopt the child. He shall be my son." He took the baby in his arms and smiled at the tiny infant, then laughed aloud at the look of wonderment on Pennatus's face. "Did you not expect that I would say yes?"

"I hoped . . . I dreamed . . . I prayed . . ." Pennatus dropped to his knees, clutched Dorso's hand, and kissed it. "May the gods bless you, master!" Reflexively, he reached to clutch the talisman of Fascinus at his breast, but his fingers touched only his own bare flesh.

The scattered exiles returned to Roma. Little by little, order was reestablished in the devastated city. The Senate reassembled. The magistrates resumed their offices.

Almost at once, the Veii Question was raised again. Camillus was determined to settle the matter, once and for all.

A few of the most radical of the tribunes of the plebs argued that the city was so ruined, and its sacred places so polluted by the Gauls, that Roma should be abandoned altogether. They proposed that the entire population should move at once to Veii, where many of the exiles had taken shelter during the occupation and had begun to feel at home. Ignoring all other possibilities, Camillus seized on this argument and decided to frame the debate as an all-or-nothing proposition: Would the citizens completely abandon Roma and move to Veii, or would they pull down every building in Veii for materials to rebuild Roma?

With the Senate united behind him, Camillus came before the people assembled in the Forum. He mounted the speaker's platform to address them.

"Fellow citizens, so painful to me are these controversies stirred up by the tribunes of the plebs, that in all the time I lived in bitter exile my one consolation was that I was far removed from this unending squabbling! To contend with this nonsense, I would never have returned even if you recalled me by a thousand senatorial decrees. But now I have returned, because my city needed me—and now needs me again, to fight an even more desperate battle, for her very existence! Why did we suffer and shed our blood to deliver her from our enemies, if now we mean to desert her? While the Gauls held the city, a small band of brave men held out atop the Capitoline, refusing to abandon Roma. Now the tribunes would do what the Gaul could not—they would force those brave Romans, as well as the rest of us, to leave the city. Is this a victory, to lose the thing dearest to us?

"Above every other concern, the will of the gods must be considered. When we follow divine guidance, all goes well. When we neglect it, the result is disaster! A voice from the heavens announced the coming of the Gauls to Marcus Caedicius—a clear warning to mind ourselves—and yet, soon after, one of our ambassadors to the Gauls flagrantly violated sacred law and took up arms against them. Instead of being chastised by the people, the offender was rewarded. Soon after, the gods punished us by allowing the Gauls to take our beloved Roma.

"But during the occupation, acts of such great piety occurred that the favor of the gods was restored to us. Against impossible odds, Gaius

Fabius Dorso performed a miraculous feat. To honor the divine founder of the city, he left the safety of the Capitoline and walked to the Quirinal, unarmed and oblivious to danger. So overwhelming was the aura of sanctity that shielded him that he returned unscathed! And though the defenders of the Capitoline suffered terribly from hunger, they left the sacred geese of Juno unmolested—an act of piety that resulted in their salvation.

"How lucky we are to possess a city that was founded by Romulus with divine approval. Those who followed filled it with temples and altars, so that gods dwell in every corner of the city. Some fools will say, 'But surely the gods can be worshiped just as well at Veii as here in Roma.' Nonsense! Blasphemy! If the gods wished to live in Veii, they would never have allowed it to be conquered. If they did not wish to dwell in Roma, they would never have allowed us to retake the city. The divine favor of a place is not something you can pack in a trunk and take with you!

"Yes, Roma is in ruins, and for a time we must endure discomfort. But even if we must all live in huts again, what of it? Romulus lived in a hut! Our ancestors were swineherds and refugees, yet they built a city in a few years, out of nothing but forests and swamps. We shall look to their example and rebuild the city better than it was before.

"This disaster of the Gauls is no more than a brief episode. Roma has a great destiny. Her story has only just begun. Have you forgotten how the Capitoline received its name? A human head was exhumed there, which the priests declared to be a mighty omen: In this place would reside one day the head and supreme sovereign power of the world. That day has not yet come—but it will! Abandon Roma, and you abandon your destiny; you consign your descendents to oblivion.

"Look to your hearts, Romans! *This* is your heartland. Let me tell you, from my own experience, nothing is worse than to pine with homesickness. In my exile, I never ceased to dream of these hills and valleys, the winding Tiber, the views from the summits, the endless sky beneath which I was born and raised. Here I belong. Here *you* belong. Here, and nowhere else, now and forever!"

The crowd was deeply moved, but remained undecided. They responded to Camillus's final words with a prolonged, uneasy silence.

Just at that moment, a company of soldiers returning from guard duty arrived at the far end of the Forum. The soldiers scheduled to relieve the company were late. The exasperated commander ordered his men to halt. "No point going elsewhere," he said. "We might as well settle right here."

The acoustics of the Forum were such that his words rang out loud and clear to Camillus's listeners, almost as if they came from the sky. People looked at one another in wonder. There was nervous laughter and cries of amazement.

"It's an omen!" someone shouted, "an omen from the gods! The voice spoke to Marcus Caedicius before this whole affair began. Now the voice speaks to us again! 'We might as well settle right here.'"

"Settle right here!" the people chanted. "Settle right here! Settle right here!"

The crowd broke into an uproar of cheering, laughter, and tears of joy. Camillus, who could see to the far side of the Forum and knew exactly where the voice came from, was acutely chagrinned. For all his eloquence and passion, it was a chance remark from an anonymous soldier that tipped the scales.

Standing in a place of honor, maintaining their composure despite the uproar of the crowd, were the Vestals. The Virgo Maxima stood stiffly upright, allowing herself a faint smile. Foslia, more smitten than ever by Camillus, gazed raptly at the dictator. Her hand sought Pinaria's and squeezed it tightly.

"Oh, Pinaria!" she whispered. "We've been through so much—you, more than any of us. And yet, all shall be well again. Vesta never ceased to watch over us, and now her servant Camillus will guide us back to virtue!"

Pinaria did not answer. The loss of her baby and her parting with Pennatus had plunged her into deep sorrow. The resumption of her day-to-day duties as a Vestal brought her no comfort. Her contemplation of the sacred hearthfire only filled her with doubt. During its hiatus from Roma—so the other Vestals assured her—the fire had never wavered in the least, but burned as steadily as ever. How could that be, when Pinaria had repeatedly broken her vow of chastity? Her transgressions should have extinguished the flame altogether!

What did it mean, that Pinaria had sinned and yet no consequence had followed? Was the goddess oblivious, or forgiving, or did she simply not exist? If a sin had been committed, Pinaria should be dead. If there had been no sin, then she should never have been separated from her baby!

Foslia squeezed her hand and gave her a commiserating smile; poor Pinaria had suffered so much in captivity, it was no wonder that she should weep! When Pinaria bowed her head and clutched her breast, Foslia thought her sister Vestal was suffering a pain in her chest, not knowing of the talisman that was hidden beneath Pinaria's vestments.

373 B.C.

The citizens voted to demolish Veii and to rebuild Roma. In celebration, a temple was built on the spot where Marcus Caedicius had received the divine warning. It was dedicated to a new deity called Aius Locutius, the Announcing Speaker.

Camillus also decreed an annual ceremony to honor the geese for saving the Romans on the Capitoline. A solemn procession would be led by a sacred goose of Juno perched in state upon a coverlet in a litter to be followed by a dog impaled on a stake.

The city was rebuilt in hurried and often haphazard fashion. Neighbors built across each other's property lines. New construction often encroached on the public right-of-way, pinching streets into narrow alleys or blocking them altogether. Disputes over property would continue for generations, as would complaints that sewer lines that originally ran under public streets now ran directly under private houses. For centuries to come, visitors to Roma would remark that the general layout of the city more closely resembled a squatters' settlement than a properly planned city, like those of the Greeks.

The son of Pinaria and Pennatus—who unknowingly carried the patrician bloodlines of both the Pinarii and the Potitii—was duly adopted into the almost equally ancient family of the Fabii. Dorso named the boy Kaeso, and raised him as lovingly as if he had sprung from his own loins. If anything, young Kaeso received greater favor than his siblings, for he was a constant reminder to Dorso of the best days of his own youth. No other time of his life would ever be as special to Dorso as those months of captivity atop the Capitoline, when nothing seemed impossible and every day of survival was a gift from the gods.

Pennatus lived out his life as the loyal slave of Gaius Fabius Dorso. His cleverness and discretion got his master out of many scrapes over the years, often without Dorso ever knowing. Pennatus especially looked after young Kaeso. Friends of the family ascribed Pennatus's special affection for his young charge to the fact that he had discovered and rescued the foundling. To see the two of them walking across the Palatine, Pennatus doting on the boy and the boy gazing up at the slave with complete trust, was a touching sight.

Pinaria remained a Vestal all her life, though she was plagued by doubts that she kept secret and expressed to no one. Not so secretly, she cherished the gift Pennatus had given her, from which she carefully removed the lead, restoring its golden luster, and which she wore openly after Postumia died and Foslia was made Virgo Maxima. When the other Vestals expressed curiosity, she explained the antiquity of Fascinus without revealing its origin.

Foslia was especially intrigued by the protective qualities of Fascinus. As Virgo Maxima she introduced the practice of incorporating Fascinus into triumphal processions. She had a copy made of Pinaria's original and placed it out of sight under the chariot of a victorious general, where it served to avert any evil that might be cast by envious eyes. The placement beneath the chariot of this object, called a fascinum, became a traditional duty of the Vestals from that time forward. Similar amulets made of base metals quickly spread into common use. In time, almost every pregnant women in Roma wore her own fascinum to protect her and her baby from malicious spells. Some had wings, but most did not.

Pinaria had become very fond of Dorso during their captivity on the Capitoline. Afterward, she was careful to keep a respectable distance from him, lest their friendship arouse unsavory suspicions. Nevertheless, at public ceremonies their paths frequently crossed. On those occasions, Pinaria sometimes caught glimpses of Pennatus. She avoided looking into his eyes and never spoke to him.

These occasions also allowed Pinaria to see her son at various stages as he grew up. When Kaeso attained his majority and celebrated his sixteenth

birthday by donning a man's toga, no one, including Kaeso, thought it odd
that Pinaria should be invited to the celebration. Everyone knew that the
Vestal had witnessed his father's famous walk beyond the barricades, and
that his father held her in special esteem.

But young Kaeso was a little surprised when Pinaria asked him to join
her alone in the garden. He was still more surprised at the gift she gave
him. It was a gold chain upon which hung a gleaming golden amulet of the
sort called a fascinum.

Kaeso smiled. With his unruly, straw-colored hair and his bright blue
eyes, he still looked like a child to Pinaria. "But I'm not a baby. And I'm
certainly not a pregnant woman! I'm a man. That's the whole point of this
day!"

"Even so, I want you to have this. I believe that a primal force—a power
older than the gods—accompanied your father and protected him on his
famous walk. That force resides in this very amulet."

"Are you saying that my father wore this when he walked among the
Gauls?"

"No, but it was very close to him, nonetheless. Very close! This is no
common fascinum, of the sort that anyone can buy in the market for a few
coins. This is the first of all such amulets, the original. This is Fascinus, who
dwelled in Roma before any other god, even before Jupiter or Hercules."

Kaeso was a little taken aback. These were odd words, coming from a
Vestal. An image of the masculine generator of life was an odd gift to receive from a sacred virgin. Nonetheless, he obediently put the necklace
over his head. He examined the amulet. Its edges were worn from time. "It
does look very old."

"It's ancient—as old as the divine power it represents."

"But it's too precious! I can't accept it from you."

"You can. You must!" She took his hands and held them tightly. "On
this, your sixteenth birthday, I, the Vestal Pinaria, make a gift of Fascinus
to you, Kaeso Fabius Dorso. I ask you to wear it on special occasions, and
to pass it on, in time, to your own son. Will you do that for me, Kaeso?"

"Of course I will, Vestal. You honor me."

Both heard a slight noise, and turned to see that the slave Pennatus was
watching them from the portico. There was a look on his face such as

Kaeso, who had known the slave all his life, had never seen before, an extraordinary expression of mingled sorrow and joy, fulfillment and regret. Confused, Kaeso looked again at the Vestal, and was astounded to see the very same expression on her face.

Pennatus disappeared within the house. Pinaria released Kaeso's hands and departed in a different direction, leaving him alone in the garden with the amulet she had given him.

Adults were so very mysterious! Kaeso wondered whether he was ready to become one of them, despite the fact that this was his toga day.

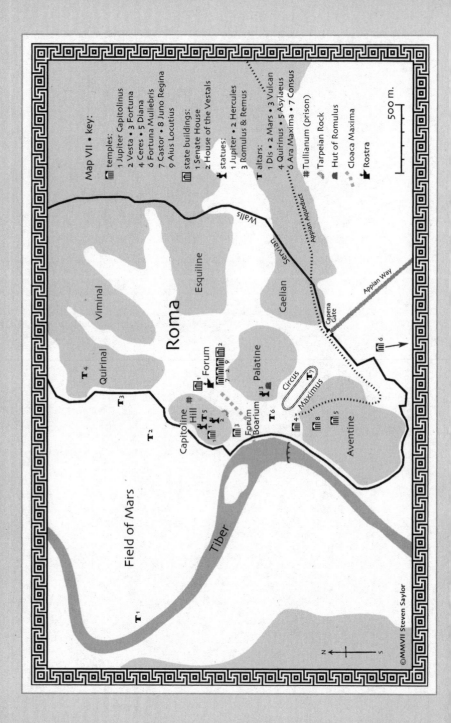

Map VII • key:

🏛 temples:
1 Jupiter Capitolinus
2 Vesta • 3 Fortuna
4 Ceres • 5 Diana
6 Fortuna Muliebris
7 Castor • 8 Juno Regina
9 Aius Locutius

🏛 state buildings:
1 Senate House
2 House of the Vestals

𝍖 statues:
1 Jupiter • 2 Hercules
3 Romulus & Remus

𝍖 altars:
1 Dis • 2 Mars • 3 Vulcan
4 Quirinus • 5 Asylaeus
6 Ara Maxima • 7 Consus

Tullianum (prison)
🗻 Tarpeian Rock
🛖 Hut of Romulus
▨ Cloaca Maxima
𝍖 Rostra

500 m.

Roma

Field of Mars

Tiber

Quirinal

Viminal

Esquiline

Caelian

Servian Walls

Appian Aqueduct

Capena Gate

Appian Way

Forum

Palatine

Capitoline Hill

Forum Boarium

Circus Maximus

Aventine

©MMVII Steven Saylor

VII

THE ARCHITECT OF
HIS OWN FORTUNE

312 B.C.

"So, young man, this is your toga day—and what a splendid day for it! Tell me, how have you celebrated so far?"

Surrounded by the magnificent gardens at the center of his magnificent house, wearing his finest toga for the occasion, Quintus Fabius sat with his arms crossed, wrinkled his craggy brow, and appeared to scowl at his visitor. Young Kaeso had been warned about his eminent cousin's severe expression; Roma's greatest general was not known for smiling. Kaeso tried not to be intimidated. Even so, he had to clear his throat before he could answer.

"Well, cousin Quintus, I rose very early. My father presented me with a family heirloom, a golden fascinum on a golden chain, which he took from his own neck to place over mine. There's a story connected with it; it was given to my grandfather long ago by the famous Vestal Pinaria. Then father presented me with my toga, and helped me put it on. I never imagined it would be so complicated, to make the folds hang correctly! We took a long walk around the Forum, where he introduced me to his friends and colleagues. I was allowed to mount the orator's platform, to see what the Forum looks like from the perspective of the Rostra."

"Of course, when I was boy," said Quintus, interrupting, "the speaker's platform was not yet called the Rostra, because it hadn't yet been deco-rated with all those ships' beaks. Do you know when that happened?"

Kaeso cleared his throat again. "I believe it was during the consulship of Lucius Furius Camillus, the grandson of the great Camillus. The coastal city of Antium was subdued by Roman arms, and the Antiates were made to remove the ramming prows—the so-called rostra, or 'beaks'—from their warships, and send them as tribute to Roma. The beaks were installed as decorations on the orator's platform; hence the platform's name, the Rostra."

Quintus scowled and nodded. "Go on."

"After I stood on the Rostra, we ascended the Capitoline. There we ob-served a Dorso family tradition—retracing the route taken by my great-grandfather, Gaius Fabius Dorso, when he walked from the Capitoline to the Quirinal, defying the Gauls. At the Altar of Quirinus, an augur took the auspices. A single hawk was seen flying from left to right. The augur declared it a favorable omen."

"Favorable, indeed! The hawk will watch after you in battle. And how does it feel, young man, to be wearing a toga?"

"It feels very good, cousin Quintus." In fact, the woolen garment was heavier and hotter than Kaeso had expected.

Quintus nodded. He thought the toga looked rather incongruous on young Kaeso, serving only to emphasize his boyish good looks—his blond curls and blushing, beardless cheeks, his full red lips and bright blue eyes. Aloud, Quintus merely said, "You are a man, now. Congratulations."

"Thank you, cousin Quintus." Kaeso forced a smile. Of all the day's events, this visit might be the most important of all; in honor of his ascent to manhood, he had been invited to dine, alone, with the most eminent of all the Fabii, the leading member of the many branches of the family, the great statesman and general Quintus Fabius. Nervous and tired, but deter-mined to make a good show of himself, Kaeso sat stiffly in his backless chair and met his cousin's steely gaze.

"Well, then, let us retire to the dining room," said Quintus. "You and I shall eat and drink like two men of the world, and talk about your future."

In fact, the discussion was almost entirely about the past. Over various delicacies—pork liver with celery in a wine sauce, tripe stewed with cinna-mon and nutmeg, mutton in fennel cream—Quintus imparted bits of family history. Kaeso had heard almost all of these tales before, but never as told by the great Quintus. Kaeso's great-grandfather had still been alive when Quintus was young; Quintus had met the illustrious Dorso on several occasions, and had heard the tale of the famous walk from the man himself.

Quintus also related the most famous and tragic exploit of the Fabii, their great sacrifice during a war against Veii, when the family raised a whole army from its own ranks, only to see all but one killed in a terrible ambush. "Out of three hundred and seven warriors, that young man alone survived to carry on the family name," said Quintus. "Like a forest of noble trees destroyed by fire, from a single seedling the family regenerated itself—proof of the gods' determination that the Fabii should play a great role in Roma's history."

Quintus was no less shy about trumpeting his own accomplishments. Early in his career, as Master of the Horse to the dictator Lucius Papirius Cursor, he had engaged in battle with the Samnites against the dictator's express orders. Though he won a resounding victory, he had faced death for his disobedience.

"There I stood in the Forum, with my father on his knees before Papirius, pleading for my life. Only a great outcry from the Senate and the people stayed the dictator from ordering his lictors to execute me on the spot with their rods and axes. Though I was stripped of my office, I kept my head—barely! But reversals of fortune can be swift. Just three years later, I became one of the youngest men ever to be elected consul. I soundly defeated the Samnites once again, and was awarded a great triumph. The very next year, the consuls who succeeded me handed the Samnites one of their greatest victories over us. For better or worse, I was not present at the disaster of the Caudine Forks. I suppose you know the shameful story?"

Kaeso quickly lowered the olive that was on its way to his mouth. "Yes, cousin. A Roman army under the consuls Titus Veturius Calvinus and Spurius Postumius, seeking a shortcut, passed through a narrow defile into a gorge that narrowed even more at its far end. When they reached the second narrows, the army found that the passage had been completely blocked with felled trees and other debris. They hastened back to the entrance, only to discover that it, too, had been made impassable by the enemy. These narrow defiles were the Caudine Forks, between which the whole army was helplessly trapped. Days passed. Rather than allow the men to starve, or attempt an impossible escape that would have resulted in a complete massacre, the consuls submitted to the terms of their Samnite captors."

"And what did those terms include?" said Quintus. "Go ahead, young man, tell me what you've been taught."

"The Romans were made to lay down their arms and their armor, and to strip off every garment. Naked, they were made to exit through the defile passing under a yoke, as a symbol of their subjugation to the enemy. Even the consuls were forced to do this. The Samnites jeered and laughed at them, and brandished their swords in the Romans' faces. The soldiers returned home alive but in disgrace. It was a very dark day for Roma."

"The darkest since the coming of the Gauls!" declared Quintus. "But rather than pretend it never happened, we must acknowledge it, and by perceiving the mistake which the consuls made—failing to scout the path ahead of them—we will make sure that such a thing never happens again. Meanwhile, the war with the Samnites continues, but there can be no doubt as to the eventual outcome. Only by conquest can we continue to prosper. Only conquest can make us secure! It is the duty of every Roman to raise his sword and lay down his life, if he must, to fulfill Roma's destiny: the domination of all Italy, and after that, expansion to the north, where we shall one day revenge ourselves upon the Gauls and make sure they never menace us again. Will you do your duty to Roma, young man?"

Kaeso took a deep breath. "I should very much like to kill a few Samnites, if I'm able. And perhaps a few Gauls, as well."

For the first time, Quintus smiled. "Good for you, young man!" His scowl returned as he began to expound on politics. As patricians, he asserted, it was incumbent on the Fabii to assert their hereditary privileges at all times, and to protect those privileges against any further encroachment by the plebeians.

"To be sure, there are some plebeians worthy of attaining high office. It is to Roma's benefit that the most ambitious and capable of the plebeians have risen to join the ranks of the nobility, intermarrying with us and ruling the city alongside us. Roma rewards merit. The rabble, foreigners, even freed slaves are given a chance to work their way up the ladder, although there are plenty of barriers to slow their advance, which is as it should be!

Democracy as practiced by some of the Greek colonies in southern Italy—giving every man an equal say—has been kept out of Roma, thank the gods! Here, republican principles reign, by which I mean the freedom of the noble elite to compete equally and openly for political honors."

He leaned back on his couch and ceased his discourse for a few moments to enjoy a plate of sautéed carrots and parsnips. "But I've strayed from the subject of family history, a more suitable topic for your toga day. The origin of the Fabii is shrouded in mystery, of course, as are all matters that stretch back to a time before writing was introduced among the Romans. However, our best authorities believe that the first Roman families were descended from the gods."

"My friend Marcus Julius claims that his family is descended from Venus," said Kaeso.

"Indeed," said Quintus, raising an eyebrow. "That might explain why the Julii make better lovers than fighters. Our pedigree is a bit more heroic. According to family historians, the very first Fabius was the child of Hercules and a wood nymph, born on the banks of the Tiber at the dawn of time. Thus the blood of Hercules flows in the veins of the Fabii even now." Quintus begrudged Kaeso a second smile, then abruptly frowned and fell silent.

There was an uncomfortable moment as both men realized they were thinking the same thought—that Kaeso's immediate branch of the family, springing as it did from an adoption, did not actually carry the ancient Fabian blood. Neither Quintus nor Kaeso had any way of knowing that the truth was considerably more complicated. In fact, the claim of the Fabii to be descended from Hercules was completely spurious, while the blood of the visitor later identified as Hercules did indeed flow in Kaeso's veins, through his descent from the Potitii, a circumstance unknown to either man.

The uncomfortable moment stretched intolerably. Kaeso's face grew hot. They had drawn close to a subject that had made Kaeso uneasy ever since the day he first learned, as a child, that his grandfather was not born a Fabius, but was an adopted foundling. The story was told with pride, for it demonstrated the piety of the great Dorso, who from the ruins of Roma brought up a newborn orphan to be his son. It had also been explained to Kaeso that his grandfather was special. Had not the gods themselves determined that the foundling should be made a Fabius? The gods set life in motion; what mattered after that was what a man made of himself. The true test of a Roman—so said Kaeso's father—lay not in his pedigree, but in bending the world to his will.

Despite these assertions and reassurances, the fact that his actual blood-line was unknown had frequently caused Kaeso to wonder and to worry about his origins. It seemed inevitable that the subject would come up on this particular day, and so it had, even if it remained unspoken.

Kaeso became so flustered that he abruptly changed the subject. "You spoke earlier of your own illustrious career, cousin, but you made no mention of an episode that has always intrigued me."

"Oh, yes?" said Quintus. "What is that?"

"I believe it happened not too long before I was born, when you were just beginning your political career. It had to do with a famous case of poisoning—or rather, many cases of poisoning."

Quintus nodded grimly. "You refer to the investigation that took place the year I served as curule aedile. A veritable plague of poison!"

"If you had rather not talk about it—"

"I'm quite willing to discuss it. As with the disaster of the Caudine Forks, there is no sense in hiding such an episode, no matter how distasteful. As you say, I was a young man, and quite thrilled to have been elected curule aedile, a magistracy that automatically admitted me to the ranks of the Senate. To me fell the responsibility of keeping law and order in the city."

"That sounds like a fascinating job."

"Does it? For the most part, it consists of tedious administrative duties—fining citizens who've damaged public property, investigating accusations of overcharging by moneylenders, that sort of thing. Not a happy post for a man who would rather be fighting! But my complaints paled beside the general gloom that reigned over the city that year. People were fearful and uneasy, for it seemed that a terrible plague of a most peculiar nature had descended on us. Its victims were all men—not a woman among them—and the symptoms varied inexplicably. Some died swiftly. Others recovered for a while and then relapsed and expired. Even odder was the fact that a disproportionate number of those who died were men of high standing. Plagues tend to strike the poor and the lowborn in preference to their betters, not the other way around. The peculiar nature and the mounting toll of this plague were only gradually perceived over a course of months, and by that time the priests and magistrates were greatly alarmed. It seemed that the wrath of the gods must be at work. What had the people of Roma, especially their leading men, done to offend them?

"Eventually, the Senate resorted to an ancient recourse in times of epidemic. As you know, there is a wooden tablet inside the Temple of Jupiter, affixed to the doorway that leads into the sanctuary of Minerva on the right. Since the founding of the temple, every year, on the Ides of September, one of the consuls drives a nail into that tablet, to mark the passage of each year; thus the age of the temple and of the Republic can be calculated. The tablet adorns Minerva's sanctuary because numbers were one of her gifts to mankind. But the tablet has another, rarer function. In times of epidemic, a special dictator may be named—a religious, not military appointment—to carry out a single duty: He must drive an additional nail into the wooden tablet. How this custom came about, no one knows, but its effect is to lessen the ravages of plague. Thus, also, the years of plague can be recalled, and the frequency of such outbreaks reckoned.

"So it was done in this instance. A special dictator was appointed—Gnaeus Quinctilius, as I recall. With the Vestals and the priests and all the magistrates in attendance, Quinctilius drove a nail into the tablet, and then, his duty done, he resigned his office. But the ritual brought no relief. The plague continued and the number of victims increased. The people grew more frightened and their leaders more uneasy. I was as concerned as anyone, of course, but as curule aedile it hardly fell to me to devise a proper means of propitiating the gods and dispelling the plague.

"Then, one day, going about my business in my chambers in the Forum, a young woman came to see me. She refused to tell me her name, but from her dress and manner, I could see she was a freeborn servant from a respectable household. She said she had something terrible to tell me, but only if I would promise to shield her from punishment by the state or retribution by those whose crimes she would reveal. Well, I thought this was going to be nothing more dire than a case of a contractor embezzling bricks from the city, or some pipe-layer charging twice for repairing the public sewer. I gave her my assurances, and she proceeded to tell me that the plague that was afflicting the city was of human origin—and perpetrated not by men, but by women. She accused her own mistress, along with some of the most highborn women in Roma.

"On its face, her story seemed preposterous. For what possible reason would so many women resort to poisoning their husbands and other male relatives? One woman might resort to poison, yes; but scores of women, repeatedly, all in the same year? And yet, by that time, hundreds of men had died, and no cause had yet been discovered. I asked for proof. She offered to take me to a house where the poisons were made. If we were lucky, she said, we might catch some of the women in the act of brewing them.

"I had to act and quickly. In that moment, the job I had considered trifling and humdrum suddenly weighed upon me as the world must weigh upon the shoulders of Atlas." Quintus sighed, but his eyes glittered; relating the grim story clearly gave him great satisfaction.

"And then what happened, cousin Quintus?"

"Speed was essential, yet proper forms had to be observed, or otherwise any evidence might be compromised. I alerted the consuls at once—how old Gaius Valerius blustered when I woke him from a nap in the middle of the day! With the consuls as witnesses, along with their lictors, I went to the house in question, the home of a patrician named Cornelius, one of the first victims of the plague. His widow's name was Sergia. Her door slave, seeing such a company, blanched and tried to shut us out. I pushed my way inside.

"At the back of the house, we found a room, which must have been a kitchen at one time, but that had been given over entirely to the brewing of potions. Herbs were hung by bits of string from the rafters. Pots were bubbling and steaming. One pot had been set on a wooden rack to cool; lined up beside it was a row of little clay bottles. Sergia was clearly in charge; the other women were merely servants. When she saw us and realized what had happened, she grabbed one of the bottles and raised it to her lips. I knocked the bottle from her hand. It shattered on the floor and spattered my tunic with a green liquid. The lictors restrained her. There was a rage in her eyes that chilled my blood.

"Sergia refused to answer questions, but, with a little persuasion, her slaves spoke readily enough. They led us to more than twenty houses where the products of Sergia's kitchen might be found. What a day that was, bursting into house after house, witnessing the outrage of the women, the disbelief of their husbands, the fear and confusion of the children. The implicated women were made to appear before the consuls in the Forum, along with the potions that had been seized.

"Before that day, there had never been a public inquest into charges of poisoning. Such matters were rare enough, and when they did occur, they had always been handled entirely within the affected household, with justice dispensed by the paterfamilias. 'It began beneath his roof, let it end beneath his roof,' as the saying goes. If a head of household's wife or daughter, or his son, for that matter, dared to commit such a crime, it was the prerogative of the paterfamilias to determine guilt and exact punishment.

"But this was clearly beyond the scope of any one paterfamilias. There was simply no precedent for such a thing—a vast web of crimes spun by a conspiracy of women! The consuls were fearful of repercussions from the powerful families involved. They were only too happy to allow me, as curule aedile, to conduct the questioning.

"Sergia at last broke her silence. She claimed that her potions were remedies for various ailments, none of them poisonous. If that were so, I said, then let every woman present swallow the potion that was found in her possession. This caused a great stir among the women. There was much weeping, shrieking, tearing of hair. Gradually, the women quieted one another. At last, they agreed to the test. In unison, following the lead of Sergia, the women swallowed their so-called remedies.

Quintus shook his head. "What a sight! What a sound! The death throes of more than twenty women, there before our eyes! Not all the potions were the same, and their effects differed. Some of the women were seized by violent convulsions. Others stiffened and died with a hideous grimace. I was a young man, but I had already fought in several battles—I had killed men and seen men killed—yet I had never witnessed anything as strange and terrifying as the death of those women by their own hands!"

Kaeso gazed at his cousin wide-eyed. The details of the mass poisonings were completely new to him. Kaeso found the tale at once thrilling and repulsive. "Was that the end of it, cousin Quintus?"

"Far from it! The friends and servants of those dead women had much more to tell us. As more women were implicated, we realized that the scale of the conspiracy was larger than anyone could have imagined. In the end, more than one hundred and seventy women were found guilty, and all were put to death. The murder of so many upstanding citizens, the shocking investigation, the executions—all cast a shadow of despair across the city. The truth was too appalling for some to accept. There were those who said I went too far, that my judgment was faulty, that I allowed wicked people to falsely accuse the wives and daughters of their enemies. Well, even the gods are not infallible! I believe my investigation was thorough and impartial, and that no other man could have done better. In any event, the poisonings stopped, and the citizens of Roma rewarded me with election to higher office in the years that followed."

Kaeso shook his head. "I had no idea the crimes were so widespread, and so bizarre. I'd heard only vague rumors before."

"I'm not surprised. When the wretched affair was over, people did their best to forget it."

"But why did those women commit such crimes?"

"The reasons they gave were as varied as the poisons they used: greed, revenge, spite, jealousy. Having committed murder once, many of the women seemed unable to resist doing so again. It was as if a kind of madness spread among them, a homicidal contagion, a compulsion to kill. The root cause of that madness, no one could determine. The only certain cure was death. I put an end to the plague of poisonings, and since that time, it has never recurred."

"What a fascinating story!"

"Do you really think so?"

"Absolutely! I should like to know even more. Who were those women? What were their names? Whom did they kill, and why, and when, and—"

Amused and a little flattered by his young cousin's enthusiasm, Quintus emitted a good-natured grunt that sounded suspiciously like a laugh. "Well, young man, as it happens, I kept a very thorough dossier of materials relating to my investigation—for my own protection, if nothing else, so that if called upon later I could show exactly what evidence I had obtained and the circumstances under which I obtained it. All the details are there—names, dates, even the recipes the women used to concoct their various poisons. Quite a few of them were able to read and write, and some of them kept copious notes about the poisons and their effects."

"Would you allow me to see that dossier, cousin?"

"Certainly. Do you know, no one has ever asked to see it before. And yet, that investigation is now a part of the family's history, a part of Roma's history."

"It shouldn't be forgotten," said Kaeso.

Quintus nodded. "Very well. Those materials must be somewhere among my memorabilia. When I have time, I shall locate them, and let you have a look."

Later that night, alone in his room in his father's house, Kaeso prepared for bed. By the flickering light of a single lamp, he removed his toga without assistance; getting out of the garment was much easier than putting it on. He carefully folded the toga and placed it on a chair. He stripped off his undertunic and loincloth, and stood naked except for the gift his father had given him that morning, the fascinum which hung from the chain around his neck.

Among the other gifts Kaeso had received that day was a small mirror. A slave had already hung it on the wall. The mirror was round, made of polished silver, and decorated around its border with images engraved in the metal. The images depicted the exploits of Hercules. No doubt the giver, a colleague of Kaeso's father, had thought the mirror would make a particularly appropriate coming-of-age gift for a young Fabius, as the Fabii considered themselves to be descended from Hercules; but the reflection of his own face, surrounded by images of the demigod, only reminded Kaeso that he was not really a Fabius by blood, only by adoption.

Kaeso stood naked before the mirror and gazed at his shadowy reflection. "Today you are a man, Kaeso Fabius Dorso," he whispered. "But who are you? Where did you come from? Your grandfather was a foundling among the rubble; was he begotten by a god, or a Gaul? Will you live and die and never know the secret of your origin—or is there an oracle who can answer your question?"

He touched the amulet at his chest. The gold of the fascinum caught the lamp's flickering light, and Kaeso was dazzled by its reflection in the mirror.

※

The next morning, Kaeso donned his toga again to pay a formal call upon a man he had never met.

Appius Claudius—the seventh of that name in the line descended from Attus Clausus—blinked in disbelief when his secretary announced his first visitor of the day. "The young Fabius?" he said. "Are you sure you heard the name correctly?"

The slave nodded.

Claudius pursed his lips and stroked his beard, which was still more black than silver. "Very well, show him in. I'll meet him here in the garden. Turn away all other visitors until we're done."

If anything, the garden of Appius Claudius, with its splashing fountain surrounding a statue of three Muses and its terraces of roses, was even more magnificent than the garden of Quintus Fabius. Kaeso was duly impressed, but not surprised. If any man was as powerful and respected in Roma as his cousin Quintus, that man was Quintus's longtime rival, Appius Claudius.

"I believe that congratulations are in order, young man," said Claudius, standing to greet him. "Your toga suits you well."

In fact, Kaeso had dressed himself that morning without the help of a slave, and had not quite succeeded in making the garment hang correctly. He was glad to take the chair which Claudius offered. Sitting disguised the awkward folds of his toga.

"Thank you for receiving me, Censor." Kaeso addressed his host by the title of the prestigious office he held. In many ways, the censorship was an even higher magistracy than the consulship, and its exalted rank was signified by the purple toga that the censor alone could wear. The censor had the power to fill vacancies in the Senate. He also kept the rolls of citizenship. He could add men to the list, or, with just cause, strike them from it. The censor's list determined the division of citizens into voting units, a tool the patricians had long used to their advantage. By manipulating the list, the censor could influence the course of elections.

Appius Claudius had also used the powers of his office to gain complete control over two public works projects of unprecedented vastness. This was the reason Kaeso had come to see him.

"If I look a bit surprised, you must understand that it's been a very long time since any man named Fabius has cast a shadow in this garden," said Claudius, who smiled as readily as Quintus scowled. Kaeso had heard that the man's charm was his most notable quality; when the Fabii said this, it was not a compliment. "Whenever a political question arises, it seems that your cousin Quintus leans in one direction and I lean in the other. The two of us can never seem to meet, either on policy or in the flesh."

Kaeso spoke carefully. "No one holds Quintus Fabius in higher esteem than I do, but I am my own man."

"Well spoken! I myself am only too well acquainted with the burden of having famous—and infamous—relatives. Fortunately, the worst of them are long dead. But like you, Kaeso, I am my own man. I am no more responsible for the criminal behavior of my great-great-grandfather, the Decemvir, than you are responsible for the dunderheaded, backward-looking politics of your esteemed cousin. We are each his own man, and each man is the architect of his own fortune. Shall we drink to that?"

A slave had appeared with two cups of wine. Kaeso, feeling a bit disloyal to Quintus but eager to ingratiate himself with his host, took a sip. The wine was unwatered and stronger than he was used to. Almost at once he felt warm and a little fuzzy-headed.

Claudius signaled that both their cups should be refilled. "Given the chilly relations between your cousin Quintus and myself, I assume you must have a very good reason for coming to see me."

Kaeso could feel that the wine was beginning to loosen his tongue; perhaps it would not be so difficult to state his desire, after all. He was just opening his mouth to speak when his host interrupted him.

"But, no—I can tell that you've come here on business of some sort, and it's still too early in the day for me to discuss serious business. Let's get to know one another a little. Perhaps we have interests in common. Do you read Latin?"

"Of course I do, Censor."

"And Greek?"

"Well . . . a little," said Kaeso.

"By which you mean not at all. A pity! I thought I might show you my library, which is the best in Roma, but since almost all the books are in Greek, it would mean nothing to you. Every Roman should learn at least enough Greek to read the great playwrights—Aeschylus, Sophocles, Euripides. And of course, the great philosophers—Plato and Aristotle. But your face remains a blank, Kaeso. Do these names mean anything to you?"

"I'm afraid not, Censor."

"Alas!" Claudius shook his head. "And do you know where *that* word, 'alas,' comes from?"

Kaeso frowned. "No."

"And you a Fabius, with family ties to Hercules! 'Alas' is a Latinization of a Greek name, Hylas. And who was Hylas?"

Kaeso furrowed his brow and shrugged.

Claudius sighed. "Hylas was a beautiful boy, the beloved of Hercules. The two of them together accompanied Jason and the Argonauts on their quest for the Golden Fleece. When the Argo dropped anchor at the mouth of the river Ascanius, Hylas was sent to fetch fresh water from the springs. But the nymphs were jealous of his beauty, and Hylas was pulled into the water, never to be seen again. Hercules was distraught beyond comforting. For a long time—long after hope of finding the boy was gone—he wandered up and down the riverbank, crying out, 'Hylas! Hylas!' And thus we still cry, 'Alas! Alas!' when confronted by great sorrow."

Kaeso raised his eyebrows. Hylas was not among the characters engraved on the mirror he had been given. "I never heard that story before. It's quite beautiful."

"There are several versions of the tale of Hercules and Hylas among my books, but you must know Greek to read any of them."

"I've never claimed to be a scholar, Censor. A Roman's primary duty is to serve the state as a soldier—"

"Indeed! And as a warrior you could surely benefit from reading Homer's *Iliad*—or, even better, *The Life of Alexander* by Cleon of Corinth. I received a copy only yesterday, by courier all the way from a book vendor in Athens. You *have* heard of Alexander?"

"Alexander the Great of Macedonia? Who hasn't heard of him? First he conquered Greece, and then the whole of the world to the south and east—Egypt, Persia, and faraway lands that lie beyond any map. My father says we're lucky he didn't turn his attention to the west, or else we'd have had to fight him on the banks of the Tiber. But Alexander won't conquer anyone else. He's been dead for ten years now."

"Eleven years, actually—but you do indeed seem to know who Alexander was. Very good!" Claudius laughed and shrugged. "One never knows what a young man is likely to know, or not know, given the dreadful state of Roman education. Many a Roman can name his own ancestors going back ten generations—not a hard feat, since they tend to all have the same name—but how many can name the reigning tyrant of Syracuse, or find Carthage on a map?"

Kaeso smiled. "My father says you're obsessed with Syracuse and Carthage."

"Indeed I am, because the future of Roma resides in the sea lanes of the Mediterranean, and those sea lanes will be controlled either by Syracuse or by Carthage—or by us."

"My cousin Quintus says our future lies to the north, not to the south. First we conquer all of Italy, then we look to Gaul—"

"Nonsense! The Gauls have nothing to offer us, not even a god worth worshiping, or a language worth learning. The wealth of the world will belong to whoever controls trade in the Mediterranean. To do that, we shall have to become a sea power, or else make subjects of those who already have a navy—such as the Syracusans and Carthaginians. Your cousin Fabius's misreading of Roma's destiny lies at the very heart of the disagreement between us. Ah, but here I am, talking politics, when I was hoping to find common ground between us." Claudius pensively tapped his forefinger against his lips. "Since you are a Kaeso, I suppose I might ask your position regarding the controversy over the letter 'K'?"

"Controversy?"

"My own opinion is that it should eliminated altogether from the Roman alphabet. What need is there for 'K' when 'C' will do just as well? Thus your name would be spelled C-A-E-S-O, and pronounced the same."

"But—I'm rather fond of the 'K' in my name . . ."

"And what about 'Z'? I say it is abhorrent and must be gotten rid of!"

"Abhorrent?"

"The sound it represents is uncouth and has no place in a civilized language. 'Z' grates on the ear and offends the eye."

"The eye?"

"Here, observe my face as pronounce it." Claudius parted his lips, clenched his teeth, and made a prolonged buzzing noise. "There, do you see? A man who makes the sound of 'Z' resembles a grinning skull. Hideous! The sound and the letter must be ruthlessly eliminated from the Latin language."

Kaeso laughed. "You seem very passionate about it!"

"Passion is life, young man. And yes, language is my passion. What is your passion?"

Kaeso abruptly felt quite sober. The conversation had arrived at his reason for coming. "I want to be a builder, Censor."

Claudius raised an eyebrow. "Do you?"

"Yes. More than anything! I'm eager to fight for Roma, of course. And if I must enter politics and learn something about the law, I will. I'll even learn some Greek, if the Greeks can teach me something about architecture and engineering—because what I really want to do is *build*. It's been so, ever since I was a child. When I was little, my favorite toys were building blocks. When I grew old enough to go about on my own, instead of watching athletes or chariot races or soldiers drilling on the Field of Mars, for hours I would stand at the site of a new temple or monument, or even at a place where the city walls were being repaired, watching the workmen and the equipment, seeing how the hoists and levers and pulleys were used, observing how mortar was mixed and bricks laid out to make arches and doorways. I admit that I have no special training, but I can draw—I know that a builder must be able to draw—and I'm very good with numbers, much better than I am with letters."

"I see. And so you've come to me."

"Yes! Men say that the road you're building, running south to Capua, is like no road ever built before—straight as a ruler, flat as a table, hard as bedrock. And everyone is talking about your brilliant idea for bringing fresh water to the city—tapping the springs near Gabii, ten miles from Roma, running the water underground, then delivering it to the city atop an elevated channel supported by arches. An aqueduct, I think you call it? Amazing! These projects are the most exciting things that have happened in my lifetime—more exciting than battles, or elections, or even stories about conquerors at the far end of the world. I want to be part of them. I know there's much I'll need to learn, but I'm willing to work very hard. I want to do whatever I can to help you build your new road and your aqueduct."

Claudius smiled. "You enthusiasm is flattering."

"I speak from the heart, Censor."

"I can see that. Strange! The Fabii have always been warriors, and a few have allegedly been statesmen, but never builders. I wonder how you came by such a trait?"

Kaeso did not care for the question, as it reminded him of his unknown origins, but he tried not to let his vexation show.

"Does your father know that you've come to me?"

"Yes, Censor. Although he disapproves of your politics—he calls you a radical populist—"

"Radical? Because I give common citizens well-paid work on public projects that benefit all of Roma? I suppose he calls me a demagogue, as well."

Kaeso cheeks turned hot. His father had indeed used that despised word, imported from the Greek, for an unscrupulous leader who exploited the unruly passions of the mob. "Despite our political differences, Censor, my father understands how greatly I desire to work for you. He will do nothing to prevent me."

"And your cousin Quintus?"

"I haven't discussed it with him. But I don't need his approval. I am—"

"Yes, I know: You are your own man." Claudius drummed his fingers on his knees for a while, then nodded and smiled. "Very well, Kaeso Fabius Dorso. I shall find a suitable place for you on one of my projects."

"Thank you, Censor!"

"And in the meantime, to please me, perhaps you will consider changing the 'K' in your name to a 'C'."

"Well—if you really think it's necessary . . ."

"Kaeso, I'm only joking—alas!"

At dawn the next day, following the instructions of Appius Claudius, Kaeso set out from his home on the Palatine. He walked past the ancient

Hut of Romulus and the fig tree called the ruminalis, a descendent of the tree which shaded Acca Larentia when she suckled Romulus and Remus. He descended the winding walkway known as the Stairs of Cacus.

He walked through the Forum Boarium (originally Bovarium, as Appius Claudius had informed him, but the letter 'V' had long ago been dropped by common usage). The workers in the shops and markets were just beginning their day. He passed the ancient Ara Maxima, where long ago his ancestors the Pinarii and the Potitii had inaugurated the worship of Hercules. The Potitii still made a sacrifice at the altar each year, but a long decline in the family's fortunes had reduced their annual feast to a paltry affair. Even with his supposed connection to Hercules through the Fabii, Kaeso was only vaguely aware of the Feast of Hercules that took place at the Ara Maxima each summer, and had no idea that it was the oldest such observance in the city. Of his descent from the Pinarii and the Potitii, he knew nothing.

His destination was a work site at the foot of the Aventine Hill, between the Temple of Ceres and the north end of the Circus Maximus. He knew he had reached the place when he saw the great piles of earth and the network of ramparts that had been built around the excavation. A small army of workers, made up of freedmen and freeborn citizens, had gathered. They milled about, joking and complaining about having to wake up so early.

The sky, growing lighter every moment, was dotted with small clouds, and there was a breeze from the east. "Looks to be an excellent day for working outdoors," said one of the men. "Too bad we'll be stuck underground!"

A foremen appeared. The men formed a queue. One by one they were issued shovels and spades, then disappeared into a cave-like hole at the base of the hill.

Kaeso waited until the foreman had a spare moment, then approached him and introduced himself, as Claudius had instructed him to do.

The man was tall and slender, but wiry with muscle. His tunic was spotless, but there was dirt under his fingernails. "So you're the young Fabius, here to learn about the aqueduct. My name is Albinius. I'm in charge of all aqueduct operations within the city walls, the most interesting part of the project from an engineering standpoint. Do you know where the city gets its water, currently?"

"From the Tiber, I suppose, and from springs here and there inside the city. And some people collect rainwater."

"That's right. And so it's been from the beginning. But the water from the Tiber's not always as clean as you might like, and some of the springs have dried up, and you can't always depend on rain. And the bigger Roma grows, the more water her people need. Water for drinking and cooking, of course, and for irrigating crops outside the city, but also for bathing. Most people like to wash a bit of themselves every day, and a lot of people want to wash from head to foot every few days. That requires a lot of water! The demand has grown so great, we've reached a point where the city can't accommodate more people unless we can somehow get more water.

"What to do? 'We'll simply bring the water we need from elsewhere,' said Appius Claudius. 'What, carry it by the wagonload?' said the skeptics. 'No, you fools!' said Claudius. 'We shall make the water flow here of its own accord, through the channel I shall build.' And thus, thanks to the genius of the censor, the aqueduct was born—first of its kind anywhere on earth, and soon to be the envy of every thirsty city on earth. Right here is where the aqueduct will end, with the water pouring into a big public fountain. Do you know where the aqueduct begins?"

"Ten miles east of the city, at the springs near Gabii," said Kaeso.

"That's right. The fresh water from those springs will pour into an underground channel lined with stones and mortar. Because it's downhill from there to here, that channel will carry the water all the way to the city walls, to a point near the Capena Gate. The underground channel is impressive in itself, if only for the amount of labor involved. Ten miles requires a lot of digging! And it's hardly a straight line; it twists and turns to follow the contours of the landscape and keep the water flowing downhill. But what happens when the water reaches the city will be even more impressive.

"Claudius wants the water to come here, to the place where we're standing. The natural way to do it—to let the water follow the lay of the land and run downhill—would mean digging a channel straight down the spine of the horseracing track in the Circus Maximus. That would be too dis-

ruptive. Instead, Claudius wants the water to make a detour around the
Circus Maximus. To accomplish that, we're tunneling through the Aventine. The channel disappears into one side of the hill and will come out the
other, right here. Amazing, no? But that's still not the most impressive
part. Follow me."

They walked along the foot of the Aventine, crossing the open area to
the south of the racing track. As they approached the city wall and the
Capena Gate, Claudius's novel solution for transporting the water loomed
before them. To bridge the space between the high ground to the left of
the gate and the high ground to the right, a channel was being built atop a
series of arches constructed of brick and mortar. The road leading to the
gate ran directly under one of these arches.

"To bring the water to Roma, Claudius will not only make it run
underground—he'll make it flow above our heads!" said Albinius. "This
elevated part of the aqueduct runs for only a few hundred feet, out of a total distance of many miles. But it's a brilliant solution—a river in the sky!
There's no reason this kind of construction can't be repeated elsewhere,
and no reason that such an elevated aqueduct can't be built on an even
larger scale, running mile after mile. Water can now be carried from any
high point to any low point. All that's required is to dig and tunnel and,
where necessary, to run the channel over a series of arches, as we've done
here. Since the beginning of the world, men have had to build cities where
there was adequate water. Now a city can be built anywhere men wish, and
the water can be brought to them. Such a possibility never existed before.
The aqueduct will change not just Roma, but the whole world!"

The foreman's enthusiasm was contagious, and Kaeso was impressed.
He would have liked to spend the rest of the day at the man's side, but, following Claudius's instructions, he took his leave of Albinius.

Walking under the immense arch of the aqueduct, Kaeso passed though
the Capena Gate and beyond the city walls. A brisk walk brought him to
the censor's other great construction project.

The site swarmed with workers busily digging, mixing mortar, and
pushing barrows filled with gravel. Kaeso asked for the foreman, a man
named Decius, and was taken to the biggest, brawniest man in sight.

"So, you're here to learn about road building, are you?" said Decius.
"Well, I've been at it all my life. Learned a thing or two in my forty-odd

years. But, thanks to Appius Claudius, this is the first time I've ever seen a road planned ahead of time with so much care and precision. The whole course has been laid out, all the proper materials have been acquired, and the best team of workers in Roma has been assembled—never mind that the boys working on the aqueduct might wish to dispute that claim! This is going to be a job we can all be proud of. Your descendents a thousand years from now will walk on this road and say, 'By Jupiter, what an outstanding job old Appius Claudius and his boys did when they laid down this road!' "

"This road will still be here a thousand years from now?"

"It most certainly will!"

Kaeso assumed the big man was exaggerating, but as Decius took him through the steps of laying down the road, he began to think the claim might have some merit.

"Your first roads were hardly more than footpaths," said Decius, "beaten into the ground by so many men passing by—or by animals, since they make trails, too, and can usually figure out the best way to get over a pass or around a rough spot. When men started using wagons, the wheels wore ruts in the ground, and that made wider roads. Finally, some unknown genius decided it was time to make a road to fit the purpose, instead of just letting it come about on its own, and so the art of road building was born.

"The road we're building follows a very old trail that's been here for centuries; Appius Claudius says it dates back to the days of the old salt traders and metal traders, before Roma existed. Here you see some workers performing the first step in the process. See how they're digging two shallow trenches parallel to each other? The trenches mark the breadth of the road. This road is fifteen feet wide, the sum of three men lying head to toe. Roman men, that is; it takes only two and a half Gauls to cover that width. They say a Gaul cut in half is the best kind, especially if it's the half without a head!"

Decius laughed heartily at his own joke, and slapped Kaeso on the back as if he could jar him into doing the same. "Now, if you'll follow me, up ahead you can see that they've moved on to the second stage. They've dug out the loose earth between the trenches, and excavated down until they've reached a solid foundation for the materials to rest on. How far down you have to dig depends on the terrain. Sometimes, if the ground's swampy or the soil's peculiar, you have to drive piles into the earth. Fortunately, that's not the case here. A strong digger can reach solid roadbed without breaking his back. These fellows hardly even break a sweat. Isn't that right, men?"

The diggers looked up at Decius and grinned. Kaeso could see that they liked the foreman.

"Keep walking. I'll show you the next stage. See there, up ahead, those big piles of stones? Those are for laying the first course of the road. These stones have been sorted for size; these are what we call hand-sized, no larger and no smaller than will fit in a man's hand. They make up the first stratum. On top of those, we lay down a mass of broken stones about nine inches deep, rammed down hard and cemented with lime—that's called rubble-work. Above that, we lay the road-core, about half a foot deep, which is made up of bits and pieces of bricks and pottery, smaller bits than the stones in the rubble-work, and cemented with lime. You can see a section where the core's been finished, up ahead."

"It's a bit higher in the middle than at the edges, isn't it?" said Kaeso.

"Very observant. We do that on purpose, to let the water run off. For now, to finish the road, we're laying down a layer of gravel. That's usually the end of the job. But on this project, the gravel layer is to be only temporary. As time and money permit, the plan is to scrape away the gravel and lay down blocks of the hardest stone we can find. Around Roma, that usually means basaltic lava. The stones aren't uniform, like bricks; they're broken and cut into all sorts of random shapes—polygonal, we call them—but skilled workmen can pick and choose among those stones and fit them together until the surface is so perfectly even and smooth, you'd be hard-pressed to find the tiniest gap, even with your fingertip. I've seen walls built that way, and there's no reason it can't be done on a road, as well. Up ahead, we've completed a small section of the road with a finished stone layer, just as a showpiece for now. Here it is. Have a look. Walk on it. Jump on it! Stoop down and run your hands over it. So flat and smooth and perfect, wouldn't you swear it was made of one solid stone that just happens to have a few seams running through it?"

"It's amazing!" said Kaeso. "And beautiful."

"And likely to last for more lifetimes than those of all your ancestors put together."

"Do you really think the entire road can be finished this finely, all the way to Capua?"

"I believe that roads this fine will some day run all up and down Italy, and far beyond—as far as any Roman dares to travel. From the Pillars of Hercules to the banks of the Euxine Sea, people will say, 'Here runs a Roman road!'" Decius laughed. "You know what Appius Claudius once said to me? 'Alexander conquered half the world with his army, but can you imagine what he might have done, if only the Greeks knew how to build a Roman road?'"

"And just how long has this been going on?" demanded Quintus Fabius, scowling.

"A month or so. Since the day after my toga day," said Kaeso.

"Just as I thought. This relationship with Appius Claudius won't do, young man. It simply won't do!"

Quintus had asked his younger cousin to pay him a visit, but he did not receive him in the garden; instead, he met him in the vestibule. Not only was Kaeso being kept from the heart of the house, like a merchant paying an unwelcome call, and being made to stand rather than sit, but here in the vestibule, following patrician custom, the wax busts of Quintus's ancestors were placed in niches in the walls, from which they stared unblinking at all who came and went. It seemed that not only Quintus was scowling at Kaeso and judging him; so were several generations of dour-looking Fabii.

"Cousin, I am aware of your disagreements with Appius Claudius—"

"The man is degenerate! He's polluted his mind with so-called Greek learning. Given half a chance, he'll pollute your mind as well."

"I don't think you need to worry about that," said Kaeso. So far, Claudius's efforts to teach him Greek had been fruitless. Happily, Kaeso's aptitude for engineering exceeded even his own hopes, and Claudius had been quite impressed with his new protégé's intelligence and enthusiasm. "I sought out Appius Claudius only because of his construction projects.

I'm learning a great deal about road-building, and also about the new aqueduct—"

"All you need to know about those wasteful and inefficient projects, you could have found out by asking me, young man. They are the result of a gross abuse of the censor's office. Somehow, Claudius managed to circumvent the Senate and plunder the treasury to finance his illegal schemes."

"But those schemes, as you call them, are surely for the benefit of all Roma."

"They are for the benefit of Claudius, a means to extend his political patronage! By giving them jobs, he buys the loyalty of the thousands of citizens he employs. No doubt he is also enriching himself!"

Kaeso frowned. "Are you accusing him of embezzling public funds?"

Quintus grunted. "I wouldn't put it past him! You're young, Kaeso. You haven't yet seen enough of the world to judge a man's character. Believe me, Claudius is not the sort of man with whom our sort should associate."

"But surely he's as patrician as you or I," said Kaeso.

Did Quintus hesitate before replying? Was he thinking of Kaeso's origin by adoption, and his uncertain bloodline? He shook his head. "The Claudii have always been vain and self-important, but at least in the old days they were rock solid in their support of patrician privilege. Appius Claudius has done an about-face and made himself a champion of the lower classes. Oh, he pays lip service to patrician ideals—the glory of the ancestors and the founders of the Republic—but at heart the man is a demagogue. He panders to the rabble. He flirts with dangerous democratic ideas, which he probably picked up from reading those wretched Greek philosophers he admires. He should never have been given control of the citizen rolls."

"But as censor, that's his duty."

"To update the rolls, yes, but not to tinker with them, and in a most irresponsible fashion. Oh, he'll tell you he's simply reorganizing the voting blocks to make them more efficient, but his scheme is to make elections more democratic and less weighted to the blocks dominated by patricians— a very dangerous idea! The founders, in their wisdom, designed the electoral process deliberately to give more influence to those families whose achievements long ago earned them a special place in the state. Nothing must be done to erode that system. It has served Roma well since the birth of the Republic. It will serve us just as well for another two hundred years.

"Even worse, young man, is Claudius's abuse of the censor's right to fill vacancies in the Senate. Every vacancy is filled with a man loyal to Claudius—and some of those new senators are the sons of freedmen! Such a degradation of the Senate would have been unthinkable in my grandfather's day. What have we come to?"

"Times change, cousin," said Kaeso.

"And seldom for the better! Once a radical idea takes root, no one can predict how fast or how far it will spread. Consider the consulship. For a very long time, only patricians were able to get themselves elected to the highest office, shutting out the plebeians. The patricians' exclusive claim on the consulship became a tradition, which eventually took on the force of law. But the so-called reformers objected, and fifty-five years ago, they managed to pass a law that allowed one of the two consuls to be a plebeian. A matter of fairness, said the reformers; if a plebeian is clever enough to get himself elected consul, then why not? But that was only the beginning. Thirty years ago, the reformers passed another law, and this one mandated that one of the consuls *must* be a plebeian! Where will it end? Such changes are always due to rabble-rousers like Appius Claudius, traitors to their patrician blood. Claudius is a dangerous man. You should steer clear of him."

Kaeso sighed. "Cousin Quintus, please understand. I share your political views. How could I not? They're the ideas my father imparted to me while I was growing up. But just as I convinced my father to allow me to work under Claudius, so I hope that I can convince you to lift your objections. I have no intention of aiding or abetting Appius Claudius in any rabble-rousing schemes. But the aqueduct and the new road are being built, no matter what objections you may have, and I want to have a hand in them. If such projects yield political benefits, then why should Claudius be the sole beneficiary? Why should there not be a Fabius involved in the projects, learning how the process works? In years to come, more roads and aqueducts will be built, and when that happens, I want it to be a Fabius who takes the credit and reaps the benefits."

Quintus shook his head. "You walk a dangerous path, Kaeso. To learn a bit about building and engineering is not a bad thing. But Claudius is a devious man, and charming. He may yet seduce you to his way of thinking."

"I assure you, cousin, he will not. Would it set your mind at rest if I were to promise you that I will not learn a word of Greek? It would be an easy promise, as I seem incapable of doing so, anyway."

Quintus begrudged him a faint smile. "Kaeso, Kaeso! Very well. Since you've convinced your father to acquiesce to this arrangement, then I shall not object, at least not publicly. I'll keep my mouth shut, and hope that you know what you're doing." He glanced at the rows of wax effigies in their niches. "Always remember your ancestry, Kaeso, and preserve the dignity of your name!" Did he once again hesitate and blink, as he looked from the faces of the deceased Fabii to the face of Kaeso, which bore no family resemblance?

"But I asked you here for another reason," said Quintus. "I have something for you—that is, if you're still interested. Come with me."

Kaeso followed him to a room where the walls were lined with pigeonhole bookcases stuffed with scrolls. On tables here and there, unfurled documents were laid flat for perusal with paperweights to hold down the corners. The library of Quintus Fabius was smaller than that of Appius Claudius, and its contents were quite different. Here there was not a Greek text to be found or any volumes pertaining to the history of foreign peoples. All the documents in the library of Quintus Fabius had to do with legal matters, property claims, monetary transactions, family history, or genealogy.

"You expressed an interest in seeing the various documents regarding the investigation I conducted many years ago, as curule aedile, into the mass poisonings in the city. They were a bit scattered, but I believe I've managed to gather them in one place." Quintus indicated a tube made of leather, into which a great many scrolls, rolled together, had been inserted. "This is the dossier pertaining to the case. Of course, I realize that your studies under Appius Claudius may be claiming all of your time and attention—"

"Not at all, cousin Quintus! I'm very grateful that you remembered my interest in the matter, and that you went to so much trouble to make these available to me." In fact, in the excitement of his work for Claudius, Kaeso had completely forgotten the discussion about the poisonings, but it would hardly do for him to say so. Did his cousin intend for him to sit here in the library, examining the documents? Kaeso did not have time; he was eager to get home so that he could perform a task which Claudius had assigned to him, recalculating the measurements for a section of the aqueduct. "Would it be possible for me to take this with me, so that I can peruse the contents at my leisure?"

Quintus frowned. "Usually, I would never allow any of these documents to leave my possession. Some contain sensitive information. Many are irreplaceable. But . . . why not? I ask only that you be very careful with them, and return them in due course. Hopefully, they'll give you some insight into the challenges and responsibilities of holding a magistracy. A life of public service can be very demanding, but also very rewarding. You must think of your future, Kaeso, beyond this work you're doing for the censor."

"This is very kind of you, cousin. I shall look at them tonight."

As it turned out, laboring under the flickering light of a hydra-headed lamp that hung from the ceiling of his room, Kaeso worked much too late that night to bother looking at the documents from Quintus. He finally fell into bed, exhausted.

But he did not sleep well. Perhaps his head was too full of numbers. Perhaps the disapproval of his cousin weighed on him more heavily than he realized.

In his dream, Kaeso was back in the vestibule of his cousin's house, alone except for the wax busts of the ancestors in the niches. Suddenly, each of the effigies blinked at once. The disembodied heads turned to stare a him, scowling, then began to speak. Their voices were sarcastic and hateful.

"He's not one of us."

"Who is he?"

"Where did he come from?"

"Who knows what sort of blood flows in his veins?"

"He might be the offspring of a Gaul!"

"The foul product of a rape!"

"Pollution!"

"Corruption!"

"Filth!"

"The blood of the noble Fabii can be traced back for centuries, but this creature comes from nothing!"

"He's like a fly that rises from a dung heap!"

In his dream, Kaeso ran from the room. He found himself in the Forum. His father was leading him onto the Rostra. A great multitude had gathered before the platform to hear him speak, but when he opened his mouth, only nonsense came out. The crowd began to laugh and jeer at him. Their heads were made of wax, like the effigies of the Fabii.

He ran from the Rostra, to the house of Appius Claudius. The censor greeted him warmly, oblivious to Kaeso's distress. He unrolled a map which showed the course of the aqueduct. The line to Gabii ran off the map, into a gray nothingness.

"But where are the springs?" said Kaeso.

"Oh, don't worry about that," said Claudius. "I know where the water will come from. What I don't know, young man, is where *you* come from!" Suddenly the censor was glowering at Kaeso, looking as stern and disapproving as the effigies in Quintus's vestibule.

Kaeso woke. His body was covered with cold sweat.

His reading lamp was still lit. In his exhaustion, he had forgotten to extinguish the tiny flames that danced upon the projecting tongues of each of the hydra's heads. Desperate for any distraction, he reached for the dossier his cousin Quintus had given him. He pulled out the documents, rubbed his eyes, and began to read.

The tale of the poisonings and the ensuing investigation was told in bits and pieces. The fragmentary nature of the material only made it more fascinating, like a puzzle with many pieces. Grateful for anything to make him forget his nightmare, Kaeso perused the documents far into the night.

※

In the months that followed, Kaeso's life settled into a comfortable pattern. He worked very hard under the tutelage of Appius Claudius, learning everything he could about every aspect of the great road, which men were calling the Appian Way, and about the water channel, which men had dubbed the Appian Aqueduct. There was no task, high or low, in which he did not take part, from digging trenches to calculating the volume of water that could pass through a given section of the aqueduct in a given amount of time.

He even managed to learn the Greek alphabet and a few rudiments of the language, but whenever Claudius set him the task of translating a passage in Greek about hydraulics or engineering, the complexity of the language continued to stymie him. "One thing is clear," said Claudius in exasperation one day, "there cannot be a drop of Greek blood in you!" The comment was entirely innocent, but set off a fresh cycle of nightmares that haunted Kaeso's sleep.

At night, after a long day of working hard with his body and his mind, Kaeso looked forward to eating a hearty dinner with his parents, relaxing for a while in the garden, and then spending an hour or so reading the documents that Quintus had loaned to him. He found it strangely relaxing to sift through the confessions of the poisoners, the lists and memoranda scribbled in Quintus's hand, the official decrees of the Senate and the consuls, and the various other pieces of evidence. An obscure reference in one document would lead him to search out another, and then another which he might already have read, but had not fully understood without the later knowledge that came from further research. The puzzle-like nature of the material amused and engaged him. From seemingly unrelated bits and pieces, an increasingly coherent picture of events began to emerge, like the creation of a mosaic from odd bits of stone.

Over and over, and utterly fascinated, he read the statements given by the women.

"I did it because my husband slept with another woman," said one.

"I did it because the shopkeeper looked at me the wrong way," said another.

"My brother and I had always quarreled," said one. "I was tired of quarreling."

And another: "I did it because my two sisters had done it to their husbands, and I did not want to feel left out."

The notorious Sergia had performed a great deal of experimentation with various plants and other substances, making notes on how the poisons could be extracted, which of them were more or less reliable, the symptoms they caused, the time they required to take effect, and how they worked in combination. Sergia had also made detailed sketches of numerous plants, to serve as guides for her servants when she dispatched them to find specimens growing in the wild.

Typical of Sergia's notes was her entry about *aconitum,* illustrated by a drawing of the flowering plant:

> *Aconitum.* A white powder derived from the plant called Pluto's helmet, because the purple flower, which grows in upright clusters, is shaped like a warrior's helmet with a high crest and cheek plates. The plant is knee-high to hip-high and grows in the shade of trees, in moist soil. A Greek merchant tells me that his people call it the Queen of Poisons. Legend says the plant first sprang from the saliva of the three-headed dog Cerberus, guardian of the underworld. All parts of the plant appear to be toxic, but most especially the roots, from which the white powder is derived. Ingestion causes death. The powder may also kill a woman if it comes into contact with her genitals. Very quick to act—death may occur within ten minutes, and almost certainly within four hours. The victim quickly experiences numbness and tingling in the mouth and throat, both of which feel parched; also there is a severe burning sensation from throat to abdomen. Tingling spreads to the hands and feet and then the whole body. The skin and extremities feel cold and clammy to the touch, yet at the same time the victim may feel as though his limbs are being flayed. Legs become weak. Sight and hearing grow dull, but the victim will be clearheaded until the moment of death. Muscles twitch and convulse. Pulse weakens. Pupils dilate. The slightest exertion results in a fatal swoon.

And so it went, with Kaeso falling asleep with details of long-ago murders in his head. Such reading matter provided an escape from the pressing problems of the day. His last conscious thought was less likely to be about some vexing technical puzzle posed by the aqueduct than about the patrician matron Cornelia, who killed her husband while they were copulating by inserting her middle finger, covered with the white powder *aconitum,* into his fundament—a method of stimulation he demanded of her and which she found distasteful. The poison killed the victim within minutes, but not, according to Cornelia, before he had attained a peculiarly violent orgasm. The dossier was full of such extraordinary details.

No amount of reading would banish the dreams that arose from Kaeso's anxieties regarding his origins. These nightmares recurred from time to time, usually set off by some chance remark made to him during the day that had nothing to do with his ancestry but that nonetheless made him feel exposed and vulnerable—an outsider, an interloper, an imposter within one of Roma's most ancient and distinguished families.

Thus, for a while, Kaeso's life settled into a comfortable pattern. Then there came a day that he knew was to change his life forever, but not for the reason he thought.

The obvious event of the day was his betrothal to a girl named Galeria. The betrothal was the culmination of intense negotiations between the two patrician families involved. On the Fabius side, it was Quintus who pushed for Kaeso to marry. The young man had shown himself to be bright and ambitious, but also stubborn and contrary; the responsibilities of marriage might be just the thing to tame his reckless energy.

Kaeso had mixed feelings about the prospect of marriage, but Galeria was a pretty girl with the figure of a Venus, and in his chaperoned conversations with her, she was charmingly shy and sweet.

The betrothal was finalized one afternoon at the house of Quintus Fabius. Kaeso, his father, and Galeria's father drank several toasts with Quintus's best wine. As soon as he could, Kaeso, feeling a bit tipsy, stole away and headed for the house of Appius Claudius, eager to share the news with his mentor.

The door slave, explaining that the censor was meeting with a visitor on official state business, asked him to wait in the antechamber next to Claudius's library. It was a warm day and the doors were open. Kaeso could hear quite clearly the conversation that was taking place in the adjoining room.

"Admittedly," Claudius was saying, "there is some precedent for what you're asking to do. The state religion has grown so large and complex, with so many rituals that must be performed every day, all over the city, that in recent years more and more duties have been delegated to temple slaves, who are owned by the state and receive special training from the priesthoods. Nonetheless, Titus Potitius, what you propose is a bit different, and sure to be controversial."

The name Potitius meant little to Kaeso. He knew the Potitii to be a patrician family—one of the oldest—but they figured little in the politics of the day and were seldom seen in the exalted social circles of the Fabii. If pressed, he might have recalled that they had something to do with the Ara Maxima, and in fact, it was that ancient hereditary duty that Titus Potitius had come to discuss with Claudius.

"Please understand, Censor." The man sounded old, and his voice was weary and downtrodden. "If I saw any other solution to the family's ills, I would never have come to you with this request. The sad fact is, the Potitii can no longer afford to maintain the altar, or to put on the annual feast in Hercules's honor. The altar itself is woefully in need of restoration. Have you looked at the site lately? It's an embarrassment to us all! The feast has become a pauper's banquet; it causes me great embarrassment to admit this, but it's the simple truth. Our inability to properly fulfill these duties does not reflect in an honorable way upon Roma, or upon the god, or upon the Potitii. Our continuing attempts to do so are only driving the family into greater poverty. Alas, in the days of our ancestors, an altar could be nothing more than a flat stone, and a feast could be a handful of beans! But Roma is no longer like that. As the city's power and wealth have grown, so have the standards of religious observance. The state can afford to restore and maintain the Ara Maxima and to honor Hercules with a feast that will make all Roma proud. The Potitii cannot."

"Your point is well taken, Titus Potitius. In return for ceding this privilege to the state, I presume you will expect a substantial payment."

"It would be proper."

"A payment large enough to get you and your kin out of the financial hole you find yourselves in."

"The state's generous recompense will be put to good use, Censor."

"So, an exclusive, hereditary religious duty, jealously guarded for centuries, is merely a commodity to be bought and sold? You realize that this is what some people will say."

"As censor, I believe you have the authority to approve this transaction."

"And if I do, what will people say of me? 'There goes Appius Claudius, abusing his office again! It's not enough that he packs the Senate with his low-born friends and fixes the elections; now he's tinkering with the most ancient religious rites in the city!' "

Potitius sighed. "I realize that the decision would be a difficult one for you—"

"On the contrary! I wholeheartedly approve of your idea."

"You do?"

"Absolutely. The old-fashioned notion that certain priesthoods and religious rites should remain under the exclusive control of a particular family is obnoxious to me. Any religious function that affects the entire state should be in the hands of the state. The people's religion should be controlled by the people. For that reason, which has nothing to do with your family's financial woes, I entirely approve of your offer to cede authority over the Ara Maxima and the Feast of Hercules to the state. Toward that end, I'm sure I can arrange for just compensation to be paid to your family."

"Censor, I can hardly express my gratitude—"

"Then don't, at least not yet. As I warned you, there will be some who rabidly oppose this change. They'll accuse me of impiety and abuse of my authority. They'll defame you and your kin. You must be prepared for their aspersions."

"I understand, Censor."

"Very well. Before we can proceed, I must ask if you truly represent the will of the entire family. From the census rolls . . ." Kaeso heard a rustling of scrolls. Claudius grunted. "I see that your numbers are smaller than I supposed. Can this be right? There are only twelve separate households of Potitii remaining in Roma, comprising some thirty males who carry the name?"

"That is correct. Our numbers have dwindled along with our fortunes."

"And you have authority to speak for them all?"

"I am the paterfamilias senior to all others. The matter has been thoroughly discussed within the family and decided."

"Very well."

Claudius called for a secretary, to whom he issued some instructions. He exchanged some parting pleasantries with Titus Potitius and escorted him from the room. As the two of them stepped into the antechamber, Claudius saw Kaeso and smiled broadly. Kaeso saw that Potitius had gray hair and a gray beard to match his elderly voice, and was wearing a toga that had seen better days. The old man gave Kaeso a passing glance, then stopped short and stared at him.

"Do I know you, young man?" he said.

"I don't think we've met," said Kaeso.

"Allow me to introduce Kaeso Fabius Dorso," said Claudius, "a young fellow with a wonderful head on his shoulders. He's helping me build the new road and the aqueduct. And this, Kaeso, is the venerable Titus Potitius, paterfamilias of the Potitii."

"One of our most ancient families," said Kaeso, simply to be polite.

"We made our mark on the city in its early days," said Potitius. "Now it's the turn of families like the Fabii to make their mark, as I'm sure you will, young man. But I must say . . ." He peered at Kaeso, squinted, and shook his head. "You do remind me of someone—my cousin Marcus, who died some years ago. Yes, you are the very image of Marcus when he was a young man. The resemblance is uncanny! You even sound like him. I wonder, is it possible that the two of you are somehow related? I recall no marriages between the Potitii and the Fabii in recent years, but perhaps—"

"I think not," said Kaeso brusquely. "I'm quite sure there's no family connection between us."

"Kaeso, your face is as red as a roofing tile!" said Claudius.

"I feel warm," muttered Kaeso. "It must be the wine I drank at cousin Quintus's house."

"Ah, well; the resemblance is merely a coincidence, then," said Potitius, but he continued to stare at Kaeso. At last he lowered his eyes, only to stare at the fascinum that hung on a chain around Kaeso's neck. Kaeso had decided to wear it that morning to mark the occasion of his betrothal.

"What's that?" said Potitius.

Kaeso stepped back, irritated by the man's scrutiny. "It's a family keep-sake. The famous Vestal Pinaria gave it to my grandfather on his toga day. Surely you're seen a fascinum before."

"Such trinkets are usually made of cheap metal, not gold, and this one appears to have sprouted wings—most unusual! Yet it seems oddly famil-iar. Yes, I'm sure it stirs some memory, but of what?" Potitius scratched his head.

Kaeso was beginning to seriously dislike the old man. Claudius deftly took Potitius's arm and steered him toward the vestibule. "I'm sure you must be eager to get back to your family and tell them of the success of your proposal," he said. "Farewell, Titus Potitius. The door slave will see you out."

"Farewell, Censor, and thank you!" The old man took Claudius's hands and squeezed them. Before he turned away, he shot a last, curious gaze at Kaeso and the amulet he wore.

"An unpleasant fellow," said Kaeso, after Potitius was gone.

"A bit scatterbrained, but harmless," said Claudius.

Kaeso wrinkled his nose. "He imagines we're related."

Claudius shrugged. "I'm related to him myself, if rather distantly. The connection goes back to the early days of the Republic. A daughter of the very first Appius Claudius married a Potitius, but the fellow turned traitor and fought against Roma with Coriolanus. For a long time there was bad blood between our two families. But all that is ancient history now, and the Potitii have fallen on such hard times that one can only pity them. But come, Kaeso, let's speak of happier things! Unless I'm mistaken, you've come to share some good news."

Kaeso told him of his betrothal. As the two of them celebrated with a cup of wine, Kaeso pushed the unpleasant encounter with Titus Potitius from his mind.

"What a large vestibule!" declared Kaeso's mother, stepping inside the front door of the little house on the Aventine.

"Mother, this isn't the vestibule. There is no vestibule. This is the house itself."

"What? Only this one room?"

"Of course not. There's a garden in the center of the house—"

"That little plot of dirt, under that hole in the roof?"

"And there's another room at the back, which serves as a kitchen and pantry. Behind that is a cubby for the slaves to sleep in, though I don't suppose we'll keep more than one apiece; they'll have to sleep on top of each other, as it is."

"Well, I suppose it won't take much to furnish the place!" At forty, Herminia was still a pretty woman, but she had a tendency to make unpleasant faces that spoiled her looks. "Really, it's hardly worth it for you to move out of the family house into such cramped quarters."

"Nonsense!" said Kaeso's father. "Cousin Quintus's wedding gift is very generous. It's not every pair of newlyweds who can celebrate the ceremony at their own house. It needs a bit of fixing up, to be sure—"

"I hope Galeria likes a challenge!" said Herminia.

"It's the location I like best of all," said Kaeso.

"The Aventine?" Herminia made a particularly unpleasant face. "Well, at least you're on the north slope."

"Come see the view from this window. Be careful of those loose floor tiles." Kaeso flung open the shutters. "Spectacular, isn't it?"

"I see a great clutter of rooftops," said Herminia dubiously.

"No, Mother, look there—between those two houses." Kaeso pointed.

"Ah, yes—you can just catch a glimpse of the elevated portion of the aqueduct, that eyesore your friend Claudius has inflicted on the city."

Kaeso's father cleared his throat. "We have much to do today, wife."

"Indeed we do! I need to draw up the list of guests."

"Then perhaps we should run along."

"I'll stay here for a while, if you don't mind," said Kaeso.

"Very well." Herminia kissed her son's forehead and swept from the room.

Kaeso's father hung back for a moment. He tapped his foot against the loose floor tiles. "Don't worry, son. We'll find the money to fix the place up."

"You forget that I have my own income, Father. Claudius pays me quite generously."

"I believe it's the state that pays you. The censor merely fixes your salary."

"Of course, Father. Hadn't you better join Mother before she grows impatient?"

Kaeso was left alone. His mother's caustic remarks did nothing to deflate his buoyant mood. The gods were smiling on him. His work for Appius Claudius was more fascinating than ever, his wedding day was fast approaching, and the gift of a house from his cousin Quintus had not only surprised him, but had deeply moved him. He recalled one of Claudius's favorite aphorisms, and said it aloud: "Each man is the architect of his own fortune." Kaeso gazed out the window at the distant aqueduct. "If that's true, then I must be a very fine architect, indeed!"

"I'm sure you are," said a voice behind him.

Kaeso spun about. His father must have left the door ajar. An old man in a shabby tunic stood in the middle of the room. Kaeso stared at him for a moment, then furrowed his brow. "Titus Potitius?"

"So, you remember me?"

"I'm afraid I do. What are you doing here?"

"Your tone is very harsh, young man. That's no way to address an elder—especially an elder kinsman."

"What are you talking about, old man?" Kaeso drew back his shoulders, but in his chest he felt a sinking sensation.

"You and I have much to talk about, Kaeso."

"We have nothing to talk about."

Potitius cocked his head and peered at him. "You're not wearing the fascinum today."

Kaeso touched the empty spot at his breast. "I wear it only on special occasions."

"Do you know where it comes from?"

"The Vestal Pinaria gave it—"

"But before that? Do you know from whom she obtained it?"

"No. But I know it's very ancient."

"It is, indeed—as ancient as the Potitii themselves."

"What are you saying, old man?"

"I'm the paterfamilias of all the Potitii. I'm also the family chronicler and historian. I understand your cousin Quintus serves much the same function for the Fabii—keeping scraps of parchment and scribbled notes about who was married to whom, and the names of their offspring, and who did what and when and how. Our families are so very old, and our ancestors accomplished so many things—great and small, wonderful and terrible—it's hard to keep track! Sometimes I think it would be a relief if we all turned to dust, so the rest of the world could simply forget us and go on about its business as if we never existed."

"I don't think Quintus Fabius feels that way."

Potitius made a croaking sound, which Kaeso took for a laugh. "I daresay you're right. But imagine the things he must know! A family chronicler becomes privy to all sorts of secrets. He knows the things that no one must ever speak of—mysterious deaths, babies born out of wedlock, bastards sired on slave girls . . ."

"If you have something to say, say it!"

"Very well. You and I are kinsmen, Kaeso. You are a descendent of the Potitii."

Kaeso's mouth was suddenly parched. "How do you know this?"

"First of all, I could tell simply by looking at you. You favor my cousin Marcus more than anyone else, but with those eyes, that chin, and the shape of your mouth, you could pass as a son or brother to any number of my cousins. At first, I thought perhaps old Marcus had spilled his seed outside his marriage bed, but as I began to track down the truth, I realized that the connection was far more complicated and went much further back in time. Just now, as he was leaving, I took a good look at your father. He, too, has the look of a Potitius, but his features are less distinctive. For some reason, the gods decreed that the family traits should resurface full-blown in you.

"It was your precious fascinum that provided the key. Somewhere in the family chronicles, I knew I had seen a reference to a winged fascinum made of gold. It was worn by an ancestor of mine, also named Titus, who lived in the days of the Decemvirs. After that Titus, there is no further reference to the golden, winged fascinum, which disappears from the family history. However, according to family legend, Titus sired a child out of wedlock, and that child became a slave. As you can imagine, this is seldom talked about. But slaves are property, and Romans keep very thorough records of property, as thorough as their genealogical records! Through diligence, and a lot of pestering, and a bit of guesswork, I was able to trace the descent of that bastard child down to a slave called Pennatus. Have you heard of him?"

Kaeso swallowed a hard lump in his throat. "It was a slave called Pennatus who found my grandfather among the ruins left by the Gauls."

"So it was! Did you know that this same Pennatus was trapped for several months atop the Capitoline with the Vestal Pinaria, who somehow came into possession of the golden fascinum, and, for reasons never explained, felt obliged to pass it on to your grandfather when he came of age? Now you wear the fascinum, Kaeso—and you are the very image of a Potitius! Do you begin to see how all these things connect?"

"Guesswork! Innuendo! You slander the memory of a pious Vestal! You have no proof of anything!"

"The gods know the truth about you, Kaeso. And now, so do you."

Kaeso felt faint. The room seemed to pitch and sway around him. "Why are you telling me this?"

"Isn't it always better to know the truth?"

"No!"

"What was it I heard you say, as you looked out the window? Something about being the architect of your own fortune? How can you build a lasting monument, a life of virtue and accomplishment, unless you begin with a firm foundation of self-knowledge?"

"You're a stupid old man, Titus Potitius! You and your third-rate family have squandered whatever good fortune ever accrued to you. You've offended the gods by selling your birthright to the Ara Maxima. How dare you come to me with such a lie, suggesting my grandfather was the bastard of a Vestal and a slave!"

Potitius sighed. "This has gone badly. I never intended to offend you. Don't worry, Kaeso. I'll be discreet. What I've discovered is for your ears only. I haven't even told any other members of the family."

"Shout your lies from the rooftops, if you dare to! You'll only make yourself a greater laughingstock than you already are."

Titus Potitius shuffled toward the door and disappeared. Kaeso violently kicked at the floor and sent a loose tile flying against the wall.

That night, sleep was slow to come. When it did, Kaeso was haunted by nightmares more vivid and disturbing than any he had previously experienced.

One dream jarringly led into the next. In each of them he felt heart-wrenchingly alone and bereft, the object of other men's ridicule and disdain. At one point, naked and covered with sweat, he sat bolt upright in his bed and reached up to discover that he was wearing the fascinum, though he had no memory of having put it on. Angry and distraught, in tears, he tore the chain from his neck and cast the amulet into the darkness, only to see it come flying back at him! He shrieked in terror—and only then awoke, realizing that he had still been dreaming.

His mother and father stood at his door, staring at him; his screams had awakened them. He felt embarrassed to be naked before his mother, but there was nothing with which to cover himself. He looked again, and in his father's place he saw Titus Potitius, clucking his tongue. "There, there, my child," said the old man, "don't be afraid of the truth . . ."

Kaeso was still dreaming.

When at last he did awake, he felt utterly exhausted. He squinted suspiciously at the sunlight that leaked around the shutters, afraid he might yet be asleep, trapped in another nightmare.

He rose from the bed. On trembling legs he shambled across the room and opened the box where he kept the fascinum. The sight of it repelled him. He should throw the awful thing away! But his father would expect him to wear it on his wedding day. To get rid of it now would only call attention to its absence. He slammed the box shut.

On the day before his wedding, Kaeso went to the house on the Aventine to make sure that all was ready to receive him and his bride the next day. In preparation for the ceremony, an altar had been erected before the front door for the sacrifice of the sheep and the taking of the auspices. Inside the house were the ceremonial chairs for the bride and groom, ready to be taken into the street for the open-air celebration. Both chairs were stacked high with dried garlands that would be used to decorate the doorway. Between them was the sheepskin rug upon which he would set Galeria after he carried her across the threshold, as if she were his captive Sabine. Kaeso's heart sped up as he considered the momentousness of the looming event. By this time tomorrow, he would be a married man.

The house was sparsely furnished, but the floor tiles had been fixed and the whole house had been scrubbed clean. The little garden had been planted with new shrubberies and flowers, and the kitchen had been stocked with pots and pans. He saw the bed that had been placed against the wall, near the window—a new bed, larger than the one in which he was used to sleeping alone—and he felt a quiver of erotic anticipation. Galeria grew more beautiful every time he saw her; soon he would see her naked, and would be naked with her, and would possess her. Any hesitation he felt about the ceremony faded when his thoughts turned to the carnal pleasures that awaited him. He crossed the room, wanting to take a closer look at the bed.

A voice that was almost a whisper said: "The house looks very nice."

Kaeso spun around. "What are *you* doing here? Get out!"

Titus Potitius stood in the doorway. "Can a kinsman not visit a kinsman on the day before his wedding, to wish him well?"

"You're a madman. The gods have made you mad, as a punishment for selling your birthright."

"Then we sold it for too little."

"Appius Claudius should have thrown you out when you came begging. He shouldn't have given you so much as a copper coin."

"It's curious that you should mention money. Along with paying my respects, that's one of the reasons I've come to see you." Potitius stood with his hands clasped before him and his eyes downcast. "Galeria's family is wealthy. I presume she comes to you with a substantial dowry. As well, I think the censor must have arranged a very generous salary for you. You even own your own house! You are a most fortunate young man, to be of independent means at such an early age."

"And you are an old fool, to have squandered everything at your age."

"The travails of the Potitii began long before my time. How typical of our misfortunes, that one of the most gifted young men of his generation, who should be the scion of the family, does not even bear the name Potitius! Still, in a time of trouble, I am hoping that young man will hear the call of the blood in his veins and will help his kinsmen."

Kaeso clenched his teeth. "What do you want from me?"

"A loan. Only that. A small loan, from one kinsman to another."

"Why now? Why must you spoil a day when I should be thinking of nothing but my wedding?"

"My request has nothing to do with your marriage—although I'm sure the bride's father would be shocked to learn that she is about to marry the descendent of a slave and a tarnished Vestal."

Kaeso's legs grew unsteady. He sat on the bed.

Potitius's voice was gentle. "It's a curious thing, that you should be a builder. Your ancestor Titus Potitius, the friend of Coriolanus, was a builder, too—did you know that? He was also the first to bring shame on the family. It would be a pity, if you should take after him in that regard, as well."

"How much do you want?"

Potitius named a sum. Kaeso drew a sharp breath, appalled at the man's greed but relieved he had not asked for more. It was agreed that Potitius would come to him in two day's time and that Kaeso would pay him then.

Amazingly, despite his excitement at his impending wedding and the anxieties aroused by his unwanted visitor, Kaeso slept like a stone that night. He experienced no nightmares. He woke early, before the first cockcrow, feeling clearheaded and refreshed. He lit a lamp.

Some time earlier he had finished reading all the documents loaned to him by his cousin Quintus. He had been meaning to return them, but in the rush of getting ready for the wedding had neglected to do so. He reached for them now. He found himself rereading certain of the documents, occasionally nodding and humming.

After a while he set the documents aside, extinguished the lamp, and slept for another hour, as men do when they have made an irrevocable decision and are at peace with the gods and themselves.

When Titus Potitius next came to call, it was ostensibly to pay his respects to the newlyweds. Kaeso received the visitor in his new home without a trace of rancor. He even spoke warmly to him, and apologized for his ear-lier harsh words, then introduced him to his new bride.

To Potitius, it seemed that a night of marital bliss had done wonders to correct Kaeso's attitude. And why not? As he saw it, there was no need for Kaeso to be unfriendly. Having convinced himself that selling the family's rights to the Ara Maxima was acceptable, Potitius had further convinced himself that his request for assistance from Kaeso was entirely reasonable. They were kinsmen, after all. Kaeso had plenty of money, and Potitius was in dire straits. The gods smiled on generosity. There was no reason the transaction should be unpleasant. Indeed, Kaeso should be proud to help an elder kinsman in need.

With his head full of such rationalizations, and his guard down, Potitius thought nothing of it when the bride offered him a portion of the tradi-tional dish of beans left over from the wedding feast, and he did not notice that it was Kaeso who actually put the bowl in his hands. He was hungry, and the beans were delicious. Kaeso discreetly slipped him a small bag of coins, then hurried him out the door. Potitius took no offense at being dis-missed so quickly. It was only natural that the groom was eager to be alone with his bride.

Patting the money bag that hung from his waist, humming a happy tune, Potitius crossed the Aventine, heading for his house on the less fash-ionable south side of the hill. Walking in front of the Temple of Juno Regina, he saw that one of the sacred geese had escaped its enclosure and was strutting across the porch, craning its neck this way and that. Potitius smiled, then felt a sudden tingling in his throat. His mouth was very dry; he should have asked for something to drink to wash down the beans.

Abruptly, a flame seemed to run down his throat all the way to his bow-els. The sensation was so intense and so peculiar that he knew something was seriously wrong. He had reached that advanced age when a man might die at any moment, suddenly and without apparent cause. Was that hap-pening now? Had the gods at last chosen to end the story of his life?

Without knowing how he got there, he found himself lying flat on his back on the ground in front of the temple, hardly able to move. A crowd gathered around him. People stooped over and peered down at him. Their expressions were not encouraging. Men shook their heads. A woman cov-ered her face and began to weep.

"Cold," he managed to say. "Can't seem . . . to move."

As if to contradict him, his arms and legs began to twitch, a little at first, and then so violently that people drew back in fright. The alarmed goose honked and flapped its wings.

Potitius realized what had happened. He hardly thought of it as murder, but rather as yet another misfortune to befall the Potitii. How the gods must hate his family! It never occurred to him to accuse Kaeso with his dying breath; to admit his extortion would only blacken his own name and further humiliate the family. His convulsions ceased, along with his breathing.

Titus, reigning paterfamilias of the Potitii, died swiftly and in silence.

Two lictors sent by the curule aedile arrived to look after the body until a family member could claim it. The lictor who took an inventory of the dead man's possessions recognized Potitius and expressed surprise that the old fellow should be carrying such a substantial amount of money on his person. "The Potitii are always crying poverty, but look at all these coins!"

"Maybe it's what left of that settlement the censor gave him for selling the rights to the Ara Maxima," said his companion. "No good could come of such sacrilege."

"No good's already come to this poor fellow!"

❁

To Kaeso's eye, Titus Potitius, the son of the deceased paterfamilias, looked only slightly younger than his father.

"So you see," said Potitius, "as far as I was able to figure out, you must have been one of the last people to see him alive. Papa told one of the slaves he would be stopping here on his way home, but he didn't say why. It's a bit of puzzle how he came to have so much money on him. No one has a clue as to where he got that bag of coins."

The two of them sat in the tiny garden of Kaeso's new house. There was no innuendo or suspicion in Potitius's voice; he sounded like a bereaved son who simply wanted to learn all he could about his father's final hours. Still, Kaeso felt a flutter of anxiety in his chest. He chose his words care-

fully and spoke in what he hoped was a suitably commiserating tone of
voice.

"It's true, your father paid us a brief visit that day. He and I had met
briefly once before, at the house of Appius Claudius. It was very consider-
ate of him to come by and congratulate us on our nuptials."

"Such a nice old fellow," remarked Galeria, who sat nearby with her
spindle and distaff, spinning wool with the assistance of her slave girl. Galeria had many old-fashioned virtues, but keeping silent was not one of
them, and the house was too small for Kaeso to conduct a conversation out
of her hearing. "He seemed very fond of you, Kaeso."

Potitius smiled. "I can see why Papa might have taken a liking to you.
You probably reminded him of cousin Marcus."

"Oh?"

"Yes, the resemblance is quite striking. And Papa was very sentimental.
And . . . he wasn't above imposing on people. He didn't . . ." Potitius lowered his eyes. "He didn't by any chance ask you for money, did he? I'm
afraid Papa had a bad habit of asking for loans, even from people he barely
knew."

"Of course not!"

Potitius sighed. "Ah, well, I had to ask. I'm still tracking down his un-
paid debts. Where he acquired that bag of coins may remain a mystery."

Kaeso nodded sympathetically. Clearly, the younger Titus Potitius knew
nothing of his father's scheme to extort money from him. And yet, the
man's fretting over the bag of coins, and his remark about Kaeso's resemblance to a kinsman, made Kaeso uneasy.

Kaeso took a deep breath. The flutter in his chest subsided. As had occurred in the early hours of his wedding day, a resolution came to him, and
with it a sense of peace.

He looked earnestly at Potitius. "Like my dear friend Appius Claudius,
I'm moved by your family's plight. That one of Roma's most ancient families should have dwindled so greatly in numbers and fallen into such
poverty should be a cause for concern to all the city's patricians. We of the
old families squabble too much among ourselves, when we should be
looking out for one another. I'm only a young man, and I have very little
influence—"

"You underestimate yourself, Kaeso. You have the ear of both Quintus Fabius and Appius Claudius. Not many men in Roma can say that."

"I suppose that's true. And I should like to do what I can to help the Potitii."

"I would be very grateful for any assistance you can give us." Potitius sighed. "The duties of paterfamilias weigh heavily upon me!"

"Perhaps I can help to relieve that burden, if only a little. Upon my recommendation, my cousin Quintus might be able to secure positions for some for your kinsman, and so might the censor. You and I should meet again, Titus, over a bit of food and wine."

"I would be honored," said Potitius. "My house is hardly worthy to receive you, but if you and your wife would accept an invitation to dinner . . ."

And so Kaeso began to insinuate himself into the household, and into the trust, of the new paterfamilias of the Potitii.

311 B.C.

The new fountain at the terminus of the aqueduct was not merely the largest fountain in all of Roma, but a splendid work of art. The shallow, elevated pool into which the water would spill was a circle fifteen feet in diameter. In the center, from the mouths of three river sprites magnificently carved from stone, water would continuously jet into the pool.

Many of the city's most distinguished citizens had gathered to witness the inauguration of the fountain. Chief among them was Appius Claudius, smiling broadly and looking resplendent in his purple censor's toga. Quintus Fabius was also there, exhibiting his perpetual scowl. He had agreed to attend only begrudgingly, and Kaeso felt obligated to stand next to him.

The auspices had been taken; the augur had spotted several river-fowl wheeling over the nearby Tiber, a sure sign of the gods' favor. There was a lull in the festivities while the engineers made ready to open the valves. Quintus began to grumble.

"So this is your friend Claudius's excuse for hanging on as censor, well past his legal term—a fountain!"

Kaeso pursed his lips. "Claudius argued that his work on the aqueduct and the road is too important to be interrupted. He asked to continue as censor. The Senate agreed."

"Only because Claudius has packed the Senate with his minions! He's as devious and headstrong as his ancestors and just as dangerous. For his own selfish ends, he's caused a political crisis in the city." Quintus shook his head. "These so-called grand projects of his are merely a diversion while he continues to press for the implementation of his radical voting schemes. He won't rest until he's made the Roman republic into a Greek democracy ruled by a demagogue like himself—a disaster that will never happen as long as I have a breath in my body."

"Please, cousin! We're here to celebrate a feat of Roman engineering, not to argue politics. Surely the aqueduct is something we can all be proud of."

Quintus grunted in reply. His frown abruptly softened. "How is the little one?"

Kaeso smiled. Galeria had become pregnant very soon after their wedding, and had recently given birth to a son. Kaeso knew that Quintus would be pleased, but he had been surprised at how avidly his cousin doted on the baby.

"Little Kaeso is in good health. He loves the gourd rattle you gave him, and all the other toys."

Quintus nodded. "Good! He's very bright and alert, that one. With those lungs of his, he'll make a powerful orator someday."

"He can certainly make himself heard," agreed Kaeso.

Claudius mounted a platform and raised his hands to quiet the crowd. "Citizens! We are almost ready to fill the fountain. But first, if you will indulge me, I should like to say a few words about how this marvelous feat of engineering was achieved." He proceeded to discourse on the importance of water to the growing city, recalled the flash of insight that had inspired him to commence planning the aqueduct, and recounted a few anecdotes about the construction. His speech, delivered from memory, was full of puns and clever turns of phrase. Even Quintus grunted an involuntary laugh at some of his witticisms.

"There are many, many men who must be thanked for their contributions to this great enterprise," said Claudius. "Lest I forget a single one of them, I have written them down." Claudius proceeded to read the names. Kaeso was flattered that he was mentioned early in the long list.

As Claudius continued to read, Quintus whispered to Kaeso, "Why is he squinting so?"

Kaeso frowned. Quintus had touched upon a matter of growing concern to him: the censor's eyesight. Quite abruptly, Claudius's vision had begun to deteriorate, to such a degree that he practically had to press his nose against his beloved Greek scrolls to read them. The list he was now reading had been written in large letters, yet still he had to narrow his eyes to make out the names.

Quintus saw the worry on Kaeso's face. "The rumor is true, then? Appius Claudius is going blind?"

"Of course not!" said Kaeso. "He's merely strained his eyes from working so hard."

Quintus raised an eyebrow. "You know what people are saying, don't you?"

"People are fools!" whispered Kaeso. He had indeed heard the vicious rumor being put about by Claudius's enemies. They said the censor, who so loved the pleasures of reading and writing, was being punished with blindness by the gods, for having allowed the transfer of religious duties at the Ara Maxima from the Potitius family to temple slaves. "Whatever you may think of his politics, cousin, Appius Claudius is a pious man who honors the gods. If his eyesight is failing, it's not because the gods are punishing him."

"And yet, the gods punished those other unlikely friends of yours, the Potitii, did they not? And most severely!"

Kaeso drew a sharp breath, but did not answer. In his dealings with the Potitii over the last year, Kaeso had been acting in his own self-interest, to obliterate the secret of his origins and to safeguard the future of his offspring. But might the gods have taken a part, making him the instrument of their wrath against an impious family ripe for destruction?

"Do you doubt that the terrible end of the Potitii was the result of divine judgment?" said Quintus, pressing him. "What other explanation could there be for such an extraordinary sequence of deaths? In a matter of months, every male in the family grew sick and died. Not a single Potitius is left to pass on the name. One of Roma's oldest families has become extinct!"

"Some said they died of plague," said Kaeso.

"A plague attacking only one family, and only the males?"

"That was what the Potitii themselves believed."

"Yes, and in their desperation they convinced the Senate to appoint a special dictator to drive a nail into the wooden tablet outside Minerva's sanctuary, to ward off pestilence. It did no good. At least they had the comfort of a steadfast friend—you, Kaeso. Others turned their backs on the Potitii, fearful of being contaminated by their bad fortune. But you, having just befriended them, remained loyal to the very end. You never stopped visiting the sick and comforting the survivors." Quintus nodded sagely. "Once, long ago, we Fabii were almost extinguished, as you well know. But that was honorably, in battle, and the gods saw fit to spare one of our number to carry on the line. History shall reflect very differently upon the fate of the wretched Potitii. Be proud of the name you have passed on to your son, Kaeso!"

"The name means more to me than life itself, cousin."

Appius Claudius finished reading the list. Amid applause, he raised his hand to order the opening of the valves. "Let flow the aqueduct!"

From the mouths of the three river sprites issued a great rush of air, as if they groaned. The gurgling sound reminded Kaeso of the death rattles of his victims.

What a great deal of ingenuity and cleverness and sheer hard work had been demanded of him, to win the trust of the Potitii and make sure they never suspected him! From Appius Claudius he had learned the arts of charm; from his cousin Quintus he had learned everything there was to know about poisons. Once it began, his quest to eradicate the Potitii had become all-consuming. Each new success was more exhilarating than the one before. Kaeso had almost regretted killing the last of his victims, but when it was done, he felt an indescribable sense of relief. His secret was safe. No man would ever tell Kaeso's son the shameful truth of their origins.

The groaning of the river sprites grew louder. The noise was so uncanny that the crowd drew back and gasped. Then water began to jet from all three mouths at once. It was a spectacular sight. Foaming and splashing, the torrents began to fill the pool.

Claudius shouted above the roar. "Citizens, I give you water! Fresh, pure water all the way from the springs of Gabii!"

The crowd broke into rapturous applause. "Hail Appius Claudius!" men cried. "Hail the maker of the aqueduct!"

279 B.C.

Before the Senate, the aged Appius Claudius, now called Appius Claudius Caecus—"the Blind"—was delivering the greatest speech of his life. More than two hundred years later, the orator Cicero would declare this speech to be one of most sublime exercises in the Latin language, and Appius Claudius Caecus would be revered as the Father of Latin Prose.

The occasion was a debate on Roma's resistance to the Greek adventurer King Pyrrhus, the greatest menace to confront the Romans since the Gauls. Just as his kinsman Alexander the Great fifty years before had conquered the East with lightning speed, so Pyrrhus thought he could invade Italy and make quick work of subjugating its "barbarians"—the term being a Greek epithet for any race that did not speak Greek.

Thus far, the Romans had confounded Pyrrhus's plans. The invader continued to win battles, but these costly triumphs stretched his supply lines, weakened the morale of his overburdened officers, and wore away the numbers of his fighting men.

"If there are many more such 'Pyrrhic victories,'" declared Appius Claudius Caecus, "King Pyrrhus may soon discover, to his dismay, that he has won one battle too many!" The chamber resounded with laughter. The unflagging wit and relentless optimism of the blind senator were much appreciated amid the gloomy debates of recent years.

"Some of you are calling for peace with Pyrrhus," said Claudius. "You want an end to the spilling of Roman blood and the blood of our allies and subjects. You are ready to offer concessions. You will allow Pyrrhus to gain the permanent foothold he seeks on Italian soil, hoping he will be content with a little kingdom here and put aside his dream of a Western empire to rival Alexander's empire in the East. I tell you, Pyrrhus will never settle for that! He will never stop scheming to rob us of everything. He will not be satisfied until he has made us his slaves.

"You all know that I am a man who treasures Greek learning and the beauties of Greek literature and art. But I will never have a Greek rule over me, and I will never obey any law that is not chiseled in Latin! The future of Italy belongs to us—to the people and Senate of Roma. It does not belong to any Greek, and not to any king. We must continue the struggle against Pyrrhus, no matter the cost, until we drive him out of Italy entirely. When the last Greek ship bears away the last remnants of his exhausted army, Italy shall be ours, and Roma shall be free to fulfill the destiny the gods have decreed for us!"

A majority of the senators sprang to their feet, applauding and shouting accolades. Seeing that Claudius had decisively carried the day, those who had argued for appeasing Pyrrhus begrudgingly joined the ovation. The war against Pyrrhus would continue.

Even as he was leaving the Senate House, assisted by a slave to guide him on the steps, Claudius was thinking ahead to his next oration. Unable any longer to read or write, he had become adept at composing and memorizing long passages in his head. The topic would be Roma's relationship with Carthage, the great seaport on the coast of Africa founded by Phoenicians at about the same time Romulus founded his city, whose rise to prominence in many ways mirrored that of Roma. The Senate had just signed a treaty of friendship with Carthage, and the incursion of Pyrrhus into their mutual sphere of interest had made Roma and Carthage allies—but for how long? Once Pyrrhus was expelled, Claudius believed that a natural rivalry between Roma and Carthage for domination of Sicily, southern Italy, and the sea lanes of the western Mediterranean was certain to come to the fore.

"Of course, once again, those fools the Fabii can't see the obvious," he muttered to himself. "They still think Roma should expand her reach northward to the Alps and beyond, and pursue a policy of moderation toward Carthage. But southward and seaward lies our destiny. A clash with Carthage is inevitable!"

The slave remained silent. He was used to hearing his master talk to himself. Sometimes Claudius carried on elaborate arguments with himself that lasted for hours, changing voices as he shifted points of view.

Now in the twilight of his life, frail and nearly blind, a lesser man than Claudius might have succumbed to bitterness. His radical attempts at reform had failed; a few years after his censorship, Quintus Fabius had seized control of the office and had ruthlessly undone almost all of

Claudius's populist enactments. Quintus Fabius was repeatedly elected consul, and his supporters dubbed him Maximus. Appius Claudius became the Blind, while Quintus Fabius became the Greatest! Claudius had been forced to realize that true popular government would never take root in Roma. But his physical monuments would endure. The Appian Aqueduct remained a marvel of engineering, and each year another stretch of the Appian Way was paved with stone that would last for the ages. After a lifetime of victories and defeats, Appius Claudius Caecus was more passionate than ever about the destiny of Roma.

Crossing the Forum, clinging to the arm of his guide, Claudius heard a voice call out, "Senator! May I have a word with you?"

Claudius stopped abruptly, almost certain that he recognized the voice—and yet, it was impossible! That voice, beloved to his memory, belonged to his one-time protégé, Kaeso Fabius Dorso. But Kaeso was no longer among mortals. He had died many months ago in a battle against Pyrrhus. Although they had drifted apart over the years, Claudius had followed Kaeso's career at a distance. His youthful interest in building had eventually been eclipsed by his excellence at soldiering; like a typical Fabius, Kaeso was born to become a warrior. Claudius grieved when he learned of his death. Hearing his voice now brought back a flood of memories.

Claudius gripped the arm of his guide. "Who speaks to me? What do you see, slave? Is it a man, or only the shade of a man?"

"I assure you, Senator, I am not a shade," said the voice that sounded so familiar. "My name is Kaeso Fabius Dorso."

"Ah! You must be the son of my old friend."

"You remember my father, then?"

"I certainly do. My condolences to you on his death."

"He died honorably, fighting for Roma. I also fought in that battle, under his command. I saw him fall. Afterward, I tended to his body."

"You can be very proud of him."

"I am. He was a fearsome warrior. Men say he killed more of the enemy in that campaign than any other soldier in the legion. My father took a fierce delight in bringing death to the invaders."

"Bloodlust has its place on the field of battle," declared Claudius. "Your father's joy in killing redounded to the glory of Roma and the honor of our gods."

Kaeso reached up to touch the talisman at his neck—the golden fascinum he had retrieved from his father's corpse on the battlefield. The amulet had failed to protect its wearer against the spear that killed him, but it was a cherished heirloom nonetheless. Kaeso wore it in memory of his father.

"Tell me, Kaeso, how old are you?"

"Thirty-two."

"And your father, when he died?"

"He was fifty."

"Can so many years have passed, so swiftly?" Claudius shook his head. "But what's that, young man? Do I hear you weep?"

"Only a little. I'm very honored, sir, to hear my father praised by a man so renowned for noble speech."

"Indeed?" Claudius beamed.

His slave eyed Kaeso suspiciously and spoke into Claudius's ear. "Master! The fellow is a Fabius."

"So he is. But his father was different from the rest of them. Perhaps the son takes after the father. He seems respectful enough."

"I assure you, Senator, I hold your achievements in the highest regard. That's why I approached you today. I was hoping you might honor a request."

"Perhaps, young man, though I'm very busy. Speak."

"My father was always quoting your aphorisms. Sometimes it seemed that half his sentences began, 'As Appius Claudius so wisely put it . . .' I was hoping, in honor of my father, that you might assist me to make a collection of those sayings. I know many of them by heart, of course, but I should hate to get a single word wrong, and there must be some I've forgotten, and some I've never heard. I was thinking that you could dictate them to me, and I could write them down, and we could group them according to subject. We might even attempt a translation of the Latin into Greek."

"You know Greek?"

"Well enough to have served as my father's translator, for the messages we intercepted from Pyrrhus's couriers."

"The son of Kaeso not only has a literary bent, but has mastered Greek! Truly, each generation improves upon the last."

"I can never hope to be the man-killer my father was," said Kaeso humbly.

"Come, walk with me. The day is mild and I need the exercise. We shall walk up to the Capitoline, and you shall describe to me the recent adornments which, alas, I am unable to see with my failing eyes."

They ambled up the winding path to the summit, where in recent years the city had indulged its fervor for grand public works. The barren hilltop where once Romulus had set up his asylum for outcasts had become a place of lavish temples and magnificent bronze statues.

"This new statue of Hercules," said Claudius. "Is it as impressive as men say? I've touched the thing, but it's so big I can do no more than grasp its ankles."

To Kaeso the statue hardly seemed new—it had been there since he was a boy—but perhaps time was measured differently by the much older Claudius. "Well, of course, my family is descended from Hercules—"

"Ah! You Fabii never miss a chance to remind us of that claim."

"So I have a tendency to favor any image of the god, and the bigger the better. Actually, the bronze workmanship is quite good. Hercules wears the cowl of the Nemean lion and carries a club. His expression is quite fierce. Should the Gauls ever dare to come back, I think his image alone might scare them away from the Capitoline."

"How does it compare to the colossal statue of Jupiter, over by the temple?"

"Oh, the Jupiter is much taller than the Hercules, as I suppose the father should be. People can see it all the way from Mount Alba, ten miles down the Appian Way!"

"You know the story of the statue's creation?"

"Yes. After Spurius Carvilius crushed the Samnites, he melted their breastplates, greaves, and helmets to make the statue. The god's enormous size represents, literally, the magnitude of our victory over our old enemy. Out of the bronze filings left over, the consul made the life-sized statue of himself that stands at the feet of the Jupiter."

"You need not describe that to me. I remember quite clearly how ugly Carvilius is! And atop the Temple of Jupiter—is the quadriga as magnificent as they say? It used to be made of terra cotta, you know, an expressive but rather delicate material. It was repaired from time to time, but some parts were as old as the temple, and probably made by the hand of the artist Vulca himself. But now the terra cotta has been taken down and replaced with an exact duplicate, done entirely in bronze."

"I remember the original terra cotta," said Kaeso. "Believe me, the bronze is much more impressive. The details of Jupiter's face, the flaring nostrils of the steeds, the decoration of the chariot, are all remarkable."

"Alas, if only I still had eyes to see! The bronze replacement for the quadriga was done by my dear colleagues Gnaeus and Quintus Ogulnius, you know. It heartens me to see men of a younger generation take up the populist banner. In the year both Ogulnius brothers served as curule aediles, they put the worst of the rich moneylenders on trial and convicted them. Out of the confiscated property, the Ogulnii paid for that new bronze quadriga. They also paid for that new statue of Romulus and Remus over on the Palatine, which has become such a shrine for the common people of the city."

"Do you know, I've never seen it."

"Really? Neither have I, but blindness is my excuse. How your cousin Quintus must detest the Ogulnii and their politics!"

"We call my venerable cousin 'Maximus' nowadays," said Kaeso.

"I suppose he's deliberately kept all the Fabii from paying homage to the Ogulnii's great monument. We must go at once, so that you can finally see it."

They descended the Capitoline, crossed the Forum, and ascended the Stairs of Cacus. The slave barely needed to assist Claudius, who knew the way by heart. At the foot of the fig tree not far from the Hut of Romulus, the statue of the Twins had been erected upon a pedestal. It was not colossal in size, but the image was striking: Beneath a standing she-wolf, two naked babies squatted and turned up their faces to suckle the animal's teats.

"Well, what do you think, young man?"

"It's remarkable. Very powerful. Very beautiful."

"Do you suppose the founder of the city and his unfortunate brother were literally raised by a wolf?"

"So legends tell us."

"And do you never question legends? Some believe the she wolf to be a metaphor, or perhaps a too-literal interpretation of a tale passed down by word of mouth. The same word, after all, can refer to a woman of the she-wolf variety—a prostitute. Is it not more likely that the Twins were raised by such a woman, rather than by a wild animal?"

Claudius was unable see the younger man's expression, but from the silence that ensued he could tell that Kaeso was taken aback. Claudius laughed good-naturedly. "Forgive my outspokenness. Obviously, such ideas are not spoken in the staid households of the Fabii!"

"Some of your ideas . . . are novel to me," admitted Kaeso. "My father said you often challenged his ways of thinking, but that you also inspired him. Thank you for showing me the statue of the Twins and the she wolf."

Claudius smiled. "We're not far from my house. Would you like to see my library? It's grown considerably since the days when I tried to teach your father Greek. New scrolls arrive every month. I can't read them myself, of course. Someone must read them aloud to me. You have a very pleasant voice, Kaeso."

"Senator, I would be honored to read aloud to you."

The slave led them homeward.

"We'll take some refreshment," said Claudius, walking through the vestibule. "Then perhaps we can get to work on that collection of aphorisms you propose."

Kaeso nodded happily, then frowned. "There was one of your sayings that my father found particularly inspiring. Something to do with architecture, and fortune . . ."

" 'Each man is the architect of his own fortune.' "

"Exactly! My father lived by those words."

"I'm sure that no man ever put those words into practice more faithfully than did Kaeso Fabius Dorso!"

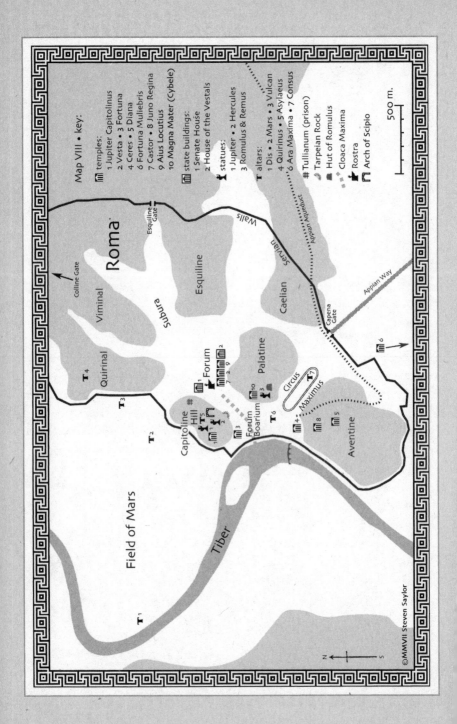

Map VIII • key:

temples:
1 Jupiter Capitolinus
2 Vesta • 3 Fortuna
4 Ceres • 5 Diana
6 Fortuna Muliebris
7 Castor • 8 Juno Regina
9 Aius Locutius
10 Magna Mater (Cybele)

state buildings:
1 Senate House
2 House of the Vestals

statues:
1 Jupiter • 2 Hercules
3 Romulus & Remus

altars:
1 Dis • 2 Mars • 3 Vulcan
4 Quirinus • 5 Asylaeus
6 Ara Maxima • 7 Consus

Tullianum (prison)
Tarpeian Rock
Hut of Romulus
Cloaca Maxima
Rostra
Arch of Scipio

500 m.

Field of Mars

Tiber

Roma

Colline Gate

Quirinal

Viminal

Subura

Esquiline Gate

Esquiline

Capitoline Hill

Forum

Palatine

Caelian

Servian Walls

Appian Aqueduct

Capena Gate

Forum Boarium

Circus Maximus

Aventine

Appian Way

©MMVII Steven Saylor

VIII

SCIPIO'S SHADOW

216 B.C.

"We brought these accursed Carthaginians to their knees once. We shall do it again!" So declared Quintus Fabius Maximus, wearing an expression stern enough to have pleased his great-grandfather, who had been the first to take the name Maximus almost ninety years earlier. With one hand he held a cup of wine. With the other he tapped his upper lip, a nervous habit that called attention to a very prominent wart. For this distinguishing feature on an otherwise homely face, his friends had playfully given him an additional name, Verrucosus.

From across the dining room, young Kaeso stole glances at his host—a man he found quite intimidating—and wished that his own physical imperfections were limited to an ugly wart or two.

One of Kaeso's legs was shorter than the other. One of his forearms had a strange bend in it and its muscles were not always entirely under his control. He walked with a slight limp and had never been able to ride a horse. He was also subject to the falling disease. The fluttering in his head occurred at the most inopportune times. At its worst it caused him to lose consciousness completely.

Despite these imperfections, Kaeso's mother had always assured him that he was nonetheless beautiful. At twenty, Kaeso was old enough to look at himself critically in a mirror and see that this was not a mother's flattery or wishful thinking, but the truth. His eyes were a rare shade of blue. His lustrous hair was the color of sunlight in honey. His face might serve as a model for a Greek sculptor. But what use was a handsome face if a man's body was unsuited to riding, or marching, or fighting, as the times demanded? Far better to have a strong body and a wart on his lip the size of a chickpea, like his great and powerful cousin Maximus—who had just caught Kaeso staring and stared back at him, scowling.

Kaeso lowered his eyes and nervously tapped at the gold fascinum at his neck, a precious heirloom that he had put on especially for this very important occasion.

The other two guests at the dinner were the same age as Kaeso. His cousin Quintus was the son of Maximus; Publius Cornelius Scipio was their mutual friend. The occasion was a somber one. Come morning, Quintus and Scipio would be going off to war. How Kaeso wished he was going with them!

Seventy years had passed since Appius Claudius the Blind had delivered his stirring speech in the Senate against the Greek invader Pyrrhus. The final retreat of Pyrrhus from Italy was now a distant memory, but there were still old fighters alive who could remember the even greater war that followed, with Carthage. As Appius Claudius had predicted, after their mutual enemy Pyrrhus was defeated, Roma's maritime rival had become her military foe. For over twenty years, in Sicily and Africa, on land and sea, the Romans and Carthaginians waged a bloody war. The peace that followed, on terms to Roma's advantage, had lasted for a generation, but now the two cities were at war again, and Carthage, led by a general named Hannibal, had brought the war to Italy.

"As you ride off into battle," said Maximus, addressing his son and Scipio but pointedly ignoring Kaeso, "never forget: It wasn't Roma that broke the peace. It was that mad schemer Hannibal, when he dared to attack our allies in Spain. The man has no shame, no scruples, and no honor. A curse on his mongrel army of Libyans, Numidians, Spaniards, and Gauls! May their elephants go mad and stamp them into the dirt!"

"Hear, hear!" said Quintus, raising his cup. Like his father, he was homely, and he displayed the same earnest scowl, which looked more like a pout on his youthful face.

Scipio raised his cup and joined the toast. Like Kaeso, Scipio had been blessed by the gods with striking looks, though his hair was darker and his features of a more rugged cast. He wore his hair long and swept back from his face—like Alexander, people said—and he was powerfully built. As a student, he had quickly matched and then exceeded the erudition of his tutors. As an athlete, he had excelled above all others. As a soldier, he had already made a name for himself. He was known for his sure, quick stride and his strong grip. Scipio made a powerful impression on everyone he met.

Kaeso belatedly raised his cup as well. Only Scipio seemed to take notice of him, tipping his cup in Kaeso's direction and shooting him a quick smile.

"As you say, Maximus, the Carthaginians are most certainly in the wrong," said Scipio. His deep voice was strong but mellow. People often remarked that he would make a fine orator when he was old enough to run for office. "But surely you misspeak when you say that Hannibal is mad. Obsessed, perhaps; we all know the tale of how his father, bitter at his own humiliation and the concessions made by Carthage after the last war, made the boy Hannibal swear undying hatred of Roma and all things Roman. Clearly, Hannibal took the oath to heart. No one can accuse him of shirking his filial duty! He deliberately broke the truce when he attacked our allies in Spain. Then, they say, he had a dream of the future: A god placed him on the back of a gigantic snake, and he rode the snake across the earth, uprooting trees and boulders and causing utter destruction. Hannibal took this dream to mean that he was destined to lay waste to all of Italy."

"So he told his soldiers." Quintus smirked. "He probably made up that dream to spur them on."

"True or not, he set out from Spain and crossed the southern coast of Gaul. Everyone said the Alps would keep him out of Italy; no one thought he could cross the mountains with his army and his elephants intact. But he found a pass, and swept down upon us like a firestorm! One drubbing after another he's given us. I was there with my father at the river Ticinus, in the first engagement of the war, when the day went so badly for us—".

"Don't be modest, Scipio," said Quintus. "You saved your father's life when he was wounded on the battlefield, and everyone knows it."

"I did what any son would do." If Scipio downplayed his own bravery, he also glossed over the magnitude of the repeated defeats the Romans had received at Hannibal's hand.

In his devastating forays across the Italian peninsula, Hannibal had acquired a reputation for almost superhuman ingenuity and resilience. He had shown himself to be a master of disguise, escaping plots to assassinate him by donning wigs and costumes. He had recovered from terrible wounds, including the loss of an eye. He had conceived and executed outrageous stratagems. One dark night he threw a Roman army into utter confusion by tying flaming torches to the horns of a herd of cattle, which in their panic created the illusion of a vast army rushing in all directions across an otherwise deserted mountainside.

Even as his implacable hatred and seeming invincibility inspired their fear and loathing, Hannibal had won the grudging admiration of many Romans, and Scipio spoke of him with a certain respect.

"Now the one-eyed Cacus and his mongrel mercenaries have penetrated to the very heart of Italy," said Quintus. "They roam and ravage at will, and pick off our allies one by one. But not for much longer, eh, Scipio?"

"Right you are, Quintus. Tomorrow we set out to hunt down Hannibal and put an end to him, once and for all!"

Maximus grunted. "You know my opinion on this matter," he said grimly. The previous year Maximus had been appointed dictator with emergency powers. While his colleagues in the Senate clamored for yet another confrontation with the invaders, Fabius had practiced a shadow war, hounding and harrying Hannibal's army but avoiding a direct engagement. His advice had been, and was still, for caution and patience. While the Romans continued to fight the Carthaginians in other arenas—on the sea, in Spain, and in Sicily—in Italy, he believed, they should avoid any more pitched battles with Hannibal, whose rampaging elephants and Numidian cavalry had so far proven invincible. Instead, the Romans should sit back and let the logistical problems of feeding and finding winter shelter for fifty thousand mercenaries and ten thousand horses take their toll. But Maximus's tactics had been ridiculed and scorned. His enemies named him Cunctator—"the Delayer"—and he had become the most unpopular man in Roma.

Now, the moment belonged to the newly elected consul Gaius Terentius

Varro, a populist firebrand determined to take the battle to Hannibal. He and his fellow consul, Lucius Aemilius Paullus, would be setting out the next morning at the head of the largest Roman army ever assembled, more than eighty thousand men. The plan was to overwhelm Hannibal with sheer numbers. In spite of his father's objections to the campaign, Quintus would be serving in the post of military tribune, as would Scipio.

Kaeso looked at the two other young men and felt acutely aware of his physical limitations. Luckily for him, his imperfections had not been immediately apparent at birth, or otherwise he might have been exposed to the elements shortly after emerging from the womb; his mother had borne two previous sons with such gross physical defects that they had been carried off to die at the behest of Kaeso's father. After Kaeso, his dispirited mother had given birth to no more children. When his father died at the battle of the Ticinus, Kaeso became paterfamilias of his small branch of the Fabii. But his freedom and status would do him little good; unable to complete the prerequisite ten years of military service, Kaeso would never be eligible to run for public office, and thus could never compete in the Course of Honor, the sequence of posts that led to the Senate and the higher magistracies.

Kaeso gazed across the room at his friend Scipio and was torn by mixed emotions. How he admired Scipio! How he envied him! Scipio's steadfast friendship made him feel quite special, and yet, whenever he compared himself to Scipio, he felt only disdain for himself. Scipio was everything Kaeso was not.

"Must we add deafness to the list of your defects, young man?" snapped Maximus. Kaeso, rudely jolted from his reverie, stared blankly at his older cousin. "It's a tedious guest who makes a host repeat himself. I asked you to make a toast. They say you're good with words, Kaeso, if with nothing else. Surely these two young warriors deserve some words of encouragement from those of us who will be sitting out this battle."

"Kaeso has been quiet all night long," said Scipio. His warm smile and gentle tone were in marked contrast to Maximus's brusqueness. "That's not like our Kaeso. He's usually so funny! I suspect my dear friend must be thinking some very deep thoughts tonight."

"I was thinking . . ." Kaeso cleared his throat. "I was thinking that my wise cousin Maximus is most certainly right. No matter what others say, the proper strategy to deal with the devious Carthaginian is to play a game of evasion and wait him out. Let him spend himself against our allies. The more territory he takes, the more he must defend. Let him tie himself down with commitments all over Italy, and spread himself thin. Let the harvests fail, then watch his troops go hungry. Let the winter storms come and spread illness among his men. As I've heard you declare on more than one occasion, cousin Maximus, our new consul Varro is a hotheaded fool. You never mince words, do you, cousin? Not even with a poor cripple like me! But . . ."

Kaeso drew a deep breath. "But, if there must be a battle, and if it must be sooner rather than later, Roma could not ask for better men to fight for her than these two." He raised his cup. "If every man in the army of Varro and Paullus was the match of you, Scipio—and of you, cousin Quintus— then Hannibal's elephants would do well to pack their trunks and leave Italy tomorrow!"

The two warriors laughed and raised their cup.

"That's my Kaeso!" said Scipio. "The one who makes me laugh!"

Kaeso basked in his friend's affectionate gaze, and forgot his feelings of envy and unworthiness.

The final course of stewed onions in a beef broth was served. Quintus suggested a final toast, but Maximus instead called for a slave to collect their cups. "You'll thank me in the morning, when you ride out of Roma with a clear head on your shoulders!"

The dinner guests made their way to the vestibule to take their leave. Kaeso trailed behind Maximus, who put his arm around Quintus's shoulder and spoke into his ear. Kaeso could not help overhearing.

"I'm glad we had this time together, son—though if you ask me, this should have been a party for fighting men only. I'd never have invited cousin Kaeso, except that your friend Scipio insisted. What he sees in that boy, I don't understand!"

Quintus shrugged. "Scipio says there's more to life than war and politics. He and Kaeso have interests in common. They both love books, and poetry."

"Even so . . ."

Kaeso's attention was suddenly claimed by a hand on his shoulder.

"I think you must have drunk too much wine tonight," said Scipio. "You look flushed."

Kaeso abruptly reached into his tunic and produced a tightly rolled scrap of parchment. He pressed it into Scipio's hand.

"What's this?"

"A parting gift," said Kaeso. "No, don't unroll it now. Read it later."

"What is it?"

"I commissioned a poem from Ennius. I know he's your favorite."

"Specially written for the occasion? But why didn't you read it aloud at dinner? You could have added some polish to the evening."

Kaeso turned even redder. The poem had not been something he was willing to share, with Maximus glowering at him. "Ennius is a fighting man, like you. The poem is a call to arms. Quite stirring, I assure you. No one does that sort of thing better than Ennius."

"He'll be as famous as Homer one of these day, mark my words," said Scipio.

Kaeso shrugged. "A bit grandiose for my taste, but I know how much you like his poetry. Read it before the battle, to screw up your courage. Or after the battle, to celebrate."

"Presuming I survive the battle," said Scipio.

Kaeso felt a chill. "Don't say such a thing, Scipio."

"In the days to come, however the fighting turns out, a great many men will die. One of them might be me."

"No! The gods will protect you."

Scipio smiled. "Thank you for the blessing, Kaeso. And thank you for the poem."

After leaving the house of Maximus, Scipio and Quintus went in one direction, while Kaeso headed off in another.

The summer night was warm. The moon was full. Kaeso glumly watched his shadow—a limping figure traversing the dark, quiet streets of the Palatine. Maximus's animosity and Scipio's talk of death had left him feeling moody and anxious, but he knew a place where he could breathe freely and relax, even at this late hour.

Kaeso reached the foot of the Palatine and headed across the Forum. Passing beyond the district of temples and public spaces, he entered a much humbler part of town. The narrow, winding streets of the Subura offered distractions of every sort, especially after dark. On this final night before their departure for war, soldiers crowded the taverns, gambling dens, and brothels. The sounds of a scuffle echoed from nearby. From elsewhere came drunken voices singing an old marching song. The whole area stank of spilled wine, urine, and vomit. The shutters of an upper-story window flew open. Bright moonlight revealed a grinning prostitute wearing a scanty tunica. She stared down at Kaeso and brazenly beckoned to him. Kaeso stared straight ahead and hurried on.

He found the alley he was looking for. The dank passage was so narrow he could touch both walls at once. No torches were set in the walls, and no moonlight penetrated the gloom; the way was very dark. Kaeso arrived at his destination. He knocked on the crudely made door.

A peephole opened. An eye peered at him. Kaeso spoke his name. The slave opened the door at once.

Kaeso stepped into a crowded room where the atmosphere was very different from the staid, patrician decorum that reigned at the house of Maximus. In one corner, a musician was playing a lively tune on a flute, but he could barely be heard over the din of conversation. A mixed assortment of guests of all ages—some richly attired, some in shabby tunics—sat close together on couches or on rugs on the floor; there were even a few women present.

Every hand held a cup. The host—a portly, bearded man in his thirties—was going about pouring wine from a clay pitcher with a cracked handle. Titus Maccius Plautus looked up from his duties, saw Kaeso, smiled broadly, and stepped toward him, sloshing wine onto one of his guests, a frail-looking youth who shrieked with laughter.

Plautus found an abandoned cup, pressed it into Kaeso's hand, and poured him some wine. "There you go, boss! Medicine for your melancholy."

"What makes you think I'm melancholy?"

"That frown on your face. But we shall get rid of that soon enough, boss." Plautus patted Kaeso on the back with avuncular familiarity.

"Don't call me that, you silly sybarite."

"But you *are* my boss! I am a playwright, and you own a substantial share of the theatrical troupe. That makes you my boss, does it not? And the boss of every fellow here. Well, the actors, anyway. Not their admirers."

Kaeso looked around the room. Although the presentation of plays was sponsored by the state, as part of various religious festivals, acting was not a profession for reputable citizens. Most of Plautus's performers were slaves or ex-slaves of various national origins. The ones who played heroic roles or girls tended to be quite young, and some were very handsome. All were extroverts; there was little evidence of shyness in the room.

One of the actors, a swarthy Spaniard, abruptly jumped up from the floor and began to juggle a cup, a copper brooch, and a small clay lamp. The spectators put down their cups and began to clap in time with the flute music. The juggler was barely sober enough to keep the objects in the air. He made a great show of staggering about and putting those nearby in peril. His companions roared with laughter every time he came near to missing one of the flying objects.

Watching this raucous buffoonery, Kaeso heaved a deep sigh and felt himself slowly relax. How much more at home he felt here than in the house of Maximus! Kaeso's eye fell on one of the younger actors, a newcomer with chiseled features and long blond hair. The youth reminded him a little of Scipio.

"I can't blame you for staring at the Greek boy," said Plautus in his ear, "but the fellow we need to impress this evening is the one sitting over there, wearing the very expensive-looking toga."

"Who is he?"

"None other than Tiberius Gracchus, scion of a very wealthy plebeian family. He's been elected curule aedile, so he'll be putting on the annual Roman Games coming up in September. Along with the religious procession and the Feast of Jupiter, and the chariot races and boxing matches, there will of course be a day of comedies to entertain the masses. As Gracchus is footing the bill, and because he's an aficionado of the theater, he's taken a personal interest in picking the program."

"I presume you've submitted a script for his approval?"

"Yes, indeed—a thigh-slapper I call *The Swaggering Soldier*. Adapted from a Greek original, as is the fashion, but I think I've managed to give the material a decidedly Roman twist. Gracchus came here tonight to return the script and give me his comments."

"And?"

"He loves it! Said he fell off his couch laughing. He sees the buffoonish woman-chaser of the title as a lampoon on our bellicose consul Varro; says the play is both timely and hilarious. A good thing, since I'm asking a bigger fee for this production than I've ever dared ask before."

"Your work is worth it, Plautus. You have the best actors of any troupe in the city, and you write the wittiest dialogue of any playwright alive. What Ennius is to poetry, you are to comedy."

Plautus rolled his eyes heavenward. "And to think, I was raised a poor country boy in Umbria. Had to make my living as a baker when I first came to Roma; thought I'd never get the flour out of my hair. For years, I was just another starry-eyed, would-be actor with a funny stage name—yes, they called me Plautus on account of my flat feet, but I figured it was a name no one would forget. But Fortuna's wheel turns round and round, and Plautus the clown is the best playwright in town. Boss, you make me blush."

"Don't call me that!"

They were both distracted by a sudden crash. The juggler had dropped everything at once. The lamp shattered against a wall. The cup skittered across the floor. The copper brooch struck one of the actors in the forehead. The fellow jumped to his feet and lunged at the juggler, fists flailing. The flute player trilled a shrill, discordant tune, as if to encourage them. Plautus hurried to break up the fight.

Kaeso heard a chuckle behind him. "I saw that coming! Got out of the way just in time. You're Kaeso Fabius Dorso, I believe."

Kaeso turned. "Yes. And you're Tiberius Gracchus."

"I am." It was hard to judge the man's age. His hair was turning silver at the temples, but his sunburned skin had few wrinkles. He had a powerful jaw and strong cheekbones, but the ruggedness of his features was softened by a mischievous glint of amusement in his gray eyes. If he was drunk, he didn't show it. He carried himself with a graceful dignity that seemed entirely natural.

Kaeso and Gracchus conversed. Gracchus did much of the talking, mostly about the challenges of mounting the Roman Games and the fine work Plautus had done on *The Swaggering Soldier*. Gracchus had a remarkable memory. He recounted long stretches of dialogue verbatim, and his deadpan delivery make Kaeso laugh out loud. There was no talk of Hannibal or duty or death. Such weighty topics would have seemed out of place in the house of Plautus.

After a while, Kaeso's eyes fell upon the young newcomer he had noticed before. The Greek youth smiled back at him.

"I believe his name is Hilarion," said Gracchus, following Kaeso's gaze. "Is it?"

"Yes. Hilarion means 'cheerful' in Greek. The name fits him. Why don't you try your chances with the boy tonight, before everyone else has him?"

"I'm not sure what you mean," said Kaeso.

Gracchus smiled knowingly. "Sporting with catamites was not the sort of thing our staid ancestors approved of, although I suspect they did their share of such things, whether it was spoken of, or not. Nor, I daresay, would your staid cousin Maximus approve even nowadays. But we live in a new age, Kaeso. We inhabit a much bigger world than did our ancestors— a bigger world than men like Maximus have eyes to see. The Spartans, who are renowned as great warriors, consider nothing more manly than the love of two soldiers; on her wedding night, a Spartan woman must cut her hair and put on a boy's tunic, to coax the groom into desiring her. The Athenians put the love of an older man and a younger man at the very center of their philosophy. Carthaginian generals make love to their young officers before allowing them to marry their daughters. Jupiter had his Ganymede, Hercules his Hylas, Achilles his Patroclus, Alexander his Hephaestion—or perhaps it was the other way around, as Alexander was the younger partner. Nature gives us appetites; appetites must be fed. If your eye should fall on a handsome and available Greek slave, why not do something about it? So long as you maintain the dominant role, of course. The Roman male must always dominate."

Kaeso nodded. The wine was hot in his veins. He gazed at the long-haired Greek youth and allowed himself to feel desire, but in his heart he longed for Scipio.

The midsummer month of Sextilis brought sweltering weather to Roma. Everyone complained of the heat; people grew listless and short-tempered. A stifling haze settled over the city, and with it an atmosphere of tension and foreboding.

Each day, the Forum was filled with people seeking news of the war, and the news was always the same: the Roman consuls and Hannibal were shadowing one another across Italy as each side maneuvered to engage in battle at the most opportune place. It was only a matter of time; the longed-for confrontation would take place any day now.

Kaeso was limping across the Forum, happily whistling a tune after an evening of pleasure at Plautus's house, on the day the terrible news arrived.

Near the Temple of Vesta, a weeping woman ran across his path. Then he came upon two elderly senators in togas. At first he thought they were arguing, for one of them was shouting at the other.

"All of them?" The man said. "How is that possible? I don't believe you!"

"Then don't," said the other. "The news is not official. There is no official news, since no officers survived to send word back to Roma!"

"It can't be true, it simply can't!"

Kaeso felt a prickling across the back of his neck. "What news?"

The senators looked at him with ashen faces. "Utter disaster!" said the quieter one. "Varro and Paullus met Hannibal at a place called Cannae, near the Adriatic coast. Somehow the Romans became encircled. The entire army was annihilated. Varro's fate is unknown, but Paullus is dead, along with most of the Senate."

"How do you know this?"

"A few survivors came straggling into the Forum this morning. Each tells the same story. A complete massacre! The largest army ever assembled—obliterated! The worst day in the history of Roma—even the capture of the city by the Gauls was not as bad as this. And there's nothing to stop Hannibal from doing just as the Gauls did, marching on the city and burning it to the ground. There's no one to stand in his way. There's no Roman army left!"

"It can't be as bad as that," said Kaeso, shaking his head.

But it was.

Hannibal's victory at Cannae was overwhelming. On the second day of the month of Sextilis, more than seventy thousand Romans perished, and ten thousand were taken prisoner. A mere thirty-five hundred escaped, and many of those were wounded. The magnitude of the loss was far beyond anything the Romans had ever experienced.

Amid the panic that threatened to overwhelm the city, it was Maximus who took charge. The wisdom of his scorned policy was now clear to all, and the steady hand with which he took control of the city impressed everyone. The remaining members of the Senate, a gray and toothless assembly, granted him emergency powers. No one opposed the appointment, if only because there was no one left to do so. Virtually every able-bodied member of the Senate had either died at Cannae or was fighting the Carthaginians abroad. No man of Maximus's experience and stature was left in the city.

For much the same reason—because he was one of the few remaining magistrates—the curule aedile Tiberius Gracchus was appointed to serve as Master of the Horse, who was the right-hand man to the dictator.

First, Maximus dispatched riders to seek out the scattered survivors, hoping that more might have escaped than was previously thought. When the riders returned, bringing home a handful of men, they only confirmed the grim truth.

To raise a fresh army, Maximus decreed that underage boys would be recruited. When their numbers proved insufficient, he declared that slaves would be eligible for military service. Eight thousand were enlisted and armed. Such a thing had never been done before, but no one could suggest a better solution.

Kaeso eagerly responded to the call to arms, but in front of the recruiting officer, in public view on the Field of Mars, he suffered a bout of the falling sickness. He was carried home unconscious, and was forbidden to report again by Maximus himself, who wished to suffer no further embarrassment from a member of his family.

Amid the general hysteria two Vestals, Opimia and Floronia, were accused of breaking their vows. The news caused riots. A mob outside the House of the Vestals accused the transgressors of bringing ruin on the city. Both Vestals were quickly tried and found guilty. Opimia committed suicide. Floronia was entombed alive near the Colline Gate while the clamorous mob looked on. The men found guilty of defiling them were publicly bludgeoned to death by the Pontifex Maximus.

Each day, by the thousands, more men were confirmed dead. Great crowds of women, gathered in the Forum to receive the news, reacted with uncontrollable grief. They ripped their garments, tore out their hair, and fell to the ground wailing. Their frenzy spread across the city. In every street the sound of sobbing was heard all night long. Roma was a city on the verge of madness.

Maximus finally declared that such extreme displays of emotion offended religious decency; the cacophony of so much weeping would drive the gods out of the city. He ordered all women to be shut indoors and imposed a rule of silence. It was decreed that the period of mourning for the dead of Cannae would be limited to thirty days. After that, the city would resume business as usual.

"The show must go on!" declared Plautus, amid the din of hammering.

"So you say," muttered Kaeso.

"So says your cousin, the dictator Maximus. So says our friend Tiberius Gracchus, who assures me that the Roman Games will proceed exactly as planned. Like everyone else, in light of the crisis, I had assumed that the plays would be cancelled. Is anyone really in the mood for a day of comedy? But the dictator believes that sticking to the regular calendar will reassure the public. Here's hoping that Hannibal doesn't show up just as we begin the opening scene of *The Swaggering Soldier*."

From above, a carpenter dropped a hammer. It whistled past Plautus's head, barely missing him.

"Idiot!" shouted Plautus. "That's what I get for hiring free labor instead of renting slaves. Ah, well, perhaps standing under this scaffolding is not a good idea."

They were in the Circus Maximus, where, in the great curve at one end of the long racetrack, a temporary stage was being constructed for the Roman Games. The curved bleachers would serve as seats for the audience, with the humblest among them crowding into the semicircle of open ground before the stage. The stage itself—an elevated wooden platform with a decorated wall to serve as a backdrop—would be thrown up quickly and even more quickly pulled down; after a single day of performances it would be dismantled overnight to clear the racetrack for the next day's athletic competitions. Accordingly, the standards of craftsmanship were no higher than they needed to be. The ornate columns and relief sculptures of the backdrop were illusions made of wood, plaster, cloth, and paint, tawdry when seen close up, but convincing enough at a distance.

"Don't the Greeks have permanent theaters, built of stone?" asked Kaeso.

"Yes, sometimes built into the sides of hills, with such remarkable acoustics that the actors hardly need to raise their voices to be heard in the back row. But the Greeks are a decadent, pleasure-loving people, sensual to a fault; Romans are not. So, while we love a good comedy, a play may be enjoyed only in the context of a religious festival, and the stage and all its trappings must vanish before the festival is over. It's a stupid policy, but it keeps these mediocre carpenters employed. You seem preoccupied, boss."

"I'm worried about my friends. There's no word yet about cousin Quintus . . . or about Scipio . . ." Kaeso wrinkled his brow.

"No news is good news."

"I suppose."

"And the best news is that there's no news of Hannibal marching on Roma. What's keeping him, I wonder?"

"Maximus made a speech the other day. He said, 'The hand of Jupiter himself has stayed the Carthaginian monster.' "

Plautus wrinkled his nose. "Is Ennius writing his speeches these day? The masses love that sort of religious hokum. It reassures them, like putting on a festival when the end of the world may be near." He shook his head. "I have to wonder whether Hannibal isn't a bit like one of his elephants—huge and destructive, but ultimately rather stupid."

"Tiberius Gracchus speculates that Hannibal, instead of heading straight to Roma, may want to win over our enemies and lay siege to our allies, so as to secure the whole of Italy while we're helpless to stop him."

"But why should he bother to conquer the limbs, one by one, when he could cut off the head? Yet the days pass, and Hannibal does not arrive."

"Nor does news of Scipio," whispered Kaeso.

"Look, here comes Tiberius Gracchus—and he does not look happy."

In fact, Gracchus looked very grim. Without the mischievous glint in his eyes, his face assumed a severe aspect suitable to the Master of the Horse at Roma's darkest hour.

"Bad news?" said Plautus.

"Bad news and worse news," said Gracchus.

Plautus sighed. "I'll have the bad news first, then."

"After a very long, very unpleasant discussion, the dictator and I have decided that *The Swaggering Soldier* is not suitable to be presented at the Roman Games."

"What? No!" Plautus was outraged. "The comedies are cancelled then?"

"No, the plays will go on, but *The Swaggering Soldier* will not be among them."

"You're throwing it out? We have a contract, Gracchus. You signed it as curule aedile."

"Think, Plautus! The comedy pokes fun at a pompous, philandering military man. Who's going to laugh at that, after what happened at Cannae?"

"You thought it was funny. You thought it was about Varro!"

"Who barely escaped with his life! People are stunned by Varro's defeat, they're appalled by his miscalculations, they're numb with fury—but no one wants to see him made fun of, not after seventy thousand men have died."

Plautus pinched the bridge of his nose. "All this incessant hammering is giving me a headache. Yes, I see your point. What shall we do, then?"

"You'll substitute another play."

"At the last moment? Impossible!"

"You must have something. Think!"

"Well . . . there is a script I've been working on. It's not nearly as funny as *The Swaggering Soldier*. It's called *The Casket*—a sweet little farce about a girl exposed at birth who's eventually reunited with her parents. Under the circumstances, I suppose it would at least have the virtue of being inoffensive. But it needs work. Several scenes need to be completely rewritten."

"You'll simply have to pull it together," said Gracchus. "You can do it, Plautus. You're funny when you write under pressure."

"No, I get indigestion when I write under pressure. But, if I must . . .
Yes, I suppose it could be done . . . if Hilarion can play the girl . . ."

Gracchus's expression became even grimmer.

Plautus stiffened. "Bad news, you said—and worse news. What is it,
Gracchus?"

Gracchus lowered his eyes. What sort of news could cause the Master
of the Horse to avert his gaze? Kaeso held his breath.

"Do you remember when the Vestals were accused of breaking their
vows?"

"How could I forget?" said Plautus. "For a few days, the whole city was
obsessed with the scandal. It took people's minds off Hannibal even while
it gave them someone to blame for what happened at Cannae. As if a couple of Vestals, by losing their virginity, were responsible for so many
deaths! If, indeed, the Vestals *were* guilty. If people wanted vengeance, it's
Varro they should have buried alive instead of that poor girl."

Gracchus drew a sharp breath. "You forget my position, Plautus. As
Master of the Horse I represent the state religion no less than does the
Pontifex Maximus. To question the verdict or punishment of the Vestals is
tantamount to blasphemy."

"If you say so. Being a country boy from Umbria, I still find Roman religion a bit puzzling—"

"I'm serious, Plautus. People are in no mood for unpatriotic or irreli-
gious talk. You must watch what you say."

The playwright clucked his tongue. "Duly noted! But, you were saying?"

"The Vestal Floronia was properly punished, but Opimia escaped her
punishment by committing suicide. Auguries were taken. An unfavor-
able sighting of birds confirmed that the gods had not been fully propitiated. Something must be done to make up for the failure to bury one
of the Vestals alive. The Sibylline Books were consulted. A verse was
found."

Gracchus quoted the chosen passage:

> *A lamb fated for sacrifice dies too soon.*
> *Kill two pair of beasts before the next moon,*
> *From fields to the north and east of noon.*

Plautus wrinkled his nose. "If only my sponsors were as indulgent of my cracked phrasing as was Tarquinius of the Sybil's! And what was the interpretation of these lovely lines?"

"The priests conferred among themselves. It was decided that, to cleanse the city of the Vestals' sins, a pair of Gauls and a pair of Greeks must be buried alive."

Plautus shook his head. "Human sacrifice is a Carthaginian vice! It's one of the reasons we look down on them as savages."

"It's neither your place nor mine to question the dictates of the Sibylline Books." Gracchus sighed. "The priests came to me for a list of names."

"To you?"

"A registry is kept by the curule aediles of all foreigners residing in Roma. So is a registry of all slaves, listing their nationality. The priests asked for the lists. I supplied them. How the priests determined which two Gauls and which two Greeks, I don't know, but they informed me of their decision this morning."

Plautus snorted. "I own a Gaul or two, myself, and more than a couple of Greeks!" His face fell. "By Hercules! That's why you're here, isn't it? The cancellation of *The Swaggering Soldier* was only the bad news. Worse news, you said . . ."

"One of the Greeks they chose was Hilarion."

Kaeso, who had listened in silence, let out a gasp.

"You'll be properly compensated, of course," said Gracchus hastily, averting his eyes.

"Compensated?"

"For the sacrifice of your property."

"But . . . why Hilarion?"

"I don't know. The priests chose the names. The Pontifex Maximus confirmed their decision."

"I suppose I have no choice in this matter?"

"None whatsoever. Lictors were dispatched to your house before I came here. I imagine they've already taken Hilarion into custody. Workmen began digging the pit in the Forum Boarium last night. The entombment will take place this afternoon."

"What's the Old Etruscan adage? 'Quickly done is best done,' " said Plautus bitterly. He gripped his head. "Oh, that infernal hammering!"

Tiberius Gracchus took his leave and strode away.

Kaeso felt unsteady on his feet. There was a fluttering in his head, such as sometimes preceded his seizures. His vision became blurry. Tears welled in his eyes. He shuddered but he did not weep.

"Madness!" whispered Plautus. "When a horror like Cannae occurs, do men react with compassion, reason, kindness? No! They blame the outsider; they punish the guiltless. And if you point out their madness, they call you a traitor and a blasphemer! Thank the gods I have a vessel into which I can pour my darkest feelings—my comedies! Otherwise, I should go as mad as the rest."

"Your plays aren't dark," said Kaeso dully. "They make people laugh."

"Comedy is darker than tragedy," said Plautus. "No laugh was ever born except out of someone's suffering, usually mine. And now—poor Hilarion!"

The two of them stood motionless for a long time, enduring the din of the hammers. Suddenly Kaeso blinked and furrowed is brow. "Is that . . . my cousin Quintus?"

A young officer wearing the insignia of a military tribune was striding purposely across the open expanse of the Circus. Kaeso ran toward him.

Quintus looked pale and haggard. There was a fresh scar across his forehead, but otherwise he appeared to be intact.

"You're alive!" said Kaeso.

"By the will of the gods."

"We've had no word. Your father has been ill with worry."

"Even so, it looks like he's managed to keep the city running. I understand he's been appointed dictator."

"Have you not seen him?"

"I only just arrived."

"What news?"

"News?"

Kaeso dreaded to ask. "What of Scipio?"

Quintus smiled. "Wouldn't you know? He proved his bravery once again, just as he did at the Ticinus. If there was one Roman hero to emerge from the catastrophe at Cannae, it was Scipio."

"Tell me!"

"The mongrels encircled us. The slaughter was terrible. Only a handful of us managed to fight our way through it and escape with our lives. We became separated. We were wounded, dazed, fearful of capture at any moment. It took days for us to find one another, one by one, all the time hiding from Hannibal's mercenaries. When we finally regrouped, and put enough distance between ourselves and the enemy to catch our breaths, a debate broke out. Where should we go, and who should lead us there? I confess, I was among those who gave in to despair and argued that we should leave Italy altogether. We assumed that Hannibal would march on Roma at once, burn the city, and enslave the citizens. There's a Roman army in Spain, and a Roman navy fighting the war on the sea. Join them, I argued, and see where the future leads us, because Roma is finished forever and there's no going home.

"But Scipio wouldn't hear of it. Even though his father and uncle are off fighting in Spain, he said he had no intention of joining them, not as long as Roma needed us to defend her. He mocked our despair. He shamed us. He made us take an oath to Jupiter never to abandon the city, to die fighting for her rather than to surrender to Hannibal. Once we took that oath, it was as if a great weight was lifted from us. We knew we could endure anything, because Scipio had given us back our honor.

"Then we watched and waited. Days passed, but Hannibal made no move to march toward the city. We were puzzled, then elated. We began the journey back to Roma, taking back roads so that no Carthaginian outriders would find us. The way was slow. Some of the men were badly wounded, and Scipio refused to leave them behind. Finally we reached the Appian Way, and I rode ahead. I'm the first to arrive."

"And Scipio?"

"He should be here tomorrow, or the day after."

"He's alive, then?"

"Yes."

"You're certain?"

"Of course."

Kaeso began to cry, weeping unabashedly with joy as he had been unable to weep with sorrow for Hilarion. Indeed, in his relief for Scipio, he all but forgot his grief over Hilarion. Quintus, who had seen terrible things at Cannae and had despaired of ever returning to Roma, had tears streaming down his cheeks as well.

Together they went to find Maximus.

On the eve of the Roman Games, the city was gripped by yet another crisis.

An emissary from Hannibal, a Carthaginian noble named Carthalo, arrived at the city gates. In exchange for a steep ransom, he offered to return a large number of Roman prisoners. A few representatives of the prisoners came with him to plead their cause, for the Romans had a long history of turning their backs on men who had surrendered to the enemy. In spite of the ban, a vast crowd of women gathered in the Forum to plead for the ransom of their husbands, fathers, and sons.

Behind closed doors, the Senate debated the matter.

The representatives of the prisoners defended their actions. They had remained on the battlefield at Cannae until the bodies lay thick around them, then had managed to break through the enemy circle and flee to the Roman camp. In the morning, rather than die on the ramparts, they had given themselves up. It was true that they had neither died bravely nor been clever enough to escape. Yet, they argued, was it not better to pay for the return of genuine Roman soldiers than to enlist yet more slaves to defend the city?

Those who opposed the ransom argued that the captives had surrendered rather than die fighting, and had therefore proven themselves cowards who deserved to be sold into slavery by their captors. Besides, any ransom paid from the public treasury would enrich Hannibal and enable him to hire more mercenaries.

In the end it was decided that the ransom would not be paid. The prisoners were abandoned to their fate. Most would be sent back to Carthage as slaves. Their relatives would never see them again.

There was bitter lamentation throughout the city. Maximus dispatched his lictors to maintain order.

In such an atmosphere, the date arrived for the Roman Games. The invocation to Jupiter on the Capitoline had an edge of desperation. The procession from the Temple of Jupiter to the Circus Maximus was a sad affair; many of the senators and magistrates who normally would have strutted before the people were conspicuously missing. The Feast of Jupiter consisted of little more than the scant daily rations allowed by the dictator for the duration of the crisis.

The company of Plautus performed *The Casket*. Their rehearsal for the new play had been rushed and chaotic, and the terrible fate of Hilarion had shattered their morale. The production was a disaster. Plautus's only consolation was that the comedy's spectators were even more depressed than its performers. The audience scarcely noticed the tardy entrances, missed cues, and flubbed lines. No one hissed or booed; nor did anyone laugh.

The athletic competitions were equally lackluster. Many of Roma's best young runners and boxers had died at Cannae, and the highly trained slaves who ranked fastest among the chariot racers had been called away to military service.

The citizens who took part in the Roman Games merely went through the motions, performing their patriotic duty to attend an annual celebration that dated back to the days of the kings. They had been rendered insensible by the massacre at Cannae, the scandal of the Vestal virgins, and the wrenching rejection of the captives' plea for ransom.

Roma was numb with grief and worry. The future of the city was very much in doubt.

212 B.C.

Four years later, the war with Carthage continued to rage, with no end in sight.

Hannibal never marched on Roma. This curious fact was to become part of the city's legend, another element of her mystique: At the city's most vulnerable moment, she was spared an assault that would surely have ended in her destruction. How and why had Roma survived? Fabius Maximus was given credit for seizing the reins when chaos threatened, and Scipio was widely praised for his inspiring example to the younger generation; but most Romans, agreeing with their priests, believed that Jupiter himself had deflected the wrath of Hannibal, allowing the Romans a chance to rally.

Hannibal and his marauding army remained in Italy. His apparent strategy—to isolate Roma and to undermine her dominance of the peninsula by winning over her allies, either by force or by persuasion—met with only limited success. The Romans steadfastly avoided another direct confrontation with Hannibal, but ruthlessly struck back at the allies who betrayed them. In regrouping their forces, marshaling their resources, and regaining their morale, the Romans proved to be remarkably resilient.

Meanwhile, the theater of war, already waged in Spain and Sicily and on the sea, expanded to the east. Philip of Macedonia, the heir to Alexander's homeland, allied himself with Carthage. To counter the threat from Philip, Roma dispatched ambassadors to seek new alliances in Greece and Asia.

As the struggle between the two cities spread across the whole of the Mediterranean world, from the Pillars of Hercules to the straits of the Hellespont, the Romans adopted an increasingly outward-looking foreign policy. The more visionary men of the Senate dared to indulge in heady dreams of empire far beyond the confines of Italy. Roma was like the legendary phoenix consumed by fire only to rise from its own ashes.

The turn of events also brought unexpected good fortune to Kaeso. Because of his lameness and his nonexistent political prospects, his parents had despaired of finding him a suitable wife. After the massacre at Cannae, and the resulting shortage of young bachelors, Kaeso's mother was able to find a perfectly acceptable patrician girl for him to marry.

Sestia was not beautiful. People said she had a mannish face, but Kaeso found her pleasant enough to look at. Like Kaeso, she had not expected to marry, and was pleased that Fortuna had allowed her to achieve the status of matron. She seemed content to confine her interests to running the household, and demanded no more of Kaeso's attention than he demanded of hers. She never questioned him about his expenses or business affairs, his abrupt comings and goings, the odd hours he kept, or the exotic perfumes that frequently scented his clothes. Her simple needs and incurious nature suited Kaeso.

Both accepted, from the outset, that the principal purpose of their marriage was to create a child. They made love on a regular basis, though without much enthusiasm on either's part. Their workmanlike efforts were rewarded. Within a year after they were married, Sestia gave birth to a daughter.

When he saw that little Fabia had been born without physical defects, Kaeso was enormously relieved. He had feared that the baby might be a monster, like the children who had preceded him from his own mother's womb, or at best flawed and ungainly, like himself. But Fabia was perfect in every regard. There and then, after giving thanks to the gods, Kaeso swore never to have another child.

To settle for a daughter was not the Roman way. Kaeso's relatives and in-laws suggested that he and Sestia should try again, to see if she could give him a son. But Kaeso, fearing to tempt the Fates, and little drawn to having sex with his wife, remained adamant that he would produce no more children after Fabia. She was now almost three years old.

Sestia had brought with her a small but useful dowry. With it, Kaeso had been able to buy out the other investors in the theater company of Plautus. Being the sole owner of a comedy troupe would never make him wealthy, and certainly would never earn him the respect of his patrician relatives, but Kaeso delighted in the role of impresario and took an active part in running the company. He consulted with Plautus about the Greek source material for his plays, he haggled with magistrates about budgets and allowances for festivals, and he particularly enjoyed auditioning the young slaves whom Plautus put forth as possible additions to the company.

❖

The fourth anniversary of Cannae came and went, stirring bitter memories of the massacre and its terrible aftermath, but also a sense of rejuvenation and hope; the unspeakable despair of those days now seemed distant and unreal, like a bad dream. As Sextilis gave way to September, Kaeso looked forward to the annual Roman Games with special anticipation, for his dear friend Scipio had been elected curule aedile and was in charge of putting on the festivities.

By law, Scipio had been too young to stand for the magistracy. But on voting day an adoring crowd raised Scipio on their shoulders and carried him through the city, demanding his election with chants, songs, and deafening cheers. The throng grew so large and unruly that the polling officials were completely overwhelmed. After a hasty conference, they allowed the unprecedented election of a twenty-four-year-old to the office of curule aedile.

Afterward, with a wink and a laugh, Scipio denied any responsibility for engineering the "spontaneous" near-riot that resulted in his election. "If all Roma wants to make me aedile," he said, "well, then—I must be old enough!" Surprised or not by his election, he seemed quite ready to take office. On the very day he assumed the aedileship, he announced a detailed plan for putting on the most lavish Roman Games ever produced. "The city needs a celebration," he declared, "an escape from months and years of constant worry. This year, let the games be not a patriotic duty, but a pure delight!"

A few grumblers complained that election laws that had served Roma for centuries had been broken to reward an upstart youth, and that Scipio's bland disavowals of self-promotion proved him to be devious and disingenuous. Well, thought Kaeso, what politician was not? And if anyone deserved to have the rules bent on his behalf, was it not the young hero of the Ticinus and Cannae? Kaeso was in awe of his friend's relentless drive and ambition, and hardly surprised by his extraordinary popularity. It seemed to Kaeso that no man was more deserving of every man's love.

For the theatrical program, naturally enough, Scipio solicited a comedy from Kaeso's company. After consulting with Plautus, Kaeso suggested *The Swaggering Soldier*.

It was a daring gamble. In the aftermath of Cannae, Gracchus had canceled the play, fearing that its portrayal of a vain, lecherous military man would be taken as a distasteful lampoon of Roma's defeated generals. But now, with the insertion of a few new puns and some hints from the costuming—would a patch over one eye be too obvious?—the character of the Swaggering Soldier might be seen as a parody of the most arrogant military man of all—Hannibal. Until now, the Romans' dread of the Carthaginian had been too great to indulge in satire, but in the years since Cannae he had shown himself to be indecisive and increasingly fallible. The Romans still loathed and despised Hannibal; were they ready to laugh at him?

When Scipio came to Kaeso's house for a copy of the play, Kaeso expected him to take it and read it at his leisure. Instead, Scipio began to read it at once. Kaeso left him alone in his study, and for a while paced nervously in his garden. Then he heard Scipio laugh. For the next hour, the laughter continued with hardly a break. Finally, Scipio stepped into the garden, clutching the scroll in one hand and wiping away a tear of laughter with the other. He flashed a mischievous grin, looking as carefree as a boy who had yet to don his first toga.

"Hilarious! Charming! An utter delight! The lovers get each other, and the Swaggering Soldier gets his comeuppance—a sound flogging, right there on the stage! 'Serve all lechers so, and lechery would cease to grow'—indeed! It's the ideal play for the occasion. By Hercules, I needed to laugh like that—and so do the people of Roma! They're going to love it, and they're going to love me for treating them to it!" He tapped Kaeso's chest with the scroll. "You're a clever fellow, Kaeso Fabius Dorso."

Kaeso lowered his eyes. "Plautus is the clever one."

"Of course he is. But without you to finance the company, the playwright would have no stage, and without a stage, all his clever lines would be no more than whispers in the wind. Don't sell yourself short, Kaeso. You have an eye for talent, just as a good general has an eye for bravery. You're a valuable fellow to know." The play had put Scipio in such a facetious mood that he tousled Kaeso's hair, then gave his backside a playful swat with the scroll.

Kaeso blushed so furiously that Scipio drew back and blinked at him in wonder, then swatted his backside again and laughed uproariously. Kaeso drew a sharp breath, then he began to laugh, too. He laughed at himself, at the absurdity of the world, at the ridiculous vanity of the Swaggering Soldier. He laughed until his sides ached and tears flowed from his eyes. He had not laughed like that in a very long time.

The splendor of the Roman Games that year was on a scale such as Roma had never witnessed before. The sacred rites atop the Capitoline exuded an air of buoyancy and optimism; men smiled as they intoned the ancient formulas to dedicate the festivities of the coming days to Jupiter, greatest of gods. The procession to the Circus Maximus became a joyous celebration, led by brightly clad charioteers on horseback, strutting boxers in scanty loincloths, and dancers twirling javelins to the music of flutes, lyres, and tambourines. Mimes in the guise of satyrs scurried in and out of the crowd, pinching bottoms and eliciting screams of laughter from the women and girls. Griffin-headed censers hung from poles were swung about, scenting the air with clouds of incense.

In the vicinity of the Circus Maximus, the perfume of the censers gave way to the aroma of meat roasting in the open air, the scent of freshly baked bread, the tangy smell of pickled fish, and the delicate odor of salted olives served in oil. No curule aedile had ever fed the citizens of Roma so well, or so copiously. There was so much food on offer, in so many places, that hardly anyone had to stand in line, and everyone could go back as many times as he wished. The Feast of Jupiter would last all day, and continue the next day as well. It was as if every man, for a couple of days, was a rich man, with a belly as full as he could want and his hours filled with leisure, secure in the blessings of Jupiter.

In the midst of the feasting, a fresh-faced youth with a powerful voice—one of Plautus's actors-in-training—stood on a box and addressed the crowd. "Citizens! Stop stuffing your faces for an hour and come see *The Swaggering Soldier*! It's a new comedy by Plautus—that's right, the flat-footed playwright from Umbria, the one who makes you laugh until you piss! Come, see the Swaggering Soldier himself, Pyrgopolynices, as he puts the make on his concubine, the ravishing Philocomasium!"

People in the crowd began to laugh, if only at hearing the boy wrap his tongue around the absurdly convoluted Greek names.

"Come, citizens, and behold the heartsick Pleusicles, a young man desperately in love, as he does his best to rescue the soldier's concubine! Come, see the angry old man Periplectomenus . . ." The boy raised his eyebrows and pressed a forefinger to lips. "And whatever you do, *don't* tell Periplectomenus about the secret passageway between his house and the soldier's, or you'll spoil the plot! Come, see the wily slaves Palaestrio, Sceledrus, and Lurcio—they always know more than they let on!"

The boy jumped from the box, produced a pipe, and played a merry tune to lead the spectators into the Circus Maximus.

Underneath the stage, Kaeso stood not far from the trapdoor—Plautus had thought of a number of ingenious ways to use it during the play—and peered through a peephole to watch the bleachers fill up. Scipio, he noticed, was among the first to arrive, taking his place in the dignitary's section along with a retinue of friends and colleagues. The day was mild and the sky was clear, with no sign of rain. The feast had put the audience in a happy mood, ready to be entertained. With full bellies and a warm sun, the danger was that they might fall asleep.

As it turned out, there was no chance of that. Any spectator who nodded off for even an instant would have been awakened by the roars of laughter around him. The players did an outstanding job. During rehearsals, Kaeso had never seen them attack Plautus's lines with such vigor; the laughter of the audience inspired them to outdo themselves. On that day, as never before, Kaeso saw the living proof of a belief that Plautus, after several cups of wine, had once confided to him: "When does comedy become sublime? When there is a collaboration in equal measures between playwright, players, and spectators, all working together in harmony to delight the gods with the music of human laughter. When men laugh, the gods laugh, and for a brief time this miserable world becomes not merely bearable, but beautiful."

The applause at the end of the play was thunderous. The audience hailed the players, especially the actor who portrayed the blustering Pyrgopolynices. Plautus ran onto the stage to take several bows. Then Scipio, laughing and genuinely taken by surprise, was swept off his feet and lifted onto the shoulders of his companions to receive the gratitude of the adoring crowd.

Kaeso remained under the stage, observing the audience through his peephole. At that moment, he wanted very much to be close to Scipio, but in such a throng even approaching him would be impossible. As he watched, Scipio dispatched a young slave, who dexterously threaded a path through the crush and made his way under the stage.

The slave found Kaeso and drew a quick breath. "My master, Publius Cornelius Scipio, says to tell you that he wishes he could congratulate you in person, but, with all the day's events, he must hurry off. However, in three day's time, when the Games are over and well behind him, he says he would be honored if you would join him for dinner."

"Of course," said Kaeso. "Of course we'll come. Plautus will be delighted."

The slave smiled and shook his head. "My master asks that you come alone. He says he'll feast the playwright on another night, but once the Games are done, he looks forward to a quiet repast in the company of an old friend."

No power on earth could have kept Kaeso from joining Scipio on the appointed night.

"What a whirlwind! I only wish my father could have been here to see it." Scipio gazed into his cup and swirled the wine. It seemed to Kaeso that his friend had drunk very little that night. Perhaps Scipio found the success of the Games intoxicating enough.

"Your father is where Roma most needs him to be, with your uncle, commanding the legions in Spain," said Kaeso. "Have you heard from them lately?"

Scipio frowned. "I received my father's last letter almost two months ago. A letter from Uncle Gnaeus arrived a few days after that. Not a word since then. No news from Spain at all. Just a long silence."

Kaeso shrugged. "Messages go astray. Your father and uncle are such busy men, I'm surprised they have time to write at all. They call Spain the viper's nest, don't they, because it was Hannibal's original base of operations? Everyone agrees there's no battleground in the war that's more important."

"Or more fiercely fought. They've been at it for years now, trying to drive out the Carthaginians. According to my father, if any man hates us more than Hannibal, it's his brother, Hasdrubal, who commands the Carthaginians in Spain."

Kaeso nodded, not sure what else to say. He would have liked more wine, but it was uncouth to drink more than one's host. Scipio's full cup seemed merely a dark mirror upon which to focus his gaze.

"In my father's last letter," said Scipio, "he complained of the cowardice of the locals. His Celtiberian allies deserted the Roman camp overnight. They claimed there was a tribal conclave that required their attendance at the far side of the peninsula, but it was obvious they were fleeing because word had arrived that an army of Suessitani was coming down from Gaul to reinforce the enemy." Scipio sighed. "Father was already feeling outnumbered by the Carthaginians and the Numidians. What a cavalry those African bastards can mount—as we learned to our regret at Cannae! Numidians are born on horseback. Father says they have a very strong leader in Spain, an audacious young prince named Masinissa, hardly more than a boy, but utterly sure of himself. It's Masinissa who worries him now, even more than Hasdrubal." Scipio sighed again.

"Perhaps this Masinissa was the true model for the Swaggering Soldier," said Kaeso. To his relief, Scipio laughed.

"What a delight that play was! Really, your troupe outdid themselves, Kaeso. They made me very proud. I sat through all the other comedies, but not one of them made me laugh half as much as yours."

"It's Plautus who should get the credit. But, on his behalf, I gratefully accept your words of praise. To Plautus!" Kaeso raised his cup. Scipio did likewise, and Kaeso was happy to see him drain his cup.

The wine seemed to affect Scipio almost at once. Perhaps, being normally so abstemious, he was more vulnerable to intoxication than a heavier drinker like Kaeso.

"A splendid play," he said dreamily. "And the athletic competitions were just as splendid. Wonderful chariot races! Excellent boxing, foot races, and javelin tosses. I especially enjoyed that exhibition of Greek-style wrestling, though the athletes were not *entirely* naked, as the Greeks prefer." He grinned. "Perhaps you would have preferred that, as well, Kaeso?"

Kaeso stammered for a moment, but Scipio didn't seem to expect an answer. Talking about the Games had excited him. "What did you think of the Feast of Jupiter?"

"It was the best public feast I can remember. Handing out vessels of olive oil to everyone who attended was a very nice touch. And the menu for the second day was even better than the first."

"It was, wasn't it? Roast pork and fowl, savory onions on skewers, and chickpeas with garum. Don't you love garum, Kaeso? I mean a really good garum, not too sweet, not too salty—not that cheap pickled fish sauce they sell in the Subura, but the kind that's been properly fermented, so pungent it pops the top of your head off. I'll wager that most people at this year's

Feast of Jupiter had never before tasted a garum as good as the one I gave them. When they think of the best garum they ever ate, they shall always think of me."

"And vote for you?"

"Exactly!" Scipio giggled like boy and raised a brawny arm to push back his mane of chestnut hair.

Kaeso blinked and tried to think of something to say. "The Games must have cost you a fortune."

"Indeed they did! Father supplied most of the money, but it wasn't nearly enough. You can't imagine all the expenses! It was like running a military campaign—logistics, supply lines, transport. I'm afraid I had to borrow quite a bit."

"Scipio! I'll feel guilty now, asking for the fee we agreed on."

"Nonsense. Every politician goes into debt to finance public entertainments for the voters. That's what moneylenders are for. Do you know, I think I shall have some more of this very fine wine. I paid for it out of the budget for the Games, after all!"

Scipio poured them both another cup. "A toast to our friendship!"

"To our friendship," whispered Kaeso, and they both drank deeply.

Scipio's eyes glittered in the lamplight. "I treasure our friendship, Kaeso. You're so very different from most of the men I associate with nowadays. They're all so relentlessly ambitious, always pushing to get ahead, concerned about nothing but fighting and politics. Their lives have no other dimension—there is the Course of Honor, and nothing else. Their marriages are only a means to an end, as are their friendships. The same applies to their education—they duly memorize a few passages so they can drop a learned quotation into a speech from time to time, but they have no appreciation of beautiful writing and lofty ideas; they don't know their Ennius from their *Iliad*. Even the worship of the gods means little to them, apart from the role it plays in advancing their careers."

He sighed. "It's the way of the world, I suppose, but you and I, Kaeso, we know there's more to life than chasing after wealth and honor. There's a spark of life inside us, unique and separate from everything else, a kind of secret flame that must be cherished and tended, as the Vestals tend the sacred hearth. Sometimes I find it hard to remember that. Sometimes I envy you, Kaeso, standing as you do outside the Course of Honor."

Kaeso managed a halting laugh. "Surely you joke, Scipio." He gazed at his friend, admiring his beauty, acutely aware of his accomplishments and the adoration he received from others, and found it very hard to imagine that Scipio was envious of any man.

Scipio's face became grave. He placed his hand on Kaeso's and gazed into his eyes. "No, Kaeso, I'm not joking. Your friendship is different from any other. It means a great deal to me. *You* mean a great deal to me."

Kaeso looked at the hand that remained atop his own. If he dared to move his forefinger, it would brush against Scipio's forefinger, in an unmistakable gesture of intimacy. "I think this must be the wine talking," he whispered.

"Perhaps. But in wine is truth, as the saying goes. Do you not feel the same about me?"

Kaeso's pulse began to race. He felt lightheaded. His mouth was suddenly dry. *Wine, give me strength to speak the truth!* he thought. But did he dare to say aloud what he felt for Scipio? He had no fear that his friend would scoff or laugh, or do anything to belittle or berate him, but even the least expression of pity or disdain on Scipio's face would be devastating to him.

Kaeso opened his mouth to speak. He looked up, intending to gaze steadily into Scipio's eyes, but his friend was looking past him, at a slave who had entered the room.

"What is it, Daphnis?"

"A messenger, master. He says it's very urgent."

Scipio snorted. "Probably a contractor for the Games, wanting a payment."

"No, master. It's a centurion. He has a message from your uncle in Spain."

Scipio withdrew his hand from Kaeso's. He sat upright. He drew a deep breath. All traces of inebriation vanished. "Show the man in."

The centurion wore a grim expression. He extended a small wax tablet to Scipio, of the type used for writing and rewriting short missives. Scipio stared at it for a moment, then shook his head. "No, read it aloud to me."

The centurion balked. "Are you sure, Aedile?"

"Read it!"

The centurion untied the lacings and opened the hinged cover. He stared for a long moment at the tiny, crabbed letters scraped in the wax, then cleared his throat. " 'To my nephew Publius, I send tragic news. Your father, my beloved brother . . .' " The soldier hesitated for a long moment, then thrust out his jaw and continued. " 'Your father, my beloved brother, is dead. Riding forth to engage the Suessitani before they could reach and reinforce the Carthaginians and Numidians, he unexpectedly encountered all three enemies, one after another. He was outflanked. In the thick of battle—fighting, rallying his men, exposing himself wherever they were hardest pressed—he was pierced through the right side by a lance—' "

Scipio gave a cry and pressed a fist to his mouth. After a moment, he waved to the centurion to continue.

" 'He fell from his horse. The Romans lost heart and took flight, but escape through the line of Numidian cavalry was impossible. The only survivors were those who managed to stay alive until nightfall, when darkness put an end to the battle and allowed them to elude the enemy.

" 'Nephew, I mourn with you, but at this moment, I can write no more. Your father's heroic death has made Hasdrubal and Masinissa bolder than ever. They press upon us. Our Spanish auxiliaries have melted away. The situation is desperate. Jupiter, be my shield! Mars, be my sword! Farewell, nephew. Your uncle, Gnaeus.' "

Having finished, the centurion again offered the tablet to Scipio, who took it but seemed unable to focus his eyes upon the wax. He put the tablet aside. His voice was hollow. "Is this all my uncle sent? Did he send no memento of my father? A scrap of his armor? Some keepsake?"

"Your uncle . . ."

"Yes? Speak!"

"Your uncle is also dead, Aedile. Because of storms, I had to wait many days to catch a ship from Spain. Even as I was boarding the ship, another messenger arrived. He brought news of the battle in which Gnaeus Cornelius Scipio perished. The enemy laid siege to his camp and overran the ramparts. He took refuge in a lookout tower. The tower was set aflame. The commander and his men emerged and died fighting. I know no other details, but I'm sure he died as heroically as his brother before him."

Scipio stared at the dancing flame of the lamp that lit the room. His voice was strangely distant. "My father . . . my uncle . . . both dead?"

"Yes, Aedile."

"Impossible!"

"I assure you, Aedile—"

"But who is commanding the legions in Spain?"

"I . . . I'm not sure, Aedile."

For a long time Scipio stared at the flame. The centurion, used to await-ing orders, stood silent and still. Kaeso hardly dared to look at his friend's face, fearful of seeing his anguish. But Scipio, with his long hair and hand-some features, might have been a statue of Alexander. Without moving, without expression, he stared at the flame.

At last Scipio stirred. He stood and looked down at each of his limbs in turn with a bemused expression, as if he had forgotten who he was and needed to take account of himself. Then he strode purposefully out of the room.

Kaeso followed him. "Scipio, where are you going?"

"Where the god calls me," said Scipio, with no further explanation. In the vestibule he paused to look at the wax effigies of his ancestors. Then, dressed as he was, in a light tunic and thin slippers, he opened the door and left the house.

He walked steadily through the dark, deserted streets, descended to the Forum, then headed for the path that would take him to the top of the Capitoline. Kaeso followed at a distance. In poems and plays, he had read of men possessed by the gods, but he had never seen such a thing. Had Scipio been possessed by a god? His reaction to the dreadful news seemed so strange, and his movements so controlled and deliberate, that Kaeso could hardly believe Scipio was acting of his own volition.

Atop the Capitoline, Scipio entered the Temple of Jupiter. Kaeso stopped at the foot of the steps. It seemed somehow improper to follow Scipio inside.

Kaeso waited. The landscape of the night seemed unfamiliar to him, and slightly eerie. The sacred precinct of temples and towering statues was ut-terly quiet, as if the gods themselves were sleeping.

But not for long. A flicker of torches caught Kaeso's eye. A group of magistrates and priests approached, headed by the Pontifex Maximus.

The priest gave him a nod of recognition. "You're Maximus's young cousin."

"Yes. Kaeso Fabius Dorso."

"Have you heard? A catastrophe! The worst defeat since Cannae!"

"I heard the news at the side of the curule aedile himself," said Kaeso quietly. "I followed him here."

"Young Scipio is in the temple?"

"Jupiter summoned him."

"Summoned him?"

"That's what Scipio said."

The Pontifex Maximus gazed up uncertainly at the open doors of the temple. Like Kaeso, he and the others chose to wait at the foot of the steps. Soon others joined them, for news of the disaster was spreading quickly through the city, as was word of Scipio's lone vigil inside the temple. Little by little, a great throng gathered. The space was filled with low murmurs of lamentation and cries of grief. The light of many torches turned night into day. If the gods had been sleeping before, thought Kaeso, they were awake now.

At last, Scipio emerged from the temple. People shouted his name, along with the names of his father and his uncle, and cried aloud to Jupiter for protection and salvation. Many in the anxious, grieving crowd believed that Scipio had been communing with the god and awaited his message.

Scipio stood for so long on the porch of the temple, unmoving and hardly seeming to notice the crowd, that Kaeso began to fear that his friend had lost his senses.

Suddenly Scipio stepped forward, raised his arms, and gave a shout. "Citizens! Be quiet! Can you not hear the voice of Jupiter speaking? Be quiet!"

The crowd fell silent. All eyes were on Scipio. He cocked his head and returned the crowd's gaze with a look of bewilderment. At last, as if solving a puzzle, he raised his eyebrows and nodded. "No, none of you can hear what I hear—but you can hear *my* voice, so listen to what I have to say. Citizens! I saved the life of my father in battle once, long ago at the river Ticinus. But when the combined fury of our enemies encircled him in Spain, I was not there, and I could not save him. When they turned their wrath against his brother Gnaeus, my father was not there to come to his rescue, and neither was I.

"My father is dead. My uncle is dead. The legions in Spain are broken and leaderless. Roma stands defenseless against our enemies to the west. If

Hasdrubal should come to join his brother Hannibal in Italy . . . if he should bring the Numidian whelp Masinissa with him . . . what shall become of Roma?"

There were cries of alarm from the crowd.

"That must never happen!" cried Scipio. "The bleeding wound of Spain must be stitched up. Hasdrubal and Masinissa must be driven out. The Suessitani must be punished. Tonight, here before you, upon the steps of the god's dwelling place, I make the vow that Jupiter demands of me. I pledge to take my father's place—if the people of Roma see fit to give me the command. I pledge to avenge his death. I pledge to drive his killers from Spain, and after that task is accomplished, I pledge to drive the one-eyed fiend himself from Italy, along with every mongrel mercenary under his command. To the east, Philip of Macedonia will be punished for allying himself with our enemy. We shall take the war to Carthage. We shall make them regret that they ever dared to challenge the will of Roma.

"It may take many years—it may take all the days that remain of my lifetime—but when I am done, I will make sure that Carthage can never endanger us again. I make this pledge to you, and I make this pledge to Jupiter, greatest of all the gods. Of Jupiter, I beg for strength. Of you, I ask for my father's command."

The crowd reacted. Moaning and weeping turned to shouts of exultation. The people began to chant: "Send the son to Spain! Send the son to Spain! Send the son to Spain!"

Kaeso looked at the faces of the magistrates and priests at the front of the crowd. They did not join in the chanting, but they did not dare to stop it. Wise men would argue that Scipio was far too young and inexperienced to receive such a command, just as he had been too young to serve as curule aedile. But he had asked the people directly for the command of Spain, and who could doubt that he would receive it?

Kaeso bowed his head, and wondered at his own audacity. How could he ever have thought, however fleetingly, that he might lay claim to the affections of a man so beloved by so many? Whether destined for triumph or defeat, Scipio had embarked on a path upon which Kaeso could not hope to follow.

"I think I must have felt as men felt in the presence of Alexander the Great," said Kaeso.

Plautus gave him a sardonic look. "Madly in love with the fellow, you mean?"

Kaeso smiled crookedly. "What an absurd idea!" Even in the uninhibited atmosphere of the playwright's house, he felt uncomfortable talking about his feelings for Scipio.

"Is it so absurd?" said Plautus. "Alexander's men were all in love with him, and why not? They say there was never a man more beautiful or more full of fire—a divine fire, a spark from the gods. And Alexander loved at least one of them in return, his lifelong companion Hephaestion. They say he went mad with heartbreak after Hephaestion died and rushed to join his beloved in Hades. Who's to say you couldn't be Hephaestion to Scipio's Alexander?"

"Don't be ridiculous! Hephaestion was Alexander's equal as an athlete and a warrior, for one thing. Besides, Greeks are Greeks and Romans are Romans."

Plautus shook his head. "Men are the same everywhere. That's why comedy is universal. Thank the gods for that! A laugh is a laugh, whether you're in Corinth or Corsica—or Carthage, I daresay. Every man likes to laugh, eat, spill his seed, and get a good night's sleep—usually in that order."

Kaeso shrugged and sipped his wine.

The playwright smirked. "Divine spark or not, your friend Scipio has fallen behind in his social engagements. Didn't you say he intended to have me over, to celebrate our mutual success? It's almost a month since the Roman Games, and I'm still waiting for *my* dinner invitation."

"You can't be serious, Plautus. Can you imagine how busy Scipio must be, preparing to take the command in Spain? He doesn't have time to entertain! I was probably the last person with whom he actually sat down and enjoyed a meal."

"You should feel lucky, then, and honored."

"I do. It will be a very long time, I imagine, before Scipio smiles again as he smiled that night—relaxed and contented and with hardly a worry. Now the weight of destiny is on his shoulders."

Plautus nodded. "He's set himself an arduous task. It will make him or break him."

"Only time will tell," whispered Kaeso. He mouthed a silent prayer to Jupiter to watch over his friend.

201 B.C.

Eleven years later, Scipio had fulfilled the vows he made to Jupiter, to the shades of his father and uncle, and to the people of Roma.

After decisive victories in Spain, Scipio took the war to Africa and proceeded to menace Carthage. This was done over the strenuous objections of Fabius Maximus, who told the Senate that Hannibal should be decisively defeated in Italy rather than lured away, and who warned against the uncertainties and entanglements of an African campaign. But Scipio's strategy succeeded brilliantly. Panicked, the Carthaginians recalled Hannibal from Italy to defend their city. Just as many of Roma's jealous allies and subjects had eagerly betrayed her, so did many of Carthage's neighbors. Scipio pressed his advantage. At the battle of Zama, some one hundred miles inland from Carthage, the long war reached its climax.

Before the battle, in a final attempt at negotiations, Hannibal asked to talk with Scipio, and the two met face to face in Scipio's tent. For a long moment, both men were struck dumb with mutual loathing and admiration. Hannibal spoke first, asking for peace despite the bitter taste of the word in his mouth. He offered terms advantageous to Roma—but not advantageous enough. Scipio craved a victory, not a settlement. Nothing less would satisfy his vow to Jupiter.

Hannibal made a final plea. "You were a boy when I began my war on Roma. You've grown up. I've grown old. Your sun is rising. I see twilight ahead. With age comes weariness, but also wisdom. Hear me, Scipio: The greater a man's success, the less it may be trusted to endure. Fortuna can turn on a man, in the blink of an eye. You believe that you have the upper hand going into this battle, but when the bloodshed and the madness begin, all the odds count for nothing. Will you stake the sacrifice of so much blood and so many years of struggle on the outcome of a single hour?"

Scipio was unimpressed. He pointed out that Roma had proposed terms of peace on numerous occasions, to which Carthage had always turned a deaf ear. Negotiation was no longer an option. As for Fortuna, Scipio was well aware of her vagaries. She had taken those dearest to him, but she had also given him a chance to exact his revenge.

Hannibal was allowed to return to the Carthaginian camp unharmed.

The next day, the two most famous generals commanding the two mightiest armies in the world advanced to battle. The closely fought contest was a test of sheer endurance for both sides. Scipio had prayed for a rout; he achieved a bare victory, but a victory nonetheless. Defeated, exhausted, abandoned by Fortuna, Hannibal fled back to Carthage.

The Romans' terms were harsh. Stripped of her warships and military stores and made to pay massive reparations, Carthage was reduced to little more than a client state of Roma. A war that had wreaked havoc on the whole of the Mediterranean for seventeen years had at last come to an end, and Roma emerged stronger than ever, a power poised to rival the fabled Egyptians or the Persians at the peak of their empires. The survivors who had fought and won the war could rightly consider themselves the greatest generation in Roman history, and the greatest among them, without question, was Publius Cornelius Scipio, forever after to be called Africanus— conqueror of Africa.

"He's cut his hair short! When did that happen? I've never seen him without his long mane of chestnut hair."

Kaeso spoke wistfully. Through the peephole beneath the stage, he gazed at the crowded bleachers of the Circus Maximus, where Scipio had finally arrived to take his seat of honor. The crowd stood and cheered him for a long time, crying "Africanus! Africanus!" Eventually the spectators began to take their seats, and Kaeso was finally able to get a clear view of the recipient of their acclaim.

"Are you disappointed, boss?" said Plautus, who was performing a last-minute inspection of the trapdoor. The simple task made him huff and puff; over the years, he had grown fat with success. "Does short hair not suit him?"

"Quite the contrary! It suits him very well indeed." Kaeso squinted slightly; his eyesight was not as good as it used to be. "He no longer looks like a boy—"

"I should think not! He must be at least thirty-five."

"But he's more handsome than ever. Not so much like Alexander anymore; more like Hercules, perhaps. He used to be almost too pretty, you know? Now he looks so rugged, so—"

"By Venus and Mars, stop swooning!" Plautus laughed. "He's just a man."

"Really? Did you see the triumphal procession?"

"Some of it. It went on too long for me to watch the whole thing."

"All those captives, all that booty! The splendor of his chariot, the magnificence of his armor! All those people shouting his name . . ."

"I'm only glad he decided to include an afternoon of comedy among the festivities—though I must admit I was a bit surprised when he requested that we revive *The Swaggering Soldier* for the occasion."

"Why not *The Swaggering Soldier*? It hearkens back to his very first elected office; people still talk about the Roman Games of that year. And it's a clever way for him to show people that he doesn't take himself too seriously. The audience can see the play as an affectionate parody of Roma's most beloved soldier, a man who's earned the right to swagger, the invincible Scipio Africanus. Giving them a laugh at his own expense will only make them love him more."

"While you, dear boss, could hardly love Scipio more than you already do."

Kaeso made no reply. He was deep in thought, musing on Scipio's spectacular success. His own life seemed hopelessly humdrum and shabby by comparison—a comfortable but loveless marriage, a daughter to whom he had never felt particularly close, an endless series of dalliances with actors and slave boys, and a merely adequate livelihood earned from his theater company and from his staff of scribes, who specialized in copying Greek books for sale to the literate upper classes.

Plautus slapped his shoulder. "Snap out of it, boss! You've been a shadow to Scipio all your life. You've admired him, desired him, idolized him, envied him—done everything, I suppose, except hate him."

"That I could never do!"

"Ah, but there you differ from your fellow citizens. They adore him now—they worship him like a god—but they'll turn on Scipio some day."

"Impossible!"

"Inevitable. The audience is fickle, Kaeso. You alone are faithful, like the keeper of a shrine. Scipio should appreciate you more than he does! Has he invited you to dinner even once since we met to talk about putting on the play?"

"He's been very busy." Kaeso frowned. Then a flash of movement caught his eye; one of the actors had forgotten from which side he needed to make his entrance and was using the passage under the stage to get across. The actor was new to the company, and quite young; they seemed to grow younger every year. He was also uncommonly good-looking, with long hair and broad shoulders. He flashed a grin at Kaeso as he hurried past.

Plautus glanced over his shoulder, then looked back at Kaeso and smiled. "Ah, yes, the new boy, from Massilia. Scipio's haircut notwithstanding, I see you haven't entirely lost your appreciation for long-haired beauties."

"I suppose I haven't," admitted Kaeso with a crooked grin.

Above their heads, the play began. The tromping of the actors across the boards was loud in their ears, but not as loud as the first roar of laughter from the audience. Amid the din, Kaeso was sure that he could distinctly hear Scipio, laughing louder and harder than anyone else.

191 B.C.

"It seems we hardly ever run into each other anymore, except at the theater," said Scipio. "When did I see you last, Kaeso? It's must have been a couple of years, at least."

The festive occasion was the opening of a temple on the Palatine, dedicated to a goddess new to Roma: Cybele, the Great Mother of the Gods, whom the Romans called Magna Mater. Her cult was said to date back to prehistoric times, but was not native to Roma or even to Italy. It had been imported from one of Roma's new allies in the East, the kingdom of Phrygia. Since the defeat of Carthage, Roma's expanding sphere of influence had resulted in an influx of new people, new languages, new ideas—and new deities. Cybele was quite unlike any goddess previously seen in Roma. The statue in the new temple depicted her wearing exotic garments and adorned from head to foot with bull's testicles. Along with her statue, the priests of Cybele had also been imported from Phrygia. They were called galli, and were also something new to Roma: eunuchs.

Games had been organized to celebrate the occasion, and a temporary theater had been erected in front of the new temple. The company of Plautus was about to put on a new comedy. For this performance, Kaeso had chosen to sit in the audience rather than remain backstage, and had invited Scipio to sit beside him. Before he could answer his friend's question, a small commotion in the audience distracted them both. The galli had arrived in a group and were filing into their seats of honor, not far from Kaeso and Scipio. The priests were gaudily attired in red turbans and yellow gowns. They wore bangles on their wrists and paint on their cheeks.

"Can you imagine our grandfathers putting foreign-born eunuchs on the sacred payroll?" asked Scipio. "Our ancestors thought of eunuchs, if they thought of them at all, strictly as the sycophants of kings, half-men who could never breed, and so would never try to put their own progeny ahead of the king's heirs. A republic has no king; ergo, no need for eunuchs. Yet now we have eunuchs in Roma, thanks to Cybele! Fascinating, aren't they? I hear they cut off their testicles themselves. They work themselves into a such a frenzy that they don't even feel it. Amazing, the acts to which religious devotion will drive a man!"

Kaeso winced at the idea of a man castrating himself, but found himself staring at one of the galli, a dark-eyed, exceptionally good-looking youth with full lips and skin like marble. He had heard that a man who was castrated in adulthood did not lose his erotic appetites. What sort of proclivities might such a young man possess, who had been willing to do such a thing for his goddess? Kaeso could not help being curious.

Aloud, he remarked, "If anyone should know about the Great Mother and her galli, it's you, Scipio. After all, it was you who officially welcomed them to the city and accepted the gift of the black stone."

The black stone, even more than the statue of the goddess, was the centerpiece of the new temple. It was said to have fallen from the sky, and its shape roughly depicted an even more primitive image of the goddess, an amorphous mass suggesting a massively pregnant female with no distinguishing features. The black stone, too, was unlike anything previously worshiped in Roma, but when the galli in the Phrygian city of Pessinus offered it as a gift, along with a request to establish Cybele's worship in Roma, a verse had been found in the Sibylline Books that called on the Roman people to accept the gift and welcome the new goddess.

Whatever its religious function, the importation of Cybele possessed a political dimension as well. Men of vision, like Scipio, believed that Roma's future now lay to the East. After Hannibal had been dealt with, the Romans turned their energies to defeating Philip of Macedonia, and had done so with help from Phrygia. Roma's embrace of the Great Mother would strengthen her bonds with her new ally. When the stone arrived by ship at Ostia, the verse in the Sibylline Books required that only the greatest of the Romans could accept it. Naturally, Publius Cornelius Scipio Africanus was chosen for the honor.

Perhaps because he was thinking of the galli and their sacrifice, Kaeso touched the golden fascinum that hung from the necklace he wore. He had put away the heirloom many years before, and had virtually forgotten about it, until he happened to come across it while going through a box of old things. The glitter of the gold caught his eye, and on a whim he decided to begin wearing it again on special occasions, as had been the practice, so he had once been told, of his ancestors.

Touching the fascinum led to another train of thought. He cleared his throat and said to Scipio, in an offhand way, "All these new religions flooding into Roma—some official, some . . . not so official. What do you think of the so-called Cult of Bacchus? They say it offers initiation into secret rites that promise an ecstatic release from the material world."

Scipio looked at him sidelong and raised an eyebrow. "The Cult of Bacchus is controversial, to say the least. Like everyone else, I've heard about it. It seems to be an offshoot of a Greek cult that worships a god of wine and madness. How much of what I've heard can be believed, or how widespread the cult's become, I don't know. I do know it has no recognition from the state."

"So it's not illegal?"

"Not technically, I suppose. But, from what I've heard, the cult's 'ecstatic' rituals are nothing more than drunken orgies where every possible sexual act is encouraged. Also . . ." Scipio lowered his voice. "The initiation of men into the cult requires that they submit to anal penetration—as if they were slave boys! I've also heard that the cult is nothing more than a front for a group of ruthless criminals. The so-called priests and priestesses are forgers, blackmailers, even murderers." Scipio took a deep breath. "I would advise you, Kaeso, to steer clear of any cult that has no official status, especially the Cult of Bacchus!"

"Yes, of course," muttered Kaeso. He hurriedly changed the subject. "I'm a grandfather now!"

Scipio smiled. "So I've heard. Congratulations."

"My daughter struck a lucky match when she married young Menenius. No man could have given her a more beautiful baby. I only wish my wife had lived to see little Menenia."

"Yes, I was saddened to hear of Sestia's death."

Kaeso shrugged. "To be honest, I was never much of a husband to her. Nor was I much of a father to Fabia. But the role of grandfather seems to suit me. I dote shamelessly on Menenia, as I never doted on her mother or grandmother. And what about you, Scipio? You've just had a daughter."

"Indeed I have! If you think you dote on Menenia, you should see me with Cornelia."

Kaeso nodded. "Curious, that your daughter and my granddaughter should be almost exactly the same age."

"Perhaps they can grow up to be friends, as you and I have been friends, Kaeso."

"I should like that," Kaeso said. "I should like that very much." He gazed steadily at Scipio. His chestnut hair, kept short, was now mixed with silver. In his rugged features, all trace of the boy was gone, except in his eyes, which sometimes glowed with youthful exuberance when he laughed. This was one of the reasons Kaeso had invited Scipio to sit beside him in the theater that day, because it would give him such pleasure to see Scipio laugh.

They were distracted by the sound of applause and a flurry of movement. Many in the audience spontaneously rose from their seats. Plautus had just entered the theater and was making his way to the empty seat next to Kaeso. At the age of sixty-three, the Umbrian playwright was the grand old man of the Roman stage. The audience knew him by sight and gave him a standing ovation.

The galli alone failed to recognize him. They looked at one another in puzzlement, then stood and joined uncertainly in the applause.

Plautus embraced Kaeso, then exchanged greetings with Scipio. The three of them sat, and the applause gradually dwindled.

"So, my flatfooted friend, what's the play today?" said Scipio.

Plautus shrugged. "Oh, a trifle I've titled after the main character, a wisecracking slave. It's called *Pseudolus.*"

"A trifle? Your masterpiece!" declared Kaeso.

"Spoken with all the conviction one would expect from the owner of the company!" Plautus laughed. "Oh, the dialogue sparkles in places, I must admit; but not nearly so brightly as words may sparkle in real life. I refer, Scipio, to the dialogue you exchanged with your old enemy Hannibal when the two of you met face to face on your recent mission to the East—if one can believe the gossips. *Can* one believe the gossips?"

Scipio had already told the anecdote to Kaeso, when they met outside the theater, but he obligingly related it again. "It's true. While I was in Ephesus, I learned that Hannibal happened to be there as well, and I arranged to meet him. Our spies say he's been wandering the East for years, offering his services to any king willing to challenge Roma. It's because of that accursed vow he made to his father; he can never stop plotting our downfall as long as there's a breath in his body. So far, he's had no takers. He's become a bit of a joke, actually."

"What did you two talk about?" said Plautus.

"This and that. At one point, I asked him which general, in his opinion, was the greatest of all time."

"A leading question!" said Plautus. "What was his reply?"

"'Alexander,' Hannibal answered. And what commander would he place second? 'Pyrrhus,' he said. And third? 'Myself!' declared Hannibal. Well, I had to burst out laughing. I said, 'And where would you rank if you had *defeated* me?' Hannibal looked me in the eye and replied, 'In that case, I would put myself before Pyrrhus and even before Alexander—in fact, before all other generals who ever lived!'"

Plautus slapped his knee. "Outrageous! Really, I could never invent a line like that, or a character like Hannibal."

"It's Carthaginian flattery, don't you see?" said Scipio. "Devious and indirect. But . . . I was flattered nonetheless." He sighed. "Someday, I have no doubt, Hannibal will be assassinated, or else driven to suicide. Not by me, of course, but by those who come after me."

Kaeso shook his head. "There'll never be another man big enough to take your place."

Scipio laughed, a little sadly and a little bitterly. "Sweet words, my friend, but alas, I grow smaller every day, and the space I occupy becomes easier to fill. I feel my influence waning. The world has grown tired of me, just as the world has grown tired of Hannibal. When people hear his name, they no longer tremble. They smirk. They hear my name, and they shrug. My political enemies circle me like wolves, waiting for the chance to bring me down on some trumped-up charge. The same small-minded men who will murder Hannibal will sooner or later drive me into exile, if they can."

Kaeso was distressed. "No! I don't believe you. Surely you're at the peak of your power. You were chosen to accept the black stone of Cybele. A magnificent arch is being built in your honor, to serve as the gateway to the Capitoline Hill. The Arch of Scipio Africanus will stand forever as a monument to your glory."

"Perhaps. Monuments last. Men don't. As for glory . . ." Scipio shook his head. "When we met for the first time, before the battle of Zama, Hannibal said something I've never forgotten: 'The greater a man's success, the less it may be trusted to endure.' We shall both be swept aside, Hannibal and I, swallowed by the rush of time. Do you want to see the future? Look there."

He pointed to a senator in the audience, a man in his forties, perhaps a little younger than Scipio. His slender face, seen in profile, was dominated by a beaklike nose. He was leaning forward with a tense posture and scanning the crowd with a predatory, birdlike gaze.

"My nemesis: Marcus Porcius Cato," said Scipio. "A so-called New Man, first of his family to hold elected office," he added, with some disdain. "But his neophyte status doesn't stop him from slandering me at every opportunity, and muttering behind my back about 'finishing' the war with Carthage—as if we had any reason to attack a crippled seaport that's been stripped of her champion, her navy, and her colonies. He says my handling of the settlement after Zama was 'lackluster, bordering on incompetent'; says I accomplished nothing in the long run because I failed to have Hannibal beheaded and burn Carthage to the ground. He slanders me on personal grounds as well; says I've 'gone Greek' because I happen to like the baths and the theater. Given Cato's loathing for all things not Roman, I'm rather surprised to see him in the audience today. What in Hades is he doing here?"

As if on cue, Cato rose from his seat. "Citizens! Citizens! Listen to me!" he cried, in such a powerful, strident voice that in short order he had the attention of everyone in the audience.

"Citizens, you know me well. I am Marcus Porcius Cato. I began my service to Roma when I enlisted at the age of seventeen, back when that scoundrel Hannibal was having his run of luck, setting Italy on fire. Since that time, I have devoted my entire life to the salvation of this city and the preservation of the Roman way of life. Four years ago, you honored me by electing me consul and sending me to Spain; subsequently I received a triumph for pacifying the revolt there. If further unrest broke out again after my departure, I think we can safely say that was the fault of my successor."

Under his breath, Scipio muttered an obscenity. It was Scipio who had taken control of Spain after Cato.

"In terms of holding high office, some call me a 'New Man,' " said Cato. "But in terms of the bravery and prowess of my ancestors, I assure you that I am as old as any man here! So, I hope you will lend me your ears for a few moments, and consider what I have to say.

"Citizens! What are you doing here today? What is this decadent spectacle in which you have chosen to take part? Think of it: Here you are, gathered to watch a play based on a Greek original, performed in honor of an Asiatic goddess imported from a land ruled by a king, all to make a group of foreign eunuchs feel welcomed! To all of this, I say: no, no, no!

"How can such an abomination have come about? I'll tell you how. Wealth and all the vices that spring from wealth—greed, love of luxury, crass opportunism—are leading you astray from the upright virtues of your forefathers. I look about me, and everywhere I see loose morals, loose living, and loose thinking. Now it comes to this: We are deliberately polluting the purity of our religious worship, diluting and demeaning our reverence for the ancient gods who have preserved us for centuries!

"Things go from bad to worse. Importing a priesthood of eunuchs is bad enough, but one hears of even stranger and more insidious foreign cults spreading among the populace. The play to which you shall be subjected today will, I daresay, be bad enough—yet another revolting compendium of Greek obscenities—but recently some senators, who should know better, have spoken of erecting a *permanent* theater in Roma, built of stone. Are we Romans to become as idle and pleasure-loving as the Greeks?

"You, there, Marcus Junius Brutus!" Cato pointed to the praetor who was sponsoring the games. "What would your heroic ancestor say, he who revenged the rape of Lucretia and brought down the last king, Tarquinius, if he could see this sorry sight? Has our beloved Roma risen to unparalleled heights of glory only to fall into an abyss of shame?

"Citizens, I beseech you! If my words have ignited even the tiniest spark of patriotism in your heart, do as I now do, and leave this place at once!"

Cato ostentatiously gathered the folds of his toga. After a few steps he halted and turned back. "Oh, and one more thing: Carthage must be destroyed!" With that, he stalked out of the theater, followed by a substantial entourage.

A handful of people scattered throughout the audience did likewise, but a greater number began to boo Cato, who disappeared through the exit without looking back. People shifted uneasily in their seats. A murmur spread through the audience.

Scipio rose from his seat. He said nothing to call for the crowd's attention, but gradually all eyes came to rest on him. The audience fell silent.

"Citizens! If the senator who just imposed on our patience by marring the joyous nature of this occasion had not seen fit to attack me personally—something he appears to do compulsively, like a man with an uncontrollable twitch—I would not presume to try your patience further by addressing you myself. However, I feel obliged, first, to say this: A man who leaves a mess behind him has no business casting aspersions on the man who comes after him. Just as I had to clean up the mess left behind by Hannibal's elephants,' so I had to clean up the mess that Cato left behind in Spain."

The audience burst into laughter. The tension left in Cato's wake was dispersed in an instant.

"Second: If, after all my years of service to the Roman people, I have any claim to speak on their behalf, allow me to apologize to our guests of honor, the priests of the goddess Cybele, for the aspersions cast upon them by the senator. I assure you, not all Romans are so boorish and inhospitable."

The galli, who had sat stone-faced through Cato's harangue, smiled and nodded to acknowledge Scipio's courtesy.

"Likewise, allow me to apologize for the uncouth words that my colleague addressed to you, Marcus Junius Brutus, generous sponsor of these festivities. Instead of citing your great ancestor to make a dubious rhetorical point, let him use the example of one of his own famous ancestors. Oh, but I'm forgetting—Cato has no famous ancestors."

Brutus laughed and called out, "Hear, hear! Well said, Africanus!"

"As for all the other drivel that spilled from the senator's mouth, I will say only this." Scipio gestured to Plautus. "In the terrible year of Cannae, all the might of Hannibal could not stop the performance of this playwright's work. Surely a temper tantrum by Cato will not stop it today. The show must go on!"

Laughing and applauding, the audience leaped to their feet and gave Scipio a joyous ovation.

The crowd's response reassured Kaeso. Here was proof, he thought, that Scipio's gloomy fears about the future were unfounded. But what a burden his friend had to bear, enduring the abuse of men like Cato! Whatever Kaeso's own petty problems, at least he did not have to worry about ruthless rivals plotting his downfall. Perhaps there was something to be said for leading an insignificant life. He thought of Hannibal's words to Scipio, but reversed their meaning. He muttered aloud, "The *smaller* a man's success, the *more* it may be trusted to endure."

"What did you say?" asked Plautus, as the ovation began to die down.

"Nothing," said Kaeso. "Nothing at all."

The play was a rollicking success.

After it was over, Kaeso declined an invitation to celebrate at Plautus's house. Limping slightly, he set off alone. The day's official festivities were over, but there were still a great many people out and about. Kaeso was jostled by the crowd. More than once he had to sidestep a pool of vomit left by someone who had celebrated too much. He only vaguely noticed these irritations; as always after seeing Scipio, he was restless and unsettled, preoccupied by thoughts of how his life might have turned out had he been a different man with a different destiny, a man like Scipio, or else a man who could have been Scipio's comrade-in-arms, worthy to share his adventures, his glory, his tent . . .

As he drew nearer to his destination, a house on the Aventine Hill, the crowds thinned. The streets were almost empty. He sighed with relief, glad to be out of the crush and knowing that the place where he was headed would offer relief from all his earthly cares.

On a respectable street in a respectable neighborhood, he came to a house where all the windows were shuttered. He rapped at the door. The peephole slid open. For a moment, he forgot the pass phrase, but then it came back to him: "Upon Mount Falernus in Campania grow the grapes from which Falernian wine is made." The phrase was changed often, but always had something to do with wine, because wine was Bacchus's gift to mankind, and essential to his worship.

The door opened, then was quickly shut after Kaeso stepped inside. The garden at the center of the house had been closed off, and all the windows had been shuttered, with heavy hangings pulled across them to keep sounds from reaching the neighbors. As a result, the interior was quite dark except for the soft illumination cast by lamps, and the sounds from within were strangely muffled.

Those sounds included exotic music played upon tambourines and pipes. The tune was by turns languorous and dreamy, then fast and frenzied. Familiar faces, male and female, emerged from the shadows. They smiled and bowed their heads in deference to him. "Welcome, high priest," they said in unison.

One of them whispered in his ear, "A new acolyte is within, awaiting initiation."

Kaeso raised his arms from his sides until they were parallel with the floor. The men and women undressed him, then anointed his naked body from head to foot with sweet-smelling oil. A cup filled with wine was pressed to his lips. He threw back his head and swallowed. Wine overflowed his mouth and trickled down onto his chest, where greedy tongues lapped it up. Hands glided over his shoulders and chest and hips and buttocks, caressing him, fondling him, exciting him.

He was taken by both hands and guided into a room that smelled of sweat and incense. Here the music was louder, and he could now discern the murmur of a low, insistent chant in which the name of Bacchus was invoked. The room was hazy with incense, and crowded with warm, naked bodies pressed close together. Presiding above the crowd, upon a high pedestal, was a statue of the god—Bacchus, deity of wine and euphoria, with grape leaves in his hair and a smile of bliss upon his bearded face.

Kaeso gazed up at the god with reverence and gratitude. The coming of the cult to Roma had marked the beginning of a new epoch in his life. In the warm, secret embrace of the god, Kaeso had at last found a purpose to his existence.

Kaeso abruptly experienced a fluttering in his head, of the sort that sometimes preceded one of his falling spells, but he felt no anxiety. The priests and priestesses of Bacchus had explained to him that his affliction was not a curse but a mark of special favor from the god. Just as Scipio had always enjoyed a special relationship with Jupiter, so Kaeso had at last discovered his own special link to the god Bacchus.

The fluttering in his head subsided. On this occasion, the god had seen fit merely to pass through him without striking him senseless.

Someone whispered in his ear, "High priest, the initiate is ready for the ritual."

His rigid sex was firmly grasped, and in his other ear a voice whispered, "And *you* appear to be ready for the initiate!"

Kaeso touched the fascinum that lay upon his bare breast. He tightly closed his eyes. Step by step, the acolytes guided him forward until his sex was met by a circle of resistance, then swallowed by a convulsive embrace. He heard the muffled cry of the initiate, followed by a whimper and a groan. Kaeso surrendered to a state of bliss.

Who was the initiate before him? Male or female, young or old? He did not know. Behind his closed eyes it was Scipio he envisioned, Scipio when his hair was still long and not a single battle scar had yet marred his perfect beauty. It was Scipio into whom he thrust all the love and longing inside him.

Even in the throes of ecstasy, he knew that his vision of Scipio was only a fantasy. But the bliss he felt was genuine. When all was said and done, only these brief moments of release were real. All else was illusion. Earthly glory was meaningless; Scipio himself had admitted as much. Scipio had reached a pinnacle of so-called greatness unknown to other men, but had Scipio ever attained the unspeakable delights that Kaeso had experienced since he joined the Cult of Bacchus?

183 B.C.

Kaeso ran his fingers through the mop of graying hair on his head and closed his eyes to rest them for a moment. How weak his vision had grown in recent years! When he was younger, even well into his forties, he had been able to read without effort all those poems by Ennius and plays by Plautus, no matter how tiny the letters. Now, squint as he might, it was almost impossible for him to read any of the documents spread before him. Reading was his secretary's job, of course, but Kaeso wanted to make sure that no mistakes were made.

He had decided to liquidate all his assets. A group of buyers had been found to purchase his theatrical troupe, and his staff of scribes was being sold piecemeal. He was going over his will, as well, though the terms were simple enough; his entire estate would be left in trust to his granddaughter, Menenia.

Kaeso opened his eyes and gazed about his study, at all the pigeonhole bookcases stuffed with scrolls. Over the years he had accumulated a considerable library, anticipating long years of retirement in which he would require many books to keep him company.

Amid the bookcases, there was a small shrine, a little stone altar upon which stood a miniature statue of Bacchus. Kaeso gazed into the god's smiling eyes for a long moment, then looked away.

"I think our work is done. You may go now," he said to the secretary. "Send in Cletus."

The secretary withdrew. A few moments later a handsome young slave with broad shoulders and long hair stepped into the room.

"Cletus, I wish to go for a walk today."

"Of course, master. The weather is quite fine." The slave offered a thickly muscled forearm for Kaeso to lean upon. Kaeso did not really need the support, but he enjoyed clinging to Cletus's arm anyway.

Together, they took a long stroll around the city.

First, Kaeso visited the arch which had been built to commemorate Scipio's victories, conspicuously located on the path that led to the top of the Capitoline. The relief carvings depicting the triumphs of Africanus were as magnificent as he remembered. It was a worthy monument to his friend.

Next, he ventured to the necropolis outside the Esquiline Gate, where he placed flowers upon the humble funeral monument of Plautus. This day was the first anniversary of the playwright's death. How Kaeso missed him—his keen insights, his piercing wit, his unflagging loyalty to his friends. At least the scores of plays that Plautus had written would live on; Kaeso had kept copies of them all.

Leaning upon Cletus's arm—for he was genuinely growing a little weary—Kaeso headed toward the Aventine Hill for the final destination of his excursion. In the vicinity of the Circus Maximus, he noticed a highly animated group of men. From the way they were all talking at once, they appeared to be discussing some highly significant bit of news. Was the news dreadful or joyous? Kaeso could not tell from their expressions.

Among the men, he recognized an old acquaintance, Lucius Pinarius, and sent Cletus to ask him over.

"What's going on, Lucius?"

"You haven't heard?"

"Would I be asking, if I had?"

"Hannibal is dead."

Kaeso drew a sharp breath. As simple as that: Hannibal is dead. It was like hearing that the sea had dried up, or the moon had fallen from the sky. And yet it must be true. What could be simpler, or more inevitable? Hannibal was dead.

"How?"

"Suicide. Sixty-four years old, and still plotting against us, trying to stir up trouble in Greece and Asia. The Senate finally had enough of his treachery and sent a military force to extradite him. I suppose he couldn't face the humiliation of being tried and executed. He took poison. But before he died, he dictated his last words to a scribe: 'Let us now put an end to the great anxiety of the Romans, who have thought it too long and too heavy a task to wait for a hated old man to die.'"

"A bitter end."

"And long overdue. Scipio Africanus—"

"Yes, I know: Scipio should have killed him when he had the chance, and burned Carthage to the ground. But I'll not hear a word spoken against the memory of my dear departed friend, certainly not on this day!"

Kaeso turned away from Pinarius. He called for Cletus to lend him his arm so they could proceed.

How prescient Scipio had been! All had come to pass just as he predicted. But what a stroke of fate, that the two great generals who once bestrode the world like Titans both should have died within a year!

With Cletus to help him, Kaeso struggled up the slope of the Aventine, finally arriving at the humble house of Ennius. The poet resided alone, with only a single slave woman to serve him. She opened the door to Kaeso and showed him in to Ennius's study. Cletus stayed behind in the vestibule.

"I suppose you've heard the news," said Kaeso.

"About Hannibal? Yes." The poet, who was careless with his dress and perpetually in need of a haircut and a shave, looked even shabbier than usual. "I don't suppose Hannibal will be needing an epitaph for his gravestone. From what I heard, he uttered his own epitaph with his dying breath."

Kaeso smiled. "What about Scipio's epitaph? Have you finished it yet?"

"I have indeed. It's ready to be chiseled on his grave monument. I was greatly honored that in his will he asked me to compose it."

"Who else? You were always his favorite poet. Well?"

Ennius handed him a piece of parchment.

Kaeso made a face. "You know I can't possibly read this. Recite it aloud to me."

Ennius cleared his throat.

> *The sun that rises above the eastern-most marshes of Lake Maeotis*
> *Illumines no man my equal in deeds.*
> *If any mortal may ascend to the heaven of immortals,*
> *For me alone the gods' gate stands open.*

Kaeso managed a crooked smile. "A bit grandiose for my taste, but just the sort of thing Scipio would have wanted. Where on earth is Lake Maeotis?"

Ennius raised an eyebrow. "It's the body of water located beyond the Euxine Sea, at the uttermost edge of the civilized world. I have no memories of it from this life, but I think in my first life I must have gone there; of course, I would never have actually seen the sunrise, since I was blind during that incarnation."

Kaeso nodded. Since becoming a follower of the teachings of the Greek philosopher Pythagoras, Ennius was convinced of the transmigration of souls. He was quite certain that he had begun existence in the body of Homer, author of *The Iliad*. His other incarnations included a peacock, several great warriors, and Pythagoras himself.

Ennius was still speaking, but Kaeso, who found such notions tiresome, let his mind wander. His thoughts returned to Scipio. How accurately his friend had foreseen his fate! In the end, his enemies overwhelmed him. He did accomplish one final military victory, a successful campaign against the upstart King Antiochus, who presumed to challenge Roma's hegemony in Greece. But it was a Pyrrhic victory; when Scipio returned to Roma he was charged with taking bribes from the king and conspiring to join him as a co-ruler. No accusation could be more damning to a Roman politician than the claim that he wished to make himself a king. It was Cato, of course, who masterminded the prosecution. Rather than face trial, Scipio retired to his private estate at Liternum, on the coast south of Roma. Behind massive walls, with a colony of loyal veterans to protect him, he withdrew from warfare, politics, and life. Heartbroken and bitter, he fell ill and died at the age of fifty-two. And now, within a year, Hannibal was also dead.

"Two giants, hounded to death by lesser men," muttered Kaeso.

"If you ask me, Scipio is well out of it," said Ennius. "Roma's become a bitter place. The atmosphere is poison. Small-minded reactionaries like Cato have gained the upper hand."

Kaeso nodded. "People's tastes have changed as well. I see it in the theater. No more comedies by Plautus. Now we have tragedies by Ennius. People leave the theater in a somber mood, to fit these somber days."

Ennius grunted. "I'd be glad to write a comedy, if I saw anything to laugh at. How did we come to this? When we finally brought down Carthage, do you remember the elation people felt, the boundless sense of well-being and camaraderie? Then came our victories in the East—heady days, with endless wealth and exciting new ideas flooding into Roma. But things changed too fast. People grew uneasy. Men like Cato manipulated their fears, and the result was a very ugly backlash." Ennius sighed. "I suppose the worst manifestation of that backlash was the appalling suppression of the cult of Bacchus."

Kaeso stiffened. He opened his mouth to change the subject, but Ennius had only begun to rant.

"What horrid days those were! The official inquiry, the flimsy accusations of crimes and conspiracy against the state, the cult and all its members outlawed. Thousands of men and women executed, forced into exile, driven to suicide! The hatred unleashed against those poor people was sickening, and absolutely nothing could be done to stop it; say a word against the inquiry, and you were branded a sympathizer and persecuted along with them! I myself was never part of the cult, but I knew men who were, and even that tenuous association put me under suspicion for a while. I was terrified.

"And yet, a remnant of the cult may yet survive. There's been a new series of arrests. Only the other day I witnessed one, just down the street. The scene was all too familiar: the accused man, dazed, trembling with fear, being dragged from his home by stone-faced lictors. Meanwhile, the household slave who betrayed the poor wretch stood off to one side, trying not to look guilty. A chilling sight!"

Kaeso could stand no more. He abruptly rose and told Ennius he must take his leave.

"So soon? I had hoped—"

"I'm afraid I have no time. I merely wanted to hear Scipio's epitaph. Thank you. But now I really must go. I'm expecting callers at my house, later today."

"Dinner guests?"

"Not exactly."

Back at home, tired after the long walk, Kaeso sat alone in his study and gazed at the many scrolls that filled his library; they were like old friends, to whom he must bid a sad farewell. He made sure his will was in the proper place. Though he could not read it, he found the passage that he had instructed his secretary to underline that morning. It mentioned the fascinum specifically, and his desire that Menenia should wear it on special occasions, and when she did so, that she should remember her loving grandfather. Kaeso removed the talisman from his neck and laid it atop the will.

He reached for a decanter and poured a cup of wine—a fine Falernian—and into the wine he stirred a powder. Holding the cup, he knelt before the shrine of Bacchus. He kissed the statue of the god, and waited.

It was not long before he heard a loud banging at the front door. A few moments later, Cletus came running into the study.

"Armed men, master. They're demanding entrance."

"Yes, I've been expecting them."

"Master?" The color drained from Cletus's face.

"Isn't this the hour at which you told them to come? I overheard you talking to that fellow in the Forum yesterday, Cletus. Why did you betray me?"

There was the sound of a commotion from the vestibule. The lictors were no longer waiting at the door. Cletus looked away, unable to hide his guilt.

Quickly, Kaeso drank the poison. He would die with the taste of the god's favorite vintage on his lips.

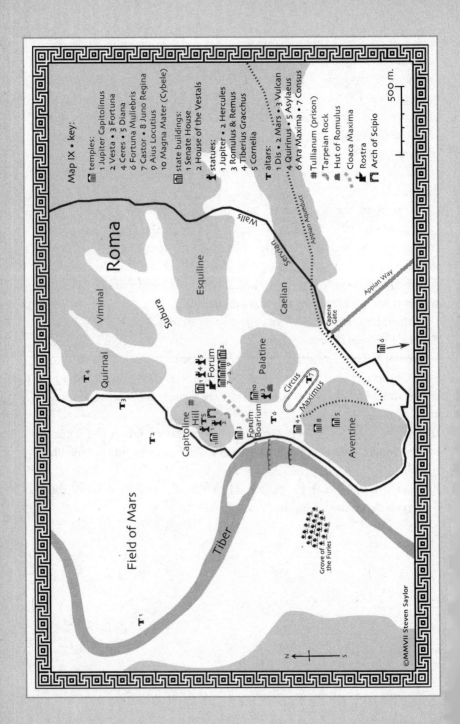

Map IX • key:

🏛 temples:
1 Jupiter Capitolinus
2 Vesta • 3 Fortuna
4 Ceres • 5 Diana
6 Fortuna Muliebris
7 Castor • 8 Juno Regina
9 Aius Locutius
10 Magna Mater (Cybele)

🏛 state buildings:
1 Senate House
2 House of the Vestals

⚵ statues:
1 Jupiter • 2 Hercules
3 Romulus & Remus
4 Tiberius Gracchus
5 Cornelia

T altars:
1 Dis • 2 Mars • 3 Vulcan
4 Quirinus • 5 Asylaeus
6 Ara Maxima • 7 Consus

Tullianum (prison)
🪨 Tarpeian Rock
🛖 Hut of Romulus
Cloaca Maxima
Rostra
🏛 Arch of Scipio

Roma

Field of Mars

Tiber

Quirinal

Viminal

Subura

Esquiline

Capitoline Hill

Forum

Forum Boarium

Palatine

Caelian

Circus Maximus

Aventine

Grove of the Furies

Servian Walls

Capena Gate

Appian Aqueduct

Appian Way

500 m.

N — S

©MMVII Steven Saylor

IX

FRIEND OF THE GRACCHI

146 B.C.

"Daughter, mother, wife, widow . . ."

As she enunciated each word, Cornelia brought together a fingertip from each opposing hand—an orator's gesture she had seen her father perform. Cornelia had been quite young when Scipio died, but he had made an immense impression on her nonetheless, and many of his gestures and facial expressions, and even some of his turns of phrase, lived on in her. She had also inherited her father's famous beauty. Now in her late thirties, Cornelia was a strikingly handsome woman. Her chestnut hair gleamed red and gold as it reflected the bright, dappled sunlight of the garden.

"Daughter, mother, wife, widow," she repeated. "Which is a woman's greatest role in life? What do you think, Menenia?"

"I think . . ." Her friend smiled a bit shyly. Menenia was the same age as Cornelia, and like Cornelia, a widow. Though not as beautiful, she comported herself with such grace that heads were as likely to turn in her direction as in Cornelia's when the two entered a room together. "I think, Cornelia, that you have left out a category."

"What would that be?"

"Lover." With one hand, Menenia touched the talisman that hung from her neck, an ancient fascinum inherited from her grandfather. With her other hand, she gently touched the arm of the man who sat next to her, and the two exchanged a long, meaningful look.

Blossius was a philosopher, an Italian born in Cumae. With his long, graying hair and neatly trimmed beard, he exuded an air of dignity to match Menenia's. Cornelia was moved by the special spark between her dearest friend and the tutor of her children. Here were two mature adults, long past the age of heady romance, who had nonetheless found in each other not just a companion but a soul mate.

"What prompts you to pose this question?" asked Blossius. As a pedagogue of the Stoic school, he tended to question a question rather than answer it.

Cornelia shut her eyes and lifted her face to the warm sunlight. It was a quiet day on the Palatine; she heard the music of birdsong from the rooftops. "Idle musings. I was thinking that Menenia and I both lost our fathers at an early age. And we're both widows, having married, and buried, husbands considerably older than ourselves. After my father's death, relatives arranged for me to wed dear old Tiberius Gracchus. And you were the second wife of Lucius Pinarius, were you not?"

"Third, actually," said Menenia. "The old dear was looking more for a caretaker than a broodmare."

"Yet he gave you a wonderful son, young Lucius."

"Yes. And Tiberius gave you many children."

"Twelve, to be exact. Each was precious to me. Alas, that only three survived!"

"But what remarkable children those three are," said Menenia, "thanks in no small part to their instruction from Blossius." She squeezed her lover's arm. "Your daughter Sempronia is already happily married, and the world expects great things of your sons Tiberius and Gaius."

Cornelia nodded. "I think we've answered the question I posed, at least regarding myself. Since I no longer have a living father or husband—and no time for a lover!—motherhood is my highest role. My achievement will be my sons. I intend for them to do such great things that when my life is over, people will say not that I was the daughter of Scipio Africanus, but the mother of Tiberius and Gaius Gracchus."

Blossius pursed his lips. "A noble aspiration. But must a woman exist only through the men in her life—fathers, husbands, sons . . . lovers?" He cast an affectionate look at Menenia. "Stoicism teaches that each man is valuable in and of himself, whatever his station in life. Citizen or slave, consul or foot soldier—all contain a unique spark of the divine essence. But what of women? Do they not also possess intrinsic value, above and beyond whatever role they play in relationship to the men in their lives?"

Cornelia laughed. "Dear Blossius, only a Stoic would dare to utter such a radical notion! A generation ago, you might have been exiled merely for proposing such an idea."

"Perhaps," said Blossius. "But a generation ago, it's unlikely that two women would have been allowed to sit alone and unchaperoned in a garden discussing ideas with a philosopher."

"Even nowadays, many an old-fashioned Roman would be appalled to overhear this conversation," said Menenia. "Yet here we sit. The world changes."

"The world is always changing," agreed Blossius. "Sometimes for the worse."

"Then it will be up to our children to change it for the better," declared Cornelia.

Menenia smiled. "And which of your sons will do more to change the world?"

"Hard to say. They're so different. Tiberius is so serious, so earnest for an eighteen-year-old, mature beyond his years. Now that he's a soldier, off fighting those poor Carthaginians, or what's left of them, I hope his outlook doesn't become even more somber. Little Gaius is only nine, but what a different fellow he is! I fear he may be rather *too* impulsive and hot-tempered."

"But very sure of himself," said Blossius, "especially for a boy his age. As their tutor, I can say that both brothers are remarkably self-confident—a trait I attribute to their mother."

"While I attribute it to their grandfather, though he was dead long before either was born. How I wish the boys could have known him, and that I could have known him longer than I did. Still, I've done all I can to instill in the boys a deep respect for their grandfather's accomplishments. They bear the name Gracchus proudly, and rightly so, but they are also obliged to live up to the standards of Scipio Africanus."

Menenia sighed. "Well, as for my Lucius, I only hope he comes back alive and unharmed from Cato's war." This was the name which many in Roma had given to the renewed campaign against Carthage. Cato himself had not lived to see the outbreak of the war, but he had never ceased to agitate for it. For years, no matter what the subject—road building, military commands, sewer repairs—he ended every speech in the Senate with the same phrase: "And in conclusion . . . Carthage must be destroyed!" Men laughed at his dogged obsession, but in the end, from beyond the grave, Cato had prevailed. It now seemed that his dream would be realized. According to the most recent dispatches from Africa, Roman forces were laying siege to Carthage, whose defenders could not hope to resist them for long.

Cornelia blinked and shaded her eyes. The garden had suddenly grown too hot and the sunlight too bright. The singing birds had fallen silent. "They say it's no longer a question of *if* Carthage is destroyed—"

"But *when*," said Blossius.

"And when that happens—"

"Carthage shall be the second city in a matter of months to suffer such a fate at Roma's hands." The philosopher resided in Cornelia's house, and the two saw each other almost daily; their thoughts often ran side by side, like horses hitched together. "When General Mummius captured Corinth, there was rejoicing in the streets of Roma."

"And weeping in the streets of Corinth!" Cornelia shook her head. "Every male citizen killed, every woman enslaved! One of the most sophisticated and opulent cities in all Greece, obliterated by Roman arms."

Blossius raised an eyebrow. " 'An example to anyone who would dare to challenge our supremacy,' according to Mummius."

"Temples were desecrated. Priceless works of art were destroyed by his rioting soldiers. Even the most anti-Greek reactionaries in Roma were embarrassed by Mummius's barbarism—"

Cornelia abruptly fell silent. She lifted one ear to the sky. In place of birdsong, another sound now floated on the air. "Do you hear? A commotion of some sort."

"From the Forum?" said Menenia.

"Closer than that, I think. Myron!" A young slave sitting on the ground nearby scrambled to his feet. Cornelia sent him to find out what was going on. While they awaited his return, the three of them sat silently, sharing the same unease. A commotion meant news of some sort. News could be good, or bad . . .

At last Myron returned, out of breath but smiling. "Mistress, tremendous news from Africa! Carthage has been taken. The war is over! A ship landed at Ostia this morning, and the messengers have just arrived in Roma. That's all I've found out so far, but if you wish, I can run down to the Forum."

Menenia began to weep. Blossius put his arms around her. The two seemed oblivious of Cornelia. Watching them, she suddenly felt very alone. The heat of the garden made her feel faint. The bright sunlight brought tears to her eyes.

"Yes, Myron, go and see what else you can discover. Perhaps there's some word about . . . Roman casualties."

"At once, mistress." Myron spun about, and abruptly collided with a man who was just stepping into the garden.

Cornelia shielded her eyes from the sun. She squinted at the newcomer, then let out a cry. "Nicomedes! Is it really you?"

The man was one of Tiberius's slaves. He had accompanied his master to Carthage.

"But Nicomedes, what are you doing here? Why aren't you still with Tiberius?" Despite the heat, Cornelia shivered.

"Rather than speak for my master, my master may speak for himself." Nicomedes smiled and produced a covered wax tablet from the pouch he carried.

"A letter? From Tiberius?"

"Inscribed by my own hand amid the smoking ruins of Carthage, as dictated by your son, mistress, who is not only alive and well, but a hero of the Roman legions."

"A hero?"

"As you shall understand when you read his letter."

Cornelia nodded. She felt strangely calm. "Myron, go and fetch young Gaius. He should be present to hear his brother's letter read aloud. Blossius, will you do it?" She handed him the tablet. "My hands are shaking, and I don't think I could make sense of the letters."

A moment later, Gaius appeared, running ahead of Myron. He was a handsome boy, the very image of his grandfather. "Is it true, mother? Carthage is taken, and there's a letter from Tiberius?"

"Yes, Gaius. Sit here beside me while Blossius reads it."

The philosopher cleared his throat. " 'To my beloved mother, daughter of the great Africanus: I write these words to you from the city my grandfather once conquered, which has just been conquered again by Roman arms. It shall never be conquered a third time. From this day forward, Carthage shall no longer exist.

" 'Along with this letter, Nicomedes also brings a memento from me. It is the mural crown, which I was awarded for having been the first soldier to scale the enemy walls.' "

From his pouch, Nicomedes produced a crown made of silver and molded to resemble a crenellated wall with towers, such as might encircle a city. He presented the crown to Cornelia. "Your son received it in a public ceremony before the troops, and wore it at a place of honor at the victory feast. He sent it home with me, so that his mother might be the first in Roma to see it."

"The first to scale the walls!" whispered Gaius, gazing at the crown in his mother's hands. "The first Roman inside Carthage! Can you imagine how dangerous that must have been?"

Cornelia could well imagine, and the thought made her lightheaded. But she managed a smile and placed the crown atop Gaius's head. It was too big for him and slipped over his eyes. Everyone laughed. Gaius angrily pushed the crown from his head. It fell to the paving stones with a clatter.

"That's not funny, Mother! The crown wasn't meant for me!"

"Hush, Gaius!" With a sigh, Cornelia bent down to retrieve the crown and placed it on her lap. "Let us hear the rest of your brother's letter. Blossius, please continue."

" 'For your friend Menenia, I also have good news: Her son Lucius fought bravely in the battle, killed many of the enemy, and sustained no injuries.' "

"Thank the gods!" cried Menenia. She reached for Blossius's hand, but he was distracted by the letter. He peered at it intently, reading ahead. His face was grim.

"Go on, Blossius," said Cornelia. "What else does Tiberius write?"

"Only . . . a bit of description . . . of the battle itself. Nothing of a personal nature."

"Very well. Let's hear it."

"I'm not sure I should read this aloud, in front of the boy. Or in front of you, for that matter. I suppose it's a mark of Tiberius's deep respect for you, that he should write to his mother as candidly as he might have written to his late father . . ."

"What were you just saying, Blossius, about the worthiness of women?"

"It's not a question of merit, but of . . . delicacy."

"Nonsense, Blossius. If you won't read it aloud, I will." Cornelia put aside the mural crown, rose to her feet, and took the tablet from him.

" 'As for Carthage,' " she read, " 'the ghost of Cato may finally rest: The city, which was as old as Roma, is now utterly destroyed. The harbor is demolished, the houses burned, the altars for human sacrifice reduced to rubble. The gardens have been uprooted. The grand mosaics of the public squares have been flooded with pools of blood.

" 'The men were slaughtered, as long as we had strength to slaughter them; the few who survive will become slaves. So far as I know, every woman was raped, regardless of her age or status. Many were killed, though they screamed for mercy; such was the frenzy for destruction that overtook the victors. The women and men who survived will be separated by sex and sold in slave markets hundreds of miles apart, so that no Carthaginian male and female may ever copulate again, and thus the race will become extinct. Before they are sold, their tongues will be removed, so that their language, and even the names of their gods, will vanish from the earth.

" 'The earth itself will be made barren. Salt is being plowed into the soil surrounding the city, so that no crops can be grown for a generation. Salt was the precious substance that gave birth to Roma long ago—so Blossius taught me—so it is fitting that salt shall seal the burial of Carthage.

" 'When Alexander conquered Persia, he chose to leave the city of Babylon intact and to make its people his subjects; for his clemency, he was exalted by gods and men. We have followed an older example, that of the merciless Greeks who sacked the city of Troy and left only ruins behind. The Greek playwrights tell of many misfortunes that subsequently befell the victorious Greeks—Ajax, Ulysses, Agamemnon, and the rest. I pray the gods will favor what we have done to Carthage, and will grant a righteous destiny to the Roman people, who have done this fearful thing for the glory of Jupiter.' "

Her hands trembling, Cornelia put down the tablet.

"If only I could have been there!" said Gaius, his eyes bright with excitement. "What a glorious day it must have been! And now it shall never happen again, because Carthage is gone, and I was too young to be there, and there'll never be another war with her. I can hardly wait for Tiberius to come home and tell me more about it."

Menenia lowered her eyes.

"War is the way of the world, and always will be," said Blossius quietly. "Clearly, the gods of Roma were greater than those of Carthage. For that, we must be thankful. And yet . . . I am fearful for Roma's future. How astute is Tiberius, when he points to the example of the Greeks against Troy. I am reminded of the Greek hero Achilles, who was very nearly invincible; yet, when he desecrated the corpse of the Trojan Hector, the gods frowned upon his hubris and withdrew their protection, and Achilles died like any other mortal on the battlefield.

"Roma has entered a new era. With the destruction of Corinth, the Romans' respect for Greek culture degenerated to wanton looting. With the destruction of Carthage, the Romans are without rival in the Mediterranean. But how will Roma bear the responsibilities of power and wealth unprecedented in the history of the world? We must pray that the gods will give Roma wise men to lead her into the future—and wise women to nurture those men as boys!"

Blossius, Menenia, and Cornelia each turned their eyes to young Gaius. Inspired by visions of the carnage at Carthage, he had dared to pick up the mural crown and was testing its fit on his brow again, oblivious of their scrutiny.

133 B.C.

"Tiberius is headed for trouble, Mother. Serious trouble. He has no idea of what he's up against. I want nothing to do with it." Lucius Pinarius, who had the auburn hair and bright green eyes typical of many Pinarii, took a bite of boiled cabbage marinated in garum. The dish, served cold, was a family favorite for a hot midsummer day.

Blossius helped himself to a bit of the cabbage as well, though it tended to give him indigestion. Though all Cornelia's children were now grown, Blossius still resided at her house, but he spent much of his time here at the house of Menenia, which was only a few steps away on the Palatine. It was unthinkable that Menenia and Blossius—a Roman patrician and a philosopher from Cumae—should ever marry, but their relationship had stood the test of time. The widow and the Stoic were growing gray together.

Menenia ate none of the cabbage. She had no appetite during hot weather; it was her lament that during the entire month of Sextilis she could eat nothing at all. A slave behind her wafted a peacock fan to stir the languid air of the garden.

"Tiberius Gracchus has always been your friend, Lucius," she said. "You should be happy for him. You might have looked upon his election to the tribunate as an opportunity for yourself. Instead, over the last year, you've deliberately avoided him. What about this legislation he managed to enact, setting up a commission to redistribute farmland? You could have served on that commission—"

"If I wanted to end my career before it's begun! The whole thing will end in disaster."

"Not necessarily," said Blossius. "To be sure, Tiberius is taking a great gamble. Frankly, his boldness astonishes me, though it shouldn't; he's the descendant of his grandfather, after all, and the son of his mother."

"And the pupil of Blossius!" snapped Lucius. "You Stoics are always claiming that the best form of government is not a republic but a just king. You've put all sorts of dangerous ideas in Tiberius's head."

Blossius held his temper, but the cabbage began to rumble in his belly. "Tiberius is a visionary. If my teachings have inspired him, I take pride in that accomplishment."

"But will you suffer the consequences along with him, when the whole enterprise collapses?"

"Tiberius is the most beloved man in Roma," said Blossius.

"He's also the most hated man in Roma," countered Lucius.

"Lucius! Blossius! Stop bickering! The day is too hot for it." Menenia sighed. "Now, I want each of you to explain to me once again, from your own point of view, exactly what Tiberius Gracchus is attempting to do, and why it holds the promise of such great success—or failure."

Blossius raised an eyebrow. "You feign ignorance, my dear, in an effort to make us defend our positions with logic rather than emotion. You could summarize the situation as well as either of us."

Menenia laughed. "If it will keep the two of you quiet, I shall! Back in the days when our ancestors were conquering Italy, piece by piece, Roma acquired vast parcels of public land. Later on, even more land was seized from the Italian cities that went over to Hannibal. Public policy has been to disburse this land to Roman citizens and to allied Italians as a reward for military service: Small farms keep the economy stable, and they supply more soldiers, since landowners are obliged to serve in the military. To keep the holdings small and to make disbursements fair, there have always been limits on how much land any single man can own.

"But, as the Etruscan proverb goes, money changes everything. In my lifetime, staggering amounts of gold and silver have poured into Roma from conquered cities and provinces, and as a result a very small group of citizens have become very, very rich. Some of those men have found ways to circumvent the legal limits, and have bought up vast tracts of public land, along with slaves to work their enormous holdings. As a consequence, free men all over Italy have been forced off the land and into the cities, where they struggle to survive, avoid raising families, and have no obligation to serve in the army. The situation benefits no one except a small number of enormously rich landholders. The poor masses of Italy are dispossessed of their land, and the available manpower for the Roman legions grows thin. Something must be done to take back the illegally acquired lands of the big owners and to redistribute that land to the people." Menenia looked pleased with herself. "There. Have I explained the general situation to the satisfaction of you both?"

"I couldn't have done it better myself," said Blossius, "though I might add that the ramifications of this situation go far beyond mere land management. There's the current war in Spain—a gratuitous, drawn-out, disastrous affair—which has been repeatedly bungled by the ruling clique in the Senate. That's led to massive dissatisfaction in the ranks and the imposition of harsh and humiliating discipline. I'm thinking of the instance when deserters from the Spanish campaign were rounded up, beaten, and sold into slavery."

He looked longingly at the cabbage, but decided to forgo another bite. "The huge influx of slaves has led to its own problems, such as the massive revolt going on in Sicily right now. Slaves are threatening to take over the entire island! And this is only the latest and largest outbreak of violence by renegade slaves. Their numbers have grown to alarming proportions all over Italy, and many of them are terribly brutalized. The situation grows more dangerous every day. Farmers pushed off the land; too little respect and recompense for the common soldiery; too many miserable, desperate slaves. The citizens of Roma are demanding that something be done—and Tiberius Gracchus has declared that he is the man to do it."

"Only twenty-nine years old, and already a tribune!" said Menenia. "Cornelia must be very proud."

Lucius took this as a slight. A smirk spoiled his handsome features. "Having an important father-in-law helps! Appius Claudius is probably the single most powerful man in the Senate."

"Ah, the Claudii, forever with us! And their politics seem to grow more radical with each generation," said Blossius. "Yes, Tiberius has a powerful ally in Claudius. But the big landholders will stop at nothing to hold on to their property. We've seen how the game has played out so far. Tiberius put forward a proposal to redistribute land, but it takes only one of the other nine tribunes to veto such a proposal, and the landowners managed to persuade the tribune Marcus Octavius to do so."

Lucius became increasingly agitated. "And now we come to the reason I want nothing to do with Tiberius and his politics. When Octavius issued his veto, Tiberius called for Octavius to be removed by popular vote, and forced him from office. But Octavius refused to stand down, whereupon one of Tiberius's freedmen forcibly dragged Octavius from the speaker's platform, and in the scuffle that followed one of Octavius's servants was blinded. Now Tiberius's detractors are calling him an enemy of the people for having done what even Coriolanus failed to do: He forced a tribune from office!"

"Tiberius's action was entirely within the law—"

"Whether the expulsion of Octavius was legal or not, I don't know.

What I do know is that Tiberius resorted to violence. Yes, he finally got his way: His proposal became law. To redistribute the land, there must be a commission. And whom does Tiberius appoint to that powerful commission? Himself, his father-in-law Appius Claudius, and his younger brother Gaius, who's barely twenty-one!"

"Tiberius needed men he could trust," insisted Blossius.

"It stinks of nepotism," said Lucius. "Mother, earlier you suggested that I might have secured a place on Tiberius's commission. I assure you, no power on earth could have persuaded me to do so!

"And now we see Tiberius's latest gambit. As you pointed out, Mother, money changes everything. King Attalus of Pergamum has died, and his will leaves the whole of his kingdom to Roma—the lands that belonged to Troy in ancient times will now belong to us. The influx of wealth will be enormous. Normally, all that gold and booty would go directly into the Senate's coffers, but Tiberius has a different idea. He proposes that it should go directly to the people, distributed along with the land allotments so as to pay for farm equipment and start-up supplies. His enemies call it public bribery on an unprecedented scale. They accuse Tiberius of aiming to make himself king."

"Never!" scoffed Blossius.

"At the very least, Tiberius is attempting a kind of revolution from the bottom up. He challenges the supremacy of the Senate by using the office of tribune to do things no tribune has ever done before."

"I think it's all terribly exciting," said Menenia. "Why are you so convinced that Tiberius will fail?"

"Because, Mother, his support grows weaker every day. The common people, whether it serves their interest or not, have bought into the argument that Tiberius impugned their sovereignty when he drove a rival tribune from office. And if he thinks he can appropriate the wealth of Pergamum for his own political purposes, circumventing the Senate, he's truly playing with fire. *Does* Tiberius want to be a king, as his enemies say?" Lucius turned his gaze to Blossius. "He already holds court like one, keeping a Greek philosopher for an adviser."

Blossius bristled. "My philosophy is Greek, but I am a native-born Italian, of noble Campanian blood. Yes, I was Tiberius's tutor when he was a boy. If he still consults me as a man, why not?"

"Because Roman magistrates do not consult Greek philosophers about matters of statecraft—unless they wish to look like Greek tyrants. I only repeat what Tiberius's enemies are saying. They also ask: When he arrived in Roma, to whom did the Pergamene ambassador deliver the royal testament and the diadem and purple cloak of the late King Attalus? To the Senate? No! He went straight to the house of Tiberius."

"Not to anoint him king!" protested Blossius. "The ambassador called on Tiberius merely as a courtesy. Diplomatic ties between the Gracchi and the house of Attalus go back a generation. It was thirty years ago that Tiberius's father headed a Roman embassy to investigate charges of sedition against the late king's father, and cleared him of all suspicion. Ever since then, the royals of Pergamum have maintained a special relationship with the Gracchi."

"Whatever the explanation, it looks suspicious."

Blossius shook his head. "Nonsense! Tiberius's enemies will stoop to any slander to bring him down. He stands up for the people, and the land-grabbers say he wants to be the people's king. The voters should know better than to believe such lies."

"We'll see what the voters think soon enough," said Lucius. "Tiberius is running for a second term as tribune. It's clearly illegal for other magistrates to hold office two years in a row—"

"But not so for the tribunate," said Blossius. "There *is* a precedent for a standing tribune to remain in office. If not enough new candidates stand for the ten positions in a given year—"

"Is *that* what Tiberius is plotting? To keep his office by bribing or scaring away other candidates?"

"The others will stand down because the people will demand it."

Lucius groaned with exasperation. "Can you not see where all of this is headed? If Tiberius is allowed to stand for tribune again by invoking some technicality, and if he wins, his enemies will only grow more determined to stop him; that means more violence. If he loses, he'll lose the immunity of his office, and his enemies will drag him into court on some trumped-up charge and send him into exile. No matter what happens, Tiberius is in a very dangerous position."

A long silence followed, finally broken by a sigh from Lucius. "It's not that I disagree with Tiberius's proposal to redistribute the land. It's a worthy objective. It must be done, and it will be done—eventually. If only Tiberius had taken a slower, more gradual approach—"

"The greedy landholders would have opposed me just the same," said a hoarse voice.

"Tiberius!" cried Menenia. She sprang up, embraced the newcomer and gave him a kiss on the cheek. "Where did you come from?"

"From speaking in the Forum, of course. Election day is coming. I thought I might find Blossius here." Tiberius Gracchus had grown into a strikingly handsome man; many who compared him to busts of his grandfather declared that he was even more good-looking. On this day he appeared a bit haggard; the unceasing demands of his reelection campaign were taking a toll. Despite his fatigue, he projected an aura that seemed larger than his physical presence, that indefinable allure the Greeks called *kharisma*. The intimate setting of Menenia's garden seemed too small to contain him.

Blossius rose and greeted him. They exchanged a few hushed words. Then Tiberius turned to Lucius, who had remained seated and silent.

"I couldn't help but overhear some of your comments, Lucius. I've grown accustomed to defending myself before my enemies. Perhaps I should spend more time explaining myself to my friends."

Lucius stood and drew back his shoulders. "I meant no offense, Tiberius. But here in my mother's house I make no secret of my misgivings. I spoke freely in front of Blossius."

"And Blossius defended me, I'm sure. But even Blossius can't speak the words that come directly from my heart, because even Blossius has not experienced what I have experienced in the last year. Menenia, might I have a little wine? My throat is dry from speaking."

A slave brought him a cup at once. Tiberius drank thirstily, but his voice was no less hoarse than before. "Lucius, a year ago, when I began my first campaign for the tribunate, I was little different from any other man running for the office. I was looking for political advancement, hoping to make a name for myself. Yes, I believed in the speeches I was making—or should I say, the speeches Blossius wrote for me—and the need for land reform, better treatment of the soldiery, and so on. But the promotion of those goals was little more than a means to an end, a way for me to find a constituency and began my ascent in the Course of Honor.

"Then I took a trip up and down the length of Italy, to see with my own eyes the situation in the countryside. What I witnessed was appalling. The rural areas have been virtually emptied of free men and their families. It's as if the whole peninsula was tilted by some Titan's hand and all those people went tumbling into Roma, and here they live piled on top of another. You can hardly pass through the streets of the Subura nowadays, it's become so crowded.

"And after the countryside was depopulated of free men, it was filled up again—with slaves. Tilling the rich farmland, toiling in the vineyards—whole armies of foreign-born slaves, working till they drop for the handful of rich men who've grabbed all the land. I mean that quite literally—these slaves fall where they work and die there. It's not unusual to see a dead slave lying in a field while the others continue to work around him under the whip of a merciless foreman. Slaves have become so cheap, so expendable, they're treated far worse than the livestock."

Tiberius shook his head. "We all know this situation exists. We all speak of 'the land problem' in the abstract, and worry over what might be done, and argue points of policy. But to see the reality firsthand, traveling day after day through the countryside, is a very different experience. I was shaken to the core by what I saw.

"But it was something else that truly changed me. I said the countryside is depopulated of free men, but that's not entirely true. Here and there you come across a small farmer who's somehow managed to hold on to his property, tilling his fields the old-fashioned way; the family members work side by side with a few slaves, and everyone pulls together. These little holdings have been surrounded by huge farms; they're like little islands of the Roman countryside that once existed. And because those small farmers acquired their land by military service, or have sons currently enlisted in the legions, you'll often see a prized piece of armor or a replica of a legionary standard proudly displayed at the gate. In a flash you see the connection between a thriving community of small farmers, a strong army, and a healthy, vibrant Roma.

"Passing such a small farm, up in Etruria, I saw a placard mounted on the gate. It said: 'Tiberius Gracchus, help us keep our land.'" He smiled ruefully. "My name was misspelled, and the letters were very crudely made, but that sign sent a jolt sent through me. And that was only the first sign I saw. After that, at every surviving small holding I passed, even those far from the main roads, I saw such placards. 'Tiberius Gracchus, restore public land to the poor.' 'Tiberius Gracchus, stop the spread of slaves.' 'Tiberius Gracchus, give us back our land and our work.' 'Tiberius Gracchus, help us.' Somehow, news of my journey had spread from farm to farm, mouth to mouth. By the time I returned to Roma . . ."

Tiberius's voice was choked with emotion, and had grown so hoarse that he could hardly continue to speak. Menenia brought him more wine. He drank it and continued.

"The mission I've undertaken is far greater than I am. Politicians come and go, with their squabbling and slanders and shameless scrambling for advancement. The destiny of Roma is what matters, and the fate of the Roman people, especially those who feed the city and fight for her, who give their sweat and blood and the offspring of their loins for the glory of Roma."

There followed a long silence. At last Blossius stepped forward. There were tears in his eyes. "My dear boy! I boast about having been your tutor, but the student has far surpassed his teacher! Always you were clever, always you were serious and disciplined—yet I never imagined that Cornelia's little boy would grow up to cast such a shadow over us all."

Tiberius smiled wanly. "Blossius, I think you're slightly missing the point. When I say that politicians come and go, while the destiny of the people endures, I mean just that. I have no illusions about my importance or about my permanence, except insofar as I may find a way to channel the power of the people for the benefit of the people, and for the greater glory of Roma."

"Of course. Well put!" Blossius dabbed the sleeves of his tunic against his moist eyes. "But you say you came looking for me?"

"Yes. There are some purely practical matters I want to discuss. Appius Claudius thinks I should propose shortening the term of military service, ahead of the election. He also thinks we should put forward the idea of allowing nonsenators to serve as judges."

"This requires serious discussion. Perhaps at your mother's house?"

"Of course. Menenia and Lucius have put up with my ramblings long enough."

"Nonsense!" said Menenia. "You're welcome in this house at any time,

Tiberius. You know I love to hear you speak! But you must do something about that hoarseness. An infusion of mint and honey in hot water can do wonders."

"I'll try it," promised Tiberius. "Good day, Menenia. And good day to you, Lucius." He smiled, but Lucius merely nodded in response. Tiberius and Blossius took their leave.

The garden suddenly seemed very quiet and still, and somehow empty. Mother and son sat apart, thinking their separate thoughts.

Tiberius's story of the placards in the countryside, apparently so heart-felt, left Lucius unmoved. To him it seemed that Tiberius must be either a compulsive politician, unable to stop emoting and speechifying even in a friend's garden, or else a genuine idealist, blinded by visions of grandeur and indifferent to the terrible dangers ahead of him. In either case, Tiberius's passionate words made Lucius feel more uneasy than ever.

Menenia was thinking of her friend Cornelia, and how very differently their sons had turned out. Which was better: to have a son who blazed a trail like a comet, with all the brilliant uncertainty of celestial fire, or to have a son as stolid and predictable as a lump of earth? Menenia had to admit that she envied Cornelia, at least for now. But would she have reason to pity Cornelia in the future?

"If only the election for tribunes wasn't held in the middle of the summer," complained Tiberius. "That's precisely when my strongest supporters are away from Roma, searching for harvesting work in the countryside. Blossius, do you think you could . . . ?"

A fold of Tiberius's toga was refusing to hang correctly across one shoulder. Blossius straightened it. "It's no accident that the elections take place when they do," the philosopher observed. "The ruling families of Roma have always arranged every aspect of every election in order to give themselves the greatest advantage and the common people the least. But if the cause is just and the candidate is steadfast, the will of the people will not be thwarted."

Cornelia stepped into the room. "Let me have a look at you, Tiberius." Her son obligingly stood back and struck a pose, clutching the folds of his toga with one hand. "How splendid you look! Your father and grandfather would be very proud. I only wish your little brother were here to see you." Gaius had been sent to scour the countryside for supporters and persuade them to return to Roma for the election.

Cornelia gave him a kiss on the cheek. "Come along, then. The augur has arrived. He's waiting for us in the garden. Stop rolling your eyes, Blossius! I know what you think of religious formalities, but this ritual must be observed for the sake of tradition. Tiberius's father and grandfather would never have appeared before the voters on an election day without consulting an augur first."

In the garden, the augur placed a cage with three chickens on the ground. He circled the cage three times, invoking the gods and the ancestors of Tiberius Gracchus. He scattered grain on the ground, some to the right and some to the left of the cage, then opened the hatch. The auspices would be determined by observing the motion of the birds, whether they moved in a group or as individuals and in which direction; to the right indicated the favor of the gods, to the left indicated their disfavor.

But the chickens did not leave the cage. They clucked and bumped against one another, ignoring the open hatch. The augur stamped his foot. He made shooing motions. Eventually, he gripped the top of the cage and gave it a good shaking. Finally, one of the chickens emerged. The bird ignored both scatterings of grain. It lifted its left wing, then turned around and scurried back into the cage.

The augur looked acutely embarrassed. "The auspices . . . are inconclusive," he said.

Cornelia frowned. "The left wing," she whispered. She felt a premonition of dread.

"Unfortunately" said Tiberius, "the science of augury is not as exact as we might wish. A veil lies across the future. The future shall arrive anyway."

Mother and son exchanged a long look. Cornelia could see that Tiberius was as uneasy as herself, but she said nothing.

Tiberius proceeded to the vestibule. He paused to gaze at the images of his ancestors. He touched the brow of the great Africanus, then nodded to the slave to open the door.

Outside, in the street, a throng of supporters awaited him. Many had spent the night in front of the house, taking turns sleeping and guarding the door. In the final days of the campaign, the rhetoric on both sides had grown so heated, and the street scuffles between the factions so violent, that many feared for Tiberius's safety. There was a rumor that his enemies were conspiring to murder him before the election; his opponents claimed that Tiberius himself had started the rumor, to whip up his supporters. Whatever the truth, a great crowd awaited him in the street, and when they saw him, they erupted into cheering.

Smiling broadly, Tiberius stepped forward. He stumbled on the threshold and lost his balance. Staggering forward, he stubbed the big toe of his left foot against a paving stone with such force that he thought he heard a bone crack. At the very least, the nail of the toe had been broken. Blood seeped through the front of his shoe and darkened the leather. He felt faint and nauseated. He reached for support, found Blossius's arm, and gripped it tightly.

"You've hurt yourself!" whispered Blossius.

"Did they see?" Tiberius kept his face down and spoke through clenched teeth.

Blossius scanned the cheering crowd. "No one seems to have noticed."

"Good. Then we shall go ahead as if it never happened."

"But can you walk?"

"If I hold fast to your arm. But first I'll say a few words. These men have been here all night, waiting for this moment."

Tiberius looked at the crowd and managed to smile. He raised his hands for silence.

"Loyal supporters, dear friends, fellow Romans: The long night has passed, and, whatever mischief our enemies might have been planning, we are all still alive!"

This was met with a great deal of cheering and laughter.

"You watched over me all through the night. For that, I thank you. And in return, in the second year of my tribunate, I promise to do my very best to watch over all of you—to restore to you the lands that are rightfully yours, to protect you from the greedy land-grabbers and their vicious gangs, and to make the Roma of your children a fairer, richer, better place for all hard-working citizens.

"To do all that, I must win today's election. And to win the election, first and foremost, I must stay alive. The threat from our enemies is very real. At any place and at any time, I might be assaulted. I don't fear a fight; I've done my share of fighting! I was the first to scale the walls of Carthage, and was awarded the mural crown. I also fought in Spain, alongside many of you brave men. But here in Roma, I am no longer a soldier, but a private citizen. I carry no weapons. You must be my guardians. Without your protection, I am defenseless."

"We'll defend you!" cried a man in the front of the crowd. "If we have to, we'll die for you, Tiberius Gracchus!" He was joined by many others.

"It will never come to that, I pray to Jupiter. But if I should perceive an immediate threat, and require a ring of brave men around me, I may not be able to cry out to you. My voice is hoarse, and the din may be too great. So, this will be my signal." Tiberius raised both arms skyward, then bent his elbows so that he pointed at his head with both hands. The sign was unmistakable: rally to the head.

The crowd began to clap and chant his name. Tiberius gripped Blossius's arm with one hand and waved with the other. He walked forward, trying not to wince at the pain. "Perhaps it's a good thing, that I stumbled," he whispered to Blossius. "The auspices indicated a bad start. Now the bad start is behind me!"

Limping slightly despite Blossius's support, Tiberius set out for the Capitoline, where the voting would take place. As he descended the Palatine, more supporters joined his retinue. Many more were waiting in the Forum. They opened a path for him, cheering and reaching out to touch him as he passed by, then joined the throng that followed behind him.

On the steps leading up to the Capitoline, Tiberius paused before the Arch of Scipio Africanus. The monument was decorated with images of his grandfather's triumphs in both Africa and Asia. Scipio had survived the battle of Cannae and shamed his fellow officers by his fortitude, had lost the father whose life he had saved in battle, and had matched wits with Hannibal and beaten him. Tiberius laughed aloud at the absurdity that a stubbed toe should give him a moment's pause. He made a silent vow to ascend to the voting place without limping or leaning on Blossius, and to show no sign of pain.

He had passed under the arch and proceeded a short distance when he heard a noise from above. Screeching and beating their wings, two ravens were fighting on the roof of a building next to the pathway, to his left. Their altercation dislodged a roof tile. The tile fell directly in front of Tiberius and shattered with a loud noise. Tiberius flinched.

"The augury, the stumble . . . and now this!" he whispered. "One bad omen after another—"

"Nonsense!" said Blossius in his ear. "Chickens behave like chickens. People stub their toes every day. Ravens squabble. Tiberius, if you start to see omens in every accident and happenstance, you will indeed be putting on the airs of a king; only a tyrant imagines the universe revolves around himself. A raven dislodged a loose bit of tile—nothing more!"

Tiberius nodded, straightened his toga, and continued the ascent.

The large open space before the Temple of Jupiter was already crowded when Tiberius arrived with his retinue. Only plebeians could vote for the tribunes, and they did so by first gathering into voting blocks called tribes. Even on the most peaceful of election days, the polling officials were hard-pressed to maintain order; for their own protection and to hold back the unruly crowd they were allowed to carry spear-shafts without metal points. News of Tiberius's arrival was met with a tremendous uproar of mingled acclamation and jeering. Jostled this way and that, some in the crowd retaliated by shoving back. Fistfights broke out. The election officials scrambled to maintain order by brandishing their shafts.

Over the centuries, the assembly area had become so congested with shrines and statues, and the number of voters had so increased, that the simple procedure of assembling into tribes had become a logistical challenge. Elections could be won or lost depending on whether a candidate's supporters were able to assemble when called on. Tiberius's supporters had arrived early and in great numbers to claim the best spots for addressing the crowd and to maintain open pathways. If the supporters of opposition candidates could be kept at the periphery of the voting area or excluded altogether, Tiberius's chances would be increased.

With Blossius at his side and surrounded by a cadre of his most ardent supporters, Tiberius was ushered through the crowd and escorted onto the steps of the Temple of Jupiter. At the sight of him, more cheering erupted from the center of the crowd and catcalls from the edges.

He had hoped to address the crowd, but the unceasing din made doing so impossible. He had never seen such a raucous election assembly. The participants seemed to be in continuous motion, shouting and gesturing. Scattered here and there, especially around the periphery or in the tight spots where a statue or shrine made movement difficult, skirmishes appeared to be taking place. It was not unlike watching a battlefield.

Some of the election officials, growing exasperated, were banging their shafts against the ground, calling for order and demanding that the gathering of the tribes begin. The voters were either unwilling to cooperate, or unable to hear them. The scene was chaotic.

A pathway opened in the crowd and one of Tiberius's supporters in the Senate, Fulvius Flaccus, rushed toward him, breathless with alarm.

"Tiberius, I've just come from an emergency meeting of the Senate. All morning your enemies have been demanding that the consul Scaevola declare today's election an illegal assembly—"

"Illegal? The people have the right to elect tribunes—"

"They claim the disorder is too great, a menace to public safety—or worse."

"Worse?"

"Your cousin Scipio Nasica says you're mustering a mob to bring down the state. After you massacre your opponents in the Senate, you'll declare yourself king—"

"Nasica!" Tiberius spat the word. The two cousins, both heirs to the bloodline of Africanus, despised each other. There was no greater reactionary in the Senate than Nasica. While Tiberius had made himself the champion of the common people, Nasica made no secret of despising them. Even when he campaigned for their votes, he could not resist insulting them. "I know better than you lot what is good for the state," he had once shouted at an unruly crowd; opponents joked that this was his idea of a campaign slogan. And once, shaking the horny palm of a farm laborer, Nasica had snidely commented, "How does one get such calluses? Do you walk on your hands?"

Blossius spoke up. "The consul Scaevola is a good man."

"Indeed he is," said Flaccus. "He's refused to sanction any attempt to cancel the election. But that hasn't stopped Nasica. 'If the consul won't act to save the state, then private citizens must do so'—that's what Nasica said. He and a number of other senators gathered outside, and then they were joined by a gang of cutthroats—the roughest sort of men you can imagine, armed with clubs."

"They planned this ahead of time," said Blossius.

"Obviously!" said Flaccus. "And now they're coming this way, with Nasica leading them. They mean to kill you, Tiberius! They think they're on a sacred mission—the senators have wrapped the red hem of their togas across their foreheads, like priests about to carry out a sacrifice!"

Tiberius's blood ran cold. He stared at the unsuspecting crowd.

"The signal!" cried Blossius. "Give the signal!"

Tiberius raised his arms in the air. The movement drew the attention of the crowd. With all eyes on him, Tiberius pointed to his head.

His supporters understood at once. They seized the shafts carried by the election officials, broke them in pieces, and passed the fragments among themselves; the longer sections could serve as cudgels and the splintered ends as daggers. There were a number of benches throughout the assembly area. They began to smash these as well, to use the fragments as weapons.

Tiberius's opponents in the crowd took the signal to mean something else. "He points at his head—he's demanding a crown!" men cried. "Look at his followers, gathering weapons—they mean to take the Capitoline by force. They'll declare Tiberius king!"

Amid the mounting chaos, there was an even greater commotion at the entry to the assembly area. Nasica and his fellow senators, with their gang of cutthroats, had arrived.

A violent free-for-all followed. On the Palatine and down in the Forum, and even on the far side of the Tiber men could hear the sounds of combat atop the Capitoline.

Several of Tiberius's supporters ran to his side and offered him their weapons, but he refused to take them. Instead he turned his back on the melee, faced the Temple of Jupiter, and raised his arms in prayer.

"Jupiter, greatest of gods, protector of my grandfather in battle—"

Blossius seized the folds of his toga and shouted at him. "Go inside the temple! Run! When they come for you, claim Jupiter's protection—"

Blossius was struck across the belly by a club. With the breath knocked out of him, he fell to his knees.

Hands converged on Tiberius. They grabbed his toga and pulled it off him. Wearing only his under-tunic, Tiberius bolted up the steps of the temple, limping because of his injured toe; he tripped on a step and fell forward. Before he could get to his feet, a cudgel struck his head and sent him reeling. He blindly struggled to his feet and stood swaying for a moment. Another club, swung with tremendous force, struck his head and shattered his skull with a sickening crack.

Blossius had just managed to get to his feet. Red gore and pale bits of brain spattered his robes. He stood aghast and gaping at the bloody remains that lay crumpled on the steps.

One of the killers recognized him. "It's the Greek philosopher—the would-be king's adviser!"

"Toss him from the Tarpeian Rock!"

Whooping and laughing, they seized Blossius by his hands and feet and carried him down the steps. They headed toward the rock, dodging clubs and hopping over corpses that littered the way.

They reached the precipice, but instead of shoving him over, they made sport of swinging him back and forth, back and forth, gaining momentum.

"On the count of three: one . . . two . . . three!"

They released him and sent him hurtling into space.

For a brief moment, Blossius appeared to defy the earth's pull. He soared skyward. Then, with a sickening twist in his gut, he began to fall.

They had thrown him clear of the precipice. Under normal circumstances, his downward plummet would have ended at the foot of the Capitoline. But many men had been pushed from the Tarpeian Rock before him. A few of these men had managed to grab hold of the rock face and cling to the sheer cliff. Flailing frantically, Blossius grabbed the garments of one of these men and broke his fall. Almost at once he lost his grip and fell upon the next man down. In such a manner, grasping at one desperate man after another, repeatedly breaking his fall and then falling again, he descended the cliff. More than once, a man above him lost his grip and plummeted past him, screaming.

At last, drained of the last vestige of will, overwhelmed with terror, with nothing left to grasp, Blossius fell in earnest.

He landed not upon hard earth, but upon a pile of bodies. More bodies fell around him, like hail dropping from the sky.

As night descended, the killers gathered the bodies of the dead, loaded them onto carts, and wheeled them across the Forum Boarium to dump them in the Tiber.

Blossius gradually woke. At first he imagined that he had been buried alive, but the confining mass surrounding him was not earth, but dead flesh. The cart jerked and bumped beneath him, sending a great throbbing soreness through every part of his body. He would have groaned, but he had no air in his lungs. The pressure against his chest would not allow him to draw a breath.

From somewhere he heard muffled sounds—women sobbing and shrieking. A woman cried out, "Let me have my husband's body! At least give me his body!" A harsh masculine voice ordered her back.

The cart came to a halt. The world began to tilt. The mass of flesh all around him shifted and gave way, like a cliff disintegrating in a landslide. He tumbled helplessly forward.

He was suddenly underwater. The shock wrenched him to full consciousness. Sputtering, flailing his arms, he found the surface and sucked in a lungful of air.

The sky above was dark and full of stars. The swiftly flowing current was littered with bodies. In his dazed state, he somehow sensed which was the farther shore and swam toward it. Again and again, he collided with floating corpses. One of them seemed to wrap its arms around him. In a panic, he struggled to free himself. The man could not possibly be alive; that was obvious from his smashed skull.

As Blossius pulled free, he glimpsed the dead man's face.

It was Tiberius.

Impulsively, he reached for the body, but it slipped away on the current, its torso spinning, its limbs bobbing, as lifeless as a floating branch.

Weary beyond hope and wracked with sobbing, Blossius pulled himself onto the riverbank and collapsed into oblivion.

"If I had followed your advice, dear mother—if I had tied my fortunes to those of Tiberius—just imagine the consequences!" Lucius Pinarius nervously paced the garden. "Now *you* must follow *my* advice. Drive this dangerous fool from our house!"

He pointed at Blossius, who sat stripped to the waist, patiently allowing Menenia to tend to his many wounds with ointment and fresh bandages. Three days had passed since his brush with death, but he was still badly shaken.

The entire city was reeling from the shock of the massacre on the Capitoline. At least three hundred men had been killed. No man alive could remember anything like it; for the first time since the fall of Tarquinius and the precarious early years of the Republic, political strife had erupted in mass bloodshed, with Romans killing Romans. The careless desecration of the bodies was grossly offensive even to many who opposed Tiberius, and had caused widespread anger and resentment. But the senatorial faction that had put an end to Tiberius, led by Scipio Nasica, was unrepentant. Having gained the upper hand, they had proceeded to order the arrest, interrogation, and execution, without trial, of anyone involved in what they called the "Gracchan sedition." New names were constantly added to the list of suspects; those arrested were tortured until they implicated others. Rumor and panic ruled the city. The Tiber was jammed with vessels taking men to Ostia, where they hoped to board ships to take them away from Italy, into exile.

Blossius winced as Menenia dabbed the stinging ointment onto a cut across his shoulder, then he took her hand and kissed it. "Your son is right," he said. "I escaped the massacre on the Capitoline, and somehow, so far, Nasica's henchmen have overlooked me. But very soon, they'll come for me."

There was a banging at the door. Blossius stiffened, then stood and covered himself.

A troop of armed lictors came striding into the garden. The senior of the lictors spared only a glance for Lucius and his mother, then glared at Blossius. "Here you are, philosopher! We went looking for you at the would-be king's house first. Isn't that your official address here in Roma, where you sponge off the daughter of Africanus? Did you think you could escape us by hiding here? Or is this how you philosophers make a living, going from the house of one lonely Roman widow to another, sucking up their wine and spilling your seed in their beds?"

Lucius bolted forward angrily, but the lictor raised his club, and Lucius stepped back. His mother was less timid. She dabbed her fingertips in the jar of ointment, then flicked them in the lictor's face. The man dropped his club and wiped the stinging unguent from his eyes.

"Bitch!" he shouted. "If you were anything but a woman, that would count as an act of sedition, and I'd see you stripped naked and flogged for it!"

The man bent to retrieve his club. Rising up, he struck Blossius hard across the belly. Blossius bent double in pain. A pair of lictors seized his arms and roughly escorted him from the garden.

Menenia covered her face and began to weep. The lictor leered at her. "Are you going to miss the old Stoic that much? He looks a bit decrepit for stud service. You're still a handsome enough mare. Surely you could find a strong young Roman to mount you!"

The man looked sidelong at Lucius; the insult was aimed as much at him as at his mother, daring him to strike back. Lucius clenched his fists and bowed his head, seething with outrage and shame.

As soon as the lictors had departed, Menenia gripped his arm. "Follow them," she pleaded. "Do whatever you can for Blossius!"

"Mother, there's nothing anyone can do."

"Then at least see where they take him and what they do to him. I won't be able to stand it, if he simply vanishes and I never know what happened. Please, Lucius, I beg you!"

Unable to stand her sobbing, Lucius ran from the house. His heart pounding, he followed the lictors at a safe distance and watched as they entered house after house on the Palatine, arresting one man after another. The prisoners were tied together and herded in single file down a winding path to the Forum.

Following the captives, Lucius witnessed a sight that seemed more appropriate to a nightmare than to the Forum in broad daylight. While a circle of well-dressed men, some of them senators, looked on and jeered, lictors forced a man in tattered, bloody garments into a wooden box that was scarcely big enough to contain him. Before they closed the lid, they emptied a jar full of writhing vipers inside. Even muffled by the box, the man's screams echoed across the Forum. The circle of watchers banged on the box with sticks and laughed.

The captives were dragged before an open-air tribunal. Lucius joined the crowd of spectators, standing toward the back and trying not to draw attention.

The judges on the platform included Scipio Nasica, who led the questioning. Blossius was the first prisoner to be interrogated.

"You are Blossius of Cumae, the Stoic philosopher?" said Nasica.

"You know I am."

"Simply answer the question. There is one protocol for questioning citizens, and another for foreigners. Are you Blossius of Cumae?"

"I am. You call me a foreigner, but I'm a native-born Italian."

"Italy is not Roma."

"Nonetheless, I am of noble Campanian blood."

Nasica raised an eyebrow. "Yes, the tribunal is well aware of your ancestors among the Blossii who betrayed Roma and induced their fellow Campanians to take up arms with Hannibal."

Blossius sighed. "That was a very long time ago."

"Perhaps. You come from Cumae, do you not?"

"Yes."

"As I said, Italy is not Roma—and Cumae can scarcely be considered part of Italy. Cumaeans speak Greek. They practice Greek vices. They send philosophers to spread polluted Greek ideas here in Roma."

"When Tiberius Gracchus was a boy, I taught him virtue, not vice. When he became a man, I offered him counsel and guidance—"

"The tribunal has no interest in your dubious career. We are investigating a very real sedition, not your imaginary philosophy. We are chiefly interested in learning what you know about the activities of the would-be king, Tiberius Gracchus, and his recent attempt to overthrow the state."

"This is absurd! There was no such attempt."

"Were you present when Tiberius Gracchus met with the Pergamene ambassador who delivered the royal testament of the late King Attalus?"

"I was."

"And did you witness Tiberius Gracchus receive the diadem and purple cloak of the king?"

"Yes. But—"

"Did he not put the diadem on his head?"

"Perhaps, briefly, as a sort of joke—"

"Did you not, at the behest of Tiberius Gracchus, draw up a ledger for disbursing the treasure bequeathed to Roma by King Attalus?"

"That ledger was purely hypothetical and contingent upon—"

"I realize, Blossius, that you are not used to answering questions with a simple yes or no. How you philosophers love to hear yourselves speak! Perhaps, to expedite this testimony, I should order your tongue to be removed. Then you can answer by tapping your foot on the ground—once for yes, twice for no."

Blossius turned pale. The spectators erupted in laughter. Standing among them, Lucius cringed and longed to make himself invisible.

As the interrogation continued, it became clear that Nasica's purpose was not so much to incriminate Blossius as to bolster his own rationale for taking action against Tiberius. To one leading question after another, he compelled Blossius to answer yes or no.

"From your answers, I believe the tribunal must conclude that any and all crimes you committed against the Roman state were carried out at the behest of Tiberius Gracchus. Is that correct?"

Blossius sighed. "How can I answer such a question?"

"I shall restate it. Any action you undertook affecting the Roman state, you undertook at the behest of Tiberius Gracchus. Yes or no?"

"Yes."

"Very well. One final question: What if Tiberius Gracchus had ordered you to set fire to the Capitoline? Would you have done so?"

"This is madness! Tiberius would never have given such an order."

"Answer the question!"

Blossius gritted his teeth. "If Tiberius had ordered such a thing, then it would have been the right thing to do, because Tiberius never gave an order that was not in the best interest of the people!"

Nasica sat back and crossed his arms, making a great show of his disgust. "There you have it—the philosopher speaks, and we can see just how corrupt and insidious his ideas truly are! My questioning is done. Is there any man present who wishes to offer testimony on behalf of the accused?" He gazed at the spectators. Lucius lowered his face and hid himself in the crowd.

The judges on the platform conferred briefly, then Nasica rose and addressed the spectators. "We declare that Blossius of Cumae has testified freely and truthfully regarding the recent sedition perpetrated by Tiberius Gracchus. We further declare that Blossius has, by his own words, discredited himself, his teachings, and anyone who was ever his pupil. If he were a citizen, he would be put to death for treason, but since he is merely a foreigner, he will be exiled from the city for life. He is free to depart from this tribunal. He must leave Roma before sunrise, or else face immediate execution. Bring forth the next prisoner!"

✦

"Not a single question about my beliefs! Not a single accusation having anything to do with Stoicism, or the values I taught Tiberius! The arrogance of those men! I, Blossius of Cumae, am too insignificant even to bother executing!"

Blossius had packed his belongings at the house of Cornelia. He had come to Menenia's house to say good-bye.

"I should go with you. There's nothing for me here." Menenia's voice was dull and lifeless. The terror of Blossius's arrest, the relief that he had been set free, and then the cruel news of his exile had utterly worn her out.

"Nonsense," said Blossius. "Your son is here. Did we not conclude, once upon a time, that a woman's greatest role is to be a mother?"

"That was Cornelia's conclusion, not mine."

"Cornelia needs your friendship more than ever. The loss of Tiberius has devastated her."

Menenia shook her head. "I should go with you."

"No, beloved. Exile is not for you."

Lucius stood nearby, saying nothing. He had been right, and here was the proof—Tiberius's radical politics had ended in disaster for himself and all those associated with him. But being right gave Lucius no satisfaction. He felt only shame and bitterness.

"Where will you go, Blossius?" asked Menenia.

"First, I'll take a boat downriver to Ostia—"

"In the dead of night?"

Blossius grunted. "That's when traffic on the river is busiest these days. I won't be the only man fleeing the city! At Ostia, I'll board the first ship heading east. There must be some monarch, somewhere in Greece or Asia who'll offer me asylum—a man who's sympathetic to Stoic teachings . . . a man who's unafraid of Roma . . ."

A fool, you mean—like you, thought Lucius. But he bit his tongue and said nothing.

129 B.C.

Lucius Pinarius took the letter from his mother's trembling hand. It was written in Greek, on parchment of the highest quality. Lucius read slowly, paying careful attention to every word.

From Blossius to Menenia, greetings and deepest affections:

What a comfort your letters are to me, like salve on a wound! Any day that a messenger arrives with a missive from you is a day of celebration for me.

I am glad to hear that you and Lucius are both in good health. I am glad that your son's business prospers. There must be much money to be made as a state contractor, especially in the building trade.

Thank you for sending news of Cornelia. That she remains in mourning, three years after the death of Tiberius, is, in my opinion, entirely fitting. The nature of her son's death, the desecration of his body, and the outrageous aftermath all justify a longer period of mourning than is customarily considered seemly.

But Tiberius's brother, you say, no longer wears black. Well, Gaius is a young man and must get on with his life. I have mixed feelings about his apparent decision to withdraw completely from political life, and to devote himself (like Lucius) entirely to money-making. In some ways, Gaius's potential as a leader actually surpassed that of his brother. What a waste, that he should forgo the Course of Honor! But after seeing what was done to Tiberius, who can blame him for pursuing a different destiny?

I wonder, though, whether Gaius will not eventually find

himself drawn back to public life. The lure of politics is so strong in his blood!

As for my career, I am proud to report that King Aristonicus takes me deeper into his confidence every day. Yes, I proudly call him King, though the Romans refuse to recognize his status and brand him a rebel. The will of the late King Attalus was rendered null and void when General Aristonicus claimed the throne of Pergamum by both force of arms *and* moral authority. How peeved the Roman senators must be, to see their dreams of laying hands on the treasury of Pergamum dashed; their greed for that treasure was one of their reasons for murdering Tiberius.

King Aristonicus is a remarkable man. I have every confidence that, with my counsel, he will attain the Stoic ideal of a just king. We speak often of the new capitol he dreams of founding—we will call it Heliopolis, City of the Sun—in which all men of all classes, including slaves, shall be free.

Aristonicus is also a military genius, thank the gods! He will boldly defend his claim to the throne of Pergamum against Roman arms. When he is seen to prevail, there is hope that other leaders across Asia and Greece will rise up and break the grip of Roma and its corrupt republic. The only hope for the rest of the world is to resist Roma's domination at every turn.

But here I am, rattling on about politics! Forgive me, my love. Without you beside me, I have little else to think about. My life is out of balance; the part of me that is most essentially alive—a corporeal man capable of love, desire, tears, and laughter—is shriveled and withered, like a once sturdy vine ripped from the rich, moist earth. How I miss you! Your words, your face, the music of your voice, the warmth of your body! Perhaps, someday—in Heliopolis?—we shall be together again. But that time is not yet, alas!

As always, I urge you to destroy this letter immediately after you read it. Resist any temptation to save my letters for sentimental reasons. Burn them! I do the same with every letter I receive from you, though afterward my tears fall among the ashes.

This is for your safety, not mine. We have seen, to our sorrow, just how ruthless the enemies of virtue have become, and how they can turn the words of the virtuous against them.

All my love to you. . . .

Lucius lowered the parchment with a shudder. He was not sure which offended him most—the Stoic's snide, backhanded compliment on Lucius's money-making pursuits, his typically self-satisfied fawning over the upstart Aristonicus, or his salacious metaphors regarding himself and Menenia. A sturdy vine ripped from the rich, moist earth, indeed!

"Promise me, Mother, that you've done exactly as he's instructed you—that you've destroyed every letter he's ever sent you."

Menenia looked up at him with tears in her eyes. She drew her eyebrows together. She shrugged with one shoulder.

"By Hercules and Hades! You *didn't* burn them, did you? You've kept them."

"Not all! Only a few," whispered Menenia. "Only the most . . . personal. There was nothing in any of the letters I've saved that could possibly—"

"*Any* letter from Blossius is dangerous, mother. Don't you understand? We must destroy anything that establishes a continuing link between him and us since he left Roma, and especially since he joined with Aristonicus. The content doesn't matter—although this latest letter could hardly be more damning! Where are the letters you saved? Fetch them! Now! Do it yourself—don't send a slave. Bring them here at once. I'll stoke the fire in the brazier."

Left alone in the garden for a moment, Lucius bowed his head and allowed his arms to drop to his side. His knees turned to water; for a moment, he thought he might collapse. For his mother's sake, he had put on a mask, showing only anger, concealing the panic that had been welling up inside him ever since he crossed the Forum that morning and heard the news from Pergamum.

Aristonicus the Pretender had been captured. His forces were annihilated. The kingdom of the late Attalus and its immense treasury had been secured at last by Roman arms. The Roman commander Marcus Perperna was already boasting of the triumph he would enjoy when he would parade

Aristonicus naked through Roma, publicly whip him till he begged to die, then strangle him in the dank prison cell of the Tullianum.

Hearing the news, Lucius rushed home, brusquely told his mother that Aristonicus was defeated, and demanded to see any scraps of correspondence from Blossius. He had not told her the news about Blossius. So far, either because she was too shocked or too frightened to ask, his mother had not inquired. How Lucius dreaded the moment!

Menenia returned with a few pieces of parchment. From their much-handled condition, Lucius could see that she had reread them countless times. Sighing, he took the letters from her.

"You're certain these are all the letters, every one?"

"Yes, Lucius."

"We must pray to the gods that Blossius did as he told you, and burned every one of your letters to him as well." One by one, Lucius laid the letters upon the flames. He and his mother watched them ignite and then crumple into ashes.

"All his letters . . . all his words . . . gone," Menenia whispered. She braced herself. "And Blossius?"

"Blossius is dead, mother. He did the wise thing, the dignified thing. If they had captured him . . ." Lucius quailed at uttering the words aloud: *torture, humiliation, lingering death*. He cleared his throat. "Rather than face capture, he killed himself. He died like a Roman."

"He died like a Stoic." Menenia closed her eyes. The heat given off by the burning letters—the last vestige of Blossius's existence on earth—warmed the tears on her cheeks.

Lucius gazed at his mother. Whatever he had thought of Blossius, he was moved by her grief. As on the day Blossius left, Lucius felt no sense of vindication, only deep shame and sorrow.

124 B.C.

"When I was a boy," said Gaius Gracchus, smiling at his listeners, "my old tutor Blossius made me read every line of Euripides. Dear old Blossius! Not much of Euripides has stayed with me, I'm sorry to say, except a few lines from his play *The Bacchae*:

> *The gods have many guises.*
> *The gods bring crises to climax*
> *while man surmises.*
> *The end anticipated*
> *has not been consummated.*
> *But god has found a way*
> *for what no man expected.*
> *So ends the play.*

Well, my dear friends, 'the play' is far from over. It's just beginning! But already, the gods have found a way 'for what no man expected.' Nine years ago, when my brother Tiberius died, who among us could possibly have foreseen this day?"

Gaius paused to allow these words to sink in. Silently, he counted to ten. The deliberate, well-timed pause was an orator's technique that Tiberius had taught him: *You go too fast, little brother. Stop now and then, especially after you've said something clever or thoughtful. Catch a breath—count to ten—allow your listeners to* think *and* feel *for a moment . . .*

Gaius was not in the Forum, haranguing a motley crowd of citizens, but in the lamplit garden of his mother's house on the Palatine, addressing an intimate gathering of his most ardent supporters. This was a victory celebration. Gaius Gracchus, who had sworn off politics forever after his brother's death, had just been elected tribune of the plebs, following in Tiberius's footsteps.

"Well, maybe my mother could have foreseen it." Gaius nodded to Cornelia, who reclined on a couch nearby. "Not a day of my childhood passed when I was not exhorted to live up to the example of my grandfather. And yet, it's my mother's example that most inspires me, that sets the greatest challenge for me. Was there ever a mortal of either sex who possessed such fortitude and courage? All of you, join me in saluting her—Cornelia, daughter of Africanus, wife of Tiberius Gracchus who was twice consul and whose statue stands in the Forum, mother of Tiberius the people's martyr!"

Cornelia smiled, so graciously that an observer might have thought she had never heard such words before. In fact, she had appeared alongside Gaius countless times during the campaign, all over Roma and up and down the countryside, playing the proud mother and beaming recipient of her son's extravagant tributes. Gaius's supporters adored Cornelia; they adored Gaius for adoring her.

In the final days of the campaign, the crowds who came to hear Gaius had increased beyond all expectations. Even Tiberius at the peak of his popularity had never mustered such multitudes. When election day arrived, such a throng poured into Roma to vote that the inns could not accommodate them. Men slept in trees, by the roadside, and on rooftops.

One result of the Gracchan massacre had been a relocation of the voting area. Elections were no longer held atop the cramped Capitoline, but on the Field of Mars outside the city walls, where there was plenty of room for the tribes to assemble. Structures resembling sheepfolds were built so that voters could pass through, one at a time, to cast their votes. But even these new accommodations proved inadequate for the number of voters who turned out to support Gaius. More than once, the crush had threatened to erupt in a riot, but in the end the voting was concluded without bloodshed. Gaius had emerged a clear victor with a mandate to carry out a platform of reforms even more radical than those of his brother.

After saluting Cornelia, Gaius turned his gaze to another who sat nearby. "And let us not forget my dear friend Lucius Pinarius. Not even he foresaw my return to politics. Yet, when I decided to run for tribune, this man devoted himself and his considerable fortune completely to my campaign. Lucius represents a powerful new force in this city: the class of men we call Equestrians, after our forefather's tradition of rewarding their finest warriors with a charger at public expense. These days, men are admitted to the Equestrian ranks by the censor, and their distinction is not horsemanship or valor, but the accumulation of wealth; they are men of means who have chosen to forgo the Course of Honor, and so they form an elite class distinct from the Senate. So fine a businessman is Lucius Pinarius that I swear commerce must be in his blood, just as politics is in mine. The Equestrians of Roma, who work hard and risk their fortunes to make this a more prosperous city, are the future. The idle senators who consume more wealth than they create—and who look down their noses at the rest of us—represent the dead past.

"Lucius is a builder, responsible for construction projects throughout the city. He has a devoted wife and a young son, and all the worldly success a man could wish for. We've been business partners for many years, Lucius and I. We know each other so well that we—"

"Finish each other's sentences?" quipped Lucius.

"Indeed! And yet, when I decided to make the run for tribune, no one was more surprised than Lucius. And no one was more surprised than I when Lucius took the headlong plunge into politics right beside me—or behind me, I should say, since he prefers to play the role of mover and shaker behind the scenes. Salute him with me, all of you—Lucius Pinarius, distinguished Equestrian, friend, financial supporter, trusted confidante!"

Unlike Cornelia, Lucius was unused to being praised in public. He was now over forty, but he blushed like a boy.

All the world knew Gaius's story: the trauma of Tiberius's murder, the withdrawal from the public arena, the eventual—now triumphant—return to politics. But no one knew Lucius's story except Lucius himself. He alone knew the tangled emotions that had led him to this night. The shame of his inaction before and after Tiberius's murder had never ceased to gnaw at him. His career had provided a lucrative distraction; family life had brought many rewards; his status as an Equestrian had given him great satisfaction. But all these accomplishments had done nothing to assuage his sense of failure. He had found redemption only by following Gaius's lead, throwing caution to the wind, and thumbing his nose at the reactionary forces that had destroyed his mother's happiness and his own sense of self-worth.

"Beside Lucius sits his mother, the virtuous Menenia. Beside her is my lovely wife, Licinia," said Gaius. "I thank both of you for sitting up with my mother on all those nights when I was late getting home after buying a round of wine for the voters."

His wife coyly cocked her head. "But Gaius, beloved, did you have to buy a round *every* night, for *every* voter, in *every* tavern in Roma?"

This elicited genial laughter from the guests, and calls for more wine.

"My friends, I could spend the whole night publicly acknowledging each one of you, and thanking every voter by name, but this is a victory party, and you are going to hear a victory speech! You've heard all my pledges already, I know, but here's the difference: Before, you heard them from a mere candidate; now you're hearing them from a newly elected tribune of the plebs!"

Gaius waited for the thunderous ovation to die down. "First, regarding the military, I propose that the state pay to clothe its soldiers, instead of requiring them to do so at their own expense. I further propose that no one under the age of seventeen should be required to serve. Most important, new colonies must be established to provide fresh homesteads for our veterans. Brave men aimlessly wander the streets, men who gave years of service and risked life and limb for the promise of a better life. That promise must be fulfilled!

"For the common good, I propose that the state should set the price of grain. I'm not saying that people should be given *free* grain, as my opponents assert, but grain at a reasonable price, stabilized by subsidies from the treasury and the building of granaries in the city to stockpile a surplus. If the state cannot make food affordable for a working citizen and his family, then what is the state good for?

"I propose a massive program of road-building, overseen by qualified Equestrians and employing able-bodied citizens, not slaves. The treasury is bloated from foreign conquests; why let that money sit idle when we can put it in the hands of the workers and get new, better roads in return?

"There must also be reform in the courts. Since time immemorial, senators alone have held the right to sit in judgment over the rest of the citizenry. They run the civil and the criminal courts. They even judge themselves; when a provincial governor is charged with extortion, his fellow senators determine his innocence or guilt. To the pool of three hundred senators eligible to serve as judges, I propose adding three hundred Equestrians. The court system will receive a badly needed shake-up, and perhaps we will begin to see true accountability!

"This, my friends, sums up the program that was overwhelmingly endorsed by the voters today. We shall win over the poorer citizens with the grain subsidy, state employment, and new colonies. We shall win over the wealthy Equestrians with lucrative public contracts and new judicial privileges. Pity the poor senators—they shall have nothing left but their dignity!"

The guests warmly applauded. Someone shouted, "What about land reform?"

Gaius grimaced, then forced a brittle smile. "Yes, what about land reform? Well, over the last nine years, much of the necessary redistribution of land has already been carried out. Ironic, isn't it? My brother Tiberius saw the overwhelming need for land reform. He bravely spoke for it, pressed for it—and for doing so, he was murdered. Then his murderers realized that reform was inevitable—either that, or a revolution—and the next thing you know, the cynical vipers were paying lip-service to Tiberius's goals, watering down his legislation and slapping their own names on it, then patting themselves on the back and congratulating one another for saving the Republic!"

Gaius's voice had risen to a shrill pitch. A servant standing behind him raised a pipe to his lips and blew a low note. The tension in the room was replaced by laughter and scattered applause. Gaius visibly relaxed. He smiled, turned about, and put his arm around the short, balding pipe player.

"You all know Licinius; he's one of my wife's freedmen. Licinius helps me practice an orator's trick my brother taught me. Whenever I start to get a little out of hand—too emotional, too heated—Licinius blows a note on his pipe, and I rein myself in. He has me well trained, don't you think?"

Gaius gave the man a kiss on his bald pate. The guests crowed with laughter.

"Well, then, back to my speech. We come to the capstone, the most ambitious project of all: to extend full citizenship to *all* of Roma's allies throughout Italy. For years, we've witnessed abuses by Roman magistrates against the subject people of Italy, who pay taxes and fight in the legions alongside us, but without the privileges of full citizenship. Give them that gift, and Roma will acquire a massive influx of loyal new citizens—and those new voters will remember the tribune who gained their rights for them. With such a power base, that tribune could guide Roma to her highest destiny."

Gaius lowered his eyes. "When I was a boy, Blossius taught me about the Golden Age of Athens, and about the great leader who made that Golden Age possible, a man of extraordinary vision called Pericles. Roma, for all her achievements, has yet to enter her Golden Age. But, with this election, I pray to the gods that Roma has at last found her Pericles."

Lucius, listening, drew a sharp breath. This was a new rhetorical flourish; Gaius had never before spoken of a Golden Age, or compared himself to Pericles. This was heady stuff. It hinted at ambitions far beyond those of

Tiberius. Listening to such talk, Lucius felt a thrill of excitement, but also a tremor of apprehension. Glancing at the faces of his mother, Licinia, and Cornelia, he saw the same mixed reaction.

Gaius ended on a somber note. "Everywhere I traveled in the campaign for tribune, men asked me two questions: What persuaded you to enter the campaign? And do you not fear the same fate that befell your brother?

"To those citizens, and to you here tonight, I give this answer: It was a dream that stirred me to put aside fear and sloth, and to stop hiding from the world. In the dream, Tiberius called my name. He said to me, 'Brother, why do you tarry? There's no escaping destiny. One life and one death is appointed for us both—spend the one, and meet the other, and do both in the service of the people.' "

All the guests had heard this story before, during the election campaign. Still, hearing it again on this joyous occasion, they broke into rapturous applause. Many shed tears.

His victory speech concluded, Gaius walked among the guests, making a point to personally thank each one. Then he withdrew to a quiet corner with his mother, his wife, Menenia, and Lucius.

"How polished you've become!" said Menenia. "Do you know, I think you're an even finer orator than your brother was. If only Blossius could hear you! It's sweet that you honor him in your speeches."

"But it does give me a shiver," said Cornelia, "to hear that story about your dream of Tiberius. To speak so lightly of death . . ."

"It's a great story, Mother. You saw how they loved it; I get that same reaction every time I tell it. Besides, it's true. I really did have such a dream, and it changed my life."

"But to prophesy your own death . . ."

"There's no oracular vision involved. Of course I'll die serving the people! Perhaps while making a speech in the Forum, perhaps while leading an army on the battlefield, perhaps while sleeping in my bed; perhaps tomorrow, or perhaps in fifty years. Like Tiberius, I'm a patriot and a politician. How else can I die, except in the service of Roma?"

"Oh, Gaius, such cynicism!" Cornelia wrinkled her nose, but she was clearly relieved by his glib answer.

Lucius, too, was secretly relieved. Perhaps Gaius's cynicism was exactly the quality that would keep him alive.

122 B.C.

"But where is everyone?" Lucius circled the peristyle, gazing across the overgrown garden and into the various rooms surrounding it.

Gaius's new house in the Subura was larger but not as lovely as the ancestral house of the Gracchi on the Palatine. For his second consecutive term as tribune, Gaius had deliberately chosen to move away from his mother and away from the Palatine, with its opulent residences. For his new home he had picked a rambling but ramshackle house in the downtrodden Subura district, so he could situate himself and his headquarters among the common citizens who most strongly supported him.

Lucius understood his friend's political motivation for the move, but still he found the neighborhood depressing, with prostitutes on every corner, maimed war veterans begging in the streets, and a miasma of unpleasant odors. And why was the house so empty? Where were the state contractors and engineers, the foreign ambassadors, the magistrates, soldiers, and scholars who had typically thronged the house on the Palatine during Gaius's first year as tribune, when his relentless legislative program and unflagging energy established him as the most powerful force in the state?

"They'll be back," said Gaius, emerging from behind one of the columns of the peristyle. He sounded uneasy, and tired. He had just returned from several weeks at the site of Carthage, where he had gone to lay the groundwork for a new Roman colony. A generation had passed since Tiberius won the mural crown for scaling the enemy walls; the salted fields around the razed city had become fertile again. The new Roman colony was to be called Junonia.

"How did things go . . . at Junonia?" Lucius asked.

"You sound a bit wary, Lucius. What have you heard?"

Lucius shrugged. "Rumors."

"And not good ones, I'll wager." Gaius sighed. "I must confess, the taking of the auspices at the foundation ceremony went badly. High winds broke the standards, and blew away the sacrifices on the altars. That damned wind! The priest said he could hear Hannibal's laughter in it."

"And . . . one hears that wolves ran off with the city boundary markers," said Lucius.

"That is a downright lie, put about by my enemies!" snapped Gaius. He shut his eyes and drew a breath. "Where is Licinius with that pipe of his, to calm me? The important thing is that, despite all obstacles, Carthage is being reborn as a colony of Roma." He smiled. "There'll be plenty of work for you down there, Lucius, if you ever run out of road-building projects here in Italy. What have you been up to while I was away?"

Lucius considered his reply, glad for a change of subject, then laughed out loud.

"If you have something to laugh at," said Gaius, "then, by Hercules, share it with me!"

"Very well. A few days ago, I was down in the Forum Boarium. There was a long line of men and women queued up with vouchers to purchase their share from the state grain supply. Who should I see standing patiently in the line but that old toad, Piso Frugi."

"Piso Frugi? I don't believe it!"

"The very senator who argued most vehemently against establishing the grain subsidy! I stood there gaping at him for a bit, then I finally asked him, 'How dare you benefit from a law you so bitterly opposed?' "

"And what did he say?"

"The old miser blinked at me, then turned up his nose. 'If that thief Gaius Gracchus had stolen all my shoes and divided them among the citizenry, and the only way to get back even a single shoe was to stand in line with everyone else, I'd do so, purely as a matter of principle. Instead, he pilfers the treasury to buy grain for his minions. So, yes, I'll stand in this line, because I intend to get back whatever share I can!' "

Gaius shook his head. "Unbelievable! Have you noticed how the men who argue most loudly against public benefits always elbow their way to the front of the line when those benefits are handed out?"

"My thought exactly!"

"What else has happened in Roma while I was away?" Gaius spoke lightly, but the look in his eyes lent weight to the question. When Lucius hesitated to answer, he grunted in exasperation. "Come, Lucius, tell me the worst! It's Livius Drusus, isn't it? What has that vile backstabber been up to?"

The trouble with Gaius's fellow tribune had begun before Gaius left for Africa. Gaius's departure should have been marked by a crowning achievement: the popular assembly's approval of a law extending citizenship to Roma's Italian allies. But at the last moment, the tribune Livius Drusus, who had always supported Gaius's reforms, held rallies against the legislation, appealing in the basest way to the mob's self-interest. "Do you think it's hard now, finding a good spot at the theater?" he asked. "Just wait until all the Italians come to town to enjoy our festivals! Do you like standing in long lines at the public feasts, or queuing for the grain subsidy? Then you'll love it when all those Italians slip ahead of you! Would you have every one of your privileges diluted, just so Gaius Gracchus can curry favor with his new friends?" When Drusus vetoed the legislation, he did so with popular support. It was a stinging defeat for Gaius on the eve of his departure.

"Drusus hasn't been idle in your absence," admitted Lucius. "In fact, he's been relentless in his efforts to undermine your support. People say he 'out-Gracchuses Gaius Gracchus.'"

"Explain."

"First, he proposed establishing colonies for veterans on even more generous terms than those which you proposed. Then he accused you of exploiting the poor—"

"What!"

"—because your laws charge the people rent if they wish to farm state land."

"The rent is nominal! It was a necessary concession to gain broader support for the law."

"Drusus proposes legislation that allows the poor to farm state land free of charge."

"And what do the hidebound reactionaries in the Senate say to that?"

"They support Drusus at every turn. Don't you see? Drusus is their straw man. By 'out-Gracchusing' you, he steals your supporters. Temporarily, your enemies are willing to legislate against their own selfish interests, to throw a few bones to the common people."

"But once I've been neutralized, they'll be free to spit in the people's faces and proceed as before."

"Exactly. Sadly, the common citizens seem unable to see through Drusus's facade. They've been won over by his blatant pandering."

Gaius's shoulders sagged. He looked utterly exhausted. "In my first year as tribune, nothing could go wrong. In my second year, nothing has gone right! I can only hope that in my third year—"

"A third term as tribune? Gaius, that's not possible. You were allowed a second year only because of the legal technicality Tiberius hoped to exploit—not enough men ran to fill all ten positions. To pull that off required the cooperation of men who would normally have been your rivals."

"And the same thing will happen again this year, because the people will demand it!"

Lucius thought otherwise, but held his tongue.

121 B.C.

"They'll goad me to violence if they can. That's what they want: to corner me, dishonor me, drive me to such desperation that I'll strike back. Then they can destroy me, and claim they did it for the sake of Roma."

Gaius nervously paced the pathway beneath the peristyle, circling the overgrown garden of his house in the Subura. Since failing to win a third term as tribune, his position had grown increasingly precarious.

"The election was a farce," he said, "rife with illegalities—"

"This is old ground, Gaius. We've covered it many times before. The past can't be undone." Lucius, who had never been one to pace, was as still as the column he leaned against. His fretting took place inside, unseen.

When would Gaius stop going on about the stolen election? The hard fact was that his support had waned considerably by election day; the undermining strategy of his enemies had worked just as they planned. After the election, during his final days in office, Gaius's influence had continued to dwindle. His frustration had given way to recklessness.

"I admit, it was a mistake—"

"A *crucial* mistake."

"—when I ordered my supporters to demolish the wooden seats erected for that gladiator match. I had good reason to do so. A paid seating area for the rich obscures the view of the poor—"

"But you resorted to violence."

"Property was damaged. No one was hurt, not seriously."

"You incited a riot, Gaius. You played into the hands of your enemies. They call you a dangerous rabble-rouser, a violent demagogue." Lucius sighed. They had been over this ground many times before.

Now that Gaius was out of office, his enemies were systematically repealing the laws he had passed, erasing his accomplishments. Today had brought the worst news yet. The Senate was scheduled to debate revoking the charter to establish Junonia. The colony that was to have been Gaius's most enduring monument—establishing forever a link from his grandfather, the conqueror of Hannibal, to his brother, the first to scale the walls of Carthage, to himself, the founder of Junonia—was to be abandoned.

Gaius was bitter. He was also fearful. He had become convinced that his enemies would settle for nothing less than his blood.

"Is it true, what people are saying about Cornelia's . . . charity?" said Lucius.

"What are you talking about?"

"Your mother set up a program to bring unemployed reapers from the countryside into Roma to look for work."

"Everyone knows that. Even Piso Frugi didn't object. The reapers provide cheap labor."

"Some say the program is only a pretext, a way to swell the number of your loyal supporters in the city—just in case."

"In case of what?"

"The violence that both sides are preparing for." Lucius looked over his shoulder. Some of the reapers were in Gaius's house at that very moment, milling about, restless, armed with staves and scythes. "What's going to happen, Gaius?"

"Whatever it is, you're well out of it, Lucius."

"You never share your plans with me anymore. Ever since you returned from Junonia, you've shut me out. You hold meetings without me. You demolished the stands at the gladiator match without a word to me. I knew nothing in advance of Cornelia's program to help the reapers."

"If I've shut you out of my counsels, Lucius, I've done it for your own good. People no longer speak of us in the same breath. If you're lucky, they'll forget that you were once my strongest supporter among the Equestrians. You're a businessman, not a politician, Lucius. You're outside the Course of Honor. You pose no real threat to my enemies in the Senate. Why should you suffer my fate?"

"I'm your friend, Gaius."

"You were also Tiberius's friend, yet you never raised a finger to help him, or Blossius, for that matter."

Lucius drew a sharp breath. Desperation brought out a petty, spiteful side of Gaius's nature. "When Fortuna favored you, Gaius, I enjoyed the pleasures of your friendship. Fortuna may have turned her back on you, but I never will."

Gaius shrugged. "Then come with me now."

"Where?"

"To the Forum. There's to be a protest against the motion to abandon Junonia." Gaius seemed to receive a burst of fresh energy. He strode about the house, shouting and gathering his entourage. "Everybody, up on your feet! What are we waiting for? Enough idleness! Let's head for the Senate House!"

On an impulse, Lucius stepped quickly into Gaius's study and reached for a wax tablet and a stylus. Gaius was still the greatest orator of his generation. On this occasion, he might utter something that should not be forgotten. The metal stylus was a formidable instrument, elegantly made but quite solid and heavy in Lucius's hand, and sharply pointed at one end.

The day was hot and oppressively humid, with thunder in the air.

As Gaius and his entourage approached the Senate House, they saw a tall, angular man leaving by a side door, carrying a shallow bowl. The man was Quintus Antyllius, a secretary to the consul Opimius. The bowl he carried was full of goat entrails. Before the start of each day's business, the Senate witnessed a ritual sacrifice and the examination of the animal's organs by an augur. The augury was done. Antyllius was disposing of the entrails.

As he passed by, Antyllius smirked at Gaius and his followers. "Get out of my way, street trash! Make way for a decent citizen."

The insult pricked at the outrage Lucius normally held in check. Blood pounded in his temples. His face turned hot. "Who do you dare to call trash?" he demanded.

"This piece of dung." Antyllius gestured at Gaius, using the bowl. Entrails sloshed out and spattered Gaius's toga. Gaius wrinkled his nose and gave a start, which caused Antyllius to shriek with laughter.

Without thinking, acting purely on impulse, Lucius sprang forward. He plunged the metal stylus into Antyllius's chest.

Men gasped. Antyllius dropped the bowl. Entrails spattered everywhere, causing the bystanders to scurry back. Antyllius clutched the stylus and tried to pull it from his chest, but the polished metal was too slippery with blood. The front of his toga turned red. He convulsed and fell backward, cracking his head on a paving stone.

Gaius gaped at the dead body, then at Lucius, unable to believe his eyes.

Someone in the street had witnessed the murder and ran inside to tell the senators. Soon they came rushing out, some from the main entrance, some from the side door, all converging on Gaius and his entourage. At their head was the consul Opimius. When he saw the body of Antyllius, his first expression was outrage. This was quickly followed by a look of barely suppressed elation.

"Murderer!" he shouted, glaring at Gaius. "You've killed a servant of the Senate while he was carrying out a sacred duty."

"The man threw bloody entrails on a tribune of the plebs," shouted Gaius. "Did you put him up to it?"

"You're not a tribune any longer. You're just a madman—and a murderer!"

Men on both sides began to shout insults. One of Gaius's men ran to bring his supporters who were mustering at the front of the Senate House. When those men began to arrive, some of the senators thought they were being deliberately encircled. They panicked. Fistfights broke out.

A flash of lightning illuminated the scene with a garish light. Gaius screamed at his men to remain peaceful, but his words were swallowed by a deafening crack of thunder. A moment later, the sky opened. Hard rain pelted the crowd. Fierce winds whipped though the Forum. The rioters scattered and dispersed.

Raised on history books, Lucius remembered a tale from the city's earliest days, and felt a shiver of dread. Romulus, the first king, had vanished in a blinding storm. Gaius had been accused of wanting a crown, and here was a storm the likes of which Lucius had never seen before. Lucius did not know the role that a previous Pinarius had played in the death of Romulus, but he knew that his mad, impulsive act had sealed the fate of Gaius Gracchus.

The next day, Lucius did something he had done only once before. He wore the family fascinum.

Occasionally, as a child, he had seen his mother wear it. When Lucius became a father, Menenia had ceremoniously passed the heirloom on to him; she explained its great antiquity and the little she knew of its origin, and she spoke of its power as a talisman to ward off evil. Lucius wore it on the day he received it, purely to please his mother, then put it away and forgot about it.

But that night, as the storm continued to rage, the fascinum appeared in his dreams, hovering before a great fire. When Lucius awoke, he searched for it among a tangle of castoff adornments he kept in a strongbox. He put the chain over his neck. The gold talisman, concealed beneath his tunic and toga, was cold against his breast. Lucius was not a particularly religious man, but if the fascinum possessed any protective powers whatsoever, of all the days of his life, this was surely the day to wear it.

To reach the house of Gaius in the Subura, Lucius had to cross the Forum. From the direction of the Senate House he heard echoes of shouting and weeping. A crowd was mourning Quintus Antyllius.

Gaius's house was more crowded than he had ever seen it. The atmosphere was one of barely suppressed hysteria. There was a surprisingly buoyant spirit among the men who rushed madly this way and that, almost a sense of celebration. The last time Lucius had seen such a mixture of dread, anticipation, and camaraderie had been when he stood before the walls of Carthage with Tiberius, just before the final siege. There was a sense that a new world, for better or worse, was about to be born, and the knowledge that many among them would not be alive the next day to see it.

Gaius, standing among a group of reapers with scythes, saw him and waved him over.

"You came by way of the Forum?"

"Yes, but I stayed clear of the Senate House. I heard shouting, but I didn't see—"

"Never mind." Gaius's tone was oddly aloof. "My surrogate eyes and ears run back and forth, bringing me fresh reports every few minutes. Quintus Antyllius has been laid on a bier before the Rostra. Various senators are competing to see which of them can deliver the most sanctimonious eulogy. The mourners weep and tear their hair. Meanwhile, I'm afraid some of my more eager supporters have gathered on the periphery. No violence yet, only some name-calling. Whenever the mourners cry 'Antyllius!' my men shout back 'Tiberius!' Of course, the corpse of my brother was dragged through the streets and dumped in the river. No one can accuse us of doing such a thing to Antyllius."

"Gaius, what I did yesterday—it was unforgivable."

"And utterly out of character!" Gaius smiled, but his eyes were sad. "The Furies themselves must have unleashed your rage—who knew you carried so much inside you? Well, Quintus Antyllius is no great loss to the world. Of course, Opimius blames me for the murder. Even now he's haranguing his fellow senators with all sorts of wild allegations, claiming that I intend to murder every one of them. 'The Gracchans are planning a bloodbath!' he cries. Curious, how his sort accuses the opposition of the very crimes which they themselves are plotting."

"Will it come to that, Gaius? A bloodbath?"

"Ask Opimius. He's doing his best to whip the senators into a frenzy. He's proposed a measure he calls the Ultimate Decree. Sounds menacing, doesn't it? It will allow the consuls 'to take all necessary measures to defend the state.' In other words, they'll be empowered to kill any citizen on the spot, without a trial."

"Gaius, this can't be happening."

"And yet, the gods have allowed it. A simpleminded fellow like Opimius doesn't realize that something like this so-called Ultimate Decree will never be used only once. They're opening Pandora's box. Allow the state to murder its citizens once, and the same thing will happen again and again and again." Gaius's glib tone suddenly gave way and his voice cracked.

"Alas, Lucius! What's to become of our beloved Republic? Our wretched, tattered, hopelessly lost Republic?"

He took Lucius by the hands for a moment, then pulled back and turned to address the reapers and the others nearby. "All of you, gather whatever weapons you have! Philocrates, bring me my sword! I'm not going to wait for them to attack me in my home. I shall go to the Forum and say a prayer before the statue of my father."

Licinia came running. She clutched his toga. "No, husband! You're safe in this house, where your supporters can protect you."

"Only the gods can protect me now."

"Go unarmed, then! If you go out armed, with armed men around you, there'll surely be violence, and they'll put the blame on you."

"I'd rather die in battle than like a sheep offered for sacrifice." He flashed a crooked smile.

"Gaius, this is no joke! The same men who killed Tiberius are determined to murder you, as well."

"While I breathe, I'm still a free citizen of Roma. I won't be a prisoner in my home." Gaius pulled away from her and moved toward the door.

Licinia was wracked with sobs. Lucius attempted to put his arm around her, but she shook him off, refusing to be consoled. As the last of Gaius's entourage disappeared from the vestibule, Lucius went running after them.

As Gaius proceeded through the streets of the Subura, shutters flew open. Men cheered him, but few of them joined the entourage. Lucius looked about nervously. Where were the vast throngs who once had promised to defend Gaius to the death? They seemed to have melted away. As the small band entered the Forum, idlers and bystanders gawked with curiosity, then scattered, sensing trouble and fleeing from it.

Before the statue of his father, Gaius paused for a long time, gazing up at the face of the elder Tiberius. His loyal young slave Philocrates stood to his left. Lucius stood to his right. Gaius spoke in a dreamy voice.

"My grandfather cast a long shadow; men know me as the grandson of Scipio Africanus, not the son of Tiberius Gracchus. But my father was also a great Roman. His victories in Spain established a peace that lasted twenty-five years. His embassies to Asia made him the confidante of kings. He was twice elected consul, twice awarded triumphs, and served as censor. My brother would have been as great, if he had lived. I had hoped that *I* might—" His voice broke. Tears fell from his eyes and streamed down his cheeks. "Did we live and die for nothing?"

Lucius heard shouting from the direction of the Senate House, followed by the sounds of a street fight. The noise came nearer. "Gaius, we must get back to your house. There aren't enough of us to take them on."

Gaius gave a start. He pricked up his ears, then shook his head. "The fighting has moved between us and the Subura. We can't go back. This is where I'll make my stand. This is where I'll fall."

Lucius's heart sank, but he took a deep breath. "I won't desert you, Gaius."

"You're a true friend, Lucius."

Armed men appeared in the distance. They spotted Gaius, gave a shout, and ran toward him. The entourage was vastly outnumbered. Men looked to Gaius for orders, but he stood as stiff and silent as his father's statue. Some of his supporters panicked and began to flee in all directions.

At last, Gaius cried out in despair. "Lucius! Philocrates! All of you, follow me!" He cast off his toga, as did Lucius and the others who were wearing them, the better to run in his under-tunic.

With the mob at their heels, they raced from the Forum. They skirted the slope of the Palatine and sprinted across the Circus Maximus. In the narrow streets of the Aventine, they lost their pursuers. Near the crest of the hill, they came to the Temple of Diana.

Gaius ran into the temple. The handful of supporters who followed watched him fall to his knees before the statue of the goddess. "Queen of the hunt!" he cried, gasping for breath. "Daughter of Jupiter, sister of Apollo! Accept this sacrifice!" He placed the pommel of his sword on the floor and pointed the blade toward his chest. Before he could fall on it, two of his followers rushed to stop him. One of them gripped his shoulders and pulled him back. The other snatched the sword and handed it to Philocrates.

Gaius wept. He beat his fists against the floor. "Ungrateful, treacherous Romans, I put a curse on you!" he shouted. "I pointed the way to freedom, and you turned against me. I risked everything for you, and now you abandon me. Be slaves forever, then, to the murderers in the Senate!"

It seemed to Lucius that a madness had come over his friend. Gaius had

always been a brave man and a fighter, yet now he seemed determined to
die by his own hand, without a struggle. Gaius had been utterly sure of his
cause, yet now he renounced it; he had been utterly devoted to the common citizens of Roma, yet now he cursed them. Lucius was appalled, but
he could not judge Gaius. He himself had been seized by a madness the
previous day, when he struck Antyllius dead without thinking.

A straggler ran into the temple. "They're close behind me!" he shouted.
"They're coming this way!"

Lucius and Philocrates pulled Gaius to his feet. They turned him toward the entrance. In a daze, he ran out into the street. His pursuers saw
him and shouted. The chase resumed.

For Lucius, the headlong flight was like a nightmare. The winding
streets of the Aventine, the old fountain at the mouth of the Appian Aqueduct, the salt warehouses along the Tiber, and the bustling markets of the
Forum Boarium, all these places were utterly familiar yet utterly strange.
Seeing them pass by, men laughed and cheered them on, like spectators
watching a footrace. Others jeered at the desperate little entourage, and
pelted them with radishes and turnips and bits of bones and hooves from
the market.

At the bridge across the Tiber, some of the men stopped and turned
about, determined to make a stand. They begged Gaius to keep running,
vowing to hold the bridge as long as they could. Accompanied only by
Philocrates and Lucius, Gaius reached the far side of the Tiber just as his
pursuers arrived at the bridge. The sounds of battle echoed across the
river.

The west bank of the Tiber was largely wild and undeveloped. The three
of them left the road, thinking to disappear amid the dense foliage. A narrow pathway led them to a stand of tall trees. The soft earth seemed to
swallow the sound of their footsteps. Amid the leafy shadows, a beam of
sunlight fell upon a stone altar in a small clearing. Lucius felt more than
ever that he was moving through a dream.

"What place is this?" he whispered.

"The Grove of the Furies," said Gaius in a hollow voice. "Tisiphone,
Megaera, and Allecto: the vengeful sisters who punish sinful mortals with
madness. Only black sheep can be sacrificed to them. Do you see their images on the altar? They carry whips and torches. Their hair is made of

snakes. They're older than Jupiter. They were born of the blood that was spilled when Cronus the Titan castrated his father Uranus—born of a crime of a son against his father. Yet I've always honored my father, and my grandfather! Why have the Furies led me here?"

He dropped to his knees before the altar. Shouts echoed amid the treetops. Their pursuers were drawing near.

"Philocrates, do you have my sword?"

The young slave quailed. "Master, please—"

"Put an end to me, Philocrates. At the Temple of Diana, I lost my nerve. I let them stop me. Do it for me, Philocrates. Do it now!" He threw back his head and raised his chest.

"Master, I can't bear to do it."

"I command you, Philocrates!"

Weeping and trembling, the young slave turned the blade on himself and fell forward. His cry of anguish reverberated though the woods. The pursuers heard and shouted to one another. They were very close.

Gaius knelt over the slave. He stroked the youth's hair, then pulled the sword from his chest. He looked up at Lucius and extended the hilt toward him.

"This is what the Furies want," Gaius whispered. "This is what they demand of you, Lucius. You brought about this crisis, when you slew Antyllius. Now you must end it."

"By doing the thing I least desire in all the world to do?" cried Lucius.

"Would you allow me to be tortured and torn to pieces by my enemies?"

Lucius took the sword. He could not look at Gaius's face. He circled him, knelt behind him, and clutched him tightly with one arm. He raised the blade to Gaius's throat.

With his last breath, Gaius hissed a curse. "Let them be slaves of the Senate forever!"

Lucius drew the blade across Gaius's throat. Gaius convulsed. Blood flowed warm and wet over Lucius's encircling arm.

Lucius drew back and staggered to his feet. Still twitching, Gaius's body fell beside that of the dead slave. Lucius dropped the blade between them.

He stepped back into the shadows and hid himself amid the foliage just as the pursuers entered the little clearing.

"Numa's balls! Dead already!" one of them shouted. "Look at the two of them—he let the slave kill him, then the slave killed himself. The coward cheated us!"

"Doesn't matter," said another. "The bounty's just as good, no matter who killed him. The consul Opimius promised a fat reward for the head of each and every citizen on his list, and the fattest reward of all is for the head of Gaius Gracchus. I claim it!"

Beating back the others with a snarl, the man raised his sword and hacked at Gaius's neck until the head came free. He lifted it by the hair and swung the trophy in a circle over his head, whooping with triumph. Blood and bits of gore spattered the onlookers and stained the altar. A few drops penetrated the foliage and struck Lucius in the face, but he did not flinch.

"What about the slave?" someone said, giving the corpse a kick.

"Worthless. Leave it for now. Back to the city, my friends, where there's plenty more killing to do!"

Nauseated, burning with anger, paralyzed by fear, Lucius remained silent and unseen in the shadows. After the men had gone, he reached up to touch his breast, and felt the fascinum beneath his tunic. Amazed that he was still alive, he whispered a prayer to whatever power had seen fit to protect him.

In the days that followed, under sanction of the Ultimate Decree, more than three thousand Roman citizens were put to death. The Gracchan movement was obliterated.

Remarkably, Lucius survived the massacre unscathed. For many days he remained secluded in his house, waiting for a banging on the door that never came. His name never appeared on the official list of enemies of the state. He could not account for this omission. To be sure, toward the end, his relationship with Gaius had grown less public and more private. For whatever reason, Gaius's enemies overlooked him, a stroke of good fortune over which Lucius never ceased to puzzle.

It seemed to Lucius there was no rhyme or reason to his destiny. He had shunned Tiberius and Blossius, and by doing so had survived their follies, to his shame and regret; he had boldly embraced the cause of Gaius, and yet had survived his downfall, to even greater shame and regret. Lucius concluded that his was a charmed life, curiously immune to ordinary reversals of fortune. In the years that remained to him, he turned his back on politics and devoted himself to his career, which kept him very busy; there were always more roads to be built. He also became more religious. Each night, before going to bed, he said a prayer of thanksgiving to the god of the fascinum who had saved his life when death was very near. It was in his bed that he died many years later, a beloved husband and father, an accomplished builder of roads, and a much respected member of the Equestrian order.

The consul Opimius was eventually brought to trial for perpetrating the slaughter of Roman citizens, but he was acquitted; the Ultimate Decree was upheld as a legal act, and thus shielded him from punishment. Later in his career, however, he was convicted for taking bribes while serving as ambassador to King Jugurtha of Numidia. Opimius became a bitter and much hated man in his twilight years, and he died in disgrace. His legacy to Roma was his authorship of the Ultimate Decree, which, as Gaius had predicted, was to be invoked repeatedly in the increasingly chaotic, increasingly bloody years to come.

Following the example of her father at the end of his life, Cornelia departed from Roma and retired to a villa on the coast, at a promontory called Misenum, taking Menenia with her for companionship. At Misenum she entertained visiting dignitaries and philosophers, and became legendary for her Stoic fortitude in the face of so much tragedy. To those who asked, she was happy to share her memories of her father, but she was even happier to talk about her sons. She spoke of Tiberius and Gaius without grief or tears, as if she were speaking of great men from the early days of the Republic. After her death, a statue of her was placed in the city and became a beloved shrine for the women of Roma.

Cornelia had often expressed her desire to be remembered not as the daughter of Africanus, but as the mother of the Gracchi. So it came to pass. In death, the two brothers remained as fervently beloved, and as viciously hated, as they had been in life, and the double tragedy of their deaths made them figures of legend. Like their mother, they were immortalized with statues, and shrines were established on the spots where they died.

Either as exemplars of evil or paragons of virtue, the names of Tiberius and Gaius Gracchus would be invoked in speeches and debates for as long as the Republic would endure.

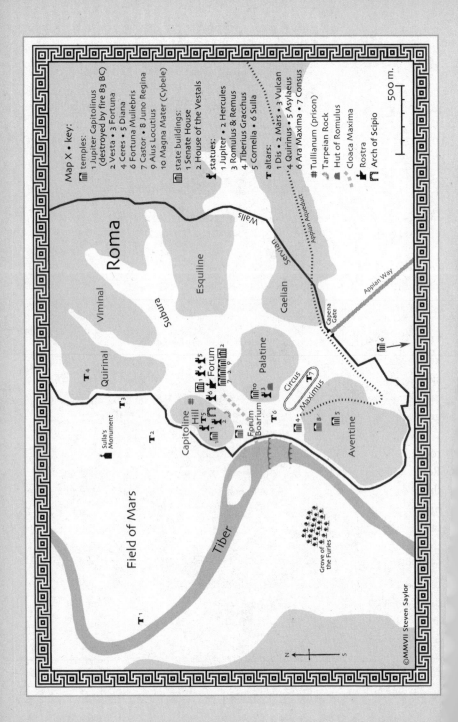

Map X • key:

temples:
1 Jupiter Capitolinus (destroyed by fire 83 BC)
2 Vesta • 3 Fortuna
4 Ceres • 5 Diana
6 Fortuna Muliebris
7 Castor • 8 Juno Regina
9 Aius Locutius
10 Magna Mater (Cybele)

state buildings:
1 Senate House
2 House of the Vestals

statues:
1 Jupiter • 2 Hercules
3 Romulus & Remus
4 Tiberius Gracchus
5 Cornelia • 6 Sulla

altars:
1 Dis • 2 Mars • 3 Vulcan
4 Quirinus • 5 Asylaeus
6 Ara Maxima • 7 Consus

Tullianum (prison)
Tarpeian Rock
Hut of Romulus
Cloaca Maxima
Rostra
Arch of Scipio

500 m.

Roma

Field of Mars

Tiber

Quirinal

Viminal

Subura

Esquiline

Sulla's Monument

Capitoline Hill

Forum

Forum Boarium

Palatine

Caelian

Circus Maximus

Aventine

Seavian Walls

Capena Gate

Appian Aqueduct

Appian Way

Grove of the Furies

N

S

©MMVII Steven Saylor

X

HEADS IN THE FORUM

81 B.C.

"How did it come to this?" muttered Lucius Pinarius, talking to himself to keep up his courage as he hurried across the Forum. Despite the mild spring weather, he wore a hooded cloak. He nervously fingered the fascinum that hung at his breast—a family keepsake from his late grandfather—and whispered a prayer to the gods to keep him safe.

The lowering sun of late afternoon loomed blood-red above the rooftops, casting long shadows. Quickening his pace, Lucius passed the Rostra. Nowadays, the beaks of captured ships were not the only trophies that adorned the speaker's platform. Lucius tried not to look, but despite himself he took a quick glance at the severed heads planted on the row of tall spikes that now encircled the platform. Some of the heads had been on the Rostra for a month or more and were in an advanced state of decay, the features no longer recognizable. Others, dripping blood, had been placed there so recently that their gaping mouths and wide-open eyes still expressed shock and horror.

Lucius scanned the faces quickly. He thanked the gods there was no one he recognized.

Looming above and beyond the Rostra, high on a tall pedestal, was the Forum's newest ornament, a statue of a general on horseback. The gilded statue gleamed with red fire in the light of the dying sun, so brilliantly that it hurt Lucius's eyes to look at it. The sculptor had captured to perfection the confident posture and bold features of the dictator, Lucius Cornelius Sulla. The statue appeared to be gazing out over the severed heads with a placid, self-satisfied smile.

Above and beyond the statue of Sulla loomed another reminder of the desperate pass to which Roma had come: the craggy summit of the Capitoline Hill, upon which the ancient temples stood in charred ruins. Two years ago, a great fire had swept across the Capitoline, destroying everything in its path, including the ancient Temple of Jupiter. The fire had been an ill omen, portending the unspeakable terrors of civil war and the victor's gruesome vengeance.

Lucius turned away from the Rostra. He hurried on until he came to the posting wall. A group of men had gathered to read the latest lists. Proscription lists, they were called, because they contained the names of those who had been officially denounced as enemies of the dictator Sulla. A proscribed man could be killed with impunity, by anyone, even in his own home. His head was worth a bounty. His property was summarily confiscated and auctioned by the state.

Reading the new lists, some of the men sighed with relief. A few stifled cries of despair. Most kept their faces hidden. Lucius did likewise, pulling the hood low across his brow as he made his way to the front of the crowd to scan the lists.

The name Lucius dreaded to see, that of his wife's younger brother, was not there. Lucius touched the fascinum and whispered a prayer of relief.

"What's this?" A man behind him leaned forward and squinted at the list over Lucius's shoulder. He spoke in an unnaturally loud voice. "Can it be? I see they're posted the name of a certain . . . Lucius Pinarius!"

Lucius spun about, his heart pounding. He recognized the speaker, but only barely—the man was a friend of a friend whose name escaped him. Seeing the look on Lucius's face, the man let out a ghastly laugh.

"I'm only joking!" he said.

"It's not funny—not funny at all!" snapped Lucius, his voice breaking. "To say such a thing, even in jest—I might have been killed, you fool! Murdered where I stand, before I could say a word!"

It was true. Such atrocities occurred every day. A man came to the posting board to read the latest list, discovered to his horror that his name was on it, gave himself away with a cry of dismay, and then, within moments, was murdered by assassins who lurked nearby, waiting for the opportunity to kill one of the dictator's enemies and claim the bounty.

Lucius elbowed his way out of the crowd and hurried across the Forum, walking as fast as he dared; walking too fast might attract attention. The straight, steep path behind the Temple of Castor took him quickly to the crest of the Palatine. From there it was only a short walk to his house.

Lucius turned down a narrow street. He gave a start. One of his neighbors was being dragged out of his house by a gang of rough-looking men. The man clutched the doorframe, clinging to it desperately with his fingernails until they pulled him clear and threw him down in the street. From within the house came the screams of his family.

The few bystanders in the street turned and fled at once, except for Lucius, who was too startled to move. He watched in horror as the assassins proceeded to stab the man to death. The sound of metal tearing flesh was nauseating. The man's wife and children ran outside just in time to see the killers hack off his head.

The leader of the group held up the severed head. Lucius recognized the killer, a notorious henchman of Sulla's named Cornelius Phagites.

"Can you believe it?" said Phagites to his companions. "This one's been on the list for more than a month. Kept out of sight ever since, until today, when he dared to come home. Thought he could slip past Phagites, the stupid bastard! There's a special premium for men who've been on the list that long. This head will be worth a small fortune when we deliver it to Sulla!"

Phagites grinned, showing crooked teeth with a gap in the middle. He saw Lucius watching and curled his upper lip, giving him a look of such malice that Lucius thought he might lose control of his bladder.

"What are you looking at, citizen?"

Lucius said nothing and hurried on.

He arrived home badly shaken. The slave who admitted him quickly barred the door behind him. His wife stood in the atrium beyond the vestibule, holding their newborn son to her breast. A nursemaid stood nearby, waiting to put the child to bed. Seeing Lucius, and the terrible look on his face, Julia pulled the baby from her breast. She kissed the child's forehead, then handed him to the slave. She waited until the girl had disappeared before speaking.

"It's bad news, isn't it? Please, Lucius, tell me at once!"

"It's not what you think." He rushed to embrace her, as much to comfort himself as to reassure her. "I saw something . . . terrible . . . on the way home. Terrible! But the new list—"

"Was Gaius on the list, or not?" Julia pulled away from his embrace. Her fingers dug painfully into his arms.

"No, Julia, no! Calm yourself. His name wasn't there."

"Not yet," said a rasping voice from the shadows. "But they *will* post my name any day now. So my informers tell me."

Julia released her grip on Lucius and hurried to the hunched figure in the shadows. "Little brother, what are you doing out of bed? You're much too ill to be up."

Gaius Julius Caesar was only eighteen, but his face was haggard and he moved like an old man, stiff and bent.

He was unshaven, and his matted, unkempt hair made a mockery of his name; generations ago, his branch of the Julius family had taken the cognomen Caesar, meaning "possessor of a fine head of hair."

"I'm feeling much better, sister. Really, I am. The fever's broken. The chills are gone."

"They'll be back. That's how the quartan ague runs its course. It comes and goes until it's entirely spent."

"Are you my physician now, as well as my sister?"

Julia kissed his forehead. "You *are* cooler than you were before. Do you think you could swallow some broth? You must keep up your strength."

In the dining room, Lucius held up a small silver dish with both hands. He bowed his head, and intoned a prayer.

"Asylaeus, we offer the best morsels of the meal to you—you, who were especially worshipped by Father Romulus; you, patron of vagabonds, fugitives, and exiles; you, whose ancient altar on the Capitoline offered a place of sanctuary to those who could find it nowhere else. Keep safe this cherished visitor in my home, my brother by marriage, young Gaius. Grant him asylum here in the shelter of my house. To you, Asylaeus, I make this prayer."

"Asylaeus, protect my brother!" said Julia.

"Protect us all," whispered Gaius.

Lucius reclined on the couch next to Julia. He picked at bits of roasted pork on a silver dish. His stomach was empty, but after the horrors he had seen that day, the sight of charred flesh revolted him. Julia likewise had no appetite, but Gaius quickly finished one cup of broth and started on another.

Gaius saw that Lucius was staring at him. He managed a weak smile. "You did a brave thing today, brother-in-law, going down to the Forum to read the new list. I thank you for it."

Lucius shrugged. "I did it for my own peace of mind. As long as you're not officially on the list, Julia and I can't be punished for keeping a wanted man under our roof."

"I shall move on tomorrow, I promise."

"Nonsense!" said Julia. "You can stay here for as long as you like."

Lucius groaned inwardly, but Gaius spared him the awkwardness of objecting.

"Thank you, sister, but for my own safety I need to keep moving. As soon as I'm able, I must leave the city and get as far away from Italy as I can. If it weren't for this damned ague, I'd be gone already. Sulla wants me dead."

Lucius shook his head. "How did it come to this? In our grandfathers' time, Gaius Gracchus was beheaded and his killer collected a bounty, and the bodies of the Gracchi were thrown in the Tiber, without proper burial, but decent Romans were outraged. Now scores of heads are added every day to the display on the Rostra, and men do nothing. The headless bodies of citizens are dumped in the river like refuse from the fish market, without a thought. Did you hear the latest outrage? Sulla disinterred and then deliberately desecrated the body of your uncle, Marius, the one man who might have stopped his madness. He cut the corpse into pieces and smeared it with feces, gouged the eyes from their sockets, and cut out the tongue. What an age we live in! Strong men no longer fear the gods. Wickedness has no limits."

Gaius turned pale. "Is it true, about Marius? Would even Sulla commit such an abomination?"

"Everyone is whispering about it. Why shouldn't it be true? Sulla will stop at nothing to punish his enemies. He tortures them while they live. Now he desecrates their corpses after they die."

Gaius stared into his cup of broth. His expression was a blank, but Lucius knew that his brother-in-law was deep in thought. By nature, young Gaius was analytical and dispassionate. Brought low by sickness and finding himself in precarious circumstances, he nonetheless held his emotions in check. Lucius envied his self-control.

"You ask how it came to this, Lucius. You hint at the answer when you mention the Gracchi. In the days of our grandfathers, the destiny of Roma lay upon one of two paths—the way of the Gracchi, or the way of their enemies. Their enemies won. The wrong path was taken. Nothing has gone right since.

"Gaius Gracchus attempted to expand the rights of common citizens, and to extend those rights to our allies. His selfish, short-sighted enemies thwarted his legislation, but the problems arising from injustice and inequity didn't go away. Instead, a long, bloody war erupted between us and our Italian allies. What the Gracchi might have accomplished peacefully was instead settled by bloodshed and brute force. What a waste!

"Because the Gracchi saw a better future, they were destroyed. Their enemies got away with murder, and ever since, men in power have never hesitated to use violence. When the Gracchi were killed, people were shocked to see Romans kill Romans. Now we've suffered a full-scale civil war, and a catastrophe that would have been unthinkable to our ancestors—a Roman army laid siege to Roma herself!"

In retrospect, the civil war of which Gaius spoke had perhaps been inevitable. Roma's expanding foreign wars led to the mustering of ever-larger armies, and the acquisition of ever-greater wealth by her military commanders. An era of conquest had given rise to a generation of warlords whose power grew to exceed that of the Senate. Driven more by personal ambition and mutual suspicion than by politics, the warlords turned on one another. In the brief but ferocious civil war that resulted, it was Sulla, surviving his rivals Marius and Cinna, who emerged as the last man stand ing. Sulla had marched on Roma, laid siege to the city, and then forced the Senate to declare him dictator.

"Now the winner holds the city in his grip," said Gaius. "He piously vows to restore the Republic and the lawful rule of the Senate, but not before he purges the state of all his enemies and potential enemies, and divides their property among his henchmen."

Gaius lowered his eyes and gazed into the cup of broth. Because Marius had been his uncle, and because Gaius had recently married Cornelia, whose father Cinna had been another of Sulla's rivals, he was certain to be counted among Sulla's enemies.

"That such a monster should rule over us is proof of our decadence," declared Julia. "The gods are angered. They punish us. In olden times, 'dictator' was a title of great honor and respect. Our ancestors were blessed to have a dictator like Cincinnatus, a man who rose up to save the state and then retired. After Sulla, 'dictator' shall forever be a dirty word."

"A monster, as you say," muttered Lucius, nervously gnawing at his thumbnail. "A madman! Do you remember when the first proscription list was posted? Men gathered at the posting wall to read the names. How shocked we were to see eighty names on the list—eighty! Eighty citizens stripped of all protection, eighty good Romans reduced to animals fit to be hunted down and slaughtered. We were outraged at Sulla's impunity, appalled at such a number. And then, the next day, there was an addendum to the list—two hundred more names. And the next day, two hundred more! On the fourth day, Sulla made a speech about restoring law and order. Someone dared to ask him just how many men he intended to proscribe. His tone was almost apologetic, like a magistrate who'd fallen behind in his duties. 'So far, I've proscribed as many enemies as I've been able to remember, but undoubtedly a few have escaped my recollection. I promise you, as soon as I can remember them, I'll proscribe those men, as well.'"

"He was making a joke," said Gaius ruefully. "You must admit, Sulla has a wicked wit."

"He's as mad as Cassandra!" said Lucius. "The killing never stops. Every day there's a new list. And anyone who gives shelter to a proscribed man is automatically proscribed as well, even a man's parents. The sons and grandsons of the proscribed are stripped of their citizenship and robbed of their property. It's happening not just in Roma, but in cities all over Italy. Men are being murdered every minute of every day, and every killer is given a reward, even a slave who kills his master, even a son who kills his father. It's madness—an insult to our ancestors, a crime against the gods."

"It's a way for Sulla and his friends to accumulate a vast amount of wealth," said Gaius. "The first men on the list were genuine enemies, men who'd fought against him in the civil war. Then we began to see other names—Equestrians who'd never taken an interest in politics, or wealthy farmers who never even came to the city. Why were they proscribed? So that Sulla could seize their property. The state sells the goods at public auctions, but the dictator's friends are the only men who dare to bid."

"It's as simple as that," said Lucius. "Men are being murdered for their property."

"Men are being murdered *by* their properties," said Gaius. "I was down in Alba the other day. I rode by a beautiful country house with gardens and vineyards, and the fellow with me said, 'That's the estate that killed Quintus Aurelius.'"

Julia groaned. "Gaius, that isn't funny!"

"Then I don't suppose you'll laugh when I tell you that men who've committed murder are arranging to have their victims inserted retroactively in the lists. They say Lucius Sergius Catilina pulled that off, after he murdered his brother-in-law. The killing was not only made legal, but Catilina received a bounty for it!"

The grim conversation lapsed for a while. Gaius drank more broth. Lucius pondered the untouched food before him. Julia finally spoke.

"Do you think we can take Sulla at his word, when he promises to lay down his dictatorship and retire to private life? He'll do so in a year, he says, or at most two years."

"We can only pray that he's telling the truth," said Lucius glumly.

"And what if he is?" said Gaius. "What will have changed, if Sulla steps down? Elections will resume, and the Senate will be in charge again—with all Marius's men dead and Sulla's men taking their places. But the state will still be crippled. The things that were broken before the civil war will still be broken, merely patched together with makeshift remedies. Gaius Gracchus, if he'd had the chance, might have sorted things out and breathed new life into the Republic; a petty, vindictive tyrant like Sulla is not the man to accomplish that. It will take someone else to save Roma, someone who can combine the political vision of the Gracchi, the military genius of Scipio Africanus, and a measure of Sulla's ruthlessness, as well."

There was a faraway look in Gaius's eyes, almost as if he were speaking of his own ambitions for the future. That was absurd, thought Lucius. The fever was giving his brother-in-law delusions of grandeur. Gaius should worry about keeping his own head, not daydream about saving the Republic.

"Perhaps," suggested Lucius, "the man you're thinking of is Pompeius Magnus." He referred to one of Sulla's protégés, a military prodigy only six years older than Gaius. Sulla, who liked pet names—he had dubbed himself Felix, "Lucky"—had taken to addressing young Gnaeus Pompeius, half in jest, half in earnest, as Magnus, "the Great." The name had stuck.

"Pompeius!" Gaius scoffed. "I hardly think so. He doesn't have the strength of character to be a true leader."

"Well . . ." Lucius raised an eyebrow. He had no affection for Pompeius, but it seemed to him that Gaius was hardly worldly enough to make such a scathing assessment. Gaius read his expression.

"Must I justify the comment? Very well, I need cite only one example to show the fundamental weakness in Pompeius's character. Other than cutting off heads, what's Sulla's most despotic behavior? Arranging marriages for those around him. And not just innocent matchmaking. Against their will, he's forced women to marry his favorites; that action turns marriage into rape, an offense to the gods. He's even dissolved existing marriages, forcing spouses to divorce each other and remarry new partners of his choosing."

"Another symptom of Sulla's madness," said Lucius.

"Perhaps. But if Pompeius thinks so, the so-called Great wasn't great enough to stand up to his master. Sulla told Pompeius to divorce Antistia—a devoted wife, by all accounts—and marry Sulla's stepdaughter Aemilia, even though Aemilia was already pregnant by her husband! And Pompeius, like the sycophant of some Asian monarch, obeyed without a whimper. This is the man to lead Roma out of the wilderness? I hardly think so!" Gaius shook his head. "I would never submit to such dishonorable, disgraceful behavior to curry favor with another man, no matter what the consequences. Never!"

"Well," said Julia, seeking to diffuse the tension in the room, "let us pray you never have to face such a dreadful choice. May your marriage to Cornelia be long and fruitful!" She smiled wanly. "When I think of a good marriage, I think of our parents, don't you, Gaius? They always seemed so happy together. If only the gods had not taken father so swiftly, so suddenly . . ."

Julia and Gaius had lost their father three years before. To all appearance, the elder Gaius had been a healthy, vigorous man in the prime of life, but one day, while putting on his shoes, he gave a lurch and fell over dead. His own father had also died young, in a similarly sudden fashion. The siblings had felt his loss deeply, and had grown even closer in the years since he died.

Gaius, seeing the look of sadness on his sister's face, leaned toward her and gently touched her shoulder.

Suddenly, there came a noise from the vestibule, so loud that all three of them gave a start and leaped to their feet. Someone was not merely banging at the door, but was trying to break it down. There was a snap of splintering wood and the shriek of hinges giving way.

Gaius turned to flee, but managed only a few steps. He was too weak to run. He swayed and would have fallen had Julia not rushed to his side.

A gang of armed men barged into the room. Lucius blanched when he recognized their leader: Cornelius Phagites.

Phagites smiled, showing the gap between his crooked teeth. "Ah, there's the very one I'm looking for—young Caesar!"

Julia stood before Gaius, like a mother protecting her young. Though his knees trembled, Lucius stepped up to Phagites, who was much taller, and raised his chin high.

"You've made a mistake. This is my wife's brother, Gaius Julius Caesar. His name is *not* on the proscription lists."

Phagites laughed. " 'Name isn't on the list!' " he said mockingly. "How often have we heard that one?"

"It's true! I checked the new lists myself, this afternoon. You saw me when I was coming back from the Forum. Don't you remember?"

Phagites squinted at him. "Well . . . if his name's not on the list yet, it can always be added later," he said, but in his voice there was a sliver of doubt. Lucius did his best to take advantage of it.

"Taking men on the list is one thing, Phagites. Taking men who aren't on the list is another. Sooner or later, by his own promise, Lucius Cornelius Sulla will resign his dictatorship. He's granted himself immunity from prosecution for life, but I doubt that he's given that sort of protection to you. Well, has he?"

Phagites frowned. "No."

"Which means that some day there *will* be an accounting of . . . of mistakes that were made. This is such a mistake, Phagites. Gaius Julius Caesar is *not* on the list. He's a citizen with full rights, not an enemy of the state. You have no right to harm him."

Phagites turned to one of his underlings, who produced a scrap of parchment, and together they pored over it for a moment, whispering and sniping at one another. At last Phagites swaggered back. He smirked and looked down his nose at Lucius. "Just how much are you willing to pay me to make sure I don't make any . . . mistakes?"

Lucius bit his lip. He thought for a long moment, then whispered a sum.

Phagites laughed. "I don't blame you for whispering! You ought to be ashamed, offering so little to make sure that nothing bad happens to your wife's darling brother. Make it four times that amount, and I'll consider your offer."

Lucius swallowed a lump in his throat. "Very well."

Phagites nodded. "That's more like it. Now, all you have to do is beg me to take the money, and I'll be on my way."

"What!"

"Beg me. I have to have some sport tonight, don't I? Go down on your knees, citizen, and beg me to accept your offering."

Lucius glanced at Julia, who averted her face. Gaius seemed to have been drained of his last ounce of strength by the sudden panic, and was hardly able to stand. Lucius dropped to his knees. "I implore you, Cornelius Phagites, take the money I offer, and leave us in peace!"

Phagites laughed. He mussed Lucius's hair. "Much better, little man! Very well, go fetch my money. But you're striking a fool's bargain. Your brother-in-law will be dead before the next Ides. Oh, I'll take your money now, and let young Caesar keep his head; and later, when I do take his head, I'll get a second payment from Sulla. I shall be paid twice for the same head—on his shoulders, and off!"

Lucius brought the money. Phagites and his men left without another word. Julia was too distraught to speak. Gaius staggered to his dining couch and collapsed on it.

Lucius felt Gaius's forehead. The young man was again burning with fever.

Despite Gaius's illness, later that night Lucius and Julia summoned a litter and took him to another hiding place. If Phagites had found Gaius, so might someone else. The fact that his name was not yet among the proscribed clearly was no guarantee of safety.

In the days and nights that followed, despite his lingering ague, Gaius moved from one refuge to another. Meanwhile, the elders of the Julii entered into frantic negotiations with members of Sulla's inner circle, trying to remove Gaius from danger. Lucius met with the Julii daily, hoping for good news.

The proscriptions continued. New names were added daily. Lucius began to fear that he himself might be added to the lists. He made sure that the door broken down by Phagites and his men was repaired and made stronger than before. He kept a dagger on his person at all times. He purchased a quick-acting poison from a dubious character on the waterfront, and gave it to Julia for safekeeping. Death by beheading would be grisly but swift, he told himself, but he shuddered to think of what might be done to Julia once he was gone. He wanted her to have a means of quick escape. What times they lived in, that a man should have to plan for such contingencies!

One day a visitor came to the house, attended by many bodyguards. He was a beautiful young man with a mane of golden hair. Lucius recognized him: Chrysogonus, an actor who had become one of Sulla's favorites. Ever since he was young, Sulla had had a weakness for actors, and especially for blonds. Chrysogonus was dressed in a tunic made of a sumptuous green fabric embroidered with silver stitching. The garment must have cost a fortune, Lucius thought. He wondered who had died so that Sulla's catamite could wear it.

"I won't stay long," said Chrysogonus, gazing about the vestibule with a practiced eye, as if scrutinizing a property that might someday be his. "My friend Felix sends you a message."

Lucius could barely stifle his disgust at hearing a former slave and actor speak so familiarly of the most powerful man in Roma. Chrysogonus, sensing his disdain, fixed him with a cold stare. Lucius's mouth turned dry. "What does Sulla say?"

"Your wife's brother will be spared—"

"You're certain?" Julia, who had remained out of sight, rushed to Lucius's side.

"*If* you will allow me to finish?" Chrysogonus raised an eyebrow. "Gaius Julius Caesar will be spared—but only on the condition that my friend Felix is able to meet with him face to face."

"So that he can see the boy beheaded with his own eyes?" snapped Lucius.

Chrysogonus gave him a baleful look. "The dictator will call on you tonight. If he sincerely wishes to receive the dictator's pardon, the young Caesar will be here." With a theatrical flair, Chrysogonus spun about on his heel and departed, surrounded by his bodyguards.

A festive retinue appeared in the street outside Lucius's house that night. Chrysogonus was among them, along with several other actors and mimes, male and female; they laughed and joked among themselves, as if out for a carefree stroll by torchlight. The bodyguards looked more like trouble-loving street toughs than staid, sober lictors. Sobriety was in short supply. Several members of the party were obviously drunk.

Perusing the group through the peephole of his front door, Lucius shook his head.

Sulla himself arrived in a curtained red litter carried by a phalanx of burly slaves. One of them dropped to his hands and knees so that the dictator could use his back as a step to descend to the street. Seeing him, Lucius sucked in a breath, appalled that the fate of the Republic and its citizens should rest in the hands of such a decayed specimen. Once strappingly muscular, the very image of a dashing Roman general, Sulla had grown jowly and fat. His complexion had always been splotchy—"mulberries covered with oatmeal," as some described it—but now a skein of spidery red veins had been added to his blemishes.

The dictator banged his fist against the door. Lucius stepped back and nodded to a slave to open it, then stood straight to greet his visitor. Sulla stepped past him and entered the vestibule without a word, alone, bringing not a single bodyguard with him. Did he think himself invulnerable? He had named himself Felix, after all.

Gaius awaited him in the atrium. Physically, the young man could not have presented a greater contrast to the dictator. Naturally slender, with a long face, Gaius had been rendered even leaner by his illness, and his bright eyes glittered with fever. Despite his weakness, his bearing was fearless. He stood with his shoulders back and his chin held high. For the occasion he wore a toga borrowed from Lucius. Even with Julia's nips and tucks, it hung on him loosely.

While Lucius stood to one side, Sulla gave Gaius a long, appraising look. He stepped closer.

"So this is young Caesar," he finally said. "I stare, and you stare back at me. I frown, but you do not blanch. Who do you think you are, young man?"

"I am Gaius Julius Caesar. I am the son of my father, who was praetor. I am the scion of the Julii, an ancient patrician house. We trace our lineage back to Venus herself."

"Maybe so. But when I look at you, young man, I see another Marius."

Lucius held his breath. His heart pounded in his chest. Did Sulla intend to kill Gaius with his bare hands?

The dictator laughed. "Nonetheless, I have decided to spare you, and so I shall—as long as my conditions are met."

Lucius stepped forward. "Dictator, you requested that young Caesar should meet you face and face, and here he is. What more . . . ?"

"First and foremost," said Sulla, speaking to Gaius, "you must divorce your wife, Cornelia. And then—"

"Never." Gaius stood still. His face showed no emotion, but his voice was adamant.

Sulla raised an eyebrow. His fleshy forehead was creased with furrows. "I repeat: You must divorce Cornelia. In your marriage, the houses of my enemies Marius and Cinna are combined. I cannot have such a union—"

"I refuse."

"You *what*?"

"I refuse. Even a dictator cannot make such a demand of a Roman citizen."

Sulla stared at him blankly. His florid complexion became even redder. He nodded slowly. "I see."

Lucius braced himself. He felt for the dagger under his toga, and wondered if he would have the courage to use it. What was Gaius thinking, to speak to Sulla in such a way? It had to be the fever, making him delirious.

And then, Sulla laughed, long and loudly.

At last he stopped laughing, and spoke in a tone of wonderment. "Is it Marius I see in you, young man—or myself? I wonder! Very well, then, you may keep your head *and* your wife. But in return for this favor, it seems only fair that *some* member of your family must remarry to please me." Sulla glanced over his shoulder. For the first time since entering the house, he looked directly at Lucius. "What about you?"

"I, Dictator?"

"Yes, you. What are you to this young man? His brother-in-law?"

"Yes, Dictator."

"And where is the boy's sister, your wife? I suppose she's skulking nearby; they usually are. Out with you, woman! Step into the atrium where I can see you."

Julia emerged from behind a corner, looking very meek.

"Why, she's the very image of her brother! Very well, she can take her brother's place. You and this fellow here—what's your name, again?"

"Lucius Pinarius, Dictator."

"You and Lucius Pinarius shall divorce at once. Since it's a patrician marriage, certain formalities must be observed. I give you two days, no more. Do you both understand?"

"Dictator, please," whispered Lucius. "I beg you—"

"After your marriage is dissolved, I don't care what you do, Pinarius. But you, Julia, must remarry at once. You're the niece of Marius, just as your brother is his nephew, and I must keep a watch on all you Julii. But whom shall you marry? Let me think." He tapped his forehead, then snapped his fingers. "Quintus Pedius! Yes, just the fellow."

"I don't even know him!" said Julia. She was on the verge of tears.

"Well, soon you shall know him very well indeed!" Sulla smiled broadly. "There, it's settled. Young Caesar's name will be removed from the upcoming proscription lists. Even so, I'd advise you to get out of town for a while; accidents happen. Also, young Caesar may keep his wife. Meanwhile, you two shall divorce—"

"Dictator—"

"Please, call me Felix."

"Lucius Cornelius Sulla—Felix—I beg you to reconsider. My wife and I are deeply devoted to one another. Our marriage is a—" He wanted to declare that their marriage was a love match, but it seemed obscene to speak of love in front of Sulla. "We have a young son. He's still suckling at his mother's breast—"

Sulla shrugged. "Then let the child stay with his mother. You shall give up all claims to him. Let Quintus Pedius adopt him."

Lucius gaped, too stunned to speak. Julia began to sob.

Gaius stepped forward, unsteady on his feet. He was the color of chalk. "Dictator, I see that I was wrong to oppose you. I shall do as you asked. I shall divorce Cornelia—"

"You shall do no such thing!"

"Dictator, it was never my intention—"

"Your intentions mean nothing here. *My* will prevails. Your life is spared. Your marriage is preserved. But your sister and her husband will divorce each other." He turned to Lucius. "Either that, or I shall see your name in the proscription lists, Pinarius, and your head on a stake!"

With a dramatic flourish worthy of Chrysogonus, Sulla turned about and left the house. His entourage welcomed him back with drunken cheers and laughter. A slave quickly closed the door to shut out the raucous noises.

Lucius stared at the floor. "After all our efforts . . . all our . . . sacrifices . . . our sleepless nights . . . the bribe I paid to Phagites . . . the humiliation . . ."

"Brother-in-law," whispered Gaius, "I never imagined—"

"Don't call me that! I'm your brother-in-law no longer!"

From the nursery, the baby began to wail. Julia dropped to her knees, weeping.

Lucius glared at Gaius. "It's Julia and I who must now pay the price for your pride. To save your neck and preserve your precious dignity, we must give up everything. Everything!"

Gaius opened his mouth, but could find nothing to say.

"You owe us for this!" cried Lucius, pointing his finger at Gaius. "Never forget! Never forget the debt you owe to my son, and to his sons, for as long as you live!"

Gradually, as thousands died or fled into exile, the frenzied pace of Sulla's proscriptions subsided, but the dictator continued to rule Roma with an iron grip.

His divorce left Lucius Pinarius a bitter and broken man. No one blamed him for his misfortune. Friends, many of whom had suffered terribly themselves, did their best to comfort him, and even praised his sacrifice. "You did what you had to, to save another man's life," they said. "You did it for the sake of your son and your wife; had you disobeyed, Sulla would have proscribed you, and your family would have been left destitute."

But no argument could alleviate Lucius's anguish and regret. To save his family, he had lost his family. To keep his head, he had surrendered his dignity.

Julia's new husband, Quintus Pedius, did nothing to bar Lucius from seeing his son, or Julia for that matter, but Lucius was ashamed to face them. To bow before a dictator reduced a man to a status hardly better than a slave; a Roman without honor was not a Roman at all.

It would be best, he decided, if his loved ones considered him a dead man. Let Julia be as a widow who had remarried. Let his son be as an orphan. How much better it would have been if Lucius had died. If only he had caught the quartan ague from Gaius and died of that!

So, like a dead man, he prematurely bequeathed to his son a precious heirloom: the golden fascinum which had been in the family for untold generations. The amulet was very worn, its shape hardly recognizable. Nonetheless, Lucius sent it to Julia with a prayer that it might protect their son from such a disaster as had overtaken his father. The talisman was passed to the next generation.

Having no desire to remarry, despondent and forlorn, he lived alone in his house on the Palatine.

As for Gaius, he took the advice of Sulla and left Roma as soon as he was able to travel. He accepted a military posting on the Aegean coast, serving on the staff of the praetor Minucius Thermus.

Lucius thought about Gaius as little as possible, but one day, while crossing the Forum, he passed a group of men conversing and overheard a stranger mention Gaius's name. Lucius stopped to listen.

"Yes, Gaius Julius Caesar," the man repeated, "the one whose father dropped dead a couple of years ago."

"Poor young fellow! I suppose King Nicomedes makes a dashing father figure, but no Roman should ever bend over to pleasure another man, not even a king."

"Especially not a king!"

This was followed by salacious laughter. Lucius stepped forward. "What are you talking about?"

"Young Caesar's escapades in the East," said one of the gossips. "The praetor Thermus sent him on a mission to King Nicomedes in Bithynia. Once Caesar got there, he didn't want to leave. It seems he hit it off with the king a little *too* well, if you know what I mean. All that high living in the royal court turned the boy's head—and Nicomedes *is* a handsome fellow, to judge by his coins. Meanwhile, Thermus is like a spurned husband, sending messenger after messenger demanding that Caesar return, but Caesar can't bear to leave the king's bed!"

"How could you possibly know such a thing?" snapped Lucius. "If Caesar's detained on a mission, there could be a hundred other explanations—"

"Please!" The gossip rolled his eyes. "Everyone's talking about it. Did you hear the latest joke? Sulla let him keep his head—but Nicomedes took his maidenhead!"

There was a great deal of laughter. Lucius, disgusted, stalked away with his jaw tightly clenched. He made his hands into fists. Tears welled in his eyes. Was it for this that he had sacrificed everything? So that a fatuous young man could desert his military post to live in luxury in Bithynia? What sort of Roman was Caesar, to speak admiringly of Gaius Gracchus and daydream about rebuilding the Roman state, and then to run off and play catamite to a Bithynian monarch? Lucius should have let Sulla take the young fool and do what he wanted with him!

78 B.C.

Belying the worst fears of his enemies—those few who remained alive—Sulla made good on his promise to step down from the dictatorship after two years.

Declaring that his work was done, he restored full authority to the Senate and magistrates. In retirement he dictated his memoirs, and proudly boasted that, having rid Roma of the worst of the "troublemakers" (as he called those who opposed him), he had instituted reforms that would return the Republic "to the golden days before the Gracchi stirred the pot and threw everything into confusion."

But could even Sulla turn back time? Since the destruction of Carthage, Roman politics had been driven by tremendous wealth and headlong expansion, and the ever-greater injustices and inequalities that resulted. Roma needed powerful generals to conquer new territories and enslave new populations; how else could more wealth be accumulated? But what was to be done when those generals grew jealous and suspicious of one another, and a citizenry riven with greed and resentment was compelled to choose sides? Civil war had resulted once. Nothing in Sulla's reforms would stop such a war from happening again. If anything, his example was an encouragement to would-be warlords with dreams of absolute power. Sulla had shown that a man could ruthlessly exterminate all opposition, declare his actions to be legitimate and legal, and then retire to live out his days in comfort and peace, beloved by the friends and supporters who had benefited from his largesse.

In the month of Martius, at his villa on the bay near Neapolis, at the age of sixty, Sulla died of natural causes. But his death was not an easy one, and in the revolting symptoms that plagued him some saw the hand of the goddess Nemesis, who restores balance to the natural order when injustice has been done.

The disease began with an ulceration of the bowels, aggravated by excessive drinking and sumptuous living. Then the corruption spread, and converted his flesh into worms. Day and night, physicians picked the worms away, but more worms appeared to take their place. Then the pores of his flesh discharged a vile flux in such quantities that his bed and his clothing were saturated with it. No amount of bathing and scouring could stop the oozing discharge.

Even in this wretched state, Sulla continued to conduct business. On the last full day of his life, he dictated the final chapter of his memoirs, concluding with this boast: "When I was young, a Chaldean soothsayer foretold to me that I would lead an honorable, upright life and end my days at the height of my prosperity. The soothsayer was right."

Sulla's secretary then reminded him that he had been requested to settle the case of a local magistrate accused of embezzling public funds. The magistrate, who wished to defend himself, was in the antechamber, awaiting an interview. Sulla agreed to see him.

The magistrate entered. Before the man could say a word, Sulla ordered the slaves in the room to strangle him on the spot. The slaves were Sulla's private servants, not assassins; when they hesitated, Sulla became furious and shouted at them. The strain caused an abscess on his neck to rupture. He began to bleed profusely. In the resulting confusion, the magistrate ran for his life.

Physicians came to stanch the bleeding, but Sulla's end had come. He became confused and lost consciousness. He survived the night, but died the next morning.

Some perverse but powerful inclination—the wish to see a dreadful episode to its bitter end, or the need to be absolutely certain that a terrifying creature is truly dead, beyond any doubt—drove Lucius Pinarius out of his house and into the streets to witness Sulla's funeral.

The entire city turned out to watch the procession. Lucius found a spot with a good view, and wondered at his luck until he realized why the spot was vacant. A ragged beggar was standing nearby, emitting such a foul odor that all others had been driven away. Lucius ignored the stench. If he could stand the sight of Sulla on his funeral bier, he told himself, then surely he could endure the smell of a fellow human being.

Heading the procession was an image of Sulla himself, a duplicate of the equestrian statue in the Forum. As the effigy passed by, it emitted an odor of spices that overwhelmed even the stench of the beggar. The man looked at Lucius and flashed a toothless grin.

"They say that thing's made of frankincense and cinnamon and all sorts of other costly spices. They took up a collection from all the rich women in Roma to have it sculpted. They'll burn it on the funeral pyre along with Sulla. The smoke from it will perfume the whole city!"

Lucius wrinkled his brow. "Sulla's to be cremated? His ancestors among the Cornelii were always interred."

"Maybe so," said the beggar, "but the dictator specified in his will that his remains are to be burned to ashes." Such men, free to spend their days eavesdropping and collecting gossip, often knew what they were talking about. "You can imagine why."

"Can I?"

"Think about it! What happened to Marius, Sulla's rival, after he was dead? Sulla opened the crypt and took a shit on his body! There are those who'd do the same to Sulla, to have their revenge, never doubt it. Rather than give them the chance, he's having himself cremated."

Lucius looked sidelong at the beggar. The man was missing his left hand and leaned on a crutch under his right arm. There was a deep scar across his face and he appeared to be blind in one eye.

Following the effigy came the consuls and the other magistrates, and then the whole membership of the Senate, dressed in black. The leading Equestrians followed, then the Pontifex Maximus and the Vestal virgins. Then, by the hundreds, Sulla's veterans came marching by, outfitted in their best armor and led by young Pompeius Magnus.

Musicians and a chorus of professional funeral singers, all women, followed. The musicians played a mournful tune on pipes and lyres, to which the chorus sang a song in praise of Sulla.

Mimes followed, breaking the somber mood with their buffoonery. Mimes were traditional at a wealthy man's funeral, and among these were some of the most famous actors in Roma, members of Sulla's inner circle since the days of his youth. The beggar felt obliged to point them out.

"Look, there's Roscius the comedian! I saw him play the Swaggering Soldier once. They say he's richer than most senators. And that's old Metrobius, who always specialized in female roles. Played the leading lady in Sulla's bed for years, they say, until that pretty-boy Chrysogonus took his place; getting on in years, but he still looks good in a stola. And of course that must be Sorex playing the archmime today, dressing up like Sulla and impersonating the dead man. He's got the walk and hand gestures down perfectly, don't you think? Let's hope he doesn't start chopping off people's heads!"

The mimes were followed by the procession of Sulla's ancestors. Men wore the wax masks of the dead and dressed in the ceremonial robes they had worn in life. They held aloft the garlands, crowns, and other military honors Sulla had received in his long, victorious career.

At last the honor guard approached, carrying the funeral bier. Sulla's body lay upon a couch of ivory decorated with gold ornaments, draped with purple cloth and garlands of cypress. His wife Valeria and the children of his five marriages followed.

The procession appeared to be headed not toward the necropolis outside the Esquiline Gate, but in the opposite direction.

"Where are they taking him?" muttered Lucius.

"Didn't you know?" said the beggar. "Sulla's funeral pyre is out on the Field of Mars. His monument's there as well. They've already put it up."

"The Field of Mars? Only the kings were ever buried there!"

The beggar shrugged. "Even so, Sulla specified in his will that his monument should be on the Field of Mars."

The last of the procession passed by. Spectators fell in behind. Lucius, grimly determined to see the burning of the corpse, joined the crush. The beggar did likewise, staying close beside him. Forever after, Lucius would remember the man's stench whenever he thought of Sulla's funeral day.

As the multitude assembled on the Field of Mars, storm clouds gathered. The sky grew so dark that the men in charge of the pyre nervously conferred. But as quickly as they gathered, the black clouds dispersed. A shaft of golden sunlight shone down on the bier atop the pyre.

"You know what they'll say," whispered the beggar, drawing close to Lucius. His smell had cleared a way for them to stand at the front of the crowd. "They'll say his good luck followed Sulla even to his funeral pyre. Fortuna herself drove the rain away!"

Speeches were made. Sulla was praised as the savior of the Republic. Tales were recounted to demonstrate his virtue and genius. The words were like the buzzing of locusts in Lucius's ears.

The pyre was lit. The flames reached higher and higher. Lucius was so close that the heat blasted his face and cinders swirled about him. The beggar pointed at the monument nearby, an imposing crypt the size of a small temple. He said something, but amid the crackle of flames Lucius could not hear. Lucius frowned and shook his head. The beggar spoke louder, almost shouting.

"What does it say? The inscription across the pediment of the temple? They say that Sulla composed his own epitaph."

Waves of heated air obscured the view, but by squinting Lucius could make out the letters. He read aloud, " 'No friend ever did him a kindness, and no enemy ever did him a wrong, without being fully repaid.' "

The beggar cackled with laughter. Lucius stared at the man, feeling pity and revulsion. "Who are you?" he said.

"Me? Nobody. Everybody. One of Sulla's enemies who received his full payment, I suppose. I was a soldier. Fought for Cinna, then for Marius— always against Sulla, though for no particular reason. And look at me now! Sulla paid me back in full. What about you, citizen? Dressed in your fancy clothes, looking spruce and sleek, with all your limbs intact; I suppose you were one of his friends. Did Sulla give you your just deserts?"

Lucius was carrying a small coin purse. He began to reach into it, then thought better and gave the whole thing to the beggar. Before the man could thank him, Lucius disappeared into the crowd. He made his way through the throng and back to the city.

The Forum was empty. His footsteps echoed as he hurried over the paving stones. Passing near the Rostra, he felt a sudden chill. He looked up and saw the gilded statue of Sulla in silhouette; the sun, behind the statue's head, gave it a scintillating halo. Even in death, the dictator cast a cold shadow across his life.

74 B.C.

The winter of that year was unusually harsh. One storm after another dropped sleet and rain on the city. On many mornings the valleys brimmed with a cold, white mist, like bowls filled with milk, and the hills were glazed with frost, making the winding, paved streets that ran up and down the hillsides treacherous underfoot.

Lucius Pinarius contracted a cold early in the winter, and could not shake it off; the ailment moved from one part of his body to another, but would not depart. He ventured out seldom, and received few visitors. Only belatedly, from a talkative workman who came to repair a leak in his roof, did he learn the news that every gossip in the Forum already knew: Gaius Julius Caesar, while traveling in the Aegean, had been kidnapped by pirates.

Lucius had not seen Julia, or his son, for many months. His rare visits were too painful and awkward for all concerned. But hearing of her brother's misfortune, he knew that Julia must be distraught, and he felt compelled to see her.

Coughing violently, Lucius put on a heavy woolen cloak. A single slave accompanied him through the dank, frosty streets to the far side of the Palatine, where Julia lived with her husband, Quintus Pedius.

The marriage had apparently worked out well for her. In its early days, however unhappy she might have been, the prudent thing had been to make the best of it, since there was no way of knowing how long Sulla would reign as dictator. Julia had adapted quickly to her new circumstances; like her brother, she was a survivor, thought Lucius bitterly. Lucius, too, had adapted, in his own fashion. Simply to keep from going mad, early on he had banished from his thoughts any notion that Julia might someday divorce Pedius and remarry him. After Sulla's death, the notion occasionally entered his thoughts, especially when his loneliness was most acute. But the act of submitting to Sulla had robbed him of his dignity as a

Roman; without dignity, he had neither the authority nor the will to take back what had been his. It was useless to blame the gods, or Gaius, or even Sulla. A man must endure his own fate.

A door slave admitted him to Pedius's house. Looking surprised and not a little wary, Julia met him in a room off the garden where a brazier was blazing and shutters had been closed to keep out the cold.

The sight of her was like a knife in his heart. Even through the loose folds of her stola he could see that she was pregnant. She saw him staring at her belly, and lowered her eyes.

The phlegm rattled in his chest. He fought against the need to cough. "I came because I heard the news about your brother."

Julia drew a sharp breath. "What have you heard?"

"That he was kidnapped by pirates."

"And?"

"Only that."

Julia wrinkled her brow. This was old news. He had alarmed her by making her think he knew something she did not, and now she was peeved at him.

"If there's anything I can do . . . ," he said lamely.

"That's kind of you, Lucius, but Quintus and I managed to raise the ransom. It was sent some time ago. All we can do now is wait."

"I see."

A faint smile lit Julia's lips. "His captors must be illiterate. If they had read what Gaius says about them in his letters, they'd never have allowed him to send them."

"His letters?"

"That's how we found out about his situation. 'Dear sister, I am held captive,' he wrote—ever so matter-of-factly! 'Could you be so kind as to raise a bit of ransom for me?' Then he went on to write the most scathing insults about his captors, how uncouth they are, how stupid. To hear Gaius tell it, he's lording it over them—ordering them about, demanding decent food and more comfortable sleeping quarters, even trying to teach them some manners. 'One must use a tone of authority with such creatures, as one does with a dog.' As if the whole experience is simply a learning exercise for him—the proper way to handle a pirate crew!" She lowered her eyes. "Of course, his bravado may be an attempt to reassure me and to keep up his own spirits. These men are thieves and murderers, after all. The things they do to people . . . the terrible stories one hears . . ."

Julia trembled and her voice broke. It was all Lucius could do not to rush to her and take her in his arms. He resisted the impulse because he had no right to do so, and because he could not bear it if she pushed him away.

"Gaius is a survivor," said Lucius; *like his sister,* he thought. "I'm sure he'll be alright." He coughed into his sleeve.

"Lucius, you're unwell."

"It sounds worse than it is. I should go home now. I merely came to offer . . ." He shrugged. "I don't know why I came."

Julia gazed into the flames of the brazier. "Did you want to see . . . ?"

"Probably it's best if I don't."

"He's growing up very fast. Only six, and able to read already! He knows about his uncle. He has bad dreams about pirates. He looks just like you."

Lucius felt a great weight on his chest, as if a stone were crushing him. It had been a mistake to come. As he was turning to leave, a slave rushed into the room. The man clutched a scrap of parchment, tightly rolled and tied and sealed with wax. When Julia saw it, her eyes grew wide.

"Is it—?

"Yes, mistress. From your brother!"

Julia snatched the letter and unrolled it. She scanned the contents, then began to weep. Lucius braced himself, thinking it must be bad news. Then Julia threw back her head and laughed.

"He's free! Gaius is alive and well and free! Oh, this is wonderful! Lucius, you must listen to this: 'Dear sister, for forty days I was held captive against my will. Thanks to the ransom you sent, I was given my freedom. The experience was most disagreeable, but left me little the worse for wear; have no anxieties about my well-being. I cannot say the same about my captors. As soon as I was freed, I set about organizing a party to hunt down the pirates. They provided little sport; the simple-minded fools were eager to spend their ill-gotten gains and headed for the nearest port with a tavern and a brothel. We captured them easily, and recovered a considerable part of the ransom; I shall return as much as I can to you now, and the balance later. As for the pirates, we set up crosses on a hillside visible to all passing ships and crucified them. During my captivity, I warned them that

I would see them come to a bad end, and so I did. I watched them die, one by one. By all means, spread this news to everyone in Roma. Between you and me, I am quite proud of how this all turned out. Justice was done and Roman dignity was upheld. The episode shall make a splendid campaign story when it comes time for me to begin the Course of Honor.'"

Julia laughed. "Dear Gaius—always with an eye to the future! I think he shall be consul someday, don't you?"

Lucius's mouth was dry. His chest ached from coughing. "Perhaps he'll be the next Sulla," he said.

"Lucius! What a terrible thing to say."

"Or perhaps the next Gracchus—except that your brother will probably succeed where the Gracchi failed."

Before Julia could respond to this, their son came running into the room. The boy's elderly Greek tutor followed, looking flustered. "Mistress, I couldn't stop him. Word's spread through the house that you've received a letter from your brother. Little Lucius wants to know—"

"Where is Uncle Gaius?" shouted the boy. Lucius noticed that he was wearing the fascinum of his ancestors. The sight of the amulet both pleased and pained him. "Where is Uncle Gaius? Do the pirates still have him?"

Julia took the boy's face in her hand. "No, they don't! Brave Uncle Gaius escaped from the pirates."

"He escaped?"

"Yes, indeed. And then do you know what he did? He hunted them down, and he killed them."

"All the pirates?"

"Yes, every one! Uncle Gaius nailed them to crosses, and gave them the terrible deaths they deserved. Those awful pirates will never bother anyone ever again."

"Because Uncle Gaius killed them!"

"That's right. So you must have no more bad dreams about them. Now, there's someone here to whom you must say hello."

Julia looked up, but Lucius had disappeared.

Out in the street, Lucius coughed violently. His breath formed streams of mist in the cold air. He walked quickly, aimlessly, his thoughts a muddle; his slave had to hurry to keep up with him. His eyes welled with tears. The tears felt hot running down his cheeks. They blurred his vision. He did not see the patch of ice on the paving stones ahead of him. The slave saw, and shouted a warning, but too late.

Lucius stepped on the ice. Limbs flailing, he fell backward. He struck his head on a stone. He shuddered and twitched, then lay very still. Blood ran from his skull.

Seeing the empty look in his master's wide-open eyes and the peculiar way his neck was twisted, the slave let out a scream, but there was nothing to be done. Lucius was dead.

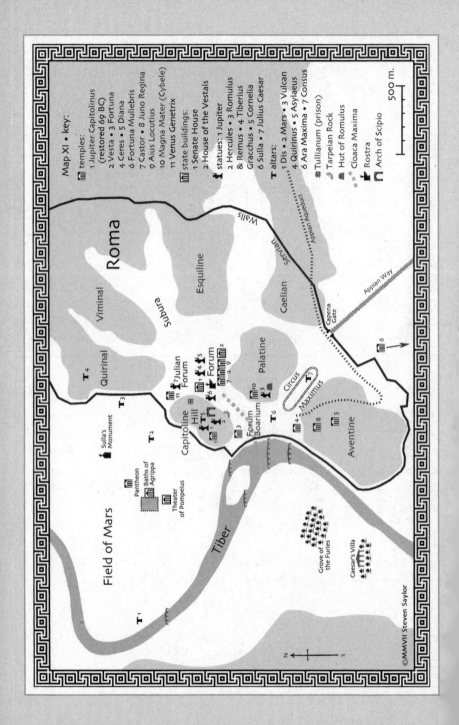

Map XI • key:

temples:
1 Jupiter Capitolinus (restored 69 BC)
2 Vesta • 3 Fortuna
4 Ceres • 5 Diana
6 Fortuna Muliebris
7 Castor • 8 Juno Regina
9 Aius Locutius
10 Magna Mater (Cybele)
11 Venus Genetrix

state buildings:
1 Senate House
2 House of the Vestals

statues: 1 Jupiter
2 Hercules • 3 Romulus
& Remus • 4 Tiberius
Gracchus • 5 Cornelia
6 Sulla • 7 Julius Caesar

altars:
1 Dis • 2 Mars • 3 Vulcan
4 Quirinus • 5 Asylaeus
6 Ara Maxima • 7 Consus

\# Tullianum (prison)
Tarpeian Rock
Hut of Romulus
Cloaca Maxima
Rostra
Arch of Scipio

500 m.

Roma

Field of Mars

Tiber

Viminal

Quirinal

Subura

Esquiline

Capitoline Hill

Julian Forum

Forum

Palatine

Caelian

Servian Walls

Circus Maximus

Forum Boarium

Aventine

Capena Gate

Appian Aqueduct

Appian Way

Sulla's Monument

Pantheon

Baths of Agrippa

Theater of Pompeius

Grove of the Furies

Caesar's Villa

N

©MMVII Steven Saylor

XI

CAESAR'S HEIR

44 B.C.

It was the Ides of Februarius. Since the time of King Romulus, this was the day set aside for the ritual called the Lupercalia.

The origin of the Lupercalia—the boisterous occasion when young Romulus and Remus and their friend Potitius ran about the hills of Roma naked with their faces disguised by wolfskins—was long forgotten, as were the origins of many Roman holidays. But above all else, the Romans honored the traditions that had been handed down by their ancestors. Paying scrupulous attention to the most minute details, they continued to observe many arcane rituals, sacrifices, feasts, holidays, and propitiations to the gods, long after the origins of these rites were lost.

The Roman calendar was filled with such enigmatic observances, and numerous priesthoods had been established to maintain them. Because religion determined, or at least justified, the actions of the state, senatorial committees studied lists of precedents to determine the days when certain legislative procedures could and could not be performed.

Why did the Romans adhere so faithfully to tradition? There was sound reasoning behind such devotion. The ancestors had performed certain rituals, and in return had been favored by the gods above all other people. It only made sense that living Romans, the inheritors of their predecessors' greatness, should continue to perform those rituals precisely as handed down to them, whether they understood them or not. To do otherwise was to tempt the Fates. This logic was the bedrock of Roman conservatism.

And so, as their ancestors had done for many hundreds of years, on the day of the Lupercalia the magistrates of the city, along with the youths of noble families, stripped naked and ran through the streets of the city. They carried thongs of goat hide and cracked them in the air like whips. Young women who were pregnant or desired to become so would purposely run toward them and offer their hands to be slapped by the thongs, believing that this act would magically enhance their fertility and grant them an easy birth. Where this belief came from, no one knew, but it was part of the great compendium of beliefs that had come down to them and thus was worthy of observance.

Presiding over the festivities, seated on the Rostra upon a golden throne, arrayed in magnificent purple robes, and attended by a devoted retinue of scribes, bodyguards, military officers, and assorted sycophants, sat Gaius Julius Caesar.

At the age of fifty-six, Caesar was a handsome man. He had a trim figure, but—ironically, given his cognoman—he had lost much of his hair, especially at the crown and the temples; the remainder he combed over his forehead in a vain attempt to hide his baldness. The men around him hung on his every word. The citizens, gathered to watch the Lupercalia, gazed up at him with fear, awe, respect, hatred, and even love, but never with indifference. To all appearances, Caesar might have been a king presiding over his subjects, except for the fact that he did not wear a crown.

A lifetime of political maneuvering and military conquests had brought Caesar to this point. Early in his career, he proved to be a master of political procedure; no man could manipulate the Senate's convoluted rules as deftly as Caesar, and many were the occasions he thwarted his rivals by invoking some obscure point of order. He had proven to be a military genius as well; in less than ten years he had conquered all of Gaul, enslaving millions and accumulating a huge fortune for himself. When his envious, fearful enemies in the Senate attempted to deprive him of his legions and his power, Caesar marched on Roma itself. A second civil war, the great fear of every Roman since the days of Sulla, commenced.

Pompeius Magnus, who had sometimes been Caesar's ally, led the coalition against him. At the battle of Pharsalus in Greece, Pompeius's forces were destroyed. Pompeius fled to Egypt, where the minions of the boy-king Ptolemy killed him. They presented his head to Caesar as a gift.

Caesar had circled the Mediterranean, destroying all vestiges of opposition. He set Roma's subject states in order, confirming the loyalty of their rulers and making them accountable to him alone. Egypt, the great grain producer of the world, remained independent, but Caesar disposed of King Ptolemy and put the boy's slightly older sister Cleopatra on the throne. Caesar's relationship with the young queen was both political and personal; Cleopatra was said to have borne him a son. At present, she and the child were residing just outside Roma, on the far side of the Tiber, in a grand house suitable for a visiting head of state.

Caesar's authority was absolute. Like Sulla before him, he proudly assumed the title of dictator. Unlike Sulla, he showed no inclination ever to lay down his power. To the contrary, he publicly announced his intention to reign as dictator for life. "King" was a forbidden word in Roma, but Caesar was a king in everything but name. He had done away with elections and appointed magistrates for several years to come; his right-hand man Marcus Antonius was serving as consul. The ranks of the Senate, thinned by civil war, had been filled with new members handpicked by Caesar. These new senators included, to the outrage of many, some Gauls, whose loyalty was more to Caesar than to Roma. It was not clear what function the Senate would serve from this time forward, except to approve the decisions of Caesar. He had assigned control of the mint and the public treasury to his own slaves and freedmen. All legislation and all currency were under his control. His personal fortune, acquired over many years of conquest, was immense beyond imagining. Beside him, Roma's richest men were paupers.

Whatever his title, it had become clear to everyone that Caesar's triumph signaled the death of the Republic. Roma would no longer be ruled by a Senate of competing equals, but by one man with absolute power over all others, including the power of life and death.

The long civil war had disrupted many traditions. As all power now attached to the dictator-for-life, it was up to him to oversee a return to normalcy. And so, on the Ides of Februarius, Caesar sat on a throne on the Rostra and presided over the Lupercalia.

Among the runners assembled in the Forum, stretching their legs and getting ready, was Lucius Pinarius. His grandmother had been the late Julia, one of Caesar's sisters. His grandfather had been Lucius Pinarius Infelix—"the Unlucky"—so-called, young Lucius had been told, because of his untimely death due to a fall on an icy street. Lucius was seventeen and had run in the Lupercalia before, but he was especially excited to be doing so on this day, with his grand-uncle Gaius presiding.

A burly man with a broad, hairy chest and powerful limbs came swaggering up to him. Some men, by the age of thirty-six, begin to soften and turn fat, but not Marcus Antonius. He carried himself with immense confidence; he appeared completely comfortable, even pleased, to be seen naked in public. Lucius still had a boy's body, slender and smooth, and felt envious of Antonius's athletic physique; Lucius thought the man looked quite magnificent. Lucius was also fascinated by the consul's reputation for high living; nobody could out-gamble, out-drink, out-brawl, or out-whore Antonius. But Antonius was such a friendly fellow that Lucius never felt self-conscious or shy around him, as he often did with his uncle.

"What's that?" Antonius tapped the pendant that hung from a chain around Lucius's neck.

"A good-luck charm, Consul," said Lucius.

Antonius snorted. "Call me Marcus, please. If I ever become so puffed up that my friends must call me by a title, stick a pin in me."

Lucius smiled. "Very well, Marcus."

"Where did you get it?" said Antonius, referring to the pendant. "A gift from Caesar?"

"Oh, no, it's an heirloom from my father's side of the family. He gave it to me on my toga day last year."

Antonius peered at the amulet. His eyes were a bit bloodshot from carousing the night before. "I can't make out the shape."

"Nobody can. We're not quite sure what it was. Father says it's been worn away by time. He says it's very, very old, maybe from the time of the kings, or even before."

Antonius nodded. " 'From the time of the kings'—that's what people say when they mean something is so far in the past it's beyond imagining. As a time of kings could never come again." He looked up at the Rostra and nodded to Caesar. Caesar nodded back, then stood to address the crowd.

"Citizens!" cried Caesar. The single utterance hushed the crowd and gained him everyone's attention. Among his other accomplishments, Caesar was one of the best orators in Roma, able to project his voice a great distance and to speak extemporaneously and with great eloquence on any subject. On this occasion his speech was short and to the point.

"Citizens, we are gathered to observe one of the most ancient and revered of all rituals, the running of the Lupercalia. The highest servants of the state and the youths of our most ancient families will take part. The Lupercalia returns us to the pastoral days of our ancestors, when Romans lived close to the earth, close to their flocks, and close to the gods, who gave to Roma the gifts of fertility and abundance.

"Citizens, in recent years, because of the interruptions of war, many rituals have been neglected or performed in a perfunctory manner. The Lupercalia has been run with a very scant contingent and with little joy. But to neglect our religious obligations is to neglect our ancestors. To perform our vital rituals with bare adequacy is to give merely adequate worship to the gods. Today, I am pleased to say, we have a very full and very robust gathering to run the Lupercalia. Our beloved city has been depopulated by the misfortunes of war; many fine men have been lost. But with the snapping of their sacred thongs, let these runners set in motion the repopulation of Roma! Let every woman of childbearing age offer her wrist! Let there be rejoicing and abundance!

"Citizens, the priests have observed the auspices for this day. The auspices are good. Therefore, with the raising of my hand, I, Gaius Julius Caesar, your dictator, declare that the Lupercalia may begin!"

To a burst of applause from the crowd, the runners set off. Their course would take them to various points all over the city, and they would run the circuit three times in all.

Lucius stayed close to Antonius. He liked the familiar way the man treated him, as if they were old drinking companions or fellow warriors, leaning in close to crack a joke about the sagging backside of one of the participating magistrates or to make lewd comments about the women gathered along the way. At the sight of Antonius, women whispered and giggled, teasing one another to step forward and present their wrists to be slapped. How effortless it was for Antonius to flirt with them!

When Antonius saw that Lucius hung back, he encouraged him to put himself forward. "Growl at them—they love that! Run a circle around them. Don't be afraid to look them straight in the eye, and up and down. Imagine you're a wolf picking out the plumpest of the sheep."

"But Marcus, I'm not sure I have the—"

"Nonsense! You heard your uncle, young man—this is your religious duty! Just follow me and do as I do. Call for some courage from that amulet you wear!"

Lucius took a deep breath and did as he was told. With Antonius leading the way, it was easy. He felt the power of his legs as they carried him forward, and the rush of breath in his lungs. He saw the grinning faces of the girls gathered along the course, and he grinned back at them. He snapped his thong in the air, threw back his head, and howled.

A sense of euphoria came over him, and the sacred nature of the ritual became manifest to him. When he had run the Lupercalia before, he had performed his duty by rote, without abandoning himself to the spirit of the occasion. What was different about this day? He was a man, for one thing, and Antonius was beside him, and his great-uncle Gaius was the undisputed ruler of Roma, presiding over the world's rebirth. The great fountainhead of the earth's fecundity, which found expression in the Lupercalia, surged through Lucius. When he slapped the wrist of a giddy, laughing girl with his thong, he felt a connection to something divine such as he had never experienced before. The sensation manifested itself physically, as well. From time to time he felt a pleasant stirring and a heaviness between his legs. He stole a glance at Antonius's sex, and saw that his friend was mildly excited as well.

Antonius saw the change in Lucius and laughed. "There you go, young man! That's the spirit!"

They finished the first circuit and ran back through the Forum, where an even larger crowd had gathered before the Rostra. People wanted to be present for the end of the run, and the public feast that would follow. As the runners passed the Rostra, Caesar remained seated on his throne but raised his arm in salute.

"Wait here for me," said Antonius to Lucius. He broke from the pack and mounted the Rostra, taking giant steps. From somewhere—he had not been carrying it before—he produced a diadem made of gold and wrapped with laurel leaves. He held the diadem aloft so that everyone in the crowd could see. He knelt before Caesar, then rose and held the crown above Caesar's head.

The crowd reacted with surprise. This was not a part of the ritual of Lupercalia. Some laughed, some cheered. A few dared to jeer and groan with disapproval. Caesar suppressed a smile. Managing to look very grave, he raised his hand and prevented Antonius from placing the crown on his head.

The crowd applauded and cheered. Caesar sat motionless. Only his eyes moved, scanning the crowd, closely observing their reaction. With his upraised hand, he made a dismissive gesture, indicating that Antonius should continue the run.

"What was that about?" said Lucius, when Antonius rejoined the pack.

In one hand Antonius still held the diadem, in the other his goat-hide thong. He shrugged. "The glare off your great-uncle's bald spot was blinding me. I thought it needed something to cover it."

"Marcus, be serious."

"To a man of Caesar's years, there is nothing more serious than a bald spot."

"Marcus!"

But Antonius would say no more. He growled and howled and leaped toward a group of young women who screamed with excitement. Lucius followed him, anxious to regain the euphoria he had experienced during the first circuit.

When they ran through the Forum to make the second pass before the Rostra, the crowd had grown even larger. Again, Antonius broke away and ran onto the platform. Again, he displayed the diadem to the crowd. A number of people began to chant, "Crown him! Crown him!" Others chanted, "Never a king, never a crown! Never a king, never a crown!"

Like a mime on a stage, Antonius made a great show of trying to place the diadem on Caesar's brow. Again, Caesar gently refused it, waving his hand as if to ward off a buzzing insect. The crowd's reaction was even more enthusiastic than before. They cheered and stamped their feet.

Antonius withdrew and rejoined the pack.

"Marcus, what is going on?" said Lucius.

Antonius grunted. "Caesar is my commander. I was thinking that vulnerable bald spot could use a bit of strategic cover."

"Marcus, this isn't funny!"

Antonius shook his head and laughed. "There is nothing as funny as your great-uncle's bald spot!" He would say no more.

They completed the third and final circuit. An immense crowd had gathered before the Rostra, made up not only of the pious and those who wished to take advantage of the feast, but of many others, for word of Caesar's refusal of a crown had spread through the city. When Antonius mounted the Rostra, the competing chants were deafening.

"Crown him! Crown him!"

"Never a king, never a crown! Never a king, never a crown!"

A third time Antonius moved to place the diadem on Caesar's head. A third time Caesar refused it.

The applause was thunderous.

Caesar rose to his feet. He raised his hands for silence. He took the diadem from Antonius and held it high above his head. The crowd watched in suspense. For a moment it appeared that Caesar might crown himself.

"Citizens!" he cried. "We Romans know only one king—Jupiter, king of the gods. Marcus Antonius, take back this diadem and carry it to the Temple of Jupiter. Offer it to the god on behalf of Gaius Julius Caesar and the people of Roma."

The applause of the crowd was deafening. Caesar again raised his hands for silence. "I declare that the Lupercalia has been well and truly run. Let the feasting begin!"

Amid the surging throng, Lucius stood before the Rostra and looked up at his great-uncle. He did not know what to think of the performance he had just witnessed, nor what to make of the crowd's reaction to it. It seemed to him that those who chanted "Crown him!" had cheered the loudest when Caesar refused the crown, as if the very act of rejecting the symbol entitled him to the power it represented. Those who had chanted "Never a king, never a crown!" had cheered as well; were they so foolish as to believe that because Caesar refused a diadem, he was not in fact their king? "In politics, appearance is everything," Antonius had once told him. Still, it was all very confusing.

Lucius was also not sure what to make of Caesar. Every man, woman, and child in Roma seemed either to revere or despise the man with great intensity, but to Lucius, Caesar had always been Uncle Gaius, a bit larger than life, to be sure, yet all too human, with his preoccupied air, his combed-over hair, and his slightly absurd habit of speaking of himself in the third person. Caesar had loomed over Lucius all his life, yet he always seemed a bit distant and aloof. Indeed, whenever the two of them had been alone together, Lucius had sensed an uneasiness in his great-uncle's manner. Sometimes Caesar averted his eyes rather than look Lucius in the face. Why was that?

A few times, Lucius's father had made veiled references to a debt owed to the family by Caesar, but he had never explained. Lucius sensed that something tragic or shameful had occurred in the past, the sort of thing that grownups never discuss in front of children. He had an idea, though he could not say why, that it involved his grandparents, Julia and Lucius the Unlucky. What had Caesar done to them, or failed to do? Probably money was involved, or an insult to someone's dignity, or both. Whatever the lapse or transgression, it was surely a very small matter when compared to the enslavement of Gaul or the carnage of the civil war. Still, Lucius was curious. Now that he was a man, would he be told what had happened in those mysterious, long-ago days before he was born?

A month later—on the day before the Ides of Martius—Lucius Pinarius attended a dinner party at the house of Marcus Lepidus on the Palatine. Lepidus had fought under Caesar and was now serving as the dictator's Master of the Horse. Caesar himself was in attendance, as were Marcus Antonius and several other of Caesar's most trusted officers.

Antonius drank more than anyone else. He showed no obvious signs of inebriation—his speech was not slurred, his gestures were controlled—but his eyes shone with a mischievous glimmer. "So, commander, what is this grand announcement you've assembled us to hear tonight?"

Caesar smiled. He had kept them in suspense through the fish course and the game course, but it seemed that Antonius would not submit to eating the custard course without hearing what Caesar had to say. "You be-

come bored and impatient so quickly, Antonius. Well, I suppose I've become a bit bored myself lately. That's why I asked Lepidus to invite this
particular group for dinner. Some of you served me in Gaul, and saw the
surrender of Vercingetorix. Some of you served me at Pharsalus, where we
took down Pompeius. Some of you were in Alexandria, where we made
peace among the bickering Egyptians, despite their treachery and their
wiles. And some of you were at Thapsus, where Cato met his end. You've
all been tested by battle—or you soon will be." He smiled and glanced at
Lucius. "You are a select band, the cream of Roma's warriors. You are my
most trusted men at arms. That's why I wanted to meet with you all tonight, ahead of the official announcement I shall make tomorrow."

"Yes!" whispered Antonius. "This is about—"

"Parthia," said Caesar, who refused to let even Antonius utter the word
before him. "I've reached my decision regarding the feasibility of an invasion of Parthia."

There was a stir of movement around the room. Everyone knew what
Caesar must be about to say, but the magnitude of it was so great that it
could not seem entirely real until the words were actually said aloud.

"And?" said Antonius, fidgeting like a boy.

Caesar laughed. "Patience, Antonius! Patience! The custard course is
on its way. We shall be enjoying tender bits of fowl and pork in an egg custard spiced with garum—isn't that right, Lepidus? Lepidus has one of the
finest cooks on the Palatine—"

"Commander, please!"

"Very well, the custard will have to wait." Caesar cleared his throat. "I
suppose I should stand up for this, and all of you should reach for your
cups. My good friends: Tomorrow, Caesar shall put forward a request to
the Senate—and the Senate, I feel certain, *will* consent." This elicited mild
laughter. "Caesar shall request a new command. The specific purpose of
this command will be a military campaign against . . . Antonius, you look
fit to burst." There was more laughter, until at last Caesar said the word
they were waiting to hear: "Parthia!"

"Parthia!" they shouted, raising their cups.

So the rumor was true, thought Lucius, draining his cup with the rest.
His great-uncle, not satisfied to have mastered the whole of the Mediterranean world, had set his sights on yet another conquest: the land of the

ancient Persians, which, since its conquest by Alexander, had become the kingdom of Parthia.

In all the known world, Parthia was the only power that could possibly rival Roma. When Lucius was nine years old, a man named Marcus Licinius Crassus, who was famous for putting down the great slave revolt led by Spartacus, led a Roman army to engage the Parthians, using Syria as his base of operations. Crassus had been the richest man in Roma and the political equal of Pompeius and Caesar; for a while the three of them formed the so-called Triumvirate, which temporarily stabilized the rivalry between them even as each plotted for a greater share of power. Crassus's bid for fortune had been his invasion of Parthia. He had hoped to accomplish there what Caesar was already accomplishing in Gaul, reaping wealth and glory—except that the fabulous spoils of Parthia would far exceed anything to be taken in Gaul.

Instead, Crassus met Nemesis. At the battle of Carrhae his army was surrounded and subjected to a relentless barrage of armor-piercing Parthian arrows. Leading a cavalry unit to try to break through the Parthian lines, Crassus's son Publius was killed; his head was cut off and used to taunt his beleaguered father. After the loss of twenty thousand Roman soldiers and the capture of ten thousand more, the Parthians offered Crassus a truce, then betrayed him and killed him, and beheaded him as they had his son. The Parthians celebrated their triumph over the invading Romans with great pomp, and presented the head of the Crassus as a gift to their ally, the king of Armenia, who reputedly used it in a production of Euripides' play *The Bacchae*. Crassus had hoped to be head of the world; instead, his head became a stage prop.

The shadow of Crassus's defeat had haunted the Romans ever since. The Parthians loomed as the great, unconquered enemy to the east. Now that civil war had settled the power struggle within the fractured Republic, it seemed only natural that the master of Roma should turn his attention to Parthia.

"Let me say outright that the military prowess of the Parthians must not be discounted," said Caesar. "But nor should it be overestimated. We must not be put off by the defeat of Crassus. To be candid, as a commander he was not the equal of any man here—and I include you, Lucius, untested as you are. As a junior officer, Crassus served Sulla well, but he was always overshadowed by Pompeius. True, he put down the slave revolt of Sparta-cus, but afterward the Senate refused to reward him with a triumph, and for good reason; it would have been unseemly for a Roman to celebrate a victory over an army of slaves. The Parthian campaign was Crassus's des-perate attempt to make his mark as a military man. He overreached."

"Even so," said Antonius, "if we're taking on the Parthians, I intend to make sure my will is in order." The grim joke was typical of his humor, es-pecially when he was drinking.

Antonius's remark was greeted by good-natured booing from the oth-ers, but Caesar dismissed their objections. "Antonius speaks wisely. My own will is kept safe by the Vestal virgins. A man must think ahead to the day when all that remains of him is his name. As long as men speak his name, his glory lives. As for worldly possessions, great or small, a man should take steps to see that they are disbursed as he sees fit." Caesar glanced at Lucius, and then at Antonius, but the significance of his glances was hard to read.

What provisions might Caesar's will contain? No one knew. Caesar was king in all but name, but he was a king with no clear heir. He had never ac-knowledged the son of Cleopatra as his own. Rumors attested that Marcus Junius Brutus, who had fought against Caesar and been pardoned by him, was Caesar's bastard, but Caesar himself had never acknowledged the pos-sibility. Caesar's closest male relations were the offspring of his two sisters—his nephew Quintus Pedius, who had served him in Gaul, and his young grand-nephews, Gaius Octavius and Lucius Pinarius. Of the three, only Lucius was present at the dinner; the other two were away from Roma on military duties.

Antonius took note of their absence. "A pity that your other two nephews couldn't be here tonight."

"Yes. But all three shall have the opportunity to cover themselves with glory in the Parthian campaign. Quintus is already battle-tested. As for Gaius . . ." Caesar's eyes lit up; he was very fond of Gaius Octavius. "He's only eighteen, but full of spirit; he reminds me of myself at that age. De-spite his misfortunes in the last year—illness and shipwreck—he managed to take part in the final push against the Pompeian remnants in Spain, and he acquitted himself well. He lost his father when he was only four. I, too lost my father when I was young, so I've done my best to look after him. He's not a bad orator, either."

"He had the best possible teacher," said Antonius.

Caesar shook his head. "Not I. It comes to him naturally. I still remember the eulogy he delivered at the funeral of his grandmother, when he was only twelve."

"And what of this fellow?" said Antonius, smiling at Lucius. For a moment Lucius was afraid that the man would reach over and muss his hair, as if he were still a boy. Listening to Caesar praise his cousin Gaius made Lucius feel acutely aware of his own lack of accomplishments.

"Lucius is only beginning his career," said Caesar. "But I have my eye on him. Parthia will give him the chance to show the world what he's made of."

"To the Parthian campaign, then!" said Lucius, impulsively seizing his cup and lifting it high.

"To the Parthian campaign!" said Antonius. He and the others joined the toast. Caesar nodded approvingly.

There was more food and more wine. The conversation shifted. Lepidus remarked on the fact that Caesar had seen fit to restore the statues of Sulla and of Pompeius, which had been pulled down and smashed by the mob in the wake of Caesar's victory. Why had Caesar put his enemies back on their pedestals?

"Lepidus, you know that it has always been Caesar's policy to show clemency; vindictiveness gains a man nothing in the long run. Sulla, despite his crimes, and Pompeius, despite his fatal mistakes, were both great Romans. They deserve to be remembered. And so, by Caesar's order, the gilded statue of Sulla on horseback will soon be back on its pedestal near the Rostra. Already the statue of Pompeius has returned to its place of honor, in the assembly room at the theater Pompeius built on the Field of Mars. That's where the Senate will meet tomorrow. The statue of Pompeius shall witness my request for the Parthian command."

He took a bite of custard, and smiled. "It was good of Pompeius, to provide Roma with its first permanent theater. We shall remember him for that, if for nothing else. As for Sulla, he was a political dunce to give up his dictatorship. But if he hadn't done so, where would Caesar be today?"

"Where would we all be?" asked Antonius, who saw the occasion fo
another toast.

Lucius at last felt sufficiently emboldened by wine and by the cama
raderie of the others to join in the conversation. "Uncle," he said, "ma
one be so bold as to ask your intentions for Roma?"

"What do you mean, young man?"

"I mean, your intentions for the city itself. There's a rumor that you ma
move the capital to the ancient site of Troy, or even to Alexandria."

Caesar looked at him archly. "However do such rumors get started
Why Troy, I wonder?"

Lucius shrugged. "My tutors claim there's an ancient link between Tro
and Roma. Long ago, even before the days of Romulus and Remus, th
Trojan warrior Aeneas survived the fall of his city, fled across the sea, an
settled near the Tiber. His bloodline flows in the blood of the Romans."

"And for that reason I should abandon the city of my birth and mak
my capital at Troy?" said Caesar. "To be sure, its location on the coast o
Asia makes it a central point between East and West, especially if our pos
sessions are expanded into Parthia and beyond. But no, I won't build
new capital at Troy. And why would I move the capital to Alexandria? Th
reason for that rumor is obvious, I suppose. Between Roma and Egyp
there now exists, shall we say, a special relationship."

"You did place a statue of Queen Cleopatra in your new Temple o
Venus, right beside the goddess herself," noted Antonius.

"I did. It seemed to me an appropriate gesture to commemorate he
state visit. As for Alexandria, it's a very old, very sophisticated city—"

"A city founded by a conqueror, and accustomed to the rule of kings,
said Antonius.

"Nonetheless, I have no intention of making it the world's capital."

"But you can see, Uncle," said Lucius, "why people become so upset b
such rumors. They're afraid that if you take the treasury and the state bu
reaucracy elsewhere, Roma will be reduced to a provincial backwater, an
the Senate will become little more than a city council."

Caesar laughed. "Amusing as that notion may be, I have no intention c
moving the capital. I suppose I should make that clear in my address to th
senators tomorrow, to allay their worries. The gods themselves decree

that Roma should be the center of the world; so it always shall be. Far from abandoning the city, I have plans to enlarge and enrich it. My engineers are working on a scheme to divert the course of the Tiber and to build break-waters along the coast, so as to make Ostia as great a harbor as Carthage was. Think what a boon that will be for Roma's commerce!"

"And speaking of Carthage . . . ," said Antonius.

Caesar nodded. "Yes, already I've begun to build new colonies at Carthage and at Corinth, the two great cities that our forefathers destroyed in a single year. The Greeks will praise the rebirth of Corinth, and the colony at Carthage fulfills the old, thwarted dream of Gaius Gracchus. Yes, great plans are afoot. Great plans . . ."

The conversation became looser as more wine flowed. Lucius noticed that Caesar imbibed considerably less than the others, and Antonius considerably more.

It was Lepidus who brought up the subject of death.

"We all know how Sulla died, in bed of a horrible disease; but to the very end, he behaved like a cruel tyrant, ordering the death of another. Crassus too met a wretched end. After Pharsalus, Pompeius sailed to Egypt hoping to make a final stand, but the minions of King Ptolemy stabbed him to death before he could set foot on shore, then delivered his head as a trophy to Caesar. After the battle of Thapsus, Cato fell on his sword, but his loyal servants found him and stitched him up; he had to wait until they slept to tear out the stitches with his fingers and finish his own disembowelment."

"And your point in recounting this grisly catalogue, Lepidus?" asked Antonius.

"Death comes in many forms. If a man could choose, what would be the best death?"

Caesar spoke at once. "Sudden and unexpected, even if bloody and painful. That would be much preferable to a lingering death. Of all the episodes you mention, Lepidus, the death of Pompeius was best. The others all saw the shadow of death long before it reached them, and must have contemplated it with dread, but up to the very last, Pompeius still possessed hope, however fragile, and his end came as a surprise, however shocking. To be sure, his body was defiled, but when I came into possession of his remains I saw to it that they were purified and given the proper rites. His ghost is at peace."

The dinner drew to an end. The guests took their leave. Caesar declared his intention to walk alone with Lucius to the house of his parents. "There's a private matter which I should like to discuss with my nephew," he said, looking at Lucius and then averting his eyes.

"Alone? Just the two of you?" said Antonius.

"Why not?"

"At least a few of us should go with you," said Antonius. "For your protection. If you need privacy, we can stay a few paces behind."

Caesar shook his head. "Toward what end has Caesar done so much to please the people of Roma, with great public feasts and entertainments, if not to make it safe for himself to walk across the city without a bodyguard?"

"That's a fine notion," said Antonius, "but in reality—"

"No, Antonius. I won't walk the streets of my city in fear of my life. A man dies only once. The dread of death causes far more misery than the thing itself, and I shall not submit to it. It's only a short walk from here to the house of Lucius, and an even shorter walk from there to my house. I shall be perfectly safe."

Antonius began to protest, but Caesar silenced him with a look.

As the two of them crossed the Palatine Hill alone under moonlight, Lucius as always felt a bit uncomfortable in his great-uncle's presence, and sensed that Caesar felt uneasy, as well. Several times Caesar began to speak, then fell silent. The world's greatest general and second-greatest orator—for even Caesar ceded the highest place to the eloquent Cicero— seemed unable to express himself.

"To Hades with this!" he finally muttered. "I shall say it as plainly as I can. Lucius, your grandfather . . ."

"The one they call Unlucky?"

"Yes. He did me a very great favor once. He saved my life."

"How did he do that, Uncle?"

"This is very difficult to talk about. In fact, I've never told this story to anyone. But you deserve to know the truth about your grandparents, Lucius, and the sacrifice they made for my sake. This was during Sulla's dictatorship, at the height of the proscriptions. I was very young, only a year or so older than you are now. I was in great danger. I was also very ill, suffering from the quartan ague." He looked up at the moon. By its soft light Lucius caught a glimpse of the youth Caesar once had been. "Maybe that's why I refuse to fear death now; I had enough of fearing death when I was young. Anyway, I was skulking from house to house, hiding from Sulla's henchmen, but at the home of your grandparents a fellow named Phagites caught up with me . . ."

He proceeded to tell Lucius about the bribe that Lucius's grandfather paid to save his life, and later, in the presence of Sulla himself, the extraordinary sacrifice that was required of Julia and Lucius the Unlucky—the dissolution of their marriage when Caesar refused to divorce his wife at Sulla's whim.

"Your grandmother was heartbroken, but she adapted swiftly; that was her nature. But your grandfather was never the same. He was a broken man. He had acted honorably, yet he felt dishonored. He saw no way to right the wrong that had been done to him. If he had lived, eventually I might have found some way to make recompense, some means to help him regain his self-respect. But he died while he was still quite young, and before I could make my mark on the world."

They had been strolling at a slow pace. Caesar abruptly halted. "Do you know how he died?"

"He fell on a patch of ice."

"Yes. Do you know where?"

Lucius shrugged. "Somewhere here on the Palatine, I think."

"It was on the very spot where we now stand."

Under the silver moonlight, it was not hard to imagine the paving stones glazed with ice. Lucius shivered. "By your reckoning, Uncle, his was a good death—swift and without warning. Perhaps the gods granted him an early death as a kind of mercy."

"Perhaps. But the debt I owed to your grandfather has weighed upon me ever since. Not even the gods can change the past, and the dead are beyond our reach. But I *can* make certain that you, Lucius, will have every opportunity to earn your own place of honor. I would have done so anyway, because you're my kin; but I wanted you to know of your grandfather's sacrifice, so that between the two of us there is an understanding of what came before. I should be gratified to see you attain the dignity that your grandfather believed he had lost."

Lucius considered this. "Thank you for telling me, Uncle. I'm not sure what else I can say." Silently, he wondered about the words Caesar had spoken with such gravity. What did "dignity" and "honor" mean now? In a world ruled by a king, the ancient Course of Honor, with each man competing against equals to become first man in the state, had become meaningless.

Caesar seemed to read his thoughts. "In the future, the Course of Honor will not have quite the same significance as it did for our ancestors. But ambitious men will still be able to earn Roma's gratitude, along with personal wealth and glory, on the battlefield. Shall I confide a secret to you, Lucius? Something I haven't shared even with Antonius?"

He commenced walking again, in the direction of Lucius's house. "My military ambitions—my ambitions for Roma—are even greater than Antonius and the others assume. The idea of conquering Parthia greatly excites them, as you saw, but that is as far as their imaginations can reach. Caesar's plans extend far beyond the conquest of Parthia. My dream is to take Parthia, yes—and then to traverse the far side of the Euxine Sea and circle back, conquer Scythia and Germania and all the lands that border them, cross the channel to Britannia, and then return to Italy by way of Gaul, ending where I began. When Caesar is finished, Roma's dominion will comprise a true world empire, bounded on every side by ocean."

Lucius was awed by the grandeur of this vision. He was flattered that Caesar should confide in him. But Caesar was not finished.

"No such empire has ever existed before; even Alexander's empire was not as far-flung. And of course, upon his death, the lands Alexander conquered did not remain unified but were divided among his heirs, with a great deal of confusion and bloodshed. Alexander's general Ptolemy did the best, when he took Egypt; Queen Cleopatra is his direct descendent. But what will happen to Roma's empire when I die, Lucius? Will it be a single kingdom with a single ruler? Will it be carefully divided into many kingdoms, all closely allied? Or will it be splintered into rival kingdoms, each at war with the other?"

"Might it not become a republic again, Uncle?"

Caesar smiled, as if at a whimsical notion. "Anything is possible, I suppose—even that! No man of my generation could find a way to make the Republic work, but perhaps men of a later day will be able to do so. Meanwhile, I think ahead. I do my best to shape the course of the future. It may be that I will live to be very old and that I will work out a means to pass on my legacy intact; or I may die tonight, as my father and his father died, struck down by the gods without warning. At present, my will provides for my heirs, and of course you are among them, Lucius. But if my power endures and if my plans come to fruition, more complicated arrangements will be required.

"I tell you all this, Lucius, because it may be that the gods have in mind for you a very special destiny. Through your descent from the Julii, you are the offspring of Venus, no less than I myself. Through your father's line, you carry one of the oldest names in Roma's history. The Pinarii are very ancient—but you, Lucius, are very young. You've accomplished nothing, as yet; but neither have you made mistakes. Prepare yourself. Be loyal to me. Prove yourself in battle. Observe the conduct of other men; adopt their virtues and avoid their vices. I'm thinking specifically of Antonius. I know you feel close to him. But you have it in you to become a far better man than he is."

Lucius frowned. "You place great trust in Antonius."

"I do. But I'm not blind to his faults."

Having been taken so deeply into Caesar's confidence, Lucius felt emboldened to ask him about the incident a month earlier, when Antonius had three times offered Caesar the diadem during the Lupercalia.

"You were there," said Caesar. "You saw all that took place. What did you think?"

"I think you staged the incident, like a play, to test the citizen's reaction to a crown. When you saw that so many disapproved, you reassured them that you had no desire to be their king."

Caesar nodded. "In politics, reality and appearance are of equal importance. You cannot attend to one and neglect the other. A man must determine both what he is, and what others believe him to be. It's a tricky business, this matter of crowns and titles. Shall I tell you another secret?"

Lucius nodded.

"Tomorrow, before the debate regarding the Parthian command, one of my loyal senators will make an announcement regarding the Sibylline Books. It appears that the priests in charge of interpreting the verses have discovered a most remarkable passage, which indicates that the Parthians can be conquered only by a king. I refused the diadem that was offered to me by Antonius at the Lupercalia, to the applause of the people. But what if the Senate should implore Caesar to accept a royal title, to ensure the conquest of Parthia?"

"You *will* become a king, then?" said Lucius. "And this will happen to-morrow?"

Caesar smiled wryly. "This is the plan: The Senate will declare that Caesar is king of all Roman provinces outside Italy, with the right to wear a crown in any place other than Italy, on land or sea. This technicality will satisfy both Caesar's need for authority and the need of the Senate and the citizens to believe themselves free of a king. Caesar will be king of the rest of the world, on Roma's behalf."

Lucius frowned. "Auguries and omens, and the Sibylline Books—are they merely tools for men to use? Do they not truly express the will of the gods?"

"Perhaps both propositions are true. Auguries and the rest are tools, yes; and the man who masters those tools does so because he is favored by the gods. It is a remarkable thing, how frequently divine will coincides with the designs of successful men." Caesar smiled. "Of course, not every omen is favorable. If I listened to every warning I receive from every sooth-sayer on every street corner in Roma, I might never leave my house, and I certainly would not venture out to address the Senate tomorrow!"

"Have you received a specific warning?"

"Too many to relate! Shooting stars, goats born two-headed, tears from statues, letters mysteriously formed in the sand—all sorts of portents have been brought to my attention in the last month. Some of these warnings specifically cite the Ides of Martius as a day of ill omen. That's one reason Antonius has been playing mother hen lately. He thinks I should be sur-rounded by a bodyguard at all times. But Caesar has decided to ignore these so-called omens and do as he wishes."

Their quiet conversation was abruptly interrupted by loud voices from a side street. A group of men was heading straight toward them. Caesar seized Lucius's arm and pulled him into a doorway.

The men began to sing, loudly and badly out of tune. They were obviously drunk. One of them spotted the two figures in the shadows of the doorway and stepped closer, peering at them.

"Numa's balls! If it isn't the spawn of Venus himself—our beloved dictator!"

"Who?" shouted one of his companions.

"Gaius Julius Caesar!"

"You liar!"

"No, I swear! Come see for yourselves."

The men crowded around the doorway. Recognizing Caesar, they were briefly awed, then began a buffoonish mime of bowing and prostrating themselves. "King Caesar!" they cried. "All hail the king!"

Caesar showed no fear. He smiled and graciously acknowledged their gestures with a nod.

One of them staggered back and flung out his arms, miming a crucifixion. "Look at me! I'm a pirate! Oh, great Caesar, have mercy on me!"

Another pulled his tunic up to hide his head. "Look at me! I'm Pompeius after he landed in Egypt! Merciful Caesar, give me back my head!"

"And I'm the Queen of the Nile!" said another, mincing about and putting his fists inside his tunic to mime enormous breasts. "Ravish me, great Caesar! Our baby will be the next king of Egypt!"

They continued with their buffoonery for a while, then seemed to forget what they were doing. Waving good-bye, they moved on and broke into another song. Only when they were out of sight did Caesar relax his grip on Lucius's arm.

Lucius looked at his great-uncle's face in the moonlight. Caesar's eyes glittered with a peculiar excitement. However briefly, Caesar had felt a moment of genuine fear. Its passing seemed to have left him neither angry nor shaken, but exhilarated.

⁂

The next day was the Ides of Martius.

Lucius awoke drenched with sweat. His room was dark. The faint blue light that precedes the dawn silhouetted the shutters drawn across his window. Somewhere in the distance a cock was crowing.

He had been experiencing one of those strange dreams in which the dreamer is both participant and observer, aware that he is dreaming and yet unable to stop the dream. In it, Caesar had died. A great multitude had gathered to hear the reading of his will. On the steps of a temple, a Vestal virgin produced a scroll and handed it to Marcus Antonius. Antonius unrolled the document and proceeded to read. Lucius stood at the front of the crowd, but strain as he might, he could not hear the names being read. The roar of the crowd was too great. He wanted to tell the others to be quiet, but he could not open his mouth to speak. He could not move at all. Antonius continued to read, but Lucius could not hear, speak, or move.

The dream was not exactly a nightmare, yet he awoke feeling shaken and covered with sweat. He staggered from his bed and opened the shutters. The cock crowed again. The view from his window showed a jumble of rooftops, the irregular spires of cypress trees, and a glimpse of the Temple of Jupiter atop the Capitoline, rebuilt since its destruction by fire in Sulla's time. All was bathed in soft light; the world might have been made of ancient, weathered marble, without color or sharp edges.

Lucius filled his lungs with cool, bracing air. The glaze of sweat evaporated from his flesh and left him covered with goosebumps. The dream had been oppressive and disturbing, but now he was awake. The world was just as he had left it, and the first glimmer of sunlight across the rooftops marked the beginning of a day like any other.

And yet, in a matter of hours, Caesar would receive the Senate's command to begin the conquest of Parthia. He would be declared king of all provinces beyond Italy. The age of the Republic would end, and a new age would begin.

Anxious to leave his room and his uneasy dream behind, Lucius quickly dressed. He put on his best tunic, which was bright blue with a yellow hem, and strapped on his best pair of shoes. When the people began cheering Caesar's decision to wage war against Parthia, it would not do for Caesar's young kinsman to be seen wearing his second-best.

He left the house and wandered aimlessly for a while, watching the city awaken. At the great houses on the Palatine, slaves opened front doors to air the vestibules, extinguished the lamps that had burned all night, and swept the thresholds. Between two houses, Lucius caught a distant view of the Forum Boarium and the Tiber waterfront. Down in the marketplace merchants were setting up shop. Many had special displays of baskets stuffed with food. Customers were already lining up to buy the baskets. Lucius had forgotten that this was the feast day of Anna Perenna, a holiday celebrated only by the plebeians.

Anna Perenna was the crone goddess, always portrayed with gray hair, a wrinkled face, and a stooped back; she wore a traveling cloak and carried baskets stuffed with food. Her legend dated to the early days of the Republic, when the plebeians staged their first so-called secession, withdrawing en masse from the city to protest the special privileges of the patricians and to demand tribunes for their protection. When the plebeians ran low on provisions, an old woman calling herself Anna Perenna appeared among them with baskets of food. No matter how much food people took from the baskets, the baskets remained miraculously full, and so the plebs never went hungry.

After the secession, Anna Perenna vanished, never to be seen again. On the day sacred to her, the Ides of Martius, plebeian families left the city to picnic on the banks of the Tiber. They gathered their own baskets of food, or bought ready-made baskets at the market. They pitched small tents and laid out blankets. Children played games with balls and sticks in the grass. Young couples courted in leafy bowers. Everyone ate and drank their fill, then dozed on the banks of the river. At sundown, the plebeian families would stream back into the city in an informal procession, singing songs of praise to Anna Perenna.

The holiday meant little to Lucius. Being a patrician, he had never taken part. Still, strolling across the Forum, passing families on their way to the river carrying food baskets, blankets, and toys, he found their festive mood infectious. It further amused him to think that among all these carefree revelers, he alone knew what a momentous and memorable day this would turn out to be, thanks to the special requests that Caesar would put before the Senate.

Thinking of Caesar, Lucius walked to the area directly north of the ancient Forum, where a large tract of land had in recent years been cleared and rebuilt by his great-uncle and named after him. The Julian Forum was surrounded by a vast rectangular portico of gleaming marble columns. At one end stood the new temple dedicated to Venus, constructed of solid marble, the fulfillment of a vow Caesar had made to the goddess before his victory at Pharsalus. In front of the temple was a fountain adorned with nymphs. Dominating the open square was a magnificent statue of Caesar armored for battle and sitting atop a white charger.

Work on the forum was not finished. When it was done, the portico would open onto courtrooms and legal offices. The comings and goings of scribes, secretaries, judges, and advocates would make the Julian Forum one of the busiest spots in Roma. As it was, on this morning, Lucius was the only person present. He walked under the statue of Caesar, amused to see the very grave look on his great-uncle's face, then past the fountain, which was full of water but not splashing. Its still face reflected the perfect proportions and dazzling marble facade of the Temple of Venus.

Lucius mounted the steps. A temple slave dozing beside the doorway stirred at his approach. Recognizing Lucius—the dictator's kinsmen were frequent visitors to the temple of their ancestress—the slave hastily opened the doors for him.

In Lucius's opinion, the inside of the temple was the most beautiful interior space in all of Roma, perhaps in all the world. The floors, walls, ceiling, and columns were made of solid marble in a staggering array of colors, and newly finished, so that every surface gleamed with a mirror-like polish. The facing walls of the short vestibule were decorated by two of the most famous paintings in the world, the Ajax and the Medea by the renowned artist Timomachus. Within the sanctuary, displayed in six cabinets, were the extraordinary collections of jewels and gemstones which Caesar had acquired in his travels. To Lucius, the most fascinating item was a savage-looking breastplate strung with tiny pearls from the island of Britannia.

At the far end of the chamber, magnificent upon her pedestal, stood Venus herself, as captured in marble by Arcesilaus, the most highly paid sculptor in the world. The goddess stood with one arm bent back to touch her shoulder and her other arm slightly extended; one of her breasts was bare. The molding of her serene features and the folds of her thin gown were extraordinarily delicate.

Next to Venus stood an equally impressive statue of Cleopatra, executed in bronze and covered with gold. The queen was portrayed not in the outlandish garb of the Pharaohs, which the Ptolemies had appropriated when they assumed the rule of Egypt, but in elegant Greek dress more chastely covered than Venus and wearing a simple diadem on her brow. To Lucius's eye, Cleopatra was not a particularly beautiful woman— certainly not as beautiful as the idealized image of Venus beside her—but the sculptor had nonetheless managed to capture that indefinable quality that had so captivated a man like Caesar. Caesar's decision to place her statue in the new Temple of Venus had sparked intense speculation about his intentions. If the purpose of the temple was to honor his ancestress, what place did the queen of Egypt have there, unless Caesar intended to make her the mother of his own descendents?

Lucius had met the queen only once, when she first arrived in Roma for her state visit. During the feasting and entertainments, Lucius had been briefly introduced to her as one of Caesar's young relatives. The queen had been gracious but aloof; Lucius had been completely tongue-tied. Since then, Caesar had installed Cleopatra at a sumptuous garden estate on the farther bank of the Tiber, where the queen had hosted a number of lavish dinners to introduce herself to the city's elite.

Staring up at her statue, Lucius felt a sudden impulse to pay her a visit. Why not? Caesar's overtures to him the previous night emboldened him. Lucius was not just one of the great man's heirs; he was Caesar's confidante. He had as much right to pay a social call on the queen of Egypt as any other Roman. To be sure, he was not formally outfitted in his toga, but he was wearing his best tunic. He turned about, left the temple, and headed for the bridge across the Tiber.

Passing through the marketplace in the Forum Boarium, he was sur-rounded by plebeians on their way to celebrate the Feast of Anna Perenna. There were so many of them heading out of the city that there was a queue to cross the bridge. On the other side, the picnickers drifted toward the public grounds along the riverbank, but Lucius pressed further on, toward the grand private estates that fronted the most desirable stretch of the Tiber. Here the wealthy of Roma had their second homes outside the city, where they could relax in their gardens, pursue the fashionable hobby of beekeeping, and go boating and swimming in the river.

At one of the grandest of these houses, owned by Caesar, Cleopatra had taken up residence. When Lucius knocked at the gate, an Egyptian slave, his eyes outlined with kohl, peered at him through the peephole.

Lucius announced himself—"Lucius Pinarius, great-nephew of Gaius Julius Caesar"—and a few moments later the slave opened the gate.

The big man peered beyond him. "Only you?" he said in Greek.

Lucius laughed. "I suppose the queen has very few visitors who arrive without an entourage, and on foot. But yes, it's only me. My uncle is otherwise engaged today, as the queen probably knows."

He was conducted to a sunny garden with a view of the river. The garden was formally laid out, with manicured shrubs, gravel paths, and carefully pruned rose bushes. Tucked amid the shrubbery were quaint pieces of Greek statuary. Lucius noticed one of a winged Eros kneeling down to touch a butterfly, and another of a young boy absorbed in pulling a thorn from his foot. Lucius sat on a stone bench and gazed at the sparkles of morning sunlight on the river.

"You're as pretty as a statue."

Lucius stood and turned to see the queen standing nearby.

"Please, remain seated," she said. "I was enjoying the sight of you. You looked like another statue in the garden: *Roman Boy Contemplating the Tiber.*"

"I'm not a boy, Your Majesty," said Lucius, bristling slightly. "I would have worn my toga, but—"

"Roman men and their togas! I'm afraid they always look slightly ridiculous to me."

"The men or the togas?"

Cleopatra smiled. "You're a sharp one," she said. "And of course you're not a boy. I didn't mean to offend you. I know how vexing it can be, when one is young but determined to be taken seriously."

Cleopatra herself was no more than twenty-five. Her statue in the temple made her look older, Lucius thought, as had her royal raiment when he first met her. On this day she wore a simple, sleeveless linen gown tied at the waist with a gold-threaded sash. Her hair, usually pinned atop her head, hung down on either side of her face. She wore no diadem. The day was early, and the queen was not yet dressed for formal visitors.

"It's good of you to receive me," said Lucius.

"I could hardly turn away Caesar's kinsman. Is there a celebration? My sentinels tell me that all sorts of people are out enjoying themselves along the river. Does it have something to do with Caesar's pronouncement to the Senate?"

Lucius smiled at her mistake. "The Feast of Anna Perenna is an ancient plebeian holiday. It has nothing to do with me or with Caesar. He won't be speaking to the Senate until later this morning."

"I see. I have a great deal to learn about Roman customs. Perhaps you could instruct me."

"I, Your Majesty?"

"By rights, the task should fall to Caesar. When he was in Alexandria, I educated him about Egyptian court protocol. But Caesar is much too busy. And there are so few people in the city I can trust."

"But you've met many people since you arrived. All the best people come to the dinner parties here at your villa."

"Yes, and they all go away utterly charmed by the queen of Egypt—or pretending to be so, to curry favor with Caesar. Occasionally, I receive word of their true reaction. That fellow Cicero, for example. To my face, the famous advocate was all smiles and flattery. Behind my back, he wrote a letter to a friend, complaining that he could hardly stand to be in the same room with me."

"How do you know this?"

She shrugged. "One didn't survive as a princess in Alexandria without learning how to discover the truth. Frankly, I don't see why Caesar allows that man to keep his head. Didn't Cicero oppose him in the civil war and fight for Pompeius?"

"Yes. Brutus opposed him, as well, but after Pharsalus, Caesar forgave them both. Caesar is famous for his clemency."

The queen narrowed her eyes. "I suppose, operating in a republic, clemency was a tool of statecraft. Caesar will learn new ways to deal with his enemies when he finally puts the last vestiges of this primitive form of government behind him."

"Primitive?" Lucius drew back his shoulders. More than ever he wished he had worn his toga; it gave a man a sense of authority. "Roma is much, much older than Alexandria. And I believe the Roman Republic predates the establishment of your dynasty by almost two hundred years."

"Perhaps. But when my ancestor Ptolemy inherited control of Egypt from Alexander, he assumed the title, the royal insignia, and the divine status of the Pharaohs who preceded him. Their dynasties can be traced back thousands of years, to the very beginning of time. By comparison, the civilization of the Romans is very young; infantile, in fact. The great pyramids were built many centuries before the Greeks laid siege to Troy, and Roma was founded hundreds of years after Troy fell."

She frowned. "The other day I hosted a group of Roman scholars, to discuss the holdings of the Library of Alexandria. We fell to talking about the origins of Roma, and they put forward a very novel theory. They said that a Trojan warrior, Aeneas, escaped the sack of the city, sailed to the shores of Italy, and settled near the Tiber, and thus the blood of Troy survives in the Romans. But when I asked for evidence, they had none. I have to wonder whether your scholars are taking a bit of license when they speak of this link between Roma and Troy."

"There are those," admitted Lucius, "who say that historians invent the past."

Cleopatra smiled. "I would rather invent the future."

She strolled to a place which afforded a better view of the water. Downriver, tiny in the distance, figures could be seen lounging on the bank. "We know so little of our ancestors, really, even we who can name them going back many generations. I suppose the Pinarii are an ancient family?"

"There was a Pinarius in Roma when Hercules appeared and killed the monster Cacus. And the Julii must be just as ancient. Caesar says the line was begun by a union with Venus."

"Which makes Caesar almost as divine as myself. He certainly behaves like a god." She smiled, then frowned. "While they are on earth, the gods do great things; but after they leave the earth, they fall as silent as dead mortals. I frequently pray to the first Ptolemy, who was most certainly a god; I speak, but he never speaks back. He fought beside Alexander, bathed beside him, ate beside him. There are a thousand questions I would like to ask him—What did Alexander's laughter sound like? Did he snore? What did he smell like?—but to those questions there are no answers, and there never will be. The dead are all dust. The past is as unknowable as the future. When Caesar and I are dust, will men of the future know only our names, and nothing else about us?"

Lucius could think of nothing to say. He had never heard a woman, or a man for that matter, speak in such a fashion. Even Caesar tended to ruminate more about troop movements than about matters of eternity.

Cleopatra smiled. "It's curious that I'm so young, and Caesar is so old—more than twice my age—while the relative ages of our kingdoms are reversed. Egypt is like a mature queen, wealthy, worldly, covered with jewels, sophisticated to her fingertips. Roma is a brawny, brash, brawling upstart. The two need not be at odds. In some ways they're natural allies, as Caesar and I are natural allies."

"Is that what you are? Allies?"

"To conquer Parthia, Caesar will need the assistance of Egypt."

"But surely there's more between you than that." Watching her graceful movements, listening to her speak, Lucius had begun to see the attraction Cleopatra must hold for Caesar. He had also glimpsed the qualities that must have been so repellent to a man like Cicero, who believed in the staid, silent, matronly virtues of Roman womanhood.

For the first time, it seemed possible to Lucius, even likely, that Caesar intended to divorce his Roman wife. Caesar had a viable excuse: Calpurnia had failed to give him a son. If the king of Roma married the queen of Egypt, would Parthia be a gift to their son? What would become of Caesar's other heirs?

A childish squeal erupted from the far side of the garden. Two handmaidens appeared, looking slightly chagrinned. Between them stood a tiny boy with upraised arms. The women held him by his hands, or more precisely restrained him, for he was eager to break from them and run to his mother.

Cleopatra laughed and clapped her hands. "Come to me, Caesarion!"

The child ran toward her. He threw himself against his mother and clutched her legs, then looked up at Lucius shyly. He seemed no different from any other child.

"How old is he?" said Lucius.

"Three years."

"He looks big for his age."

"Good. He needs to grow up fast." The queen gestured to the handmaidens, who came to fetch Caesarion and then set about amusing him in the garden. "Now you must excuse me, Lucius Pinarius. Caesar will call on me later today, after his pronouncement to the Senate. I must prepare myself. I'm glad you came to visit. You and I should know one another better."

✠

Lucius headed back to the city.

He chose a path that led him through the Grove of the Furies. The secluded holy place was deserted and quiet except for the distant singing of revelers along the riverbank. Passing by the altar, Lucius recalled the story of Gaius Gracchus and the terrible fate he had met in this very spot, chased to ground by his enemies and killed by a trusted slave, who then slew himself. Lucius's great-great-grandfather had been a friend of Gaius Gracchus, or so Lucius had been told; of the two men's actual dealings with one another, Lucius knew nothing.

He recalled something that Cleopatra had said: *We know so little of our ancestors, really, even we who can name them going back many generations.* It was true. What did Lucius know about those who had come before him? He knew their names, from the lists kept by his family of marriages and offspring, and from the official records that listed the magistrates of the Republic. About some of them he had heard an anecdote or two, although the details often differed depending upon who told the story. In the vestibule of his father's house there were wax images of some of the ancestors, so that Lucius had an idea of what they had looked like. But of the men and women themselves—their dreams and passions, their failures and triumphs—he knew virtually nothing. His ancestors were strangers to him.

Until the previous night, he had not even known of the terrible sacrifice made by his grandparents to save Caesar's life. How much more did he not know? The magnitude of this ignorance overwhelmed him—so many lives, so full of incident and feeling, lost to his knowledge completely and forever. What had Cleopatra said? *The past is as unknowable as the future.* He suddenly perceived his existence as a tiny point illuminated by the thinnest crack of light—the *now*—poised between two infinities of darkness— *before* and *after*.

He left the grove, crossed the bridge, and wandered across the Forum Boarium. Close by the Temple of Hercules stood the Ara Maxima, the most ancient altar in all of Roma, dedicated to Hercules, who had saved the people from Cacus. Had there really been a Hercules and a Cacus, a hero and a monster? So the priests declared, and the historians agreed; so the monument attested. If the story was true, there had been a Pinarius among the Romans even then, and the Pinarii, up until the early days of the Republic, had been assigned the sacred duty of maintaining the Ara Maxima and celebrating the Feast of Hercules. They had shared this duty with a family called the Potitii, which no longer existed. Why had the Pinarii abandoned the duty? What had become of the Potitii? Lucius did not know.

From the Temple of Hercules he heard a man calling, "Shoo! Shoo!" A temple slave appeared at the open doorway, wielding a horsetail whisk to drive a fly from the sanctuary. Everyone knew that flies were forbidden to enter the temple, because flies had swarmed about Hercules and confounded him when he fought against Cacus. Nor could dogs come near, because the dog of Hercules had failed to warn him of the monster's approach. These things must have occurred, or else why did rituals exist to commemorate them, many lifetimes later?

Lucius recalled the story of the Romans trapped by the Gauls atop the Capitoline; the geese raised the alarm, while the dogs failed to bark. To commemorate that event, each year a dog was impaled on a stake and paraded through the city, along with one of Juno's sacred geese carried in a litter. The first time Lucius had witnessed this spectacle as a child, he had been puzzled and revolted by it, until his father had explained its meaning. Now when he saw the ritual each year, Lucius found it reassuring, a reminder both of the city's past and of his own childhood and the first time he had seen the procession.

Thinking of all the many rituals that took place during the year, and all the traditions of the ancestors which had been so scrupulously preserved over the centuries, Lucius felt comforted. Religion existed to honor and placate the gods, but did it not also make the past and the future a little less mysterious, and therefore less frightening?

Lost in thought, Lucius wandered homeward. Turning a corner, he realized that he was very near the house of Brutus. An impulse had caused Lucius to call upon Cleopatra. An equally spontaneous impulse now prompted
him to pay a visit to Brutus, who, according to rumor, was another of Caesar's possible heirs.

Everyone knew that Caesar had been the lover of Brutus's mother,
Servilia. The fact had come out before Lucius was born, and on the floor of
the Senate, of all places. Servilia was the half-sister of Cato, grandson of
the famous Cato who had called for the destruction of Carthage. Cato had
been one of Caesar's bitterest enemies. Twenty years ago, during a heated
debate in the Senate regarding an alleged conspiracy by the populist
Catilina, Caesar had been seen to receive a note from a messenger. Cato,
suspecting it might implicate Caesar in the plot, insisted that he read the
note aloud. Caesar refused. Cato grew more suspicious and more vehe-
ment, until finally Caesar relented and read the message aloud. It was a
love note from Servilia, Cato's sister. Cato was humiliated. Caesar was
much amused. From that day, his affair with Servilia was public knowledge, and the speculation began that he might be the father of her son,
Marcus Junius Brutus. The special regard in which Caesar had always held
Brutus, even when Brutus sided with Pompeius, had further fueled this
speculation.

Whatever their relationship, Brutus was among the men whom Caesar
had chosen to fill various posts when he began rebuilding the government.
Currently Brutus was praetor in charge of the city, but in the coming year
he would leave for Macedonia to serve as provincial governor. Because
Caesar's Parthian campaign might keep the dictator from Roma for an in-
definite period, all such appointments had been made not for the usual
one year but for five years.

Brutus was also a key member of the Senate, and it occurred to Lucius
that he might already have left home, heading for the Field of Mars and the
meeting of the Senate at the assembly hall in the Theater of Pompeius. But
evidently Brutus was still at home, for as Lucius drew nearer to Brutus's
house, he saw several men in red-bordered senatorial togas being admitted
at the front door. Lucius assumed they must be gathering before heading
off in a group to the assembly hall. Clearly, it was not a good time for Lu-

cius to pay a visit. Nonetheless, he continued in the same direction, toward Brutus's house.

Suddenly he heard the sound of many footsteps behind him. A large group of men caught up with him and swept past him. Lucius saw a blur of togas, and glimpsed several familiar faces. Some of the senators must surely have recognized him, but not one of them uttered a greeting. They averted their eyes from him. As they hurried on, whispering among themselves, he thought he heard them speak his name. It was very strange.

The senators reached the house of Brutus, rapped on the door, and disappeared inside.

Lucius arrived at the threshold and stared dumbly at the door. What was going on in the house of Brutus? Something was not right. It occurred to him that the senators might have been bringing bad news—something to do with Caesar, perhaps? Lucius gathered his nerve and rapped on the door.

A peephole opened. Lucius gave his name. He was perused by a pair of unblinking eyes. The peephole closed. Lucius was left waiting for so long that he decided he had been forgotten, and was about to leave. Then the door opened. A grim-looking slave admitted him to the vestibule.

"Wait here," said the slave, and disappeared.

Lucius slowly paced back and forth. He looked at the busts of the ancestors in their niches, paying only scant attention until he saw one that was clearly honored above all the others, placed in a special niche with votive candles in sconces at either side. The mask looked very, very old. It was a famous face, known to every Roman from public statues all over the city.

"That's only a copy, of course," said a voice. "Wax masks don't last forever, and more than one branch of the family lay claim to him, so there had to be duplicates. Still, that mask is very ancient, and very sacred, as you can imagine. The candles are kept lit always, day and night."

Brutus stood before him. Curious to see if he could detect a resemblance, Lucius looked from the face of Brutus to the face of his famous ancestor and namesake—the man who had been the nephew of the last king, Tarquinius, who had revenged the rape of Lucretia, who had helped to overthrow the monarchy and had become first consul, who had watched his own sons be put to death for betraying the Republic.

Lucius frowned. "You don't look anything alike, as far as I can see."

"No? Even so, I think we may share a similar destiny. At any rate, his example inspires me, especially today."

Was Brutus feverish? It seemed to Lucius that the man's eyes glittered unnaturally.

"Why have you come?" said Brutus.

"I'm not sure. I happened to be passing. I saw your visitors arriving. It seemed to me that something . . . that perhaps something was wrong . . ."

His voice trailed away as another man appeared behind Brutus. Gaius Cassius Longinus was Brutus's brother-in-law, married to his sister. He was one of the senators who had swept past Lucius in the street. Lucius nodded to him. "Good day to you, Cassius."

Cassius did not return the greeting. He whispered in Brutus's ear. He looked tense and pale.

The two exchanged more whispers, and cast furtive glances at Lucius. They appeared to be arguing and trying to come to some decision. Lucius began to find their scrutiny unnerving.

Brutus gripped Cassius's arm and pulled him to the far side of the room, but his whisper was so loud that Lucius overheard. "No! We agreed already—Caesar and *only* Caesar. No one else! Otherwise, we show ourselves to be no better than—"

Cassius cast a cold gaze at Lucius, silenced Brutus with a hiss, and pulled him into the next room.

If they were still whispering, Lucius could not hear; his heartbeat was suddenly so loud in his ears that he could hear nothing else. He looked toward the front door. It was blocked by the grim-faced slave. From the atrium, more slaves appeared, followed by Brutus.

"Don't harm him!" Brutus shouted. "I only want him restrained. We'll hold him here until—"

There was no time to think. A thrill of panic ran through Lucius and he acted purely by instinct. He bolted toward the door, but hands on his arms and shoulders held him back. He tried to shrug them off, but the hands gripped him more firmly. With all his strength he pulled free, turned around, and swung his fists. His knuckles connected with the hard jaw of one of the slaves and sent a painful shock through his arm. The slave took a swing at him in return and struck a glancing blow across his shoulder. Lucius struck the man square in the face. The slave staggered back, blood pouring from his nose.

Now only the slave barring the door stood in his way. Lucius ran toward him, lowered his head, and butted the man in the stomach. The slave cried out in pain and bent forward, clutching his belly. Lucius pushed him out of the way and managed to slip through the doorway, into the street.

He meant to run in the direction of Caesar's house, but there were already men in the street, blocking his way. He turned about and ran in the opposite direction, away from the Forum, away from the Field of Mars and the Theater of Pompeius.

Lucius was young and quick, and he knew the streets of the Palatine well. He gained a good lead on his pursuers. He rounded a corner, and then another, and could not see them behind him at all. But he was growing weary; he needed refuge. He realized that he was near the house of Publius Servilius Casca. Surely he could trust Casca, who was deeply indebted to Caesar. The rotund, red-cheeked, bumbling Casca was something of a buffoon. It was impossible to imagine him as a menace to anyone.

Lucius paused for a moment to get his bearings, then sprinted to the end of the street and rounded a corner. There was Casca's house—and Casca himself standing in the open doorway, evidently on his way out but pausing to make sure he hadn't forgotten anything. He was reaching into the folds of his voluminous toga, searching for something and looking befuddled.

Exhilarated by the run and by his narrow escape, Lucius drew a deep lungful of air. Casca, startled by his sudden approach, gave a jerk and stumbled against the doorjamb.

"Casca! What are you looking for?" said Lucius, gasping. "If you can hide me half as well—"

Even as Lucius spoke, Casca produced the thing he had been searching for. In his fist he held a short but very sharp dagger. The look in his eyes raised the hackles on Lucius's neck.

Lucius heard shouts behind him. He had not escaped his pursuers after all. He bolted, but Casca grabbed his arm. The man was stronger than he looked. He called for slaves to come and help him. Lucius struggled. As he sprang free, he felt a searing pain across one forearm. Casca's blade had scraped him, just deeply enough to drawn a line of blood. Lucius felt sick, but he did not dare to stop running.

The flight continued across the valley of the Circus Maximus and up the winding streets of the Aventine. Near the Temple of Juno, Lucius was sure he had lost them. He hid in a doorway, his heart pounding and his lungs on fire. The trail of blood had thickened on his forearm. The shallow wound burned as if he had been seared by a brand.

Where was Caesar? He must be on his way to the meeting of the Senate by now. Antonius would be with him, surely, along with others who would defend him. But could even Antonius be trusted? And what if Caesar insisted on leaving his bodyguards behind? Lucius thought of the risk the two of them had taken the previous night, walking alone across the Palatine, and trembled.

He must reach Caesar and warn him, but how? Lucius was a fast runner, but even if he sprouted wings and flew, Caesar would almost certainly arrive at the Theater of Pompeius ahead of him, and if Brutus and the rest were already waiting for him . . .

Lucius had to try. He took a deep breath and began to run again.

Down the Aventine he ran, around the fountain of the Appian Aqueduct and past the Ara Maxima. He was suddenly very weary. His legs turned to lead and his chest seemed to have a tight band of iron across it. There were blisters on his feet. The shoes he had put on that morning were not good for running.

Still he ran, faster than he had thought possible.

At last, the massive facade of the theater loomed before him. To avoid accusations of decadence, Pompeius had dedicated the complex not as a theater but as a temple. By a clever architectural trick, the rows of theater seats also served as steps leading up to a sanctuary of Venus at the summit. Branching off from the theater itself were several porticos decorated with hundreds of statues. These arcades housed shrines, gardens, shops, and public chambers, including the large assembly room where the Senate was to meet.

The public square and the broad steps leading up to the main portico were empty. Lucius had hoped to see the area awash with red and white; here the senators in their crimson-bordered togas were accustomed to mill about before going inside. They had gone inside already.

But no—not quite all of them were inside yet. Lucius spied two figures on the steps, near the top. They stood close together, apparently engaged in a serious conversation. Lucius hurried across the square and reached the bottom of the steps. Looking up, he could see that one of the men was Antonius. The other was a senator he vaguely recognized, a man named Trebonius.

Lucius bounded up the steps. The men saw him approaching and broke off their conversation. Lucius drew near, dizzy and gasping for breath. He staggered. Antonius seized his arm to steady him.

"By Hercules, you look a fright!" Antonius smiled. He seemed more amused than alarmed by Lucius's appearance. "What's the matter, young man?"

Lucius was so out of breath it was difficult to speak. "Caesar . . ." he managed to say.

"Inside, along with everyone else," said Antonius.

"But why—why are you not with him?"

Antonius raised an eyebrow. "Trebonius here drew me aside—"

"To discuss an important matter—*privately*." Trebonius gave Lucius a stern, threatening look.

"But we're done with that, aren't we, Trebonius? We really should go in. They haven't shut the doors yet, have they?" Antonius looked over his shoulder, toward the entrance to the assembly hall. In front of the massive bronze doors, which stood open, priests were clearing blood and organs from the stone altar where auspices were taken before the start of each day's business. Antonius, whose buoyant mood seemed unshakable, smiled and laughed.

"You wouldn't believe the slaughter that just went on over there," he said to Lucius. "One poor creature after another sacrificed and cut open, to take the omens. The first chicken had no heart, which rather alarmed the priests. Caesar ordered another sacrifice, and another, but the priests kept telling him that the entrails were twisted and all the omens were contrary. He finally told them, 'To Hades with this nonsense, the omens before the battle of Pharsalus were just as bad. Let the Senate get on with its business!' "

Antonius grinned. Why was he in such a jovial mood? Lucius stepped back from the two men. Could even Antonius be trusted?

Lucius felt faint. Spots swam before his eyes. The moment seemed unreal and dreamlike. He stared at the nearby altar, where a priest was mopping up remains. The sight of the rag, saturated with blood and dripping gore, sent a thrill of panic through him. He pushed past the two men and raced toward the entrance.

The hall was an oval-shaped well, with seats on either side descending in tiers to the main floor. The session had not yet commenced. There was a low hubbub of conversation. Most of the senators had taken their seats, but others were milling about on the main floor in front of the chair of state—no one yet dared to call it a throne—on which Caesar was seated. How serene Caesar looked, how confident! In one hand he held a stylus, for marking documents. He turned the stylus this way and that with nimble fingers, the only sign of the nervous excitement he must be feeling on such a momentous day.

One of the senators, Tillius Cimber, stepped toward him, bowing slightly as if importuning Caesar for a favor. Caesar apparently found the request inappropriate. He shook his head and waved his stylus dismissively. Instead of withdrawing, Cimber stepped closer and clutched Caesar's toga near his shoulder.

"No!" Lucius shouted. His voice rang out high and shrill, like a boy's. Heads turned toward him. Caesar looked up, saw him and frowned, then immediately returned his attention to Cimber.

Caesar spoke through clenched teeth. "Take your hand off me, Cimber!"

Instead, Cimber yanked at the toga, so forcefully that Caesar was almost pulled from his chair. His toga was askew. The naked flesh of his shoulder was bared.

Holding fast to Caesar's toga, Cimber looked at the others nearby. As Caesar tried to pull free, Cimber's expression became frantic.

"What are you all waiting for?" cried Cimber. "Do it! Do it now!"

The portly Casca stepped forward. His forehead was beaded with sweat. A grimace bared his gums. He raised his dagger high in the air.

The sight elicited gasps and exclamations from all over the hall. Only Caesar appeared not to realize what was about to happen; he was still staring at Cimber, looking angry and confused. He turned his head just as Casca plunged the dagger downward. His face registered shock as the blade struck the exposed skin below his neck. There was a sickening sound of metal cutting into flesh.

Caesar let out a roar. He seized Casca's wrist with one hand. With the other he stabbed his stylus deep into Casca's forearm. Casca bleated in pain, withdrew his bloody dagger and scurried back.

Others stepped forward, baring their daggers.

Caesar jerked free from Cimber's grip. His toga was in such disarray that he tripped on it. He was bleeding profusely from the wound at his neck. The look on his face was of outrage and disbelief.

Even then, Lucius thought that disaster might be averted. Caesar was wounded, but on his feet. He had a weapon of sorts—his stylus. If he could hold the would-be assassins at bay long enough for the other senators to rush to his assistance, all might be well. If only Lucius had a weapon!

And where was Antonius?

Lucius looked back toward the entrance. Antonius had just appeared. He stood in the doorway with a puzzled look on his face, realizing from the sudden uproar that something was terribly wrong.

Lucius called to him. "Antonius! Hurry! Come quickly!"

But when Lucius looked back toward Caesar, he lost all hope. The assassins had converged on their victim. Caesar had dropped his stylus. He held up both arms, desperately trying to fend off his attackers. They stabbed him again and again. In all the confusion, a few of them appeared to have stabbed one another by accident.

Blood was everywhere. Caesar's toga was drenched with it, and the togas of the assassins were spotted with red. There was so much blood on the floor that Casca slipped and fell.

Amid the flashing daggers, Lucius caught a glimpse of Caesar. His face was barely recognizable, contorted with agony. He let out a scream that seemed to come from an animal, not a man. The sound chilled Lucius to the marrow.

Caesar broke free from the men surrounding him. He reeled backward, tripping on his toga and stamping his feet as he staggered past the chair of state, toward the wall, where a statue of the hall's founder stood in a place of honor. Caesar fell against the pedestal of Pompeius's statue. He slid downward, smearing the inscription with blood. He ended up slumped on the floor, his back against the pedestal, his legs outstretched.

His disarray was indecent; his undertunic was twisted and pulled aside so as to bare a patch of flesh where his thigh met his groin. Jerking like a spastic, flailing grotesquely, he seemed to be trying with one hand to cover his face with a fold of his toga, and with the other to cover his nakedness. Caesar was dying, yet he still sought to preserve his dignity.

Some of the assassins looked horrified at what they had done. Others looked exhilarated, even jubilant. Among the latter was Cassius, who was covered with blood. He strode toward Brutus, who stood at the edge of the group and had not a drop of blood on him. Nor was there any blood on the dagger in his hand.

"You, too, Brutus!" said Cassius.

Brutus looked numb. He seemed unable to move.

"You have to do it," insisted Cassius. "Each of us must strike a blow. Twenty-three brave men; twenty-three blows for freedom. Do it!"

Brutus stepped slowly toward the twitching, bloody figure at the base of Pompeius's statue. He seemed horrified by Caesar's appearance. He swallowed hard, clutched his dagger, and knelt beside him.

With blood spilling from his mouth and running over his chin, Caesar managed one last utterance. "You, too . . . my child?"

Brutus appeared emboldened by the words. He gritted his teeth, pulled back his dagger, and plunged it into the exposed place where Caesar's thigh met his groin. Caesar thrashed and convulsed. Blood bubbled from his lips. He stiffened, uttered a final grunt, and did not move again.

Lucius, watching from a distance, saw everything. He was transfixed with horror, oblivious to the stampede of senators rushing to the exit. He felt a hand on his shoulder and gave a start. It was Antonius. The man's face was ashen. His voice trembled.

"Come with me, Lucius. You're not safe here."

Lucius shook his head. He was rooted to the spot, unable to move. He had come to warn Caesar. He had failed.

Brutus walked slowly and calmly toward them. The feverish glimmer had left his eyes. His held his shoulders back, his chin up. He had the look of a man who had done a difficult thing and done it well.

"No one will harm you, Lucius Pinarius. You have nothing to fear. Neither do you, Antonius, as long as you don't raise your sword against us."

The chamber was almost empty. The only senators who remained were those too old to run.

Brutus shook his head in disgust. "This wasn't the reaction we anticipated. I meant to give a speech after it was done, to explain ourselves to the others. But they've all run off, like frightened geese."

"A speech?" said Antonius, incredulous.

Brutus reached into his toga and produced a scrap of parchment. His fingers smudged the document with blood. He frowned, displeased that he had marred it. "I was up all night working on it. Well, if not today, then I'll deliver it tomorrow, when the Senate resumes normal business."

"Normal business?" Antonius shook his head in disbelief.

"Yes. The normal business of the Senate of Roma, freed from the rule of a tyrant. The Republic has been restored. The people will rejoice. Five hundred years ago, my ancestor Brutus freed Roma from a wicked king. Today we followed his example—"

"Give your speech to somebody else!" shouted Lucius. He shoved Brutus aside and ran toward the exit, weeping.

Antonius caught up with him. "Come with me, Lucius. No matter what Brutus says, we're not safe. My house has strong doors, high walls . . ."

They were on the steps, descending to the public square. There was not a person in sight.

"But . . . his body," said Lucius. "What if they throw him in the Tiber, as they did the Gracchi?"

"That will not happen," said Antonius grimly. "I won't let such a thing happen. Caesar will have a proper funeral. On my honor as a Roman, I promise you that!"

When he was annoyed, Gaius Octavius's voice could become quite shrill. He needed oratorical training to overcome the defect, thought Lucius. In the days since Caesar's assassination and Gaius Octavius's return to Roma,

Lucius had grown very tired of hearing that shrill note in his cousin's voice.

"From this day forward, Antonius, you will address me as *Caesar,*" said Octavius, sounding even more shrill and annoyed than usual. "I don't ask it of you. I demand it!"

"Demand it? *You* make a demand of *me?*" Antonius leaned back in his chair and crossed his arms. He wrinkled his nose. "In the first place, young man, this is my house; here, *I* give the orders. I used to take orders from Caesar, because he was my commander, but Caesar is dead. He was the last man I'll ever take orders from. I certainly won't take orders from his niece's brat—and I won't call you by his name! As long as we're discussing titles, perhaps you should address me as Consul, as I'm the only one of the three of us here in this room who actually holds a magistracy."

"Only because Caesar saw fit to appoint you—as he saw fit to name me his son and heir!" snapped Octavius.

Antonius bristled. "This is my house, Octavius. You are my guest—"

Lucius rose to his feet. "Marcus! Cousin Gaius! Does this meeting have to be so contentious? The whole city is a viper's nest. If I want to be subjected to vicious arguments and hateful words, I have only to step outside the door. Can the three of us not speak to one another with some degree of decorum?"

"A good idea, cousin," said Octavius. "Decorum begins with addressing a man by his rightful name. Caesar's will made me his son by adoption, and I have taken his name. I am now Gaius Julius Caesar Octavianus."

"I understand," said Lucius. "But if Antonius happens to address you by your old name, why not allow it? Octavius is an honorable name, a patrician name, and he honors you and your ancestors when he speaks it. Antonius is our friend, cousin. We need him. He is the shield between us and the men who murdered our uncle. Are we not allies? Do we not share a common purpose? Are the three of us not close enough to call each other by first name, or family name, or whatever name we wish? Can you not simply drop the point for now, cousin Gaius? The question at hand isn't what we call each other, or yet another discussion of Caesar's will, but how to keep our heads!"

For the moment, Octavius was silenced, and so was Antonius. It still surprised Lucius that he could command their attention and argue with such self-confidence. Almost overnight, after the initial shock of Caesar's assassination had passed, Lucius had felt himself transformed. He was no longer a callow youth who hesitated to assert himself in conversation with his elders. He was one of Caesar's heirs, engaged in a desperate struggle for the future.

When it came down to it, Octavius was only a couple of years older and only slightly more experienced than himself. True, Octavius had seen a bit of battle, but not enough to prove himself a gifted strategist, much less a hero. His overbearing pride sprang from vanity, not accomplishments. In some ways, at least in Lucius's opinion, his cousin was quite deficient. To begin with, Octavius's oratorical skills were not at all impressive, no matter what Caesar had thought.

Antonius was a far more polished and persuasive speaker, as he had shown when he delivered Caesar's funeral oration before a huge crowd. The speech had been intensely dramatic yet remarkably subtle. Antonius never said a word against the killers, but by praising Caesar he moved his listeners to tears of grief and cries of outrage. Without directly saying so, he made the case that Roma had been defiled by the murder of a great leader, not liberated by the assassination of a tyrant. Antonius had also revealed one of the terms of Caesar's will: From his vast personal fortune, Caesar had decreed a generous disbursement of seventy-five Attic drachmas to every citizen living in Roma. This had done much to sway the crowd against Caesar's assassins.

But Antonius, too, had his faults, as Lucius had become all too aware in recent days. For one thing, he drank too much. In happier times, the man's appetite for debauchery had impressed and even awed Lucius. Now it struck him as foolhardy; the jeopardy in which they found themselves demanded clear thinking. Antonius also had a streak of pettiness. His refusal to address Octavius as Caesar was perhaps understandable, because it raised a sore point: Octavius was the chief benefactor of Caesar's will, while Antonius, to everyone's surprise, had been left out of the will entirely. Nonetheless, Antonius's repeated and deliberate baiting of Octavius served no one's purpose.

The will was the crux of the matter. In it, Caesar posthumously adopted Octavius as his son, and bequeathed to him half his estate. The other half he divided equally between his nephew Quintus Pedius, who was still away from the city, and his great-nephew, Lucius Pinarius. So much for the special debt that Caesar had owed to Lucius on account of his grandfather's sacrifice; Octavius had merited adoption, but not Lucius! Lucius had his own reasons to be resentful of Octavius, but he was determined to move past them.

The will had made no mention of Caesarion, Cleopatra's son. Immediately after the assassination, the Egyptian queen vacated Caesar's villa and sailed back to Alexandria.

Politically, it was left to Caesar's long-time subordinates, Antonius and Lepidus, to uphold his edicts and maintain the order he had imposed on the state, but without the benefit of his dictatorial powers. The cooperation of Caesar's heirs was vital to their cause. Each of the three cousins had inherited an enormous fortune, and each could exert a tremendous sentimental appeal to those who had supported Caesar and now mourned him. In return, the heirs needed the protection and experienced advice that Lepidus and, especially, Antonius could provide. Driven by necessity, this alliance had been uneasy from the start, rife with mutual suspicions and resentments, especially between Octavius and Antonius.

In the aftermath of Caesar's assassination, Roma had become a cauldron of intrigue. The conspirators against Caesar numbered at least sixty men; some had taken part in the actual killing while others had only lent support. Should those men be declared criminals and brought to trial, or applauded as saviors of the Republic? Three days after the Ides of Martius, the Senate voted an amnesty for the assassins, drafted in careful language that neither acknowledged their guilt nor praised their patriotism.

Despite the Senate's amnesty, fierce partisans on both sides had resorted to violence. An innocent tribune named Cinna, unlucky enough to be mistaken for one of the conspirators, had literally been torn apart by an angry mob; pieces of his body were scattered across the Forum. After gangs threatened to burn down the houses of Cassius and Brutus, both men left Roma to prematurely claim the provincial governorships that Caesar had scheduled for them.

This raised a further question: Were Caesar's appointments still valid? Brutus and Cassius argued that Caesar was a tyrant and usurper. If that were so, how could any of his decrees be legally valid, including their own provincial appointments?

The legitimacy of every act by every magistrate was now routinely called into question by partisans of one side or the other. Who possessed legal authority, and by what right? Those who had hoped that Caesar's death would result in a quick and harmonious restoration of senatorial power were bitterly disappointed. Roma was poised on a sword's edge, ready to fall into chaos. After so many years of death and destruction, the outbreak of another civil war was an almost unbearable prospect, yet increasingly it seemed inevitable.

The future was fraught with uncertainty. The future was what Lucius and his cousin had come to the house of Antonius to discuss. Yet the discussion seemed to circle back endlessly to recriminations about things already past.

It was Octavius who broke the strained silence. "The conspirators should have been dealt with at once, immediately following the murder. You, Antonius, as consul, had the power to arrest them. You could have invoked the Ultimate Decree—"

"There were no senators left in the chamber to vote on such a proposal!"

"Even so, if, instead of fleeing to your house, you had taken immediate action against the men who killed my father—"

"If you think it would have been as easy as that, young man, then you're even more naive than I thought, and you are certainly *not* Caesar's son!"

"Enough!" said Lucius. "You both need to stop this squabbling and return to the matter at hand. Namely, the need to deal with Cassius and Brutus. It may or may not be possible to convince the Senate to declare that Caesar's murder was a criminal act. Most of the senators seem inclined to mimic Cicero. They'll avoid taking sides as long as possible, until they see how things fall out. For now, the Senate's amnesty protects the assassins.

"However, it seems to me that the premature seizures by Cassius and Brutus of their provinces were unquestionably illegal. Those actions could be construed as hostile acts against the state, and thus lay them open to military action by you, Antonius, acting as consul."

"If any military action is taken, Caesar must take part as well," said Octavius, adopting his great-uncle's habit of referring to himself in the third person—to Antonius's disgust, as evidenced by the gritting of his teeth. "It's Caesar's fortune that can raise the troops. It's Caesar's name to which his veterans will swear loyalty. And if I am to command troops in the field, I must be given full consular authority."

"Impossible!" said Antonius. "You're far too young."

"By what reckoning? My great-uncle appointed men to magistracies who were under the required age. Thus there is legal precedent—"

"An important point, cousin," said Lucius. "We must be seen to follow the law. Any military action must be perceived as just and necessary. There must be no grounds for anyone to assert that we have initiated"—he hesitated even to say the words—"that we have initiated a civil war for personal gain or private revenge. We must win the support of the Senate, the legions, and the people. But how? It's the sort of challenge at which Uncle Gaius excelled so brilliantly."

Lucius took a deep breath. He looked from one man to the other. He had no illusions that he could assume Caesar's mantle of leadership, but increasingly it seemed to him that neither Antonius nor Octavius was fit to do so either, no matter that one had been Caesar's right-hand man and the other was his adopted son. They were barely able to keep peace between themselves.

As if to prove him right, both men began to speak at the same time. Neither would yield. Instead they raised their voices. Lucius clapped his hands over his ears.

"Marcus! Cousin Gaius! Be quiet and listen to what I have to say. You're both ambitious men. You both have a craving to rule the state. Good for you! The gods admire ambition, especially in a Roman. But my ambition—my only ambition—is to avenge Caesar's death. All the assassins must be declared outlaws. They must be hunted down. They must be killed. Brutus and Cassius are our foremost concern. I'm eager to take up arms against them. Put a sword in my hand, and I'll readily serve under either of you—you, Gaius, or you, Marcus, I don't care which! But I don't believe either of you can see the task to completion without the other. I beg of you, stop this bickering and bend your wills to the common purpose!"

He stared at Antonius, who finally shrugged and nodded.

He stared at Octavius. His cousin raised an eyebrow. "You're right, of course. Thank you, cousin Lucius. Such a clear-sighted sense of purpose is just what we need to keep us on course. Well, Antonius? Shall we get back to business?"

The discussion that followed was fruitful. Lucius was glad to have spoken out. But as he looked from Octavius to Antonius, he knew his words had not been entirely truthful. He had said he didn't care which man he served under, but in his heart, there was no question which of them he preferred: the hot-blooded, plain-spoken, pleasure-loving, sometimes crude Antonius. Partly this was because of the affection the man had shown him. Partly it was because his cousin Gaius was so vain and cold-blooded. Antonius he could serve with enthusiasm. Octavius he would serve if he must.

Lucius prayed to the gods he would never be forced to choose between them.

1 B.C.

Lucius Pinarius dreamed an old, recurring dream. It was a nightmare he had first experienced on the Ides of Martius long ago, when he was young.

In the dream he was both participant and observer, aware he was dreaming and yet unable to stop the dream. Caesar had died. A great multitude had gathered to hear the reading of his will. A Vestal virgin produced a scroll. Marcus Antonius unrolled the document and proceeded to read. Though Lucius stood at the front of the crowd, he could not hear the names being read. He heard only the roar of the crowd in his ears, like the crashing of waves. He wanted to tell the others to be quiet, but he could not open his mouth to speak. He could not move at all. Antonius continued to read, but Lucius could not hear, speak, or move.

With a start and a shiver, he woke from the dream. He was trembling and covered with sweat. The dream was like an old enemy, still hounding him after all these years, taunting him with memories of his youth and of the bright promises that had been shattered by Caesar's death. But the dream had been visiting him for so many years it had almost become an old friend. Where else but in the dream could he see again the face of Antonius, alive and in his prime?

Lucius wiped the sleep from his eyes. Slowly, he came to his senses. The dream faded.

Against all odds, Lucius Pinarius had become an old man. He was sixty.

So many men of his generation had died in the civil wars that followed Caesar's death. If they survived the wars, accident or illness had eventually taken them off to Hades. But Lucius was still alive.

He rose from his bed, relieved himself in the chamber pot, and slipped into a tunic. Later he would put on his senatorial toga, for this was an important day, but for now a tunic would do.

The cook prepared for him a simple breakfast of farina cooked with a little milk and water and sweetened with a dab of honey. Lucius still had strong teeth, but his digestion was not what it used to be. Nowadays, the blander the food, the better. Chewing a mouthful of mush, he thought back to the days of endless feasting in Alexandria. Wines from Greece, dates from Parthia, crocodile eggs from the Nile; serving girls from Nubia, dancers from Ethiopia, courtesans from Antioch! Whatever else people said about Antonius and Cleopatra, no one could deny that those two had known how to mount a banquet—especially in their final months and days, as the end drew near for them.

It was the dream's fault, that he should be thinking of Antonius. Remembering made Lucius sad. The mush turned bitter in his mouth.

But today was not about the past. Today was about the future. His grandson was coming.

Even as he thought about the boy, the door slave announced that young Lucius Pinarius had just arrived and was waiting in the vestibule.

"Already?" said Lucius. "He's early. Ah, well, he can spend a few minutes contemplating the effigies of his ancestors while I force a bit more of this mush down my gullet. Meanwhile, order the bearers to bring a litter around to the front door."

"Which litter, master?"

"Oh, the fancy one, I should think, with the yellow curtains and embroidered pillows and all those brass baubles hanging off it. Today is a special day!"

"Once upon a time—before this blasted stiffness in my knees—I'd have walked to the Baths of Agrippa, no matter that they're all the way out on the Field of Mars. But here we are, two Roman males, taking a litter through the streets. I blush to think of what our ancestors would have thought of such an indulgence!" Lucius smiled at his grandson, who sat beside him and seemed to be enjoying the ride. The boy leaned forward and turned his head this way and that, peering at the passing sights with the insatiable curiosity of a ten-year-old. Ideally, Lucius would have waited until his grandson's toga day for this occasion, but that was years away. Lucius might not live to see it. Better to tend to his duty now, while he still had his wits and a pulse.

"Why do they call this the Field of Mars, Grandfather?"

"Let me think. Very, very long ago, I believe it must have been called the Field of Mavors, because that was the ancient name for Mars. I suppose someone built an altar to the god, so naturally they named the whole area for Mars—"

"Yes, but why is it called a *field*? There's no field here. All I can see are streets and buildings."

"Ah, I see what you mean. Yes, it's all built up now. But it wasn't always so. I can remember a time when the Field of Mars, or at least a large portion of it, was still open to the sky, a place for soldiers to drill and for large groups to assemble. Now the city's spread outward to fill up every patch of land between the ancient walls and the Tiber. I see we're passing by Pompeius's theater now. I was about your age when that opened."

Lucius's eyes followed the steps leading to the main portico. He never passed the theater without remembering what he had witnessed there, but he was not in a mood to speak of it and was grateful that the boy did not question him about it. "Up ahead is the Pantheon, of course, which was built by the emperor's right-hand man, Marcus Agrippa. And near the Pantheon are the baths, which Agrippa built at the same time. When the baths opened, twenty years ago, it was quite an event, because there had never been anything like them in Roma before. Once the baths were open, all sorts of shops and arcades were built in the vicinity."

The boy furrowed his brow. "If the Baths of Agrippa were the first baths built in Roma, did no one ever bathe before that?"

Lucius smiled. At least the boy was curious about the past. So many people nowadays seemed oblivious of all that had come before, as if Roma had always been at peace and ruled by an emperor—as if there had never been a republic, or a series of civil wars, or a man named Antonius.

There he went, thinking of Antonius again . . .

"The Baths of Agrippa weren't the first baths in Roma, but they were much bigger and much more beautiful than any of the previous baths. They were also the first to be open to everyone and free of charge—a gift from the emperor to the people—which made them very popular. Half the reason for going to the baths is to see and be seen, and to mingle outside one's class. Economic and social disparities between citizens tend to dissolve when everyone is naked and wet."

Young Lucius laughed. "You say the funniest things, Grandfather."

"I try. Speaking of the baths, here we are."

Lucius enjoyed the morning immensely. Time spent with his grandson was always precious, and the diversions offered by the baths were among the greatest pleasures of city life. The day began with a shave from his most trusted slave. Young Lucius watched the procedure with great interest. His father wore a beard these days, so the boy was not used to seeing the skillful application of a sharp blade to a man's face.

After the shave, they went outside to the open-air pool—a man-made lake, some called it, on account of its size—where the two of them swam a few laps side by side. The boy's stroke was choppy, but his breathing technique was good. Wherever life might take him, young Lucius would surely have occasion to travel by ship, and it would behoove him to know how to swim. How many of Antonius's soldiers had drowned at the decisive naval battle at Actium, not because their armor pulled them under, but because they simply did not know how to swim?

Again, he found himself thinking of Antonius . . .

A gymnasiarch organized a series of competitions on the long racing track beside the pool. Lucius encouraged his grandson to take part. He was delighted to see the boy win his first two heats. Young Lucius was beaten in the third race, but only by a nose. His grandson was a strong runner.

Another gymnasiarch organized a series of wrestling matches. The competitors were all older and bigger than young Lucius, who sat with his grandfather among the spectators. The wrestlers competed in Greek fashion, naked and with their bodies oiled. Such a diversion, like being carried in a litter, struck Lucius as slightly decadent. What would his ancestors think? True Romans preferred to watch gladiators fight to the death.

Lucius recalled how the emperor, in his heated propaganda war against Antonius and Cleopatra, had railed against the dangerous influx of foreign vices, saying the Greek-blooded queen had corrupted Antonius with the appetites of the luxurious East. Yet, once he triumphed over his rivals, the emperor had made Roma a more cosmopolitan city than ever before. He allowed Agrippa to build the baths. He imported the worship of exotic gods. He catered at every turn to the citizens' appetite for entertainment and pleasure.

Finished with their morning exercise, Lucius and the boy bathed. They began by scraping the sweat from their bodies, using strigils. They did so in the shadow of the famous statue by Lysippus which depicted a naked athlete doing exactly the same thing, bending back one muscular arm to run his strigil over the other arm, which was extended before him. Agrippa had installed the statue at the baths with great fanfare. Lysippus had been the court sculptor to Alexander the Great. Though many copies had been made of the *Apoxyomenos,* as *The Scraper* was known in Greek, the original bronze was of incalculable value. The statue was yet another lavish gift from the emperor to the people of Roma.

Lucius and the boy went back and forth between pools of varying temperature. The coolest was quite bracing after their exercise. The hottest was obscured by a curtain of steam and required a gradual process of immersion. Even the floors were heated, by water piped beneath the tiles. The walls were of marble, and even in the wettest areas Agrippa's decorators had found means to adorn them with paintings, infusing dyes into beeswax, then fixing and hardening the images with heat. The paintings depicted gods, goddesses, and heroes. Scenes of legend appeared to hover in the mist.

After bathing, they wrapped themselves in linen cloths and took a light meal in an adjoining arcade. The boy ate pieces of bread slathered with garum. Lucius abstained from the spicy garum and ate fig-paste instead.

They discussed the boy's studies. He was currently reading *The Aeneid* by the late Virgil, who had been the emperor's favorite poet. When the emperor asked Virgil to create a Roman epic to match *The Iliad* and *The Odyssey* of the Greeks, *The Aeneid* was the result. The long poem about the adventures of Aeneas celebrated the Trojan warrior as the son of Venus and the founder of the Roman race. Aeneas, it turned out, was the ancestor not only of the emperor and his uncle, the Divine Julius, but also of Romulus and Remus. If Lucius had doubts about the historical validity of *The Aeneid,* he did not express them to the boy. There was no denying that Virgil had created a work of art that greatly pleased the emperor.

After eating, they rested. A few old friends and colleagues stopped to say hello, and Lucius was delighted to introduce his grandson. The talk turned to foreign imports, the cost of slaves, the advantages and disadvantages of transport by land or by sea, and who had been awarded contracts for various construction projects in the city. "As you can see, my boy," remarked Lucius, "these days, more business is done here in the baths than in the Forum."

In the old days, of course, all the talk would have been about politics and war. Nowadays, war was an activity on the distant frontier that might or might not affect trade, and politics—true politics, as their forefathers had understood the word, with everyone freely arguing and shouting to make themselves heard—no longer existed. One might speculate about intrigues within the imperial family, or conjecture about the relative influence wielded by members of the emperor's immediate circle—but only in whispers.

Exercised, bathed, and fed, the two retired to the dressing room. Young Lucius slipped into the tunic he had worn earlier, but his grandfather, assisted by the slave who had shaved him, put on his toga. While the boy watched, he pontificated on the proper wearing of the toga.

"A man isn't simply wrapped in his toga," he explained. "He carries it as he carries himself, with a show of dignity and pride. Shoulders back head up. And the drapes should fall just so. Too few folds, and you look a if someone threw a sheet over you. Too many folds, and you look as you're carrying a bundle of laundry to the fuller."

The boy's laughter delighted Lucius. It meant that his grandson was paying attention. He was watching, listening, learning.

The slave handed his master a shiny trinket on a golden chain. Lucius slipped the necklace over his head and tucked it beneath his toga.

"What's that, Grandfather? An amulet of some sort?"

"Not just any amulet, my boy. It's very old, and very important, and today is the very last day I shall ever wear it. But we'll talk of it later. For now, I want to show you a bit of the city. There are some places I should like you to see through my eyes."

"Shall I summon the litter?" asked the slave.

"Actually, I think not. The hot plunge has so loosened my knees that I think I might be up for a bit of walking. But you must be patient, young Lucius, and not run ahead of me."

"I shall stay by your side, Grandfather."

Lucius nodded. How polite the boy was, always respectful and well-mannered. He was studious, as well, and very clean and neat. The boy was a product of his times. The world had become a much more orderly, peaceful, settled place than it was in the old days of the civil wars. His ancestors would be proud of young Lucius. They would be proud of the harmonious world that their descendents, through much bloodshed and toil, had finally achieved.

As they headed out from the baths, a flash of excitement crossed young Lucius's face, then he bit his lower lip nervously.

"What is it, my boy?"

"I was thinking, Grandfather, as long as we're taking a walk, and we're so close—but father says it's something you don't like to talk about. Only, he says you were actually there, when it happened . . ."

"Ah, yes. I think I know what you're trying to say. Yes, that will be our first stop. But I have to warn you, there's nothing to see."

"Nothing?"

"As you shall observe."

They strolled to the Theater of Pompeius. Lucius took the steps slowly, but not on account of his knees. As they reached the top, he could feel his heart pounding in his chest. His skin prickled and his breath grew short. Even after all these years, he felt a sense of dread as they drew near to the spot.

They came to a brick wall. "It was here," he said. "This is the place where the Divine Julius, your great-great-granduncle, met the end of his mortal life."

The boy frowned. "I thought it happened in some sort of assembly hall, at the foot of Pompeius's statue."

"Yes. The entrance to the hall was here, and the place where Caesar fell was perhaps fifty paces from this spot. But the hall has been sealed. Some years ago the emperor decreed—or rather, the Senate voted, at the emperor's behest—that this place should be declared an accursed site, never to be seen or set foot upon. The statue of Pompeius was removed and placed elsewhere in the theater complex. The entrance to the hall was walled up, like a tomb. The Ides of Martius was declared a day of infamy, and it was forbidden that the Senate should ever again meet on that date. As I told you, there's nothing to see."

"But it's true, Grandfather, that you were here? That you saw it happen?"

"Yes. I saw the assassins strike. I saw Caesar fall. I heard his final words to the infamous Brutus. Antonius was here, too, though he arrived after I did. They purposely detained him outside, partly to prevent him from shielding Caesar, but also, I think, because they didn't wish to kill him. The assassins did possess a certain sense of honor. They truly believed that what they were doing was for the good of Roma."

"But how can that be? They were bloodthirsty killers."

"Yes, they were that, as well."

The boy frowned. "And Antonius; I thought he was—"

"But let us speak no more of this," said Lucius. "There's so much more I want to show you."

They walked toward the older parts of the city. In the Forum Boarium, Lucius showed the boy the Ara Maxima, and informed him of the role once played by the Pinarii in maintaining the cult of Hercules. Long ago, that religious role had been abandoned by the family, but it marked the first appearance of the Pinarii in history, and so was never to be forgotten. They had shared the duty with another family, but the Potitii were long extinct, as were a number of the original patrician families, whose name now existed only in annals and inscriptions.

CAESAR'S HEIR   541

They ascended the Palatine, walking slowly up the ancient Stairs of Cacus, which took them by a recess in the stone reputed to have been the very cave where the monster once dwelled. They paused beneath the shade of the fig tree said to be a descendent of the legendary ruminalis, beneath which Acca Larentia had suckled the infants Romulus and Remus. They visited the Hut of Romulus, which even the boy could see was too new to be the actual hut where the founder had lived; the civic landmark had been rebuilt many times over the centuries.

They descended to the Forum, which in recent years had become even more crowded with monuments and temples.

"Once upon a time, all of this was a lake, or so they say," remarked Lucius. "Hard to believe, isn't it? The first temples were made of wood."

"Everything I can see is made of marble," said the boy.

Lucius nodded. "The emperor's proud boast: 'I found Roma a city of bricks, but I shall leave it a city of marble.' During his reign, a great many buildings have been restored, refurbished, even rebuilt from the foundations up. The quaint shrines have been dusted, the ancient glories have been burnished; everything has been made bigger and more beautiful than before. The emperor has given us peace and prosperity. The emperor has made Roma the most resplendent of all the cities that ever existed, the undisputed center of the world."

They came to a statue of the emperor, one of many in the city. This one depicted him as a young warrior, handsome and virile and armed for battle. The inscription referred to his great victory at Philippi, in Macedonia, when he was only twenty-one years old: "I sent into exile the murderers of my father, and when they made war on the Republic, I defeated them in battle." It seemed to Lucius that the statue flattered his cousin. Octavius had never been quite that handsome, and he certainly had not been that muscular and broad-shouldered.

The boy gazed up at the statue with a less critical eye. "Father tells me that you were at Philippi, too, Grandfather, when the assassins Brutus and Cassius were brought to justice. He says you fought right alongside the emperor."

Lucius raised an eyebrow. "Not exactly." Octavius, as he recalled, had been sick in bed for most of the battle, except for the time he spent hiding in a marsh after his camp was overrun by Brutus. "I myself inflicted no bloodshed at Philippi. I was in charge of supply lines for the legions led by Marcus Antonius."

"Antonius?" The boy frowned. "But he was the emperor's enemy, wasn't he? He became the willing slave of the Egyptian whore!"

Lucius winced. "That happened later, much later. At Philippi, Octavius and Antonius—"

"Octavius?"

"I misspoke. Octavius was the name that the emperor received at birth. Later, of course, he was adopted by the Divine Julius, and was called Caesar from that time forward. Later he took the majestic title of Augustus, and so we call him Caesar Augustus. But I digress. As I was saying, at Philippi, the emperor and Marcus Antonius were allies. They fought together to avenge the Divine Julius. Cassius and Brutus were defeated, and they killed themselves. But Philippi was only the beginning. Some sixty senators took part in the conspiracy against Caesar; within a few years, every one of them was dead. Some died by shipwreck, some in battle; some took their own lives, using the same dagger with which they had stabbed Caesar. Even some who had not plotted against Caesar were dead, like Cicero; he made an enemy of Antonius, and he lost his head and his hands for it."

"His hands?"

"Cicero made vile speeches against Antonius, so when Antonius ordered him killed, he commanded that Cicero's hands should be cut off along with his head, for having written such offensive words. There is no denying that Antonius had a vindictive nature."

"Was that why the emperor killed Antonius, because he murdered Cicero?"

"No." Lucius sighed. The truth was so very complicated, especially when large parts of it were not to be spoken aloud. "The two of them remained friends—well, allies—for a number of years. Then Antonius threw in his lot with Cleopatra, and some thought that Antonius and Cleopatra would rule Egypt and the East, and the emperor would rule Roma and the West. But—so philosophers tell us—just as the heavens are one under the rule of Jupiter, so the earth naturally desires to be united under one emperor. Antonius's dreams came to ruin."

"Because of the Egyptian whore?"

Again Lucius winced. "Come with me, young man. There's something else I want you to see."

They made their way to the Julian Forum. Left unfinished by Caesar, the arcades for courtrooms and offices had been completed by the emperor. Still dominating the open square was the magnificent statue of Caesar sitting atop a charger. How much more at home in his armor the Divine Julius looked than did his successor, thought Lucius.

The square was crowded with men going to and fro, talking to one another and carrying documents. Under the emperor, the legal codes had grown more complicated than ever, and lawyers were kept even busier than they had been under the Republic, settling private disputes, adjudicating bankruptcies, and negotiating contracts.

Lucius and the boy walked past the splashing fountain and into the Temple of Venus. Lucius still considered it the most beautiful interior in all of Roma, unsurpassed even by the emperor's most lavish projects. Here were the famous paintings of Ajax and Medea by Timomachus; here were the cabinets containing the fabulous jewels and gemstones that Caesar had collected in his travels.

Holding the boy's hand, Lucius strode before the two statues at the far end of the sanctuary. The Venus of Arcesilaus remained unsurpassed. And beside the Venus, despite the misfortunes that had befallen the flesh-and-blood original, stood the gilded statue of Queen Cleopatra, last of the long line of the Ptolemies who had ruled Egypt since the time of Alexander the Great. Some had thought that the emperor would remove the statue, but here it remained, where Julius Caesar himself had installed it.

"Despite what you may have heard, she was not a whore," said Lucius quietly. "As far as I know, she slept with only two men in her entire life: the Divine Julius and Marcus Antonius. To both she gave children. The emperor in his wisdom saw fit to execute Caesarion, but he spared her children by Antonius."

"But everyone says that she—"

"What everyone says is not always the truth. It served the emperor's purposes to call her a whore and a seducer, but she was far more than that. She considered herself a goddess. For better or for worse, she behaved like one."

The boy frowned. "And when she lured Antonius to join her, you sided with the emperor to fight against them?"

"No. Not in the beginning. At the start of the war between them, I fought for Antonius."

"For Antonius? *With* Cleopatra? *Against* the emperor?" The boy was incredulous.

"Antonius was my friend. He was my protector when I was very young, in the perilous days after Caesar was murdered. He had always been loyal to Caesar; I felt obliged to be loyal to him. So I served under him at Philippi, and I remained in his service afterward, even when another civil war broke out and the emperor declared him the enemy of Roma. Antonius posted me to the city of Cyrene, to watch his west flank. Do you know where Cyrene is?"

The boy frowned. "Not exactly."

"It's on the Libyan coast, west of Alexandria, which was Cleopatra's capital. If she and Antonius had won, my boy, Alexandria—not Roma—would have become the capital of the world. Roma might have become nothing more than a provincial backwater."

"Impossible!"

"Yes, you're right. I once heard the Divine Julius himself declare that the gods chose Roma to rule the world; how could I forget? But back in those heady days, when I was young and Antonius and Cleopatra were riding the serpent's tail, anything seemed possible. Anything!" He sighed. "At any event, there I was in Cyrene. I was to be Antonius's watchdog should his enemies attempt to sail toward Egypt hugging the Libyan coastline. In the meantime, while I watched and waited and drilled my soldiers, I minted coins for Antonius to pay his debts. War is expensive! That reminds me, I have a silver denarius for you, one of the coins I minted for Antonius." Lucius reached into his toga. "They're rather rare these days. Many of them were melted down and recast with the image of the emperor."

The boy accepted the heavy coin and gazed at it with great interest. "I recognize Victory, bare-breasted in profile with her wings behind her and carrying a wreath . . . but there's something else I can't make out . . ."

"A palm frond," says Lucius. "Palms grow wild along the Nile."

The boy turned the coin over. "But who is this fellow, with the flowing beard?"

"None other than the king of gods, Jupiter."

"But he has ram's horns!"

"That's because this is Jupiter Ammon, his Egyptian manifestation, who is called Zeus Ammon by the Alexandrians, who speak Greek. Alexander the Great worshiped Zeus Ammon. So did his general Ptolemy, who inherited Egypt. It was Ptolemy who founded the dynasty that ruled Egypt for almost three hundred years, until the royal house ended with Cleopatra."

"And . . . she was not a whore?" The boy remained dubious.

"Her enemies in Roma alleged that she was, while she lived. Everyone seems to believe so now, long after she's dead. But Caesar didn't think so. Nor did Antonius. Cleopatra considered herself the manifestation of the goddess Isis. A woman tends to take procreation rather seriously when she thinks that carnal union might result in a god or goddess springing out of her womb!"

"Whatever she was, she lost everything, didn't she, and she took down Antonius along with her?"

Lucius nodded. "Antonius and Cleopatra gathered a great navy and sailed off to Greece, to meet the Emperor in battle. I stayed behind in Cyrene, and waited for news. The sea battle took place at Actium. The navy of the emperor, under the command of Marcus Agrippa, destroyed the navy of Antonius and Cleopatra. It was all over then, and everyone knew it. Antonius sent me a desperate message, saying he was coming to collect my troops."

"And then what happened?"

Lucius's face grew dark. "I killed the messengers. I sent word to Antonius that he would not be welcome in Cyrene. I finally came to my senses, you see. I saw that the gods had sided with the emperor, that they had sided with him all along, and only an ungodly man would continue to stand against him."

The boy nodded gravely, as at the outcome of a moral tale, satisfied that his grandfather had at last seen reason. But the look on Lucius's face was grim.

"Antonius and Cleopatra retreated to Alexandria, to await the end.

Some say they spent those final months indulging in every possible vice, squeezing life for the last vestiges of pleasure. Perhaps that tale is only another slander against them, but to me it has the ring of truth. How those two loved to drink and carouse! Cleopatra also set about testing various poisons on her slaves, to determine which caused the least painful death. When the emperor and his legions arrived in Egypt, and all hope was gone, Antonius fell on his sword. But Cleopatra . . ."

"Yes, Grandfather? What happened to Cleopatra?" The boy studied his grandfather's face. His eyes grew wide. "Were you there, Grandfather? Were you there in Alexandria when . . . ?"

"Yes, I was there. Octavius—the emperor—insisted that I accompany him. He was determined to take Cleopatra alive. He wanted to bring her back to Roma and parade her in his triumph. But the queen had other plans."

How much should he tell the boy? Certainly not all of the story. He had never told that to anyone . . .

Antonius was dead. Cleopatra's army had vanished, like smoke on the wind. Occupied by Octavius's forces, the city of Alexandria held its breath. The queen remained in the royal palace, holed up with two handmaidens in a sealed chamber that could be entered only by climbing a rope through a trapdoor from below. She could not flee, but nor could she be taken by force.

On a terrace of the palace with a splendid view of the harbor and the famous lighthouse, Lucius was summoned before Octavius. The commander dispensed with greetings and got straight to the point.

"You have a long association with the queen. She knows you, cousin. She trusts you."

"Not anymore. I betrayed her."

"Even so, you stand a better chance of coaxing her out of her lair than I do. I want Cleopatra alive, not dead. Go to her. Talk about Antonius and the good old days, and what might have been. Flatter her. Cajole her. When you've regained her trust, say whatever you have to say to convince her to surrender to me. Assure her that I intend to treat her with all the re

spect due to her rank and lineage. She will appear in my triumphal procession, but she will not be mistreated."

"Is that the truth?"

Octavius laughed. "Of course not. I intend to see her completely broken and humiliated before she dies. Roma demands nothing less than the
complete destruction of the Egyptian whore. She'll be raped and beaten,
kept in chains, starved, and tortured. When people see her crawling naked
behind my chariot, they'll wonder how such a wretched hag ever seduced
a man like Antonius. Then she'll be strangled in the Tullianum, but not before she sees the boy Caesarion killed before her eyes."

"He's only fourteen," said Lucius.

"And he shall never be fifteen."

Lucius had no choice. He agreed to act as Octavius's emissary.

Through the trapdoor, in whispers, he negotiated with the queen's
handmaidens, Charmion and Iras. Cleopatra agreed to see him the following day, but only if he arrived alone, with no other Roman in sight.

The next day, Lucius arrived at the appointed time. He brought a gift
for the queen. She had expressed a craving for figs. The basket that Lucius
lifted up through the opening was full of plump, ripe figs nestled atop a
bed of fig leaves. Iras accepted the basket. A little later, Charmion lowered
a rope, and Lucius was allowed to climb up.

He had expected to find the three women cowering in a squalid little
room, but the chamber was magnificent. Small openings high in the walls
admitted beams of sunlight. The floor was black marble. The columns
were red granite. The walls were painted in dazzling colors. Cleopatra sat
on a magnificent throne in the shape of a vulture with its wings spread, or-
namented with gold, silver, and lapis. She wore a cobra-headed diadem
and a robe encrusted with jewels. Iras sat at her feet with the basket of figs.

"Will you not change your mind, Your Majesty?" said Lucius.

"Too late for that," said Cleopatra. In one hand she held a fig. On her
wrist were two puncture marks—the bite of the asp, which Lucius himself
had obtained from one of the queen's agents and hidden beneath the fig
leaves. "Thank you, Lucius Pinarius. When I see Antonius in Elysium, I
will tell him of the great favor you did me."

Her eyelids fluttered and closed. Her head fell to one side. The fig
dropped from her hand.

Lucius's eyes filled with tears. "Was this a fitting end? Was this worthy of your mistress?" he demanded of the handmaidens.

Iras was silent. She had already joined her mistress in death. Charmion, beginning to stagger and sway, was using her final moments to straighten the queen's crown, so that in death her appearance would be perfect. "It was very worthy," she whispered, "as befits the last of all the Pharaohs."

Lucius wept, but only briefly. He braced himself to deliver the bad news to Octavius. . . .

❈

To his grandson, Lucius merely said, "The queen submitted to the bite of an asp. The emperor wanted her for his triumph, but she cheated him of that victory, at least."

"But even so, they say it was the greatest triumph of all time," said the boy.

"So it was. A very great triumph, indeed. On that day, my cousin Gaius, who had been born Octavius but had become Caesar, took the name Augustus, to celebrate his elevation to divinity. The whole world was made to see that the emperor was worthy of worship—not just a king, but a god on earth."

Lucius gazed at the statue of Cleopatra for a long moment, then reached for the boy's hand and led him away.

As they were leaving the Temple of Venus, there was a stir of excitement in the square.

"The emperor! The emperor!" men shouted.

A litter appeared, splendidly appointed with purple and gold and surrounded by a veritable army of attendants. Onlookers fell back in awe. Within the litter, Augustus could clearly be seen, reclining on purple cushions. To Lucius, despite the jowls and wrinkles and all the other ravages of age, Octavius still looked like the callow boy who boldly laid claim to Caesar's legacy, rode the whirlwind to greatness, annihilated every rival, and never looked back.

The ways of the gods were capricious and impossible to predict, thought Lucius, and their methods were often maddeningly obscure; and yet, surely, steadily, the story of mankind progressed. After many convul sions, the world had at last attained a state of stability and peace, perhaps even of perfection: one empire, ever expanding, to be ruled by one emperor, from one city, Roma.

Men like Romulus or Alexander or Caesar could seemingly arise from nowhere and change everything. If men could become gods, anything was possible. Might the older gods, like men, someday perish altogether? Who could say what might be occurring at that very moment somewhere else in the world—perhaps in some obscure backwater at the empire's edge—where the birth of a certain man or movement might alter the world's destiny once again? Perhaps Jupiter himself might be thrown down, to be replaced by another king of heaven! Not only one empire and one emperor, but one god: Might such a world not represent an even greater state of perfection?

Lucius banished the blasphemous thought, and concentrated instead on the earthly splendor of the receding retinue of Caesar Augustus, emperor of Roma, surely the greatest of all men who had ever lived or ever would live on earth.

But Lucius had almost forgotten the most important thing! He reached inside his toga and removed the necklace he was wearing.

"This is for you, my boy. I should have liked to wait until your toga day to present it to you, but I think you're ready for it."

"What is it, Grandfather?" The boy gazed at the amulet in his hand.

"Its origin is uncertain. I don't even know the name of the god it represents. But when I received it, I was told that this talisman is older than Roma itself. It's been handed down in our family for many generations, since before the days of Romulus."

Young Lucius peered at the object curiously, unable to discern what it was meant to represent. After so many years and so many wearers, the details of the winged phallus had worn away. In outline, the shape appeared to be little more than a simple cross—not dissimilar, the boy thought, to the crucifixes upon which the Romans executed criminals.

"As it was handed down to me," said his grandfather, "so I now hand it down to you, my namesake. You must vow to do the same thing yourself, in a future generation."

The boy gazed at the pendant, then solemnly placed the necklace over his head.

AUTHOR'S NOTE

The origins and early development of Rome represent one of the most exciting areas of historical study in the world today. Through most of the twentieth century, it was fashionable to dismiss the foundation accounts of the ancient sources as fabrications, but recent archaeological discoveries have given fresh credence to stories once dismissed as legends. Thus the epigram from Alexandre Grandazzi's *The Foundation of Rome: Myth and History* that opens this book: "Legend is historical, just as history is legendary."

I began my research for *Roma* by reading and rereading T. J. Cornell's *The Beginnings of Rome: Italy and Rome from the Bronze Age to the Punic Wars (c. 1000 to 264 B.C.)* (Routledge, 1995). If you want to know the specific sources for this period, and to understand the state of current Roman studies, read Cornell's book.

In its opening pages, I was struck by the author's comment that "all history contains an element of fiction," and his observation that ancient historians, as opposed to their modern counterparts, openly practiced certain techniques in common with modern historical novelists. In the historical novel, Cornell notes, "and in pre-modern historiography . . . writers are permitted to reconstruct, from their own imaginations, the feelings, aspirations and motives of persons and groups, to conjure up plausible scenes—on the battlefield, on the streets, or in the bedroom—and even to put their own words into the mouths of persons in the drama. These conventions were accepted without question in antiquity, when history was at least in part a rhetorical exercise."

R. M. Ogilvie (as quoted by Betty Radice in her introduction to *Livy: The War with Hannibal*) explicitly compares the great Roman historian to a writer of fiction: "Like a novelist," Livy "subordinated historical precision to the demands of character and plot. He indulged freely in invention and imagination in order to present a living picture." Even so, as Radice wryly notes, Livy "never falls into the error of trying to create atmosphere by lifting pages from Baedeker—George Eliot and Lord Lytton earnestly did their best with Florence and Pompeii, but the dead stones never speak. Instead, he keeps descriptions to a minimum and recreates the spirit of Rome by entering into the feelings of the people of the time . . ."

Titus Livius, known in English as Livy, lived in the reign of Augustus. His monumental history, *Ab Urbe Condita* (From the Founding of the City), is our principal source for the first several hundred years of Roman history, from its mythic origins to the beginnings of its Mediterranean empire. For sheer pleasure and escape, reading Livy straight through is an experience comparable to reading Tolkien, Tolstoy, or Gibbon; in other words, it is one of the great reading experiences of a lifetime.

Other ancient sources for early Roman history include the biographies of Plutarch, Cicero's *De Republica,* the *Geography* of Strabo, the histories of Dionysius of Halicarnassus, Diodorus Siculus, Cassius Dio, and Polybius, the plays of Plautus, and the *Fasti* of Ovid, a lesser-known work by the great Latin poet that gives fascinating details about the practice and origin of various Roman customs and religious rites. Our sources for the later Republic include the history of Appian and Suetonius's biography of Julius Caesar.

Books by modern authors which I found especially stimulating included Augusto Fraschetti's *The Foundation of Rome* (Edinburgh University Press, 2005; first published in Italy as *Romolo II Fondatore* in 2002), T. P. Wiseman's *Remus: A Roman Myth* (Cambridge University Press, 1995), Jacques Heurgon's *The Rise of Rome to 264 B.C.* (University of California Press, 1973), Nigel Bagnall's *The Punic Wars 264–146 B.C.* (Osprey, 2002), and Keith Richardson's *Daggers in the Forum: The Revolutionary Lives and Violent Deaths of the Gracchus Brothers* (Cassell, 1976).

I also found inspiration in Thomas Babington Macaulay's *Lays of Ancient Rome,* an imaginative nineteenth-century "reconstruction" of ancient Roman ballads, Shakespeare's tragedy *Coriolanus,* and Shakespeare's long narrative poem "The Rape of Lucrece."

William Smith's *Dictionary of Greek and Roman Antiquities* (I own a copy of the 1869 edition, as well as Smith's three-volume *Dictionary of Greek and Roman Biography and Mythology* from 1870) and Samuel Ball Platner's *A Topographical Dictionary of Ancient Rome* (mine is the 1928 edition) were my daily companions. Both books can be found online, along with many other texts, maps, and additional information, at a Web site called LacusCurtius maintained by Bill Thayer; during the research and writing of *Roma,* my visits to this extraordinary horn of plenty were too numerous to count. When I needed to borrow a "real" book, I visited the libraries at the University of California at Berkeley.

Readers who want to know the precise location of monuments and landmarks should consult the book *Mapping Augustan Rome* (Journal of Roman Archaeology Supplementary Series, 2002), largely produced by scholars at the University of Pennsylvania. The large-scale maps that accompany their book are works of prodigious research and exquisite design. For sheer pleasure, readers may want to have a look at the map *Roma Arcaica* (a publication of the Museo della Civiltà Romana available from the American Classical League), a bird's-eye view of the city as it might have appeared in the early days of the Roman Republic.

This novel has been the largest and most complicated project I've ever undertaken, and I'm grateful to those who've helped me along the way. The earliest origin of *Roma* can be traced to Nick Robinson of Constable, my publisher in the U.K., who proposed that I should attempt a novel beyond the scope of my Roma Sub Rosa series; it was at Nick's flat in London that I first put forth the idea that became this book. It was during a walk along Barton Creek in Austin, Texas, that I further discussed the idea with my editor at St. Martin's Press, Keith Kahla, who understood at once what I was attempting to do; a few years (and roughly 200,000 words) later, I gratefully received Keith's insightful comments on the first draft. Krystyna

Green, my editor at Constable in the U.K., also played an active role in following the book's development. I'm also grateful to Gaylan DuBose, teacher of Latin and author of *Farrago Latina,* who read the galleys and gave me valuable feedback.

Special thanks, as always, to my partner, Rick Solomon, and to my agent, Alan Nevins, both of whom never fail to buoy me up when I need it.

※

The sometimes uncannily familiar political struggles and partisan machinations in *Roma* are not my invention, nor have I done much to modernize the terms of the debates. The long tug of war between the patricians and the plebeians, the cynical tactic of the war-mongering ruling class to exploit religious rhetoric and fear of outside threats to their own advantage, the political shift of the descendents of Appius Claudius from far right to far left, the witch-hunt that eradicated the "subversive" Cult of Bacchus, the appeal of the high-born Gracchi to the disenfranchised rabble—each of these incidents is given to us in explicit detail by the sources. The republic of the Romans endured almost twice as long as has our own, so far, and they confronted the paradoxes and paradigms of class struggle long before we did. Whether the American republic will end with the rise of an all-powerful executive, as did that of the Romans, remains to be seen.

Was Fascinus the first deity of the Romans, as recounted in *Roma*? According to Pliny's *Natural History* (28.7), Fascinus was the name of a god worshipped by the Vestal virgins, who placed his image (a fascinum, or phallus amulet) under the chariot of those who triumphed as a protection against "fascination" (what we would call the evil eye). Varro tells us that phallic amulets were often hung around the necks of Roman children to protect them; they were also placed in gardens and on hearths and forges. Anyone who visits Pompeii will notice phallic graffiti and sculptures, but few may realize that an image that may appear obscene to the modern eye was sacred to the ancients.

The mystical phallus that rises from a hearthfire appears in the original myth of the Roman king Servius Tullius, and, even earlier, in a variant of the origin story of Romulus as related by the historian Promathion. Early

Greek authors like Promathion were the first to speculate on the beginnings of Rome, upon which they tended to superimpose their own myths; eventually the Romans themselves would link the foundation of their city with a Greek legend, the fall of Troy (the subject of *The Aeneid* by Virgil). "What is extraordinary" about Promathion, as T. P. Wiseman notes in *Remus,* "is that this early Greek author evidently reported a native Roman story. The phantom phallus is a totally un-Greek concept. Greek gods do not manifest themselves in such a way."

If Promathion's depiction of the divine phallus is drawn from an authentic and very early Roman myth, and if this phallus from the hearth is the same deity that later became known as Fascinus, then it may indeed be that Fascinus was the first Roman god. Livy, I suspect, would understand my reasons for making it so.

Reading Group Gold

ROMA
by Steven Saylor

About the Author

- A Conversation with Steven Saylor

Historical Perspective

- "What Made the Matrons Murder?"
  An Essay by the Author

Keep on Reading

- Recommended Reading
- Reading Group Questions

A
Reading
Group Gold
Selection

For more reading group suggestions
visit www.readinggroupgold.com

 ST. MARTIN'S GRIFFIN

A Conversation with Steven Saylor

What was it like to do the research for such a big project?

Sheer pleasure. When you dive into the research required for a historical novel written on this scale, it's tremendously exciting; whole new worlds unfold as you follow one fascinating link to another, going further and further back in time to unravel the story of Rome's origins.

The research was anything but dull, because the ancient historians had a keen sense of storytelling. They wanted to keep their audience enthralled from first page to last, so the accounts they've given us are full of all the "good stuff"—tales of heroism and treachery, rape and revenge, hope and heartbreak. The people who built Rome into the greatest city on earth—warlords, slaves, vestal virgins, rabble-rousing politicians, scheming millionaires—still live for us today because the human drama of their lives still touches us.

> *"The ancient historians had a keen sense of storytelling."*

How did you move beyond the research into the actual writing?

Creating the novel presented a great challenge, given the immense sweep (a span of a thousand years), the sheer number of characters, and the huge historical and political issues involved. I chose to split the big story into a number of smaller stories set a few generations apart, linked across the centuries by following the fortunes of two of the founding families of Rome. Their personal dramas allowed me to hit the very highest points of the historical saga, episodes such as the sack of Rome by the Gauls—a humiliation the Romans never forgot or forgave—and the terrifying threat the Romans faced when Hannibal crossed the Alps with his elephants, determined to destroy Rome forever. There are several critical points when Rome might have been wiped from the face of the earth and forgotten, but

thanks to the gods, and the sheer determination of her citizens, Rome always survives.

We first see the site of Rome as nothing more than a stop on a trade route, but by the end of the book it's become the world's biggest and most powerful city. How did that happen?

Relentless military conquest was always the key to Rome's success, but so was Roman innovation. It was a man named Appius Claudius who gave Rome the world's first aqueduct, the Aqua Appia; without water from distant sources, Rome could never have grown to accommodate a million inhabitants. He also laid down the famous Appian Way, which revolutionized road building. Roman roads not only allowed armies to march across Europe, they also allowed the wealth of conquered lands (including slaves) to be brought back to the capital. Those ancient roads were so finely built that they still exist all over Europe today.

As Rome grows richer and more powerful, Roman culture becomes more sophisticated. We see the birth of the Roman theater, for example, and the importation of foreign artists and sculptors to decorate the magnificent temples that will make Rome the most opulent city on earth. As their sphere of influence expands, the Romans also begin to import exotic religions, including the infamous Cult of Bacchus, which included orgiastic rituals, and the worship of Cybele, whose priests castrated themselves. The more religiously conservative Romans begin to think the city needs a thorough cleansing, and the result is one of history's bloodiest witch hunts.

The details about Roman religion are eye opening. You're also clearly fascinated by the politics of ancient Rome.

Endlessly fascinated, because they're still so relevant today. Rome moves from a small community of traders to a walled city ruled by kings. Then, after driving off a particularly nasty king called Tarquin—the famous rape of Lucretia causes his downfall—the upper classes establish a new form of elected government they call a republic. The kings tended to balance the interests of the have-nots against the power of the rich, but in the new republic, it's every man for himself. The elite class, the patricians, ruthlessly stack the electoral process to favor themselves, but the unruly have-nots, the plebeians, have their own hand to play—they're needed to harvest crops and fill the ranks of the army—so there's a constant tug of war between the classes.

"The American republic has so far lasted only about half as long as did Rome's."

All the issues Americans deal with today in our polarized republic, the Romans dealt with first. Conservative politicians preached patriotism and religious piety and whipped up xenophobic hysteria; over and over we hear them say, "Do as your betters tell you and Rome will be safe; disobey us and your treason and sinfulness will let outsiders destroy Rome." At the other end of the political spectrum, rabble-rousers—whether driven by idealism or personal ambition—exploited the resentment of the struggling classes. Both sides used lawsuits and sexual scandals to drag down their opponents. Doesn't all this sound familiar?

**Yet, despite all that turmoil, the Roman Republic
managed to last for almost five hundred years.
Why did it finally fail?**

It was the imperial success of the Republic that doomed
it. The staggering wealth brought in by foreign conquests only served to increase social and economic
inequality—the poor became poorer, the rich became
super-rich. And at the very top, a handful of men (like
Caesar) became far too powerful. The social order was
fractured and destabilized to the point of civil war, and
when the wars were over, Rome essentially had a king
again, the emperor Augustus. The Republic was dead,
never to rise again.

The American republic has so far lasted only about half
as long as did Rome's. Whether it will end with the rise
of an all-powerful executive, as happened in Rome,
remains to be seen. There are certainly forces at work
leading us in that direction.

What sort of characters populate the book?

I wanted Rome itself to be the leading character of the
book, which is why I've tried to include the full sweep
of the city's history. But it's the people of a city we care
about, and I've tried to show these momentous events
through the eyes of the men and women who actually
experienced them.

Perhaps my favorite character is the vestal virgin Pinaria,
who becomes trapped along with a handful of defenders
atop the Capitoline Hill when the Gauls conquer the city.
Like all the vestals, who came from leading families, Pinaria
has led a very privileged, sheltered existence, and her
values are completely proper and pious. But in a world
turned upside-down, this vestal virgin finds herself falling
in love with a slave—something utterly unthinkable!—
and she faces some wrenching choices.

*About the
Author*

You also include Romulus and Remus, the founders of the city. Were the twins real, or just legendary?

No one can say for sure. Modern historians used to dismiss the twins as mere legends, but that attitude has begun to change in recent years, thanks to new archaeological discoveries in Rome that date almost exactly to the supposed era of Romulus and Remus. More and more, it appears that the basic details given to us by the ancient sources are accurate, after all.

For all the regal trappings that Romulus took on in his later years, he and his brother essentially started out as ruthless young gang leaders who raided the countryside until they eliminated all the competition. They issued an open invitation to every brigand in Italy to come join them—which is how Rome ended up with too many men and not enough women, leading to the rape (i.e., abduction) of the neighboring Sabine women. Putting up walls around the settlement of Rome—making it a proper city—was just a way to protect their loot. When you read between the lines, the story of Romulus the founder is more gritty than glorious; it has the ring of truth.

You also tell the story of Coriolanus. His name is familiar...

That's because Shakespeare wrote a tragedy about Coriolanus—T. S. Eliot declared it a greater play than *Hamlet*. As I researched the story, I saw what drew Shakespeare to such dramatic material. In the first years of the Republic, Rome's greatest war hero is driven to become a traitor, then marches on Rome at the head of an invincible army. Only one force on earth can stop him and save the city. The story of Coriolanus provides one of history's great twist endings.

"When you read between the lines, the story of Romulus the founder is more gritty than glorious; it has the ring of truth."

Who else is in the book?

One of the characters commits one of history's first mass murders—I don't want to give away any details, but I promise they come straight from the historical record.

Another character becomes the impresario for the first great Roman playwright, Plautus; he's also hopelessly infatuated with his boyhood friend, who happens to become the greatest of all Roman generals, Scipio Africanus, the conqueror of Hannibal.

Then there are the brothers Tiberius and Gaius Gracchus, charismatic politicians who fearlessly try to revolutionize Roman society from the bottom up—and who meet a tragic fate that may remind readers of two Irish-American brothers named Kennedy.

The last descendant in the bloodline traced by *Roma* is Lucius Pinarius, one of the three heirs named in the will of Julius Caesar. As the Republic ends and the age of the emperors begins, Lucius faces a very personal test of loyalty. Should he bow to the inevitable triumph of his despised cousin Augustus, or remain faithful to his friends, the doomed lovers Antony and Cleopatra?

There's a gold talisman on a necklace—an image of a god called Fascinus—that's handed down through the generations in *Roma,* linking the first characters and all their descendants. Some readers may find this talisman a bit far-fetched.

And yet, the worship of Fascinus is one of the most authentic details in the book. The form taken by this god may indeed strike readers as unusual: Fascinus appears to the worshipper as a detached human phallus levitating in a fire, and the talisman worn by the characters is a gold image of a winged phallus.

Anyone who's been to Pompeii has seen phallic images on buildings, and museums have many examples of such amulets. To the ancients, these images weren't prurient or even sexual; they represented the god Fascinus, who protected wearers from the so-called "evil eye" or "fascination" (the word comes from Fascinus). The vestal virgins placed such an image beneath the chariot of a general when he celebrated a triumph, and phallic trinkets were widely worn, especially by women in childbirth and by infants.

Fascinus is significant because the ancestors of the Romans had no gods in the strict sense; they believed in tree spirits and such, and only later adopted the gods of others, especially the Greeks. But the very first deity of the Roman ancestors, uniquely native to Rome, may have been Fascinus, who appears in their earliest myths. That's why I put Fascinus at the heart of *Roma*— though by the end of the book, the god's talisman, worn by time, has subtly changed shape, setting the stage for a new millennium and a new era of the Eternal City.

"I shall relate the sordid details just as they've been handed down to us."
—Livy

"What Made the Matrons Murder?"
An Essay by the Author

Rome is my bread and butter. When I was a boy growing up in rural Texas, watching gladiator movies, playing with my battery-operated Roman galley, sword fighting with my brother, and dressing up as Cleopatra (just kidding!), I could never have guessed that I would someday make a living writing about ancient Rome, but so it goes.

My mystery series featuring Gordianus the Finder, sleuth of ancient Rome, is now up to twelve volumes (ten novels and two collections of short stories), translated into twenty languages. Gordianus returns in 2008 in *The Triumph of Caesar*.

None of the episodes in *Roma* are, strictly speaking, a murder mystery. But of course, amid all that research, it was inevitable that I would come across some criminal mayhem. One of the most intriguing tidbits involves what may be the first recorded mass murders in history. Here's a loose translation of the tale as recounted by the Roman historian Livy (Book VIII, chapter 18), writing about Rome in the year 332 B.C.:

> This year gained an evil notoriety, either because of pestilence or human guilt. Since the authorities are not unanimous on the point, I would gladly believe it was disease, not poison, that carried off so many victims. But lest I impugn the credibility of our sources, I shall relate the sordid details just as they've been handed down to us.
>
> The foremost men in the state were being attacked by the same mysterious malady, which in almost every case proved fatal.

A maidservant went to the city magistrate, Quintus Fabius Maximus, and promised to reveal the cause of these suspicious deaths, provided the state would guarantee her safety. Fabius went at once to the consuls, who referred the matter to the senate, which authorized a promise of protection and immunity.

The maidservant then accused certain women of concocting poisons. If officers would follow her at once, she said, they could catch the poison makers in the act. The officers followed the informant and did indeed find the accused compounding poisonous substances, along with batches of poisons that were already made up.

The evidence was seized and brought into the Forum. Twenty high-born matrons, at whose houses poisons were discovered, were brought before the magistrates. Two of the women, Cornelia and Sergia, both from ancient patrician families, contended that the concoctions were medicinal preparations. Accused of lying, the maidservant suggested that the women should drink some of the supposed medicine themselves, if they wished to prove it was harmless.

The court was cleared of spectators. The accused women consulted among themselves. All consented to drink the potions, whereupon they all died.

Reading
Group
Gold

Their attendants were arrested at once, and informed against a large number of matrons. Eventually, 170 women were found guilty.

Up to that time there had never been a public investigation of poisoning in Rome. The whole incident was regarded as a evil portent, and the women were thought to have acted out of madness rather than deliberate wickedness.

Historical Perspective

No wonder Livy couldn't resist relating this episode— he knew a good story when he heard one! Here we have multiple murders among the high born, betrayal by a servant, mass suicide, and an ever-expanding circle of accusation and guilt. There's even an attempt to explain the event as the result of mass hysteria. But in ancient Rome, there was no insanity defense.

I come across such extraordinary material all the time in my research; when there's murder involved, my interest is especially piqued. Naturally, I had to find a way to incorporate this incident in *Roma,* and so I set about uncovering all I could about the poisonings. (See Chapter VII, "The Architect of His Own Fortune.") In the end, the tale is only a tiny ingredient in what I hope will be a rich banquet of a book—but a little murder, like a powerful spice, goes a long way.

(First published in *Mystery Readers International* © 2006)

Recommended Reading

Ancient Authors

Livy (Titus Livius). *The History of Rome from Its Foundation.* **Penguin Classics.** Four volumes:
I. *The Early History of Rome,* translated by Aubrey de Sélincourt, 1960.
II. *Rome and Italy,* translated by Betty Radice, 1982.
III. *The War with Hannibal,* translated by Aubrey de Sélincourt, 1965.
IV. *Rome and the Mediterranean,* translated by Henry Bettenson, 1965.
Living in the age of Augustus, Livy recounted the story of Rome with intense drama and majestic sweep.

Plautus. *The Pot of Gold and Other Plays,* **translated by E. F. Watling. Penguin Classics, 1965.**
Take parts and read a comedy aloud! This collection includes "The Swaggering Soldier," mentioned in *Roma.*

Plutarch. *Lives.* **Various translations and editions.**
The brief, individual biographies include those of Romulus, Coriolanus, Camillus, Tiberius Gracchus, Gaius Gracchus, Julius Caesar, and Marc Antony. Plutarch was the chief inspiration for Shakespeare's magnificent *Coriolanus, Julius Caesar,* and *Antony and Cleopatra* (also highly recommended).

Modern Historians

Cornell, T. J. *The Beginnings of Rome.*
Routledge, 1995.
The single most essential book for understanding
early Rome.

Wiseman, T. P. *Remus: A Roman Myth.*
Cambridge University Press, 1995.
From the tale of Romulus and Remus, a challeng-
ing historian wrests startling new ideas.

Matyszak, Philip. *Chronicle of the Roman
Republic.* **Thames & Hudson, 2003.**
A copiously illustrated survey of Rome and its
rulers from Romulus to Augustus.

*Keep on
Reading*

1) What did you know about ancient Rome before reading this novel? Did this book teach you something new or change your impression of this important chapter in the world's history of civilization?

2) Which characters in the book are the most memorable, and why? Which characters were makers of history? Which characters were victims of history?

3) In what ways is the city of Rome itself a character in this novel?

4) Why *do* modern readers enjoy novels about the past? Which is more important, the ability of a historical novel to educate or to entertain? How does *Roma* compare with other historical novels you've read (as a group or on your own)?

5) What comparisons can be drawn between Roman politics, religion, and foreign policy and those of the United States?

6) How, if at all, do you think the rise and fall of Rome can be used as a cautionary tale—or history lesson—for today's world superpowers?

7) In *Roma*, certain ceremonies—like the celebration of the sacred geese and ritual punishment of a dog to mark an episode in the capture of the city by the Gauls—endure through the centuries, even when their original significance becomes hazy. Are there any rituals we practice today, even though we can't explain what they mean or how they began?

8) Two thousand years later, why is there still such a widespread fascination with Rome? What elements of that enduring fascination are captured or evoked by the novel?

9) We are taught, as young readers, that every story has a moral. Is there a "moral" to *Roma*? What can we learn about our world—and ourselves—from this book?

10) Who has ever been to Rome? Discuss your impressions of the imperial city and how its history is seen through the eyes of those who visit.

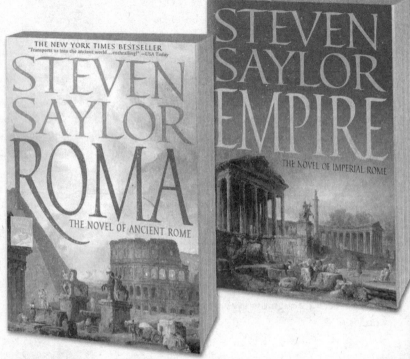

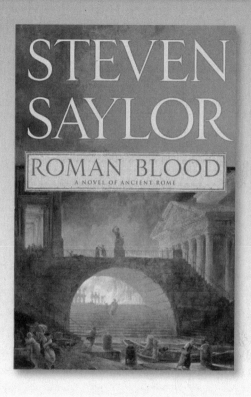